Touchdown for
Walt Loves the Bearcat!
The epic novel that dares to dream

"Boyd's imaginative epic embraces serious topics: interracial relationships, homophobia in professional sports, gay culture, black life on the down low, and living with AIDS. But *Walt Loves the Bearcat* is first and forever a love story, one written with a roller-coaster brio and a magical intensity that demand—and deserve—the reader's perseverance."
—*San Francisco Bay Times*

"Warm-spirited...more than a mere jock romance. Fans of the exuberant spirit of college football will appreciate Boyd's description of football games. Its lighthearted tone keeps the pace going, [and the] expansive confection of existential characters reverberates with soulful queries into the nature of love and life." —*Bay Area Reporter*

A Lambda Literary Finalist for Best Romance

WALT LOVES THE BEARCAT
by Randy Boyd

WEST BEACH BOOKS

This novel is strictly and entirely a work of fiction and fantasy. All references to real people, events, establishments, organizations or locales are purely and solely intended to give the novel a sense of reality and authenticity. All other names, characters, incidents, organizations or locales are strictly the product of the author's imagination, as are those fictionalized events and incidents that involve real persons and entities. Of the fictional characters, any resemblance to actual persons, living or dead, is entirely and purely coincidental.

A story known as "Little Bearcat's Racist Nightmare" appeared in the anthology *Freedom in this Village* and is not part of the *Walt Loves the Bearcat* novel.

Designer: Alan Bell
Cover Illustration: Hedri W.

LCCN: 2005932414
ISBN: 9781931875264
ISBN may vary on eBook editions

First Paperback Edition: October 2005
Second Paperback Edition: September 2006
Third Paperback Edition: May 2007
First ePub Edition: August 2015 v1.0
Fourth Paperback Edition: August 2021
Second ePub Edition: August 2021 v2.0
Fifth Paperback Edition: October 2021
Third ePub Edition: October 2021 v3.0
Sixth Paperback Edition: December 2021
Fourth ePub Edition: December 2021 v4.0
Seventh Paperback Edition: April 2022

To my buddy,
come what may

WALT LOVES THE BEARCAT
by Randy Boyd

On the Road of Life...

I have dreamed half a life.
So far, this much is true ...

1

Upon Further Reveal

"Dancing ... Bear?" asked a voice from nowhere.

"What?" Marcus emerged from his reverie. The interior of the plane came into focus, as did his Asian female seatmate who spoke very little English.

"The football people!" said the Asian woman, pointing to the crude illustration on the paper atop his tray table.

"Oh ... yeah." Marcus chuckled at the two figures he had sketched to pass the time. He could see why she thought the quarterback and the mascot were dancing, especially with his minimal drawing skills. "Football people ... right," added Marcus.

"They dance on eggbeater?" asked the Asian woman, eyes full of wonderment. "True? Gold? Love?"

"Love?" laughed Marcus. "I ... how do ... *yo no se?*" Pleading ignorance in Spanish was the best he could do. Her smile faded. Her attention did not.

"Ladies and gentlemen, we are now beginning our initial descent ..." said the PA system.

"Oh, goody." Marcus folded the drawing and stowed away his tray table. Then he pointed toward the window next to his shoulder. "Landing soon, see."

"Perfect," said the Asian woman, surveying the landscape. "Always perfect pretty pictures."

Faraway in the distance, the skyscrapers of Chicago sprouted toward the heavens in a jagged cluster. The towers appeared minuscule compared to the vast expanse of Midwestern flatlands in front of them, and a sunny but hazy Lake

Michigan behind them; but the scene *was* a perfect pretty picture, especially if the *picture* were a movie where the main character was about to find himself knee-deep in adventure in the Windy City.

Opening shot, thought Marcus, ever the Great Filmmaker, if only in his mind.

The Asian woman became lost in her own reverie beyond the window. Marcus closed his eyes and imagined that the plane was flying directly over Soldier Field, the venerable home of the city's football team, seemingly since men played the game in leather helmets without faceguards. The stands used to be filled with working-class men who yelled their lumberjack guts out during gladiator-like clashes in windswept snowstorms. Now, to keep up with the times, the stands had been transformed into a big corporate playground, glistening with the perks of the elite: gourmet menus, waitresses in the club seats, and luxury suites that served as a comfortable buffer from the chaos and disorder of the game. But Marcus was a stadium buff and had a certain affinity for all stadiums, and Soldier Field certainly possessed its share of classic gridiron memories.

The touchdown passes of Walt Yeager alone.

The thought resonated. Marcus took a deep breath. Eyes still shut, the words came to him the way they might come to anyone preparing for the speech of a lifetime, say, for example, at the induction of one's husband to some sort of football hall of fame:

I am not a religious man. Not in the "dress up and go to church every Sunday" sense, not in the "pray before meals and bedtime" sense, and certainly not in the "eternal damnation" sense. But I do consider myself spiritual. And I do believe that there are forces greater than mankind, and powers far beyond our confused little brains' ability to comprehend. Sometimes, I give these forces a name, not a very original one, but a name just the same: God.

To me, God's not a man. Or a woman. Or a tree or a dog. God's not even a He. God is everything beautiful, powerful and majestic. Everything worldly and otherworldly, and everything in between. God truly is ... All That.

With that preface, I say the following:

As a young child, when I gazed into the big pupils of our family dog, a black beagle named Benito, I saw the eyes of God.

As a preteen, standing on the swaying deck of a tour boat, my aging grandmother holding my hand, I stared up at Niagara Falls, its vast expanse consuming my entire line of sight, and I saw the face of God.

As a 21-year-old college student, when I saw Walt for the very first time, his golden blond aura brighter than his pale yellow polo shirt, I saw the soul of God ...

Marcus gave the thought a few more seconds of free airtime, then opened his eyes.

God, I'm such a ... fill in the blank: Idiot? Complete loser? Retard?

He became conscious of the surroundings in his periphery. The seatback in front of him returned to the upright position. The Asian woman handed her plastic cup to a flight attendant. A voice on the PA made another announcement about their arrival. Marcus unfolded the drawing, then turned it over, revealing a printout from his computer.

The miracle of the Net. All you need is a couple of dreams you've kept to yourself for 21 years, and some desire, guts and determination.

The thought resonated. He took a deep breath and closed his eyes once more. The words came to him the way they might come to anyone preparing for the speech of a lifetime, say, for example, to the stranger who's been the star of one's lifelong fantasies:

Way back when—in the prime of our youth—I was a cheerleader at UCLA while you were a quarterback at the University of Georgia. Our schools played one another on a rainy night in Athens, in a big season opener on national TV. I'm not even sure if you were in the stadium that night, or what happened after your college career, or anything else about you, for that matter; but a few months after the game, I became captivated by your picture in the game program. I'm a writer, a storyteller. I've always planned to create a story inspired by the beauty of the man in the photo, a kind of "what if." What if we had met and fallen in love? What if you had gone on to become a great NFL quarterback? What if I were by your side—your rock—and we became an openly loving couple that changed the world, true golden heroes of our time?

He gave the thought a few more seconds of free airtime, then opened his eyes once more.

Oh, and I just happened to be in Chicago for the first time ever, and I remember that the program said you were from Winnetka, Illinois. Wassup, man? Wanna hang out with a black male ex-cheerleader who's had a crush on you for 21 years?

An admonition came over the PA to turn off all electronics. The cornfields below gave way to suburban sprawl and long roads with tiny cars. The Windy City and Walt Yeager were closer than ever.

Cut to the 42-year-old professional black writer fidgeting like the high school geek he used to be, thought Marcus, head bowed to the window.

He wasn't sure which landed first, the plane or his stomach, but while his mind was racing with his thoughts, his body had touched down in Chicago. He was filing out of the aircraft now. Beyond the gate, his Asian seatmate vanished and his surroundings became as blurry as they were in his dreams. His mind was consumed with a single purpose, moving in search of open space and a path to his goal. His pupils took care of the details of the journey—making sure the literal path was clear—but his sights were focused on a much grander vision. Even the frenetic energy circling about wasn't gonna stop him now.

Nothing was gonna stop him now.

A confident smile crept across his face. He journeyed through an elevated pathway that led toward the temporary land of his dreams. The morning sun flooded the round glass tunnel with an intense glare that radiated through his soul like golden light through a prism. When he was on the other side, his shoulders dropped and relaxed for the first time in ages. The breath he exhaled was much more than relief for safely reaching his destination. Upon further reveal, it was the breath of newborn hope and anticipation, ripe with the knowledge that anything, truly anything, was possible. True?

2

Warriors United

"And now, let me introduce our distinguished guests," said the dark-haired lesbian at the podium. Marcus put his smile on autopilot and glanced at the other panelists. Initially, he had declined the offer to speak at the writer's conference on a Friday afternoon before most of the participants had arrived. But once he realized he'd be free for the remainder of the weekend, he was just fine with being part of the warm-up act. That way, he could be ready on a moment's notice should he need to leave the hotel in downtown Chicago, say, for example, to meet Walt Yeager—should Walt Yeager, for some crazy reason, want to grab a beer after hearing Marcus' crazy tale.

"... author of some 'unique' novels so far," said the dark-haired lesbian at the podium, reining in his attention, "Marcus Coleman hails from the LA area and has been nominated for several book awards. So far, he has been *Lucci'd* at every award ceremony—his words, not mine."

Laughter rippled across the small gathering in the large conference room. The turnout belied the topic of the panel: WHY GAY AMERICA CARES ABOUT GAY LITERATURE. Marcus sat the farthest away from the podium. His mind stayed in the room for a little while and even heard an interesting point or two. But eventually, as it so often did, his imagination took him elsewhere. He envisioned a handsome blond man in his early forties, driving a sedan or luxury SUV down the highways of Chicago on a late Friday afternoon. He figured Walt to be a white-collar professional who made lots of money the way white, ex-college quarterbacks do. Maybe Walt was on his cell at that very moment, checking with his secretary, or giving his wife and kids an update on his arrival time home. Then again, maybe he was single. Divorced, single and hetero, wondering where to head tonight to look for divorced, single and hetero women without too much baggage. Maybe he was a lover of men, and single and heading home from a tough day at the office, dreaming of an adventurous weekend in the city, not far from the conference hotel.

Just to know what happened to the beautiful man in the photograph.

And what if, by some wild chance ...

"Our literature is our backbone, our gay history," said the female panelist adjacent to Marcus, alerting him that he was on deck ...

... Meanwhile, Marcus thought about all the years imagining a life with a total stranger. He had told himself the daydreams were just for the book he was going to write one day; but if it was just for the book, he now possessed 21 years' worth of stories in the form of daydreams. And 21 years' worth of memories he'd never shared with another soul.

There was the beach house in Malibu and all the games all over the NFL. Marcus had been there for almost every snap at every venue, from those cool, windy stadiums up North, to the dome that was their home for a good while. From Walt's debut as an NFL starter on a rockin' Monday night in Denver to the Frozen Tongue Playoff Game in Buffalo. From the Doak Minnefield sack that threatened to end Walt's career, to the Hail Larry pass that threatened to end Walt and Marcus' cool and dreamy life. From the playoffs and the Super Bowls to the unidentified flying object that came from the cheap seats in Pittsburgh. From the highest of accolades to all the other missiles launched at both men, especially after Walt Yeager became the first superstar athlete to admit his love for another man while still in the prime of his pro football career ...

"We conquered the world, or tried to," said Marcus aloud to the audience at the writer's conference. "In my dreams, we did great things and stood by one another like warriors united, always and forever. This much is true."

Suddenly he realized that the room might not be interested in hearing about Walt Yeager, and that maybe he should utter something about the topic at hand.

"*That* was my dream for this community," said Marcus, continuing onward, "that we band together. Like warriors united. But it's a dream unfulfilled. This 'gay' community I see in the early part of the 21st century is nothing that I can personally identify with *or* relate to. Somebody hijacked the word *gay*. Now it means you're a *Queer Eye Guy*, or Will or Grace. If that's what being gay is, I'm no longer a homo."

Murmurs of approval filtered through the audience.

"Not knocking anyone," said Marcus. "We all should be who we are. But when I signed on to this *whole gay thing*, I did so with the understanding that it was an easy way to convey to the world my number one draft pick for the gender of my sex partners and eventual love of my life, nothing else."

Laughter replaced the murmurs.

"*Sex life* and *love life* were the *only* things I signed up for," said Marcus. "No behavioral tendencies, no special icons and divas, no particular clothes or labels or activities or lifestyle—although I must say, I've probably tried them all on for size in the name of finding who I really am. And this is who I really am: the only reason I'm *gay* is because there are certain things about a man that I don't wanna live without. Daily, preferably. The first of those is another man's soul. After that, everything else is details. That's the *only* reason I check *gay* on the census form, so to speak. And as far as labels, I learned a long time ago to let 'em go. So the *Queer Eye Guys* can keep *gay*. And I hope all their dreams come true, just like mine. But I'll just say ... I'm sexual ..."

Silence ensued in the room as if time were momentarily suspended.

"Thank you very much. Enjoy your weekend," concluded Marcus.

"Uh, excuse me," said the dark-haired lesbian at the podium. "Just exactly how does this relate to WHY GAY AMERICA CARES ABOUT GAY LITERATURE?"

Marcus collected himself. "Because this new gay world does not care about gay literature. How many here today tell people you write gay lit, and they automatically assume you do porno? Yeah, see, if I had a dollar for every hand in the air right now, I could afford to stay at this hotel on a regular weekend. This new gay world doesn't care about gay literature because, even though we have great stories, they don't have pretty pictures, like all the other sources for gay media." Then it dawned on Marcus for the very first time. "We've got to give them pretty pictures!" He folded his hands and cracked his knuckles. "*Then* all of America will care," said Marcus, smiling at the dark-haired lesbian, who still didn't seem convinced.

"Perhaps we'll leave that discussion for the Q&A," she said, sounding quite bewildered.

MARCUS SAT ON THE BED IN HIS HOTEL ROOM and wondered what the rest of Chicago was doing on an early Saturday morning. He imagined husbands running errands for their wives, fathers chauffeuring kids to soccer, single men arriving home, sweaty and pumped after a good workout at the gym.

What other kind of man could Walt possibly be?

Marcus toyed with the printout from his computer. Years ago, when the

Internet was a newfangled way to look up people's contact information, he had found Walt's phone number via Yahoo! People Search—just for kicks, he told himself, to find out if the man actually existed beyond the game program. Sure enough, Walt Yeager was real, and in the 'burbs of Chicago, just like the program said. Marcus held onto the printout for years—thought he had lost it for most of that time. Then came the invitation to appear at the writer's conference. He discovered the tattered paper once again in a very old folder marked *Walt Loves the Bearcat.* The printout made the road trip, but calling Walt would be, as they say in sports, a game-time decision. As if Marcus didn't know himself any better.

A college football game was playing on the hotel television. He turned off the set, then decided to raid the minibar. "This is my movie and I'll have a cliché shot of courage if I want." He poured himself a shot of tequila in a plastic cup, then retrieved his cell phone, sat on the bed and cleared his esophagus. The hacking made him dizzy, but he continued onward.

I'm looking for a Walt Yeager who played football for the University of Georgia in the early 80s ...

His plan was to be perfectly honest. There was nothing to fear. He dialed the number and pressed TALK, then held his breath. The combustion within his soul forced him to stand. A wave of nausea boomeranged in his head, followed by a sudden eruption of blaring music and a shrill female voice:

"—*oooooooooo ...*"

He spun around in a panic. The clock radio on the nightstand had turned itself on, drowning out the cell phone in the process.

"*... where would I be?*" sang the female. It was Belinda Carlisle, *the former lead singer of the Go-Gos.*

"This is ..." came from the deep, penetrating voice of a man on the phone.

Marcus reached for the radio's cord, traced it behind the nightstand, and yanked it out of its socket, getting the silence he wanted. Too much silence. A man who sounded mature enough to be in his forties—like *Walt*—had answered the phone and was waiting for a reply. But Marcus needed a moment, during which, the man—who might be *Walt*—said hello again. Marcus remained mute. Belinda Carlisle had thrown him off. He needed one more second—

"I'm Marcus," came out of his mouth.

"Hold on," said the man. The commotion in the background suggested he was multitasking. "Marcus ... when you coming home?"

Marcus exhaled and waited for the man to finish what appeared to be a conversation with someone else who was physically present.

"Well?" said the man. "Do I get a hint?"

Marcus remained quiet, wondering if the masculine, sexy voice belonged to the man of his dreams.

"Are you there?" asked the man. "Lotta construction here."

"I'm still here," said Marcus.

"So when are you coming home? Hold on ... okay ... I'm back. Well, are you? Hello? Are you coming home? Marcus? ... bear ... you there?" The man waited for an answer. Marcus listened for another voice but heard none. Then something within demanded he speak:

"Are ... are you talking to me, Walt?" asked Marcus.

"You're Marcus," said the man, but the signal began breaking up. "When ... home ... are you coming home?"

"When should I?" Marcus heard himself say.

"Where are you now?" asked the man.

"Chicago," said Marcus, head spinning from all the energy combusting within. "I've just come from home near Malibu."

"You're breaking up," said the man.

"I live near Malibu," said Marcus. "I've just come from home near Malibu."

"Bear, I love Malibu," said the man. "I love Malibu and ... you."

"Did," Marcus paused, but failed to stop the words from escaping his heart. "Did you just call me Bear?"

"Bear ... cat ... your name ... right?" said the man. "I love Malibu and ... you."

"You do?" said Marcus. "You love me or Malibu? Or both? You know about Malibu? And the Bearcat? You know that's my nickname—our original nickname?"

"This is twisted," said the man. "Marcus? Do we know each other?"

"I think I have the wrong number," said Marcus. "I was looking for someone, but I think I screwed up. Sorry to bother you."

Marcus pressed END twice, then pressed it again to make sure the connection was severed. Whatever had just happened with whomever that was on the other end of the phone instantly killed any visions of having a beer with a golden blond stranger. Now, the bigger priority was his own sanity. He picked up the drawing from the airplane, the quarterback and the dancing bear, according to his Asian seatmate.

"Are they in love?" she had asked.

"Not even living in the same worlds, we regret to inform you." Marcus balled up the paper and sent it flying like a comet into the black hole of a wastebasket.

A short time later, he was sitting in that same seat on that same plane, this time going in the opposite direction without a seatmate. He had checked out of the hotel early and paid an astronomical fee to change his flight. Such was the price to pay for possibly losing one's mind and believing, even for a few fleeting seconds, that a lifelong fantasy had any roots in reality. He lowered his forehead on the window and felt the stirring of jet engines beneath him. A half-hour later, the plane was chasing the sun westward.

EDWINA BEGAN READING THE DNA RESULTS clutched in her trembling hands, just as the cell phone started ringing. "Off!" cried Daddy Rent from his Lay-Z-Boy. His eyes were glued to the fading close-up of his favorite heroine on *All My Loves*.

"Show's over, but my bad." Marcus rose up from the couch, plugged in his earbud and pressed TALK. "Eve, give me a minute. Daddy Rent just got some shocking news that's gonna rock Mellow Valley."

"Quiet!" said Daddy Rent, using the remote to fast-forward through the commercials. "Gotta see the previews."

"You're not talking about the soaps, are you?" Eve Abercrombie was one of Marcus' best friends. In her mid-30s now, she was a sexy blonde personal trainer with whom he had shared life's up and downs for over 15 years. Because she lived halfway across the country, she was an Ear Bud mostly, someone he spent more time talking to than seeing in person.

"My life should be so realistic," said Marcus. He stood in front of the French doors just off the living room. Mama Rent was on the patio with the dogs (a golden mutt and a chocolate Lab). His mother was doing one of the things she loved most in the world: feeding them as much food as humanly possible. This time it was bits of her lunch, which she was having with Helen, her 88-year-old white neighbor who had the energy of a 58-year-old.

This is to you, and you alone, Walt, and nobody else. Because that's how much I love you.

Marcus swung around and steadied himself against the glass doors, which rattled Daddy Rent's already heightened nerves. "Quiet!" cried his stepfather.

Or was Marcus still delirious from the weekend?

Since returning from Chicago an hour ago, all Marcus had to do was conjure up an idea about a blond, 6'3", former college jock from Winnetka, Illinois, and his mind traveled to very strange places at the same time that his stomach sensed a rumbling as real as any earthquake he had ever felt. And he had felt earthquakes. Earthquakes had changed the direction of his life. And these *Walt* tremors were beginning to have a life of their own as if they could happen at any moment. Think about Walt, don't think about Walt—it didn't matter. His mind kept coming back to Walt, and his soul wanted to shake, rattle and rumble.

"I have to go any minute now," said Eve, "but your message was kinda creepy. Do you have privacy now?"

"Dream on," said Marcus. "Speaking of dreams, have you ever had something happen to you in real life that felt like a dream? Or maybe a dream come true? Only it wasn't a dream come true because things didn't turn out like you dreamed? Or hoped? Or imagined? Maybe because you went retarded at the worst possible moment?"

"I can still hear you, Coleman," growled Daddy Rent.

"What happened in Chicago?" asked Eve.

"One sec," whispered Marcus. "Mama Rent and her friend are about to vacate the patio."

Outside, Helen gave the dogs their requisite affection and disappeared through the tall wooden gate that led to her condo. Oxnard Bay was a seaside nook of senior living, just far enough north of Los Angeles not to *be* Los Angeles. The Rents were one of the few black families of over 700 residents, but that didn't bother Mama Rent. She was a retired librarian residing blocks away from the Pacific, living her Southern California dream after selling the family home of 33 years in the Bay Area.

"I forgot why you call your mother Mama Rent," said Eve.

"Long story," said Marcus, stepping outside. "Some other time."

"So Chicago," said Eve. "What's up with this experience where you thought you might be crazy, but won't tell me the details?"

The dogs followed Mama Rent and the dishes into the house. She passed her son with a triumphant smirk, as if proud that she had graduated from the soaps to Maury Povich and the afternoon court shows.

"I wasn't insane, Eve," said Marcus, reclining in his favorite lounge chair. "Just caught up in a perfect storm of no sleep and too much stress."

Hip, his sensitive golden mutt, came to the patio door to make sure Marcus was still around, then disappeared. Dad came in second to Granny's crumbs in the kitchen.

"Did your mom freak out to see you back so soon?" asked Eve.

"Does anything I do surprise you *or* her?" asked Marcus.

"My next client just walked in," said Eve. "You okay?"

"Dreamy," said Marcus, followed by goodbye. Inside the living room, Hip and Comet wrestled one another as they always did after eating. They were two neutered adult males and had been the best of buds since bonding as puppies.

Because Marcus had been single his whole life, he took great comfort in knowing his dog had a soul mate. That thought alone put a smile on his face as he drifted off to sleep under the midday October sun.

No dreams of Walt Yeager, daydreams or otherwise. Let it go. Let him go ...

A tickling on his nose interrupted his descent into reverie. He tried to swat away the distraction, hitting his face instead. Upon further reveal, 88-year-old Helen had used a long blade of grass to stimulate his nostrils.

"You punk'd me," whined Marcus, sounding childlike.

"I've got a surprise for you." Helen's face was directly above him, as was the sun, which was behind Helen and eclipsed by her head. The effect created a halo around Helen's head, which was shaking due to a nerve problem. The halo shifted and flickered on the outskirts of her face, causing Marcus to think of angels.

"A surprise?" asked Marcus, using his knuckles to rub the corners of his eyes. "I won money?"

"Something better," said Helen. A postcard replaced her face in the halo. "Somebody is reaching out. That's much more important, don't you think?"

"I'll get back to you on that one." He snatched the card and squinted to read it against the sun's glare. "Something about: GET FIT: NO ENROLLMENT NECES-SARY." He scoffed and tossed the card from his mind. "Whatever amount they want, I can't afford it."

"The new guy put it in my box," said Helen. "I thought maybe you could use the exercise."

Marcus sat upright to avoid the luminance of Helen's halo. "I'm happy with my body the way it is, if that's what you're trying to tell me."

"So maybe it's not your body they're after," said Helen, getting a big laugh from him. Mama Rent's dear sweet neighbor was one of the few people on earth who could take his volley and slam it back over the net with the ferocity of the Williams sisters. Before he could react to her comeback whizzing by his ear and hitting the back wall of the patio, he was saved by the bell, literally, as the cell phone in his shorts rang out like an old-fashioned telephone.

"Thanks for the special delivery," said Marcus to Helen, indicating the postcard before casting it aside.

"Answer your phone. You're a good son," said Helen before disappearing. Briefly, he wondered if she knew he was a man who loved men, and that his mother accepted him; but the Illinois number on the caller ID became the more curious mystery. The number wasn't familiar; the name was absent. He thought of the hotel, pressed TALK and said hello.

"Marcus?" asked the deep, sexy voice of a self-assured man.

"This is he."

"This is Walt Yeager ..."

For Marcus, it felt like Santa Claus calling, as in fulfilling his prepaid, prearranged duty to give you a personal jingle from the North Pole. You talk to him awhile. Tell him what you want for Christmas. Take a photo—in your mind, in this case. Then, when your visit with Jolly Saint Nick is over—after your allotted prepaid time runs out—the call ends and you resume the hell that is your life.

Only it wasn't Christmastime. And Marcus had never told anyone *anything* about his own personal Santa Claus, let alone given the North Pole his credit card numbers. And his cell *had* rung. Helen had been a witness, which only meant that Marcus Coleman had entered into a whole new world, one where Walt Yeager existed beyond his own mind. He was real, and he was on the phone. This quake was the big one. Northridge, 1994, literally shifting his landscape and causing all matter in his world to come crumbling down.

"... reached my cell phone earlier this morning," Walt was saying. He was already moving faster than Marcus with this whole new reality. " ... wondering why you called."

"I was looking for a Walt Yeager who played football for the University of Georgia," said Marcus. The idea of lying to this man was inconceivable, or at least, comparable to lying to himself. And by 42, Marcus had long ago ceased the practice of lying to himself and the world. There was nothing to hide, especially from your own personal Santa Claus.

"*I* played at Georgia," said Walt.

That is so Walt, ladies and gentlemen, that tone, that cool, confident and in-control attitude that those who fail to understand his true nature call "high and mighty."

Don't do this now, speak!

Marcus tried to keep his mind from exploding with thoughts that were shooting off like fireworks from some unknown origin. This new world was speeding by much more rapidly than the old one. He wanted to utter words but instead, simply exhaled: "Walt."

"Are you sure we don't know one another?" said the baritone, youthful, exhilarating voice on the other side.

"I don't think so," said Marcus. "Do you?"

"Maybe it's thinking about Georgia," said Walt, "but you've definitely been on my—how are you doing?"

"Uh, travel fatigued?" said Marcus.

"Do you remember ever meeting in the past? I can almost swear we've met, can you?" said Walt.

"Now that you mention it," said Marcus. "But have we?"

"Not that I recall," said Walt. "That's why it's kinda ... twisted. Why did you call me again?"

Marcus felt his head rise and his body fill up with air. Leaves rustled on the patio. The earth started to move again.

What do you have to say for yourself now, Dreamer Man?

"No wait!" said Walt, followed by silence. The leaves grew still again. The earth stopped moving, or rather, the earth slowed back down to its legal speed.

"Waiting," said Marcus, steadying himself on the lounge chair.

"Let's do this in person," said Walt. "When are you going home?"

"Home?" asked Marcus, feeling a legitimate sense of déjà vu from this morning's conversation, when it was: when are you *coming* home.

"You caught me on my way outta town this morning," said Walt. "I'm in your neck of the woods now, not far from Malibu. How crazy is that?"

The earthquake swallowed Marcus whole, but it felt more like an amusement park ride than a disaster.

"I—this—I flew back this morning, too!" said Marcus, almost scared to admit it.

"*Whoa,* hold on, you're kidding. You showed up here in LA? You're not kidding," said Walt. "Twisted."

"How crazy is that?" said Marcus. The world became a blurry exchange of two distant voices on opposite sides of his head, one voice probing for directions, the other offering coordinates and logistics. Marcus agreed with whatever Walt wanted, more concerned with the images floating like asteroids in his headspace.

Marcus being ambushed by cops and men in white coats while Walt Yeager stands tall on a distant hill, overseeing the capture of his lifelong stalker, unbeknownst to Mr. Yeager until very recently.

Marcus being ambushed by Mr. and Mrs. Walt Yeager and the 12 Yeager children, all of them holding hands as they march toward the crazy black man trying to detonate the perfect nuclear family.

Marcus being ambushed by Walt Yeager alone, a man who's man enough to take care of this matter on his own, because Walt Yeager, former college QB, can handle anything that comes his way.

One voice confirmed something about being at a nearby park in about an hour. Not long after, the connection was lost. It took a while, but eventually Marcus realized it was because the conversation had concluded and they had hung up. And a man named Walt Yeager was about to show up in Oxnard.

To meet Marcus Coleman.

"I am about to experience something that I dreamed possible, but never imagined. I am about to meet my fantasy lover of the last 21 years, the literal living embodiment of my deepest dream, the man, if God came down from the sky, or a genie came out of a bottle—or whatever devil I had to sell my soul to—if whoever had the power in this universe asked me who to cast as my soul mate, Walt would be the man ...

"Physically anyway. After all, who knows what this man is like in the real world—*but guess who's about to find out?!*—but for better or for worse, for richer or for poorer, Walt would be the man I'd choose to get to know, to see how far we could go and how high we could fly together in this twisted and crazy world of ours ...

"And I wouldn't care about why I chose him over another kind of man or whether my choice was based on: *feeling like a nigger in need of a white man's approval vs. wanting to bond with a white man to make the ultimate political/ sexual statement vs. just wanting to love and be loved by a man whose appearance, at least, sets every particle of my soul on fire.* I wouldn't care about the why. I would just want to get to know the man I've been thinking about for half my life. I would want to know what his life has been like the last 40-some years, to share my dreams and see if we can't make each other smile a little more."

Should've brought Kleenex.

Marcus wiped his eyes. Towering palm trees and a seemingly endless stretch of green grass came into focus, reminding him he had left the Rents and was already sitting on a park bench, waiting for Walt.

Sometimes life literally blurred by like the landscape in dreams, reminding him of the lyric from "Row, Row, Row Your Boat." *Life is but a dream.*

To meet Walt, Marcus had chosen a gem of a park on the coast in Oxnard. The beach beyond the dunes was clean and friendly, but the huge oval park bordering the dunes was the true scenic treasure. Large enough to hold a football field, the grassy commons was surrounded by an oval pathway for pedestrians and bicycles. The pathway was lined with tall, thin palm trees that swayed in the ocean breeze. Marcus and the Rents brought the dogs there often, and it seemed like the perfect place for dreams to come true.

In his mind, he tried to age the photo of Walt, but didn't get very far, nor did he really care to. He hadn't seen the photo in years and never really spent much time looking at it. Except, of course, in those first few moments of the photo's existence in his life. Like a sonogram, in a way ...

The season opener between UCLA and Georgia had come and gone by the time Marcus Coleman first laid eyes on Walt Yeager. In fact, football season was over, basketball season was off to a rocky start, and Marcus was in exile, miles away from the sidelines. The Rose Bowl at the dawn of 1984 had done him in. The holiday flu inside his weakened body did not appreciate cheerleading eight miles along a parade route in Pasadena, then cheering for an entire football game in a stadium full of 100,000 folks. By nightfall, UCLA had routed the Illinois Fighting Illini, 45-9, and the "holiday flu" had KO'd the Bruins' first black male cheerleader in years.

By morning, Marcus was half-dead at Student Health.

"Are you gay?" asked the ancient female doctor after he relayed his symptoms.

"No," scoffed Marcus, taking up the tone of an indignant New Yorker. "What—is this, like, similar to ..."

Those four little letters—a i d s—were cropping up more and more around the periphery of his world, slowly replacing herpes as the Sexual Disease of the Day. "Yeah, and they have this new thing that can kill ya," said a man at a bathhouse once. Another time, while driving with the other cheerleaders, they had spotted hundreds of men walking at night, holding candles by the Federal Building near campus.

"Those are the fags doing a vigil because they're all dying," said Heather, the girl with the highest hip quotient of anyone on the squad.

They have this new thing that can kill ya. The fags are all dying. Those were the only two things anyone ever said to 21-year-old Marcus Coleman about the disease until 125-year-old Dr. Battle Axe asked him: "Are you gay?"

Of course, he said no. He was the 6'4", athlete-looking, "straight" black cheerleader in a decent white fraternity, the cheerleader some of the football players respected, according to their cheerleader girlfriends. "Yeah, Coleman's the only cool one," was one lineman's glowing review. Marcus was living a life-long dream, and in his dream, he wasn't gay and everybody played along.

"Have it your way, cheer queer," Dr. Battle Axe may as well have said as she stared into his jaundiced eyes. She sent him away that day with a truth he couldn't deny, hepatitis B, which left him a lone option: return home to Hayward in Northern California, to recover from his very first STD.

Leaving school, even temporarily, felt like dropping out, just as his brothers had done before him. Their downfall had been broken hoop dreams. Marcus' downfall had been the lofty sport of fag sex. His secret junkets to the dark places where grown men hunted for anonymous sex had finally caught up with him.

And if he had contracted hepatitis from a stranger, and if Dr. Battle Axe had immediately thought of *aids,* he wondered what else might he have acquired? And if hepatitis made him feel this ill, what about this thing called *aids* lurking around, not even identified as a virus yet, only as a killer of the males he was having sex with when he wasn't busy living the college high life.

At 21, he felt mortal, more so than he ever imagined. And if he was mortal, his dreams were mortal, including his deepest dream, the one he survived high school for, came to LA for, and was secretly being a fag for. College had been his transformation from high school geek to fraternity material. The ride had been entertaining so far, but missing still was the one thing he wanted most: the college buddy of his dreams, the one with whom he was going to have all that collegiate fun, then ride off into a sunset called the rest of their lives together, always and forever. Hep B sacked him during the fourth year of his five-year plan. His college days were numbered. Time was running out on making his dreams come true, and he wasn't even in the game anymore.

Upon landing in his childhood sickbay in Hayward, his body shut down and he slept for days. Two weeks later, he claimed he was well enough to return to school, but some lab results said otherwise. His winter quarter was officially canceled. He had the house to himself much of the time, which gave him plenty of chance to rest, watch television and be bored out of his restless young mind. Then one day, he came across the UCLA-Georgia game program while browsing through the magazine rack in the den. The previous September, Mama Rent and her two sisters had attended the game in Athens, Georgia, their first time ever seeing Marcus cheer live. He had barely seen his mother during that rainy and chaotic weekend, but she had obviously bought the game program as she often did at sporting events. Or perhaps Marcus had handed over *his* copy for safekeeping during all the rain.

Sitting on the floor of the den, he thumbed through the Georgia program with a renewed enthusiasm for his wild and crazy college life, reminiscing about the road trip, one of the all-time highlights of his college experience. He also did what he did with every program from every game: he checked out the football players.

And then I saw him ...

As if by magic, the most beautiful, captivating, stunning, pure and godly image of a man stared into his eyes, peering deep into his soul. Everything about him was so perfect and perfectly in place: the right amount of radiant, youthful hair; the right amount of distinctive yet soft facial features; the right amount of gold poured into his golden skin; the right amount of love beaming from his smiling eyes, which never wandered from his own and instantly became eyes that would peer into the far reaches of his soul forever. One glimpse. One glance. One moment was all that was necessary to see the exact opposite of his reflection, yet the perfect duplicate of his soul.

He's so perfect, whispered something from inside, softly, without a trace of doubt. The words echoed back, just as softly, and sounded like, *You're so perfect.*

But the message got twisted inside his very fallible brain.

Me perfect? *You're* perfect! Or is that, perfectly put together?

Perfect was not a word his star-struck soul had ever used on himself, only others, so the other man, who was already known to be perfect, became not *perfect,* but *perfectly put together,* as if to achieve a calculated effect that essentially said, "I'm perfect and you're not." And so the star-struck soul glanced away, remembered who he was, and decided that perfect was simply out of reach.

"It's a lot of hard work," said a young Latina passing by on roller skates with a cell phone to her ear. The interruption brought Marcus back to the park by the ocean, mind, body and soul. His eyes had already spotted the blond aura in the distance, a football field away at the polar opposite end of the oval pathway. If Walt Yeager was at the North Pole, Marcus Coleman was at the South. They acknowledged one another with body language, Marcus waving a hand high in the air, Walt giving a barely perceptible nod of the head backward.

The voice of a woman scolding her hound dog in the parking lot pierced the air. Marcus used it as an excuse to look away and collect himself. He began moving, relieved to discover the blond aura moving as well. They circumnavigated the oval pathway and played a game of nonchalant peek-a-boo. Occasionally, the orbit of a jogger or skateboarder passed close enough to give them a reason to glance elsewhere, but they never lost sight of one another for very long. Still, they got halfway around the park before realizing they had circumnavigated the oval in what *appeared* to be opposite directions: clockwise. By the time Walt arrived at three o'clock on the pathway, Marcus was nearing nine o'clock.

Having read the situation moments earlier, Walt was now cutting across the grass from three o'clock. Marcus did the same from nine o'clock. The two men walked in a straight line toward one another until they found themselves standing at the center of the park, face to face.

His beauty is as real as his handshake and his smile.

"Walter Yeager," said the former Georgia football player.

"Marcus Coleman," said the former UCLA cheerleader.

"Now," said Walt, taking a step or two back. "First impressions, okay?"

It's him! It's him! It's him! It's him! It's him! It's him! It's him! More beautiful than—

"Okay," said Marcus with a calm smile. Walt's face raised and drew backward, his eyes narrowing. Marcus' face lowered and leaned in closer, his eyes widening.

Keep it together. Don't be a retard now.

"Marcus," said Walt, his half-smile belying the bewilderment in his eyes. "*Do* we know each other?"

How? Can? This? Be?

"We've never met," said Marcus, unable to censor the silly grin on his face. "At least not in this lifetime. Unless you've seen me?"

"No, I'd remember you," said Walt, his head recoiling to better assess the situation. "I'm pretty sure we've never met ... I *knew* I didn't know you." He inhaled, then exhaled with great relief. Their mutual nervous laughter confirmed that they were strangers. "Sometimes the mind ..." said Walt. "For a second, on the phone in Chicago, I had this weird kind of déjà vu. How strange is that?"

"Very," chimed Marcus.

"So you were looking for me," said Walt, a statement of fact. "Here I am."

"Just like that, Santa Claus comes to town," said Marcus, letting out a laugh that could have been mistaken for cocky. "Mind if we sit over there?" He indicated a small cluster of stone picnic tables on the east side of the park.

"As I stated," said Walt, moving toward the tables, "I had to be around, and I figured the only way to know if I truly knew you was to meet you. So what'd ya want?"

"I guess the phone call was kinda weird, huh?" said Marcus, cringing.

"No kidding," said Walt. "Is your nickname Bear or Bearcat?"

Marcus hesitated, hoping to reach their destination before spilling his guts.

"And I'm guessing you're having trouble with some guy?" asked Walt. "It's none of my business. I just hope I didn't inconvenience you. Did you go to Georgia?"

"Not exactly," said Marcus. "When you were at a quarterback at Georgia—"

"Hold on." Walt froze and waited for something to happen. When it didn't, he sighed with relief. "Sorry, earthquakes. Thought for a second." He reclaimed his cool, then kept moving.

"Do you remember," said Marcus, "a season opener on a rainy Saturday night in Georgia, prime time ABC?"

"The UCLA game," said Walt.

"Funny, I call it the Georgia game," said Marcus. "Remember what happened that night? Anything about it?"

In the waning seconds of the game, Georgia's Charlie Dean picked off a Rick Neuheisel pass to halt UCLA's potential game-winning drive, and the 86,000 Bulldawg faithful erupted as one in the pouring rain as Dean turned the interception into a touchdown and Georgia victory.

"I was there," said Marcus as they found themselves between two stone picnic tables. "I was a Bruin."

"You played on the team?" asked Walt.

"I cheered for the team," said Marcus.

"Really," said Walt, unable to hide the shock of finding out the tall, athletic black man was a former cheerleader. Walt decided to sit on the stone bench behind him, elbows resting on his knees, eyes focused straight ahead.

"I saw your picture in the game program around that time," said Marcus. "I've always wanted to write a story inspired by the beauty of the man in the photo. A story about a handsome blond quarterback and a black cheerleader and how they met the weekend of the game, fell in love and had a lifetime of wacky adventures in football and filmmaking—that's my dream career in that life, screenwriting."

Walt remained motionless, staring at the dunes in the distance.

"I had to be in Chicago for my first and only time," said Marcus. "I thought we both might get a kick out of acknowledging that I remembered you after all this time. So I looked you up on the Net. That's where you came in, this morning."

"It's funny," said Walt, allowing himself a mild laugh. "I watched a football game on TV this morning for the first time in years, pretty ironic."

"I hope it's not too ironic to find out the person who had a non-stalking, secret crush on your photo all these years was a man," said Marcus.

"I've been exposed to homosexuality," said Walt. The thought hung in the air like dead weight. "And it is somewhat flattering," he added.

"I haven't known anything about you all these years," said Marcus in his own defense.

"I understand," said Walt, shifting positions on the bench.

"And I'm not implying anything about you or your life," said Marcus, "or who you are."

"I get that," said Walt, sounding rather calm for a man in his situation.

"It's not every day a guy gets a phone call outta the blue from someone who was captivated by your photograph 21 years ago," said Marcus, sitting atop the stone picnic table opposite Walt.

"As I stated, I'm somewhat flattered," said Walt, more focused on the near-by playground, which was crowded, even for a Saturday.

"My mind was a little fried from the travel when I called," said Marcus. "I was so out of it, I thought I heard you say, '*Bearcat is your name, right?*'"

"That was: '*Bear? Did I catch your name right?*'" said Walt. "The reception was lousy, I'll give you that. I was in the midst of some construction commotion, trying to deal with some defective nails at my former junior high school."

"Is *that* what was twisted?" asked Marcus.

"Did I call something twisted?" laughed Walt. "Could be. A lot of them were."

"Maybe it was all a big misunderstanding!" said Marcus, feeling stupidity and relief. And a little less insane than previously feared. "I thought you meant *I* was twisted."

"Why would I say that?" asked Walt, letting out a mild laugh.

"To top it all off," said Marcus. "I kept hearing you ask the other person you were talking to: *when you coming home?* So I was extremely confused for a second."

Walt stopped laughing. "What other person?"

"And each time I heard you ask that," said Marcus, "I got this strange feeling in my gut. Like you were talking to me, and I was supposed to answer because you really wanted to know when *I* was coming home."

"To Malibu," said Walt, the words erupting from some unknown origin. "*When you coming home to Malibu? I love Malibu and you.*" He stood up. "That's what I kept hearing *you* say! I was trying to figure it out all morning. It drove me nuts! You have a very deep and distinctive voice on the phone—intimidating to some people, I'm sure—but anyway, I couldn't get your voice out of my head."

"Really?" asked Marcus.

"Not that I was thinking about it much," said Walt in his own defense, "but I was trying to remember what you said. Or what I thought I heard you say between the reception breaking up. That was it! *When you coming home to Malibu? I love Malibu. I love Malibu and you!*"

"That's what I thought you were saying to *me*," said Marcus.

"We both heard bits and pieces that sounded like that, talk about crazy," said Walt. "Bear, I tell ya."

There was a rumble in every direction.

"Did you just say Bear?" asked Marcus. "Or boy?"

Walt turned to him abruptly, his face strained with bewilderment. "I don't know."

The rumble turned into a roar. The oval park turned into a disc that tilted and swayed from side to side. On the swing set, children flew toward the heavens. On the merry-go-round, frenetic bodies flew out of orbit and were sent spinning into the gathering dust. In the sandbox, a golden brown boy and a golden blond boy were huddled in their own world, seemingly nonplussed by the change in gravity.

Our powers are amazing.

What do you want to play?

Whatever you want to play. You know that's the way we do it.

I wanna play whatever you wanna play, that's why I showed up.

The park righted itself almost as quickly as it had taken them for a ride.

"Was that just me?" asked Marcus, gasping for air.

"You tell me," said Walt, also gasping for air. "You live here."

Their eyes locked, their lungs calmed. They looked around them. The park was running at regular speed, the population of their panic ... two.

"That *had* to be a quake," Walt and Marcus said together.

"How can no one else be running around screaming their heads off?" asked Walt. "It can't be just you and I—first this weird telephone mix-up in Chicago, then a few hours later, this quake that no one around us felt in California? What—we're supposed to have entered some cosmic dimension?"

Marcus laughed because it was funny and because it sounded more rational than anything he could come up with on his own.

"Where were you calling from in Chicago?" asked Walt. "I thought I heard a woman screaming."

"She was singing," said Marcus, "an old Belinda Carlisle song."

"What song?" asked Walt.

"Actually, one of my favorites of hers," said Marcus, "called 'World Without You.'"

"Who was singing?" asked Walt, "if you don't mind my asking."

"Belinda Carlisle," repeated Marcus. "My alarm clock went off accidentally."

"Oh, I thought ..." Walt paused, "never mind. I thought maybe that was one of *our* songs or something, since someone was singing for you at that moment—but obviously you didn't hire the ex-lead singer of the Go-Go's. Forget I said it."

"We have our songs," said Marcus. "We probably have at least 500 songs—in my daydreams, of course. But that's not one of them. 'In a World Without You' by Belinda Carlisle? No, definitely not. At least as far as I can remember. We are talking 21 years of ... memories here."

The look on Walt's face was far from judgmental, but it also said, *I have never met anyone like you.* "How far along is this story of yours?" asked Walt.

"I've been writing it in my mind all these years," said Marcus. "Recently I started putting it all down on paper, a sketchy rough draft, more or less."

"Does the couple have a fight in Chicago?" asked Walt.

"I never imagined it," said Marcus. "Why?"

"Do they have a house in Malibu, by chance?" asked Walt. "It's just down the road from here, right?"

"About 30-35 miles straight down the coast," said Marcus, sounding a bit sheepish. "And yes, the famous version of you and me has a dream house in Malibu. On this beautiful ridge overlooking the beach. It's similar to my all-time favorite house on Pacific Coast Highway, modest but big enough—white adobe, great balconies and decks."

"What else have you imagined, if you don't mind?" asked Walt.

"The kind of life and relationship I envisioned having someday with a buddy whose inner and outer beauty matched that of the Georgia quarterback in the picture: a relationship built on camaraderie, trust and a sense of adventure; a relationship full of wild and crazy times for a college cheerleader and a college quarterback; a relationship between two great kids who both grew into awesome, mature adults and came out to the world and dealt with the mass hysteria like true heroes for the entire universe. That's all. And I'm not saying you're that man, just the man in the photo who inspired the man. And the dream."

"You don't have to keep reassuring me," said Walt.

"I want you to understand, talking to the real-life Walt was never part of the equation, realistically anyway," said Marcus.

"I don't even remember taking the picture that year," said Walt, "or what I looked like."

"You were wearing a pale yellow polo shirt," said Marcus. "It was a full-color picture. You were only visible from the chest up ... with this handsome half-smile and bright smiling eyes."

"No offense," said Walt, "but I've had three strange occurrences today, and you're part of two of them."

"The phone call and the tremors," said Marcus. "What was the other one?"

"Watching a college football game for the first time in years," said Walt.

"So in a way, I was part of all three strange things," said Marcus, prompting both men to scan their surroundings in anticipation of another quake.

"This is kinda crazy of us, don't you think?" asked Walt.

"For one of the few times in my life, I don't know what to say." Marcus fell silent and waited for the quarterback to call the play.

"Tell me what happens in this story of yours," said Walt.

"You don't want to hear all that, do you?" said Marcus, his grin betraying his protest. "It's syrupy and crazy and—"

"Great!" said Walt. "Crazy seems to be the order of the day."

"I was a romantic fool in another life," said Marcus. "I was young and innocent with all these headstrong dreams, daydreams and fantasies. *That* Marcus is the one you need to contact. He's the one who produced all this."

"Well," said Walt, "maybe *that* guy can tell us what the fuck is going down—pardon my French."

"What if it all has to do with earthquakes and cosmic dimensions?" asked Marcus, trying to keep things light-hearted.

"I can't think of a better way to find out, can you?" asked Walt. "Tell me about your story. Does it have a name?"

"*Walt Loves the Bearcat.*"

"You're using *my real name?*" asked Walt.

"Walt is a great name, Walter," said Marcus. "It has to be Walt. Walt is so strong, so true. Both Walt and Walter are strong and true."

"But never Wally," warned Walt.

"Never!" said Marcus. That this man wasn't the Wally-type was merely a truth Marcus had always possessed. No fantasizing. No daydreaming. Just true. But the last few hours had been strange enough, so he kept quiet about his soul's intuition.

"So what happens to this Walt and this Bearcat?" asked Walt.

Having done his part, the quarterback returned to the bench and waited for the cheerleader to begin.

3

The Aspirin Incident

The year was 1983. Madonna was not Like a Virgin yet, just on the Borderline. Prince was cruising in a Little Red Corvette and had yet to baptize the world in his Purple Rain. And the king of the day, without needing an official proclamation, was Michael Jackson, who was providing a Thriller of a reality shift in how we felt music, especially on that other fascinating new reality shift, MTV.

Politically, the country had agreed to let President Reagan do anything he wanted, as long as we saw him awake in a few meetings from time to time, and as long as he kept us feeling good about being strong Americans again after the international bitch-slapping the USA's pride took during the previous administration. There were whispers and jokes that some of the nation's citizens were being neglected, or failing altogether to feel any of Reagan's trickle-down economics, but the country was too busy getting high off of savings and loans and cocaine to really care. As long as Grandfather Ronnie kept the Commies and evildoers at bay.

And in sports ... professional athletes were starting to make "serious money," as more and more jocks were crossing over to careers and endeavors the guys of the leather helmet days could only dream of. Years before, shooting stars like Joe Namath and Jim Brown had paved the way for athletes marketing themselves as entities to be parlayed into ventures as diverse as pantyhose commercials and black cowboy movies. The 80s, in its toddler stage, was beginning to see an even greater sea-change, as more and more athletes were crossing over to careers and endeavors Joe Namath and Jim Brown could only dream of.

Magic Johnson and Larry Bird were building an East Coast/West Coast rivalry that would save the NBA and create global superstars able to sell and be anything to anybody anywhere in the world as we knew it. The NFL was abuzz with talk of brand new stadiums to replace barely old stadiums in order to take advantage of the nascent concept of luxury boxes, club seats and personal seat licenses. And television, led by the sometimes amateurish Entertainment and Sports Programming Network, was putting more TV cameras on more sporting events than ever before. As a result, college and pro athletes in all sports dreamed dreamier dreams. Football players started asking for *big* salaries. Basketball players dreamed of living even larger, demanding *bigger* salaries. And thanks to a black athlete named Curt Flood—who dared to dream the *biggest*—baseball players had been emancipated altogether. By 1983, some professional athletes were earning over a cool and dreamy one million dollars.

Life was on the move in every single way possible.

Of course, none of this was going through the mind of Marcus Coleman—our fearless main character's name—that first and fateful night that Walt met the Bearcat, Marcus' eventual nickname. That night, the new wave music was way too loud, the living room of the antebellum mansion too packed, and Marcus' senses were already overwhelmed by the fact that he was the only black man at a raging, all-white frat party in the Deep South. It was his first time ever below the Mason-Dixon line, and he wasn't even sure of the name of the frat. Phi Hang a Negro, for all he knew. Kappa Kappa Konfederate flag, perhaps.

UCLA was opening the 1983 football season on the road against Georgia, a powerhouse program only a few months removed from the three most glorious years in school history. All-Everything running back Herschel Walker had just trampled through the Southeastern Conference for three seasons, during which Georgia had won one national championship and lost only three games. Walker had forgone his senior season to make a million dollars a year for "personal services" to Donald Trump and his New Jersey Generals in the upstart United States Football League, but Athens and the rest of the Peach State were still high on the fumes of success.

They weren't the only ones. The UCLA spirit squad had been pointing to the trip since their first spring meeting. "We're going to Georgia, we're going to Georgia!" they told one another, their parents, their friends, anyone who'd listen. "Saturday night in September, primetime, national television, ABC, we're there!"

Oh, Walt, I can't do this without your help.

You've always had it.

"*Whoa, stop right there,*" said Walt from the stone picnic table in Oxnard, California. "Another tremor?"

"I don't know," said Marcus from the opposite stone picnic table in Oxnard, California. "Kinda felt one, too."

"This is weird," said Walt. "Onward." He gripped the bench underneath him, knuckles tightly wrapped around the edge.

"Since I do want the story to be a movie someday," said Marcus, "why not think of it all happening like a movie? Or a really wacky novel with a warm and fuzzy message of hope?"

"I think your novel or movie might be better if the quarterback wasn't from Georgia," said Walt. "Maybe he could go to USC. That might work better. But it's your story. Just a suggestion."

"I promise to consider it," said Marcus. "Can I tell you about my daydreams first? Then, if there's anything you want me to cut out, delete or edit out of any book or movie, it's as good as gone. You have my word. I'm open to whatever Walt wants."

"Deal," said Walt.

"So, if you're ready," said Marcus, "cut to the song 'What I Like About You' by the Romantics, the kick-ass dance tune that was quickly becoming one of *the* new wave party anthems of that time. Our time."

... The Bruin cheerleaders stood in a cluster, watching Southern frat boys carrying mugs of beer high over their heads, Southern frat boys consuming large quantities of alcohol through funnels, and Southern belles trying their best to look appealing and aloof to those same Southern frat boys. The cheergirls didn't have to do much to secure party invites on the road, which was why all 16 members of the UCLA spirit squad were standing in a frat house on a Friday night in Athens, Georgia, 24 hours before their primetime debut. (The guys on the squad weren't fools. They accepted the fact that people included them because they came with the package. They were experts at riding the girls' tails—*er*—coattails.)

Marcus was the only black brother in a fraternity back home, but being the only *Negro* at an all-white frat party in the South was a dicey prospect. As far as he knew, no one had ever been lynched near UCLA because of the color of their skin, and his frat did have two Asians and two Latinos to round out the rainbow coalition. This party, however, was lily-white except for him and the two black girls on the squad.

"Stay with the group," admonished Jenny, his tall, brunette stunt partner. They had become close since practice started in August. Trust is a good thing when you're throwing someone in the air and she's counting on you to catch her each and every time.

"I heard you before," said Marcus. "And the time before that."

"We're *all* sticking together," said Holly, a redhead with a permanent stern expression. To some, she was a perfectionist, to others, a bitch.

"You think I'm a fool?" Marcus bobbed his head to the music and scanned the boys—of course, not *too* much. He was, after all, deep in the closet and on foreign soil. And being thoroughly scrutinized. All around the cheerleaders, young Georgians gawked as if in the company of Hollywood celebrities. This kind of "fishbowl" existence was old news for the vets on the squad. At hallowed places like Notre Dame and Michigan, where snowdrifts ruled over beach tans, it was easy to feel like a zoo animal, especially around the male students salivating over the California Girls Exhibit.

"What position you play, guy?" slobbered a voice in Marcus' ear. A drunken frat boy was so close, they could have kissed. He had dark hair and a smooth, narrow face.

"Cheerleader," yelled Marcus over the music. The drunken Reb laughed, then eyed the rest of the males in the California contingent. They were all white and in good shape, but they weren't 6'4", 215 pounds and black. And mistaken for a football player almost every day of their lives. Drunken Reb shot him a brief glare of suspicion, then took a swig from his beer bottle.

"So y'all got *quizzes* out there?" he asked.

"*Quizzes*? What school doesn't?" asked Marcus. "What kind of *quizzes* do y'all have?"

"You know, fruitcakes, fairies," said Homophobic Reb.

"Oh," said Marcus. "You can't get rid of *queers*. They're everywhere."

If he was going to be a straight frat rat, at least he was going to be a straight frat rat who didn't downgrade gays. Anymore. Most of the time.

Homophobic Reb started rambling about California Girls, but Marcus tuned him out. Matter of fact, everything *but* Marcus' body left the conversation. His eyes found a group of eight football players, all white, all unfamiliar, and all momentarily paused just inside the doorway. Their presence captured the room. Some sort of rebel yell went up, but the players barely acknowledged the gesture. They looked attractive, confident and proud, their skin tanned from the summer just passed. Their shoulders were broad, their pecs firm under preppy shirts. Marcus scanned their faces, which was easy to do since, even though they were at polar opposite ends of the room, many of them were close to his height, especially ...

And then I saw him ...

As if by magic, the most beautiful, captivating, stunning, pure and godly image of a man stared into his eyes, peering deep into his soul. Everything about him was so perfect and perfectly in place: the right amount of radiant, youthful hair; the right amount of distinctive yet soft facial features; the right amount of gold poured into his golden skin; the right amount of love beaming from his smiling eyes, which never wandered from his own and instantly became eyes that would peer into the far reaches of his soul forever. One glimpse. One glance. One moment was all that was necessary to see the exact opposite of his reflection, yet the perfect duplicate of his soul.

He's so perfect, whispered something from inside, softly, without a trace of doubt. The words echoed back, just as softly, and sounded like, *You're so perfect.*

But the message got twisted inside his very fallible brain.

Me *perfect?* You're *perfect! Or is that, perfectly put together?*

Perfect was not a word his star-struck soul had ever used on himself, only others, so the other man, who was already known to be perfect, became not *perfect,* but *perfectly put together,* as if to achieve a calculated effect that essentially said, "I'm perfect and you're not." And so the star-struck soul glanced away, remembered who he was, and decided that perfect was simply out of reach.

"It's a lot of hard work," Holly was saying, bringing Marcus back to the frat party, mind, body and soul. She was schooling Homophobic Reb on the rigors of college cheerleading, but Marcus needed to see *those eyes* again. When he found them, they were still peering into his soul, wider but smiling less, then less even more. Marcus turned away, head and all. Moments later, he was there again, and so was the perfect one. But this time not in sync. Others commanded their focus with collegiate folly, requiring them to look away, then glance back when afforded the opportunity. They began dancing, eyes only, at various tempos. Stare deep, get bashful, then look away. Peek again, laugh while pretending it's something someone else said. But there was no one else. This was a *pas de deux* of the pupils—pupils who knew they were destined for a rendezvous but didn't know *how* to rendezvous.

Their friends would help solve the problem. The Georgia football players and the UCLA cheerleaders became aware of one another instantly, but no move was made by either group to acknowledge the other. Duran Duran was singing about a Reflex. The natural reflex of tomorrow's opponents was to circumnavigate the party in what *appeared* to be opposite directions: clockwise. By the time the players arrived at three o'clock, the cheerleaders were nearing nine o'clock. The room was just big enough so that each group could feign aloofness yet check for reactions. But there was also the matter of the rest of the party, which now had two sets of stars to orbit. The focus of energy on these two clusters of stars sent both galaxies spiraling toward the center of the room, eventually causing a merging of the galaxies into one—players and cheerleaders together—surrounded by a fraternity party.

Conversations swirled in the new constellation—questions about Hollywood, shoptalk with some Georgia cheerleaders who were also there—until Marcus found himself standing next to the one who mattered more than anything else around them. It was a miracle they found each other at all, because during the last moments of the merge, each man became invisible to the other. The only reason they knew they were standing next to one another now was because each man could feel the presence of *him*.

They remained speechless as the chaos ensued around them. Teammates, cheermates, frat boys and sorority girls dipped in and out of their consciousness like comets and asteroids, never commandeering their focus for long. Life became about the space between them. But these were two nascent stars when it came to revealing their deepest dreams to another soul. They had no idea what to say. Still, they hung in there, never leaving one another's side. They'd both played eye contact games with others before and lost, but this time, nothing was gonna stop them now. It felt too right to walk away, and eventually, their persistence paid off.

"Walter," said the Georgia football player.

"Marcus," said the UCLA cheerleader.

"*Whoa, stop right there*," said Walt from the stone picnic table in Oxnard, California.

"What'd I do now?" asked Marcus from the opposite stone picnic table in Oxnard, California.

"It's *weird* hearing you use my name," said Walt, staring at the dunes in the distance. "I didn't say, 'Hi, my name's Walter.' Your dream man did. This could get confusing. Can't you call me something else? Elway. Favre. I don't know. Boomer Esiason. I'm joking, call me what you want."

"In my dreams, you said your name was Walter," said Marcus. "I took you at your word from word one."

"Walter is fine," said Walt. "Most people call me Walt, so *Walter* can be your dream guy, cool?"

"Cool," said Marcus, barely suppressing his grin.

"But what about you?" asked Walt. "Are you going to be Marcus? I don't know if that feels right. When do you become this Bearcat?"

"At the Sugar Bowl," said Marcus.

"The Sugar Bowl?" laughed Walt. "Georgia didn't go to the Sugar Bowl that year."

"In my dreams Georgia did," said Marcus. "Hail Larry dropped the touchdown pass that blew it for Auburn."

"Hail Larry?" laughed Walt. "Who's Hail Larry?"

"You'll see," said Marcus. "*You* started that."

"Me?" said Walt. "If he played at a different school—" Then it dawned on Walt. "In your dreams, in the pros, Walter throws this Larry a Hail Mary touchdown pass, right?"

"If I tell you now, it'll spoil it," said Marcus.

"You brought up his name," said Walt.

"Because you doubted getting to the Sugar Bowl in my dreams," said Marcus.

"My bad. I'm still learning the rules here, okay?" said Walt.

"You and me both," said Marcus. "Anyway, to answer your question: the Marcus of my dreams becomes the Bearcat at the Sugar Bowl. Later, he becomes just Bear, for a very good reason, or so we think. I met this guy in a cave—"

"Got it," said Walt. "So *Walter* and *Bear*, even though that's not Marcus' nickname yet, introduce themselves at a Georgia frat party. Take it away."

"So you cheer for the Bruins," said *Walter*. He was looking over *Bear's* shoulder, moving his head to "Now," a rockin' "powerpop" song by the Plimsouls.

"And you play for the Dawgs," said Bear, looking at Walter's thick neck.

"Quarterback," said Walter.

"I know," said Bear.

"Really?" asked Walter. "How?"

"I just knew." Bear looked down to the fuzzy haze of shuffling shoes. The collegiate chaos surrounding them began swirling at a faster pace. The bodies in their periphery interacted with them increasingly, which only served to keep the two young men from talking or making eye contact, but not from feeling one another's presence. And wanting more of that presence in a space minus the chaos. They both searched for ways to reach out, then the topic of football caught their attention, as voices began raving about the school's stadium, specifically, the intimidating crowd noise and the hedges.

"What are the hedges?" asked Bear, looking past a faceless fraternity boy.

"Bushes around the stadium," answered Walter, looking past that same faceless fraternity boy.

"I love stadiums," said Bear. "I used to draw them as a kid all the time. I still doodle them in lectures. I think, in another life, I would have been an architect, just to build stadiums."

"Stadiums can be pretty cool," said Walter.

And so the boys began to communicate through others, for had they been forced to gaze so deeply into one another's eyes at that party, during the birth of their souls' common journey, their undeniably magnetic attraction would have been instantly exposed. So they kept in verbal contact only. But after a precious few moments, they heard the stirrings of teammates and cheermates on the move, mentioning words like "making it an early night." This was the boys' two-minute warning: the other soul that felt so good was about to vanish.

"I feel a headache coming on," said Bear, looking in the vicinity of Walter's eyes. "Would you happen to know of a drugstore that's open late?"

"Probably," shrugged Walter, looking straight ahead.

"Mind showing me where it is?" asked Bear.

"Sure."

A conspiracy was born. No other plans were needed. They were going to find themselves a drugstore, Bear figured, then find themselves a secluded hilltop and talk under the starry Georgia night. Were they going to do more than talk? Oh, yes, indeed, much, much more! Bear was going to somehow confess his attraction and pray a similar confession would come boomeranging right back at him. Maybe they would seal their mutual fate with a meaningful handshake. Maybe, if Bear were really lucky, a long, tender hug. And in his wildest of wildest dreams, just maybe, Walter had the courage to initiate a kiss. No matter what, they were going to walk back down that hilltop as buddies, not opponents. The details would work themselves out. Or so Bear dreamed.

"Time to go, Coleman," said Holly. "Back to that crappy guest dorm for some sleep."

Bear nodded casually toward Walter and said, "He's gonna take me to get some aspirin." Then he stood poised, waiting for Holly to turn on her heels and leave them be. Instead, the referee known as God threw a yellow flag skyward and blew a whistle so loud, the music stopped.

"I've got aspirin in my purse at the dorm," declared a female voice.

Thank you, Jenny, the considerate brunette stunt partner of one Marcus "Bear" Coleman. She had swooped in like a meteor, detonating the hopes of two souls who had yet to dream of a Plan B.

"Perfect," barked Sergeant Holly with a smug, knowing smile. Bear made vague eye contact with Walter, who remained mute. To do anything other than separate would have meant revealing themselves to be a quarterback and a cheerleader in the midst of a covenant they themselves didn't fully understand.

"Thanks for the offer, anyway," said Bear to Walter.

"Sure," said Walter to Bear.

The gravity that held them together for most of the night evaporated. Before they had a chance for anything more, they found themselves in alternate galaxies once again.

"THAT KINDA BITES," SAID WALT from the stone picnic table in Oxnard, California, "getting torn apart like that."

"How does all this make you feel so far?" asked Marcus from the opposite stone picnic table in Oxnard, California.

"What's with the celestial bodies and orbits?" asked Walt, dodging the question.

"Dunno," said Marcus. "It just kinda came out of me that way. I never thought of it like that before. Or to be accurate, I've never articulated these dreams to another soul. You're pretty much getting an exclusive. Meeting you is affecting my dreams, I know that."

"I have to admit something." Walt paused, then called an audible. "*Nah.*"

"What?" insisted Marcus.

"I can see myself back there," said Walt. "I feel it. Kind of like a home movie of something I haven't thought about in years, know what I mean? You do, don't you? And you've never done this before?"

"I've had other dreams in my life, sure," said Marcus. "Dreams are what keep us alive, from the standard 'orphaned child in a new and improved family,' to scoring the winning touchdown in the big game."

"Do I do that?" asked Walt. "Sorry, does *Walter* do that?"

"If I told you now, that would spoil it," said Marcus. "How much fun would a big game be, if you knew the creator of the game had already decided the outcome?"

Walt emitted a short laugh that sounded more like a *ha!* Then he rubbed his face as if to wash away the weariness. "I'm starting to get the feeling I can't win with you," said Walt.

"What do you mean?" asked Marcus, giggling. "Do you want to know that, in the near future, you throw an unforgettable, 99-yard pass when you're in Atlanta for the Super Bowl? Do you want to know that for a fact before the actual pass? Or now? You'd miss living in the moment, the rush, the sudden shocking twist to the game, the spontaneous combustion that comes from moments that end up becoming headlines, like: DEAN'S INTERCEPTION STEALS UCLA's HOPES."

"When you put it that way," said Walt with a mild laugh. "I did have the talent back then. I was the top-rated quarterback in America coming out of high school my senior year."

"There's no doubt in my mind that's what Bear and I both saw in you," said Marcus. "Greatness."

"You hungry, by the way?" asked Walt, dodging the compliment.

"No, surprisingly," said Marcus.

"No kidding," said Walt. "Normally I'd be starving by now—don't tell me, this is another weird phenomenon?"

Marcus laughed. "Time does seem to ... I don't know ..."

"... go by differently," said Walt. The sun above was still in afternoon mode, the park less crowded than before. Not that it mattered. When they talked, the rest of the world faded into the blurry background.

"You're pretty easy to talk to," said Marcus, "especially considering."

"I keep seeing this image," said Walt, again dodging the compliment. "It's of you and me at the stadium. During a game, there's no way I would ever go near a male cheerleader. I'm sorry if that sounds callous, but that was just my mindset at that time, if you want me to be honest."

"I only want you to be honest with me," said Marcus.

"Cool," said Walt, moving onward. "I'm much more open-minded now, but we'll get into that some other time. Getting back to Walter and the Bear ..."

"It's just Bear," said Marcus, "not *the* Bear."

"You'll never hear it out of my mouth again," said Walt. "So why do I get the feeling Bear's hoping Walter will come and spring him out of that guest dorm?"

"Maybe because Bear knows the chances of him and Walter interacting during the game are virtually nil," said Marcus.

"Maybe Walter should be in my little red sports car from back then," said Walt.

"Oh yeah?" said Marcus, grinning ear to ear. "Like the car you rented?"

"I'm not trying to alter your dream," said Walt, "just offering a suggestion for your story—use it or don't, doesn't matter to me."

"I'm open to anything you suggest," said Marcus. "Daydreams are like ever-changing landscapes anyway, just like real life. New truths come along and alter your landscape, especially when you review things under a microscope."

"Or in the instant replay booth in football," said Walt.

"Maybe that's why I like to call it *upon further reveal*," said Marcus.

Walt let out a mild laugh. "But that would be cool if you gave me my little red sports car."

"Whatever Walt wants," said Marcus.

THE 16 MEMBERS OF THE UCLA SPIRIT SQUAD were so close, even the subtlest mood changes became everybody's business. This was, after all, the start of the yearlong cheerleading season and the honeymoon period where everyone went around asking "how are you?" with such sincerity. By Thanksgiving, that very same phrase would be hijacked by anyone wanting to mimic and attack any person on the squad who still possessed a sunny disposition. But during Labor Day weekend in the Peach State at the start of football season, all was bliss. Until Bear was pissed.

"He was trying to meet some girl," said Jenny. "That's why he's being such a sourpuss." She stuck a finger in Bear's ear as she spooned his backside. They were on his twin bed in what amounted to a guest dorm on the Georgia campus.

"Coleman's sulking because of some chick at the party?" asked Drew Miles, who was on his own bed, flipping through the game program. He was the hardbodied captain of the squad and Bear's roommate for the night.

"I am not sulking," said Bear. "If anything, it's these sorry accommodations."

"Poor baby." Sergeant Holly, who was practically sitting on his head, pinched his cheek.

"Come on, Bear, smile," said White Donna. She was hovering between the beds, eyeing him through the lens of a camera.

"Thought he was gonna get a little Southern Hospitality," teased Black Donna. She was sitting on Bear's legs, her large chocolate gymnast ass weighing heavily on his knees.

On the way back to the guest dorm, Bear had found out that Sergeant Holly and Jenny hadn't bought the aspirin jig for a second. "I saw that look in your eyes," Jenny had told him as they walked through the night. "You and that gorgeous blond guy were going to go off and get into some kind of trouble, probably go meet some Donna Summers' Bad Girls, huh?" He had said yes, like a guilty husband. "I knew it!" she had exclaimed. Now, the few squad members still awake were having the time of their lives, ridiculing his futile attempt to score the night before the big game.

"I could see the headlines tomorrow," said Sergeant Holly, "CHEERLEADER MISSING."

"*That's the night that his lights went out in Georgia,*" sang Black Donna. "*That's the night that they hung an innocent ... Bruin.*"

"One more shot to capture this incident," said White Donna. "The Aspirin Incident."

"This dorm sucks. I would have been fine," said Bear, playing up the curmudgeon act to hide his true frustration.

"Then smile!" said White Donna. Bear and the three cheergirls on his bed paused long enough for the flash to flash and the camera to click, then untangled themselves.

"One more," said White Donna.

"No more!" growled Bear, grabbing his toiletries and heading for the bathroom down the hall. "FYI, when I get back, I'm getting naked."

"Night, party pooper," said Jenny.

"*Rightbackatcha,*" said Bear, disappearing into the hallway. Once in the men's bathroom, he brushed his teeth and dreamed of running into Walter at tomorrow night's game. The notion gave him a sudden chill—didn't feel right. He imagined Walter glancing his way with vague recognition, then turning away. He imagined himself doing the same in all likelihood. He was bold, but that bold?

Just then, he heard a faint rattle to his right, giving him a start. An arm reached into one of the tall, vertical windows in the bathroom, a golden blond arm, shaking a tiny tin box of aspirin. Bear spit up a mouthful of toothpaste into his hands, then quickly rinsed the rest of the Crest away. When he reached the waist-high window, the quarterback on the other side put his hand to his own mouth, as if to silence the home crowd. Bear obeyed, then followed the quarterback's prompt to sneak through the window. It was narrow, but nothing was gonna stop them now. With Walter's help, Bear's big prototype athlete body made it through to the other side, a landscaped grounds full of magnolia trees.

Together they ran a sweep to the right, Walter out in front, Bear following. Ahead, two alley cats crossed their path, left to right, giving Walter and Bear a start—Walter flinching backward, Bear flinching forwards. Once the cats were passed, they started to run again, but Walt slowed things down with his hand when he saw a dark-haired man walking two small dogs past a little red sports car near the sidewalk. A bicyclist passed the dogs at the axis of the car, but after the passing ships were a sufficient distance away, Walter said *now* and took off. Bear followed, to the little red sports car, upon further reveal.

"Hop in," said Walter. He was standing over the driver's side, Bear, the passenger's side.

"Where we going?" asked Bear.

"Wanna know now or when we get there?" asked Walter.

Bear laughed, all giddy, then looked around to make sure this wasn't a dream. "Is it unlocked?"

"Get in." Walter started up the engine as Bear closed the passenger door. "If you want a fast getaway," Walter told Bear as they took off, "ya gotta leave the doors unlocked. A free tip on this very quick tour. I've got literally minutes to do this."

"Do what?" giggled Bear.

Like I care. I'll just enjoy the rush of being in a car with you, going anywhere. I'll take you there.

"What's the one thing in Athens you'd rather see than anything else this weekend?" asked Walter.

"You throwing a long bomb under the night lights of Sanford Stadium," said Bear. Walter let out a series of breaths that sounded like the suppressed laughter of a young boy who had suppressed his laughter for far too long. Bear tugged at the shirt covering his own chest, as if to free up more space for a heart bursting with joy. "Not that I'm saying I want you guys to win," said Bear, clarifying his wish.

"Understood." Walter reached into the tiny compartment behind the seats. "Generals and Majors," an upbeat, peppy new wave song by a group called XTC was playing on the radio. A football appeared near the vicinity of Bear's ear, like a magic trick. "I can't guarantee seeing me throw a long bomb *tomorrow* night," said Walter, playfully tossing the ball with his golden blond hand. "Tonight, you just might be in luck."

"You're taking me to see the stadium," said Bear, statement of fact. "We saw it coming back from dinner—it's all lit up." He laughed incredulously. "We're going there, man? Really?"

"We're going there, man," said Walter. "Is that cool?"

"Ah, Walter." Giddy laughter trickled out of Bear. "Thanks, man, thanks. Man ... thanks."

They came to a stoplight at a dark intersection on campus. An ambulance and a cop car raced by, right to left. After they disappeared, Walter looked both ways, then accelerated forward, even though the light was still red. "I'm not a big red-light runner normally, but my time is limited."

"How are you even out like this?" asked Bear. "You guys stay in a hotel the night before a game, right?"

"Correct," said Walter. The little red sports car swung around a corner. The outside world blurred by. "I snuck out of this old movie house. We see something supposedly inspirational before every game. Those players you saw me with at the party—we all ditched the movie and we gotta sneak back in before Rambo's final death blow to some helpless wimp who's about to die."

"How much time is that?" asked Bear.

"Not much," said Walter.

"I don't want to cause you any trouble," said Bear.

"Not to worry. I got it all under control," said Walter.

"How did you know how to find me?" asked Bear.

"I overheard the redhead," said Walter. "My family made the mistake of staying at that dorm once. But I gotta tell you, I just got lucky and saw the back of this tall black man passing by the glass doors in the hallway. I was trying to come up with some reason for having the front desk get you down to the lobby. All I could think of was this." He held up the tiny tin box of aspirin. "You want these, by the way?"

"No thanks," said Bear. "Headache's gone."

"I figured they were just watching out for you, like they should down here," said Walter.

"I don't need anybody's protection," said Bear. "Do I? Does stuff still go on here?"

"You have to understand, I'm not from the South," said Walter. "I was born and raised in Chicago. Things are very different here."

"What do you mean?" asked Bear ...

"When I first got there," said Walt, interrupting the story from the stone picnic table in Oxnard, California.

"Something happened?" asked Marcus from the opposite stone picnic table in Oxnard, California.

"I knew from the start I had landed in a whole other world," said Walt. "Man, talk about a culture shock. Playing football in the South and traveling around the Southeastern Conference was like nothing I ever imagined. I couldn't believe some of the things still happening, like segregated showers in the locker room."

"That was 1983," said Marcus. "I thought times had changed."

"This is 1983," said Bear. "Haven't times changed?"

"I don't know," said Walter, cruising in the little red sports car through the dark streets of the Georgia campus. "My eyes have really been opened. Let's just leave it at that for now. I don't want to scare you. I'll tell you stuff some other time."

"You're sure it's okay, you taking this little black cheerboy to the stadium at night?" asked Bear, sounding like a Southerner.

"What say we find out," said Walter. They sped down an elevated roadway adjacent to the stadium, which sat below, as if in a gorge. "If we run into anybody, let me do the talking. Oh, and you're one of my teammates. You definitely fit the part."

Beyond the passenger window, Sanford Stadium beamed like a lit spaceship that was parked for the night. They eyed the 86,000-seat horseshoe, attracting them like an open-ended magnet.

"How does it feel?" asked Walter.

"Like a dream come true," said Bear.

"Not yet." Walter parked and got out of the little red sports car, Bear followed. They climbed over a tall fence—Walter landing on his feet, Bear doing a clumsy tuck and roll. From there, the journey was dark and hasty, some grass at their feet, a concrete tunnel or two, Walter's golden blond hair, signs promoting the Bulldawgs, another hallway or two, Walter's golden blond hair, then suddenly they were inside the enclosed end of the horseshoe, standing in the end zone.

"Amazing," said Bear, star-struck.

"Cool?" asked Walter.

"And dreamy," said Bear, rotating 360 degrees while gazing toward the upper reaches of the stands. "Where's my camera when I need it?"

"I hate to break this up, but I gotta get back," said Walter.

"This is way more than I ever imagined," said Bear.

"Hey, you wanna do a cheer?" asked Walter.

"A cheer?" asked Bear.

"*Nah.*" Walter called an audible. "I still gotta park my car somewhere safe, then get back to the movie house."

"Tell me you're starting tomorrow," said Bear.

"If I had a chance of playing at all tomorrow, no way would I have been at the party." Walter grabbed at the back of his neck and tried to wrangle out a kink. "I was injured in the spring and couldn't compete for the job." He indicated the football in his hand. "So if you wanna see me throw a pass, this is the only guaranteed chance you got."

Bear broke into his announcer's voice: "The Bulldawgs are backed up near their own goal line. Let's see if Walter—what's your last name?"

Walter lined up underneath an imaginary center. "Yeager."

"Let's see if Walter Yeager can get *dem Dawgs* outta trouble," said Bear.

Walter hiked the ball, then dropped back and launched a missile that sailed long and high, torpedoing back to earth near midfield.

"The Dawg receiver snags it!" said Bear. "*Whoa,* nelly, he's going all ... the ... way! Touchdown, Yeager!" He cupped his hands together and made crowd-cheering noises. Walter let out that suppressed boyish laughter again, then Bear stopped himself before he did something really embarrassing like a cheer. "Do it for real someday in the pros and I'll make a movie about you. I'm gonna be a great filmmaker."

"Do it, man," said Walter. "I'm gonna change the world."

"*The Walter Yeager Story,*" imagined Bear.

"Directed by—what's your last name?" asked Walter.

"Coleman," said Bear. "My real name is Marcus, but I've been called Bear for as long as I can remember, for some reason."

"Directed by Bear Coleman." Walter paused, then decided: "Deal."

Bear extended his hand. Walter looked both ways, then extended his. Their first touch was electric, reigniting the radiant smiles not seen since the early moments of the fraternity party. Bells went off, but the bells sounded more like a stuttering police siren, followed by stuttering static from a police bullhorn:

"*Big Norse Yeager, oft-injured Yankee QB, what are you doing down there?*" asked a very drunken and Southern voice from the upper deck of the stadium, just beneath the press box.

"Shit," said Walter.

"What is it?" asked Bear.

"Teammates, with the police—don't worry, it's not serious," said Walter. "The cops'll do anything for us. But I gotta go. I'm really late now. Would you be cool if you—"

"I can make it back on my own," said Bear.

"You sure?" asked Walter. "I feel bad."

"Show me the way—wait, what about the ball?" Bear indicated the football resting near midfield.

"It'll be returned to its rightful owner," said Walter. "The Georgia Athletic Department. Come on."

They weaved their way through the underbelly of the stadium, stopping when they reached the ticket booth outside the closed end of the horseshoe. It was time to split up, Walter to the left, Bear to the right. Walter's plan was for them to circumnavigate opposite sides of the horseshoe, then continue on their separate ways, Walter to the left, Bear to the right.

"Now you understand what to do?" asked Walter.

"Yeah, man, I got it," said Bear. "Thanks for the mini-tour, it was awesome."

"That makes me feel good." Walter started to leave but checked himself. "I won't see you at the game. I'll be way too ... uptight. But a lot of people eat at Snaky Lu's Roadhouse Cafeteria afterwards. Think you might show up?"

"Sure," said Bear, conjuring on the fly. "If that's *the* place. The squad loves going to traditional stuff. That's what road trips are all about."

"Sweet." Walter backed away. "If you show up, I'll show up."

Bear eyed him with a curious smile, then gave him a thumbs up. Walter ran, then turned back.

"Make sure you show up. Cool?" said Walter.

"Cool," said Bear, watching until Walter vanished from sight. The world around him turned dark and unfriendly, the shadows on the concrete surrounding him more ominous than before. He began his own circumnavigation around the right half of the horseshoe, knowing Yeager would already be gone by the time Coleman reached the other side.

"YOU CAN SKIP GOING INTO what happened at the game, if you want," said Walt from the stone picnic table in Oxnard, California. "I barely broke a sweat, no story to tell, for me anyway. How about you?"

"When I walked into that stadium on Saturday night, it was like a dream come true," said Marcus from the opposite stone picnic table in Oxnard, California ...

Sanford Stadium was the center of the entire college football universe that night. This was the very first game of the season for all of college football on national television when national television aired about 10,000 games *less* than they would come to broadcast in future seasons. Coming off three straight years of Ultimate Glory, the Georgia Bulldawgs were the peachiest of programs, and UCLA, well, UCLA was UCLA, a four-letter word that evoked so many California dreams for so many people the world over.

But Bear Coleman knew that whatever Walter Yeager wanted from him, game time was not the time. The Dawgs' backup quarterback had enough on his mind, no doubt. And so did Bear. On top of everything, Mama Rent and her two sisters had driven to the game from Alabama, where they were visiting family. Bear had left their tickets to the game in his room in his fraternity house, 2,000 miles away. Brother Kehela had overnighted them, but so far, the delivery was lost in space. His family, however, did arrive at the dorm guesthouse as planned, just in time for Bear to hug them before giving them the bad news and taking off with the spirit squad for the game.

As the stadium filled up with the Bulldawg faithful, Bear stood in the same end zone from the previous night and imagined his family somehow getting into the sold-out contest. He was also trying to soak up as much atmosphere as possible since pre-game was the best time to appreciate his surroundings. At the moment, that meant taking pictures, with the cheerleaders from both schools, the mascots from both schools, and of course, an actual bulldog named Uga. As pre-game warm-ups came to an end, Bear found himself arm in arm with Harry Dawg, the Georgia mascot who looked like an overgrown football player with a gigantic gray bulldog head. The photo op was about to be captured by White Donna ... until a female voice in the vicinity yelled, "Walter, quick!"

Like a cloud of steadily moving stardust, the entire Georgia football team passed through the end zone, heading for the locker room for their last hurrah before kickoff. Bear's whole world shifted. Again. He turned and caught sight of the blond aura underneath a red helmet 10 yards away. A pretty young female cheerleader from Georgia wrapped her arms around Walter's waist and signaled for a pretty young male cheerleader from Georgia to snap a picture. Walter kept moving and unintentionally knocked the girl off balance. The male cheerleader caught the moment. Walter steadied the girl until she was standing on her own, then he merged with his teammates and vanished.

"Bear, you looked away!" cried White Donna, upset for the ruined photo op with Harry Dawg. "One more."

This time, White Donna got her photo op and a big ole grin from Bear ...

"THE GAME ITSELF WAS HECTIC AND CRAZY," said Marcus from the stone picnic table in Oxnard, California. "It started pouring rain, then there was my ticket crisis. My family did make it into the game—FedEx never came through, but someone from UCLA did—but it all flew by like a swiftly moving dream. There was halftime under the stands to keep dry, then next thing you know, Georgia's Charlie Dean picks off that interception and runs it back for a touchdown. Game over."

"I'll never forget it," said Walt from the stone picnic table in Oxnard, California.

"The thing I remember most," said Marcus, "was the way the whole stadium, minus a handful of Bruins, erupted as Dean ran down the sideline. For a moment, there was no rain, no opponents, no home team, no visitors, just the power of 86,000 humans experiencing the exact same joy at the exact same moment. Everyone rose to their feet with such a spontaneous eruption of pure joy, the stadium practically blasted off like a spaceship. I felt so grateful to experience the moment *in* the moment." Marcus sighed. "Then time expired and what mattered most was the fact that we were soaking wet, 0-1, and our season of dreams was off to a rocky start."

And then there was the matter of Walter Yeager ...

Bear didn't have to convince the squad to go to Snaky Lu's Roadhouse Cafeteria after the game. The challenge, however, was getting there at the right time in light of a host of variables completely out of Bear's control. By the time he arrived at the restaurant, it was past one a.m. He had driven there with his family to rendezvous with the squad, but his mother had gotten lost on dark roads in the middle of nowhere. As they entered Snaky Lu's, the weary squad was settling up their tabs. Had they seen anyone from the game? Bear wondered aloud. "No one from his dreams," was all he inferred from their vague recap. He made plans to rendezvous with them at their next destination—a hotel in Atlanta—then had a late dinner with his family. It wasn't until he was standing in the foyer, preparing to leave, that he saw Walter approaching from the parking lot, his golden blond hair wet from the rain.

"He showed up!" said Bear, unable to suppress his joy.

"Who?" asked Mama Rent, not privy to his deepest dreams.

"He plays for Georgia," said Bear, battening down his emotions.

"There he is," said Walter, entering the restaurant's doors. "You showed up. Cool." The quarterback was joined in the foyer by the blonde female Georgia cheerleader who tried to have her picture taken with him in the end zone. Another girl also crowded her way inside. She was a short, dark-haired girl who didn't look too happy. Bear played the part of UCLA ambassador and introduced his family. Walter introduced the girls, but Bear never heard their names. He was too busy imagining best-case scenarios for the rest of the night while everyone mused about the game, the rain and their plans. To his amazement and his delight, whatever was said worked to his advantage. The final verdict of the exchange in the entryway: his family would head back to Alabama now that the rain was letting up; the girls would get the slices of the pie à la mode they were craving, and Walter would drive Bear to the hotel in Atlanta for his rendezvous with the squad.

But there was one catch, a catch Bear didn't consider until it was too late to conjure up an alternative: the nameless girls and their pie à la modes were coming to Atlanta.

Who *are* they? Bear wondered, sitting in the front seat of the little red sports car while the two females sat all twisted up in the tiny compartment behind them. The blonde cheerleader came off as more of a good friend, but the dark-haired girl seemed to harbor resentment toward everything and everyone, including Walter. "It always pours down raining at the worst times in my life," she said as they took off from the parking lot of Snaky Lu's.

"*You* didn't have to do stunts in the rain tonight," said the blonde.

"I would have, had I tried out for the squad," said the dark-haired girl. Walter turned on the radio and Bear knew it was to give the front seat a better choice of ambiance. A pop station came on. Michael Jackson started to Beat It, and before long, they were flying down the highway toward Atlanta. Walter and Bear didn't say much, just a comment now and then to touch base verbally. "Yeah, I like this song." "Me, too." "It was a good game tonight." "Yeah, it was." "The rain wasn't so bad." "*Nah.*" "Glad it let up now." "Yep." The girls were in their own world, and there wasn't much time until the flight, but Bear possessed a quintessential feeling of well-being anyway.

I'll just enjoy the rush of being in a car with you, going anywhere.

I'll take you there.

The more they saw ATLANTA, the more an uneasiness crept into the front seat of the little red sports car. The boys hadn't uttered one word about keeping in touch, or the meaning of all this hanging out together. Bear had envisioned resolving any lingering mysteries on a hilltop under a starry night—last night. Now they were about to receive yet another two-minute warning, and Bear had no idea if he would get a chance to articulate his desires.

The exit for the hotel came into view. He felt the headache from last night's fraternity party returning and heard an uneasy rustling in the driver's seat.

"Guess this is it," said Walter.

"I'm glad you could show me the stadium," said Bear.

"Glad you liked it," said Walter.

The car slowed at the red stoplight at the bottom of the exit. The girls woke up from a temporary slumber. "It's five in the morning," said the blonde. The squad's wake-up call was at six. Bear had one hour to get some sleep before he had to be an ambassador for UCLA again.

"Where are we?" yawned the dark-haired girl. No one answered. "I hate this song," she added.

"I don't," said Walter.

"I don't either," said Bear. "I love it."

Walter looked both ways, then accelerated onto the thoroughfare and turned up the volume. The song was "True," the melodic ballad by Spandau Ballet, an English group enjoying its time in the sun.

"I never know what they mean," said the dark-haired girl. "Why do they keep saying, 'I think this much is true?' What's true? What do they want to be true? *Soooooo* stupid."

"Listen," said Walter, turning the volume a little louder. "Maybe you'll learn something. Right, Bear?"

"Exactly."

They drove in silence down otherwise empty roads. The lead singer's baritone voice was clear and golden, his lyrics vague and dreamy and backed by a sweet-sounding saxophone. Bear didn't know what the words were supposed to mean any more than the dark-haired girl, but he loved the song anyway, long before tonight, when he knew that now, he would forever be "True."

They pulled into the hotel parking lot as the music faded and the dark-haired girl's whining took over: "I know this is true, I want to tell the truth," she said, full of ridicule. "For Christ's sake, just tell the truth."

"*This* much is true," said Walter, bringing the car to a halt in front of the lobby. "I'm gonna make sure Bear is cool, then take you girls back home, cool?"

Walter and Bear emerged from the little red sports car. Bear's heart palpitated like never before. Walter seemed harried. An 18-wheeler truck passed as he retrieved Bear's bag out of the trunk and made the handoff.

"I guess I need to go find out which room I'm staying in," said Bear, wishing Walter would come with him. "I hope I don't wake up whoever I'm staying with."

"I gotta get them back." Walter nodded to the back window of his car. "They weren't too happy about coming up here in the first place."

The passenger door opened. A female's ass in jeans emerged, followed by the rest of the dark-haired girl. "Walter," she said agreeably, clutching her stomach. "Can we go now? I don't feel so well." She approached the quarterback, reaching for his waist.

"I don't wanna catch your cold." Walter absently pushed her away, then extended his hand to Bear. "Got everything?"

"Think so," said Bear, full of doubt. They shook hands under the watchful eye of the dark-haired girl, who was right by Walter's side. "Thanks, big time," said Bear, still holding onto the QB's massive hand and strong grip.

"Great weekend." Walter released his hand and pointed at him. "True?"

"True." Bear squelched every impulse he possessed to do or say more, which wasn't too hard since squelching impulses was all he'd done his entire life. "Go Dawgs," he said and turned away. He didn't look back until he was inside the lobby. By then, the little red sports car was speeding toward the dawn of another new day in the Peach State.

4

If You Were There, You'd Know

"**M**an, you've got a vivid imagination," said Walt from the park in Oxnard, California.

"Forgive me if I tend to indulge myself when dreaming about my favorite two people in the whole world," said Marcus from the park in Oxnard, California.

"When did you find the time to daydream all this?" asked Walt.

"At night a lot, putting myself to sleep. Or watching a football game, thinking about you." Marcus cracked his neck side to side. His bones were loud. They (yes, the bones) had no idea of the time, just that it was still Saturday.

"And you did this for 21 years," said Walt, statement of fact.

"Not exactly," said Marcus. "It was kinda like a long-running TV series that I could tap into anytime and get a brand new episode. Or watch a rerun. Or sometimes, when I changed my mind about something in their lives, I'd go back and re-create what I'd already dreamt to be true, because, upon further reveal, there was more to the story than I previously imagined."

"I'm sure your fantasies must have went on the backburner, say, when you had a relationship, if you've ever had one," said Walt.

"I've been just as much of a *man,* or male sexual dawg, as any other male sexual dawg on the planet, but I've never known true love, and not because I've been off in fantasyland," said Marcus. "I just never met the right buddy, the one who wanted exactly what I wanted. It just never felt right. He never showed up. And I was never the type to be in a relationship just to be in one, though after 42 years, sometimes I don't know if that was such a great idea."

The park in Oxnard, California grew still. A warm breeze snaked through the dunes, causing the palm trees on the oval pathway to sway. Marcus arched upward, the sunlight warming his face. Something collided with the back of his head.

"Sorry," said Walt with a mild laugh. The back of his head had collided with Marcus'. Upon further reveal, the two men were no longer sitting face to face on opposite stone picnic tables. Sometime during ... this time ... Walt had joined Marcus. They were sitting back to back on top of Marcus' stone picnic table, their bodies resting against one another like chair backs.

"I don't remember doing this," said Marcus.

"I got up to move around," said Walt. "Thought I was going to be stiff, but I wasn't. Sorry to interrupt."

"I was just saying, I've had a very decent life," said Marcus. "I've realized a lot of my dreams, just about everything I ever set out to do, well, except ... but I've also had a lot of free time at night. Walter and Bear spent a *lot* of time together, keeping me company in my dreams."

"And obviously Bear finds a way to get in touch with Walter after the big weekend," said Walt.

"What makes you so sure it wasn't Walter finding a way to get to Bear?" teased Marcus.

"If you know Walter like I know Walter," said Walt.

"I guess I do," said Marcus. "Bear's the one who had to get in touch with Walter."

"Good Bear," said Walt with a mild laugh. Then he stood promptly. Quarterback scramble. "How in the world did I sit this long without my back giving out? It's a miracle."

"I feel pretty good, too." Marcus also stood and stretched, his body restful and at peace.

"Where's this picture of me?" asked Walt. "Do you still have it? I gotta see this."

"A short drive away, if you're ready and willing," said Marcus.

Walt inhaled and considered it. "Wanna check out the ocean first, or head straight there?"

"Whatever Walt wants," said Marcus.

"Wouldn't mind seeing the Pacific while I'm here," said Walt. They headed down the oval pathway together toward the dunes. "You sure you're six-four? We look about the same height, six-three."

"Could be," said Marcus. "Six-four was just a number I dreamed up."

"You and your dreams," laughed Walt. A family of six passed, all of them on bicycles, down to the last little girl on training wheels.

"Mind telling me about the real-life Walt Yeager?" asked Marcus.

"Married twice, divorced twice," said Walt. "Four kids total from both marriages. Daughters. I finally had a son this last time. My boy's a rough and tumble little linebacker, the opposite of me at his age. I left football the day I retired from it in college and never looked back. As I stated, I only saw a game for the first time this morning. Georgia was not a good time for me."

"Why is that?" asked Marcus.

"There was that whole Deep South thing," said Walt. "Plus I transferred from Illinois, where I left a not-so-good situation. I had two back surgeries in college."

"Did you ever think about going pro?" asked Marcus.

"The second back surgery ended my career," said Walt.

"I'm sorry to hear that," said Marcus. A concrete pathway veered off from the oval and led beyond the dunes. They traveled to the very edge of the offshoot, coming to a stop half a football field away from the Pacific.

"I parlayed the drive and ambition I had for football into the financial world," said Walt. "I was fortunate enough to grow up comfortable, and I'm still fortunate in that way. I don't miss football. I never think about it." The sound of the calm ocean waves filled their world for a moment. "And the real-life Marcus Coleman?" asked Walt.

"I write books," said Marcus. "I've pretty much been a professional writer of some kind my whole adult life. Now I just tell my own stories, my way. I've published three novels, so far. They're kinda like *my* kids. I'm happy with the way they turned out."

"Sweet," said Walt, barely nodding, almost smiling. While the former cheerleader possessed an expressive face, the former quarterback's countenance gave away little about his innermost thoughts. Yeager would make a good gambler or cowboy.

"I hope all these football memories aren't taking you on a bad trip down memory lane," said Marcus.

"So our boys are at their separate schools," said Walt, still in possession of his scrambling skills. "What now?"

"My emotions were running high in those first few months after the UCLA-

Georgia game," said Marcus. "Everything took off like one gigantic amusement park ride. Not only did I have cheerleading, but I was living in this big white frat house—literally and figuratively—in a basement alcove with three other brothers. And *no*, I didn't have one single fraternity sex experience actualized in my entire collegiate life, just to clear that up. I think I had sex with one other college student the whole time I was in college."

"I don't have to know all your business," said Walt.

"I want to tell you," said Marcus, "so you can know what this crazy cheerleader guy who's been thinking about you for 21 years is all about. I have to tell you, for you and for me. That's the only way we can decide if any of this is a few hours of strange coincidences or some twilight cosmic dimension, right?"

"Onward," said Walt. He sat on the stone bench next to the pathway, Marcus followed.

"I learned how to have sex with other males in adult bookstores," said Marcus, "then bathhouses, then back alleys and dark places like that. Sometimes, I think the sex helps keep me alive and gives me this great connection. Sometimes, I feel like it's eating away at my soul. Lately—we're talking years—I've come to love and accept myself for who I am and all that I do, but getting there has been one very long and winding journey."

He wanted to tell Walt right then and there that he was HIV-positive, so Walt could see that he, too, had carried a heavy load in life, just like the heavy load Walt must carry for only being the top-rated quarterback in America out of high school his year, not the top-rated quarterback in the world out of all the top-rated quarterbacks in the universe, at least for a few shining seasons in the sun. His *years*.

Walt had dreamed that big as a kid. Marcus could feel it, understand it. He also knew the devastation of finding out that *no*, dreams don't necessarily come true, even the ones you let seep out of your soul when you're still young and not so distracted by what the rest of the world is telling you about yourself. He imagined Walt in bed as a kid, tossing the football in the air, daydreaming in those moments, however brief or often, when you don't need another soul, when all you need is a place to dream, and a dream to keep you company, when you only need the feelings that come from your dreams, because when you are young, you and your dreams are like soul mates ...

"Marcus? Marcus? You okay?" asked Walt.

"I'm fine," said Marcus, the ocean coming into focus once again.

"What did you want to be when you were a kid?" asked Walt.

"I grew up in a sports family, so I had my sports dreams," said Marcus. "I played the big three—basketball and football, from little league to junior high, baseball just in little league. Then in my late teens, I dabbled in soccer and tennis. But I never got that much joy from actually playing sports."

"Why?" asked Walt.

"There was always something in the way, my body, my mind ... I was six-four, 215 when I was *six*," joked Marcus. "One time, I was at an alumni function as a cheerleader and this UCLA assistant football coach told the audience that recruiting was all about getting guys with prototype bodies like mine. I always had the form, just none of the grace. When you're a kid, that means they stick you underneath the basket in basketball and on the line in football."

"So true." Walt let out a series of breaths that sounded like the suppressed laughter of a young boy who had suppressed his laughter for far too long. Marcus smiled, tugging at the shirt covering his own chest.

"Call it what you want," said Marcus, "but Marcus Coleman never wanted to be on the court or the field, and *not* have a legitimate turn in the spotlight. I was not born to block for somebody else. Or to attack somebody on defense. I was born to carry the ball, maybe not literally, but I was born to be ... center stage, at least for part of the time, in the game of life. I warred with my coaches over it, especially in football. Guess what position I wanted to play?"

"QB." Walter let out that suppressed boyish laughter again.

"I finally gave up trying to fit into the 'team' concept in junior high," said Marcus, "coincidentally around the time I was getting a major jones for this very tall, hot blond guy trying out for the 9th-grade basketball team. The coach had envisioned us as twin towers. Between the blond kid and my exploding feelings for guys in general, it was all looking like a nightmarish train wreck where I was going to be the only victim."

"What'd you do?" asked Walt.

"Instead of risking my life as I knew it, I quit basketball," said Marcus. "Forever. I joined this peer tutoring program where I got paid helping other kids do their homework. I had served my official notice to the world—my basketball family included—that I was no longer a jock-in-training." Marcus sighed. "I got out of sports because I was scared of everyone finding out I was starting to become a fag. Boy, that gave me a pain in the gut to admit."

They sat for a while without words, listening to the hypnotic rhythm of the waves tickling the shore. Walt repositioned himself on the stone bench so that his back was reclining. Marcus remained upright and still, eyes focused on some other world.

"That was also about the time I got straight A's," said Marcus, "something

I swore never to do again after the whole school treated me like the biggest geek this side of Steve Urkel. And I didn't have the benefit of a sitcom laugh track and network marketing."

"You told other students?" laughed Walt.

"They posted it at the top of the freakin' honor roll bulletin board!" said Marcus. "The school outed me! As a brain! For the rest of my academic career, I purposely never did that well again."

"So what did you want to be when you grew up?" Walt asked again.

"I don't know if I've ever thought about that," said Marcus. "Good one, Yeager. I'm usually the one who stumps people." Marcus considered the question, then debated revealing the answer. But they were here for the truth, and so he gave the truth: "I wanted to be somebody's buddy."

The revelation forced an exhale, followed by a new revelation.

"Somebody's buddy," laughed Marcus. "I just realized that's why I loved that song by Jackson Browne, 'Somebody's Baby.' Back then, I was a horny boy—who'd've guessed?—and I wasn't *gettin' nuttin'* at school, no boys, no girls, not even any Rosie Palm and the Five Fingers with my living situation. I used to sneak out of the big white frat house under the cover of darkness to get some physical contact at the anonymous sex zones in LA. I'd hop into my lime green Oldsmobile Omega, slip Jackson Browne into the cassette deck, and head away from campus, singing, 'I've got to be somebody's buddy tonight.' God, that's so fucking sick. See, Walt, I told you this was going to be a sappy story."

"But in your dreams, you had Walter, so you didn't need those places, right?" asked Walt.

"Those days were over," said Marcus. "We were as good as engaged in my mind. I just had to dream of a reason for Bear to get in touch, and lo and behold, a miracle happened."

"How many miracles can one story have?" laughed Walt.

"As many as you want, as I learned from Peter Benchley when I was a kid."

"The author of *Jaws?*" asked Walt.

"In the book version," said Marcus, "the wife is flirting with some guy, telling him her fantasies but trying to be too logical. The guy says something like: *In your fantasies, anything can happen. That's what fantasies are for.* Those words were like a gift I've never forgotten. So dreaming up a way for Bear to get in touch with Walter was easy, even though those days were nothing but crazed. Being a cheerleader was not just showing up on game day and trying to look straighter than the football players, because, at some point in time, at least 110% of the population will question your sexuality based on the fact that you once were and always will be: a male cheerleader."

BEAR COLEMAN'S CHEERLEADER DREAM had been born in his formative years, and had seeped out around his family and caused countless hours of commotion in Hayward. As a young boy, he would watch sporting events on TV, and during appropriate moments—including timeouts—he would cheer because that's what cheerleaders did. His two basketball brothers, both older, gave him hell for it until he put the dream back in the bottle of his imagination, knowing he would uncork that bottle at a big-time school someday.

His brothers had possessed their own hoop dreams but had failed to make it past the "I'm still in JC because I can't get my shit together" level. On the other hand, Bear was now seen on national television at the very same arenas his brothers once dreamed of ruling. By college, cheerleading was as natural to Bear as sitting at home and watching a sporting event. Now, unlike his brothers, he had been involved in big-time games between big-time schools; he had traveled the country; and most importantly to everyone back home, all it took was a half-second shot of his small Afro on national TV for the Coleman phone to start ringing as if Bear had just appeared on *The Tonight Show Starring Johnny Carson*. Bear's dream had come true after all, and the whole Coleman family was feeling better about the harassment they'd subjected him to for all those years, all those years ago. Now, even his brothers possessed a certain amount of admiration and respect, if not pride, for the youngest Coleman. Upon further reveal, Bear had won that particular civil war. Despite their early attempts to crush his dream, he had become what the family used to deride him for pretending to be: a cheerleader.

Of course, as a young cub, Bear had always pretended to be a female cheerleader. More precisely, a cheerleader who did the things female cheerleaders did. Those were the only cheerleaders Bear ever saw as a child. But for Bear, it wasn't about being a female. It was about being able to feel comfortable in his skin. He couldn't impersonate great athletes, whose greatness comes from spontaneous creations on the fly. Bear's body didn't work that way, for the most part. The cheerleaders, however, offered an alternative for his physical spirit. Their movements were playful, exuberant creations that were repeated over and over, game after game. He could learn the routines. He could rehearse. He could mimic. He could still run free on the very same basketball courts and football fields where he was a clumsy player never afforded the spotlight.

In his own world at home, when he was alone, Bear cheered and it didn't matter how clumsy he looked. His head was up high, proudly commanding an imaginary crowd that gave him the perfect response every single time while watching the games he loved. On top of that, athletes valued cheerleaders, the team's vital link to the in-game fuel reserve that was the crowd. It was a perfect match and a way for Bear to be a shining star.

Of course, none of this was going through the mind of a 21-year-old Bruin Bear who had just fallen in love in Athens, Georgia, and was now back at UCLA, living college life at warp speed. The spirit squad was in its busiest season, each week a series of grueling practices and events in preparation for the Church of College Football every Saturday. As such, Bear had little time to do anything about Walter, except dream. Until the day two angels in the form of two cheer-girls paved the way.

One afternoon, half the squad was sitting on the steps of the men's gym, while the other half stood on the lawn in front. Midway through stunt practice, White Donna had called Sergeant Holly a bitch before bursting into tears and running inside the gym. Bear had volunteered to retrieve White Donna while the others formed two separate and not-so-subtle camps of support.

"She'll be out in a second," said Bear, emerging from the ancient gym. "I had to go into the women's restroom and talk her into not quitting."

"*Oops*," said Black Donna. She was sitting on the gym steps—in support of White Donna—going through a stack of photos. "Ah, here's Bear and Harry Dawg in the end zone at Georgia."

"Speaking of paradise lost," said Bear. He was also in the White Donna camp, so he sat beside Black Donna and regarded himself in the photo with Harry Dawg, the Georgia mascot.

"She blew this one." Black Donna flipped backward through the stack, showing him the previous attempt to capture the same shot, which only managed to get a fuzzy red corner of Harry Dawg's jersey. The lens had strayed from its original target and had found—

There he is!

He was wearing his red Georgia helmet, his red Georgia jersey, and his silver Georgia "britches." Best of all, Number 13 was sportin' a whole lotta golden blond aura. He was also running over a blonde Georgia cheerleader, the same one from the ride to Atlanta in the little red sports car. Instantly, Bear realized what had happened: White Donna, while about to take the photo of Bear and Harry Dawg, moved her camera from her face to shout at Bear for turning around (to gaze upon Walter passing in the end zone). The errant lens had captured *Walter!*—oh, and the blonde Georgia cheerleader trying to pose for a photo with him.

Bear wanted to leap off the steps and do a fight song routine. His quarterback was back in his life. Lately, Walter had been on his mind, but not *in* his life. Bear couldn't locate the game program from that weekend. Maybe it was lost in the fraternity. Or maybe he'd given it to the Rents during the game to keep safe during the downpour. If the latter were true, it would take a miracle for the program to end up back in his hands, considering it would have to travel from Athens to Alabama to Northern California, then back to Bear again. The program was all but lost. And Bear hadn't even had a chance to open it and gaze upon his golden boy's official photo. Nor was he afforded any real opportunity to hunt down another copy.

He did, however, get one glimpse of another image of Walter. On the flight from Atlanta, Bear noticed another cheerleader browsing through a Georgia newspaper supplement. When Bear got a chance to borrow it, he saw a black and white team photo that he guessed was from spring ball. Walter was in the middle of the group, near the front. He was a much younger-looking Walter, his hair much shorter, his posture more erect, his eager grin suggesting he was ready to leap out of the photo and *go play some football!* This alone made him stand tall over the other Bulldawgs around him. Some of his teammates beamed just as brightly, but none brighter. Walter Yeager looked like a kid ready to take on the world.

But Walter Yeager of the pale yellow polo shirt and Labor Day weekend looked like a kid morphing into a man, a man who had responsibilities and the ability to have something on his mind other than the moment in which he was living, a man who had lost a little of his youthful, piss 'n' vinegar smile and was struggling with something.

After practice, Bear knew exactly what he had to do. Life became a blur until he was standing next to the postal kiosk not far from the gym. White Donna had agreed to let him keep the photo of Walter, which was now inside an envelope addressed to "Walter Yeager, Quarterback, c/o University of Georgia Athletic Department, Football Team, Athens, Georgia." He hadn't bothered with a zip code. From the looks of Athens, *Football Team* was plenty enough address. The note he included was simple:

> Look who showed up in a cheergirl's camera. Brought a
> smile to my face during an intense moment at practice. If
> you were there, you'd know I was remembering that great
> weekend, even though we lost. Go Dawgs. Go Walter!

No sense in getting all flowery in case the sentiments fell into the wrong hands, or Bear was wrong about Walter wanting to be buddies. He let the envelope fall into the rabbit hole of a mailbox, then came back down to earth and continued onward.

Life became a blur again, until a few weeks later when an envelope just like his arrived in his mail slot at the fraternity. The return address told him it was from a nameless person in Athens, Georgia. As if he needed visible confirmation for the anticipation simmering from the moment he grabbed his mail that day. He opened it right there in the foyer of the big white frat house. Inside, there was a picture of Bear and Harry Dawg, the same shot White Donna had taken but from a slightly different angle. And a note:

> Thanks for reaching out. Guess what Cindy gave me to give to you if I ever got your address. You showed up in *her* camera! Big laugh after shitty day. If you were there, you'd know. Time limited. Hope all is well @ UCLA.

Upon further reveal, when the male Georgia cheerleader tried to take the shot of Walter and Cindy, Cindy's fall caused the male Georgia cheerleader to lose his focus. The errant lens had captured *Bear!*—oh, and Harry Dawg—at the exact same time that White Donna's lens had caught *her* errant subject. The two lenses had acted like klieg lights crossing in the sky and had captured the other's intended photo.

An ear-to-ear grin lit up Bear's face as he stood in the foyer of the big white frat house. Three brothers passed by on their way to class. One of them mentioned Coleman's Cheshire cat grin. Bear lied to get rid of them. When they were gone, he left the house alone, knowing exactly what he had to do.

Life became a blur again until he was once again standing next to the postal kiosk near the men's gym. This time, he used Walter's mailing address. The thank you card was simple. Just the word *thanks* on the front, then Bear's handwritten note inside:

> You are the best, simple as I can put it.

The previous eleven drafts were long-winded and contained all kinds of "let's get married" code between the lines. Those drafts were now shredded into an infinite number of unreadable pieces.

"Please feel me," said Bear, dropping the card into the rabbit hole of a mailbox. "Please show up again in my mail slot."

Life became a blur again until a week later when a large manila envelope showed up in Bear's mail slot in the big white frat house. The envelope was crumpled and stuffed with something that was meant to be crumpled—a shirt, Bear figured right away. No return address this time. As if he needed proof. He bolted from the frat and escaped to his only private space in the physical world: his lime green Oldsmobile Omega in the parking structure near the frat. He waited until he was in the driver's seat to open the package. Inside was a red t-shirt with the words GO DAWGS in collegiate-style block letters. And a note:

> Saw this in a store and thought of you and your *Go Dawgs*. Had to laugh, even though no one I was with understood. If you were there, you'd know.

This is getting very serious, thought Bear, joy and panic rising in equal measures. He couldn't send Walter a UCLA shirt—didn't feel right. Walter Yeager would never walk around Athens advertising the Bruins. An idea came to him, but it seemed risky. It also put another Cheshire cat grin on his face.

Life became a blur again until he was at the post office, handing the female clerk a big white envelope containing a thank you card a hundred times the size of his original one. The card itself was plain, just the word *thank* on the front and *you* on the inside. Bear's intuition told him to keep it simple, no paw prints, no personal note, not even a return address. He smiled a confident smile as he released his heart into the hands of the United States Postal Service.

Relax, he told himself, you're getting good at this game.

Two weeks went by without anything showing up from Georgia. Calling was not an option. They'd never exchanged phone numbers. Bear tried his best not to lumber around campus in a daze, but he was failing. He was also failing a hellish statistics class required for his Soc major: Stats 666. He had never been a numbers guy, and intuitively, he understood that Walter would be the one to take their money and perform the financial wizardry necessary to live their dreams. As such, Bear saw little use for Stats 666, which was one insufferable hour that blurred by daily, *if* it blurred by at all. It was also the class where he doodled the most, drawing the sports stadiums of his dreams.

If sports were Bear's religion, stadiums were his temples. He drew them on the side of everything. All he required was a narrow margin of the material world to carve out a church of his own, always starting with the field of play for the chosen game. Lately, that meant his doodles began as rectangles that morphed into gridirons that morphed into stadiums inspired by the horseshoe magnet in Athens.

One fall afternoon in Stats 666, Bear was putting the finishing touches on a rather nifty, futuristic horseshoe magnet stadium when a curious commotion gathered steam among the other students. Glancing up from his seat high atop the lecture hall, he saw three of his frat bros encouraging a shy clown to approach the ancient female teacher. The shy clown was holding a bouquet of helium balloons. "Way to go, Coleman!" shouted one of his frat bros, pumping a fist in the air. The students buzzed. The ancient female teacher shooed away the frat bros, who scampered out of the lecture hall, abandoning the clown. Bear fought off the part of him that said things like this didn't happen to guys like him—from any guy, but especially from a guy like Walter Yeager.

"You young people and your infatuations," said Professor Battle Axe. "There's no song and dance, is there?" she asked the clown, using her reading glasses to examine the man's clipboard. "Is there a Marcus *Bob* Coleman?"

"Bear!" cried Bear. "Bear Coleman!" He started to get up, but the clown came bounding up the lecture hall steps, big red clown shoes and all. The clown tripped on the second step, unintentionally, but recovered before falling, then swayed as if still off-balance, intentionally offering a glimpse of his act.

The students laughed like children.

"Young clown man, you come back here." Professor Battle Axe pointed to the right corner at the bottom of the lecture hall. "Leave those there. Bob Coleman can get them after class."

Bear sank in his seat, radiant nonetheless. After the clown disappeared, the students settled down, many of them eyeing Bear with curious smiles. But that was nothing compared to the journey home after class. It was the middle of the day; campus was packed. Between cheerleading and the fraternity, Bear was always running into people he knew. But today, the rest of the world had to settle for a beaming smile and a furtive wave. Bear felt like the most special boy in the world and simply flew away with his balloons. It was the first time anyone had ever done anything like that for him. In fact, Walter's gifts were the first and second gifts he'd ever received from anyone in college. In high school, he'd always been envious of people who were popular enough to have their friends decorate their lockers for birthdays or big days. In college, Bear was active and known, but he was still something of a loner, still trying to find a social life that fit. There had never been anyone in his life who did things like throw him a birthday party, or send him balloons, birthday or not, until now. Now he had Walter, and it didn't matter that Walter was 2,000 miles away in another world ...

"*Hmmm*," said Marcus from the bench facing the ocean in Oxnard, California. "I remember that little gift exchange sequence pretty well after all these years. And I think for the first time, I just realized why I dreamed it up in the first place."

"Tell me about it," said Walt, sitting next to him on the bench facing the ocean in Oxnard, California.

"I first saw your picture around my 22nd birthday." Marcus sighed, adjusting to the new light shed on his dreams. "I was at home sick, missing college, and my sister's asking me if I'm gay because she did some checking and found out Hep B was common among gays. Of course, I lied. All that pressure. I guess around my birthday, I dreamed of Walter sending me—*Bear*—balloons. I warned you this was the sappy story of one lovesick puppy."

"Sounds to me like it was good medicine," said Walt. He inhaled the ocean air and stared at the horizon. "So you're a year older than me. You're the older one."

"Hey, watch it there," said Marcus.

"I mean, like, to be respected more," said Walt, "as in wiser."

"Oh ... well ... since you put it that way," said Marcus, then added like a proud black man: "That's right!"

"So I wanna see how you're gonna top our dashing romantic hero's fantastic balloon surprise," said Walt, the dashing romantic hero's alter ego.

Marcus let out a big Bear laugh to go along with his big Bear grin. "If you were there, you'd know."

THE BOUQUET LASTED ONE NIGHT in the basement alcove of Bear's fraternity, but Bear didn't mind. In their short time in his life, the balloons forced him to answer countless inquires, all of which he fielded awkwardly until he got the idea to say they were a gift from his sister. That controlled most of the damage but not all. His heart was bursting with joy and he had no one to share it with, not even Walter. He also didn't know how to respond to the quarterback's latest move. That is, until he decided to be a little honest and write Walter a letter.

> Don't wanna say too much but have so much to say. You
> Dawgs were scheduled to come out here next year, season
> opener. Game canceled. Dunno why. Would have been a
> dream come true to hang. True?
> PS: 12 thanks for ... if you were there, you'd know.

Lick the envelope. Seal our fate. Drop that fate in the rabbit hole of a mailbox at the postal kiosk near the men's gym. Deep breath.

There went Bear's fate. Had he said too much? Been too sappy? Come off as faggy, talking about dreams?

"I had plenty of social skills," said Marcus from the bench facing the ocean in Oxnard, California. "I just didn't have any experience when it came to talking to a guy to find out anything important about him, or telling him anything important about me. I had zero experience dating, going steady, asking someone out, looking a person in the face and feeling love. There were some dates with women, but that wasn't the real me. I had a dream of finding a buddy, not being gay or straight, just finding a buddy. Women didn't make it past central casting. Men did, just for being men. But men in the dark don't do social skills. So I had plenty of mates, but no soul. And when it came to Bear and Walter loving one another, at first it was all soul. But I did get to see you again," said Marcus, forgetting he wasn't supposed to be Bear, "and sooner than I thought, even though I didn't find out about your visit until you hit me on the jaw. And hard."

"I hit you?" asked Walt, forgetting he wasn't supposed to be Walter.

"Two nights before the USC-UCLA game," said Marcus, rubbing his chin in memory of Yeager's uppercut.

"Tell me about it," said Walt, still incredulous.

"It was a crazy week," said Marcus. "Alumni events, TV appearances, practices, a pep rally, then finally, a frat party. So, if you're ready, cut to 'Pump It Up' by Elvis Costello, the upbeat new wave song jamming throughout the big white frat house. An exhausted Bear is passed out, asleep or drunk, on top of the nameless, faceless brunette he was making out with—you know, to prove to the bros what a black stud he is."

... The couch rumbled like an earthquake, swaying back and forth and taking Bear and the nameless, faceless brunette on a tilt o' whirl of a dream. When it was over, Bear jumped off the ride in search of the pranksters, but as he landed on solid ground, the nameless, faceless brunette grabbed him in the name of trying to pull herself off the couch. As a result, Bear started to fall again and grabbed the only thing within reach, a man's gray sleeve. But Bear's descent was already in progress. The gray sleeve was sucked into his gravitational pull, as was the rest of what turned out to be a very heavenly body. The one that wore #13 for the Georgia Bulldawgs.

The boys continued the fall together. Their practically identical bodies landed simultaneously, sending the couch flying backward. The result: Walter and Bear went over the couch, the couch went over Walter and Bear, and the brunette, her legs still entwined with Bear's legs, went over everything. The boys did a tuck and roll and landed next to one another like a pair of dice.

"Walter!"

"Bear!"

They jumped up and stood face to face.

"You showed up!" shouted Bear over the music.

"This ain't no dream, baby!" shouted Walter.

"Gross!" cried the nameless, faceless brunette. The couch-quake had been courtesy of Beamer, one of Bear's more rowdy brothers, who was trying to let Bear know he had a visitor. After the somersault, the nameless, faceless brunette had landed on top of Beamer. She sat on his gigantic beer gut, trying to get her bearings, while Beamer regurgitated a steady stream of beer that coated his face like a water fountain.

"You're really here?" asked Bear.

"True, baby, true!" said Walter.

"Bear, who's your gorgeous friend?" asked Roxanne. She was Joe Bruin, the UCLA mascot, and a member of tonight's invited sorority.

"My bud!" Bear's face lit up with joy. Walter and he were about to explode, but the party came into focus long enough to remind them of their surroundings. Their bodies combusted with restlessness, arms flailing, faces contorting. Finally, one of Walter's hands made a fist and hit Bear square in the jaw. Bear was as stunned as Walter. Their eyes locked, their mouths agape. Bear felt the stares of his brothers and the sting in his jaw. He touched his chin. It felt exhilarating. He smiled at Walter. Walter grinned. With that settled, they returned to being their regular selves. "What was that all about?" said Bear for show. In truth, everything was fine. His bud had made contact.

"It's good to see you, Bear!" shouted Walter. "What it be like?"

"It be like—*you* are wasted, Walter Yeager," said Bear, gazing at the most beautiful drunken college student he'd ever laid eyes on.

"And you're fucked up, too, Marcus 'Bear' Coleman!" said Walter.

"What are you doing here, man?" asked Bear.

"Long flight, long story, not much time," said Walter. That was all Bear needed to hear. He made sure the nameless, faceless brunette was all right, then whisked his man away from the big white frat house. It was a cool night in late November. Bear shivered as they headed for campus, his purple polo shirt not enough for the chilly wind. "Want this?" Walter indicated his hooded grey sweatshirt, which bore the logo of a junior college over the left breast.

"Of course," said Bear.

"You can keep it, if you want," said Walter, revealing another sweatshirt underneath.

"I want. *And* I have a million questions," said Bear.

"I get two of those. You only get 999,998," said Walter.

"Go for it," giggled Bear, halting at an intersection.

"How the hell's my boy? I'm mean, my Bear? I mean, my buddy?" Walter put his hand on Bear's shoulder. "How's my buddy, Bear? You feel good?"

"Like the spaceship is taking off again," said Bear.

"Spaceship?" laughed Walter.

"Sanford Stadium," said Bear. "When Charlie Dean sealed the game with that interception return for a touchdown, the whole crowd exploded with so much energy, the stadium looked like it wanted to blast off and orbit the moon, or go wherever it wanted to go."

"Did you tell me that before?" asked Walter. "I'm having déjà vu."

"Don't think so," said Bear.

"Show me the campus," said Walter.

"That's one of the great things about the SC-UCLA rivalry," said Bear as they made their way down a hill leading toward the track stadium. "The crowd's pretty evenly split between the reds and the blues, so nothing that happens is neutral. Everything is either good or bad for half of the stadium, and because most of the reds are packed together and most of the blues are packed together, it's very easy to see who's on whose side. It's amazing when a big play happens because one side is completely elated and the other is completely deflated. Then all of a sudden, sometimes, on the very next play, the reverse happens. All those blues feeling so much elation are suddenly feeling deflation, and all those reds feeling deflation are suddenly feeling elation. Man, that is the SC-UCLA rivalry."

"Or us and Tech next week," said Walter.

"Did I tell you I cheered at both schools?" asked Bear ...

"Whoa. One second there," said Walt from the bench facing the ocean in Oxnard, California. "You went to both schools?"

"I started out at SC, transferred and graduated from UCLA," said Marcus, sitting next to him on the bench facing the ocean in Oxnard, California. "Cheered two years for both with a year off in between due to transfer status."

"Onward," said Walt ...

"UCLA's basketball team cost me a six-pack last week," said Walter.

"You should know better than to bet on the Bruins," said Bear.

"It's not like I have time to follow hoops to the last detail," said Walter, sounding defensive and wounded. Bear felt stupid for deriding him, realizing he didn't have to put up a tough veneer just because Walter was a jock.

"Sorry there's no spaceship stadium here," said Bear. The Rose Bowl, football home of the Bruins, was miles away. Bear had taken Walter to the track stadium, where they sat at the top of the stands, looking out over the intramural fields and the rolling hills of campus.

"Why'd you leave SC?" asked Walter.

"I'm not rich and my father doesn't own a department store," said Bear. "Not to mention half my financial aid drying up as soon as Reagan got in office. Plus, it didn't help being called nigger while walking by the Sigma Chi house the week before school started."

"That's not right," said Walter.

"And not what I want to talk about with my—bud," Bear paused to recalibrate his sensors. "Hey, you made me forget my a million questions."

"Is that a bad thing?" asked Walter. "You have so many."

"And you have so few, " said Bear.

"Cut it down to half a million and shoot," said Walter.

"How did you get here?" asked Bear.

"One of my coaches helped me out," said Walter. "I told him I wanted to visit a sick great aunt in LA, since this is the bye week before the Tech game. He excused me from some stuff in the morning. He's a black guy; he's pretty cool. I'm here tonight and back on a plane at the crack of dawn."

"You came all this way for a few hours?" asked Bear.

"Needed the break," said Walter.

"Is that why you got drunk?" asked Bear. "Pissed off at not playing?"

"How do you know I'm not playing much?" asked Walter.

"I check the Sunday paper for the Georgia box scores," said Bear. "I rarely see your name, and when I do, it looks like Coach Dooley has no idea what Walter Yeager is capable of. How come?"

"You don't really have to know right now, do you?" asked Walter. "Show me your car, it's freezing here."

They headed for Bear's lime green Oldsmobile in the parking structure near the frat. Once they were seated and warmed by the heater, Bear brought up football again: "We need to get you some playing time. So they know how great you are. So they see what I saw when I looked into your eyes the first time."

"What did you see?" asked Walter.

"A man destined for greatness," said Bear. "A born winner and leader."

"Dream on," said Walter, snuggling into the passenger door.

"I mean it," said Bear.

"How could you see all that?" asked Walter, yawning.

"I did," said Bear, yawning. "I'm just realizing it now, maybe because I'm so tired, I can barely keep my eyes open and can't ... fake ... truth ... when I saw you, I knew you ... had the ... capability of being ... any, every, whatever Walter wants ... to be."

"*Rightbackatcha,*" said Walter.

"True," said Bear.

Night morphed into morning. "True," the song, came to them in their dreams. They awoke in the lime green Oldsmobile Omega, which was still in the parking structure. Bear was playing "True" on his cassette deck, the sound of which gently awakened Walter.

"Remember this?" asked Bear.

"No doubt," said Walter.

They listened in silence, Bear looking down to his left, Walter looking up to his right. They were in a car, saying goodbye again. Matter of fact, they were at the airport now, parked curbside in front of Walter's terminal. The time had flown by that fast.

"I hope you're glad you showed up because I am," said Bear.

"If you are, then I are." Walter got out on the passenger side, Bear followed from the driver's side and met him on the curb.

"Thanks for this," said Bear, pausing to smell the hooded gray sweatshirt he was wearing.

"It probably reeks," said Walter.

"Yeah, it does," said Bear, heady from the whiff of stale sweat.

"So we got each other's numbers now," said Walter, "but I live in a house with a bunch of crazy guys, so bear that in mind, Bear."

"I live in a house with a bunch of crazy guys, too," said Bear, "and I share a house payphone in the mailroom. If you ever call, it might take a miracle to track me down."

"Likewise," said Walter. "We'll be in touch."

"Hey, speaking of miracles," said Bear, "what about that crazy scenario where UCLA and Georgia could meet in the Sugar Bowl?"

"Highly unlikely," said Walter. "So much has to happen. Washington over Washington State. Arizona State *ties* Arizona. You guys beat SC tomorrow."

"Which we'll do," said Bear. "Then you guys beat Georgia Tech next week, LSU falls to Tulane so their overall record loses in a tie-breaker, Auburn loses to Alabama, and presto, see you in New Orleans in a little over a month."

"You forgot about Ohio State beating Michigan so the Sugar Bowl doesn't want them anymore," said Walter. "So you're saying you'd rather see UCLA go to the Sugar Bowl as Pac-10 runner-ups, not to the Rose Bowl as Pac-10 champs?"

"I would never cheer against my own team," said Bear, "but I also want to see you in New Orleans in a month."

"If I'm the starting QB, who would you root for?" asked Walter. "Why is your face contorting like a puzzle about to fall apart?"

"I can't imagine rooting against my bud," said Bear. "I guess I wouldn't do any KILL THE QUARTERBACK cheers, that's for sure. If we get to the Sugar Bowl and you're in the game, we'll see what happens."

"On that note," said Walter. "Be seeing ya, buddy."

As Walter vanished through the airport doors, Bear took another whiff of the ripe gray sweatshirt. Something told him it was pungent, and that his nose should be offended. Just to make sure, he smelled it periodically while driving to the LA Coliseum for an appearance on a local morning talk show ...

"That morning at the Coliseum changed the course of the year for me and the squad," said Marcus from the bench facing the ocean in Oxnard, California. "The whole setup was a recipe for disaster. We were all freezing and crabby. The Georgia honeymoon was but a memory. We barely acknowledged one another, but when the camera's red light came on, we put on these happy masks and did a stunt-filled routine to the fight song.

"Who the fuck wants to see cheerleaders cheering first thing in the morning? To an empty stadium? I guess that was my attitude, and I guess that didn't help Jenny and me on our final stunt, a difficult maneuver in the best of times. I was supposed to throw her straight up in the air, then catch her by her inner thighs, sort of like a star—the split catch, or star catch, a stunt the NCAA later outlawed because it was too dangerous at games, let alone at seven a.m. in a cold and empty LA Memorial Coliseum.

"I only caught the left split. Her right leg hit my head and she fell right in front of me and an undetermined number of viewers getting their LA morning started right. The fight song ended as I lifted her off the ground. She was shaking. I held onto her until somebody yelled, *Cut!*, as in that's a wrap. It was also a wrap for Jenny and me. Our partnership could have survived that one fall. It was a fairly neutral timing mistake. Thing was, that was our second major breach of trust in a matter of weeks.

"The first accident happened in practice. I'd come up with this idea for a new stunt sequence. The guys line up in an "I" formation, then we toss the girls over our heads, cradle to cradle. We're trying it out. It's going pretty good. I've got Jenny cradled in my arms, then I throw her over my head for the guy behind me to catch. Only *I* wasn't supposed to throw Jenny to Tad, the guy behind me! I was supposed to *keep* Jenny cradled in my arms because she was *my* partner."

"Was she all right?" asked Walt, sitting next to him on the bench facing the ocean in Oxnard, California.

"Luckily, but still," said Marcus. "I became infamous. I was already a cocky, hotshot transfer yell leader from USC. From day one of that particular UCLA spirit squad's inception, I had led this swiftly moving revolt to modernize and *masculinize* the squad. My first victory came easy: I eliminated all arm motions for the guys while making sure our choreographed movements only involved hoisting up a hot chick in a partner stunt, something the frat boys were in awe of anyway. This wasn't about homophobia, either. It was about doing my job: harnessing the crowd's energy in the most efficient way possible, glory, glory to Westwood.

"I mean, who wants to look down on the field and see a bunch of glitter boys next to these big-assed linebackers? Football is a brutal and masculine game, pure and simple. It only works if almost all the elements are extremely masculine or the exact opposite. In the space that is a football field, only the celestial bodies working the game—the refs and such—possess neutral energy. The rest of the game consists of nearly identical polar opposite forces battling one another. Head coach to head coach. Quarterback to quarterback. Mascot to mascot. Home announcer to visitor announcer. All in support of the hyper-masculine cause. It's a perfect balance. Where does the glitter boy fit in?

"In *this* world, a feminine male cheerleader has a much greater challenge getting the job done, at least until the elements of the game or the perception of male cheerleaders change. I was all about getting the *true college experience* of my day, from frats to homecoming floats. That meant getting in touch with the male cheerleader within. It wasn't like I tried to be anything I wasn't or hyper-masculine. I was just a different side of me. And I liked that side, and the thrill of my *demonstratively baritone voice* on the microphone at the Rose Bowl, commanding the Bruins to: *"Hold that line on the count of three ... ready!"*

"*Ha!*" said Walt, letting out a big laugh. "I can see it now."

"It was fun while it lasted," sighed Marcus. "Jenny's fall to the cold Coliseum grass sealed my fate for the year. Jenny fell. Marcus dropped Jenny. Those were the only two ways the squad described it. I couldn't win either way. My cocky black ass was no longer the Shit, just full of shit. Sometime after the Rose Bowl, Jenny completed her own downfall by quitting or getting kicked off. I was never sure because it happened while I was in Hep B rehab. But I do know that she was very much in love, and cheerleading had taken a backseat to a man she believed was the One. I ran into her after graduation at a UCLA-Stanford game in Palo Alto. She was living in the Bay Area and happily married to that same college sweetheart. Boy, did that make me feel a little better about what happened between her and I. You know how some shrinks will tell you there's no such thing as an accident? Sometimes, I've wondered: did I drop Jenny out of resentment?"

"For?"

"She put the aspirin in the Aspirin Incident," said Marcus. "She stopped us from finding a drugstore and a secluded hilltop under a starry Georgia night. Maybe my subconscious played a role in our downfall. But if that's the case, I'm glad to have given her something in exchange. The college sweetheart she married? I set them up. He was a pledge brother of mine who was just a handsome stranger to her until, upon Jenny's request, we all went out on a double date—me and Black Donna, a pledge party or something. If I did drop Jenny because of you, I hope my frat bro was her soul mate and still is."

"You're mixing realities," said Walt.

"Yes and no," said Marcus. "Bear dropped Jenny because of the Aspirin Incident, too, but he merely dropped her from his dream squad, the harmonious group of 10 studly males and 10 gorgeous females who materialized and cheered whenever Bear needed them in his imagination."

"You're telling me the Aspirin Incident happened in this life, too?" asked Walt.

"Sure," said Marcus. "Me and a guy at the Georgia frat party tried to hook up in the same way, at least from where I was standing."

"Who?" asked Walt.

"*Huh?*" asked Marcus.

"In your infamous life," said Walt. "Who did you meet instead of me?"

"Oh," said Marcus, more focused on the horizon over the ocean. "Some Reb, short, furry, shy ... opposite of the man they call Big Norse. Didn't lead to anything. The Aspirin Incident was the beginning and the end of it. That's the difference between Bear and me sometimes. Sometimes, we're in sync, other times, we'll be in the same exact place and time, having polar opposite experiences."

5

The Infatuations

... pretty cool stuff ... in here
... a treasure chest
... three treasure chests!
... look at you ... all excited ... brown-eyed girl
"*Huh ...* Walt?"

"Listen," said Walt in Oxnard, California. "The song 'Brown-Eyed Girl,' coming from some radio in your parents' neighborhood ... you sure your mom doesn't mind us messing up her garage like this?"

"How else are we gonna find the buried treasure?" asked Marcus, also in Oxnard, California. "The sacred document that foretold our future, which is present, which is all about the past, that foretold our future, which is present, which is all about the past, that foretold our future ..."

"Man, now you're just plain scaring me," said Walt.

"Welcome to my world," said Marcus.

Walt was sitting on a pile of old spare tires, sifting through a cardboard box full of college mementos, UCLA this, USC that. Marcus was squatting nearby, rummaging through another box full of college mementos, USC this, UCLA that. The garage door was up, letting in the warm afternoon sunlight. The house on the other side of the patio was empty. Miracle of miracles, it was *dogercise* time, and the two- and four-legged varieties of the Coleman family were now at the seaside park recently vacated by Walt and Marcus. As if both parties had agreed to pull some sort of cosmic reverse and switch positions. Marcus couldn't have dreamed of a better scenario for their exploratory mission to find the game program. For now, it was best to keep things as family-free as possible. Perhaps there'd be a chance in the future to dream a better dream.

"You're my ... brown-eyed ..." sang Walt, more focused on sorting through the box. "... remember us ..."

Marcus fell backward as if knocked off balance. Luckily, another pile of old spare tires cushioned the fall of his 42-year-old big black ass. He covered his clumsiness with a smile and a laugh, which prompted Walt to return the same.

"Did you ever *not* smile when you were in college?" asked Walt, the photos in his hands taking him back to Marcus arm in arm with football players, Marcus arm in arm with Bill Cosby at a basketball game, Marcus arm in arm with female cheerleaders from Nebraska, Arizona State, Notre Dame, Penn State, Georgia.

"Gotta smile," said Marcus. "The squad signed a blood oath, especially me. I can definitely look and sound like the kind of brutha ladies fear on empty streets at night."

"You did play some ball, I see." Walt picked up the football that was buried under more treasure and flipped it to Marcus. The former cheerleader was caught off guard but freed his hands of the trash he was holding in time to catch his first-ever shuttle pass from the real Walt Yeager.

"My brother insists I could have been a good fullback if somebody had just worked with me," said Marcus.

"I wouldn't doubt it." Walt picked up the card Marcus had dropped to catch the ball. When he saw some kind of colorful drawing, he tossed it back on the garage floor.

"I guess I'll have to dream that dream another day." Marcus tossed the football back into the box.

"When I was a kid," said Walt, "I used to throw rocks at telephone poles for hours, dreaming I was a QB. I never got tired. I could do it all day. I only missed to make it interesting." Walt picked up the football again, along with a new batch of photos, taking him back to Marcus in a dorm with three boys. All of them appeared masculine, even though they were mimicking a cheergirl dance pose.

"I could get those guys to do anything," said Marcus. "Wish I had known that back then."

"Looks like you lived the college high life." Walt grabbed another batch of photos, taking him back to Marcus all over the country in different stadiums and arenas, followed by Marcus in a fraternity "team photo." Much like Walt in his spring ball photo, Marcus stood out over the rest. "Looks like you're ready to beat somebody up here," said Walt with a mild laugh.

"We were all supposed to be posing like male models," said Marcus. "You do what you gotta do to survive, right?"

"This much is true," laughed Walt. "This much is very true."

"You sure this trip down memory lane isn't taking you for a spin you're not ready for?" asked Marcus, face filled with concern.

"I'm good," said Walt, grabbing a stack of old term papers. "So where's this game program been all these years? Where is it now?"

"Told you, I haven't seen it in ages," said Marcus. "I've moved so many times, and this stuff has gone back and forth between here and my mom's old home in Northern Cal a time or two—I'm not even sure it's here."

"Geez, thanks for taking care of my sacred picture so well," said Walt.

"I didn't need to keep referring back to it," said Marcus. "I probably had a good stretch of 10-15 years without even thinking about looking at the program, or caring where it was."

Your image went straight from my eyes to my heart. And when I started imagining our life together, 2,000 miles apart, you entered into my mind, literally.

"Unbelievable."

"*Huh ... Walt?*"

The former quarterback held in his hands the program from the UCLA-Georgia game, circa a lifetime ago. The front cover was simple: an aerial view of Sanford Stadium, the original horseshoe magnet of Marcus' dreams. The stadium was lit for a night game. The rest of the cover was as black as space, but because the program was worn and crinkled, the pitch-black space around the stadium was full of white specks that looked like distant stars in the night sky and faded scratches that looked like stardust swirling about the universe. *Heaven Gazing Down at One of Its Celestial Bodies.* Very few words graced the cover, just a red, black and white box at the top, giving the who, what, where and when.

Walt went deep and inside, only pausing if a page of the program happened to pause on its own. Whatever caught his eyes was simply followed by a barely audible ... *hmmm*. Marcus was about to combust, so he talked: "I always thought I randomly picked the most attractive guy I saw at the time. But you being here and being this open-minded, it makes me think I didn't just pick any ole guy, like maybe my intuition was working behind my back."

"Where's this photo that did all this?" asked Walt, more focused on the program.

"Near the first half of the book, I think," said Marcus. "Been years since that day I opened it up and said: let's pick out a blond god to fantasize about for the rest of my life. Joking."

Walt's browsing came to a halt. The quarterback had found himself. He paused, then blurted: "Who is that guy?" Then he let out a mild laugh, then raised the image of his face to his face. "Man, will ya look at how young I look."

"The picture is so tiny!" said Marcus, truly astonished. "It's smaller than a postage stamp! You can't even see *your eyes* from the shadows. How did I ever ... notice you out of all ... how did I ever blast off with my daydreams from such a tiny image?"

"Man, this takes me back." Walt slammed the program with a thunderous clap of his massive hands. But the sacred document that foretold their future was weak and tattered, unable to withstand the natural force that was Walt Yeager. Pages spilled onto the garage floor like violently felled leaves. "Man, I'm sorry. Now I feel bad," said Walt.

"It was already like this, don't worry," said Marcus, casually retrieving the scattered pages.

"I didn't mean to do that," said Walt.

"I know."

"I would never, ever want to take anything away from your experience and what you value," said Walt.

"I know."

"I hope you understand that," said Walt.

"Of course, I do." Marcus stood and began re-organizing the pages.

"Good." Walt exhaled a sigh of relief. "On that note, it's been real flattering, but I have to get going." He stepped out of the garage and into the sunlight in the back alley. Then he broke left. Marcus tossed the program back in the box and followed, wondering if he should mention the fact that they were going the long way.

"It's been too much for you, huh?" said Marcus, trying to keep up with Walt's fast pace. The quarterback's eyes were focused straight ahead as if consumed with the single task of getting his big blond ass back to his rental car.

"As I stated, I'm flattered," said Walt, "but looking at the picture and talking to you more—I think it's just due to your wild and amazing imagination that we met, not some cosmic phenomenon. Agreed?"

"Meeting you has been incredible," said Marcus. "I know you didn't have the pro career you always dreamed of, and that we both know you were capable of, but maybe having a pro career in *Walt Loves the Bearcat,* maybe it can be like a little—maybe it can serve to ... well ... as ..."

"You mean, like a gift to me," said Walt, statement of fact.

"Exactly. Even though it might not be exactly how you dreamed it up when you were a kid throwing rocks at telephone poles disguised as receivers," said Marcus.

They came to a stop at the end of the alley. All they had to do now was take a counterclockwise journey on the oval pathway that led to the visitors' lot, then go their separate ways once again. Walt broke left, Marcus followed.

"I hope it goes well for you," said Walt, moving steadily down the path. "My hands are pretty full, but I'll help in any way I can. Keep me in the loop."

"I'd love to," said Marcus, immediately regretting his choice of words. "I hope this hasn't been too overwhelming."

"Try welding," said a voice from nowhere. "Welding is always better."

Their surroundings came into focus. The voice belonged to a Latino gardener, who was near the oval pathway. He was moving in the same counterclockwise direction, practically right alongside Walt and Marcus. But instead of using the sidewalk, he stayed on the grass, even as it morphed into the miniature golf course that lay inside most of the oval pathway.

"So I'm guessing it's been overwhelming," said Marcus to Walt.

"Try welding," repeated the Latino gardener. "Welding is always better."

Walt and Marcus eyed one another curiously, then stole glances at the intruder to their space. He was an older man with specks of gray in his jet-black hair. His skin appeared to have seen a million too many suns in its day, no doubt from a lifetime spent working in the great outdoors.

"Anyway, Marcus," said Walt, quickening his pace. "I wish you the best with everything in your life, really, I swear."

"He's not good enough," said the Latino gardener, "not on his own."

Walt and Marcus eyed one another again, their curiosity morphing into something less inviting. Marcus shrugged, as if to say, *Beats me*. Then the quarterback reassessed the situation and mouthed the words: "Cell phone ... other ear." As if to remind them that nowadays, crazy people are only crazy if they're talking to themselves without the benefit of a wireless plan.

"So, Walt," said Marcus once the mystery was solved, "this is overwhelming, admit it. It's okay, I swear."

"I'm not overwhelmed, I swear," said Walt.

"Welding is always better," said the Latino gardener, keeping pace, "and swearing is like saying your word isn't good enough on its own. Aren't you good enough on your own?"

Walt slowed to a crawl and told the Latino gardener: "You go ahead of us, buddy. We're kinda in the middle of something."

"Not even close," said the Latino gardener, who kept moving.

"I got a suggestion for your book," said Walt to Marcus. "If you want to make the quarterback more realistic, make him real moody, so moody that most people don't understand him and it causes a lot of problems for him and everyone else. Give him this—this *thing* that nobody can deal with. Then Bear—your guy—comes in and fixes it. But I guess you've probably already thought about something like that, haven't you?"

"I wouldn't be Marcus 'Bear' Coleman if I didn't," giggled Marcus. He returned Walt's smile, which evaporated on contact.

"I'm outta here," said Walt, continuing his orbit around the golf course.

"I hope I can do the story justice." Marcus followed, trying to say anything to keep Walt from leaving. "We're talking 21 years of daydreams about that dream man from that oh-so-dreamy weekend that kicked off that dream season in Athens, Georgia, the dreamiest of college towns."

"*Ha!*" said Walt, letting out one of his rare big laughs. "Anyone ever tell you that you use the word *dream* a lot?"

"The most beautiful words should be spoken as often as possible, to remind us why we're here," said the Latino gardener, once again traveling parallel to them.

"Not only that," said Walt to Marcus, as if ignoring the intrusion, "you daydream a lot, too."

"The most beautiful acts should be done as often as possible, to remind us why we're here," said the Latino gardener.

"All right, guy, what's the deal?" Walt asked the Latino gardener, halting the journey. "Did you want to talk to us? Because we're kinda busy right now. I've got stuff on my mind. He's got stuff on his mind."

"What about the stuff on both your minds?" asked the Latino gardener.

"How's that?" asked Walt.

"You obviously have a lot to talk about," said the Latino gardener. "Keep talking. How else are you going to make up, if you don't communicate?"

"Make up?" laughed Marcus. "And I thought *I* was crazy."

"Uh, not that it's any of your business," said Walt to the Latino gardener, "but you're way off base."

"No worries, man," said the Latino gardener. "I don't own a television or nothing. I don't know much about what's happening socially, or what you want me to call you these days. But you gotta believe, I'm a man of the times."

"Cool, man, we wish you all the best." Walt continued onward, Marcus followed.

"I gave away my TV the day JFK got shot," said the Latino gardener, staying behind as his audience moved farther and farther away. "I sure love my music though. Don't you? I bet you two are song men. I bet you got a thousand songs together, am I right?"

"He's half right," said Marcus to Walt.

"Keep going," said Walt to Marcus.

"And out of those a thousand songs, there's probably *ooooooone* song ... that means *mooooooore* than anything. I bet ... I can even name it."

Walt stopped in his tracks. A twisted smile full of piss 'n' vinegar crept across his face. He cracked his neck, both ways, then turned to face his challenger, the grin of a gambler on the quarterback's face.

"I'll give you five hundred bucks if you can tell *us* our song," said the gambler.

"Walt!" cried Marcus.

"This guy thinks he knows *our* song," said Walt. "Let's see what he's made of."

"I'm never wrong," shrugged the Latino gardener. "I've spent a whole lotta time doing this."

"Knock yourself out," said Marcus, enjoying Walt's enjoyment.

"Three guesses," said the Latino gardener. "I get it wrong, I walk away without another word, ever, so help me, Father. You boys game?"

"Game," the boys said together.

"Okay ... first let me put on my special baseball cap. It's got magical powers." The Latino gardener appeared to put on a baseball cap, doing everything necessary but with empty hands.

"He's a mime!" said Walt, as if that explained everything.

"Oh, you don't believe," said the Latino gardener. "You gotta believe in the magical cap to see the magical cap. That's the way everything works. There. It's on."

"Great," said Walt. "What's our song?"

The Latino gardener began a slow orbit around the boys, sizing them up from head to toe. "I'm feeling a lot of good times between you two ... *hmmm* ... and a lot of romance in the air around us, sweet ... *hmmm* ... oh ... you boys have been little devils at times, too, huh?"

"He's stalling," said Walt.

"He's also right," said Marcus.

"Just try not to be Big Devils," said the Latino gardener. "But I will say your song ... is ... 'True ... Blue.' Yes. 'True Blue' by Madonna. Did I get it right?"

"Sorry, that is wrong," said Walt, relieved until he noticed the consternation on Marcus' face.

"Well," said Marcus, "we do like that song. We even shot our own 50s-style, black-and-white video in a very special fantasy episode of the weekly TV series. But it's not *our* song."

"Not now," said Walt.

"But you were so cool in your leather jacket on that motorcycle with your blond hair in the wind," said Marcus.

"That was a whole different person," said Walt. "That *we* was not the we that we are today."

"Well, *we* can't fight about it in front of *others*," said Marcus, nodding to the Latino gardener, "not if *we* are going to play this silly game."

"Two more chances and I'm outta here," said Walt.

"Not Madonna, *hmmm*," said the Latino gardener, sizing up their backsides. "I won't dare say anything by Wham!." He stole a sideways glance at their reaction to hearing the name of the gayest band of the 80s. But Walt remained poker-faced, and Marcus simply averted the man's gaze. Having gleaned nothing, the Latino gardener uttered: "Second choice: 'Celebration' by Kool and the Gang!"

Marcus shook his head as if to say, *Sorry*.

"That was almost my first choice, too," said the Latino gardener.

"Final chance," said Walt, ready to close out the victory. "Need a hint?"

"Nope," said the Latino gardener.

"We'll give you a hint, if you *truly* want one," said Walt.

"Don't need a hint, just my third chance," said the Latino gardener, making another orbit around them.

"We *truly* don't mind giving you a hint," said Walt. "True, Marcus?"

"I guess it's true, Walt," said Marcus, "seeing as how you're about to give away a wad of cash if you keep this up. Truly."

"I truly believe," said the Latino gardener, ending his orbit and landing in their faces, "your song is ... 'World Without You' by Belinda Carlisle."

"*Ha!*" Walt turned on his heels and continued onward. "Have a nice life. Come on, Marcus, walk me to my car."

"Walt!" said Marcus when he caught up. "Walt, where are you going?"

"He didn't say 'True' by Spandau Ballet," said Walt. "That was our song—from the Athens weekend, right?"

The quarterback held up, then froze in his tracks. It was coming back to him. "World Without You" ... from this morning in Chicago.

"You don't think ..." Marcus fell silent, not knowing what to think.

"Is this our song after all?" whispered Walt, refusing to glance backward and acknowledge the Latino gardener. "Is this—is this one of your Upon Further Reveals?"

"I have no idea what this man is talking about," whispered Marcus.

"First the strange phone call in Chicago this morning," said Walt, pacing back and forth. "Then we happen to *both* fly from O'Hare to LAX around the same time. Then we feel things no one else can, rocking 'n' rolling. Then there's *time,* passing by like *time* doesn't exist. To top it off, we haven't eaten all day, yet we're not hungry; and now, a Latino gardener in the old folks home has just named—out of the wild blue yonder—the song that woke us up this morning. Do I have all the so-called bizzaro facts right? I just want to make sure ... before I go to the nearest gun store to blow my fucking brains out."

"Can I come?" asked Marcus. They turned to the Latino gardener.

"Who *are* you?" Walt moved closer but not too close, Marcus followed.

"How did you do that?" asked Marcus, feeling like the nerdy kid who'd caused trouble for the jock.

"My story doesn't matter," said the Latino gardener, "not if you want to untwist whatever's twisted between you and you."

"Twisted?" said both Walt and Marcus, not quite together.

"Like a nail," said the Latino gardener. "A twisted nail can't do what a nail is supposed to do."

"Nail something," said Walt.

"This man is brilliant," said the Latino gardener to Marcus. "I hope you plan to hold onto him."

"Man, this is crazy," said Walt.

"Anything's possible with love," said the Latino gardener. "Do you believe in miracles?"

"I don't know what to believe," said Walt.

"That makes two of us," said Marcus.

"That's all you need," said the Latino gardener. "Now go create some beliefs of your own."

The boys stood with blank expressions, unable to speak.

"So how did I know you were song men?" asked the Latino gardener. "It's the infatuation feeling that's coating the air."

"He's a psychic!" said Walt, as if that explained everything.

"Do you know what infatuations are, young man?" asked the Latino gardener. "Try to remember your very first one."

The boys stood motionless.

"Now unless you met as teenagers, you probably weren't each other's first infatuations," said the Latino gardener, "but no matter ... go back in your minds and remember the *very first* time your *heart burst* with something you didn't know existed until you *felt* it coming alive from deep within your soul ...

"But your *heart* wasn't big enough to hold this joyous *burst,* which gave you a joyous feeling. So the joyous feeling *burst* from your heart and *filled* your entire body, head to toe. But that still wasn't enough to contain the joyous *feeling*—this brand new life form that kept *feeling* you like helium *filling* a balloon, expanding until the *feelings* and the *filling* seeped out into the air around you ...

"If you fed the *feeling,* gave it enough love and energy, that *feeling* ended up *filling* your whole world, and your whole world became that *feeling.* What *filling* was that again? Infatuation. What is infatuation? Pure. Unconditional. Love. He's perfect. He can do no wrong. Every single thing he says and does is the single most perfect thing he can say or do at *any given moment in time.* His voice alone can bring tears to my eyes. The idea of him using his lips to form the sound of my name is enough to send my senses reeling toward the stars on a fantastic voyage from which I never want to descend. And stuff like that there. You feel me?"

"Yeah," said Walt with a mild laugh. "I've had a couple of those in my lifetime."

"Ditto for the black cheerboy," said Marcus.

"So why do we get infatuations?" asked the Latino gardener. "What's the point of them, supposing you believe everything has a point?"

"So you can go around thinking someone is absolutely perfect for you," said Walt, "before you rejoin the real world after knowing 'em a couple weeks."

"Give or take 21 years," said Marcus.

"*Nah,*" said the Latino gardener. "Infatuations are here so we know what *the most perfect, perfect* is like. You see, once the *feeling* becomes your world, *every*thing in your world becomes the *feeling. That* means *every*thing is perfect, every song, every task, every situation, *every*thing anybody around you does. When you're infatuated, the world makes perfect sense, down to the last detail. That, boys, is pure unconditional love. The receiver of this love can do no wrong, say no wrong, be no wrong. That person, in your eyes, is like—"

"God," said Marcus, lost in his own headspace.

"*The most perfect, perfect,*" said the Latino gardener. "And that person stays *like God* until the infatuation leaves you. Then the receiver becomes a normal human being, capable of doing wrong, saying wrong and being wrong."

"Because you get over the infatuation," said Walt.

"Get over?" asked the Latino gardener, "or forget about the *feeling,* which makes the *filling* inside start to deflate, like a helium balloon you don't keep *feeling* from time to time."

"So what good are The Infatuations?" asked Walt, followed by a mild laugh. "That outta be the name of an old-fashioned singing group."

"Glad you asked," said the Latino gardener. "In the game of life, when you ask questions, you always get answers. The Infatuations ... you nailed it. They're a musical group. They're just about every single musical group that ever existed. They sing songs just for you, you and everybody else in the world, songs that remind us how it *feels* to be *filled* with pure unconditional love. Otherwise known as infatuation. You feel me?"

"This is crazy," said Walt.

"No doubt," said the Latin gardener. "You boys have a lot of songs, together and separate. True? But I'm thinking Belinda Carlisle's 'World Without You' is the big one. It made some serious impact that changed your world. You mentioned something about 21 years. If you've been together that long, who knows what you've forgotten and what you remember."

"This guy still thinks you and I are together right now," said Walt.

"That's why you gotta talk," said the Latino gardener, "and remember how you got here, so you can work your way back. The only way to do that is to talk it *alllllll* out of you. Go somewhere, be alone together, get to know each other all over again. Go someplace you both love. Play the games you love. I can tell you two boys love your games. Songs and games, that's you two, songs and games. Go play. Go talk. Go be boys again. Go. Go. Stop hanging around an old man in an old folks home."

The back of the Latino gardener began moving away, and the boys realized it was because he was leaving. "Should we go after him?" asked Marcus.

"What for?" asked Walt.

"He got the song right," said Marcus.

"Coincidence," said Walt.

"Walt," said Marcus, droning it out. "I know you don't believe that."

"Dream on," said Walt.

"I know you," said Marcus, "better than you think."

"One sec, sir," yelled Walt. The Latino gardener turned and waited. "What do you want me to say to him?" whispered Walt to Marcus.

"I dunno," said Marcus, sounding like a kid.

"One sec, sir," said Walt. "My friend and I here need a—"

Huddle!

Walter's eyes grew wider and wider. The deafening roar made him dizzy, so he covered his ears. Suddenly, he was a midget amidst skyscrapers—the stands at Mile High Stadium were so damned mile high, the crowd stomping and swaying and yelling for his—the visiting QB's—guts ...

"Whoa," said Walter, grabbing the shoulder to his left. "This is nothing like the hedges."

"Walt?" said a wary voice. Walt looked to his right. A black man stood there, looking ... just like ...

"Marcus!" said Walt, releasing his grip on the cheerleader's shoulder. "Did you feel that one, that quake?"

"Probably," said Marcus, still coming out of his own haze. "You, too?"

"The gardener!" said Walt, looking up. "Hey, sir, did you feel that—"

The Latino gardener was gone, vanished from the oval pathway. Near where he had been standing was something the boys hadn't noticed until now: a football.

"Holy ..." Walt paused, figuring he'd might want to hold off on completing that phrase. Marcus went over and picked up the ball and the postcard lying next to it. "What's it say?" asked Walt.

"On the front it just says, LIFE IS A GAME, PLAY IT," said Marcus, looking at the artist's rendering of an airplane hangar surrounded by green fields.

"What's that mean?" Walt took the postcard and flipped it over. "The Complex, whatever the heck that is," he said, more focused on the directions, which appeared to lead into the hills over Malibu and the Pacific.

"So we're supposed to believe the magic cap has magical disappearing powers, too?" asked Marcus, more focused on looking around for the Latino gardener.

"I have no idea," said Walt, "except to go to this Complex and find out."

6

Why Walt Loves the Bearcat

"Where are we going again?" asked Walt, more focused on driving.

"The Complex," said Marcus, glancing at the postcard on the dashboard of the little red sports car. "Whatever that means. And we're gonna play the game of life, whatever that means."

"And why are we doing this again, other than the possibility that we've gone insane?" asked Walt.

"Because Sanchez, a musical expert and Latino gardener, gave us a football and told us we should go there to make up, his words, not mine," said Marcus.

"How can you make up if you're not together?" asked Walt. "*That's* what you call twisted."

"Maybe if we only believed in his magic cap," said Marcus, half-joking, half-serious. Walt accelerated faster, as if putting the car in TURBO MODE. They were heading south on Pacific Coast Highway, the mountains to the left, the ocean to the right. The sun was still high, the air warm, the skies clear. Another dreamy day in the fantasyland known as Southern California.

"So you didn't have any plans today? Or tonight?" asked Walt.

"Maybe a movie tonight," said Marcus. "Or just hanging with the dogs if I decide I'm not in the mood. You?"

"Something tonight, which is why I flew to LA," said Walt.

"When do you need to get going?" asked Marcus.

"I'll let you know when it's time to jet," said Walt, changing the radio to get rid of "Gambler" by Madonna, which had been playing on an easy-listening radio station.

"You know how you suggested the QB in the book be a moody guy?" asked Marcus. "Okay, so I get that you can be moody, and I can relate more than you know. But I gotta tell you, Walt, you've had this *phenomenal* reaction to this black, male ex-cheerleader calling you out of the blue because he saw your picture in a game program a whole other lifetime ago. Literally, kinda."

"Ah," said Walt, moving his sun visor to deflect the ray of sunlight. "I know you're cool."

"I know you do, and that's the thing," said Marcus. "It's like ... hard to put into words, but ... you understood right from the start that I meant you no harm. I was more scared of me than you were. And this whole time, I haven't felt one negative vibe from you. Truly amazing."

"So where are these two knuckleheads now?" asked Walt, obviously a great scrambling quarterback in his day.

"Don't knock 'em," laughed Marcus. "*Walter* Yeager and *Bear* Coleman become world-famous. *Their* lives are about to take off, while *this* Marcus Coleman just became infamous as the cocky black cheerleader who dropped poor little Jenny. Twice."

Marcus wondered if Walt felt infamous for being the top-rated quarterback who took a different path in life than Elway, Marino, Kelly, Young, and the other great QBs of his day, the golden era of great QBs.

"I wish things could have been different for you, Walt," said Marcus, feeling a dull ache in his lower left abdomen.

"It is what it is," said Walt, shifting in the driver's seat.

"I know you had the talent to compete with the best," said Marcus. "You probably envisioned yourself doing just that, going up against Favre, Testaverde, Aikman. I just want you to know, you weren't the only one."

Walt did a double-take. "You didn't."

"Oh, yes, I did," grinned Marcus. "You went up against all of them on a ton of Sundays in my dreams, which sometimes happened to coincide with me watching a football game on television."

"Really?" said Walt, full of doubt. "Dream on."

BEAR COLEMAN WAS CONTENT JUST TO HAVE A BUDDY, even though his buddy was miles away at another school. To Bear, the relationship was perfect. He had always imagined falling in love with a smile, followed by a romantic first date ending with a handshake, followed by dinner-and-movie dates ending with hugs, followed by a starry magical night and a spontaneous ... kiss. From there, he and his buddy would agree to wait a whole year to have sex, which would finally happen on their unofficial wedding night. Of course, once they'd progressed to the kissing stage, there'd be a lot of dry humping and wet stains on the fronts of their jeans. And once they were bonded in "marriage," there'd be no territory out of bounds, and nothing the buddies wouldn't do for one another.

The cheerleader had lots of ideas about those future days, many of which began to permeate his senses after the quarterback's brief visit to UCLA in November. Bear wore Walter's ripe gray sweatshirt like an eighth layer of skin so that he was never far from a strong whiff of his man. Of course, smelling Walter only put more ideas into Bear's swelling head, which made concentrating on the rest of life quite a challenge. Not that it mattered to the 21-year-old Bear in love. He had been single for life but had finally found his buddy. All that mattered was their friendship and the ideas percolating inside Bear's head, ideas that came to a boil after it was announced that the Bruins and the Bulldawgs, who had met in the season opener, were set for a rematch in the season closer, at the Sugar Bowl!

An angry fist banged on the glass door to the phone/mailroom. "Come on, Coleman, stop hibernating, gotta make a call!" yelled the voice of an impatient frat bro. Bear backed up against the door to keep it from opening, then said to Walter on the other end of the phone:

"I told you miracles happen, Big Norse Yeager! We're *Sugarbound!* What should they call the game? *Dawgs-Bruins II: This Time It's Personal?* When are you guys getting there? Walter, are you there?"

"One of my roomies almost tripped over the cord," said Walter. "Hold on, lemme go out to the balcony. Can't somebody make a phone that doesn't have to be attached to a cord?"

"Dream of it," said Bear. "Somebody will."

"Bear! Need my mail!" yelled the voice of another impatient frat bro.

"Fuck, it's freezing out here," said Walter. Bear could hear him warming his hands before adding: "So I'm number two on the depth chart. You might get to see me throw a few in New Orleans."

"Talk about a dream come true," said Bear.

"But unfortunately, as much as I'd like to hang out ..." said Walter.

"Talk about an even bigger dream coming true," said Bear, "but I know. That would take a boatload of miracles. Several boatloads."

"I'll run into you, at least," said Walter, "or you into me. Dream of that.

We'll make it happen. I gotta get inside. I'm starting to ache—*two minutes!*—well, bud ..."

"Yeah, bud?" said Bear.

"You're a very cool bud," said Walter. "A good friend."

"*Rightbackatcha.*"

"We'll run into each other, brother," said Walter, "but only when it's cool, right? Gotta go, roomies buggin', but Bear, I'll see you in New Orleans. I'll show up, if I know you're there. I mean, if you show up, I'll show up. Later, bud."

The line went dead, ending their first-ever phone call, and their last communication before blasting off for the Sugar Bowl in competing rockets ...

"That's what you call a crazy college life," said Walt, driving down Pacific Coast Highway in Southern California.

"It's about to get a little crazier," said Marcus, riding down Pacific Coast Highway in Southern California. "So, if you're ready ... cut to the song 'Shook Me All Night Long' by AC/DC, the kick-ass, guitar-riffin' jam that was quickly becoming one of *the* hard rock party anthems of that time. Our time."

... The Bruin cheerleaders stood in a cluster, watching Southern men carrying mugs of beer high over their heads, Southern men offering beads to look at titties, and Southern belles trying their best to look appealing and aloof while flashing said titties. The cheergirls had gotten the entire squad through the VIP door in minutes, which was why they were all standing in a crowded Bourbon Street bar a few hours after landing in New Orleans. The squad had been pointing to the trip since the announcement soon after Thanksgiving. "We're going to the Sugar Bowl!" they told anyone who'd listen. "Primetime, national television, ABC, we're there!"

At the heart of every true college cheerleader is a true passion for big road trips and big games, period.

But Bear Coleman was also living for something else now: his very own quarterback. Both schools making it to New Orleans was a miracle, maybe enough of one to speed along Bear's sexual timeline for his buddy dream. After meeting Walter, Bear had said goodbye to the dark venues where anonymous men roamed. As a result, the head above his neck felt freer, but the rest of him was as calm as a grizzly bear wrestling with a steel picnic basket, the goodies inside locked away for what truly seemed like forever.

"Bear, over here!" yelled White Donna. The rest of the squad had descended on the bar. He joined her near the outer regions of the group. "You've been a total space cadet all day," she said, "Forget about finals. Go get you some sugar now!"

"God willing," said Bear.

Everywhere Bear went in New Orleans, he dreamed of running into Georgia football players, one of whom would happen to be Walter Yeager. But Bear knew Walter had little free time. There were practices, media events, pep rallies, bonfires, barbeques and banquets. Plus there were the tourist excursions with various configurations of the football team, not to mention Walter's family, whatever that meant. But Bear was always on the lookout for his buddy. A few times, he thought he caught a glimpse of the golden blond aura ... just past a corner ... getting into an elevator ... near the lawn outside the hotel ... even at one of Bear's TV appearances on the field at an empty Superdome. He could feel Walter closer than ever. He just couldn't see him.

At the same time, Bear dreamed that Walter was dreaming the very same dream, that everywhere Walter went in New Orleans, he dreamed of running into UCLA cheerleaders, one of whom would happen to be Bear Coleman. But Walter knew Bear had little free time. There were practices, media events, pep rallies, bonfires, barbeques and banquets. Plus, there were the tourist excursions with various configurations of the spirit squad, not to mention Bear's family, whatever that meant. But Walter was always on the lookout for his buddy. A few times, he thought he caught a glimpse of the golden-brown aura ... just past a corner ... getting into an elevator ... near the lawn outside the hotel ... even at one of Walter's TV appearances on the field at an empty Superdome. He could feel Bear closer than ever. He just couldn't see him ...

"These guys are never going to get some Sugar at the Sugar Bowl," said Walt, driving down Pacific Coast Highway in Southern California.

"Bear wouldn't let his man down," said Marcus, riding down Pacific Coast Highway in Southern California. "All he needed was a little miracle, and he got one at the First Annual Snaky Lu's-New Orleans Crab Grab and Battle of the Sugar Bowl Bands Contest."

"Thank *Godddddddd!*" Bear roared so loud, the entire hotel lobby stopped to notice the handful of cheerleaders under the marble archway.

"*Bear, hush!*" said Candi, the feminist faculty advisor. Candi Mandonato had very short hair and was rumored to be a lesbian. *Rumored* being the key word, for there was no evidence she was anything more than a divorced woman who sometimes dated men and sometimes hated men. More often than not, Bear fit into the *hated* category, which was the case in New Orleans, even before his outburst. "Do something insane like that again, Bear Coleman, and you won't be cheering come game time," said Candi. A chill overcame the hotel lobby at the mere mention of her signature ultimate weapon: suspending a cheerleader on the spot, anywhere, anytime, any day.

"Sorry," said Bear, not sounding sorry.

Georgia and UCLA had been orbiting around one another all week, but the galaxies were scheduled to merge at an old-fashioned honky-tonk on the Mississippi River. The bands would battle. Each football team would try to out-eat the other team. And Walter Yeager and Bear Coleman would ...

"This is gonna be impossible!" cried Bear, getting off the bus and panning the setup at Snaky Lu's-New Orleans. The restaurant was a series of tin boxes of various sizes, all connected in a circular fashion to the largest tin box in the middle. To the left was a long, wide dock fronting the Mississippi River. Against the backdrop of the river, several bleachers full of fans were enjoying the music of the bands. The UGA Redcoat Marching Band was playing "Bulldog March Medley," stirring Bear's heart almost as much as the prospect of seeing Walter.

"Impossible to do stunts, for sure," said Captain Miles, the next one off the bus. The two bands were seated in folding chairs facing the bleachers. Between the band and the bleachers were two large vats filled with crabs. Directly in front of the vats sat two salivating football teams in the bleachers, one team wearing red jerseys, one team wearing blue. Bear scanned the reds but was too far away to locate the golden blond aura.

"Impossible to get excited about," said Roxanne, the next one off the bus. She was the female student underneath Joe Bruin, the UCLA mascot.

"Don't tell me you *and* White Donna are on the rag," said Bear.

"If only," said Roxanne. "Carry this?"

"Got the holiday flu that's going around?" asked Bear, taking possession of the plastic bag containing Joe Bruin's head. "That bug missed me, thank God."

"Just things on my mind," said Roxanne, moving forward.

"Join the club," said Bear, moving forward. "*Me*, too."

"This is a critical week for me," said Roxanne.

"*Me*, too," said Bear.

"I'm in love with *the* Georgia Bulldawg," said Roxanne.

"*Me*, too," said Bear, then caught the slip-up and froze in his tracks.

"Bear, I'm sure!" Roxanne snatched Joe Bruin's head in disgust. "You haven't been listening to a word. And people think *I'm* the one who's out of it."

They entered one of the tin boxes of Snaky Lu's-New Orleans, a restaurant storage area turned makeshift dressing room. Roxanne/Joe Bruin was the only member of the spirit squad who wasn't in uniform, so the cheergirls used the facility for last-minute touchups in their mirrors, while the guys took turns using the adjacent can. Before long, Captain Miles, who was near the door, heard the rousing intro to the fight song and yelled: "'Sons!'"

The squad piled out of the tin box and flew toward the bleachers, morphing from road-weary travelers to the most energetic beams of light in UCLA history. Instinctively they gravitated toward the stands colored in blue and landed before *their* choir like angels sent from the heavens to help worship *their* gods.

At the heart of every true college football fan is a true passion for big road trips and big games, period.

Bear clapped along to "Sons of Westwood," his aura *juuuuuust* this side of robotic and demonstratively masculine. Being a college cheerleader wasn't about censoring the feminine cheerleader from his boyhood. It was about setting free the masculine cheerleader within his manhood. It was about being a participant, not a spectator, a leader, not a follower. And yet he felt the same exact joy he had felt as a child, dancing in the imaginary stadiums of his youth.

After the initial rush of the "run-on" subsided, Bear clapped on autopilot and looked for his buddy. The hunt didn't take long. Cheering in front of 50,000 people on a regular basis makes finding your personal golden blond aura out of 100 men relatively easy. Walter was a few rows up in the bleachers, a good distance farther to the right ...

"Bear's not going to try to make contact, is he?" asked Walt, driving down Pacific Coast Highway in Southern California.

"That's exactly what Bear saw in his quarterback's eyes," said Marcus, riding down Pacific Coast Highway in Southern California. "Neither Bear nor I would ever be so stupid as to think a male cheerleader from UCLA could approach Walter Yeager in a situation like that."

"*Whew,*" said Walt, rolling down the window and letting in the ocean breeze ...

Walter's posture grew less nervous as he sat in the bleachers on the dock of the Mississippi in New Orleans. After the fight song ended, the spirit squad stood in a cramped, two-line formation between the band and the stands. A local radio announcer guy popped up on the stage between the two bands. He said something about being "wild and *k'waaaay-zy,*" then he explained the rules of the Crab Grab. Each school would send up 10 football players at a time to eat as much crab as possible for 10 minutes, followed by another 10 players and so on. The football team that emptied its crab vat first would be declared the winner. Meanwhile, the bands would alternate turns entertaining the crowd (thus the "battle of the bands" portion of the First Annual Snaky Lu's-New Orleans Crab Grab and Battle of the Sugar Bowl Bands Contest).

"Do we even need to be here?" asked Sergeant Holly.

"Roxanne must not think so," said Black Donna.

"She does not want to piss off Candi this week," said White Donna.

"Bear, go find her," said Black Donna.

"Why me?" asked Bear. Black Donna flashed him one of her sweet innocent smiles that, had life turned out differently, made him want to do more than just partner stunts with her. "Be right back," said a reluctant Bear. The local announcer guy encouraged the players to line up for the Crab Grab. Bear did his best version of the "respectful cheerleader exit," then accelerated when he cleared the staging area.

"Bear? Where do you think you're going?" asked a voice from nowhere. It was Candi, the feminist faculty advisor, halting him near the tin boxes.

"Restroom," said Bear.

"Hurry," said Candi. "And next time, go beforehand. And also ..."

"Great." Bear took off, pretending not to hear. His first impulse was to steal a closer look at Walter, but wandering around all that red while wearing all his blue was beyond his wildest dreams. Instead, he went to the tin box dressing room to find Roxanne. "Joe Bruin, you're on," said Bear, peeking around the door in case she was still getting dressed. Upon further reveal, he saw no humans, just animals. Joe Bruin lay crumpled on the floor, void of life. Next to him lay Harry Dawg, also void of life. Roxanne was with the Georgia Bulldawg. The moaning coming from the other side of the storage shelves was definitely that of mixed breeding. It also provided a love-starved Bear with a little inspiration ...

At the heart of every true college football athlete is a true passion for big road trips and big games, period.

Outside, the Bruins and the Dawgs were having such a good time being pigs, the players descended on the crab vats *en masse,* 100 red jerseys around a vat of crabmeat, 100 blue jerseys around an adjacent vat of crabmeat. The players morphed from fine young men to ravenous boys, moving about frenetically while remaining within the confines of their own atom, 100 red jerseys combusting around a vat of crabmeat, 100 blue jerseys combusting around an adjacent vat of crabmeat. Then there was Harry Dawg among the reds. His football uniform seemed a bit small, his big gray dog head a bit wobbly. But the Georgia mascot was right there in the trenches of the Crab Grab, permanent scowl and all.

Bear had always disliked the idea of being inside a mascot's uniform, so much so that he resisted the urge to even try on a head for curiosity's sake. But that was before he had a chance to be Walter's mascot, and hopefully stand next to his bud for a few harmless minutes. If only he could see through the big gray dog head eyes and find the blond aura. But Bear/Harry Dawg was being knocked around like a bumper car, propelled by elbows, shoulders, butts, and the general outbreak of rowdy boyish combustion. Between the virtual blindness and the dizzy ride, he became lost in his headspace. When he did feel something, it was because the bumper car that was his body collided with the very comfortable backside of a Georgia football player.

At the heart of every true college football romance is a true passion for big road trips and big games, period.

"Walter," said Bear into the void of his headspace. One of the bands was playing "Gimme Some Lovin'." The mass of players swayed in every direction, pressing the two bodies together as if on a crowded subway. The Dawgs began howling. Bear arched toward the heavens and surrendered. The Georgia player fell into him deeper. *His* backside fit perfectly with *his* front side. The howling intensified. A wave of bodies pushed them sideways, rotating them counterclockwise until they had reversed positions. The Georgia player arched toward the heavens and surrendered. Bear fell into him deeper. *His* backside fit perfectly with *his* front side. Howling pierced the skies. A wave of bodies pushed them sideways again, this time sending them spiraling in opposite directions.

The local announcer guy called for order, informing everyone the contest was over. Tension evaporated among the red jerseys and the blue jerseys, but the clock had struck midnight for the big gray dog head. Bear/Harry Dawg fought his way through the red jerseys until he was free, then slipped behind the bleachers and headed for the tin box dressing room.

"Joe Bruin, are you here?" asked Bear, peeking around the door in case she was still getting dressed. Upon further reveal, he saw no humans, just one animal. Joe Bruin was still crumpled on the floor, void of life. Bear removed the big gray dog head and Harry Dawg's football jersey. He contemplated his naked upper body, which was covered in sweat, but he didn't get too far because a pair of strong hands grabbed his naked waist from behind, as if to say, *Gotcha.*

"I *knew* it was you," said Walter. He spun Bear around and covered his mouth to keep him from making noise. "Man, you're fucking crazy. You make me wanna ..." Walter paused and Bear wasn't sure if it was to choke him or hug him. Turns out, it was neither. Still covering Bear's mouth, Walter kissed the back of his own hand, bringing them nose-to-nose, and bugged-out eyes to bugged-out eyes. Then suddenly, Walter jerked away his hand and replaced it with his mouth, which inhaled Bear until *his lips* found *his lips.* Their very first kiss: cool and refreshing yet warm to the soul, replete with the understanding of why God created the mouth: to taste, to savor, to flavor. The boys kissed roughly, then softly, then broke away, exhilarated and breathless.

"I can't live without you," said Walter, holding Bear's face.

"Really?" said Bear, holding Walter's forearms.

"I gotta go," said Walter.

"I know," said Bear, wishing he had said more than, *Really?*

Walter took one more look at Bear's sweaty chest, shook his head in frustration and disappeared. Hastily, Bear removed the last of Harry Dawg: his football pants. He was just about done when Roxanne came bursting into the tin box.

"Bear, give me those!" She snatched Harry Dawg and stuffed him into a body bag. "You went out there in my boyfriend's costume, I can't believe it."

"Your boyfriend?" asked Bear, naked except for his holey draws.

"We've been dating since the season opener," said Roxanne. "I told you that earlier when I said I was dating the Georgia Bulldawg."

"I thought you said you were dating *a* Georgia Bulldawg," said Bear.

"You are in so much trouble," said Roxanne.

"*Rightbackatcha*," said Bear with a knowing grin.

"We're not finished." Roxanne took off with her boyfriend's body. Bear shrugged off her threat, then turned toward the corner and his cheerleading uniform. Which wasn't there. Which wasn't anywhere in the tin box.

"Roxanne," uttered a devastated Bear, realizing Roxanne's naked boyfriend was no longer naked. Now Bear was the only one naked at the Crab Grab. He rifled through the squad's bags and found nothing helpful. He gave the room a thorough scan, but all he saw were cans of food and Joe Bruin, still crumpled on the floor. Voices echoed from the world outside, coming closer and closer. There was only one choice other than standing there in his holey draws ...

The UCLA spirit squad headed for the tin box dressing room, bewildered by Bear and Roxanne's disappearing act. "... and there's Roxanne!" said White Donna upon seeing Joe Bruin emerge from the dressing room. "Where have you been? And where's Bear? You guys are in big trouble!"

Because mascots never speak, Joe Bruin put his Bear paws to his Bear mouth and shrugged his Bear shoulders. Then Joe Bruin sauntered past the rest of the squad with his Bear paws over his floppy Bear ears. Once the coast was clear, it was time for Bear/Joe Bruin to figure out his next move: find someplace to hide to figure out his next move. His best shot was the tin box of a men's restroom on the other side of Snaky Lu's-New Orleans. He ambled inside, took off his head and camped out in one of the stalls. He stayed there for what felt like a whole hour, then put on his head and ambled outside. The dock was peaceful and quiet. A check of the parking lot told him the squad was gone. He checked the tin box dressing room for his own clothes, hoping Roxanne had returned them, but it was locked.

Bear/Joe Bruin sat in the empty bleachers next to the Mississippi River with no money and no wallet. A cleaning crew was getting rid of all evidence of the Crab Grab. A few fans lingered behind, but Bear/Joe Bruin didn't see one person from UCLA. He stood, intent on searching for a compassionate person wearing blue. Instead, he discovered one in red, standing next to a Winnebago in the distance, signing autographs for a handful of Bulldawg fans.

A young boy shoved a Georgia helmet in Yeager's face, forcing Yeager to glance upwards. Yeager caught sight of Joe Bruin and absently took hold of the helmet. Another fan snapped a photo. Yet another offered up a shoulder of her jersey for him to sign. Walter's audience became a blur to him. The QB excused himself and made his way toward the UCLA mascot with a curious expression.

"Do we know each other?" asked Walter upon reaching the bear.

"Better now," said Bear/Joe Bruin, his voice muffled under his big Bear head.

"I've been looking for you all over," said a relieved Walter. "I ditched my teammate twice. Why the bear suit now?"

"Holey draws," said Bear/Joe Bruin. Walter eyed him nonplussed, as if Bear were beyond shocking him at this point. Intuitively, the quarterback reached in his wallet and gave the mascot two twenties for a taxi.

"I gotta give this kid his helmet back," said Walter, pulling the headgear over his golden blond locks. "How do I look?"

"Can't see much with mesh eyes," said Bear/Joe Bruin, "but now I know your Sugar tastes great."

"You fucking animal you, don't get me started," said Walter with a mild laugh. "For a third time."

"Paranoid here. And off balance. We safe? What's that I hear?" asked Bear/Joe Bruin, head tilting upstream.

"A fish in the river, maybe a bass," said Walter.

"What's that on the ground?" asked Bear/Joe Bruin, head tilting downward.

"Somebody's breakfast, maybe a Danish," said Walter.

"What's that I see?" asked Bear/Joe Bruin, head tilting skyward.

"A bird overhead, maybe a hawk—put that aside, I gotta go," said Walter. "You think it would be cool for me to hug a Bear in a bear suit goodbye?"

"Joe Bruin is female underneath," said Bear/Joe Bruin, full of hope.

"Quick, gimme me some more Sugar." Walter led them into the shadows of the bleachers until they were near the edge of the Mississippi. They hugged, quarterback to mascot. "When are you leaving town?"

"Morning after the game," said Bear/Joe Bruin.

"Meet me here, day after, same time," said Walter. "I gotta take care of my family, but I'll be done by then. Just show up. I'll make sure you get back to school, okay. Okay?"

"If you show up, I'll show up," said Bear. Walter laughed, hugging deeper.

"Yankee Yeager!" yelled a voice from nowhere. "Stop sucking face with the enemy!"

It was one of Walter's teammates, a gigantic redheaded lineman. The boys untangled so fast, they pushed one another away. Bear, with his Joe Bruin equilibrium, stumbled backward and found himself teetering on the edge of the dock, his overwhelming headspace leaning toward the Mississippi River. Walter reached out as Bear reached out. They caught one another, and momentarily, remained off-balance together, suspended between water and land. To the outside observer, they were tilted and sure to fall. Instead, they remained in perfect *off-balance* balance, their center of gravity apparent but unseen.

"*Brilliant!*" yelled a nasally voice from nowhere.

It was a light-skinned Creole kid with a camera. He had just taken Walter's picture with Bear/Joe Bruin. The moment lost, Bear began to fall again until Walter pulled him away from the edge.

"Great shot," said the Creole kid. "The player and his mascot."

"That's not a Bulldawg, dimwit," said the gigantic redheaded lineman, standing next to the Creole kid.

"I don't do sports, just extra credit," said the Creole kid.

"What is this?" asked Walter, moving in front of Bear/Joe Bruin, as if to conceal his identity.

"Dimwit's a reporter," said the gigantic redheaded lineman. "Some pissant high school."

"So, that's not *your* mascot?" asked the Creole kid, indicating Joe Bruin. "He was kissing his opponent?"

"*She!*" said Walter, moving aside from Bear/Joe Bruin, as if to reveal her identity. "She's a girl! That's girl I was hugging. Underneath. A girl."

"Roxanne," mumbled Bear/Joe Bruin under his breath.

"Roseanne!" said Walter.

"So, Roseanne," said the Creole kid. "You're the what? Bears? Bearcats? Which is it?"

"She can't talk," said Walter, covering Bear/Joe Bruin's Bear mouth.

"Don't you know mascots never speak, dimwit?" said the gigantic redheaded lineman.

"Well, can you speak to me?" asked the Creole kid. "I need a story. Otherwise, I've blown the Sugar Bowl edition and don't pass journalism this semester. Please, Mr. Bear? Bearcat?"

"Roseanne's gotta go," said Walter.

"The Bearcat's gotta go, dimwit." The gigantic redheaded lineman smacked the Creole kid on the back of the head.

"Roxanne," mumbled Bear/Joe Bruin under his breath.

"Roseanne's got UCLA business," said Walter. Bear/Joe Bruin nodded his Bear head in demonstrative agreement, then shrugged.

"If I don't pass journalism, I don't get into film school," said the Creole kid. "If I don't get into film school, I'll never make great films that change the world."

"Sorry, kid," said Walter.

"*I'll* give you the scoop, dimwit," said the gigantic redheaded lineman, putting an arm around the Creole kid, "but you gotta buy me a beer. You of age?"

"Got a fake ID," grinned the Creole kid.

"Big Norse," said the gigantic redheaded lineman to Walter. "Out front, 10 minutes, cool?"

"Cool." Walter waited until they were gone, then let out a gigantic redheaded exhale.

"He took our picture?" asked a worried Bear/Joe Bruin. "*My* picture as Joe Bruin? With a Georgia football player?"

"A high school newspaper," shrugged Walter. "Put it aside. How big a deal can one pissant little photo turn out to be?"

7

Late Night Bus to Georgia

The little red sports car was parked on a ridge high above the Pacific. Walt stood at the very edge of the cliff, sizing up the massive scoop of a canyon between his feet and the ocean. Meanwhile, Marcus stood near the car, sizing up Walt Yeager. The former cheerleader had so many questions for the former QB, but the former QB played it close to the vest, like an out-of-town gambler at the roughest saloon in the West. And yet the man was sharing so much of himself, so generous with his time, his ear, his open mind. For now, at least, Marcus was content with those gifts and showed his gratitude with respect for the man's privacy. As much as he was dying to know everything ...

"When you woke up this morning in Chicago," said Marcus, "which would you have thought was more improbable: getting a call from a black male cheerleader who's had a crush on your photo for 21 years, or driving to a place called the Complex because a Latino gardener with a magic cap told you to go there?"

"The question alone twists my mind," said Walt. "What would have been more improbable when *you* woke up this morning in Chicago: you and I shooting the breeze here in Malibu, or a total stranger telling you that we should get back together again?"

"You're right," said Marcus. "It's too twisted to try to untwist."

"Fuck it. Let's just get to this Complex and put an end to this." Walt headed for the little red sports car, Marcus followed. "There's gotta be a logical explanation, I know it," added Walt, putting the car into gear.

"Whether there is or not, I'm glad we're figuring it out together," said Marcus from the passenger seat.

"So the famous boys," said Walt, steering away from the ocean and deeper into the hills, "the *Walter and Bear* that are gonna make it big—they're still at the Sugar Bowl, right? The Crab Grab zanies are over. They got their little Sugar. Please tell me Walter does something good in the actual game, like, wins it."

As if any other outcome was even more improbable and twisted.

"THIS IS THE SUGAR BOWL." It finally hit Bear as he sized up the Louisiana Superdome from a nearby parking lot. "It looks like a big golden mushroom."

The spirit squad was unloading their megaphones and gigantic flags from the side of the charter bus. "Bear!" said Black Donna. "You getting ready to cry? Bear's getting ready to cry."

A Winnebago roared past, forcing them to jump back to save their lives. The entire body of the RV was painted red, silver and black, and kept going as if the cheerleaders were never in danger. HOW BOUT DEM DAWGS? asked the sign between the taillights.

"Bring it on, Dawgs!" yelled Bear as the question retreated.

"Save some of that, Bear," said Sergeant Holly.

"Yeah, what happened to his hangover?" asked Black Donna.

"Plenty more energy where that came from," said Bear. "All the Sugar I'll ever need to keep me going is right there in that big golden mushroom."

Game time was eons away, but Bear's spirits were just as high a short while later, as the squad loitered in the concrete underbelly of the stadium. Some were stretching, others were eating, and a good percentage of the cheerleaders were getting over too much fun in the French Quarter all week.

"So are you stoked?" asked Roxanne. She was still dressed as herself, not Joe Bruin.

"Aren't you?" asked Bear, arms raised over his head, torso twisting side to side. Since the Crab Grab, the two of them had struck a deal: she wouldn't reveal *his* mascot escapades at Snaky Lu's-New Orleans, and he wouldn't reveal *her* mascot escapades at Snaky Lu's-New Orleans.

"Did you hear about their number one quarterback?" asked Roxanne. "Isn't it hilarious?"

"Walter Yeager? What happened?" asked Bear, full of panic.

"Who's that?" asked Roxanne.

"Their number one quarterback," said Bear, stating the obvious.

"No, Trent Stacey," said Roxanne, eyeing him curiously. "He's still sick. From the crabs? The starting Georgia quarterback? Bear, where have you been? Trent Stacey's been sick since the Crab Grab, the only player out of both schools to come down with food poisoning! It's all anybody's been talking about. You—you're, like, living on another planet, aren't you?"

He's starting! My bud is starting! My buddy is starting the Sugar Bowl for the University of Georgia! And I bet I know what he's thinking ...

I'm starting! Man, the look on my buddy's face when he finds out I'm the starting QB! And I bet I know what he'll be thinking ...

"—and Bear, we have a serious situation," said a voice from nowhere. "It's getting more and more out of control, and I'm putting an end to it right now."

It was Candi, the feminist facility advisor. She was standing in front of Bear and Roxanne in the underbelly of the golden mushroom. The agenda of this impromptu meeting was understood. For days, Candi had been furious that both Bear and Roxanne/Joe Bruin went AWOL from the Crab Grab, at least from Candi's point of view.

Bear and Roxanne had cooked up some story about helping out an elderly alumni man who had fallen ill, prompting Candi to demand details and names. Bear and Roxanne had bluffed their way this far, but their alibi was crumbling like a house of cards, and the issue had yet to reach a satisfactory conclusion, according to Candi.

"This Mr. Milton, or Mr. MacLitton, or Milltown is not turning up," said Candi. She had that "you can't cheer" look on her face. Everyone on the squad knew the look, whether they'd been victims or eyewitnesses, or whether they'd yet to see it at all. Everyone knew and understood the look. "I'm gonna make this quick." Candi turned to Bear. "You can't cheer." Then she turned to Roxanne. "You can't be Joe Bruin."

Bear's spirits fell beneath the underbelly. Roxanne dropped to the floor. The Georgia cheerleaders came streaming by, waving a big red flag high in the air. They were practicing the run-on (running onto the field with the team right before kickoff). Their rehearsal was loud for the sake of the UCLA cheerleaders, most of whom countered with cheers and jeers of their own. Only Bear, Roxanne and Candi, the feminist facility advisor, failed to join in.

"Thing is," said Candi once the Georgia cheerleaders disappeared. "We can't be on national TV without Joe Bruin. So, Bear, as punishment ... because I remember you telling me once that you'd rather die than be a mascot ... since the costume fits ... don't expect you to be as good ... or as funny ..."

The rest of her words blurred by Bear's spinning head. Candi had exacted her revenge on him for being a man, and one who usually stood up to her at that. She had won and he had lost everything. Not only would he not be able to see Walter play from a bar or elsewhere in the stadium (yes, his quick-thinking mind had already gone down those paths), but now he wouldn't be able to *see* Walter play at all. A blindfolded man could take in a football game better than Joe Bruin, with his wire mesh eyes and that space helmet of a head, which incidentally reeked from years of different kinds of nasty, funky, unwashed, sweaty, college-student hair.

On the outside, Joe Bruin was anything but nasty or mean. He was a cross between a teddy bear in an animated movie and a cool and dreamy guy who always had a smile on his face. Joe Bruin wanted to go surfing in Malibu. Or dance on the sidelines. He could even entertain people throwing a football or shooting a basketball and it didn't matter how athletic or unathletic he appeared. Joe Bruin could move just about any way he wanted and make people feel good. Unlike Georgia's Harry Dawg, there was no permanent scowl on Joe Bruin's mug, just a goofy grin anyone with an open heart could love.

Joe Bruin was created to make people feel good.

Of course, none of this was going through the mind of the new Joe Bruin, who by kickoff was plenty dizzy from the years of nasty, funky, unwashed, sweaty, college-student hair. The entire space around his head was dark except for the mesh eyes. The one-piece bearskin body was tailored to fit Roxanne, who was four inches shorter. It was as if he were walking around in a world made too small for him, and he had to crouch just to exist. He also had to do those cute little Joe Bruin things that Joe Bruin did, but he was determined to be defiant to the end. He planted himself in one corner of the golden mushroom, and only performed a minimum of mascot duties. That way, he could preserve his equilibrium and find out how Walter was doing by listening: to the clashing of the pads, the crowd, and most of all, the game announcer's play-by-play:

"Starting at quarterback for Georgia ... Walter Yeager."

"Pass is complete. Yeager to Fields. First down, Dawgs. Gain of 21 yards on the play."

"Masters is the ball carrier. Gain of four yards."

"Yeager's pass is incomplete. Third down and six."

"Georgia is too far to the right—their field goal attempt, that is. The attempt by Del Kicko is no good. First down, UCLA."

The announcer told Bear the story, and the crowd and the bands provided the soundtrack. Occasionally, the golden mushroom erupted for one side or the other, prompting him to turn suddenly, as if to get a glimpse. The motion would render him dizzier and turn the game into a heady dream, only becoming less heady when he gave in to the rush and let his body go where it wanted to go. Most often, his body wanted to right itself by flailing his arms freely or kicking his legs in different directions, as if to work out the kinks. When he did, the audience laughed, so he assumed they were being entertained by his actions, though he really didn't concern himself with their needs.

"Pass is complete. Yeager to Fields. Gain of 14 yards. First down, Dawgs."

Bear didn't care about UCLA at the moment. Candi, the feminist faculty advisor, and by extension, UCLA had deprived him of a once-in-a-lifetime experience: watching the man of his dreams in the Sugar Bowl. He didn't hate the Bruins or want them to lose. He merely wanted to soak up the idea of his quarterback buddy playing football.

"Turnover. Georgia ball."

"Percy is the ball carrier. Gain of 1."

"Franklin with the sack of Yeager. Loss of 17 on the play. Third down, 26."

The Georgia offense was backed up near Bear's end zone, where Bruin fans were trying to rattle the Dawgs. Bear spun around to see through his mesh eyes, but became heady and could only locate *whooshes* of the crowd. The decibel level went up: the center had just hiked the ball to Walter.

The ground rumbled. "Pass!" echoed a thousand voices in his headgear. Adrenaline exploded like the big bang from somewhere inside his chest. His feet took over for his feet. His arms took over for his arms. His eyes didn't need to see. His mind didn't need to think. He surrendered thought. He released. He let go, let it go. He let it go, then flopped gracefully backward to the turf.

The nearby crowd exhaled devastation. The distant crowd sang out. And kept singing. More of their kind joined them, while the nearby crowd fell silent, their hopes momentarily dashed. The other end of the universe erupted in utter bliss, complete with music, bells, cannons and all sorts of explosive and magical sounds. The reds were celebrating. Walter had done them right.

"Seventy-four yards on the pass, complete from Yeager to Masters. Touchdown, Georgia."

Bear/Joe Bruin danced as if he were in *seven heaven*. The UCLA band even provided the audio: "Gimme Some Lovin'," the soul classic made popular again by the Blues Brothers and the song from the Crab Grab. The squad had a great routine for the song. Bear himself had bestowed it on them. The combination of thoughts made him dance with glee, laughing aloud inside his headspace and visualizing the long bomb his buddy had just completed.

"You're an awesome bear!" said a voice from nowhere.

Bear/Joe Bruin spun around and felt something hitting his big Bear head—a fuzzy black ball, upon further reveal, held by a rather tall man whose hair was dotted with ice cream sprinkles.

" ... normally with KWAZ Mighty Mouth Radio," said the man, looking in the direction of a bright red light. "We're *k'waaaay-zy*. Get it?"

The band finished giving the crowd some lovin'. Bear/Joe Bruin bowed to the applause, then turned around to pretend he could see the kickoff, all while dismissing some very *k'waaaay-zy* words drifting through his dizzying headgear.

" ... *live* on the air... get the *dirt* ... Georgia quarterback ... you listening up ... Bearcat?"

Bear/Joe Bruin's headgear rotated a quarter-turn. Those weren't ice cream sprinkles on the other side of his mesh eyes. Upon further reveal, they were flakes of snow. And Bear/Joe Bruin had never dreamed of seeing snow inside the golden mushroom, otherwise known as the Louisiana Superdome. The funky-haired ghosts of mascots past were haunting him for mocking their passion, he decided.

"You are the Bearcat, aren't you?" asked Evil Announcer Guy.

"*Whoa, stop right there,*" said Walt, steering his way through the hills overlooking Malibu, California.

"What'd I do?" asked Marcus from the passenger seat, eyes roaming the hills overlooking Malibu, California.

"Evil Announcer Guy?" asked Walt. "The guy's name is Evil Announcer Guy?"

"You bet," said Marcus, "especially after a certain, very pissed-off quarterback warned to never, *ever* mention his name again."

"What's the guy's name?" asked Walt, sounding impatient.

Marcus remained silent, lips not budging.

"Come on," said Walt. "What's his name? Just say it."

Marcus remained silent, lips not budging.

"I can't win with you, can I?" said Walt.

"With good reason," giggled Marcus. "We're on the same team."

"So anyway," said Walt, sounding like a frustrated gambler. "Evil Announcer Guy is about to rock their dreamy little world. Dream on."

... Bear/Joe Bruin's limited vision became coated in a strange mix of blond aura and newsprint. On top of that, he was now hearing things, like people calling him Bearcat. He was dehydrated or just plain delirious. Either way, he needed out of his headspace. He staggered toward the wall bordering the underbelly of the stadium, fanning himself with his big Bear paw, as if to inform the faithful: *I'm going on break.* Had they wanted to know the real reason, he would have had to have mimed: *I'm hearing some very scary things inside this big head on my shoulders.*

"... announce to the world ... holy union ... your man ... this photo ... listen up! We're on the air live, you little—Bearcat."

Bear/Joe Bruin stopped in his tracks, having sworn someone just called him a little bitch. He rotated slowly, wondering if this was the moment in his life where he had to choose between preserving his world as he knew it, or beating the senseless crap out of someone because they called him a bitch. He paused to ponder the two roads, and more light was revealed on the fork.

"You're *this* Bearcat, right?" asked Evil Announcer Guy. "Can you see the photo in front of your eyes? Here, look closer."

It was all mesh-mash to Bear/Joe Bruin, who shrugged his Bear shoulders while an uneasy rumble stirred inside his Bear stomach.

"It's my daughter's pissant high school newspaper," said Evil Announcer Guy. "According to the caption, *you*, Roseanne, Last Name Unknown, and *that guy*, right over there—who's coming out of the huddle to try to get into your end zone on fourth down—met here earlier this week, and are getting hitched after the game, am I dreaming here or what? Can't you see the picture? It's right here on the front cover, special Sugar Bowl edition!"

Bear/Joe Bruin choked down the vomit trying to erupt in his headspace, then tried to will his Bear feet forward.

"How about the damned headline?" asked Evil Announcer Guy, his voice rising with the crowd's anticipation. "Can you see the damned headline? True or false: QB LOVES THE BEARCAT. Tell our worldwide audience!"

Bear/Joe Bruin shook his head and covered his mouth, as if to say, *Me No Speak.*

"We got two damned billion people watching!" said Evil Announcer Guy. "Never mind that. Blow your man a kiss. He's about to snap the ball! There he is, do it! Go! We're live! Show your love!"

Breakfast recycled, Bear/Joe Bruin focused on the next biological challenge: vanishing.

"Nobody else has this story!" yelled Evil Announcer Guy. "Give a radio guy trying to bust into television a break. It's for my reel, okay? We're not really live. Come on ... wait ... where are you going ... Roseanne Bearcat, come back here!"

The UCLA crowd was merciless and unforgiving, punishing him for simply wanting to penetrate their territory. He lunged forward, staggering but staying off the turf. He willed himself onward despite throbbing pain within. Get under, get under, instinct told him, dive, dive ... a tunnel ... cut, dart ... slice ... been hit, twisting, falling, fallen ... didn't make it, short.

Bear/Joe Bruin picked himself off the floor of the golden mushroom, just short of his goal: the exit tunnel. "Coleman, you all right?" asked Captain Miles, helping him stand. Bear/Joe Bruin insisted he had merely stumbled and continued onward. Even in the underbelly, the blues could be heard celebrating. They had stopped Walter on fourth and goal. Judging by the tempo of the play, Walter must have tried a quarterback sneak, which had failed as miserably as Bear's mascot sneak. But Bear knew that Yeager wasn't down for the count, and neither was Coleman.

Roxanne was sitting on a staircase in the underbelly, still unable to move from where she had received the devastating news from Candi.

"I'll make this quick," said Bear/Joe Bruin upon finding her. "I feel really bad for everything, so let's pull a switch. You be Joe Bruin the rest of the game, and no one will be the wiser. Deal?"

Roxanne's face lit up like a little girl whose Christmas wish had come true. They made the switch in a stall in a women's restroom, where Bear promised to remain in order to avoid the watchful eyes of Candi, the feminist faculty advisor. "Wish I would have thought of a change-of-clothes clause before I made this deal," said Bear, only wearing a sweaty grey t-shirt, a sweaty pair of white underwear, and his sneakers and socks.

"I owe you, Bear," said Roxanne, finishing her transformation to Roxanne/Joe Bruin.

"One more thing," said Bear. "If some *k'waaaay-zy* announcer guy starts bugging you, keep away from him. He's evil."

"Whatever." She was halfway out the door. "Thanks."

Bear sat in the stall while the Sugar Bowl went on without him, his only updates coming from the commentators in the women's restroom:

"Offense is doing better. Now, if only my husband would when he's in *my* end zone."

"Bruins got a field goal, 7-3 Georgia."

"If I don't have my period, it's hello Mom and Dad in Pittsburgh."

"What a punt return! Bruins kicking butt now."

"I had some good butt in the French Quarter last night. Four of them."

"How 'bout dem butt cheeks on the Georgia quarterback? Makes me wanna run on the field and plant one on his lips."

Bear learned a lot about the women, but very little about the game, unlike a men's restroom, where it was all about the game and very little about the men themselves. His first meaningful contact with the action on the field came courtesy of a small radio he swiped from the floor of the adjacent stall:

"Georgia could sure use a stop right here on third down," said the broadcaster. "Stevens back to pass, rolls right, going to try to keep it—no, he fires it to Grasshoff ... Grasshoff catches ... Grasshoff dives for the first down. The Bruin drive is still alive to open the second half ..."

The score was: Walter 7, UCLA 17. The Bruins put two more field goals on the board to make it: Walter 7, UCLA 23 with five minutes to go in the third quarter. Bear sank deeper into the toilet, the broadcast a dull hum from his lap as his mind tried to will Walter onward. He imagined Number 13 fading back to pass, calm and confident, but his concentration was broken by a rapping on the stall door.

"Bear, say something!" It was Roxanne.

"Something!" said Bear, then added: "What?"

"I'll make this quick ..." Roxanne explained that Candi, the feminist facility advisor, had approached Joe Bruin, wondering if Joe Bruin had seen Roxanne, who was missing. Roxanne/Joe Bruin had shrugged her way out of it, but now Roxanne had a new plan. "Switch again," she said inside the stall. "I'll make a cameo with Candi as myself, then we can switch back, okay?"

Before Bear/Joe Bruin knew it, he was staggering out of the women's restroom and wandering around in the underbelly of the stadium, the game announcer's voice descending from speakers on high:

"First down, Georgia. 20-yard line."

After sitting for so long, he was still getting his bearings. He was back in the action so abruptly after that turnover. His world was like a dream again, the eyes not the best of senses to guide him. He closed his eyelids just enough to blur the world before him and find a sense of balance inside his head. When he did this well, he found the sense of balance inside his soul.

He moved like a lost star in the night sky, finding its way in the darkness by floating at the speed of his surroundings. Was he going to faint from the rush? He could only hope someone was there to catch him should he fall. He wanted to keep going, but he could have easily fallen right there ... right here as well. But no, he kept onward, then to the right, then a little farther, then to a safe place, a safe space ... out of space, out of bounds. He could rest now. Maybe the pain would stop.

Bear/Joe Bruin stood against a wall near the sidelines, clutching his stomach. His big Bear head was bowed, as if out of respect. As if there were an injured player on the field. "The injured player on the play ... quarterback Walter Yeager," said the game announcer.

You said you can't live without me. I can't live without you either.

Don't go getting dramatic. It's just a minor, minor, I'm ... give me a few ... rest ... catch wind.

I can see you now, getting checked over. A black coach has got your back. A black coach has always got your back. Relax. Black Coach got your back.

Bear/Joe Bruin dreamed it so. Whether it was true or false, the dream kept him calm until he reached a safe port: in this case, the UCLA sideline. Soon after, there was good news.

"Yeager the ball carrier, loss of two yards."

Walter was just fine and back in action. But he was still down, 7-23, and the game was in the fourth quarter. Yeager needed two touchdowns and a field goal, and a little help from the Junkyard Dawgs on defense.

"Yeager to Masters for the completion up the middle, 38 yards on the play. First down, Dawgs. Ball at the 49-yard line."

The crowd of blues on the other side of Bear/Joe Bruin's mesh eyes sensed a power surge. Moments later, Bear/Joe Bruin felt one in his head, swaying in all directions. The stands lifted toward the dome, then the distant crowd erupted with jubilee. The "Battle Hymn of the Republic" filled his headspace. "Glory, glory (to Georgia)" filled the golden mushroom. Same song, different deity. Bear hummed along merrily, worshipping his own divine being.

"Extra point is good ... touchdown run by Simmons of Georgia, a 51-yard, end-around double reverse."

The score was now Walter 14, UCLA 23.

"Bear!" cried White Donna, suddenly next to his head. "Roxanne told me to get a message to you—don't worry, I won't tell—she said she ran into Candi, now let her be Joe Bruin again for the rest of the game."

"Five more minutes," said Bear/Joe Bruin, more focused on the ruckus on the field. UCLA had recovered its own fumble on the kickoff. Clearly, Yeager had the blues rattled. The Junkyard Dawgs held the Bruins to three and out. Walter got the ball back on his own 14-yard line, 86 yards away with a few minutes to go. Bear/Joe Bruin looked as nervous as Yeager must have felt.

He needed water, but there wasn't time. There was work to be done. He had to focus, execute, concentrate, will it to happen. He could do it. He could do anything. There's no doubt. No doubt. We can do this. Keep it up. We can do this. Let's make this happen.

"Yeager is the ball carrier. Gain of twelve yards. First down, Dawgs."

"Penalty is on UCLA, roughing the passer. First down."

Stay cool. You know you want to throw it in the fucking end zone right now just to shove it back up their asses, but stay calm. Focus on what you gotta do.

"Pass is complete, 18 yards on the play. First down, Dawgs."

"Bear!" cried White Donna, back and bothering him again. "Roxanne says meet and swap now!"

"Tell Roxanne after this drive," said Bear/Joe Bruin.

"Touchdown, Dawgs! Pass is complete. Yeager to Dawson, 34 yards."

"Great!" said White Donna. "Now she won't be pissed if you let her see the end of the game."

"Let me keep the crowd going until the defense comes on," said Bear/Joe Bruin.

"We're on offense, Bear," laughed White Donna, "who are you rooting for?"

Walter was down 21-23 with under two minutes to play. When the television timeout ended, the crowd rose to its feet for the onside kick. Bear tried to savor the moment by panning the crowd, but his mesh eyes landed on snow again, the same snow he had mistaken for ice cream sprinkles in the first half. He squinted for better focus now, and upon further reveal, realized that the snow wasn't snow at all, but dandruff coating the hair of a very *k'waaaay-zy* man.

"Roseanne!" said Evil Announcer Guy. "If your fiancé wins the game, we're gonna get you and him in a victory smooch, okay? Talk about a career maker, boy, I'll never forget you two for this. What do you mean, shaking a finger no? You just said the quarterback was your boyfriend. I just asked you—where's the scoreboard ... in the third quarter—I asked you if you're in love with the #1 Bulldawg. You nodded yes. You started dancing and covering your heart up like you're happy and in love. Now you're changing your story? Which is it? What's the big secret? I need this. I'm trying to make it big here!"

"Kickoff recovered by UCLA. Penalty on the play."

The blues erupted with joy.

"Where are you going?" shouted Evil Announcer Guy. "Roseanne?"

"Penalty is on UCLA."

The reds erupted with joy.

"Hey, Bearcat, I'm talking to you!" yelled Evil Announcer Guy. "God dammit. College kids."

He staggered backward. Reprieve. At least partially. There was still a chance this could turn out all right, but they had to recover the kickoff this time. He stood patiently and waited for the action to unfold and determine if his next step was forward or backwards.

The crowd rose again, louder than before. Something popped, then soared in the air, but only for a moment before landing below and causing an earthquake on the field. But it was good, it was good, it was good for the reds! The reds had a shot! The reds had a shot! Somewhere near midfield, the reds had a shot! Distractions flew at him from every angle! Voices, choices, noises, chaos, confusion!

"Quarterback for the Georgia Bulldawgs, Walter Yeager."

Got that right. In good hands. No doubt. And good arms and shoulders and everything else. Walter Yeager is ready to go play some football! *and throw a couple spirals to some buds.*

"First down at the Georgia 45."

"Bear! Joe Bruin!" yelled White Donna from somewhere.

"Don't you want to be on TV with your boyfriend?" yelled Evil Announcer Guy from somewhere.

Always playing it close to the edge, keeps life entertaining and keeps 'em guessing. Let's do this, come on, let's do this.

"Pass is complete. Seven yards on the play."

These people are going nuts, all for this, for what I got to say about this game, this game right here, right now.

"Yeager to Simmons on the pass action, gain of 14. First down, Dawgs."

That's right. Let the clock run down. You think you're getting a chance to see the ball again? Dream on.

"Pass is incomplete. Second and 10 from the 32."

You're crazy if you think we're settling for a field goal from this far out. Still got some clock to piss away. We know how to work it, get us some Sugar ... that Sugar ... had a taste of Sugar, and that Sugar was oh, so, sweet!

"A loss of 15 yards on the play. After the extensive scramble, Yeager is eventually sacked by Wyatt and Gibson. Third down, 25, from the UCLA 47-yard line. Timeout, Georgia, their last time out."

Okay, we fucked up. Too much Sugar, need to regulate the Sugar. Listen up, people are telling you things.

"Roxanne is about to barge out onto the field and rip your head off, literally, if you don't switch with her now!" said White Donna.

"After you guys kiss, we'll rip your head off and show the world the love-birds," said Evil Announcer Guy.

Listen, then walk away and do what you know you have to do. Onward. Focus. Third and 25 from their 47. Two or three offense plays left at best. Gotta get back in field goal range. Fuck, why can't I see him? Why haven't I seen him all game? What are they doing to him? This one's for you.

He moved on autopilot. The top blew off the golden mushroom. The space in his headgear was perfectly aligned, no darkness, no light, just clarity of knowledge and purpose, two forces merged with one common goal. The roaring in his headgear sent him flying higher and farther until he'd done what he needed to do. He'd covered his ass, all his bases, all the ones he could think of anyway—in fact, he could say that about the whole Sugar Bowl week. He'd survived, more than survived.

"Please reset the game clock to :04. The ball carrier, Number 13 for Georgia, retained possession before going out of bounds. When play resumes, it will be first down, Georgia. Ball on the 20. Timeout, UCLA, one remaining."

Walter Yeager had scrambled 27 yards for a first down. The field goal unit ran onto the field. The Sugar Bowl was to be decided by Del Kicko, the smallest player on the team. The great equalizer or practical joke, depending on one's point of view. The blues called two timeouts to ice the kicker, but they couldn't forestall fate.

Didn't watch. The crowd would tell him ... blue.

Bear found out who won from the voices streaming into the women's restroom. He was dressed as himself again, soaking wet in a gray t-shirt and white briefs. The news caused him to fall back against the stall wall. The last time he was in contact with the game, Walter had just run for big yardage to set up the game-winning field goal, which must have gone astray. Game, blues.

Walter 21, Bruins 23.

THE MISSISSIPPI WAS CALM in the still of the night. The Crab Grab vats and Battle of the Bands bleachers had vanished from the large dock between Snaky Lu's-New Orleans and the river. In his mind, Bear played "True" by Spandau Ballet. He was moving down the dock, left to right, as Walter moved down the dock, right to left. They came together slowly and stood in the moonlight. They were just college boys now, no uniforms, no mascots, just themselves.

"I don't want to talk about it," said Walter.

"I know," said Bear, knowing he meant the game.

"We should be safe here," said Walter, scanning the empty dock. "Smells fishy but then again ... where were you?"

"I don't want to talk about it," said Bear.

"I looked for you everywhere I saw blue," said Walter.

"I was brown," said Bear. "My punishment for being black and assertive."

"I passed out for a second when I got hit outta bounds," said Walter. "I thought I saw bear feet. Was I dreaming?"

"God knows," said Bear. "God also knows more women at the game were dreaming of your butt over their second favorite, some young DB on your team with a name like Showman. Oh, freak, never mind that ..." Bear told him about the QB LOVES THE BEARCAT headline and Evil Announcer Guy.

"*That's* what he meant," said Walter.

"The announcer?" asked Bear.

"The redheaded lineman," said Walter. "Claims he told the Creole kid everything he needed to know. Dimwit! Guys never stop acting like boys."

"I did my best to cover," said Bear.

"It's still just a high school paper, and that announcer sounds like your average *k'waaaay-zy* local idiot," said Walter. "Don't sweat it. Wanna get something to eat or drink?"

Underneath the tin boxes of Snaky Lu's-New Orleans was a restaurant with sawdust on the floor. The jukebox was playing "I Want You to Want Me" by Cheap Trick as the boys drank beers at the bar.

"This is for your flight," said Walter, handing Bear a wad of cash.

"We're not flying around the same time?" asked Bear.

"I'm busing it," said Walter. "Your ticket cost a mint. I could only scrounge up so much on such short notice without raising eyebrows. We're both outta here pretty soon."

"We're always leaving each other," said Bear.

"I need some more Sugar," said Walter, causing Bear to look downward and blush. "What's funny? Why are you laughing, Bear Coleman?"

"Where can we go to get some Sugar?" asked Bear.

"What kind of Sugar you want, Bear Coleman?" asked Walter. As an answer, Bear stood up and disappeared. Moments later, he was waiting in yet another stall in New Orleans. On the other side of the restroom, the jukebox was playing "Anyway You Want It" by Journey. Walter entered the stall. Bear started to speak, but Walter grabbed him and planted some Sugar on his lips. Seconds later, Walter tore himself away, his lips anyway. "We shouldn't do this here, Bear Coleman."

"Where then?" asked Bear, running his hands through Walter's golden blond hair for the very first time.

"Somewhere." Walter started consuming Bear's tongue until they heard the sound of the restroom door. They froze in place, forehead to forehead, lips to lips. The threat smelled fishy. It peed, washed its hands for minutes on end, then disappeared as if down the drain.

Walter slammed his way out of the stall, then slammed his way out of the restroom altogether. By the time Bear joined him, the QB was hunched over the bar, drinking another beer, while the Rolling Stones crooned about never being a Beast of Burden.

"Ever notice how most love songs sound like infatuations?" asked Bear. "*Baby I loved you from the moment I saw you, can't live without you, you are my world, you are every single thing to me.* My father used to say, 'Those are punks, singing those songs with the falsetto voices, pussy-whipped by bitches.' Good ole Daddy Coleman."

"I'm real sorry, Bear," said Walter, meaning his mood change.

"Nowhere else I wanna be right now. Or ever," said Bear. The QB let out a mild laugh, then rotated on his stool so that his back was to the bar.

"Being friends won't be easy, Bear. You know that, don't you? Of course, you do." Walter made sure the bartender was out of earshot. "You're gonna have to put up with a lot of shit being with me. A lot of shit."

"Are you saying ... you want to be with me?" asked Bear.

"Haven't we been together since—" Walter nodded to a man passing by wearing a Georgia t-shirt.

"—the Aspirin Incident," said Bear. Walter eyed him curiously, hearing the reference for the first time, yet knowing exactly what Bear meant. They smiled: Walter, a half-smile; Bear, a Joe Bruin-sized grin.

"This is good," said Walter, taking a breath and a good look at the honky-tonk. "Takes my mind off the game."

"I got something else that will," teased Bear, reaching in his duffel bag.

"Don't start something you don't think you can stop," warned Walter. "Once I get started, I'm not gonna wanna stop, so consider that fair warning when that day comes, because I know you want it to come, don't you?"

"Like a dream come true," giggled Bear, glancing shyly toward the floor.

"I'm going to use the can for real this time, then we gotta get to the airport." Walter hopped off his stool, wincing from some hit his body took 24 hours ago at the Sugar Bowl. Alone, Bear had an idea. He searched the jukebox for "True" by Spandau Ballet. But Snaky Lu's-New Orleans was not "True." Much to his delight, however, Snaky Lu's-New Orleans did have a little soul, and that soul sounded so heavenly in the form of the introduction to "Midnight Train to Georgia."

Bear sauntered into the restroom and past the partition. Walter was leaning like a cowboy with his back against the wall to the left, the R&B classic throbbing from the jukebox on the other side. The QB shook his head, his shit-eating grin saying: *I knew that was your doing.* Bear smiled and started singing, accompanied by the Infatuations, featuring Gladys Knight and the Pips:

LA—as in Louisiana, folks—had enough! said my man
He couldn't make it—the freakin' field goal kicker!

... Bear threw up his hands in frustration and got slightly off track.

So Walter's leaving the Sugar Bowl
Not 1-0

... Walter had so much bittersweet joy in his eyes, Bear fell out of sync with the rest of the Infatuations.

Walter is going
Walt's gonna be fine
Because he is so fine

... The restroom door started to open. Walter leaped to shut it and lock it in one fluid motion. Then Bear found his place again.

Walter's leaving
On a late night bus to Georgia (leaving on a late night bus)
'Cause he's gonna get back
To a better dream in his mind

... Walter pulled Bear into him.

I'm gonna be with him—in spirit!
On that late night bus to Georgia

... And Walter started filling in for the Pips:

Leaving on a late night bus to Georgia. Woo. Woo.

... Which made Bear tear up.

I'd rather be in Walter's world

... Which made Walter calm Bear with a finger to Bear's lips.

Than live without Walt ... in mine

... Which made Bear point at Walter's chest with a determined finger.

You keep dreaming
Because someday you'll be a star (a superstar, 'cause you *will* go far!)
And let's not find out the hard way

That dreams *do!* always come true! (I'm gonna make sure, Walter!)

So don't burn all your hopes
And don't you ever sell that sweet old car
Because there is no ticket back
To a life ... without me or you

... Bear was overcome with more emotion and lost his place again, which prompted Walter to sing indecipherable words, which made Bear laugh until he found his place again.

Walter, I'm gonna be with you!

... and Walter the Pip sang:

I bet you will

... and Bear broke out in tears for Walter, his rock star.

Oh, Walter
On that late night bus to Georgia

... and Walter the Pip sang:

Leaving on that late night bus to Georgia. Woo. Woo.

... and Bear lost it altogether.

Oh, Walter,
don't go,
just be here,
be right here with me,
Walter ... don't go back ... without me ... take me with you,
 take me with you ... take me ...

... Eventually Bear calmed down. His breathing became regulated, his tears subsided, and he found peace in the bosom of his buddy, holding him in his arms, calming his soul. The Sugar Bowl was still a dream come true.

THE AIRPORT WAS RELATIVELY QUIET. Walter and Bear had a whole row of seats to themselves in the area outside Bear's gate.

"Del only missed one kick in the last four games of the season," said Walter, slumped so far down, he was practically horizontal.

"You put them in position to win, bud," said Bear, sitting upright.

"I shouldn't have gotten sacked for that big loss," said Walter.

"Why do I get the feeling Walter Yeager is always hardest on himself?" asked Bear.

"It's my job to nail it," said Walter.

"And be the Man, which you were. But let's see how good you really are at football." Bear reached into his duffel bag and pulled out a little green box made of hard plastic—a handheld game. At the very top was a small screen in the shape of a football field, which was sunken in to accommodate a stadium around the perimeter, along with a "high tech" digital scoreboard along one sideline. The lower portion of the little green box contained a small group of color-coded buttons and an on/off switch with two speeds, PRO 1 and PRO 2. Eight buttons, two speeds, and a handful of frenetic red dashes trying to outwit other frenetic red dashes, the most important of which was the quarterback. Bear was holding in his hand the golden treasure of many a boy of their time: Mattel Electronics Football.

"Version 2!" said Walter.

"But of course." Bear flipped on the on/off switch and pushed KICK. The digital *charge!* sounded, the kickoff commenced, and Walter absently took the game from Bear, who was beaming ear-to-ear.

"Man, I haven't played this in ages," said Walter.

"Same here. I got bored, then burnt-out," said Bear.

"I never lose," the boys said together, then laughed.

"How'd you know I'd love this? asked Walter, more focused on running his offense.

"I know my quarterback," said Bear.

The boys played Mattel Electronics Football for the rest of the night, boasting and bragging and kidding one another like two boys who planned to share a lifetime of joyous moments just like this one. Only the boarding call was able to bring them out of their reverie. "Thanks, man, that took me back," said Walter, handing over the game as they joined the back of the passenger line and moved slowly toward the gate.

"You can have it, if you want," said Bear, hoisting his duffel bag over his shoulder.

"*Nah*, I wouldn't do that," said Walter.

"You sure?" said Bear. "Anything mine is yours."

"*Rightbackatcha.*"

"From here on out," said Bear, "when I play Mattel Electronics Football by myself, I'm gonna imagine I'm playing with you."

"Just don't imagine beating me," said Walter, more focused on scanning his surroundings—the other passengers, the ticket counter, the baby in front of them, smiling over his mother's shoulder at Walter.

"Walter, I only want to see you," said Bear, looking down.

"Man, you read my mind," said Walter, looking ahead. "So you're cool with that?"

"More than cool," said Bear. "That's the way I like it."

"Don't go busting out in an old disco song," said Walter.

Bear's laughter calmed them. "So, it's just us?"

"You know Ellen?" asked Walter, then he saw the confusion on Bear's face. "The dark-haired girl from the ride to Atlanta."

"If you say so," said Bear.

"She was—we were seeing each other," said Walter. "Long story, another time. Point being: it's over, completely, never to darken my—correction, *our*—lives again, okay?"

"Got it," said Bear, still processing.

"So we ..." said Walter, indicating him and Bear, "together, right?"

"Signed, sealed and delivered," said Bear.

"What do we call each other?" asked Walter with a mild laugh. He had reached a rope and had gone as far as he could go. Bear had to keep going but wanted to leave his quarterback on a high note. He was, after all, his spirit leader. Moving forward, he glanced over his left shoulder. Walter was fading away from him, his beautiful blond arms extended on either side of him, still waiting for an answer.

"We're buddies," said Bear with a proud, confident smile. Then he disappeared into the tunnel.

8

Le Sucre

... running underneath the stadium, me and my brown-eyed Bear ...
... wake up, sleepyhead ... little Bearcat?

"We home yet, Walter?"

The car slowed to a crawl, then stopped altogether.

"No, but welcome to hell," said Walt, surveying the landscape outside.

"You mean heaven," said Marcus, surveying that same landscape.

"Heaven?" scoffed Walt.

"The eggbeaters," said Marcus, "both of them."

"Eggbeaters?" laughed Walt.

Marcus opened his eyes a little wider. The world came into better focus. He saw what looked like a junior high school football stadium in the foreground, and dilapidated, boarded-up school buildings in the background—all nestled in a canyon in the mountains overlooking Malibu and the Pacific.

"Did we take a wrong turn?" asked Marcus.

"Depends," said Walt. The little red sports car was parked next to a fence bordering the stadium, or rather, the half-stadium. There were worn wooden bleachers along the far sideline, but only tractors, construction equipment and a shed on the near sideline. A sign by the side of the road said: THE COMPLEX: COME PLAY THE GAMES OF LIFE TODAY. COMING SOON (NOT TODAY).

"Where's this airplane hangar?" Marcus grabbed the postcard on the dashboard, then studied the directions. A vague recognition permeated his senses until it morphed into a disheartening revelation. He started to tell Walt the news, but the former quarterback had vacated the car and was roaming the nearest end zone. Marcus followed with the postcard in hand.

"That was the only gate open on the campus," said Walt. "Man, this place needs work." He tossed the Latino gardener's football to himself and scanned the field. "There's your airplane hangar." He pointed behind the bleachers to a long narrow building with a round roof: the gymnasium.

"Which explains this even more," said Marcus, indicating the postcard.

"How so?" asked Walt.

"I'm not sure Sanchez left this after all," said Marcus. "Long story short: Helen, a neighbor, gave this to me. I saw something about enrollment fees and dismissed it. I never looked at the side with the artist's rendering. I don't know what I did with the card after that, but I remember seeing it in the garage with you at some point. When we found it on the walkway, I only paid attention to the artist's rendering, which was new to me. *You* were the one who focused on the side with the directions and the written information, which was cool with me because you were driving."

"I saw this in the garage, too," said Walt, indicating the postcard. "I had the ball, I think. Remember? Is that familiar?"

"Instant replay," said Marcus. "We're back at the garage, going through my stuff."

"I flipped the ball." Walt flipped the ball.

"I had the card in my hand!" Marcus dropped the card and caught the ball. "That's what happened!"

"Then I picked up the card, saw the drawing and tossed it," said Walt, "or thought I did. I dropped it on the golf course! When we picked it up, I only paid attention to the side with the written information, which was new to *me*. We both did the same thing in reverse. Marcus, why are you looking so weird?"

"I think that explains this, too." Marcus held up the football, which said: PROPERTY OF UCLA REC. DEPT. "This is the ball from the garage. I must have had it and dropped it, without realizing it, just like you and the postcard."

"Then I'm *not* crazy!" said Walt. He decided to inform the canyons surrounding them by yelling at the top of his lungs: "I'm not *k'waaaay-zy!*"

"Whoever said you were?" laughed Marcus, shocked and exhilarated.

"Don't you see?" said Walt. "This place is just a new gym in the works. There's no magic cap, no magic phenomenon, no magic nothing! Just our—just your—hey, it's just been a crazy day. *Whew!* Glad we did the instant replay."

"The things you find out upon further reveal," said Marcus, picking up a rock.

"*Ha!*" said Walt with a rare big laugh. "I love it. You do have a way with words, I'll give you that. Man, what a day this has been, eh?" He took the football and heaved it as far as possible, as if he could release all the madness and frustration with one missile.

Something within told Marcus: *go chase that ball!* So he did, by throwing the rock after the ball.

The football sailed toward the sideline opposite the bleachers. The trajectory was more like a rocket than a forward pass, but the rocket flew erratically and crash-landed near the top of a telephone pole not far from the vicinity of the 50-yard line. The landing caused a spark on the pole. Around the same time, the rock disappeared into the commotion, and the spark turned into a small fireworks display. The small fireworks caused a strand of wire to break free from the top of the pole and come swinging down like a rope. The end of the rope was still shooting off fireworks when it hit the shed on the sidelines between the telephone pole and the 50-yard line. The small shed went up in flames that lasted for but a few moments. The flames disappeared. The shed was still standing, its sides only slightly charred from the instant barbeque.

"Let's get out of here," said Walt, sounding like a kid trying to escape a broken window rap.

"I think it's okay," said Marcus, meaning the shed. "Miraculously."

"Let's get out of here anyway," said Walt, not about to take on another miracle. "We got our answers. It was both of our overactive imaginations."

"Don't you want to hear the rest of the story?" asked Marcus.

"You bet," said Walt, heading for the little red sports car. "As I stated before, keep me in the loop. I hope the book/movie deal goes well."

"Walt! You can't just walk away now," cried Marcus, surprising himself. "Not when I'm about to kick your telephone-pole-killing blond butt."

The gunslinger stopped in his tracks, then rotated slowly. "Come again?" said Walt, staring down the man and his threats.

"You heard me right." Marcus reached for his weapon in the pocket of his shorts, then aimed it at the cowboy in the distance. Walt eyed him with a crooked grin, then slowly moved forward. When he was a heartbeat from the chosen weapon, he broke into his biggest smile of the day.

"Version 2!" said Walt, beaming at the little green box that was Mattel Electronics Football, the golden treasure of many a boy of their time.

"But of course." Marcus flipped on the on/off switch and pushed KICK. The digital *charge!* sounded, the kickoff commenced, and Walt absently took the game from Marcus, who was beaming ear-to-ear. "*This* I purposely brought from the garage to surprise you," said the former spirit leader. "Amazingly, this little green box has survived my crazy life."

"Man, I haven't played this in ages," said Walt.

"You and me both," said Marcus.

"I never lose, just like Walter," said Walt, more focused on running his offense.

"I never lose, either, just like Bear," said Marcus.

"We need shade to see the screen," said Walt, surveying the rickety old school. "Wanna kick back under the bleachers and play? You can tell me what happens to the famous boys while I open up a can of whoop-ass on you."

Marcus grinned a Joe Bruin-size grin, eyes full of wonderment and joy, as if to say, *I'll play whatever you wanna play. That's why I showed up!*

"I JUST WANNA SEE YOU HAPPY, WALTER," said Bear, turning away from the payphone in the dark. The Sugar Bowl was ancient history, having happened one whole month ago. The boys were back to their separate lives, and all Bear could think about was finding a way to be with Walter, who sounded very unhappy in Athens.

"I don't burden people with my troubles, even my buddy," said Walter on the phone. "Just know I'm fine and we're gonna see each other soon."

Two weeks later, on a sunny winter day in Southern California, the lime green Oldsmobile Omega came to an abrupt halt at the curb at LAX. Bear jumped from his car and ran to Walter, just as Walter came shooting out of the terminal doors. They met, hugged and spun around once, only untangling after noticing the sea of humanity around them.

"That's the last time we're ever doing *that!*" said Walter, looking through the rearview mirror heading away from the airport. "In public at least. Bear, how ya doing, man? How's my little Bearcat?"

"In heaven for two whole days," giggled Bear. *He called me little Bearcat!* The boys held hands for the first time ever, which made them laugh.

"I've never held anyone's hand before," said Walter. "I mean, a guy's."

"How does it feel?" asked Bear, gazing into his man's eyes.

"Like—*pay attention!*" Walter unhanded Bear just in time for Bear to steer away from the median divider heading into their lives. They drove the rest of the way to Malibu without touching—that much—and made it safely to the Seaside Inn. They told themselves they were staying in a motel because it made more sense than dealing with Bear's basement alcove in the big white frat house; but as they settled into the room, the fringe benefits became too hard to ignore.

"So you're cool with this deal, right?" asked Walter, standing on one side of the bed.

"Whatever's cool," said Bear, standing on the other side. Walter sized up Bear, who wasn't quite ready to look his buddy in the eye, so Walter asked if they should check out the beach. Bear thought it was a fantastic idea. Walter agreed after he saw the relief in Bear's eyes. A short time later, they were walking on the sand, northbound. The Pacific was calm, the afternoon comfortable. "You look like a different person than the airport," said Bear. "More relaxed already. Walter, what's going on? Something with football?"

"Same old," said Walter, more focused on the sand in his immediate path.

"They gotta be happy with the Sugar Bowl," said Bear. "Let's see the guy who got sick with crabs throw for 312 yards on 21-28 passing, with two TDs and one pick—all with a day's notice before the start."

"I had two picks," laughed Walter.

"Ah," said Bear. "Hail Mary passes right before halftime should not count toward a quarterback's interceptions. Neither should tipped passes."

"I like that you know my stats," said Walter. "You saw them in the paper?"

"I *saved* the paper," said Bear.

"That makes me feel kinda good," said Walter with a mild laugh.

"That's my job," said Bear.

"In all ways?" asked Walter, pausing in the sand.

Bear savored the thought, then said with utter faith: "Whatever Walter wants."

"Walter wants to eat. He's famished."

They wandered farther down the beach to a hamburger shack and stuffed themselves with chili cheeseburgers and chili cheese fries on a patio facing the ocean. "Growing up, I wasn't ever sure I could be this happy," said Bear, watching Walter scarf down a burger in three bites.

"What was it like for you?" asked Walter. Bear swallowed some kind of groan, then paused until a belch erupted and made them laugh like boys half their age. "So? Your childhood?" asked Walter afterward.

"Ah, man." Bear looked toward the sky. "When I'm with you, none of that stuff even matters."

"What does?" teased Walter, nudging Bear's leg under the table.

"Whatever Walter wants," said Bear, swallowing the last of his burger.

The quarterback's face grew serious and decisive. "Follow me," said Walter before heading down the beach toward the Seaside Inn. Bear hastily bussed their table, then made the same journey, thrilled to discover that Walter Yeager had a full back—not a quarter back—in the seat of his faded blue jeans. It was the first time Bear had dared noticed, and he was very pleased. Walter kept his pace, not looking back. Bear followed, in no hurry to catch up right away.

By the time Bear entered the room, Walter was removing his shirt, exposing his naked chest for the first time. "We left the heat on," said the QB with a chagrined smile, as if he had created the excuse. He started to leap backward on the bed, but changed his mind and lay down gently, then pointed the remote at the TV and said, "Anything good on?"

"Nothing is as good as this," said Bear, joining him. The boys kissed, first in haste, then in deep exploration. They went from vertical to horizontal, first side by side, then Walter on top of Bear. Walter's left knee pinned the remote to the bed, inadvertently changing the bowling highlights to a non-working channel with a white fuzzy screen. Now, there was both a snowstorm and a heatwave in room 104 of the Seaside Inn. Walter melted into the golden-brown body beneath him. Bear clung tightly to the golden blond body above him, as if holding on for dear life, as if caught in an avalanche. Suddenly, the QB tore himself away, then rolled over and collapsed on his back.

"Bear, I need to know something," said Walter, out of breath.

"Okay," said Bear, turning on his stomach, mouth pressed against the bed in exasperation.

"How long? What's your idea? How long before we, you know, in your mind?" asked Walter.

"What makes you think I want to wait?" asked Bear.

"My powers are amazing," said Walter. "It's cool, don't worry. It's probably the best thing for my mind, too, right now. But what are you thinking, as far as, how long?"

"Well," said Bear, "I used to think a year—"

"A *year!*" gulped Walter. *"I've waited 21 already!"*

"That was before I met the buddy of my dreams," laughed Bear. "I don't think I can wait a year now."

"I wouldn't wanna try!" said Walter.

"You don't have to," said Bear.

"Nope, we ain't waiting no year, no way, no fucking way, cool?" said Walter.

"You're the signal-caller," said Bear.

"That's what I wanna hear from my little black cheerboy," said Walter.

"Little black *who?*" cried Bear, his voice rising several octaves.

"You called yourself that in my car in Athens," said Walter.

"Never!" laughed Bear.

"What else don't you remember, trying to handle my stick shift?" asked Walter.

They were at it again, kissing, caressing, Bear running his hands all over Walter's golden blond hair, Walter running his hands all over Bear's golden brown body. They began wrestling in the name of swallowing one another whole yet resisting temptation. The sheets got caught up in the fracas, the pillows flew off the bed. Walter's foot knocked over the lamp on the nightstand. Bear's head hit the wall behind the bed so hard, the painting of the ocean would have collided with their heads, were it not for Walter's quick hands. "Timeout," said the quarterback after the recovery, then he disappeared into the bathroom. A while later, he emerged, looking like a man with a lot less stress on his mind.

"Brush my teeth," said Bear, making his way to the bathroom, passing Walter on the way. A while later, he emerged, looking equally relieved. Walter was lying in bed, playing Mattel Electronics Football, which had been on the nightstand. Bear joined him and they played into the night. They were competitive, but only to make the game interesting. Walter played like a true quarterback, focused at all times (and usually going for it on fourth down). Bear was part football player, part cheerleader, part game announcer, relishing the chance to visualize his QB in action.

"The Dawgs are in the Dawg House. Can Yeager be the comeback kid again?"

"Boy, that defense of Walter Yeager really sucks. Coleman's able to penetrate anytime he wants."

No egos were involved, and Bear made a point of never saying anything to betray their common reality: Walter Yeager was the top-rated quarterback, period. No qualifiers like *year, team,* or *league* needed. There was Walter Yeager, and there was everybody else. Forever. That weekend, Bear made a covenant with himself: as his QB's spirit leader, he would only accentuate the positive, just as he'd done for whole universities his entire college career. It was the least Bear could offer in return for Walter's gift of being the first man who wanted Bear for more than just sex. By three a.m., they were suffering from Mattel Electronics Burnout and falling asleep, Walter spooning Bear's backside.

"We're cool?" asked Bear, just before dozing off.

"Always," yawned Walter. "All ways."

"You think you can put up with me for a while?" asked Bear.

"Longer than that," said Walter.

"Think you can put up with me forever?" asked Bear.

"Gimme another 21 years to figure it out, little Bearcat," said Walter, falling deeper into his dreams. "I should know something by then."

"So *every*thing's cool?" asked Bear.

"Three times cool," mumbled Walter.

"Three?" giggled Bear. "Twice here."

"You owe me one," said Walter as they drifted off.

They spent most of Sunday on the beach or in bed. They also allowed themselves to dream about the future, especially while watching highlights of the just-past NFL season. "That's gonna be you real soon. I know you're that good," Bear told Walter.

"You haven't even seen me play with your own two eyes," said Walter.

"Neither have you," said Bear.

"I don't have to see myself to know I'm good," said Walter.

"Then why should I be any different?" asked Bear. Walter let out a big laugh, and kissed Bear, but not for long. They were in bed, only in their underwear. The slightest friction between them made them want to fuck around like horny college boys. This restraint thing was going to take work. Neither man was used to waiting for or going without sex.

"We might have to make this wall higher," said Walter, leaning over the row of pillows between them to plant one more kiss on his buddy.

THE SPRING BREAK GODS WERE UNKIND TO Walter and Bear, not granting them rollicking days and nights filled with surf, sand and each other's company. Not that either one had the time. Spring meant spring ball for Walter and spirit squad tryouts for Bear. Walter's prospects were solid after his Sugar Bowl heroics. His voice over the phone reminded Bear of Piss 'n' Vinegar Walter from the spring ball photo the previous year. On top of that, Bear's own outlook was just as sunny. Right before tryouts, he met the cutest drunk little blonde girl at his frat party. She cornered Bear, not for sex, but for advice. "Do I look like college cheerleader material?" asked the freshman.

Bear, who was also intoxicated, became intoxicated with the drunk little blonde girl, who looked as if she were sixteen going on fifteen, and viewed Bear as the *Mighty Cheer God.* She was also from Orange County, California, the place where beautiful white people came from (as Bear learned during his very first week of college). That night at the big white frat house, Bear Coleman cast his next cheerleading partner, a girl right out of his frat brother's dreams ...

"That was true in this life, too," said Marcus from underneath the bleachers of the football stadium nestled in the hills overlooking the Pacific Ocean.

"The little blonde girl?" asked Walt from under those same bleachers. They were sitting side by side in a golf cart. Walt was in the driver's seat, trying to beat Marcus at Mattel Electronics Football.

"The girl *and* the sunny outlook that spring," said Marcus, reclining in the passenger seat, legs on the hood of the cart. "The squad had this huge turnover. So many people graduated, the Legend of Jenny's Fall faded from the air. Naturally, my drunk little blonde girl made it. She had what it takes, but I'm also a good teacher. It was all about visualizing game situations, then reacting to them as if you're in front of the crowd. Practice, practice, practice the simulation of the game, so when you're in there, it's like riding a bike, not a roller coaster."

"Yes, first down!" said Walt, happy with his play calling. "In a way, cheerleading sounds like football."

"Same goal, different path," said Marcus. "Touchdowns, enough to lead to ultimate glory."

"Speaking of TDs ..." Walt handed Marcus the little green box, which began playing the digital ditty that meant *touchdown!* "I'm up three with a second to play. Your ball."

"There's that piss 'n' vinegar, ladies and gents," said Marcus.

"*Ha!*" said Walt. "Start another game. I'll give you a chance to redeem yourself."

"We had a blast—my little blonde girl and me," said Marcus, punching the buttons on the game. "Her parents loved me, taking us to dinner, videotaping us from the stands with one of those newfangled camcorders the size of a small building."

"Ah, Yeager's defense just picked off Coleman," said Walt upon hearing the *turnover!* whistle. A chagrined Marcus handed him the little green box, then began rambling on as a way of rattling the quarterback:

"So basically, Marcus Coleman has Walt in his dreams, and Bear Coleman has Walter in his life, which is but a dream. Of course, Bear Coleman has no idea he's only dreaming. It's as real to him and Walter as you and me sitting here. Freaky, eh?"

"You can't distract me," said Piss 'n' Vinegar Walt, more focused on the game. "Give it up."

"But neither one of us black cheerboys knew how his bud was doing in spring ball," said Marcus. "Plus, Bear was starting to crave more Sugar."

"*Ha!*" blurted Walt, still focused on the game. "He's a Sugar addict!"

"Not yet," said Marcus. "However, Bear finally became one in France. The boys finally got all kinds of *Le Sucre* in France. I dreamed that you had an uncle who was eccentric by American standards and lived on a yacht in the Mediterranean."

"Slow down, little Bearcat," said Walt. "Yeager's supposed to go from fighting for the QB job in spring ball to enjoying himself on a boat?" Then he changed his tune. "Pretty cool way to unwind after school gets out. Tell me more."

"AWESOME WAY TO UNWIND after school gets out, little Bearcat," said Walter on the phone from Georgia.

"Tell me more!" said Bear on the phone in the big white frat house. *He called me little Bearcat!*

"My uncle and his wife are somewhat different from what I remember—"

"No, no!" said Bear. "Where do I show up? That's all I need to know!"

The South of France was everything the boys dreamed it would be. Walter's Uncle and Walter's Aunt hadn't seen the rest of the family in years but welcomed Walter and Bear as if they were old friends, and treated them as adults. For two glorious weeks, they sailed the Côte D'Azure, only stopping for supplies and an occasional night at an expensive restaurant, courtesy Walter's Uncle. The boys spent their days tossing the football and diving into the Mediterranean, then repeating as necessary. Some days, they fished with Walter's Uncle, catching big scaly sea creatures that Walter's Aunt turned into dinner. The Yeagers retired early each night when Walter's Uncle said to his wife: "Come on, sweetie, time to go dreamin'." This afforded the boys their own dreamtime, alone on the deck. It was during one of those nights that Walter brought up something he knew had been on both their minds.

"I'm not saying we are, but you know everybody else would see us as being fags," said Walter. They were on their backs, hands behind their heads, staring up at the starry sky.

"Do you care what people think?" asked Bear.

Walter knew this was a trick question. He paused for half a lifetime, then let out a guilty laugh and said, "Yeah, I do. It's a reality."

"I know," said a resigned Bear. "We can't mess up your career."

"We're gonna have to be careful," said Walter.

"I won't let anything happen," promised Bear.

"I know you won't," said Walter. "You sure Roseanne knows nothing about the QB LOVES THE BEARCAT story?"

"Her name is Roxanne, but she didn't even make Joe Bruin again," said Bear. "She's clueless. And out of our lives."

"*Hmmm*," murmured Walter, as if unconvinced. They fell silent, their attention drifting upward to the world above. They floated away to separate parts of the universe until Walter brought them together again. "I was thinking you could come to the Georgia Tech game after you guys finish with SC the week before that."

"You mean that, Walter?" asked Bear, rising up on his elbows.

"I might not be able to see you at all that weekend," said Walter, "but you could be there for me, that cool?"

"And dreamy," said Bear. "*Hello?* I can finally erase the misery of not seeing you with my own two eyes in the Sugar Bowl."

"Tell me about it," said Walter, rising up on his elbows and reaching for Bear's hand. "Bear, buddy, after college, I want you to come to all my games."

"In the pros? For sure," shrugged Bear.

"Every one," said Walter, "but only if you want to. We'll have to come up with some kind of red-alert security plan."

"No way! I'm gonna be like: *Would somebody please point me in the direction of my man's cheering section?*" said Bear, all faggy.

"Now, Bear!" said Walter. A hint of wariness flashed in his eyes, then evaporated. "Oh, fuck, that's pretty funny!" Just like that, the unspoken fear vanished. Bear had confirmed in a comical way the polar opposite of what was acceptable around football people. "Seriously, though. I want you there," added Walter.

"Put me down for any chance to see my buddy *go play some football!*" said Bear.

"I want you there all the time, Bear," insisted Walter, as if Bear wasn't getting it. "I want *us* to be there, wherever I am ... together. Every step."

"Every pass?" asked Bear, face coming closer to his buddy's.

"Every snap," said Walter, face coming closer to his buddy's.

"Every touchdown?" asked Bear.

"Every Bear Coleman movie premiere," said Walter.

"Every game-winning, fourth-quarter drive?" said Bear.

"Every night going to sleep with you," said Walter, looking into Bear's eyes. "Sometimes, I dream of being the one to change sports, with you, so we could be open, so I could just be myself and play and hang with you, and it's no big deal."

"Dream of it," said Bear. "Walter Yeager can do anything he sets his brilliant mind to."

"*Rightbackatcha,*" said Walter.

They melted into the moonlight and one another. For a moment, they laughed their way through the nervousness, then Walter regulated their heartbeats by kissing the back of Bear's hand, then kissing his forehead. That night, they finally got all *Le Sucre* they desired, and it was everything they dreamed it would be. The Mediterranean provided their rhythm; the nature of boys did the rest. When the sun rose on the sea the next morning, they were asleep naked on the deck, coiled around one another like pieces of the same rope.

Bear found himself dreaming of a pair of hairy and weathered blond legs that certainly didn't belong to Walter, who was drooling on Bear's chest. To escape the dream, he opened his eyes, only to find a pair of legs standing over him—hairy and weathered blond legs that didn't belong to Walter, who was drooling on Bear's chest. In a panic, Bear grabbed his buddy's blond locks and pulled backward, giving the quarterback a clear view of his uncle's face.

"Waking up on the deck like this, guys?" said Walter's Uncle, thoroughly disgusted. "Are you nuts? Wrong word choice."

"Sweetie," said Walter's Aunt, emerging from below, breakfast platter in hand, "the sausages and sticky buns are ready—oh! Boys! ... Seconds?"

"It's not what you think." Walter scrambled to his feet and into his swim trunks.

"He's a mind reader *and* a quarterback now," said Walter's Uncle.

"I've never done this before," said Walter, avoiding all eye contact, even with his naked and motionless Bear. "Not here, or together, I don't know what to say, I'm sorry."

"And now he's apologizing for it!" said Walter's Uncle, truly astonished. "Bear, put on your shorts. Both of you, stand together. Wife of mine, take your sticky buns downstairs. And keep 'em nice and toasty."

After the boys did as they were told, Walter's Uncle lit up a cigar, sat on a crate behind them, took a puff, savored the flavor, glanced at the sea, decided to do more than glance, then took an easy breath and let out some smoke.

"Uncle," said Walter, looking back with his head and shoulders. "We didn't mean for it to happen like this."

"It was the first time," said Bear, looking back the same way.

"As big a pigs as *you two* were last night? That'll be the day," said Walter's Uncle, taking another puff.

"We were *that* loud?" gulped Walter. "Sir?"

"That loud? My wife and I were right in front of you! How could we not notice? How could *we* not be in the line of fire?" Walter's Uncle dabbed at the corner of his eye, wiping away the memory of an errant shot of something.

"We pigged-out that much?" the boys said together.

"Your gluttony is not a shock to me," said Walter's Uncle, standing up and taking another puff. "My wife and I live in the South of France, where it's copasetic to follow a different path in life. The rest of the family lives in a country where taking a different route makes you crazy, one way or another. Not hard to figure out which side of the ocean is repressed and which isn't, not to mention who in the family is living their dreams and who's not. But that wasn't my point."

"What is?" gulped Walter. "Sir?"

"That you two were pigs last night, pig-eating pigs," said Walter's Uncle. "I should have known something like this would happen, that you two hungry young bucks would end up breaking the one rule we have on *The Fair Lady.*"

"The one rule?" asked Walter, sounding confused.

"Bear, what's the one rule?" asked Walter's Uncle, standing in front of them.

"Sunscreen at all times," said a bewildered Bear. "Sir?"

"You're still boys and all, but you should have known that scarfing down a big fat barbeque-roasted pig between the two of you at dinner was gonna make you pass out on the deck like stuffed pigs yourselves, then get caught sleeping under the morning sun without *this.*" Walter's Uncle snapped a bottle of sunscreen into Walter's naked stomach and said, "Do me a favor. Don't tell your father about this. I know what it's like to be young with an insatiable appetite, but I get the feeling my brother forgot a long time ago. I don't want him thinking I'm over here letting you go off all half-cocked, so to speak." Walter's Uncle caught a whiff of something in the sea air. "*Hmmm*, I think suddenly I'm in the mood for some sticky buns," he said, then disappeared below deck.

"I don't know if that was about sunscreen, or sticky buns, or us!" said a wide-eyed Bear.

"Exactly!" said a fired-up Walter, sporting a grin that was a cross between Joe Bruin and a big country boy just admitted to the all-star jamboree of lust. Apparently, they were off the hook for having sex on the deck, and in theory, off the hook for having sex in their cabin, and on the docks at night, and under the docks in the morning, and in the deserted alleyways in the coastal villages, and in back of the fishing supply stores, and everywhere else the boys breathed for the rest of the trip.

They dropped all rules in France. No deodorant. No shaving. No showers until they felt like a change of pace. France was where Bear learned how Walter smelled and tasted, and where Walter learned how Bear smelled and tasted. During those two weeks, Bear imagined that Walter inhaled more black man's funk than all his years of being in locker rooms, for Bear sure inhaled more dirty white man's hair than all his years of school buses, locker rooms and frat houses. It was that scent that was the first thing Bear missed upon landing at LAX.

Buddy, do you know how much I want to be back in your arms? I'd give anything to smell your hair right now ...

"That was the first thing Bear told Walter that night when they spoke on the phone from opposite sides of the country," said Marcus from underneath the bleachers of the football stadium nestled in the hills overlooking the Pacific Ocean. "I won. Rematch?" He handed Walt the little green box that was Mattel Electronics Football.

"Man, this is still overwhelming," said Walt, taking the game.

"Try welding," said Marcus.

"What?" asked Walt.

"Try welding. Welding is always better," said Marcus. "That's what Sanchez said. You said *overwhelming* and he said, 'Try *welding.*'"

"Yeager for the first down," said Walt, more focused on the football game.

"Try welding ... try welding," said Marcus, more focused on the word game. "Overwhelming ... over-welding ... don't over-weld ... don't overwhelm ... don't be overwhelmed ... try ..."

"Whelming!" said Walt. "Being *whelmed* is better than being *overwhelmed.* Sorry, didn't mean to steal your thunder."

"Your thunder is my thunder," said Marcus.

"So try whelming," said Walt. "Do you think ... *nah!*"

"That he was giving us advice?" asked Marcus.

"Can't be," said Walt, getting back to the football game. "Coming here was our own fault."

"That doesn't mean Sanchez wasn't giving us advice," said Marcus.

"Yeah, like us getting back together?" said Walt. "This is *still* overwhelming."

"Try whelming," said Marcus with a sly smile.

"This is whelming," said Walt. "Not overwhelming, just pretty freakin' whelming." He paused to see if it did any good. "*Hmmm,*" he said, then decided to start up the golf cart. "Go for a spin?"

Walt drove the cart out from under the bleachers, then toward the football field. "So did you gloss over the guys being intimate for my benefit? Just curious," said Walt.

"What do you mean?" asked Marcus.

"I kinda expected fireworks over the Mediterranean," said Walt.

"Back then, I didn't have sexually graphic fantasies. I've never imagined Walter and Bear's first time beyond what I just told you," said Marcus.

"Amazing, considering everything else you've thought of," said Walt.

"I don't think it's a feeling I can imagine," said Marcus. "Nor want to—imagine, I mean. As in *only* imagine. If you want me to be honest."

"So why France?" Walt took them for a loopy ride all over the football field, reminding Marcus of the dizzying antics of Fran Tarkenton, the legendary Viking QB who drove people crazy doing exactly what Yeager was doing now, scrambling.

"Why France? That's an easy one," said Marcus. "Summer after sixth grade, Daddy Coleman saw some ad in some paper for Madame Karnowsky's French lessons. Next thing you know, I'm learning how to *parlez vous.* Next thing you know after that, I'm enrolled in Private Parks Academy, the K-12 private school where Madame Karnowsky taught. On scholarship. The public school system in our area was one of the best in the nation, but for some reason, I spent seventh and eighth grades at this private school that was 99.99% white, a big change from my previous world, which was very diverse."

"Hold onto the rails!" said Walt, stopping on a dime, then going backwards in a swirling circle.

"There are no rails!" cried Marcus, laughing nervously until they were going forward once again. "Anyway, those two years in the private school pen changed everything. I went in a 12-year-old kid who liked race cars and playing football, basketball and baseball, and came out a collection of questions, all starting with Who the Fuck Am I: Big Guy Marcus, valued for his barely athletic body; Faggy Marcus, secret admirer of the junior high and high school boys, all of whom shared the same locker room; Class Clown Marcus, the distracted student; and the list goes on.

"On the football team, I was a big-ass lineman who played every down, both ways, but was never recognized along with the stars: the boys who touched the ball. On top of that, I was the basketball player who started but was his team's equivalent to the underachieving big man on an NBA team with stellar athletes like Jordan and Kobe, who also happened to be black at my 99.99% white private school."

"That bites," said Walt, crossing midfield and heading toward the left corner of the end zone

"I returned to public school for ninth grade as a pure act of rebellion against my father," said Marcus. "I remember Daddy Coleman standing in the kitchen, demanding that I make a choice: the private school for a third year, or the public school, whose deadline for registration was that day. I knew where *he* wanted me to go, so I looked him straight in the eye and said the exact opposite."

"Public School, USA," said Walt.

"Exactly," said Marcus. "My father said something like: fine. Next thing you know, we're on our way to registration. It's funny, when I see some teenager in a movie making some huge life decision just to spite their parents, I always think to myself: how realistic is that?"

"There's your answer," said Walt.

"Have you ever done anything like that?" asked Marcus.

"This is your story," said Walt, crossing the faded goal line.

"Touchdown, Yeager!" said Marcus.

"So was your father upset?" asked Walt with a mild laugh, steering the cart toward a cliff not far from the edge of the football field.

"Dunno, probably," said Marcus. "But whatever they did to me in private school turned me into a straight-A student in public school. I was a good student before, but now, suddenly I'm doing the work in my sleep! Once the other students found out, I was toast. Just one more label to hang on me: brainiac."

"Perfect," laughed Walt.

"I got straight A's a time or two that year," said Marcus. "It was a tough habit to break, but after that, I vowed never again. I wanted friends, not straight A's. I already had too many strikes against me. For the rest of my academic career, I never tried my best, only well enough for a B average, give or take. I ended up taking French for *beaucoup de years,* which is about how well I speak it now. But the times I've been to France, as an adult, *les Français* claim I speak it pretty good, if they say so themselves."

"So you went to France, just like Bear," said Walt, stopping the golf cart just short of the canyon below.

"*Mais oui!*" said Marcus, gazing out at the world beyond the Complex. "France paid us all back, and either way you look at it, it all turned out *très bien.*"

9

Game Within the Game

"This is still overwhelming," said Walt. He was sitting in the driver's seat of the golf cart parked at the edge of the canyon. "I know, try whelming." He placed his big blond forearms on the steering wheel and surveyed the rolling hills beyond the Complex. "This whole day that has gone by like no other, pretty whelming."

"I promise you won't regret this," said Marcus from the passenger seat. He was a little nervous about peering down at the valley below, or the horizon beyond, so he raised his head and squinted toward the heavens.

"I'm not worried," said Walt.

"You and me meeting like this is not just an accident, I'm convinced now," said Marcus.

"The coincidences earlier today? This long and winding day?" said Walt, his tone a mix of boyish wonderment and adult bewilderment. "We settled all that."

"What about the song? 'World Without You' by Belinda Carlisle," asked Marcus, shielding his eyes from the afternoon sun.

"It's not our song. Correction, it's not *Walter and Bear's* song. You don't remember it," said Walt.

"We're talking 21 years of memories," said Marcus, "I mean, story-scripting—oh, fuck, who am I kidding—we're talking 21 years of fantasies about you. Or rather, the man in the photo, which I guess would be you. Man, this *is* some crazy cosmic dimension, even sitting here talking to you. Look at you, you're real! You're a real person! What's up with that? Who let the real guy in?" Marcus looked offstage as if he were sparring with his pesky morning talk show producer. "Gellman, did you do this?"

"*Ha!*" Walt laughed so hard, the golf cart rolled forward just enough to cause the front tires to tickle the edge of the canyon. "We're falling!" gasped Walt, moving an arm in front of Marcus.

"For real!" whispered Marcus, mouth agape, eyes fixated on the blond arm beneath his chin.

"*Every*body loves the cart!" said a voice from nowhere.

The boys felt themselves retreating from the edge. "But you two are the cream of the crop," said the voice, a mature-sounding man who groaned as if he were pulling them backward using his arms. Walt and Marcus couldn't turn around to look, lest they tip their fate one way or another. "Never seen anyone," said the man between breaths, "actually ... try to fly ... you two ... certifiable ... will go places ... I can only imagine what it'll be like ... when you get there." The golf cart came to a halt a safe distance from the edge. "But you'll have to take that leap when I'm not around to see it with my own two eyes," said the man as the boys jumped out and faced their rescuer.

"*Noooooo!*" said Walt, as if his plea could make Sanchez, the Latino gardener, disappear right then and there. "Not Merlin the Magician, back for more magician-ing! Where's the pixie dust, for Christ's sake?"

"Helen thought you might want some fruit instead." Sanchez held up a small brown paper bag. "She figured you boys would start playing around in these hills and forget to eat, even if you aren't hungry."

"You know Helen, my mother's neighbor?" asked Marcus.

"Met her this morning before I met you, when I was delivering those." Sanchez indicated the postcard in Marcus' hand.

"He works here!" said Walt, as if that explained everything.

"Wherever, whenever," said Sanchez.

"So you're not a gardener?" asked Marcus.

"I love to garden," shrugged Sanchez.

"This is crazy," said Walt, turning to the canyon.

"Real crazy or made-up crazy?" asked Sanchez.

"What difference does it make?" asked Walt, looking like he wanted to take another stab at driving off the cliff.

"How did Helen know we were coming here?" asked Marcus.

"Overheard you in your mother's garage," said Sanchez, "something about me telling you to come here—which was kinda strange. She said you were in such a rush, you didn't notice her trying to give you this bag, so she tracked me down just as I was leaving."

Marcus took the bag and examined its contents. "All this to give us two apples?"

"She appreciates you," said Sanchez.

"I put her closet door back on track one time, months ago," said Marcus.

"They put expiration dates on good deeds now?" asked Sanchez.

"So you just happened to be coming by," said Marcus.

"Saturday. The best day for the soul to play." Sanchez inhaled the mountains and canyons around them.

"And you just happened to see us over here," said Marcus.

"Did you come here to sweat the details or fix things between you?" asked Sanchez.

"There's nothing to fix," said Walt, turning from the edge.

"You rescued us at the exact moment we needed it. How can that be?" asked Marcus.

"The skeptical one who needs analytical proof," said Sanchez, regarding Marcus. Walt chuckled, prompting Sanchez to regard the former quarterback.

"Which means you're the one who goes on instinct. What does your gut instinct tell you about me?" asked Sanchez

"There's more to you than you're telling," said Walt.

"You can say that about every other person you've ever met, yes?" said Sanchez. "And every person who's ever met you can say the same. True?"

The boys remained silent.

"What's your intuition tell you about getting away from this cliff?" asked Sanchez. Moments later, the golf cart was heading across the football field again, Walt in the driver's seat, Marcus in the passenger seat, and Sanchez riding behind them, standing like a general, or some kind of proud and somewhat cocky coach.

"So what is this Complex all about anyway?" asked Walt, eating his apple and driving.

"Place for people to play games, I guess," said Sanchez.

"What kind of games?" asked Marcus, eating his apple and enjoying the ride.

"What kind of games can you think of?" asked Sanchez.

"How about the game where one person asks a simple question, and the other person gives a smart-ass, vague answer in return?" said Walt.

"Oh," said Sanchez, "and I bet you're the reigning world champ at that game, aren't you, golden blond one?"

"I can still swing back around to that cliff, if you keep it up," said Walt.

"You win," said Sanchez. The Latino gardener turned delivery boy kept his mouth shut for the rest of the ride, which stopped in front of the bleachers. "You boys playing nice so far?" asked Sanchez as they disembarked.

"That's an affirmative," said Walt.

"Getting along famously," said Marcus. "*And* infamously."

"Mind if we ask something?" said Walt.

"Please, please." Sanchez motioned them like a conductor, urging them to join him in the bleachers. "Ask questions, get answers. That's rule number one in the game of life."

"We're going through something, the two of us," said Marcus, entering the stands and rising higher. "Do you know anything about it?"

"Can't say I do," said Sanchez, rising but not as high.

"You're not plugged in at all?" asked Walt, entering the stands and rising higher.

"Who am I plugging? What are you trying to ask me?" Sanchez stopped and stood with his back to the field. The boys went a little higher before sitting on the same row, more than an arm's length apart. "How about this," said Sanchez. "You're searching for answers, right? How about I tell you what I know to be true. Then you can keep it and use it, or throw it in the trashcan, just like you do at home. Either way, it'll be recycled, okay?"

"Go for it," said Walt, leaning forward, elbows resting on his knees.

"You boys are powerful," said Sanchez. "Energy radiates off you both like a whole galaxy of stars. I have not seen two lights as bright as yours in a very long time."

Marcus emitted a deep breath and leaned backward. Walt remained motionless.

"You're here because you love games," said Sanchez. "We human beings love all kinds of games, big ones, small ones, tough, rough, tender, smart, physical, sexual, mental, emotional, spiritual—have I left anything out? Oh, I guess a billion more games, give or take."

Marcus leaned forward. Walt reclined backward.

"You two can play any game known to humanity, and it would be a rout, as long as you are on the same team and at the top of your game," said Sanchez. "That's the power I see when you two are gathered together. That's what pulled me to you twice today. Your energy is like a magnet. But you two need to be on top of your game to get where you're going, especially with the way you two drive."

"You've misunderstood something: *we're not together,*" said Walt. "We're here because he's been—how do I say this?—putting a lot of time and energy into the idea of us having this perfect life together. I hope you don't mind me saying that, Marcus."

"Be my guest," said Marcus, "please."

"You're saying you didn't have any part in all this?" Sanchez asked Walt.

"Let's just say, I wasn't around much," said Walt.

"Where were you?" asked Sanchez.

"Uh, kinda busy, doing my own thing," said Walt. "You might say I was in a whole different world. And Marcus here wasn't exactly my top priority. I hope you don't mind me putting it this way, Marcus."

"Be my guest," said Marcus, "please."

"So this perfect life was only in his mind, not yours?" Sanchez asked Walt.

"Exactly, and that's pretty much how we wound up here," said Walt. "Right, Marcus?"

"So what part did you play in this perfect life?" Sanchez asked Walt.

"I didn't," said Walt.

"You're sitting here. You had to have played some part," said Sanchez.

"None," said Walt.

"You didn't do anything to promote or encourage his thoughts?" said Sanchez. "You had absolutely nothing to do with his feelings?"

"Correct," said Walt.

"It was all in his mind?" asked Sanchez.

"He's getting it!" said Walt.

"How did you get in his mind?" asked Sanchez. Walt ran out of obvious answers and went momentarily blank. Marcus tried to respond, but Sanchez put up a hand. "Let the golden blond one speak for himself."

"The only thing I did was show up for a photo session because of who I was 21 years ago," said Walt.

"So you *did* have a hand in the creation of this perfect life." Sanchez turned to the field and raised his arms straight in the air. "Touchdown for the golden boys! They know how to get in the end zone instead of flying off the cliff after all!"

The cheerleader thought of celebration music and cheers. The quarterback just laughed. "You don't understand," said Walt. "I wasn't aware of any of this until today. One little ... *look* ... 21 years ago did all this."

"Wow." Sanchez turned to Walt. "You're amazing, do you know that? One look ... you weren't even paying attention ... one vision of you is all it took for him to fall in love with you, and give you 21 years of his life, come what may. How amazing is that? How powerful is the golden blond one?"

"I wasn't there!" said Walt.

"Have it your way," said Sanchez. "If that's the game within the game you want to play."

"It *is* all my doing," said Marcus.

"Have it *your* way," said Sanchez. "If that's the game within the game *you* wanna play."

"I had my own life, too," said Marcus. "I made the best of it and never stopped following my own dreams."

"And you still see him as perfect. I can see it in your eyes," said Sanchez. "The golden blond one could have driven you both off that cliff, and your love for him would not have changed. How powerful is the golden-brown one?"

"You have this all wrong," said Walt.

"Not from where I'm standing," said Sanchez.

"You don't have all the facts," said Marcus.

"And you do? You both do?" asked Sanchez, sounding like an eager child.

"*His* putting energy into this perfect life thing has caused all this," said Walt. "It's just a fantasy. Sorry, Marcus, this guy has it too twisted."

"Where is all this energy now?" asked Sanchez.

"What do you mean?" the boys asked together.

"Let's do 'parking spaces' for a moment," said Sanchez. "You know how sometimes you're driving someplace and you just know you're gonna get a great parking space? Why is that? Because your mind created that space, as in conceived of it. And your belief in its existence was so strong, that energy was set forth into motion. And what did that energy go out and do? Get you your parking space. What kind of energy was it? Positive energy, because you had faith in getting that space, that little piece of empty space you needed to borrow from the universe for a little while."

"Then sometimes you get there and the space is gone," said Walt.

"Because you lose faith, or never really had it, meaning you were playing a little mind game with yourself," said Sanchez.

"Been there, done that," said Marcus.

"But there's more to the story and the game," said Sanchez. "Because, for you to get to that empty space, first you had to conceive of it, then have faith it's gonna be there when you need it. *Then* you have to do everything in your power to get there. Besides all that, the world has to cooperate a little to make it happen. How? By helping to create the space for you, starting with your basic needs. Who can tell me the basic things needed to create a parking space?"

"The ground," said Walt.

"The curb," said Marcus.

"Exactly," said Sanchez. "The ground beneath the space, so your car won't fall to China, and the curb, so your car won't crash into the window of the grocery store. What are those things? Matter from the material world, created by material boys and material girls. Sorry, can't help myself sometimes. Did I tell you I love music? Anyway. Your parking space needs matter—all co-creations of humanity. So getting your space is a cooperative effort between you and the rest of the world."

"What does this have to do with us and his daydreams—sorry, Marcus—his energy?" asked Walt.

"Energy, daydreams, thoughts, fantasies—they're all the same," said Sanchez. "They're all just different words for the mind's creations. And the mind, what a creation itself, yes? The mind can create anything from parking spaces to whatever you two are dealing with right now."

"What if what we're dealing with is all in one person's mind?" asked Marcus.

"Not possible," said Sanchez. "You're both here, in this space, sitting on matter, trying to *fly matter* off cliffs, eating fruit, sent by Helen, matter of fact."

"But we're talking about a fantasy world," said Marcus.

"You're here. Is that fantasy?" asked Sanchez.

"Man, we're talking about a whole other life!" said Walt, growing impatient. "Not this one, a whole other realm, another dimension, another world, understand? A separate reality."

"I love that game!" said Sanchez.

"Say what?" asked Walt, about ready to give up on the guy.

"This isn't a game," said Marcus.

"Humanity is all about games," said Sanchez, "from Peek-a-boo, to Hide and Seek, to Guess My Sexuality, to that little green box on the bleacher there. What about all the games you played as a child? What did they all have in common?"

"I usually won," the boys said together

"More alike than you know," said Sanchez.

"More overwhelmed than I know is more like it," said Walt. "I know. *Try whelming.*"

"Try leaning back against the bleachers," said Sanchez. "I wanna take you someplace, only in your mind—I ain't going over any cliffs with you. Go ahead. Golden brown one, the analytical one, look to the intuitive one, the golden blond one, for the lead. That's what he brings to your life."

Marcus glanced at Walt, who shrugged and reclined backward. Marcus followed.

"Now close your eyes," said Sanchez. "The bleachers in your mind are gonna shift a little, in your mind only now. If you get a little unsteady, reach out and hold one another's hand ... or not. Anyway. The bleachers in your mind are gonna become more comfortable and more like your favorite deck chair. Lean back, take a breath, have a smile on me—and keep those eyes closed—because we're gonna go stargazing. That's right, it's nighttime in your mind. Think about all the infinite number of stars flickering in the night sky ...

"Think about what scientists believe: that those tiny blips of light are—in another reality—massive infernos of energy, raging balls of fire, each one hotter than we can imagine and bigger than we can imagine. On top of that, the light you see coming from those massive infernos is light that left those infernos thousands of years ago and is only now twinkling in your eyes ...

"If you can absorb that concept, my dear sweet golden boys, you can handle anything that comes your way in life. And when it looks like life is gonna wash over your heads and drown you, think about the idea that the known universe is just an itty bitty peek at all that's out there, that space goes on infinitely in all directions, and we can't even truly imagine All There Is. Potentially overwhelming, huh? Now. Do you really think whatever's going on inside your two little heads is all that *over*whelming? To you *or* All There Is?"

The boys regarded one another, then looked away, smiling a little more.

"Eyes closed," said Sanchez. "Now, if the universe can do all that fiery inferno and infinite space stuff, the universe can probably handle *your* needs, don't ya think? And wouldn't you rather think?"

"Meaning?" asked Marcus.

"Until you find out otherwise for sure," said Sanchez, "wouldn't you rather think the universe has nothing to lose, and maybe even something to gain, by granting you your deepest dreams? And why wouldn't the universe do that? God—that's another name I use for the universe—God can do anything, right? So why wouldn't God grant you your dreams? What's it to God? God created all this in the blink of an eye, and can take all this away in the blink of an eye, right? Sort of like, *poof,* it's there. Then, *poof,* it's gone—everything, people, buildings, planets, solar systems—don't laugh, golden blond one. Humanity has already figured out how to make people, buildings, and planets go *poof* into thin air. You think God didn't pass that course? You think God didn't *create* that course?"

"Who is your God, Sanchez?" asked Walt.

"Close your eyes and I'll tell you," said Sanchez, pausing to let the air breathe. "God is like a mind. A great, powerful, super-intelligent mind. *The mind* is the *only* thing that exists in the entire universe. There is nothing else outside this mind. *The mind* is all there is and knows it is All There Is, therefore *the mind* knows it is all-powerful and can be anything. But what is there to be? There is nothing because there is *nothing else*. There is only *the mind* and the darkness inside. But *the mind* wants to know more about itself than the mere fact that it is All There Is, so *the mind* summons up all its power and explodes into an infinite number of pieces that are off in search of whatever the mind can think of and create, all so that *the mind* may know itself and what it is capable of. *The mind* called these pieces *energy*. And *the mind* told the energies: 'Go make something of yourselves, so that I may know what *my mind* is capable of; and what I am capable of, so that, by separating myself into pieces, I may know myself, and myself in relation to another form of me, which is merely a reflection of myself, *the mind*, God.'"

The massive infernos of raging balls of fire blurred and dimmed, then faded altogether. A warm breeze moved through the bleachers, as comforting as an airy blanket, as the boys drifted off to sleep. Naptime.

SOMETIME LATER, MARCUS AWOKE to find himself lying on his back, parallel to the bleacher beneath him. The sun had shifted toward the ocean but was far from making its descent. Wilson, his former writing professor, discouraged the use of cliché lines, like: "for what seemed like an eternity." After spending time with Walt Yeager, Marcus was inclined to believe in clichés.

The former quarterback was asleep on his back, parallel to the bleacher beneath him, two rows directly above Marcus. How they ended up horizontal was blurry like a dream, but one thing was clear: Marcus had picked a good man to be the man of his dreams, not some jerk of a jock who turned out to be some uncaring monster. Marcus had no idea how Walt treated others and didn't care. They were both in their 40s, which meant they'd had their share of lovers and haters, supporters and detractors, and horror stories and great moments, depending on the teller of the tale. Details that were neither here nor there, literally. What mattered most to Marcus was what Walt Yeager offered to Marcus from Moment One: an open heart without judgment. That and the fact that it felt so good and so natural to be in the former quarterback's company.

To think Marcus once had a nightmare about a cabin in the woods and a Walt Yeager who was racist, like so many of the men Marcus encountered.

"What's on your mind?" asked Walt, eyes now open.

"*Walt Loves the Bearcat*," said Marcus. "Meeting you has definitely altered my dreams and the story."

"Have I been a distraction?" asked Walt.

"Never. It's still the story of a classic love that unfolds over the years, partially told in flashbacks," said Marcus.

"Kind of like one of my favorite movies, *The Way We Were*. You know that movie?" asked Walt.

"Of *k-k-kourse*," said Marcus, stuttering like *K-K-Katie*, Barbra Streisand's character. He wanted to tell Walt it was one of his favorite movies, too, but didn't. There was just so much to say, sometimes he didn't know where to start. "Then again, Redford and Streisand didn't end up together. Walter and Bear have to end up together. I've never written a book where the guy gets the guy and rides off into the sunset. You can bet the big league boys are gonna end up happily ever after. Though I've never imagined how the story actually ends."

"So if I'm altering your dreams, maybe there's a surprise ending?" teased Walt. "Maybe Walter goes off with the other bearcat, Roseanne."

"He's more than welcome to try to hunt down a girl named Roseanne," said Marcus, sounding a bit defensive.

"Come on," said Walt. "Do you want to know the outcome of the Super Bowl of your life? Didn't some wise little Bearcat say that to me once?"

Marcus failed to come up with a comeback. Walt Yeager was one of the few people in this world who could shut him up.

"See," said Piss 'n' Vinegar Walt.

"Right back at me," said Marcus. *He called me little Bearcat!* "By the way, we did get a visit from Sanchez, right?"

"Affirmative," said Walt.

"*Whew*," said Marcus. "Glad that wasn't a dream. Sometimes, it gets hard to tell."

"Do what Coach Sanchez says," said Walt. "Don't sweat the details."

"Coach Sanchez also says God is like a mind that can blink worlds into and out of existence," said Marcus.

"You—you're not about to go there, are you?" Walt reached for the little green box on the bleachers. "Game?"

"Go where?" laughed Marcus. "Game on."

The quarterback is perceptive, assessing any situation based on gut feeling, much more so than the cheerleader, who must analyze any situation by getting as much factual information as possible, then reacting.

"You know what I'm talking about," said Walt as the two began a new round of Mattel Electronics Football.

Both boys understood that Marcus had conceived of the notion of his day-

dreams happening in another dimension. But the idea was much too fragile to con-
taminate with words, for the fallible minds of both boys had stockpiles of weapons
of mass doubt to destroy any notion so infantile and out of this world.

"I have no idea what you're talking about, QB," said Marcus.

"Dream on," said Walt, more focused on the little green box.

"Don't mind if I do," said Marcus. "So the famous boys are back to their separate lives after getting all that *Le Sucre* in France. For Walter, it was crunch time at Georgia. His college career had been full of fits and starts, and now, he had every reason to believe he was finally gonna get his shot. For Bear, *and* his infamous alter ego, *me*, it was the last dance. I was a fifth-year senior and definitely over the *rah! rah!* collegiate life, well, except for the actual *rah! rah!* part. I said goodbye to the big white frat house because all it had ever been to me was a place to get drunk and pretend I'm something I'm not, all while sleeping in a basement alcove. I moved into an awesome apartment still in the heart of campus life. I loved the building and it had always been a dream of mine to live there, but it was a tough building to get in. I persisted and got in—I made shit happen back then. I found these two non-Greek roomies and we lived my dream."

"Ah, man, interception, just as I was about to score." Walt handed him the little green box.

"At the three-yard line, folks!" said Marcus upon seeing the display. "Settle in for a while. I'm gonna take my time driving down the field for this touchdown while I dream on ... I was pretty much done with college except for one last thrill ride on the football and basketball express. On the sidelines, I could live in the moment and always, always experience parts of myself that I've always been fully in love with, minus a shred of doubt ... still going, still going, yes, first down, Coleman!

"I was raring to go out on top with a shining season full of great moments, all reflecting what a great and experienced spirit leader I was by then. I didn't even apply for captainhood, though some thought I was a shoo-in. I didn't want the drama to get in the way of my last moments of joy on the sidelines. I even made up with Candi, the feminist faculty advisor, in a drunken meeting of the minds at a bar near campus. And sure enough, I had a great football season and the greatest of basketball seasons. I got along famously with my partner, the little blonde girl. Man, I was at my best. It was as much of a dream come true as I could have made it, considering ... Coleman to the 50-yard line, what a stud!

"Miracle of miracles, I even did schoolwork! I busted my ass to make a clean break from college. It was a challenge, being a student again, but I managed. Socially, I was low-key. A few times, I shared a beer or three with some football or basketball players. That year, I got the feeling that a lot of them were more comfortable around me, and me more comfortable around them, beyond the games, I mean. It was pretty cool. I look back now and I think how young and naïve I still was, but if you look at 23 from 18, I guess I'd aged eons since my freshman year in terms of finding my own skin ... and Marcus Coleman is the man after that long scamper all the way down inside Walt Yeager's red zone!"

"And the big-league boys," said Walt, sounding irritated by the effort of his defense, "how'd they fare?"

"*Huh?*" asked Marcus, more focused on the game. "Oh, them. They were on their two separate roller-coaster tracks again, one going one way, the other going the opposite direction, like two carts that start at the North Pole, split up and then travel the world in opposite directions, one to the right and clockwise, one to the left and counterclockwise ... ah, had to settle for the field goal. Yeager's ball."

"Who goes which way?" laughed Walt, taking control of the little green box.

"Dunno, just thought of it," said Marcus. "I guess Walter goes to the right and clockwise, and Bear goes to the left and counterclockwise. That's what it looks like in my dreams."

"Time for Yeager to do some damage here," said Walt, more focused on getting back in the game ...

In the fall, Bear dreamed of his quarterback's sense of well-being based on the stats from Georgia's games, which he found in the Sunday paper. The name Yeager appeared from time to time, but not enough to satisfy Bear. The Dawgs were not doing Walter right, but Walter had a way of not wanting to talk about it.

"How's my QB?" asked Bear during one of their phone chats.

"Carrying a heavy load, but hearing your voice makes it much lighter," said Walter.

"Wish I could relieve things for you," said Bear, "and I don't mean—"

"I know," said Walter. "Another thing: as much as I wanna see your handsome face in the stands at the Tech game, it's not worth coming. Limited snaps—all I can say for now. If something changes, I'll call ya."

Nothing changed. Bear didn't attend the Georgia Tech-Georgia game. There was no Sugar at New Year's either. Walter and the Dawgs were in the Cotton Bowl in Dallas, while Bear and the Bruins were in the Fiesta Bowl in Phoenix. They did, however, experience a first, their first New Year's Eve together—on the phone, hours before midnight, but it was theirs.

"You're gonna get you some Cotton tomorrow, Walter," said Bear, lying on his hotel bed in Arizona. "I can feel it, you're gonna play."

"So, you pumped?" asked Walter from his hotel bed in Texas. "Your last football game, bud, how you feeling?"

"Bittersweet," said Bear. "But the good news is: tomorrow's the last time I'll ever miss seeing you play in person. You'll be the only quarterback I'll ever cheer for the rest of my life."

"On that note, Bear Cole-man the Soul Man, Happy Freakin' New Year."

Yeager did get playing time in the Cotton Bowl. The sports section the next day proved it. The numbers themselves were a blur. What Bear felt inside was what he imagined Walter must have felt inside: the adrenaline burst every time *you're on!* The thrill of commanding others to *let's do this!* The awe of being the center of attention of an entire stadium of people, waiting for *you* to *make something happen!*

Walter was a shining star who caused the action on the field. Bear was a shining star who led the reaction to the action on the field. He knew Walter thrived on the rush as much as Bear, and that Walter wanted that rush to be a big part of both of their lives. And Bear wanted every single one of his quarterback's deepest dreams to come true.

The spirit leader held onto those dreams as winter progressed and basketball season wound down, signaling an end to college as he'd known it. Miraculously, the Bruins basketball team bestowed upon Bear the best senior gift possible: a championship run, albeit in the National Invitation Tournament, the little dance for those not invited to the bigger dance that was March Madness.

For Bear and the spirit squad, the NIT Final Four was a road trip from heaven: Spring Break in New York City on somebody else's dollar. On top of that, Indiana was there, and Bear had followed his beloved Hoosiers since childhood, thanks in part to Indianapolis being Mama Rent's former hometown. Earlier in this particular season, legendary Hoosier Coach Bob Knight had thrown a chair across the court and become the Sports Clip of the Year. The Hoosiers were engulfed in hysteria, but Bear loved IU, and for the last game of his cheerleading career, he witnessed Reggie Miller and UCLA beat Steve Alford and Indiana in the finals of the NIT ...

"THAT GREAT BRUIN TITLE RUN might have saved my life, and definitely my sanity," said Marcus, lying in the bleachers at the football stadium nestled in the hills overlooking the Pacific.

"How so?" asked Walt, lying two rows higher in the bleachers at the football stadium nestled in the hills overlooking the Pacific.

"I suffered a very big gaping wound that spring," said Marcus, back in control of the little green box and his offense. "A hurt that would take some time to heal—now I'm not gonna get all misty and sentimental and there are no sad love songs. Anymore. Just something that happened to a 23-year-old kid named Marcus Coleman in the spring of '85 ... damn, turnover, Yeager ball, but you're gonna have to go long."

"Piece of cake," said Walt, taking back the game. "Tell me about the big hurt, only if you want to."

"My dream of finding a buddy in college officially died," said Marcus, closing his eyes. "To make a long, not-so-fun story short: remember those two roommates in my dream apartment? I confessed to one of them that I was—I don't even know the word I used—but we both understood it as gay. Or he probably understood it as queer, since he was from the South—blond, by the way. Anyway, I told him I was queer and in love with him—again, in whatever inarticulate words my 23-year-old mind used. He moved out the next day, breaking my very adolescent heart and leaving me without a good friend and a roommate."

"Ah, man, I just got sacked on fourth down," said Walt, handing over the game. "That sounds pretty heavy."

"It all happened toward the end of February," said Marcus, working the offense. "The basketball team was in a heated battle with about three other Pac-10 schools for an at-large berth in the NCAA. Both SC and UCLA were doing well enough to be talking March Madness in late February when we met at Pauley Pavilion, UCLA's historic gym. In the matchup earlier in the month, SC beat UCLA by a point in two overtimes. This time, we slugged it out in four overtimes before the cutest white boy on our team missed a couple of free throws and UCLA lost. I've been to countless basketball games in my life, as a fan, as a player, and as a cheerleader, but that was the greatest basketball game I'd ever experienced. The arena was packed—both bands, both cheerleading squads. Everyone stood for hours, leaning in so intensely, the gym felt like one of those high school barns you see in the movie *Hoosiers*. And I was right there, Walt, and I knew it was my last USC-UCLA battle of any kind as a participant. Even though we lost, it never mattered. I had just witnessed the collective energy of two universities move through my soul, starting with the 13,000 people in the joint that night. Moments like that were why I chose a big-time school. Times like that were why I had been a cheerleader ... fuck, missed a field goal from five yards out! How can life be so cruel sometimes?"

"I would never kick from five yards out," said Walt, taking back the game. "Sounds like a good distraction from your personal life at the time."

"It was, until I got home that night, after the four-overtime donnybrook," said Marcus. "The apartment was eerily quiet. Next thing I know, I'm sitting at the kitchen table and reading this very long and angry letter on yellow legal paper. The note was from the *other* roommate, the one I hadn't been in love with. He wasn't even a student, just a Hawaiian guy on some Christian missionary-type voyage. Our apartment had been his temporary harbor. Turns out, the *beloved* roomie—who had moved out recently—had ratted me out as a fag, so the evangelical roommate moved out while I was at the basketball game, leaving me a vitriolic note telling me all the reasons I was going to hell. Life became a blur. I had literally days to come up with all the rent, and before that, coming up with my third was already a monthly challenge."

"Man, that bites," said Walt. "Touchdown. Your ball."

"From the moment I read that letter until I graduated a few months later, I went into survival mode," said Marcus, taking back the game. "My landlords were an understanding elderly couple. They gave me a few extra days to pay the rent and I recruited two strangers who each needed a mattress on the floor—same arrangement, different cast. This time, I kept my mouth shut and concentrated on surviving until graduation. The basketball team's NIT run was a godsend, a place to live the last of my boyhood dreams, the only one I had left ... Yes! Coleman goes for it on fourth and 21 and scores! How about that, ladies and gents. His powers are amazing, too!"

"Finish your story," said Walt, taking back the game with a little more determination.

"After the climax of the hoop season, Candi, the feminist faculty advisor, wanted us to cheer at some volleyball games," said Marcus. "I didn't even bother responding. My work was done. I'd given two major universities my life and times and my heart and soul for five years, all while searching for one other male student who thought like me, felt like me, and was compatible enough to be my buddy-for-life. The closest I ever got was a guy at USC who once told me he was gay when he was drunk, then later told me he had no recollection of that disclosure when he was sober; and a guy at UCLA who was from the South and thought so much of me that he moved out the day after I told him I was in love with him and very confused about it all. I don't blame him, mind you. He did what he had to do to move on, and eventually, so did I. I spent my last months of college making sure I passed my classes so I could get out of there and never, ever have to look back. Strangely enough, Walter and Bear did the same."

... BEAR SAT LAZILY ON A COUCH in the hotel lobby in New York with White Donna, Black Donna, and Kathy, his little blonde girl. The NIT championship game between Indiana and UCLA was hours away and they were relaxing before the literal last hurrah of the basketball season.

They were all laughing at something silly when Bear noticed his golden blond aura moving in the distance, right to left. Walter was supposed to be in Georgia. Something was not right. The spirit leader steadied his nerves, then casually excused himself and headed toward his buddy. Their eyes met while their bodies were still approaching. Even though it was spring, the quarterback's face was pale and drained of all piss 'n' vinegar.

"I'm done with football," said Walter upon reaching Bear. "My career. Is over."

10

Sexy But Sexless in Seattle

Walt sat upright on the bleachers in the football stadium nestled in the hills overlooking the Pacific. His eyes were focused on something only visible to his mind. The little green box that was Mattel Electronics Football lay beside him, facedown. Two rows beneath him, Marcus also sat upright, straddling his row and wondering what was going through the former quarterback's headgear.

What happened to "from the Sugar Bowl to the Super Bowl?"

"In my dreams, Walter Yeager's career was over at age 22," said Marcus. "We both left college and everything about it behind us. I never dreamed you went straight to the pros, or ever intended to after our last year in school, never."

"Why?" asked Walt, his mind barely there.

"Bear wasn't the only one who checked for your stats in the paper," said Marcus. "When I didn't see your name as much as I'd hoped, for your sake, well, I knew that, for whatever reason, you didn't have the opportunity to show your stuff and get enough exposure for the pros to go crazy over you."

"Go on," said Walt, glancing skyward. The sun, which had seemed immovable all day, wavered away from its zenith, hinting at beginning its initial descent into the horizon over the Pacific.

"But I did hold out a little hope for you," said Marcus. "Not that I ever intended to be a part of your life, but I kept an ear and eye out for your name in the sports world, thinking you might turn up as a late bloomer at Georgia, or even in the NFL. You know how names slip through the cracks until you catch some highlight or read some clip? For the first couple of years after college, I imagined seeing WALT YEAGER linked to some pro team and thinking: 'Oh, yeah, that's where he ended up.' Just to know, you know, and I guess to have a little lifeline to my dream buddy, just to know where he was in the world. But I never saw WALT YEAGER again anywhere, and since I knew your football dreams had ended in this life, Walter and Bear's football dreams ended, too."

The bleachers rattled. WALT YEAGER was on the move. "I feel like riding the dune buggy again," said the former QB, descending the stands and heading for the golf cart. Marcus remained motionless, eyes frozen in suspense. "You coming?" asked Walt from the driver's seat. "Hop in," said Walt after getting no response. Marcus unfroze himself and sprang into action, bouncing down the bleachers until he bounced right up into the passenger seat. "Let's just ride for a while," said Walt.

The golf cart took off across the football field, straight down an imaginary 50-yard line. Walt put the ride in TURBO MODE. Whatever TURBO MODE was, it was enough to take Marcus' breath away, especially when he realized they were heading straight for the storage shed on the opposite sideline.

"Check out the shack?" asked Walt, shouting over the roar of the engine.

"Why not?" said Marcus, noticing they were getting closer but not slowing down.

"Check it out now?" asked Walt, speeding up.

"Ready if you are!" yelled Marcus.

"Or you wanna check it out later?" shouted Walt, not slowing down.

"Whatever Walt wants," said Marcus, staring straight into his eyes with a big ole Joe Bruin grin. Walt decided he wanted to jerk the steering wheel to the right to miss the storage shed by the narrowest of margins. The golf cart did a wheelie, rising in the air on the driver's side while remaining on the ground on the passenger side. The maneuver worked. They cleared the shed, then Walt decided he wanted to come back down to earth with all four wheels, so he righted the world, but kept speeding through it just as swiftly.

"Wanna check out the cliff now?" asked Walt, not hiding his *I-dare-you* half-smile.

"Why not?" said Marcus, not hiding his *I-double-dare-you* grin.

"You think Sanchez is right?" asked Walt, speeding toward the cliff.

"About?" asked Marcus, trying to hide his fear.

"Everything!" yelled Walt, trying to hide his enjoyment of Marcus' fear.

"I have no idea," shouted Marcus. "Wanna find out now?"

"Ready if you are!" yelled Walt, not stopping or slowing.

"Or you wanna find out later?" shouted Marcus.

Walt decided to bring the cart to a slow but grinding halt a safe distance away from the cliff. Marcus exhaled when Walt killed the engine, then the former spirit leader grabbed the keys and said, "The biggest single thing the famous boys learn in their lives is: *as a duo, never make life-changing decisions without first discussing it and taking it as seriously as you do buying a house.* Not bad for a guy who's been single his whole life, huh?"

"Dream on," said Walt, as if the fun had been taken out of the moment. "Wait—first you need to know something: I would never, ever choose a Belinda Carlisle song to be our song. No offense, but I can't stand her whiny, nasally voice."

"I'm not offended," said Marcus. "It's not my whiny, nasally voice."

"Just thought you should know," said Walt. "Now, dream on."

WALTER NEVER GAVE BEAR a complete picture of the events that led to the end of his football career. There were some vague references to an injury and never getting the chance to prove himself, but Walter didn't feel good talking about it, and Bear didn't want Walter not feeling good. Bear was already sensitive to great athletes not getting a true crack at their dreams. Bear's basketball brothers were such men. Now, Bear's husband was such a man.

And husband is exactly what Bear thought of Walter when they agreed to move to Atlanta upon graduating. They didn't have a plan, just a dream: huddling up to figure out the rest of their lives now that their days on the football field were over. Details aside, Bear was quite confident as he sold his car and most of his possessions, and said goodbye to California, land of his dreams, and hello to Atlanta, and the man of his dreams. Getting off the plane that night, he even allowed himself to dream about the next few years in the Peach State. They'd make tons of cool friends their age. They'd do the occasional tailgate party for big Bulldawg games. Walter would get the itch and make a glorious comeback with the Falcons—

Walter jumped on the curb and ran to Bear, just as Bear came shooting out of the terminal doors. They met, hugged and spun around once, only untangling after noticing the sea of humanity around them.

"Who cares now?" said Walter of their public display. "I'm a fucking washed-up nobody!"

"Not to me," said Bear before that ridiculous notion was given any more time to exist. "I love you just the same ... What's wrong?"

"That's the first time you said it," said Walter, eyes crinkling.

Bear rewound his mind, then smiled. "I wouldn't be here if I didn't love you, Walter."

"Don't get all teary-eyed," said Walter, throwing a playful punch to Bear's arm.

"*Rightbackatcha,*" said Bear, throwing a playful punch to Walter's arm.

A horn honked, bringing their surroundings into focus again. They were standing near the back of a truck bed that was packed with clothes, sneakers, tattered books, and a whole lot of disorganized belongings.

"Somebody's on the run," laughed Bear.

"Hop in," said Walter.

"Hop in what?" asked Bear. "Where's the little red sports car?"

"You trust me, right?" Walter took Bear's bags and stuffed them into the chaos of the truck bed, which belonged to a black pickup truck.

"You know I do," said Bear, helping Walter add to the chaos in the truck bed. A horn honked in the rear. It was a cop car. Walter held up a hand, as if to say, *hold on,* then he grinned at Bear.

"I love you, too, buddy. Hop in my new ride." Walter made a dash for the driver's seat, Bear followed by making a dash for the passenger seat.

"You know I'll go anywhere with you," said Bear once they were seated.

"I'll take you there," said Walter, starting the engine.

"Ready ... break!" said Bear, as if they were in a huddle.

"And by the way," said Walter, speeding off. "No football analogies. Got it?"

"Check," said Bear. "Any other rules you want to inform me of, sir?"

"One." Walter drove for a moment, then pulled over to the side of the road. "Kiss me before I fucking explode."

They grabbed each other like two desperadoes, frantically searching for truth via their mouths, their necks, their hands, their souls. Headlights flashed across their faces, breaking the moment. They unhanded one another hastily; then Walter drove off again.

"Finally I get to see Atlanta!" said Bear.

"What if I promise to show it to you another time?" asked Walter.

"I don't mean tonight," giggled Bear.

"I can't live in Atlanta, Bear," said Walter. "I gotta get as far away as possible from Georgia."

"So where are you kidnapping me to?" joked Bear, not ready to take him seriously.

"Seattle," said Walter, statement of fact.

Bear scoffed, then glanced outside his window. The truck fell silent. Slowly Bear rotated toward his man, who was still waiting for a reaction. Bear turned to the dark road ahead, his eyes getting wider, his smile growing bigger, his breath becoming more and more breathless.

"Say something!" Walter's half-smile had a hint of piss 'n' vinegar. "There's no radio in here. Did you sell your boom box? Shake your head, yes or no? Bear, are you all right? Hold on, lemme stop the car ... okay, I'll be right back, don't move ... good job!"

No Atlanta, no Bulldawg tailgating, no Falcons, no Atlanta.

"I'm back, Bear, you okay? ... hold on one sec ... road trip started in the right mood ... radio station on your boom box ... man, I'm worried about you ... hold on, Bear, you with me or not? Good ... shaking your head is good, but say something, man of a thousand words! Or close your mouth ... man, I love this song ... Earth to Bear Coleman ... Bear, it's Steppenwolf, man, it's our song for the trip ... Bear, you're freaking me out ... Bear, can you hear me?" Suddenly, Walter decided to sing along with Steppenwolf: *"Born to be wiiiiiild!"*

And Bear came out of his trance to echo his man, right in time with Steppenwolf's next line: *"Born to be wiiiiiild!"*

Piss 'n' Vinegar Walter Yeager let out a rebel yell, cranked up the music and blasted off for Seattle. "See ya, Georgia Goddamned Bulldawgs!" shouted Walter, sticking his arm out the window to give the whole state the finger.

"Seattle, I'm coming with my man!" roared Bear, prompting another rebel yell from the former quarterback. The boys started hooting and hollering as if they'd just won the Super Bowl, while Steppenwolf's rock classic, "Born to Be Wild," blared from Bear's old boom box. "Seattle, I'm coming with my man!" Bear repeated several times until Walter noticed a strange look on his buddy's face and pulled over once again.

"Bear, what's wrong now?" asked Walter.

"Nothing," said Bear, face all contorted, eyes full of tears. "I'm coming with my man."

Walter eyed him curiously with a mild laugh, then put the truck in gear and blasted off again. This time they took off for real, heading out of the past and into a whole new world. The Georgia highway passed beneath them in the Georgia night. Life had infinite possibilities, every one of them destined to include two buddies-for-life, some classic rock and some classic male bonding.

"You know, you can trade me if you want," said Walter in the dark of the night, somewhere over Tennessee. "I Was Made for Loving You" by KISS was playing on the boom box.

"*Huh?*" asked Bear, snuggled cozily against the passenger door.

"Trade me for a QB who's not retired at 22," said Walter. "You can get Elway, Montana, anybody."

"I'm happy with the QB I have, thank you very much," said Bear. "Sincerely."

"You didn't sign up for this kind of setback when we met," said Walter.

"Neither did you," said Bear. "Don't think you can get rid of me just because you're on a different career path."

"Hope not," said Walter.

"Playing football was your dream, Big Norse," said Bear. "Mine was having a buddy who makes me feel as good as Walter Yeager does."

"I know," said Walter.

"And helping you shine," said Bear.

"I know," said Walter.

"Then you know I hurt for you," said Bear. "Big time."

"Let's not talk football for now, cool?" said Walter.

"You're just my freshman boy delivered late," said Bear.

"Your what?" asked Walter with a mild laugh.

"I came to college to find my buddy," said Bear, drifting off to sleep. "Thought I was gonna meet him first week, freshman year. You showed up, just late. I don't care what you play, or if you do. I'm always gonna love ... my buddy."

"So you sold our little red sports car," said Bear from the driver's seat in the dark of the night, somewhere over southern Illinois. "Keep On Loving You" by REO Speedway was playing on the boom box.

"Man's gotta do," said Walter from the passenger seat.

"What does your family think of the move?" asked Bear

"You'll be the second person to know," said Walter.

"Do they know anything?" asked Bear.

"Nope. Yours neither, right?" said Walter.

"Correct," said Bear.

"You think we're gay?" asked Walter

"I couldn't be gayer than when I'm around you," giggled Bear.

"I mean the modern definition," laughed Walter.

"So do I," giggled Bear.

"What does that mean?" laughed Walter.

"Now that you mention it, what does *gay* mean?" asked Bear.

"I dunno, that we fuck around with each other, I guess," said Walter.

"If that's all it means, I couldn't be gayer being gay with you," said Bear.

"YOU THINK WE'RE FAGS?" asked Walter. He was in the driver's seat again as the truck passed through Missouri near dusk. "Don't Do Me Like That" by Tom Petty and the Heartbreakers was playing on the boom box.

"We're buddies," said Bear from the passenger seat.

"What would you do if someone called you a fag?" asked Walter.

"Probably say fuck off," said Bear.

"You realize some people would call us fags," said Walter. "They'll say we have fag sex and live together like fags."

"Having that fag sex, you mean," said Bear.

"Right. Probably lots of fag sex," said Walter.

"Are we gonna have that much fag sex, Walter?" asked Bear.

"All kinds of fag sex," said Walter. "You do wanna have all kinds of fag sex, right?"

"Well, *geez*, Walter, I'm open to any kind of sex," said Bear. "I like sex."

"Sex likes you." Walter indicated a billboard on the highway. "Look, Fag Sex Motel, five miles. Let's go have some fag sex."

The next morning, Bear was at the ice machine of the Fag Sex Motel, filling up the Styrofoam ice chest, when Walter approached and murmured in his ear: "I gotta be a fag again before we check out." The ice chest hit the floor, its contents melting in the simmering sunrise.

Later, in a restroom at a gas station in rural Iowa/Nebraska/Kansas, Walter was washing his hands in the lone basin as Bear waited his turn. "Are you a fucking fag?" asked Walter, eyeing Bear suspiciously through the mirror.

"What if I am a fucking fag?" asked Bear.

"Prove it then, fucking fag," said Walter, making sure the restroom door was locked. The boys played *fucking fag* constantly through the Plains States. By the time they reached the Pacific Northwest, they were beginning to lose interest. By the time they reached the outskirts of Seattle, they stopped playing *fucking fag* altogether, as if some unspoken accord had been struck to enjoy their Sugar without further additives.

"GO FOR ANOTHER RIDE? A smoother one this time," said Walt, sitting in the driver's seat of the golf cart that was parked near the edge of the canyon.

"Take me there," said Marcus from the passenger seat.

"So what the fuck—pardon my French—did the boys do in rainy Seattle?" asked Walt, reclaiming the keys and starting up the golf cart.

"Got wet a lot," said Marcus.

"Take me there," said Walt, embarking on an aimless journey around the grounds of the Complex ...

... Walter and Bear's first weeks in Seattle were spent holed up in a cheap motel, looking for two jobs and one apartment. They didn't know a soul in the state of Washington, but that didn't keep them from calling their college friends and asking them if *they* knew of any souls in the state of Washington.

"Think," said Walter one day. He was pacing their motel room, ignoring the steady rain pouring outside their door, which was open.

"About what?" asked Bear. He was sitting on the bed, more focused on the pavement outside and the pounding it was taking.

"Between cheering and football, we've got connections up the wazoo," said Walter. "Come on, brother! Where's that brilliant mind when we need it? What kind of job would you have gotten if you and I never met in college? Where in the world would Bear Coleman be right now?" Walter watched as Bear's eyes became transfixed on some blur beyond the door. For a moment, the former spirit leader went elsewhere, only returning to Seattle when Walter said, "Bear ... Bear?"

Bear looked up at the blond aura that kept him centered, then remembered who and where they were. "Did I faint?" asked Bear.

"No," said Walter, sitting next to Bear. "You okay, bud? What were you thinking?"

"What my life would be like had we never met," said Bear.

"You're regretting this," said Walter, slumping forward.

"Never!" said Bear. "It's just, the concept never even occurred to me, but anyway, I came up with a great idea!"

"Then you're *not* regretting this," said Walter. "I'd hate to ruin your life, of all people."

"You didn't put a gun to my head and make me follow you. I'm following you because this is my dream," said Bear. "Come true."

"To be running around the country with a broke, 22-year-old, washed-up ex-jock?" asked Walter.

"To be with my buddy. Can we talk about my good idea?" asked Bear.

"BEAR'S GOOD IDEA TURNED into their first break in Seattle," said Marcus from the passenger seat of the golf cart in the hills overlooking Malibu.

"He got his bud a tryout with the Seattle Seahawks," guessed Walt from the driver's seat of the golf cart. He was taking them on long, lazy loops and spirals through the athletic fields of the former junior high school.

"Sorry, that is wrong," said Marcus, sounding like a game show host. "Bear and I had the same post-college idea, which had to do with a job for us—me—him—us."

"I get it," said Walt, using the cart to run the bases of the baseball field.

"Thanks to another dream of my youth," said Marcus, enjoying the breeze on his face as he gazed at the mountains and valleys passing in the distance. "As a teen of the 70s, I developed this fascination with TV promos. You know, 'Tonight on *The Love Boat*, it's a cruise from hell as the devil pays Captain Stubing and the crew a visit and it's more than they bargained for.'"

"Got it," said Walt, rounding first base.

"Cut to college, where I took a class taught by one of the promo gods of Hollywood," said Marcus. "I absorbed his teachings like a grateful fanatic, which landed me a job one summer as a promo writer/producer for cable TV."

"Impressive," said Walt, heading toward third.

"Cut to a few years down the road," said Marcus. "Two weeks before graduating UCLA in 1985, I came out of my posttraumatic-roommate-situation-survival-mode and decided that it was time to think about the future, which was beginning in 14 days. That meant a place to live and a job to pay for that place, among other things."

"Better late than never," said Walt, making an extra-wide turn for home.

"A black female writer/producer at one of the networks happened to be going on maternity leave for six months," said Marcus. "Her baby gave birth to my career. And the career of one Bear Coleman of Seattle, Washington, as well."

"Let's hear it for the newlyweds," said Walt, sliding into home plate sideways with the golf cart ...

... The black pickup truck pulled to a stop in front of KSEA.

"One down, two to go," said Walter, referring to their to-do list, which now read: ONE JOB AND ONE APARTMENT.

"All our dreams are gonna come true, buddy," said Bear, bypassing the doubt in his man's downcast face. "Here's an invisible kiss."

The former spirit leader went off to his first day on the job, thankful he had called his old promo contacts. Coincidentally, a woman at the station was going on maternity leave for six months, and Bear was the perfect replacement. Over the next few weeks, Walter borrowed money and found them a tiny one-bedroom apartment. The former QB also received several job offers but turned them all down. Bear knew the real reason behind the flimsy, stated reasons: Walter Yeager was a football player. Putting on a coat and tie for work meant giving up his dream. The high-powered desk job was supposed to come later, after a long and successful career on the field, not as a substitute for it. Bear also knew Walter didn't want to talk about it and refused to press the matter.

Thus began the boys' humble life in Seattle, the center of which was their barely-furnished one-bedroom apartment. For fun, they overcooked (or under-cooked) dinner on the grill on the balcony and watched movies on that still-newfangled toy, the VCR. They also shopped for cheap furniture and went out to the movies. One night, they were coming out of the hit movie of the summer, *Back to the Future*, when they had their own blast from the past.

"Bear? Is that you?" asked a voice from nowhere.

It was a former Asian cheergirl from one of the other Pac-10 schools.

"From Stanford," she said. "We did that thing together for TV once."

"TV!" said Bear, more focused on how to introduce his buddy and/or hus-band. The Asian cheergirl rambled on about living in Seattle now, talking to Bear, Walter and her female Asian friend, who was by her side. From what Bear gathered, she was also a former cheergirl from a different Pac-10 school, but Bear was too busy admiring the way Walter was charming them with talk of *Back to the Future* and the nice weather Seattle was enjoying. The former quarterback was so enchanting, the girls were still giggling as they disappeared into the the-ater for the next showing.

"You're hilarious, Bear," said Walter as they moved down the sidewalk.

"How so?" asked Bear.

"For a guy who loves to talk, sometimes you clam up like ... a clam," said Walter. "Give me their number. I have a feeling you might lose it." Walter took the crumpled-up paper from Bear's hand. "So you realize they're lesbos, right?"

"Oh ... right," said Bear, wondering to himself: *really?*

The boys had dinner at the girls' apartment, and the lesbo ex-cheergirls admitted to being just that, as well as a couple. A short time later, during that same dinner, the boys admitted to being a couple as well, and a foursome was born—for board games and movie nights ...

"Their names?" asked Walt from the driver's seat of the golf cart. They were parked behind home plate on the baseball field in the Complex.

"*Huh?* Oh, Wendy Jiu and Lisa Wu," said Marcus from the passenger seat, more focused on the hills overlooking the Pacific.

"Which was which?" asked Walt.

Marcus laughed and shook his head in agreement. "Tell me about it!"

... For Walter and Bear, the easiest part of their new life in their new town was getting along. They had similar tastes concerning what was important to them, and a similar indifference about what wasn't. "Doesn't matter to me," they would say more often than not about the logistics of the household. For 22 months, they had lived 2,000 miles apart, barely able to communicate, only granted fleeting moments of physical and emotional intimacy. One thing mattered: how good it felt to be in each other's presence.

Their previous lives felt like prison compared to their new world. They talked openly in the living room, lapsed into kisses in the kitchen, wrapped themselves around each other watching TV in the bedroom. Most notably, they started referring to themselves as a couple, though in Bear's mind, they were more like a duo, or a couple of superheroes. Not that their lives were heroic. For the most part, Bear toiled away, creating TV promos, while Walter half-heartedly searched for a new identity.

In August, Bear came home from the station to find Walter at the kitchen table, organizing a brand new briefcase.

"If I can't be an athlete, I'm gonna make all the fucking money in the world that I can," declared the former QB. Thus began Yeager's career as a financial wizard. Walter was a numbers guy, and Bear took comfort in the fact that his man was using his high-powered brain to make high-powered decisions for some high-powered company in the financial district. Sometimes, Walter would even talk about a successful deal with more than a hint of that old piss 'n' vinegar.

"You're a born leader," said Bear on one such occasion. They were having undercooked hamburgers on the living room couch, watching some financial news on television. "The deals that end up being successful are the ones where you follow your gut instinct, and your peeps rally around you and your gut feeling. The deals that end up going south are the deals where either you or your peeps don't follow your gut feeling. And I pity the fool who doesn't listen to Walter Yeager's gut instinct. Pity the fool."

"You think you know how Walter Yeager wheels and deals, huh, little Bearcat?" said Walter.

"I know Walter Yeager," said Bear. *He called me little Bearcat!*

"Dream on and gimme some Sugar, you animal," said Walter.

Life in Seattle was off to a nice and easy start. They had their 9-to-5s. They had the occasional get-together with the lesbo ex-cheergirls, and mostly, they had one another's company, day after day after day.

"They say be careful what you ask for," said Walter one night in bed. They were nose-to-nose, heartbeat-to-heartbeat.

"Oh, I was very careful," said Bear, causing Walter to laugh. "Seriously. When I was a child, really, really young. I don't remember the age, but my life was much more about what was going on inside my mind than the stuff around me."

"Kinda like now," said Walter, playfully biting Bear's nose.

"I asked God for you," said Bear. "I remember feeling like the only boy in the world who felt like I felt and wanted what I wanted, a buddy to love and be loved by. I dreamed that, out of this world of billions of people, there had to be one other boy who was just like me, and when I found him, we'd be buddies for life. Period."

"You believe this was destiny?" asked Walter.

"I believe dreams come true," said Bear. "Look at me: wanted to go to school in LA; went to school in LA. Wanted to be a cheerleader; became a cheerleader. Wanted to work in promos; working in promos. Wanted to meet the buddy of my dreams; presto."

"Man, you're all outta dreams," said Walter.

"Storytelling," said Bear. "Being a great screenwriter of great movies."

"If anybody can do it, it's my Bear," said Walter. "I'm just sorry one of your movies won't be *The Walter Yeager Story,* not after my demise."

"*You* didn't demise," said Bear. "Your career ended—stopped. I don't like the word *ended.* Are we sure it's over? It doesn't look like it's over in your eyes, Walter."

The superhero paused, then broke down and cried in the arms of his buddy. For the first time in their relationship, Bear was the dry-eyed one, holding onto his partner who finally let out some of his grief. Thus began a nightly scene during their first months in Seattle. The lone variation was simple. No matter how they started out in bed, Walter cried facing away from Bear, who ended up spooning Walter's backside through the night. The intimacy felt better than raw sex, which was a good thing, since, although they were more in love than ever, there was an uneasy shift in the winds of the sexual universe, and the debris from the growing storm was becoming too big to ignore ...

"I HOPE YOU DON'T MIND me dreaming of you crying," said Marcus from the passenger seat of the golf cart, still parked behind home plate. Walt was sitting in the driver's seat but didn't answer. "I suspect you rarely do it," said Marcus, "and when you do cry, it's for more joyous occasions, as in joy for others, but I digress. I was the one who was crying around that time, every morning on the way to work, grieving the loss of that beloved roomie, but in reality, grieving the bigger loss that was five years of college down the drain without fulfilling my deepest dream."

"You still had the rest of your life," said Walt.

"Ah," said Marcus. "Tell that to the boy whose life is nowhere near where he dreamed it would be at the end of college. Then introduce that boy to a much scarier world. Whose reality would you rather visit first, mine or Bear's? They're both going to feature boys forced to grow up a little faster."

"You make the call," said Walt ...

... Bear Coleman stood on a street corner in downtown Seattle and glanced skyward. It was a cool and gloomy day, but at least it was dry. On top of that, all the golden blond sunshine he needed was approaching from a block away, ready to take him to Snaky Lu's Seafood Market in honor of their five-month anniversary, living together.

"I *thought* that was you," said a voice from nowhere.

It was a beautiful brunette woman from the station, some sort of reporter *slash* intern. "Hey, you!" said Bear, unable to remember her name. A gust of wind smacked his face, giving him a chance to take note of the striking man with black hair standing next to her. He was tall with a toned physique that made Bear think of skill position football players.

"You work at the station, right?" asked the woman, pulling the flap of her jacket from the corner of her mouth.

"Bear," said Bear. "Bear Coleman."

"Right." The woman said her name, but Bear was busy absorbing the sight of the handsome, masculine man. "This is my husband."

"And you are?" Bear asked the man, but just then, the man's attention was commandeered by—

"Walter Freakin' Yeager," said Hail Larry. "It's about time—"

"*Whoa, stop right there,*" said Walt from the driver's seat of the golf cart behind home plate in the hills overlooking the Pacific.

"What'd I do?" asked Marcus from the passenger seat of the golf cart behind home plate in the hills overlooking the Pacific.

"This must be the guy Walter throws a Hail Mary touchdown pass to, right?" asked Walt.

"Maybe," shrugged Marcus.

"The guy's name is Hail Larry?" asked Walt with a mild laugh.

"In my dreams it is," said Marcus. "Of course, people just call him Larry, but when I, Marcus the dreamer, see him, he's Hail Larry."

"Dream on," said Walt. "Can't wait to see what you call Hail Larry's wife."

... On the street in downtown Seattle, Hail Larry gave Walter a hard punch to the arm, and said, "About time I ran into your golden boy ass, so you can get down on your freakin' knees and thank me."

A sly smile crept across Walter's face. Hail Larry McPherson was the Auburn wide receiver who dropped the pass that should have beaten Alabama and sent Auburn, not Georgia, to Walter and Bear's Sugar Bowl.

"You got yours," said Walter. He meant the fact that Hail Larry was playing for the Kansas City Chiefs, but his eyes were on the beautiful brunette.

"Meet the wife," said Hail Larry. "She lives here. I popped in for a quick celebration. Our sixth-month freakin' wedding anniversary. We're doing Snaky Lu's."

Walter and Bear extended their congratulations to Hail Larry and Hail Larry's Wife, who accepted them, then paused politely for the *fourth* introduction. "Oh, uh," said Walter, as if just now realizing the oversight. "This is Bear Coleman."

"You played at Georgia, too?" asked Hail Larry, trying to place Bear's face.

"No, honey, he's the cheerleader!" said Hail Larry's Wife. "UCLA, right? You did that great promo about pet adoptions with the Husky Band. Someone was saying they really like your *rah! rah!* enthusiasm—in a good way."

Bear gritted his teeth and flashed a Joe Bruin half-smile.

"You guys met in Seattle then?" asked Hail Larry, eyeing freakin' Yeager and trying to figure out the connection between a white quarterback from Georgia, a black male cheerleader from UCLA, and a downtown street in the Pacific Northwest.

"Oh," said Walter, ready to scramble for his life. "I used to date this girl at UCLA—Roseanne, who was best buds with Bear, who was looking to get into sports management, and was going to be my personal assistant while I was making my millions in the NFL."

"Yeah, man, sorry to hear your career went in the freakin' toilet," said Hail Larry.

"The good thing," said Walter, not done scrambling, "after I retired so abruptly and screwed up Bear's future, I told him to come work for me in Seattle and we'll make our fortune another way, right Bear?"

"Pretty freakin' cool of him, huh?" said Bear.

Hail Larry seemed satisfied and Hail Larry's Wife seemed hungry. The boys pretended they had dinner reservations elsewhere, and the former SEC football rivals made a casual promise to keep in touch through Bear and Hail Larry's Wife.

"Way to prevent a potential turnover," said Bear, watching the happy couple enter Snaky Lu's Seafood Market. "Sorry, no football analogies. My bad."

"Forget about that," said Walter. "You heard the news at the station, right?"

"I was swamped all day watching tape, what happened?" asked Bear, bracing himself.

"Rock Hudson died." Walter's face looked as if he'd just witnessed a bad car accident. Bear stood frozen, as if the car accident had yet to happen ...

"IT WAS 1985 AND THE KNOWN WORLD went through a sexual reality shift," said Marcus. He was out of the golf cart and standing on the other side of the backstop, fingers interlaced with the fence separating him and Walt, who was still in the driver's seat, facing the outfield. "That strange new disease that kills fags killed a movie star and turned *aids* into AIDS. The media alone—so many shots of dying men, so few answers. I was just as shocked as the public, and just as ignorant. Before then, AIDS was a whisper in the dark.

"Doctors couldn't agree on the name or nature of the virus yet, but they knew the symptoms. I saw them on a newscast. One of them was feverish sweats that appeared like magic in the middle of the night. One minute, you're in dreamland; the next, your entire existence is drowning in your sweat. I got night sweats right after college. I'm not 100% sure how they got there, inside my body, or when they were put there, but it was probably sometime during my last days of school. The exact details are not important. But as the world was forced to adjust to the new reality of AIDS, I had to adjust personally.

"I buried the night sweats incident in the back of my mind and hoped that it was just the bad timing of some flu-like bug. Part of me went into a holding pattern. Part of me just held my breath. Outwardly, I was the happy-go-lucky, UCLA grad, hotshot promo guy, Joe Bruin on cruise control. Inside, I was terrified. I shut down parts of me just to keep on living day to day, always wondering if I was going to end up looking like those men dying on the news, losing half my body weight, fading away in a hospital bed at 23 ... 24. Sometimes, it was too much to think about. Those were the nights I turned to Walter and Bear to live my dreams."

Marcus sighed nostalgically, remembering the times when the boys were closest to his heart, the times when he stumbled upon "True" by Spandau Ballet on some easy-listening radio station. He imagined Walter and Bear having the same moment. The boys would pause from whatever they were doing, if only for a moment, to acknowledge their first song. If they were close enough in proximity, in the car perhaps, Walter would give Bear's hand a tug, or if they had privacy, a gentle kiss. Then, having paused to say grace, they would continue onward, living their lives ...

... Sexually the boys went on lockdown, but became more physically intimate than ever, sharing massages after work, hugging just for the sake of hugging while fixing dinner, sleeping more often in their favorite spooning position, Bear's front to Walter's back. Before Rock Hudson, they watched TV sitting apart. After Rock Hudson, they watched TV tangled up in each other's limbs.

Over the next year, scientists conceived of HIV and an HIV test, but gay activists discouraged everyone from taking the test, citing conservative politicians and their visions of quarantines and concentration camps. The new world was scary and frustrating for the boys, especially after the sexual freedom of France. But if there was an upshot to their lack of sex, it was the fact that Walter and Bear got to know one another better than ever, as best friends. On top of that, they also discovered they could have *almost* as much fun being sexy as opposed to sexual.

Sexy meant goofing off on the basketball court, then coming home and having a beer and a nap, content to fall asleep surrounded by the heavenly smell of one another's sweat and funk. Sexy meant wearing the same sweat pants and gray t-shirts time after time without washing away their sexy scents, then wearing each other's clothes because of those very same sexy scents. Sexy meant watching Bear inhale Walter's scent, and Walter inhale Bear's scent. Sexy meant shopping at the sporting goods store for toys and the casual athletic wear they loved so much, the same athletic wear they lived in on the weekends and found so sexy on the other man. Best of all, sexy meant savoring each and every moment afforded them in this ever-changing world. Together.

"EVENTUALLY, THE BOYS weren't the only ones to breathe again," said Marcus from behind the backstop of the baseball diamond.

"Marcus Coleman, too? Good man," said Walt from the driver's seat of the golf cart.

"But Marcus and Bear take really divergent paths around the world now," said Marcus. "He's got Walter. I got ... life after college. I wanted to get as far from UCLA as possible, so I moved to the San Fernando Valley, the shopping mall haven just north of the LA basin. UCLA was outta my life. You weren't the only one aiming for a clean break from college dreams gone south. I was all about the promo dream now. After a while, the tears over school dried up, the media's hysteria over AIDS subsided, and I started to do the things college grads do: make money, spend money, move up in the career, live in a quirky apartment, buy a new car, spend more money, and look for love and sex, not always in that order.

"I was still looking for my buddy, too. I even got my feet wet meeting guys, not college guys, or guys in the dark sex zones—which were pretty much run out of town by AIDS—but *guys,* who were also looking for love and sex, not always in that order. I found them in some personal ads, I think. And in the gay world. Where else was I supposed to look? Some guys became tricks. Some became friends. Some just kept passing in the night. I became real good at living while holding my breath. And best of all, I got to live some of my dreams through Walter and Bear."

... One night, Walter's tears vanished so abruptly during his nightly grieving session, both men understood that was that: Yeager was done crying over football. Life brightened instantly. The boys explored Seattle more, and connected more often with the lesbo ex-cheergirls, although they argued over which lesbo ex-cheergirl was Wendy Jiu, and conversely, which lesbo ex-cheergirl was Lisa Wu. During one particularly drunken night of cards, Walter and Bear came *thisclose* to revealing their ignorance.

"I have never seen you guys fight about anything," said Wendy Jiu or Lisa Wu as she dealt up a new hand. They were on the floor of the girls' living room, each partnered with his or her partner in some card game Bear barely understood.

"We fight about one thing," said Bear, meaning the girls' names.

"Bear!" warned Walter, arranging his cards. "Shut your trap."

"See, that's a fight," giggled Bear.

"Oh, please," said Wendy Jiu or Lisa Wu. "Her and I—we break dishes."

"Over what?" asked Bear, taking another dizzy sip of his bottle of Bud.

"Doing the dishes, for one," said Lisa Wu or Wendy Jiu.

"Problem solved," said Walter.

"How can you guys not argue?" asked Wendy Jiu or Lisa Wu.

"I'd be a basket case if I didn't have him around," said Walter, more focused on the cards he was dealt. "The rest is details."

"We waited 21 years to be together," said Bear, clutching his bottle of Bud tenderly and swaying as if on a roller coaster. "I don't care what we do. As long as I can reach out and touch him. Or at least, smell him."

"What do you mean, 21 years?" asked Wendy Jiu or Lisa Wu. "You haven't dated since you were babies."

"Not what I'm saying," said Bear, putting his bottle of Bud between his legs. "Any way you look at it, we're depraved—I mean, *deprived*. It was *Walt at first sight*, then we had to wait 22 whole months and a couple of days—how many was it? I forget—and a couple of days, just to spend more than a few *seconds* together! I don't care how this man *screws the toothpaste*, or which side of the bed he wants, and by the way, *he can sleep on either side*," whispered Bear. He scooted across the floor to his blushing buddy. "Walter Yeager can have *whatever Walter Yeager wants*. I'll go *anywhere* with him."

"I'll take you there," said Walter. A kiss became their holy communion, one which they permitted the world to witness for the very first time. A short time later, they walked home through a light drizzle and had drunken college masturbation sex, imagining they were back in LA in Bear's old lime green Oldsmobile Omega.

By morning, they were strewn across the bed in opposite directions, not spooning as they usually did to start and end their nights. It was a Saturday. They were sleeping in until the sound of two lesbo ex-cheergirls pounding on the door roused them out of bed. Both Wendy Jiu and Lisa Wu insisted they become a foursome for today's Apple Cup, the big rivalry football game between Washington State and Washington.

"You call it," Walter told Bear as they stood in the doorway in their underwear. Bear relished the idea of going to another big rivalry matchup reminiscent of USC-UCLA. He chose to *go watch some football!*

The girls had a whole tailgate setup in the back of their Jeep Cherokee, which was parked amongst a sea of tailgaters. The four of them ate, drank and got caught up in the revelry of the rivalry. *Correction:* three of them got caught up in the day. The former quarterback put on a good game face, but Bear knew his man and understood why he was laughing and smiling only when necessary. Bear knew what Walter wanted, but didn't know how to give it to him. He also realized that 22-year-old Walter Yeager didn't want to be at any football stadium dressed as anything but a quarterback.

If only there were a way to make my man's dreams come true, thought Bear. *If only there was somebody looking out for us, somebody who could make miracles happen for two buddies, very much in love.*

11

The Universal Space Halftime Report

"Hold on, boys, I'm coming to the rescue." Marcus dried his eyes with his gray t-shirt. He was lying on his back in the bleachers of the football stadium in the Complex. The sun was high above the hills overlooking the Pacific. If there was still such a thing as time, he figured it to be around one in the afternoon, whatever that meant.

"How you gonna get me—*Walter*—back in the game?" asked Walt. He was lying on his back in the bleachers on the same row as Marcus. Their two heads— one golden blond, one golden brown—were separated by the gap in the bleachers that was the exit to the ground beneath the stands. Otherwise, they were polar opposite pillars, resting horizontally.

"I'll get you in the game if you have the time to go there," said Marcus, talking to the heavens but not blinded by the light.

"I have time if you have time," said Walt, talking to the heavens but not blinded by the light.

"What about your thing tonight? The thing you said you came here for?" asked Marcus.

"I have time," said Walt, plain and simple. "You have time?"

"Nothing but," said Marcus.

"Didn't you say something about a movie tonight?" asked Walt.

"*Me?*" said Marcus, perhaps a little too dramatically. He mumbled something indecipherable, then found a response inside his head. "So far, the only thing I *had* to do was make sure the dogs are taken care of. Glad I got through on your cell phone. Mine doesn't work at all up here."

"What'd your mom say about the boys?" asked Walt.

"Did I mention they were both boys? Anyway," said Marcus, "she was on her way to some function or something. I dunno—my mind's been elsewhere, if you get my drift."

"Getting it," said Walt.

"The dogs are with Helen, whom they love, so all is well with the boys, at least those boys," said Marcus.

"So what was Walter's injury that he never wanted to talk about?" asked Walt.

Marcus chuckled. "*He's* asking *me!*"

"You're the dreamer man," said Walt with a mild laugh.

"I like the sound of that," giggled Marcus.

"So tell me what happens, dreamer man," said Walt.

"A black hole, and not the kind that's sweet as Sugar," said Marcus.

"*Whoa, stop right there,*" said Walt.

"You can't '*whoa, stop right there*' in this life!" said Marcus, laughing like a kid whose buddy just broke the rules of the game.

"Oh, fuck, you're right," said Walt, sounding like a kid whose buddy just caught him breaking the rules. "So what's up with your black hole—pun not intended."

"No doubt," said Marcus. "The black hole I'm talking about is the one in my dreams. You see, Walter Yeager shared so much of his life with Bear, but there was one part of the quarterback that Bear wasn't privy to at the time: the deepest reaches of Yeager's football soul."

"Getting lost here," warned Walt.

"We're talking about my dreams from almost 20 years ago," said Marcus. "I remember stuff, but the way a really old black man remembers the great love of his life. It's kinda blurry, some of it, just like real-life memories. Sometimes, the details are sketchy, but how you feel about someone or something is always just a flash away."

"Got it," said Walt.

Marcus sighed. "I tried to tell myself all that time you had some kind of leg injury, maybe knee, hip, something that wasn't too painful physically, something that didn't keep you from living a full life." Marcus fell silent, listening to the faint sounds of nature from the canyons. "I should have known better."

"How's that?" asked Walt.

"It would have taken a lot more than a nagging injury to keep Walt Yeager from living his dreams. I know my quarterback," said Marcus. "He's just like me. It took a lot more than striking out in college to keep me from living my dreams, you'll see."

"My back problems ended my football career," said Walt.

"I'd love to resurrect your football dreams in ways I don't think you can imagine," said Marcus. "Yet."

"So you knew I didn't have a minor injury, then what?" asked Walt.

"The big league boys walked through the fire and made the miracle happen," said Marcus.

"How?" asked Walt, full of doubt.

"I just remember the fire ... in the hole ... everything else is lost," said Marcus.

"What does *that* mean?" asked Walt.

"I don't know, that's the black hole," said Marcus.

"The black hole," repeated Walt.

"Need a shovel or a flashlight?" said the voice of Sanchez, the Latino gardener turned delivery boy. He was standing between the boys in the exit to the ground beneath the stands.

"What's up, Coach?" asked Walt, not stirring from his horizontal position.

"Checking up on you fellas while I do some work around here," said Sanchez. "Folks got some big deal happening here tonight."

"What kind of work?" asked Marcus, not stirring from his horizontal position.

"Raking, weeding, sandblasting, scraping, whatever it takes to get the gunk off," said Sanchez. "Gotta remember the original beauty of something every once in a while."

"What's this about a shovel or a flashlight?" asked Marcus.

"Heard you saying something was lost in a hole," said Sanchez.

"This is a hole in his head," said Walt.

"More like a hole in my dreams," said Marcus.

"So what's it gonna be, shovel or flashlight?" asked Sanchez.

"Say what?" the boys said together, laughing like little kids.

"Close your eyes, like we did before. Time to use your imagination again," Sanchez paused until the boys morphed from restless to restful, their eyelids slowly turning the world pitch black. "A dream is like a moving landscape, like the night sky, full of the mystery and magic of the entire universe. That universe is never still, and neither are dreams. Dreams breathe ... move ... shift ... dreams reveal themselves, just like the sky moving across the night, or the whole universe, moving in all directions."

Infinite space in every direction, not just above and to either side. In reality, there is no above, no below, not even side to side. Only here and there, and the space between.

"Picture space and the universe moving in all directions," said Sanchez. "That is the moving universe in which you exist, the same universe in which your dreams reside. Everything single thing in that universe is in constant motion, you and your dreams included. Your mind, body and spirit creates itself anew in every single moment of your life, right down to your thoughts, your skin, and how you create yourself in each and every moment. The universe does the same. Your dreams do the same. As the universe shifts, the light within shifts, shedding light (that is new to you) on the world around you. Of course, you have to choose to see that new light."

"What if there's no light, just a black hole?" asked Marcus.

"Do you wanna know what's inside the black hole?" asked Sanchez.

"If Walt does," said Marcus.

"Go for it," said Walt.

"If the black hole were in the ground, you'd need a flashlight, right?" said Sanchez. "Same deal with your dreams, you need a flash ... light, as in ... a flash of light."

"Come again?" asked Marcus.

"Absolutely, especially if you both keep your golden-boy eyes closed like I tell you to," said Sanchez. "Now ... imagine the night sky and the universe again. Now imagine voids in space where there is no light, only darkness that humans currently comprehend as black holes. The black hole in your mind is the same. Shine some light into the hole. What's inside will reveal itself to you, if you truly wanna see it."

"Like the magic cap," said Marcus.

"Man can't explore black holes," said Walt.

"My sincerest apologies. I assumed you weren't just *any man*," said Sanchez, descending the stairs.

"What's that supposed to mean?" asked Walt.

"Where you going, Coach?" asked Marcus.

"I thought the golden blond one was a man who looks at life thinking: *how to get the job done*, not, *it can't be done*," said Sanchez.

"He is that way," said Marcus. "He wouldn't be here otherwise. That goes for both of us."

"Thanks, bro," said Walt.

"You da man, QB," said Marcus.

"So where do we get this light to shine into this black hole?" asked Walt.

"Keep sharing your memories and stories," said Sanchez. "Talk. Dream. Together. Fill in the blanks with the energy of your golden light, both of you."

"*He's* the storyteller," said Walt, indicating Marcus.

"Be grateful for that gift," said Sanchez. "The storyteller is a valuable person in a duo, the person in charge of the archives. Those archives are your source of light and power."

"Power?" asked Walt.

"How do you define power?" asked Sanchez.

"Control," said Walt.

"Guess again," said Sanchez. "What does the world run on?"

"Money," said Marcus.

"What does your world run on?" asked Sanchez.

"Power," said Walt.

"What kind of power?" asked Sanchez.

"Gas!" said Marcus. "Coal. Energy. Oil. Electricity."

"The world runs on energy!" said Walt.

"Eyes closed, lie still." Sanchez paused until the boys settled down again. "Your memory—another name for your archives—is full of stories. Your stories are full of life. Your life is full of stories. The stories give your life meaning, which gives you the energy to keep going. Your energy is your source of power. Your world runs on your power. What happens in your world becomes your stories. Your stories are your energy. Your world runs on energy. Your energy is your source of power. Your *power* powers your world. Jump in here anytime. We can even make it a song if you want."

"What if the energy is all in one person's mind?" asked Walt.

"Then that person is like God, imagining what the mind can do," said Sanchez. "But that's not the case with you two."

"Thank God," said Marcus.

"You're like *two* gods imagining what the mind can do," said Sanchez.

"Say what?" asked Marcus.

"*He's* the one!" said Walt, indicating Marcus.

"Until you understand that *you* created the world in which you live, you will be lost in it," said Sanchez.

"We don't *live* in that world," said Walt.

"Maybe you better get your golden butts back there then, if you wanna see what's inside the black hole," said Sanchez.

"That world is in my head," said Marcus.

"Golden blond one, do you know anything about this world?" asked Sanchez.

"I do now," said Walt.

"There—golden brown one—*your* world is not just in your head alone anymore," said Sanchez. "Feel better now?"

"Hard to say," said Marcus.

"There's a black hole that has you both in a dither," said Sanchez. "Take a trip to that world, shine your golden light, don't be afraid."

"You are talking a trip down memory lane, right?" asked Walt, in search of clarification.

"If that's what you wanna call it," said Sanchez. "It's all space."

"Space?" the boys said together.

"Remember: our planet is in a solar system, which is in a galaxy of billions of stars, which is part of a universe of billions of galaxies, right? And some believe it's possible our universe is merely one of billions of universes."

"*Whoa! Stop right there,*" said Marcus. "Just kidding. You're talking a lotta space, Coach."

"You doubt a supreme being we'll call God—you doubt God's ability to create that?" asked Sanchez.

"No doubt here," said Marcus.

"If God can create an infinite number of universes, why would God sweat giving you some space in space?" asked Sanchez.

"For what?" the boys said together.

"That's all God wants to know," said Sanchez.

"So we can build whatever life, world, universe we want," said Marcus.

"I knew you weren't just *any* men," said Sanchez.

"So now you're saying we're all just 'minds' imagining whatever the hell we want?" asked Walt.

"Do me a favor: sub *heaven* for *hell* and repeat the question," said Sanchez.

"So we're all just 'minds' imagining whatever the heaven we want?" asked Walt.

"Which version makes you feel better, one or two?" asked Sanchez.

"Heaven," said Walt.

"Heaven," said Marcus.

"Congratulations," said Sanchez. "You are now in heaven. Enjoy your stay."

"You don't mean the real heaven, do you, the cloudy one?" asked Marcus.

"You can open your eyes now," said Sanchez. "See any clouds in the sky?"

"I just see the sky," said Marcus.

"Welcome to heaven on Earth," said Sanchez.

"What does *that* mean?" asked Walt with a mild laugh.

"Tell me about it," said Sanchez. "But first, get back to telling each other your stories. You need light for this black hole. And what is light?"

"Energy," said Walt.

"And what do ya need to shine inside that black hole in your memory?" asked Sanchez.

"Light," said Marcus, "which is energy, which is our stories, which we have to share to shed light on the black hole—damn, I'm good!"

"Not if you're gonna *damn* yourself," said Sanchez.

"In that case, I'm just *gooooood!*" said Marcus.

"But what if the life is but a dream?" asked Walt.

"Dreams, thoughts, stories, songs—it's all energy. Remember: worlds run on energy. If you've been together 21 years, that's a big world with a lot of memories. No wonder you got some black holes," said Sanchez.

"You still don't understand," said Walt.

"I don't need to. You do," said Sanchez. "Find those holes and light 'em up. They're out there, just like your parking space at the mall. You gotta conceive of the possibility, do your part to get there, and believe that space will be there just when you need it most. Do your part, have faith. There's space for you."

"Define doing our part," said Walt. "Coach? Still there?"

"Gone," said Marcus, "but I think our part would be to shed light, as in share the story."

"Would you be offended if I said: dream the fuck on?" asked Walt.

"I'm not sure it's genetically possible for me to be offended by anything that comes out of you, just for the record," said Marcus.

"In that case: dream the fuck on," said Walt, his voice somewhere between utter amazement and complete sarcasm.

12

Double Reverse

Walter and Bear began to dream bigger, as in bigger circle of friends and bigger apartment. They got together weekly with the lesbo ex-cheergirls, even meeting some of their friends at the occasional birthday party. They also searched for a dwelling with enough room for a home office for two. Walter was adamant about Bear getting a jump on his screenwriting dreams, always telling the former cheerleader: "You can do this! Your mind is amazing!" Bear kept those dreams close to his heart but was also enjoying the niche he'd carved for himself at KSEA, where he had landed a permanent staff position. Meanwhile in downtown Seattle, Walter proved to be an instant master of financial wizardry and the business world, as if he were meant to lead men into action, one way or another. He made deals on hunches, and those hunches were fruitful for his investors, as well as Walter and Bear. A year after graduating college, there was food on the table, gas in both cars (yep! they bought one for Bear!), and an apartment full of furniture and love.

The boys even learned how to breathe in a world filled with AIDS, and found their way to back to sexy *and* sexual. Their lovemaking was "laboratory safe" and guarded, as if there were a third or fourth party in the room, silently watching. Yet they were still boys, and they did manage to share passionate moments where they forgot about the potential traveling companions inside their bodies. They were healthy but untested, still siding with the decreasing number of activists wary of the world's intentions. They'd have to face the music someday, but for the time being, they were free to ignore *that* particular band playing on.

At least while together. When Bear was alone, AIDS would float into his dreams like an uninvited asteroid. One day at KSEA, he was putting the finishing touches on a batch of promos in the sound studio, which meant making sure the announcer and the sound guys carried out his vision. To that end, he was sound asleep on the couch. Lawrence the Sound Guy (at the mixing board), and Jimmy the Announcer (inside the glass booth) had worked with Bear long enough to know the deal: "Do your job, then wake me when it's done." Upon waking, Bear would either make changes, or more often, bark out his now-patented: "*Perfect!*" After which, the guys would all laugh and wrap up the session. The skilled crewmen appreciated the chance to do their job without interference, plus it gave Bear time to dream.

With HIV so present in Bear's mind, he often wondered how life might have turned out had he not met Walter. Had their monogamous union saved them from AIDS, or had they been too late? Where would Bear be without Walter? How could Bear have ever made it through this whole AIDS epidemic as a single man?

"*Not the real life!*" cried Bear.

"Change something, Mr. Coleman?" asked Lawrence the Sound Guy, staring at Bear from the mixing board.

"Change who?" asked Bear, the studio coming into focus.

"Did you say, *not my real line,* as in the script here is wrong?" asked Lawrence the Sound Guy.

"Bad dream," said Bear, waving him onward.

Lawrence the Sound Guy went back to work, and Bear sat up and reminded himself to thank God every day for Walter. The same Walter who magically appeared on the other side of a dark glass partition. He was standing in the tape room with Hail Larry's Wife, who must have assisted the visitor in search of Walter Yeager's buddy. It wasn't the first time Bear's thoughts had conjured up his husband in the flesh, just the first time at KSEA. Walter was smiling more than his usual half-smile, too, which made Bear grin like Joe Bruin. Hail Larry's Wife waved hello and goodbye to Bear, who saw his own hand wave in his own periphery as the golden blond aura approached, radiant as ever.

"It couldn't wait," said Walter.

"Mr. Coleman, we're ready for you," said Lawrence the Sound Guy.

"*Perfect!*" said Bear, whisking Walter out of the studio. They flew to the outdoor patio behind the station, a round concrete clearing with two stone picnic tables. It was past lunch; they were alone.

"Took a client to nine holes of golf this morning," said Walter, leaning on the edge of one of the tables. "I'm in the locker room changing, kinda sore, trying to massage my back."

"Were you dressed?" asked Bear, standing in front of his man.

"Doesn't matter. This guy and I start talking about my injury," said Walter.

"Was *he* dressed?" asked Bear.

"He was checking me out," said Walter, "because he's this homeopathic, pathogenic, cryogenic, photogenic chiropractor-genic or something, I don't know—*details!* The guy gives me a good feeling."

"I don't blame him," said Bear.

"Bear! He saw how my back is fucked up, from the way I moved," said Walter.

"From football," said Bear, still catching up to speed.

"You look sleepy. What were you dreaming about?" asked Walter.

"Nothing important right now," said Bear. "You never talk about your back. How fucked up is it, Walter?"

"See, that's why I hate to talk about it. Look at you, getting all upset. Please don't start crying," said Walter.

"This is not about how *I* feel," said Bear, trying to check his emotions.

"I hate to burden you," said Walter.

"I know you're hurting, you know how I know?" said Bear. "Every time I think about you in any kind of pain, no matter where I am, my lower left stomach starts hurting. It's killing me right now. What's wrong with your back? You're my hero, let me be yours."

"You and this chiropractor can help, okay?" said Walter, exhaling as if relinquishing control of his life. Unwillingly.

"What's this chiropractor's name?" asked Bear, drying his eyes.

"Bass derVanderkerplunkendorph, more or less. He's Danish," said Walter.

"Good looking? Young? Athletic?" asked Bear.

"All the above," said Walter. "Will it hurt?"

"It's starting to," said Bear, reaching for his lower left abdomen.

"I wish I could give you a hug right now, you big, lovable, baby Bear, you," said Walter.

"Bass," said Bear, as if getting used to the idea of a man with a fishy name.

"The Dane, yes," said Walter. "Why don't we wait until after I see him tomorrow in private before we get all hot and bothered, okay, little Bearcat?"

BEFORE HIS APPOINTMENT with Bass the Dane, Walter was cautiously optimistic. Seems as though the photogenic chiropractor saw something in the way Walter moved that indicated a common back problem. According to the Dane, if the problem were "reversed," it might make all the difference in the world, enough difference, perhaps, to return a quarterback's back to its previous piss 'n' vinegar, *let's go play some football!* condition. The course of treatment was no walk in the park, but that was all the boys knew. When Walter came home after the private consultation, he informed Bear that the "reverse" was more akin to a journey through the lower gates of hell.

"We're talking months of painful manipulation of my entire body," said Walter. He was lying on the couch on his side, head resting in Bear's lap. "Bass, the Dane guy, stumbled on some ancient, holy, pre-Tibetan, Sacred Band of Homo Mud Wrestlers Lost World Haiku Scrolls found in an excavation of some lakebed cave in 1972 or something, I don't know—*details!* He's been studying the stuff his whole life and happens to be looking for the perfect human to be his guinea pig in the States. Lucky me."

"In the States?" asked Bear, gently stroking Walter's hair.

"Apparently, he had an arrangement with some zookeepers in a country I've never heard of," said Walter. "And you know how good I am with history and geography."

"Almost as good as your black buddy," giggled Bear.

"Yeah, right," said Walter. "Anyway. This Dane guy, who's like our age, wants to break my body apart and put it back together again—internally that is. Claims he can substitute the weak energy in my back for stronger energy elsewhere in my body, and redistribute that weak energy in a place that needs less energy—but not my sex drive! Made that perfectly clear!—but anyway, if it works, this process will heal *and* strengthen my back. How about that, little Bearcat?"

"The photogenic chiropractor said all that?" asked Bear.

"It was like a dream come true, or too good to be true," said Walter. "What if I'm just being conned?" Walter struggled to sit upright, then he struggled to find a comfortable sitting position.

"It's been the back," said Bear. "All this time. My big strong hero has had back problems. You never said a word. You kept it all inside."

"I've got my pride," said Walter from the opposite end of the couch.

"And I've got a lot of love to give," said Bear. "I'm begging you, Walter, please let me give it. I live to give you love. Please let me help you feel better."

"Right now, this is all so overwhelming," said Walter, eyes crinkling.

"Try whelming," said Bear, stopping his own floodgates.

"Try what?" asked Walter.

"Whelming," said Bear, more focused on double-locking the floodgates.

"You mean, like, downgrade my emotions to whelming? Like a weather alert?" asked Walter with a mild laugh.

"I dunno, just thought of it," said Bear.

"My boy and his imagination—my *Bear,* I mean," said Walter. "I know how some black guys don't like a white guy calling them *boy.*"

"Whatever Walter wants to call me, as long as he calls me," said Bear, lying on his side and placing his head in Walter's lap.

"The treatments could take months, with no guarantee of success," said Walter. "And the further I get into it, the more external pain."

"External?" asked Bear.

"According to Bass and the pre-Tibetan Haiku Mud Wrestlers, pain is mental," said Walter, stroking Bear's head. "The brain tells the body how to turn itself into a headache, the flu, cancer, HIV, chronic back pain. They claim nothing happens without the brain and the body's cooperation. Normally that means the brain telling the body what to do."

"Scratch your nuts, grab lunch, put one foot in front of the other," said Bear.

"Reach out and touch someone's worried, golden brown forehead," said Walter. "Use a finger to ski down your man's beautiful black nose; stick a finger in between your man's beautiful black lips; take your finger ... back before a big grizzly Bear bites it"—Walter reclaimed his finger—"*off,* and so on. But this ancient, pre-Tibetan Holy Zookeeper Scroll thing puts the traffic in your body in reverse."

"*The body* telling *the brain* what to do?" asked Bear.

"Imagine energy normally flowing from the brain to the body," said Walter. "Bass is gonna put me in reverse every other day, see if my body can convince my brain that my back is in great shape. Eventually, if the brain thinks the back is fine, the body will think—"

"Cool, dreamy, what chronic back pain?" said Bear, completing the thought.

"Is that crazy or what?" asked Walter. "All this with no pain killers, except some natural, herbal, homeopathy arsenic extract or something—*details.*"

"Bottom line?" asked Bear.

"I could turn into a monster," said Walter. "You haven't seen the Yeager-monster, but I know you know about him."

"I'll go anywhere with you *or* him," said Bear.

"I'm serious, boy—Bear. You have no idea. We're still practically in our honeymoon stage. When the pain hits, it's unbearable," said Walter.

"So let *me* bear some of it," said Bear, sitting upright.

"What's your gut instinct tell you on this one?" asked Walter.

"Honest?" asked Bear, taking a deep breath. "When this decade started six years ago, I was so ready for the 80s. I mean, the very first dream of the sports world became one of the greatest Olympic dreams in history ..."

"Short version, bro, just this once," said Walter.

"Do you believe in miracles?" asked Bear.

"*That's* my Bear!" yelled Walter. "Man, I love you!"

THE NEXT DAY, WALTER YEAGER began reversing his energy flow every other day. The routine seemed simple enough. Bear dropped him off at the photogenic chiropractor's office, then picked him up an hour later. Walter couldn't talk about what went on during the actual visits. The pre-Tibetan Homo Mud Scrollers forbade expending verbal energy on the treatment details. Apparently, talking about pain had the ability to bring on more pain for those not of higher consciousness. Whatever that meant, the Homo Wrestlers backed up their threats. Whenever Walter tried to tell Bear anything about the therapy, Walter's pain doubled instantaneously. Not that Walter felt like talking much. That one hour every other day left him vacant and drained.

"Can't you tell me *anything?*" asked Bear one day while having breakfast at the kitchen table.

"If you could only *see* how much I want to," said Walter, more focused on scribbling something in the margin of the financial section. "You're the only soul I trust with this stuff. You're gonna just have to read between the lines, okay?— fuck, *hint*—of a spasm—*ouch!*" Walter bolted from the table. Bear picked up the financial section that fell to the floor. A second before placing the newspaper back on the table, he paused. Something told him to read the three words Walter had just scribbled on three separate lines: WORLD. HUBBLE. SUN.

Each word was written between the lines of a newspaper article. Was Walter trying to tell Bear something about the treatment? Or had he just been scribbling down notes to himself? "Bear! We're never talking about this again, right?" yelled Walter from the bedroom.

"Roger!" said Bear, tearing off the scribbled note for future investigation.

Walter's pain itself was no mystery. As the treatments wore on, he reminded Bear of a boxer whose spirit was taking a beating every other day at sparring practice. On top of that, Bass the Dane warned that Phase 2 was much more painful and challenging. "How many phases are there?" asked Bear, spooning his man's backside in bed one night.

"You keep going until you're ready to get off the wheel—*ouch!* Just said too much." Walter winced and pulled away from Bear. "Gonna be hard work. You're gonna have to put up with all my shit."

"Don't I already?" asked Bear. The objection was canceled midstream:

"You ... I guess you do," said Walter, as if just now realizing.

During Phase 2, "the wheel" flattened Walter, who was forced to take a leave of absence from his job. His only excursions from the bed became his hobbling to and from therapy, and Bear received a very personal introduction to chronic back pain syndrome: the stress of living with physical pain as a steady companion; the struggle to perform tasks previously taken for granted; the spasms that rocked their world without notice. Bear saw sides of Walter he never knew existed. Walter in constant mental anguish. Walter who ached, just because he was alive and possessed a spine. Walter who hated to ask for things, even of a willing servant like Bear. Walter who, when he did ask for things, often forgot about asking for them politely because his back was literally killing him. And then there was the Walter who turned away Bear because of the pain.

"Can I spoon you?" Bear would ask, hovering over the bed.

"Hell, no!" Walter would say before returning to his private purgatory.

One night, the pain was so intense, Walter insisted that Bear call the man responsible for the former QB's suffering. A short time later, a photogenic Danish man with horned-rimmed glasses and sunken cheeks was standing in the doorway. Bear noted that he was definitely gay, then showed him to the bedroom. "Two choices, Dane," said Walter, looking like a lump of broken dreams in sweaty, crumpled linens. "Stop the pain, or die. Which?"

The chiropractor felt Walter's head for a fever and took his pulse. "With any luck, tonight will be the worst night of his life," said Bass the Dane, a hint of Danish in his voice.

"Dead man!" yelled Walter. "Bear! Kitchen! Knife! Self! Defense!"

"Walter, what are you saying?" asked Bear.

"He wants you to kill me and say it's self-defense," said Bass the Dane. "If you decide not to, and if tonight *is* the worst night of his life, tomorrow will be the second-worst. The day after that, the third-worst, and every day after that, less and less worse, until worse becomes better, then better, then better."

"Kill the fucking Dane!" cried Walter. "What's the derogatory term for fucking Danes?"

"That's a good sign," said Bass the Dane. "If he's ready to commit murder, he's ready to be reborn."

"Bear, so help me, if you don't fucking slit his throat or get him out of here!" yelled Walter. "Fucking wheel of death! *Ouch!* Out! Out!"

"That's all you're going to do?" asked Bear, herding the photogenic chiropractor into the living room. "What about something for the pain?"

"The brain needs the pain, but soon it will need it less and less," said Bass the Dane.

"Bear! Is he dead yet?" cried Walter from the bedroom.

"What's this wheel?" whispered Bear, moving toward the front door, "and what about this scribbled note I got from him? I think he was trying to tell me something about his therapy."

Walter screamed bloody murder from the bedroom.

"Words deep within his soul," said Bass the Dane, "but you must never invoke those words in the name of the wheel, only if they come up in the natural course of life."

"Shut up about the freakin' wheel in there!" yelled Walter.

"One other thing." Bass the Dane sized up Bear. "If he has a significant other, tell that significant other to sleep close to Mr. Yeager in the night, as close as possible to the lower back region to give it positive energy. That too can work miracles."

After the photogenic chiropractor vanished, Bear retrieved the scribbled note from his pocket and went to find a match. He read the words one last time. WORLD. HUBBLE. SUN. Three things Walter was trying to tell Bear. Three things important to the man's hurting soul. Three things Bear could only bring up in the natural course of life. The scribbled note went up in flames, then the fire went into the black hole of a wastebasket in the kitchen.

Dreams are as infinite as the stars we see and the stars we don't see.

Bear went back to the bedroom. Walter was on his side, trying not to exist for fear of more pain. This time, Bear didn't ask if he could spoon his man. He simply melted into Walter, who winced in protest, then fell silent. Walter lay in bed for several days, and so did Bear, who spooned his man until his own body ached from the motionlessness. They barely spoke, save what was necessary. Walter was in too much pain to even use the toilet, so Bear told him to use the toilet in bed, which Bear kept spotless, just so his man could "heal instead of deal."

"Did you call the Dane?" asked Walter one day as they were spooning. It was the first time he'd spoken in over two days.

"Again?" asked Bear, too exhausted to talk.

"Been here already?" asked Walter.

"Days ago," said Bear, falling asleep.

"Not hurting ... as bad," said Walter, falling asleep.

Bear opened his eyes and lifted his dizzy head. It was no dream. The beginning of the end of the pain was near for the filthy, shivering man of men lying next to him. If Walter were a superhero, his powers were meaningless at that moment. The supervillains and archnemeses who lived for his demise could have gone in for the kill. In fact, Walter Yeager could have died just fine on his own. It was Walter's choice to live. No one else had a vote. And Walter had chosen life.

Walter. Chose. Life.

Were Bear not so exhausted with so much to do, he would have sobbed. Taking care of Walter was hell. *Correction:* taking care of Walter was heaven. Seeing Walter hurt was hell. Bear was having his heaven and hell on a platter in equal doses. Now, just maybe, there was some heaven to pay.

OVER THE NEXT FEW weeks, their expectations were confirmed. Walter had run a reverse. The wheel, however it worked, had convinced his brain that his *back* was *back* to the way it was *back* when Walter Yeager was an uninjured, top-rated quarterback. The pain morphed into soreness, which morphed into a dull ache, which morphed into nothing. Once again, Walter could tie his own shoes, use the facilities, pick up trash on the floor—all without struggling. Bear had never noticed Walter's so-called limitations before. When he looked at Walter, Bear was more focused on *Walter being Walter,* and that made Bear glow. So Bear didn't know all the details about his man. He had never even taken note of Walter's eye color. As he once explained to the lesbo ex-cheergirls:

His eyes aren't a color to me. They're a feeling in my soul.

So even though Bear felt Walter's back pain in his own abdomen—the place where Bear stored his own emotional junk—he had never *seen* Walter's back pain, just Walter, the beautiful child of God. And still, the pre-Tibetan reverse changed Bear and Bear's life. He had never imagined taking care of a demanding and disgruntled white man who could be the most sensitive man in the world one minute, then the most insensitive beast the next.

At times, Bear felt like a Negro slave. Other times, he feared a day when his man might have to take care of him. Still other times, he felt such an intense devotion, he wanted to take on the back injury himself to set his man free of the pain. It was a balancing act for the 6'4" Bear, but when he gave love in the form of patience and compassion, he felt love in return. During those moments, even the pain in his own abdomen subsided.

Together, the boys survived the reverse. With Bear studying Walter's every motion, they were equally amazed at the quarterback's progression from a life of pain management, to a life of pain-*free* management. A few months after Walter's darkest days in purgatory, he was even allowed 10 minutes of tossing the football in the park.

"How's it feel?" asked Bear after catching a few easy passes.

"I'll be cool." Walter was a short distance away, loosening up his arms and torso. "What?" he asked, noticing Bear's silly grin.

"Looking like a QB stud already," said Bear.

"You're just saying that," said Walter.

"I only speak the truth," said Bear.

"Throw me the ball," commanded Walter, saying wassup to that piss 'n' vinegar simmering inside. The next day, he was a little sore, but that was to be expected. He kept pausing throughout the day, expecting trouble, but trouble never came. "I think I got a shot," said Walter from the living room couch. The man his teammates called Big Norse never showed much emotion on the outside, but Bear was beyond having to scrutinize his buddy's outer body language. The extra lift in that sexy half-smile and the brighter shade in those soulful eyes were the only forecasts needed: cool and dreamy skies ahead.

"Timeout!" Bear raced to the living room closet where they kept his old college stuff. He began rifling through the boxes, butt sticking out of the doorway.

"What now?" laughed Walter.

"Perfect song." Bear came out of the closet and popped a cassette tape in the stereo on the fireplace mantle.

"We haven't had one of those in ages!" Walter recognized the dramatic intro, already popular at pro sports stadiums. "He nailed it!"

"We both still got it, brother!" Bear danced like Joe Bruin trying to be a boxer. Walter sat on the couch, hands on his knees like an athlete resting on the bench, laughing his ass off. The stereo pumped out "Eye of the Tiger" by Survivor, the rock anthem of many a warrior of the time. Their time.

If it was good enough for *Rocky III*, it was good enough for *Walter II*. Yep, it was cliché, but that was one of the games within the games known as sports: clichés battling one another to the finish. Number 13 was gonna *go play some football!* again. How crazy was that? Piss 'n' Vinegar Yeager, getting one last shot to show how the top-rated high school QB of his year can still create magic with a piece of pigskin, a childhood dream, and a whole lotta desire, guts and determination.

"Don't call him the comeback kid," barked Bear. "His heart never left the game. His dream never died. Walter Yeager is alive and well and is never gonna die *againnnnnn!*"

An exhausted Bear collapsed on the couch, making sure not to land on the healing athlete, who was laughing for the first time in a very long while.

THE BOYS BEGAN THROWING THE FOOTBALL daily, and Walter continued reversing himself every other day. He also aced the series of weekly strength tests in the Dane's private gym, and eight months after beginning the treatments, Walter Yeager was pain-free. He could sit anyway he wanted, bend anyway he wanted, walk anyway he wanted, and sleep anyway he wanted (though Bear and he spooned more often now, not doubting the potential of their love to move mountains). Nine months into treatment, Walter was done reversing. His energy was balanced. Once again, his brain was in charge of his body, even his back, which had recycled itself, according to Bass the Dane. Details aside, Walter and Bear were grateful, but also anxious. Walter had full use of his back, but NFL combat was not rolling around in bed with your buddy. The tests showed that Walter was fit for contact drills, but Walter's mind wasn't so sure.

"What could be worse than all the pain you've already faced?" asked Bear one night, washing the dishes.

"More of it," said Walter, drying the dishes.

"You survived so far. Is there anything you can't handle?" asked Bear.

"Of course not," said Walter.

"Can you handle not playing football?" asked Bear.

"Already have," shrugged Walter.

"Can you handle not playing, now that you, me, and the Dane have rehabilitated yo' ass and put up with *all yo' shit* just because *yo'* high and mighty ass is Walter *Freakin'* Yeager, man of my freakin' dreams, who's put me through more mutha-fuckin' mind-spinning moments than I'll ever be able to *rightbackatcha* in a million lifetimes? You ungrateful mutha-fuckin' white man, can you honestly tell me you don't wanna *go play some football!?* Don't make me get Black on yo' ass, man, *sheeeeeet.*"

Walter eyed him, his face void of emotion.

"Pretty good, huh?" asked Bear.

"Yeah," said Walter. "You got the gene."

"Cool," said Bear. "This has been a test of the Emergency Blackcast Network. Had this been an actual emergency for black people in America ..."

THE TURF. INNOCENT BLADES OF GRASS. Their crime: growing on the field where the gladiators roam. Their punishment: hours of constant trampling by the gladiators themselves ...

"If this is how you describe a park in Seattle, what are you going to say about the real deal, if I make it the pros?" asked Walter, tossing the football to himself at Wok-Knee Park.

"*When* you make it to the pros. I wouldn't dream of it any other way," said Bear, standing within arm's reach of his man at Wok-Knee Park. It was a cool spring day. They had the long rolling hills of the park to themselves, save some Frisbee throwers in the blurry distance.

"If only it were all up to your dreams." Walter flicked the ball into Bear's chest.

"That would be a dream come true," said Bear, grabbing onto the ball.

"Larry is gonna be here any minute," said Walter, performing a security check.

"Hail to the Kansas City Chief," said Bear, flipping the ball back to the quarterback. "And thank God his wife works at KSEA, whatever her name is."

The former spirit leader found a tall oak tree half a football field away and climbed high to watch his man throw his first passes in years to a true wide receiver. Larry McPherson, the black-haired white boy from Auburn, was fast, the fastest white boy Bear had ever seen outside of Walter. Hail Larry ran route after route, and Walter fired the rock like shots from a cannon, his accuracy and confidence growing with each passing moment. The farther the one white boy ran, the farther the other white boy threw, mesmerizing a wide-eyed Bear in the oak tree. He had never seen two white guys in their own private world of athletic supremacy. They didn't need blacks to play in their games after all, he realized. The games were just more interesting that way.

Thank God for the integration of life.

Sometime during the glorious display of two men being men, a hound dog started howling at Bear in the oak tree, perhaps mistaking him for an overgrown squirrel. The ruckus alerted a female jogger on the trail in the nearby woods. She called the hound dog, who peed on the tree before joining her. The disturbance commandeered the attention of the two white guys playing football in the distance. By the time Bear descended his perch, the hound dog was gone, but in its place were a Tiger and a Bulldawg, waiting next to the tree trunk.

"Bear, you remember McPherson," said Walter, as if stopping by the tree was all part of the day's plan.

"I was looking at camera angles—for *The Walter Yeager Story*," said Bear, shaking hands with Hail Larry.

"This guy's got it!" said Hail Larry, looking at Walter with stars in his eyes. A carload of girls gone wild in a convertible zoomed by. Hail Larry waved, his eyes following their rear. "Man, I love women," he said. Walter and Bear tried to conjure a response, but the wide receiver beat them to it: "And one in particular. Gotta go. See ya, Bear."

"That hound dog was barking up the wrong tree," said Bear, watching Hail Larry jog away.

"Did you see me? I was awesome!" said Walter.

"Hell, we can still tell Larry I'm your assistant, right?" asked Bear.

"Not a thing!" said Walter, probing his back. "Bear, I don't feel a thing. Except ... good!"

All Bear could do was smile a big Joe Bruin smile.

Walter's workouts with Bear morphed into Walter's workouts with Hail Larry, which morphed into Walter's workouts with Hail Larry and some of the Seattle Seahawks hanging around in the off-season. Before long, Yeager was doing everything a quarterback does, except getting his golden blond ass tackled. He knew the day was coming, he just didn't know when.

One evening, Bear was in the bedroom while Walter was on the phone in the living room, giving his family in Chicago the weekly rehab report. Bear heard whiffs of the conversation, something about two years away from contact sports, most of it spent in pain. Like a perturbed roomie, Bear cranked up the music, as if to drown out the interference. A song or two later, the station played "True" by Spandau Ballet, a tune that had escaped their orbit for quite some time. Bear turned up the volume even higher, then waited.

As "True" began to fade, the door to the bedroom swung open, revealing a pissed-off Yeager-monster, angry for the interference with his phone call. He didn't find his man on the bed, so he came deeper into the room, just as a big black Bear came flying out of the bathroom. He grabbed the quarterback, threw him to the bed and fell on top of him.

"Yeager is sacked at the two-yard line!" yelled a triumphant Bear.

"Man, fuck!" shouted Walter, more focused on being spooked. Bear jumped to his feet. Walter felt his back. "You're lucky I'm not hurt."

"I'm also grateful," said Bear, vanishing from the bedroom.

The next day, Walter was coming out of the bathroom after a shower and was attacked once again by a big black Bear, who picked him up, hauled him into the living room and slammed him down on the couch.

"God dammit, Bear!" shouted Walter. "Don't ever do that again!"

"I'll never repeat that move again, promise," said Bear, vanishing from the living room.

The next morning, Walter was browsing the headlines in the front doorway when he was attacked yet again by a big black Bear, who sprang from the hallway, picked up the quarterback, wrestled him into the living room and slammed him down on the loveseat.

"Motherfucker!" yelled Walter. "This is not helping! Your tackles aren't shit compared to the real deal!"

"I promise to do better." Bear wiped strands of blond hair from his mouth and turned away, strutting like a badass.

"You sonafabitch!" Walter rose up and charged Bear, bulldozing him into the bedroom and onto the bed. "You like this kind of shit?" asked Walter, pressing Bear's face into the mattress.

"I fucking love it!" Bear twisted around and grabbed Walter's neck as if to choke him. They wrestled, not knowing if they were playing around or killing one another. There were no punches, just chokeholds, pins, scissor holds, and a lot of breathless, wordless woofing. When it was over, their clothes were ripped to shreds, two lamps were broken, and the boys lay exhausted on their backs on the hardwood floor, covered in sweat and grime. The bedroom came back into focus. So did the radio in the shower, which was still on. The station was playing "Midnight Train to Georgia" by Gladys Knight and the Pips, otherwise known as "Late Night Bus to Georgia" by Bear Coleman and his One Pip in New Orleans. The boys' eyes were glued to the cottage cheese ceiling of the tiny one-bedroom apartment. Walter's hand found Bear's. Bear squeezed Walter's hand. Walter squeezed back. The wrestling match became a detail. They were back on the same track once again.

A FEW DAYS LATER, Bear was at his desk at KSEA when suddenly, he looked up and smiled a comfortable, confident smile. His eyes were filled with tears, his mind ripe with visions of a field on the University of Washington campus. Walter was on that field that very moment, getting the shit knocked out of him. Bear pictured his QB in full pads, scrimmaging for the first time in eons with Hail Larry and Bass the Dane looking on. Bear grabbed his lower stomach. There was no pain, more like an explosion of joy, making him feel as pregnant as a man can get.

By the end of the summer, Walter Yeager was ready to be a quarterback on the football field again. A few well-placed phone calls landed him an agent, who landed him a tryout for the Edmonton Eskimos of the Canadian Football League. The CFL season started after the ground thawed in the spring and ended before the ground re-froze in the fall. Edmonton had a handful of games remaining in an unspectacular season and the boys were forced to make some quick decisions. "It's not like I dreamed of being a CFL QB as a kid," was Walter's first reaction, "but I know, I know. The road of life is full of detours, I'm thankful, I'll shut up and stop being a dickhead now."

Because being apart was not an option, the easiest thing to do was to sell Bear's car and haul their entire world to Edmonton, Alberta. If the tryout didn't work ... well, it was just going to. As Walter put it: "I can throw in the CFL in my sleep."

To celebrate and say goodbye to Seattle, the boys had a picnic on the rolling hills of Wok-Knee Park. After eating, they threw the football around one last time before taking off. As Bear was about to catch his last pass ever in Seattle, a lesbo ex-cheergirl came out of nowhere, intercepted the ball, then spiked it in an imaginary end zone.

"I thought you boys vanished," said Wendy Jiu or Lisa Wu afterward.

"Give us a few seconds," said Bear.

"You guys leaving?" asked Lisa Wu or Wendy Jiu. She was looking at the black pickup truck parked alongside the curb. The truck bed was loaded with what little they were taking with them to Edmonton.

"Hey ... ladies," said Walter, joining them, prompting an awkward silence. The boys had stopped calling the girls during Walter's reverse treatments, for fear of the girls thinking Walter had AIDS. Now the boys kept their distance for fear of their friendship with the lesbos coming back to haunt Walter's career.

"Where you moving?" asked Wendy Jiu or Lisa Wu.

"We'll know when we get there," said Walter.

"Nice knowing you," said Wendy Jiu or Lisa Wu, then nodded for her and her partner to continue jogging. Walter and Bear paused, then, not knowing what else to do, hopped in the truck and took off for Canada.

"I've got the perfect song to start the trip," said Bear, cueing up the music.

"Already?" asked Walter from the driver's seat.

"When else do you play a *Get the Trip Started* tape?" laughed Bear.

"All right," said Walter. "I can't win with you, can I?"

"That's because we're on the same team," said Bear. "So, if you're ready, it's time for the us-against-the-world rock anthem of our time."

The intro for "Nothing's Gonna Stop Us Now" by Jefferson Starship came blaring over the speakers. The black pickup truck had its own cassette deck now, which made it easy for Walter to quickly kill the music, which is exactly what the quarterback did.

"Not a good time for that, do you mind?" asked Walter.

"To set the mood," begged Bear.

"My mood is fine," said Walter, dialing up the radio. "How about something a little less grandstandish right now?"

"Cool," said Bear, looking out his window.

"You're all pumped up and ready," said Walter, placing a hand on his man's thigh.

"You know me," said Bear, exhaling with Walter's touch.

"Yes, I do." Walter rubbed Bear's thigh on the way out of Seattle. By nightfall, the mellow rock station had them both in a comfortable groove, so much so that Bear snuggled against the window, not minding the absence of Walter's reassuring hand.

"You feel shitty about the way we said fuck off to the girls?" asked Walter.

"Don't you?" said Bear, inhaling the smell of the damp mountains in the dark of the night. "Hysteria" by Def Leppard was playing on the radio.

"So, Bear-man," said Walter. "Let's say I turn pro. Our families are going to become much more involved in our lives, you realize."

"You mean, no more holidays on opposite coasts?" asked Bear.

"Maybe no more telling them we're just friends and business partners through my ex-girlfriend, Roseanne," said Walter.

"Roxanne, dammit. You're supposed to have fucked this girl, now you can't even say her name." Bear rose up. "Fuck, that's brilliant!"

"The Bear-man catches on," said Walter.

"You call her Roseanne. If anyone tries to check up on your story, it's all twisted," said Bear.

"What if the guys at the lesbos' parties recognize me on TV?" asked Walter, then he said mockingly: "There's the blond homo from Seattle."

"Walter, we're on a deserted highway in the middle of the night in the middle of nowhere. Now is not the time to get all dark," said Bear.

"We can never go back to Seattle," said Walter. "My God, what if I have to play for Seattle? What about a road trip there? Fuck, Bear, what did we just do?"

"Lived our lives," said Bear, massaging Walter's neck and shoulders, "and we want to keep on living, so relax, or let me drive."

"I know," said Walter, focusing on the road instead of his rage. "We didn't do anything wrong. Loving each other is not wrong. The rest is details." He put his hand on Bear's thigh. "Thanks, buddy."

"Always and forever," said Bear.

DEEP INTO CANADA, BEAR WAS behind the wheel, driving through the night. "Waiting on a Friend" by the Rolling Stones was playing on the radio, and Walter decided to break a long silence:

"What do you think you'd be doing, if you weren't following me all over the place, like, if we'd never met?" asked Walter.

"Not feeling as good as I am now," said Bear.

"You can't say that for sure," said Walter.

"I'd be missing you," said Bear, "and missing a part of me."

"I wouldn't have a chance to play football if I hadn't met you," said Walter.

"How do you figure?" asked Bear.

"I wouldn't have moved to Seattle and met Bass," said Walter. "I would have probably married Ellen and moved back to Chicago."

"Who in the world is Ellen?" asked Bear.

"The dark-haired girl from the ride to Atlanta. Talk about not remembering names," said Walter.

After 800 miles, give or take, the black pickup truck rolled into a gas station in Leduc, Alberta, just outside Edmonton. Bear went inside the station to call KSEA about his last paycheck while Walter gassed up. When Bear hung up, he came shooting out of the station, out of breath and in shock.

"What is it?" asked Walter from the driver's seat.

"Hail to the Chief and his wife!" said Bear, hopping in the passenger seat. "She left a message for me, *for you.* The quarterback coach in Kansas City wants to see you!"

Piss 'n' Vinegar's eyes became as big as saucers as he cranked up the engine. "Where's the song? The song?" asked Walter, pulling out of the gas station.

"What song?" giggled Bear.

"Your song! Play it now, if you want!" Walter pulled onto the highway, going in the same direction. "Our song!" He stuck his head out of the window and let loose one long rebel yell of relief. Bear fetched the tape from the glove compartment, then cued it up. The intro for "Nothing's Gonna Stop Us Now" came blaring over the speakers. Jefferson Starship started singing about building dreams together and how not even the world falling apart around them was going to get in their way. Zooming down the highway, Walter cranked up the music and played the drums against the steering wheel, while Bear sang along to the chorus with one notable substitution:

Nothing's gonna stop Walt now.

The QB reacted every time with either his mild laugh, his mild headshake, or that sexy half-smile. Midway through the song, the black pickup truck came across a legal U-turn and made it. Moments later, the truck was heading away from Edmonton, toward a dreamier flavor of the dream.

The boys were pulling another reverse.

13

Wet Week Waiting in Kansas City

The golf cart was on its own roller-coaster ride in the canyons and hills overlooking the Pacific. The piss 'n' vinegar quarterback turned gambler turned mad driver was at the wheel, looping around the Complex as if he were a bumblebee on acid. In the passenger seat, Marcus held on for dear life, but he was holding his own just fine. His head was arched toward the sun, the wind smacking his face like a fresh gust of God.

This must be what dogs in the car feel like, or figure skaters high on the ice.

Abruptly, the cart came to a summit, then descended the steep hill. "How's the stomach?" asked Walt.

"Cool and dreamy," said Marcus. They made a sharp turn to the left. The edge of an endless cliff sped past, a breath away in the blur beneath them. "How's the back?"

"Primed and ready," said Walt.

"Just like our boys, our crazy fucking boys," said Marcus. *Or was he Bear? And was that Walt or Walter in the driver's seat? Oh, who the fuck cares? He's got the same aura. So do you, somewhere inside. Go find it.*

"So my boy Bear sets fire to my boy Walter's note, and puts the fire in the hole of a wastebasket," said Walt, steering into a narrow alleyway between two buildings of the former junior high school. "What's up with that?"

"Bear's life, Bear's hole," said Marcus.

"Lost me," said Walt, accelerating through the alleyway, as if putting the golf cart in TURBO MODE.

"Sometimes, I let the boys alone to do their own thing," said Marcus. The sides of the two buildings sped past like a hazy tunnel, reminding him of the *Star Wars* movies. "The single black college grad known as Marcus Coleman had some dreams of his own, ya know."

"Good for him," said Walt.

"I wanted that kind of magic with a real-life buddy," said Marcus. "Now and then, I let the famous boys live on their own and caught up with them later. Sometimes, a man's job is to follow his own dreams. Sometimes, a man's gotta stop dreaming altogether and just go along for the ride."

"This much is true," said Walt, pressing onward with their dizzying trek.

WALTER AND BEAR ARRIVED at a service station in Kansas City in the dead of a rainy Missouri night. Walter replenished the fumes in the gas tank and secured their belongings in the truck bed under a tarp, while Bear bought food and supplies, including medicine for their miserable colds. The heater had broken over North Dakota. They had been coughing and sneezing since Iowa.

"The clerk in the store thinks the Chiefs' QB is a pussy," said Bear once he was back in the passenger seat.

"Who was he talking to?" asked Walter from the driver's seat.

"The customer before me," said Bear.

The lite jazz radio station played something soft and mellow. It took Bear a while to feel the soothing hand on his thigh, and just a beat longer to rub his hero's neck. They drove in silence in the pouring rain. Bear tried to fall asleep and dream, but the road was too bumpy. Plus, he knew Walter was having second thoughts about their impulsive U-turn because of their ill-timed sicknesses. They had abandoned a good shot at making a Canadian team for what was essentially a look-see by the Kansas City QB Coach. "I need the NFL to see what I can do, not the CFL," Walter had said more than once. "Whatever Walter wants," Bear had told him each time. Now, Bear knew words wouldn't help. Only not getting sicker could help. Neither one of them could ever get sick.

"You make it all right?" asked Walter when the pickup truck pulled in front of the door to motel room 104.

"Nothing stop us." Bear got out. The rain was misty and somehow warmer. He exhaled a stressful breath, then inhaled a peaceful one. His head fell back to a dark navy sky full of stars winking at him. Moments later, he joined Walter, who was waiting for him in the doorway to their space for the night. A short time later, they climbed into bed, exhausted from driving up and down the continent in a few blurry days. They found themselves face to face, which prompted Bear to object, which prompted Walter to calmly put a finger to his buddy's lips.

"If we get sicker, we get sicker together," said Walter. Bear knew what Walter was feeling: the 2500 mile whirlwind tour had them on the verge of a health crisis, and Walter felt like shit for putting Bear at risk.

"No regrets," said Bear, drifting off to dreamland.

... Bear's world turned to a blur. The mist in Kansas City morphed into a downpour that pelted the world outside. A calm voice said, "Keep dreaming. I'll take care of our stuff in the truck." Bear went deeper into his headspace, so deep, the rain pelting the world outside pelted the world inside his dreams, melting away that world and revealing a whole other landscape in its place. The new world was also rainy, but not in Kansas City. The new world was in Hollywood. And Bear wasn't Bear. Voices were calling him Marcus, his birth name.

He, Marcus Coleman, was on a couch in a sound studio, dreaming away. Lawrence the Sound Guy was waiting for Marcus' patented "*perfect!*" so they could wrap up the day's batch of promos for the network. But Marcus wanted to dream a little longer. With HIV so present in his mind, he often wondered how life might have turned out, had he actually met Walt Yeager, the man of his fantasies. Would their union have saved Marcus from AIDS? Did Marcus have AIDS? Should he get tested? Why was he having so much trouble finding love and happiness after college? Why was he 60 pounds overweight?

"*Want that life!*" cried Marcus.

"On or off?" asked Lawrence the Sound Guy.

"Too dark," said Bear, the room not yet in focus.

"So you want the light *on,* not off, right?" asked Walter, his hand underneath a lampshade. He was standing next to the nightstand in the motel room in Kansas City.

"Bad dream," said Bear. "No light."

Walter and Bear endured their miserable colds with a sense of calm, as if intuitively, they understood that this wasn't their time to get sicker. However, it was their time to sit in a motel room in Kansas City and watch the rainfall. Monday's workout with the QB coach was postponed; something about flooding and a family emergency. Tuesday was more of the same, along with a lot of channel surfing on the motel TV.

"This is where we cut to the song 'Raindrops Keep Fallin' on My Head' in *The Walter Yeager Story,*" said Bear from the bed that afternoon. "We'll have a montage of you and me sitting here, hour after hour with the door propped open while it rains outside. I'm reading, watching TV, and tossing a football, while you're standing right there, leaning against the door, looking like a restless cowboy who can't go cowboying until the rain stops."

"There's no comeback story if the rain doesn't stop," said Walter, leaning against the door.

"Do you honestly think we drove all this way *not* to get a shot?" asked Bear. "It's gonna happen, buddy. We just have to let it."

"I just wanna play a little football," mumbled Walter.

"Then bring your fullback over here," giggled Bear.

"What'd my Bear bring?" said Walter, getting on the bed like an eager kid.

"A blast from our past." Bear held in his hands the little green box that was Mattel Electronics Football. He flipped on the on/off switch and pushed KICK. The digital *charge!* sounded, the kickoff commenced, and Walter absently took the game from Bear, who was beaming ear-to-ear.

"How long has it been?" asked Walter, taking command of his offense.

"Not so long that I still can't kick your blond butt," said Bear.

"Dream on with your brown ass, boy," said Walter. With the door to their motel room open, they played football while the rain washed away the outside world. Of course, Bear had to provide the soundtrack as the occasional cheerleader, band or announcer, especially as a way of distracting the QB:

"Fourth and nine ... Yeager scrambles for 44 yards, what a crazy kind of quarterback, folks."

In the closing minutes of a tie game, Walter added his own commentary: "Yeager can't concentrate due to hot black Bear breath all in his face."

"You're on the road, baby, consider this the Bear's Den." Bear cupped his hands and cheered like 80,000 fans screaming for blond meat. Walter focused on marching down the field. Bear messed with the QB's hair, bumped into the QB's elbow, blew into the QB's ear. Yeager played on, never wandering from his mission. When he neared the goal line, Bear chanted *defense!* and waved his hands in front of the QB's eyes.

"I'm gonna sock you," warned the QB, mildly distracted. A beat later, they heard the game's *touchdown!* jingle. "Your defense sucks," said Walter, handing over the little green box. "You've got :04 seconds to beat me."

They played Mattel Electronics Football for several days straight, most of it through the driving rain. Their spirits became restless, their cash flow low. "Maybe I can bite the bullet and borrow from the family," said Walter one night. He was sitting in the doorway with his back against the doorframe.

"We've still got my last check from the station coming," said Bear. He was resting on his stomach on the bed, half-asleep.

"And why the hell does Larry's wife have to be here this week?" asked Walter. "Fucker doesn't have a second for me ... Bear, when's it gonna stop raining?" Getting no answer, Walter beat the back of his head repeatedly against the doorframe, then he started singing "Nothing's Gonna Stop Us Now" by Jefferson Starship. The song was stuck in his brain, but instead of singing the words in the chorus, he sang: "The rain's gonna stop Walt now."

"Nothing's gonna stop Walt now," came from the groggy Bear on the bed.

"The rain's gonna stop Walt now," insisted the quarterback.

"Nothing's gonna stop Walt now," insisted the cheerleader.

"The rain's gonna stop Walt now," insisted the quarterback.

"Nothing's gonna—*ahhhhhh!*"

The cheerleader was attacked by the quarterback. The boys wrestled around the bed for control, but whenever the boys wrestled, Bear always ended up laughing and Walter always ended up winning. This time, Walter gained the upper hand by sitting on top of Bear's chest, knees restraining Bear's arms.

"What's gonna stop Walt now?" asked Walter, daring Bear to say anything but *the rain.*

"Nothing!" said Bear, cocky and insubordinate. Walter's lip curled upward, then descended onto Bear's mouth. The kiss was short and passionate.

"So, Bear," said Walter, rolling on his back. "It's been all about me lately. Once we settle down, I wanna see you get going on your writing. You can do it."

"I have an idea for a movie called *My Whole Other Life*," said Bear. "It's a kinda 'what if.' What if we had never met during that one magical weekend in the prime of our college days?"

"A great guy like you would have met someone by now," said Walter, pulling the covers over both of their shivering bodies.

"Yeah, right," said a sarcastic Bear. "This great guy was doing so well meeting guys before he got lucky and met you. I never told you this, but I was kind of a geek in high school."

"I knew you didn't feel good about yourself," said Walter.

"I never told you that," said Bear. "Did I?"

"I know my Bear," said Walter, massaging Bear's neck. "You don't tell me half the stuff I know about you. I just know."

"Then you know that guys like you were way outta my league in high school," said Bear. "I can count the times a god like you acknowledged me back then. Really, I can. Sometimes I still ... never mind."

"I know what you're gonna say," said Walter.

"There's a part of me that wonders how in the world a guy like you ever came to love a guy like me," said Bear.

"What if I told you I wonder the same thing but in reverse?" asked Walter.

"You'd blow my mind," said Bear.

"*Rightbackatcha*," said Walter.

"If you hadn't showed up at that fraternity party and we never met, I'd still miss you," said Bear, reclining on his side and facing his buddy.

"You wouldn't know me to miss me," said Walter, kissing Bear's hand.

"Trust me," said Bear. "I dreamed of having a buddy like you long before I looked deep into your soulful eyes and realized you were the One. If I didn't have you, I'd still be looking for my buddy."

"Maybe you would have found him by now," said Walter.

"Or maybe I'd be eating my way through the sadness of not finding him in college," said Bear, rolling on his back and staring at the ceiling. "Maybe I'd be 60 pounds overweight and miserable. I'd probably be doing promos in Hollywood, still feeling like a fucking fag, living as far away from UCLA as possible."

"Why would you hate the Bruins?" asked Walter.

"I wouldn't hate them. I just wouldn't be so high on college, if I was 25 and still alone," said Bear. "If you would have told 18-year-old Marcus 'Bear' Coleman he was gonna graduate college without meeting his buddy, he would have laughed in your face as if you said Santa Claus was alive and living on Mars."

Walter laughed his mild laugh, then said, "If you would have told 18-year-old Walter Yeager he was gonna graduate college without making it to the NFL, he would have thought you were fucking crazy."

"Anybody who doubts Walter Yeager is fucking crazy," said Bear.

"Ditto for anybody who doubts Marcus 'Bear' Coleman," said Walter.

"If I hadn't met you during that Georgia road trip," said Bear, "I would have probably tried to reach out to someone in some desperate, last-ditch attempt to make the college buddy dream come true. It would have ended in disaster, no doubt."

"This *Whole Other Life* doesn't sound like a feel-good movie," said Walter.

"It's all the rain, I guess. I don't want it to be a downer," said Bear. "I just know I'd be missing what we have, even if I wasn't missing you. And I might even be missing the real you. I always looked in the game programs. Maybe I would have seen your picture and fallen in love with you."

"From a photo?" asked Walter, nibbling on Bear's ear. "Now who's crazy?"

"If I saw you in the game program, I'd feel something," said Bear. "Wouldn't you? Come on, I'd feel something for the love of my life, right?"

"Then what?" asked Walter. "Call me up and say—"

"Hey, I'm a cheer queer from UCLA," said Bear. "Can you imagine? Bear Coleman is not *that* crazy!"

"Wanna bet?" said Walter.

"Man, there's no way," giggled Bear. "I think I would have just kept you in my heart all these years. Maybe, if nothing else, your image would have inspired *that* Marcus to find a love as beautiful as ours."

"*That* Marcus should be so lucky to have a love like ours," said Walter. "So would I, if I didn't have you."

"*That* Marcus should also be so lucky to taste something as good as this." Bear grabbed his favorite physical part of Walter, but the motel phone was guilty of pass interference.

"Talk to me," said Walter, answering the call. "Larry, hell, what's up?"

Bear dove under the covers for some Sugar while Walter talked football with Hail Larry. The quarterback's attempts to swat away the distraction didn't dissuade the spirit leader. Finally, Walter relented and conducted his football business while Bear conducted his QB business. A short time later, Walter hung up and said, "I can't win with you, can I?"

"That's because we're on the same team," said Bear, coming up for air. "Sorry, buddy, when I'm getting a taste of you, I'm like a great athlete in the zone. Can't stop me."

"This Monday, it's on," said Walter. "Gimme the Mattel box, then get back to work. You need some more face time in the zone."

It was a Friday night. Last Friday, they were in Canada. Two Fridays ago, Seattle. What was another weekend in Kansas City? For the next two days, they kept their expenditures low and their spirits high. "Nothing's Gonna Stop Us Now" remained stuck in both their heads, the one lyrical change turning the song into "Nothing's Gonna Stop Walt Now." They found themselves subconsciously singing or humming it everywhere: the ice machine, the laundry room, the burger joint, the shower.

Nothing's gonna stop Walt now.

If only one of them had the song on the brain, their downfall as a duo would have been imminent. But the lyrics burrowed themselves into both men's minds, leaving them no choice but to surrender. All weekend long, "Nothing's Gonna Stop Walt Now" was their number one hit single, as much a part of their ambiance as the sound of the rain.

THE RAIN WAS STILL COMING DOWN on Sunday for the Chiefs' home game against Tampa Bay. The black pickup truck was parked near Arrowhead Stadium. Bear was in the passenger seat, waiting for his buddy, who came charging into the driver's seat, soaked from the downpour. "This bites," said Walter.

"No passes?" asked Bear, shivering from the rush of wind.

"*That's* why that secretary asked me if I was here with my wife," said Walter, referring to a phone call earlier in the week. "She only left one freakin' pass, and I couldn't get hold of anyone who can do anything about it."

"You go be Walter," said Bear. "I'll go find some warmth."

"Bear, I feel bad," said Walter.

"*Or* you can feel good about taking care of football business, then giving me all the Sugar I need later," said Bear. "I'm easy. For you, that is."

"Take some more money, see if you can't get in the game," said Walter.

"We need that money for whatever happens after tomorrow," said Bear. "Now, will you get your fullback out of here and go shake some football hands? Your buddy will be just fine, but not if my man doesn't follow his dreams, now get the fuck outta here!"

After his husband left, Bear took a walk in the rain around the perimeter of the stadium. On his way back to the truck, he stumbled upon all the warmth he needed in an unopened bottle lying under the wheel of a parked Winnebago. "You're gonna get run over, little guy," said Bear, picking up his new friend, Jack Daniels. "I can't get in the stadium either. Let's talk about it." The conversation was one-sided, but it did make waiting in the truck a drunken and dizzy dream. At one point, he had visions of a small red light and a female in a suit. He danced with her momentarily, interrupting her dance with a man dressed like a real Chief, not a football Chief.

"Some players have husbands, not wives," Bear told them, then passed out against his rainy passenger window.

THE BLACK PICKUP TRUCK pulled up next to a basketball arena on a Missouri college campus. Monday was yet another rainy day in Kansas City, but the football people were willing to put aside their wet lives for a few minutes with a man who, six years ago, was the best of the best. "Not even my family knows about this trip," said Walter from the passenger seat. It was his way of expressing his appreciation for Bear being there.

"I'm proud of you, come what may," said Bear from the driver's seat.

Walter performed a quick security check, then kissed Bear on the cheek and jumped out of the truck. He sprinted in the rain against the backdrop of the brick arena. A fire truck sped by in the same direction, racing him momentarily. Walter ran faster as if enjoying the thrill of one last challenge before the biggest challenge of his life. The siren screamed. The fire truck kept going. Walter came to a stop at the double doors to the indoor track facility next to the arena. Before entering, he bent over and caught his breath, having just blown away any remaining shreds of doubt.

Bear waited awhile, then made his way to the elevated pathway between the arena and the track facility. Once he was above the track, he remained on the pathway, just this side of a large glass window to the action below. One thing the week of waiting had been good for was scouting out the location for both boys. Walter was already throwing passes to Hail Larry and two other receivers. Three men, who appeared to be coaches, watched from an imaginary sideline. Two of the coaches gravitated toward a heavyset man—the QB Coach, Bear presumed. He made gestures about which types of routes he wanted the receivers to run, then Walter would drop back and fire away. In between, they took breaks, limbered up more, and seemed to do a lot of joking and laughing.

At one point, however, things grew more serious. The QB Coach put Walter and the receivers through a series of drills. Walter threw a dozen long bombs, each one hitting his intended receiver with precision. Only a dropped ball by Hail Larry ended the streak, causing them all to react with various degrees of disbelief. "Just like the Auburn-Alabama game back in the day," Bear imagined one of them joking.

Walter threw a few more bombs, then it was over. The coaches had seen enough. Their postures weren't as enthusiastic as Walter's, but it was Walter's posture that mattered. His body was full of movement, as if he'd just gotten off a roller coaster full of loops and thrills. His gestures were demonstrative, especially for Walter. It was the liveliest Bear had ever seen his man. Before escaping the pathway, Bear etched the moment in his mind. Twenty minutes later, Walter jumped into the passenger seat of the truck and said, "Drive off now! Before I kiss the fuck out of you. Or fuck the kiss out of you, I'm not sure which."

"Foreplay: what happened?" Bear slammed on the gas. The truck blasted off, as if in TURBO MODE.

"They loved me like you said they would. We're checking out of the Rainy Days Inn and getting the fuck outta Kansas City like we planned," said Walter.

"Say *what?*" said Bear, his voice rising several octaves. "Then what?"

"They don't have a spot like we figured, but they know I'm back. Now we follow our next hunch. Where's the song?" Walter searched frantically through the trash on the floor.

"In the deck already," laughed Bear. "Where are we going after the Rainy Days Inn?"

"To see an assistant coach who loves me, Bear, buddy, 'cause nothing's ever gonna stop you and me now!" yelled Walter.

"Where's that?" yelled Bear.

Jefferson Starship came on full blast. Piss 'n' Vinegar started hooting and hollering while Bear drove in the rain, shouting a million questions over the music. Walter was too hyper to calm down, so he answered by making up his own words to the Song of the Week.

> And we will live this dream together
> Plus have better weather
> Nothing's gonna stop Walt now
>
> So hit the road to San Diego
> And give me mashed potatoes
> Nothing's gonna stop Bear
> Or Walter Yeaaaaaa-ger now

"Pull over! Pull over!" yelled Walter, pointing to an overpass. "Get out! Get out!" Walter jumped out of the passenger seat, Bear followed. They met up under the bridge, and sung the rest of the song in the pouring rain, with one lyrical change. "Nothing's Gonna Stop Walt Now" reverted back to "Nothing's Gonna Stop Us Now." And raindrops weren't the only thing on the quarterback's face. Walter was crying. Walter cried for joy, rarely for anything else, and usually joy for others. Bear grinned and sang minus the tears. Bear didn't cry when Walter cried. Bear only cried when he needed to cry for the both of them, something he realized as the boys sang out at the top of their lungs, finally putting an end to their wet week waiting in Kansas City.

"SO THEY'RE DRIVING ALL THE WAY to California on a hope and a prayer?" asked Walt from the passenger seat of the golf cart in the hills overlooking the Pacific.

"That's all you need when you're young and full of piss 'n' vinegar," said Marcus from the driver's seat. He was taking them on a spin through the Complex at half the speed of the former quarterback's tour.

"What's with Bear dreaming about your life?" asked Walt.

"Don't remember that personally, but that's real sweet of him," said Marcus.

"How accurate is he? Were you overweight after college?" asked Walt.

"Overweight, outta shape, and feeling like shit, for a couple of years anyway," said Marcus. "I was trying to find myself all over again, living in LA, working in Hollywood, calling myself gay, trying to meet gay men for love and sex.

How else was I supposed to find my buddy? I was spinning my wheels. I finally said fuck it and went to see a shrink, told him something like, 'I want to work on my self-esteem.' I did most of the talking. After about a year of yammering on, I started to realize I wasn't a psycho, criminally insane, child-molesting, perverted, hell-bound deviant just because I wanted to be with a man. Of course, the actual psychological journey wasn't nearly as casual as I'm making it sound, but those are just details now. Point being: I exorcised some serious demons inside my mind that said I was a bad person. Once I did that, I was able to climb outta rock bottom. I quit overeating, quit feeling like shit, and started to get my life together."

"Call you the Phoenix," said Walt.

"The famous boys would be the ones calling Phoenix," said Marcus ...

... Before reaching California, Walter and Bear stopped in Phoenix, Arizona, to take the Test. With football a reality, they needed to know their HIV statuses. They found an anonymous testing clinic and went in at separate times, each one wearing a cap and sunglasses. Shortly thereafter, they continued westward.

The San Diego Chargers were in the midst of an intense, two-game road trip when the boys arrived. To survive, the QB finally asked his family for money, admitting to them he was pursuing his football dream in the US, not Canada. The Yeagers were supportive, emotionally and financially. Walter and Bear rented a studio apartment by the month in Ocean Beach, a funky community full of hippies and homeless kids. Rent was cheap and the beach was a block away, along with plenty of athletic fields. Right away, Walter networked with some local football people and began arranging workouts.

Meanwhile, when the time came, the boys placed two very nervous phone calls to Phoenix. After both results were in, they turned to one another. When they made eye contact, they knew. Whenever they made eye contact, the whole world was open to them, especially their own private world, which was now officially HIV-negative ...

"I warred with that one for years," said Marcus, bringing the golf cart to a halt on a summit in the hills above the Pacific.

"Their test results, you mean," said Walt from the passenger seat.

"Would I be negative? Should I be negative? But in reality, timing was everything," said Marcus. "Not being in a relationship—a monogamous one at that—during college was the difference. By the way, I'm HIV-positive. But I'm guessing your brilliant mind already figured that out."

"You look great," said Walt.

"I got tested in 1988," said Marcus, exhaling toward the canyon. "I had risen up from that emotional rock bottom and was ready to face the music. The results just confirmed what I already knew from the post-grad night sweats: sometime during my last days of college in '85, I became infected. Right away I called my mom. She did her cheerleading, then I hung up and hit the gym. I was getting in the best shape of my life. I wasn't gonna be late."

"Talk about balls," said Walt.

"Kinda like surviving back surgery that ends your football dreams in your early 20s," said Marcus.

"Doesn't compare," said Walt.

"Doesn't have to. Doesn't even have to mean either one of our dreams had to end," said Marcus ...

... Bear Coleman drifted off to sleep, feeling like one very lucky Bear.

Thank you, God, for sending me the buddy of my dreams when you did. You saved me from AIDS. I'm so grateful to You and to Walter. All my deepest dreams have come true and can keep coming true. My God, if I hadn't met Walter during that Georgia weekend, where would I be right now? Probably would have just tested positive. And would still be alone ...

But that *Marcus would be strong in the face of a positive HIV test. He'd be smart enough to face his fears. He'd join support groups and attend AIDS information meetings. He'd do research, form his own opinions, take charge of his health.*

Bear dreamed of Marcus Coleman swimming and working out religiously, just like Bear. Bear did it for his buddy. Marcus would do it in the name of being healthy, athletic and a good catch for a good man someday. Marcus would still believe all his dreams could come true. Bear made sure of it by dreaming that Marcus discovered the photo of Walter from the game program for inspiration. That way, Marcus would know good men like Walter Yeager exists. They were out there. Somewhere ...

... Marcus Coleman drifted off to sleep, feeling like one very hopeful man.

Man, if only I had met Walter Yeager during that Georgia weekend. Where would I be right now? I wouldn't have the virus. I would have met my buddy right before the storm hit home. But I'm gonna face my fears, do what I gotta do. Still have hope. Still want my buddy, whoever he is, wherever he is.

And now more than ever, he wanted to find a way to make all of Walter and Bear's dreams come true, just like his own deepest dreams.

14

The Snowman Cometh

Walter Yeager finally got a job, and it was the only job Walter Yeager wanted at age 24: NFL quarterback. As fate would have it, another ex-Georgia Bulldawg was the catalyst. Reggie Snowman was a dark-skinned defensive back who played for the Washington Redskins. Way back when, Yeager only knew him as the loudmouth sophomore who picked off a lot of his passes in practice during Yeager's senior year. In the first week of December, Reggie Snowman returned the favor for all that time honing his skills against Number 13.

The Redskins were battling the Dolphins in Miami. On the final play of the game, Reggie intercepted a Dan Marino pass in the end zone. In the post-game interview, Marino said something vaguely insinuating about his team's defense. A war of words ensued in the media. The team held a players-only meeting before their next game, at San Diego. The united Dolphins had a feeding frenzy on the lifeless Chargers. Marino threw for four touchdowns. The Dolphins defense took out two of the Charger QBs, re-injuring the starter's throwing hand and breaking the backup's leg.

San Diego was out of playoff contention and down to one QB, an ailing third-stringer named Norm Presbo. Because they knew Yeager was in town and raring to go, Walter was invited to take a crack at emergency backup. After two days of showing them what he could do, Piss 'n' Vinegar signed his first pro contract and was set to be in uniform for their next game, at home vs. Green Bay.

Life changed instantly. Walter disappeared into the vortex known as the football world. This was still in the prehistoric days before mass public consumption of mobile phones, so Yeager ended up leaving a lot of notes to keep Coleman in the loop.

AGENT, THEN PHYSICAL, BACK LATER. #13

TURN ON LOCAL NEWS AT NOON, DON'T KNOW WHICH ONE. #13

EXTRA FILM SESSION. WAKE YOU? #13

WHERE'S MY BEAR HUG? #13

All that in the first week of their new lives, all thanks to Reggie Snowman's interception. Like Walter, Bear didn't have much time to savor the high. The Yeagers were coming to San Diego to see the blond prodigy stand on his first NFL sideline. Their son would only play in the event of a franchise catastrophe, but that didn't matter. The Yeagers wanted to see Walter on the field as much as Bear did, and because Walter was busy transforming himself into a pro quarterback, Bear became the link between family and son.

To the Yeagers, Bear was Walter's good friend turned business partner turned houseguest, all through their son's ex-flame, Roseanne/Joe Bruin. The night before the game, Bear waited at the airport with a minivan and a Joe Bruin smile. Mr. and Mrs. Yeager were just as he imagined them to be, the dad's masculine bravado softening with age, the mom self-assured but deferring, as if running the show from the wings. There was also Walter's Sister. Bear sensed she had the ability to get under her brother's skin with very little effort and was proud of her special gift. He could feel the ghosts of battles past, reminding him of his own sister and her powers.

The quarterback's ambassador drove the family to their hotel and explained the Seattle to Edmonton to Kansas City to San Diego trek in his own words—downplaying the spontaneity of it all. "I'm glad he has you to bring him back down to earth once in a while," said Mrs. Yeager from the passenger seat.

Bear smiled a Walter Yeager half-smile. He was the *cool black guy* this weekend. His goal was for the Yeagers to leave San Diego knowing their son was in good company, no matter the details. The four of them sat together at the game and watched their hero stand on the sidelines for an entire professional football game. It didn't matter that Walter didn't play. Or that they never made "official" eye contact with him. What mattered was that their golden boy was standing tall and proud, healthy, happy, and full of headstrong dreams again. Walter Yeager was golden, whether he threw another touchdown pass or never suited up again. But they all wanted to see him shine like the brilliant star they knew him to be in their hearts, and they also wanted the world to experience that brilliance.

Walter and his #1 fans celebrated with a hearty post-game meal at Snaky

Lu's Lobster House, a quaint restaurant adjacent to the calm waters of San Diego Bay. Over dessert, the family got a hint as to how much their son's houseguest meant to their son. Bear and the Yeagers were worshipping their warrior hero. In true Walter fashion, QB deflected all the adulation and spotlight away from himself. "*This* guy got me through the madness and the rehab," said Walter, indicating Bear with a bottle of Bud. Mr. Yeager raised his glass, Mrs. Yeager and Walter's Sister followed. "To Bear," said the Yeagers. The toast was Bear's favorite moment of the weekend, second only to seeing his buddy on the field.

That night in bed, the boys were exhilarated and exhausted. Their first week in the NFL was behind them. The Yeagers were jetting through space to Chicago. And Walter and Bear were alone for the first time in ages. They spooned—Walter's front to Bear's back—and watched highlights of today's loss on ESPN.

"I need to be in the game," said Walter.

"What did it feel like today?" asked Bear.

"Like I want more," said Walter, using the remote to turn off the TV.

"Dream of it," said Bear, kissing his man goodnight.

IF WALTER'S DREAMS INVOLVED endless hours of football practice, his dreams were coming true. The Chargers scrambled to acquire a veteran to help finish out the season, which made Yeager third on the depth chart. He was there in case of emergency, in case another angry defense put the hurt on the other QBs. The practice experience was the gift for now. To take full advantage, Yeager started "talking a little shit" in scrimmages to piss off the defensive linemen. Getting knocked around cranked up his adrenaline and helped knock out any lingering doubts about his reversed back in combat.

One day, Yeager got it in his head to piss off a defensive tackle who weighed as much as three of his teammates. Doak Minnefield was a black rookie whom the vets called Babyface. Another rookie like Yeager, however, didn't possess the privilege. Naturally, Piss 'n' Vinegar was aware of this, but he was also a little restless. While scrimmaging, he kept calling Minnefield "Babyface" and Minnefield kept warning Yeager: "Say it one more time, man, I'm tellin' you." Walter complied and Minnefield hit him harder each time. The coaches were also restless that day and sat back and enjoyed the show. The antagonism spread to the rest of the offense and defense. At one point, an offensive guard was knocked down as a result of a Minnefield-Yeager collision. The guard charged after Minnefield. A scuffle broke out, forcing the coaches to separate the players. When calm was restored, Walter explained he was just trying to get Minnefield to hit him for real. "Why didn't you say so, fool?" said Minnefield. Then he knocked

Walter so far off his ass, the quarterback landed 10 yards away. "First down, Yeager!" said Minnefield, his right arm making the ref's forward hand signal.

"What about the black eye?" asked Bear that night. He was sitting on the
couch, sizing up his man's shiner.

"The brawl afterward," said Walter, sitting next to him, pressing the ice
pack deeper into his swollen right eye. "Offense versus defense."

"You sure know how to stir shit up, don't you, PV?" said Bear.

"My face hurts, gimme some Sugar," said Walter. For the rest of the Chargers season, Piss 'n' Vinegar kept his piss 'n' vinegar to a minimum and learned
the ropes of the NFL. "Backup is kinda like vice-prez of the White House," said
Walter. "Nobody remembers your name until somebody gets hurt."

Minus the lack of playing time, though, it was a mini-football season in
heaven, albeit one that came to an abrupt end when the Chargers finished a dismal year with a road loss at Washington. "Just getting started, baby," said Bear,
pulling away from curbside at the airport hours after the defeat.

"I think we can afford a new car now," said Walter, exhaling against the
passenger door. "And a real place to live."

"Hey, what were you and Reggie Snowman talking about after the game?"
asked Bear, noticing the sputtering of the engine for the first time. "In the middle
of the field, after Reggie left the prayer circle."

"Same thing as everyone else." Walter did his imitation of a black man raising his voice several octaves: "*Man,* how'd you rehab? *Man,* I'm coming out to
Hollywood!"

"*Man,* what'd you tell him?" asked Bear, imitating Walter's imitation.

"*Man,* same as everyone else," said Walter, then added in his own voice:
"Revolutionary Tibetan Danish Archeological Chiropractor Zookeeper Therapy,
et cetera."

"How do you feel?" asked Bear. Walter cracked his neck and moaned. The
quarterback had just called a personal timeout. Bear let the mellow jazz on the
radio fill their space and drove his warrior home.

DURING THE OFF-SEASON, the boys moved into a small two-bedroom house not
far from the beach. The spare bedroom morphed into their very first home office,
where Walter performed his financial wizardry, and Bear learned how to use the
newfangled word processor that was a gift from his buddy. "You supported me
during rehab," Walter told Bear. "Time to get your dreams going."

One weekend, Mama Rent flew down from Northern California. Perhaps
because she hadn't seen her son's best friend since the original Athens weekend,

Mama Rent's eyes lit up upon Walter at First Sight, reminding Bear of himself. Near the end of the visit, the boys took her to dinner at Snaky-Lu's Lobster House by the bay. After they left the restaurant, Walter went to fetch their new SUV in the parking lot while Bear and his mother stayed behind.

"I can tell you like Walter, Mom," said Bear, gazing up at the moon.

"You've found a really nice friend," said Mama Rent.

"I love him, Mom," said Bear, breaking into tears. "We've been in love since the day we met. We're gonna be in love forever."

"Are you both gay?" asked Mama Rent.

Bear paused, then cried and smiled some more. "If gay means being happy, I'm the gayest man on the planet."

"I love you no matter what," said Mama Rent. The two biggest floodgates in the Coleman family opened. Mother and son hugged one another in a river of tears until headlights illuminated them.

"Everything cool?" asked Walter once they were settled inside the SUV.

"And dreamy," said Bear from the passenger seat. They drove Mama Rent to the airport. She hugged both boys before disappearing into her plane.

"I told her," said Bear from the passenger seat on the way home.

"I know," said Walter from the driver's seat.

"How?" asked Bear.

"She told me she loved me," said Walter, "at the airport."

In January, the boys rented a secluded bungalow by the beach on the Baja California peninsula of Mexico. For eight glorious days, they unwound in the sun and reclaimed their right to be *two as one*. They also rediscovered sides of their sexual souls long buried in the fear of AIDS.

"Sex is so fucking good," Bear would say.

"Man, I love sex! I gotta have sex!" Walter would say. They'd spent two years equating their physical love with sickness. Now it was time for the chains to come off their minds. When they weren't declaring their sexual freedom, they were drinking Coronas on the beach. They spent countless hours under a gigantic red umbrella, Walter bobbing his head in time to the music on his cassette headset, while Bear drifted off to fantasyland.

Bear often dreamed of a better script for Marcus Coleman of *My Whole Other Life*. That Marcus was single and HIV-positive, but like Bear, *that* Marcus had heart and determination, and thus wouldn't give up on life just because the college buddy thing didn't work out.

Bear imagined Marcus vacationing on the other side of Mexico, perhaps in

Cancun. By now, Marcus would be a 26-year-old, muscular, athletic, intelligent black man who happened to be openly gay. People would gravitate toward his confident, bright light, all kinds of people from different ethnic and sexual backgrounds. And he'd still be searching for his own dream man, one just as real as Walter, or so Bear Coleman believed. Staring out at the sea, the spirit leader wondered: *how would the world treat a man like me, who happens to be HIV-positive and still trying to find his buddy-for-life? How would the gay world treat me? How would the guys at the gym—the studs like Walter—treat me? Would any of them want to be my buddy? Would Walter?*

ONCE THE BOYS RETURNED FROM MEXICO, it wasn't long before their world began to gravitate toward football again. In the spring, the Chargers had a mini-camp for players who had something to prove. Piss 'n' Vinegar had the mini-camp of his life. Of course, it was his *only* mini-camp, but that was just a detail. Afterward, the Chargers were high on Yeager's chances for making the team during the regular training camp. On top of that, Walter and his agent were high on QB making *some* team should San Diego fail to see the light.

Bear was also taking care of business, setting aside *My Whole Other Life* for a new screenplay. *The Bridges Between Us* was a heartwarming story about a diverse group of international tourists forced to get along while stranded in a Mexican resort. Among them, an intelligent, athletic, black gay man with HIV. While Walter trained for training camp, Bear made steady progress building *Bridges*. That is, until he was interrupted by the doorbell one day.

The peephole revealed an intriguing black man. Opening the door revealed: "Reggie Snowman!"

"Yeah, you got it," laughed Reggie. He remained on the porch, searching for a street number on the house. "Do I have the wrong place? I'm looking for a friend of mine, plays football."

"Walter. Come on in," said Bear.

"Cool, cool." Reggie Snowman became the first of the football people to ever enter their domain. He was even more handsome in person, his dark chocolate skin as smooth as his personality.

"This is his place," said Bear, putting on his tough voice. "I work for him, part assistant, part manager. I'm Bear."

They went to shake hands, but Reggie's urban "finger-tug" didn't fit Bear's traditional handshake. They tried to connect by mimicking the other's position, rendering them right back where they started.

"Fuck it," said Reggie with an amicable laugh. "So my boy's not here?"

"Out doing cardio. Was he expecting you?" asked Bear.

"I told him I'd drop by while I was in Hollywood, shooting my rap video." Reggie surveyed their sparsely decorated living room, then rapped: "Smack it, flip it, rub it on down."

"Rap video?" asked Bear.

"For my new song, 'Jacuzzi Freak'," said Reggie. "Gonna do thangs they ain't never seen a brutha do in this world, my own cable network, my own movie studio, my own sports teams, you name it ... freak, freak, freak of the week."

"Cool, cool," said Bear, not one to shit on other people's dreams, no matter how dreamy.

"You play ball somewhere?" asked Reggie, sizing up Bear, who was in the best shape of his life, thanks to a strict regimen at the gym. "Seem like I seen you somewhere."

"Me? *Nah*," said Bear. No need to tell him any more than that.

"Tell yo' boy I came by," said Reggie. "I'll be at my uncle's for ..."

Reggie's words were upstaged by Walter's voice entering the house before the rest of him because the front door was still open. By the time Walter was through the door, he had finished saying with mock bravado: "I need me a Bear hug!" Then he saw two tall black men standing in his living room, only one of whom knew anything about Bear hugs. "Reggie Snowman the Showman!" said Walter, suddenly sounding a little black himself. He extended his hand, and *he* got the urban handshake right.

"Snowman the Showman, I like that," said Reggie, storing it in his mind.

"You met my back cracker Bear?" asked Walter, casual as ever. "Reggie, I'm telling you—you were wondering how I rehabbed? It was him!"

"Thought it was a Danish dude," said Reggie.

"Ah, but I was the Dane's assistant, ya," said Bear, adding *just a touch* of Danish to his voice.

"The Dane—he's off on a pilgrimage," explained Walter, "but my manager here—did he tell you he was my manager, too?"

"*And* assistant," said Bear. "Ya."

"He's the maintenance man, so to speak," said Walter. "I pay him big bucks to crack my back like the Dane."

"Really?" Reggie rolled his shoulders. "I could use some cracking."

"But you can't!" said Walter. "You see, it's part of the ancient Haiku Scrolls that the back cracker only crack one back during his time of service. To that back. He can't crack anyone else's back until I no longer need it."

"*What?*" said Reggie, the octaves rising off the charts.

"Man, I'm telling ya, it's some crazy shit," said Walter, sounding like the blackest white man on the planet. "It's some crazy ancient pre-Tibetan shit, but the shit works!"

"I ain't gonna fuck with that," said Reggie. "Gone ahead and get yo' back crack on. Whatever it takes to get you in the game, man. I need the picks."

"You know," said Walter, "the Mud Wrestling pre-Tibetans didn't say anything about Bear cracking another person's neck, did they, Bear?"

"It's your eyes, man," laughed Reggie. "You glance at your primary receiver out of the huddle. At least you did your last year in school."

"No fucking way!" Walter began pacing the room, astonished, pissed, yelling to himself: "That is not acceptable. That cannot happen to me. How the fuck could I let that happen? That does not happen to Walter Yeager. No fucking way! Pisses me off! How could I?"

"So where do I know you from?" Reggie asked Bear, "if it ain't from football?"

"Not sure," said Bear, raising his voice to be heard over his ranting quarterback. "I don't think he's gonna be in the mood for a back cracking now. I'm gonna head home—to where I live, my own place, an hour from here. Bye."

"YOU DIDN'T HAVE TO PRETEND you don't live here," said Walter when Bear returned a short time later. QB was sitting on the couch, slumped over.

"I panicked," said Bear from the doorway.

"We both did," said Walter. "We escaped AIDS and we're still not breathing any easier."

"Why was Reggie Snowman here anyway?" asked Bear, sitting next to Walter.

"Party invite," said Walter. "Babes and Jacuzzis in the Hollywood Hills. I thought that talk about visiting me was all bull. I should have known better."

"You sound like you mean that," said Bear.

"You know the black assistant coach that was my first contact in San Diego?" said Walter. "He's Reggie's uncle. Of course, Reggie would come down here to visit him. They're tight. Coach helped raise him."

"You think Reggie's gonna tell his uncle about us?" asked Bear. Walter jumped up and paced the living room in fits and starts.

"You learned the back-cracking technique I need," said Walter, getting the story straight in his mind. "That's a Bear Hug. Fuck, I'm a dead man."

"From everything you said about this coach on the way to San Diego, he doesn't sound like the kind of man who would judge you," said Bear.

"You're right," said Walter, sitting back on the couch. "We'll play it out and see what happens. What's really pissing me off right now is Reggie telling me I have a weakness."

THE BOYS INTENDED TO COME UP with a standard cover for surprise visitors but didn't anticipate needing such a plan a mere 48 hours later, when the second of the football people appeared at their door. "It's Coach!" whispered Walter after looking through the peephole. "Reggie's uncle."

Bear leaped from the couch and tiptoed toward the bedroom.

"Stay." Calm and steady, the quarterback opened the door. "Coach!"

Walter and Black Coach exchanged greetings and (traditional) handshakes.

"*Whoa, stop right there,*" said Walt from the passenger seat of the golf cart parked on a hill overlooking the Pacific.

"He doesn't have a name other than Black Coach in my dreams, at least not yet," said Marcus from the driver's seat.

"Okay, I get that," said Walt, "but that's not that same black coach who helped me at Georgia, is it?"

"Nope," said Marcus. "Want to know the biggest personal question I had about you all these years? How you felt about blacks. I gave you a black coach at every level of your career as my way of sensitizing you to ... black people. I guess my way of explaining how a golden boy like Walter Yeager could be attracted to Bear—sounds stupid, I know. Remember, I was a kid."

"Not stupid," said Walt.

"Thanks," said Marcus. "So *this* Black Coach is from youth football. He helped teach you all the good stuff sports teaches. You guys are meeting up again, farther down the playing field of life."

"Dream on, you crazy dreamer man," said Walt with a mild laugh ...

... While Walter and Black Coach exchanged greetings and (traditional) handshakes, Bear stood mesmerized by the sight of the distinguished-looking Negro in their San Diego living room. Black Coach had dark weathered skin, big auburn lips and a small Afro with airy traces of gray. He looked like a man who would never dream of hurting the boys, yet the pained expression on his face said otherwise. "Coach," said Walter, leading him into the living room, "I'd like you to meet Bear—"

"The back cracker. My nephew Reggie says he knows you," said Black Coach. The two black men shook hands. Walter offered them drinks. "I don't wanna pussyfoot around," said Black Coach, sitting in the sofa chair. "You know I'm here for a reason, and I know you wanna hear it, *aiight?* As the kids say."

"Lay it on us," said Walter, nodding for Bear to join him on the couch.

"You knew you had a long shot with the team before mini-camp, but you used the opportunity like a winner," said Black Coach.

"I'm hearing a big fat *but* coming," said Walter.

"*True dat,* as the kids say," said Black Coach. "San Diego can't use you. My advice: go to Canada and prove yourself. Then, let 'em come after *Yeager.*"

Walter stewed for a moment, then said, "What about Kansas City? Or San Francisco?"

"Denver and Miami have slots," said Bear.

"Was he born to be a backup?" Black Coach turned to Walter. "Were you born to carry around somebody else's jock on a clipboard? Or were you *special* as a kid, a kind of *special* most of us can't understand and won't understand, at least not in this lifetime? Because if Walter was born a regular Joe, you can have all my contacts in the NFL, right now."

"Great, lay 'em on me," said Walter.

"But I've never lied to you," said Black Coach. "This is my advice. Figure out what you are, and who you are. And if you're different—or special, or *all that,* like the kids say, or whatever you want to call yourself—go to Canada. Otherwise, your life here will be more hell than you can imagine." Black Coach eyed Bear. "Ditto for everybody around you."

The boys remained mute, not knowing what to say.

"Bear," said Black Coach. "As a chiropractor's assistant who happens to be black, I bet you have to be twice as good as all the other chiropractor's assistants. I got a niece in the medical field. She tells me stories all the time. Shame it's gotta be that way."

"Is it that way in the NFL, too?" asked Bear, feeling the rising tension in his periphery. "How backward is pro football?"

"Fools are everywhere," said Black Coach. "You just gotta know which fools are on your team, your personal team, *feel me?*"

"Trying to," said Bear, stone-faced.

"So you're saying Canada or hell?" asked Walter. "Canada *is* hell."

"If you say so," said Black Coach.

"Come again?" said Walter.

"Repeat what you just said, but substitute *heaven* for *hell,*" said Black Coach.

"Canada is heaven," said Walter.

"Which feels better?" asked Black Coach.

"Canada is not my idea of heaven," said Walter.

"You know he's way overqualified for the CFL," said Bear.

"And *you* know it's not just about talent," said Black Coach.

"What else besides talent is in play here?" asked Bear, imagining Walter's eyes rolling like a Vegas slot machine.

"Your buddy is still young," said Black Coach, "younger than most QBs his age, in terms of NFL maturity. Those guys are settling down, getting married, having families, getting *real* about life. If the league saw that kind of maturity in Yeager, they'd factor that into taking a chance on him."

"My back is hurting. I'm going to lie down." Walter disappeared into the bedroom. A dazed Bear got up to show their guest out.

"If he listens to you, I hope you tell him to go North," said Black Coach.

"I hope he listens to his intuition, always and forever," said Bear, then shut the door and went into the bedroom. "How's the back?"

"It's fine, I lied," mumbled Walter, lying on his side on the bed.

"Did he just say what I think he said? That he knows about us and so does the rest of the NFL?" Bear sat next to his husband and massaged his neck.

"That was my first impression," said Walter.

"Or did he just mean: go prove yourself because you're young and full of piss 'n' vinegar?" asked Bear. "So settle down in Canada and focus on football?"

"That was my second impression," said Walter. "Now I don't know what to believe."

Bear spooned Walter's back. No words were needed. They were undergoing another reality shift, and there were no words for reality shifts, just feelings that transfer from one reality to the next.

THE SWEET-SOUNDING HARMONICA from a bluesy folk song hummed on the radio as the SUV rolled into a gas station in a small Canadian outpost. The time was daylight, that was all the boys knew. They were weary road travelers and feeling the blues.

Walter went inside to call his agent while Bear serviced the vehicle. Their next stop was a town called Regina, where Walter was going to become a Saskatchewan Roughrider, unless ...

The quarterback emerged from the station.

"Any news?" asked Bear, checking the oil.

"Yeah," said Walter. "I'm a Roughrider."

Translation: his agent had struck out finding them another decent offer. This time, there'd be no last-minute clemency from the football gods.

"Where the hell are we?" asked Walter, standing near the front of the SUV.

"Where the *heaven* are we?" Bear paused to enjoy the collision of the hood with the rest of the car, then surveyed his surroundings. Were it not for the stoplight, the intersection was like something out of the Wild West. Two-story brick buildings. A barren landscape beyond. Tumbleweed blowing down the street. Bear squinted at the words painted on the window of the barbershop that was adjacent to the gas station. "Cut it close in Moose Jaw. Saskatchewan. Canada. North America. Planet Earth. Your Universe."

"Thank you, Professor Coleman," said Walter, more focused on the brochure in his hands.

"Thank the barbershop," said Bear. "I wonder if they cut black men's hair."

"They'd better learn," said Walter, still focused on the brochure. "Moose Jaw is the perfect place for a guy's Bear to hibernate. They've even got tunnels!"

THE SASKATCHEWAN ROUGHRIDERS played their home games at Taylor Field, a cozy stadium with a gridiron wedged between two long and narrow grandstands, reminding Bear of a functional office item, like a paperclip. Adjusting to Canadian football took some time for the boys. The field was wider and longer, the end zones deeper, the rules slightly different. (Yeager only had *three* downs to perform his QB wizardry!) The Canadians were protective of their little niche in the football world. They were quick to inform Americans that Canadians had introduced the sport to North America, and that the CFL had been around as long as, if not longer than, the early iterations of the NFL.

It was all amusing to Bear, who enjoyed most of the Northern neighbors he encountered. Canadians possessed an inner peace most Americans didn't. Canadians weren't always looking over their shoulder or glancing sideways, or through you. They had ambition but weren't power-hungry. They enjoyed modern comforts but not to the point of obsession. Canada was like America with the edge taken off, and as the season moved into fall, Bear figured out exactly how to take his own edge off ...

The sellout crowd at the paperclip exhaled in disappointment at the incomplete pass, bringing Bear back to the stadium, mind, body and soul. He took another sip of his hot toddy and savored the buzz of watching his very own Roughrider jogging toward the near sideline in his sexy green and whites. Yeager had a brief but intense discussion with the head coach about the failure of the previous play. After the punt, the head coach slapped Yeager's ass with his clipboard, as if to say, *Keep believing.*

Saskatchewan was hosting the Calgary Stampeders, the Western Division leaders. The Roughriders hadn't made the playoffs in the six years prior to Walter's arrival, just one reason Yeager nailed the starting QB job in his mind long before the boys landed in Canada.

Matt Strickland, another gorgeous blond quarterback from the States, threw a 38-yard bullet to a Calgary receiver streaking down the sideline. First down, Stampeders.

The province of Saskatchewan was a black hole for most players, but a void was just what the boys needed. Walter focused on football from day one in training camp. His body was as strong as ever, maturing in all the ways an athlete needs his body to mature as he advances toward his physical and mental prime.

Bear glanced inside the game program at the photo of Matt Strickland. Who knew the CFL was such a hotbed for handsome blond QBs? This guy would be perfect for Marcus Coleman of My Whole Other Life! *And he just threw for another first down. Maybe it's time to focus on my own quarterback. Defense, Roughriders, Defense!*

Walter lived in a rented house in Regina with a handful of teammates, some of whom slept on mattresses on the floor because they were either too poor or couldn't predict their whereabouts week to week. Yeager was barely around though. He spent his days honing his skills and his nights seeing some Canadian chick in nearby Moose Jaw.

The Saskatchewan defense sacked Matt Strickland's blond ass twice, forcing Calgary to punt. One last possession for the Roughriders, who were down by six.

While Walter was throwing TD passes all over Canada, Bear worked on *The Bridges Between Us* in a rented room over a saloon in—what a coincidence—Moose Jaw! Barney, the owner of the saloon next to the barbershop, had insisted on renting to Bear after meeting the "black American writer doing top-secret research for a film featuring the town's underground tunnels."

Yeager ran a sweep to the right on that extra-wide Canadian field, flipping the ball to the tailback at the last minute and taking a shot to the chops as a reward from the defensive end.

Each night before Bear went to bed, he left his second-story window open, no matter the weather. Closed, the window jammed. Open, it allowed Walter to slip inside after climbing the fire escape. Bear would fall asleep alone, the night air cool on his bare shoulders. Sometime later, in his dreams, the chill would vanish, the still of the night replaced by the rustling of garments being stripped from his man's tired body—sweatshirts, jeans, sneakers, underwear. The blond aura would slip into bed and gently rock Bear's world with a tender kiss on the shoulder. Then, his man having peaceably invaded his senses, Bear would fall deeper into his deepest, most soulful dreams.

Yeager rolled to his left, a stampede of defenders following him. Number 13 lobbed the ball over their heads. Screen pass. The squat black running back inhaled the ball and scampered for 15 yards. First down, Roughriders at their own 40. A minute to go. Saskatchewan was down by six.

Game time, home or away, was the only time Bear was guaranteed to see Walter. They were never together in public, but that wasn't a problem, thanks to some dead criminals turned angels. Decades ago, Al Capone and his homies created passageways underneath Moose Jaw to bootleg liquor all over Saskatchewan. With the help of Barney the Saloon Owner, the boys had their own private parties for two, just below Canada.

"I think this makes us certifiable," said Walter on one such occasion down below. "You realize you're one of four player's wives—or whatever—crazy enough to be up here. Or down here, in our case."

"Good crazy, right?" asked Bear, sitting on a barrel in a room that looked like an old wine cellar.

"If you like dark, musty tunnels while you're trying to get some face time in the zone," said Walter, holding onto vertical bars that looked like they belonged in a jail cell.

"I wouldn't dream of it any other way," said Bear, taking a sip of his Bud.

"The tunnels, or the face time in the zone?" asked Walter, approaching his buddy.

"Whatever Walter wants," said Bear, pulling Walter closer.

"Walter wants to know if Reggie and his uncle stabbed us in the back," said Walter. "Coach is with Denver now. Sometimes, I feel like calling him up and saying, *What the hell is the deal?* I know, stay cool. I won't blow this. Things are going well."

"I got faith in you, QB," said Bear. No need to state aloud what they both knew: Yeager's superstar potential was turning the right football heads northward. His CFL days were numbered.

"I could still wring Reggie's neck," said Walter, "if I just knew whether or not he hung me out to dry."

"Either way, he gave us a gift," said Bear.

Yeager took the snap from the shotgun. The Calgary middle linebacker blitzed from the right. Walter sidestepped him and let the ball rip toward the corner of the far sideline. The team's leading receiver, a lanky vet from the Yukon, caught the ball in stride at the five and didn't stop until he collided with the mini-bleachers in the end zone. Touchdown, Roughriders. Game over.

Reggie Snowman's gift was one the quarterback used wisely. Now when Yeager emerged from the huddle, his focus was on Yeager, not his primary receiver. The difference was astounding, even to Yeager, who was morphing into a professional athlete in so many ways.

The body belongs to the boy until the boy gives the body to the man within.

In Canada, Walter's body became that of a man's. Bear saw him less often, so Bear saw the change more dramatically. Every morning in Moose Jaw, Walter looked like a different person, the piss 'n' vinegar kid morphing into an athlete who was primed and ready for greatness.

Yeager led the Roughriders to a 12-6 season, their best in years. Not even a playoff loss a few weeks later to those very same Calgary Stampeders could dampen the boys' spirits. Their dreams were coming true. Soon after the season ended, the football world south of the border came calling, just as Black Coach had predicted.

15

Mile High Monday

"I finally get my chance," said Walt from the passenger seat of the golf cart. They were parked on a hill overlooking the Pacific.

"Yes you do," said Marcus, smiling in the driver's seat.

"Correction," said Walt. "Big-league *Walter* gets *his* chance."

"Yes you do," giggled Marcus.

"Dream on," said Walt with a boyish laugh, "but lemme drive."

"Ready, break!" said Marcus. The boys jumped from the cart in unison. Walt orbited counterclockwise around the front. Marcus orbited in the same direction around the back. Walt, the swifter in body, landed in the driver's seat a tad before Marcus settled in the passenger seat.

"So did Marcus—*you*—have a good time in Cancun?" asked Walt, cranking up the engine.

"You're good," giggled Marcus. "While the big league boys were having their Sugar-coated Coronas on the west side of Mexico, I was having my own adventures on the east side."

"Where you met your cool dream guy!" said Walt, taking off from the hill.

"Not quite," said Marcus, "but I did meet a pair of cool and dreamy teenage brothers, circa ages 14 and 16."

"*Whoa!*" said Walt, hitting the brakes at the bottom of the hill.

"I was on a soul-searching mission, not a jailbait getaway," said Marcus.

"Good man," said Walt, easing his foot off the brake.

"But then again, I'm betting Walt Yeager's intuition knew that all along," said Marcus.

"So what happened on the east side?" asked Walt, the great scrambler.

"I had just tested positive and turned my life around, all for the better," said Marcus. "I went to Cancun for a break. Strangely enough, these two golden white boys in the prime of their youth stuck to me like glue for an entire week. I was 26, in great shape, and probably glowing from all that personal growth. Seems they had it in their minds I was this *cool black dude*. They hero-worshipped me—how else can I put it? We played hoops, tennis, hung out in the Caribbean, did sports trivia. We had these *Hardy Boys* adventures, looking for aliens in the night skies. I even bonded with their very cool yet shrewd single mom."

"Sweet," said Walt, embarking on another journey through the hills.

"It wasn't that simple," said Marcus. "I was a man and a lonely one. The oldest brother was a Jock God to me, like the guys I worshipped when I was his age. Thing is, before Cancun, I wasn't even aware I had this lifelong jones for Jock Gods. But *this* Jock God was as naïve as a Norman Rockwell painting. And worshipped *me!* The whole thing was a twisted mind trip."

"Like this one," said Walt.

"Not even close," said Marcus. "This is a ride through the universe. *That* was the long line to get on the ride."

"*Ha!*" laughed Walt, accelerating and taking them on a loopy loop in a never-ending meadow.

"Of course, I ended up being honest with the whole family about myself, including my sexuality and my attraction to the oldest brother," said Marcus. "These people really loved and respected me, in their own way. I owed them *and* myself the truth. Honesty was keeping my soul alive."

"What happened?" asked Walt.

"A wonderful story that inspired one of my novels, which wouldn't be published until years later," said Marcus. "The details are on a bridge I gave to the world in the form of a book, but here's what matters most: Cancun was where I began to realize that there wasn't much difference between the golden gods of my youth and little ole black me. We all had our hopes, fears, dreams, nightmares, insecurities, questions. And need for heroes."

"Was Matt Strickland one of your heroes?" asked Walt.

"Did I mention you're good?" giggled Marcus. "Matt was a CFL QB who lived in LA and seemed like the perfect choice for *my* slice of *Walter and Bear.* Only, while I was dreaming of Matt, Matt wasn't dreaming of me, or other guys, period, like a lot of the men I gravitated toward on the road of life."

"You were out there trying," said Walt.

"And not always with unattainable Jock Gods," said Marcus. "Matter of fact, I pretty much crossed that bridge and moved on to more fruitful pastures. I opened myself up, dated all kinds of men of all colors. It was about the feelings Walter and Bear shared. That's what I wanted with my buddy. They were like my role models, lighting the way."

OF ALL THE TEAMS INTERESTED in Number 13, the Los Angeles Rams were the best fit. The franchise had a winning tradition and an unproven quarterback—just like Yeager. In addition, Bear would be close to Hollywood, where he intended to sell *The Bridges Between Us,* his just-completed screenplay about the tourists in Mexico.

The NFL season was still in progress when the SUV took off from Saskatchewan and landed in Southern California. The Rams were out of playoff contention and giving their current unproven QB *his* shot at removing the *unproven* from his name. Jim Everett was a high-profile draft pick out of Purdue who was the same age as Yeager. Many in the football world believed Everett possessed the potential for greatness, but so far, he had yet to set the football world on fire. More importantly for Everett, he had yet to impress his ultimate boss, who was anything but a pussycat. The Lioness was a brassy, white-haired woman who inherited the club years ago, after her champion swimmer husband drowned off the Florida coast. Her first act as owner had been the firing of the team boss, her stepson. Her replacement: herself. No job was secure in Ramsland, except hers.

Yeager inked a deal to be on the team's practice squad for the remainder of the season. Eighteen-year-old Walter never envisioned being on a lowly scout team, but 25-year-old Walter knew better than to look down on the opportunity. He was still full of piss 'n' vinegar, but a little humility had been injected into his veins, the kind of humility that comes from realizing: sometimes, The Powers That Be have a different path in store for you, one you may have never imagined or dreamed of.

Bear was learning his own version of this very same revelation. Never in his wildest dreams had he envisioned living in Orange County, home of the Rams and the place where beautiful white people came from. But this was no dream. This was a nightmare. "Talk about a ticking time bomb," said Bear from the passenger seat as the SUV roared down the California highway. "A big-ass black man, hunkered down amidst a bunch of conservative white people while secretly loving one of their own—the most golden one of all. Kinda overwhelming."

"Try whelming," said Walter from the driver's seat.

"Kinda whelming," said Bear, staring at the blur of malls on the other side of the passenger window. "Orange and whelming."

"Think of all the great stadiums you'll get to visit now," said Walter.

"You remember that I like stadiums," said Bear, always astonished at Walter's memory of intimate details Bear scarcely remembered about himself. His quarterback might not make a big deal of an anniversary or birthday, but he never forgot a dream or a feeling people shared with him. "We haven't talked about that in years, QB."

"Next year this time, you'll be in the stadiums of your childhood dreams," said Walter, rubbing his buddy's thigh.

"So will you." Bear reached for his man's blond locks until an entirely different universe came into sharp focus beyond the SUV. They were now behind the Orange Curtain. Both men sat upright, not touching.

"I wonder who else knows about *us*," said Walter, continuing past the blur of malls, "besides Reggie and his uncle."

"You gotta play football, PV," said Bear. "That's all Coach told you to do. That's all we know for sure. Focus. Recalibrate."

"You're right." Walter reached over and once again, massaged his man's thigh. "That's my Bear. Man, I love you."

The boys set up two different residences in the area. Walter lived part-time in a condo in Newport Beach near the football world, while Bear lived full-time in a condo in a sleepy little town farther inland, a town appropriately named ... Corona. They also decided the bachelor quarterback should be seen dating women, and since Walter merely had to breathe to attract the opposite sex, the dates were easy. In addition, the boys agreed that Bear should become a full-time aspiring screenwriter who worked at home. Walter was big on helping others achieve their goals, but the added benefit was unspoken and understood: a hibernating Bear was less likely to be a target in open-hunting season ...

"QB liked dating those women," said Marcus from the passenger seat of the golf cart. "Especially the dark, exotic ones."

"*Ha!*" said Walt from the driver's seat. The golf cart snaked up and down over a series of hills and valleys that reminded them of a miniature roller-coaster ride. *The Serpent.*

"I never saw me or my man as gay or straight, or even bi," said Marcus. "I just saw him as ... my man, and vice versa. We made our own rules."

"No doubt," said Walt.

"And my—correction, *Bear's*—man impressed the Rams enough to get an invite to training camp the following spring."

"Yeager's the man!" said Walt.

"No doubt!" said Marcus. "So is Bear. An independent British production company bought the screenplay for *The Bridges Between Us*. To celebrate, Walter came out to Corona carrying candles and a romantic dinner for two from Bistro de Snaky Lu's, some fancy restaurant near the football world."

"What a guy," said Walt.

"What a man," said Marcus, placing his hands behind his head and enjoying the ride ...

DURING TRAINING CAMP the following summer, 26-year-old Walter Yeager became a bona fide NFL quarterback. His performance: assertive. His attitude: *how do I get better?* His aura: radiant. Even a simple task like getting the car washed could result in a deep conversation with a total stranger drawn to his light.

"All from being a pro athlete," said Walter, sitting in bed one night, commanding the remote.

"Hardly," said Bear, sitting next to him. "That's just your natural glow when you feel good about yourself."

"*Shh*, listen," said Walter, indicating the report in progress on ESPN:

"... *coach of the Rams, won't call it a quarterback controversy, but veteran Jim Everett might have a dogfight on his hands for the starting job. That's because Walter Yeager—a former high school standout who meandered his way through Illinois and Georgia, but has yet to take a snap in the NFL—impressed coaches at mini-camp, training camp, and again tonight in the preseason opener at home against the Broncos.*"

"He didn't say I had a year in Canada!" yelled Walter. "Dimwit."

"*Shh!*" said Bear, bug-eyed at the clip of his man throwing passes in the pregame warm-ups. "Looking all good in his blue and gold. He didn't meander!"

"*Shh!*" said Walter, squinting at the clip of himself fading back to pass in the first quarter.

"*The pocket's collapsing ... Yeager's gotta eat it or throw it. He decides he isn't hungry right now ... or better still ... he'd rather eat touchdowns! Flipper Anderson, former UCLA Bruin, was open over the middle and caught Yeager's 59-yard, first-ever NFL touchdown pass. So what if it's preseason, still counts to his mom.*"

"And his buddy!" shouted Bear.

"*Shh!*" laughed Walter.

"*Yeager, who played in the frozen tundra of Canada last year—*"

"Thank you!" yelled Walter.

"*—threw for another TD in the fourth quarter, a 14-yard screen ... then got*

*over on this two-yard keeper to account for three scores, compared to just one for
Everett. In other notes, the Rams won, 31-16, and John Elway did not play in tonight's game."*

"I'll kick Elway's ass," said Walter.

"No doubt!" said Bear.

In reality, there was no quarterback controversy in Ramsland. Everett had
signed a big contract. It was his team by default. For now, Walter had his eye on
the number two spot and made his case with a solid preseason. But a few days
before the season opener at Detroit, the Rams made a startling announcement.
And Walter was pissed—

The door to the condo in Corona opened, then slammed shut. Bear was
waiting on the couch in the living room. They had cell phones now, and he was
up to speed with the latest headline in their world. Everett was out for the opener
with a bum ankle. The start was going to Holmes Easley, a professional backup
acquired a half a second ago.

"The job was mine," said Walter, storming through the condo.

"I know," said Bear.

"I had *the* preseason," said Walter, pacing the living room.

"You're right," said Bear.

"Can you fucking believe it?" said Walter, looking for something to throw.

"I wish I didn't have to," said Bear.

"What the fuck am I supposed to do now?" asked Walter.

"What do you want to do?" asked Bear.

"Blow somebody's fucking head off," said Walter.

"And after that?" asked Bear.

"Go back and prove I'm their QB," said Walter.

"With a murder rap," said Bear.

"Just once," said Walter. When Bear didn't respond, Walter added, "Don't
you ever want to blow somebody's head off, just once?"

"Just once was all my brother Stefan needed when we were kids," said Bear.
"If he had found Daddy Coleman's gun just that once, while he was stark raving
mad at me, you wouldn't have anybody here to calm you down right now."

"What were you guys fighting over?" Walter paused behind the couch.

"Who knows? He was a hot-head. He exploded," said Bear. "I ran outside in
my holey draws and waited in the dark until my mom said it was safe, however long
that was. I think her running interference is what kept him from finding the gun."

"You never talk about your family," said Walter, squeezing his man's shoulder. "I wish it hadn't been so bad for you."

"It wasn't so bad," said Bear, massaging his man's hand. "It was life. *Then.* Which led me to you. I'll never call anything that led me to you *bad.*"

"I don't know what to say," said Walter.

"How about: you won't waste one ounce of your energy thinking about blowing somebody's head off?" asked Bear. "Because that's one ounce of energy I'd rather you'd spend loving me, or letting me love you."

"Sometimes I don't know if I deserve you," said Walter.

"Then it's a good thing it's not your call," said Bear.

"My crazy Bear," sighed Walter, bending over the couch to hug his buddy. "You know I'm better than Everett."

"No doubt," said Bear. When it came to football, Walter's reality was Bear's reality. No other truths need apply.

HOLMES EASLEY GOT THE START and the win at Detroit. The following week, Easley and a partially hobbled Everett steered the Rams to a narrow loss at Atlanta. The good news: Walter Yeager stood in the state of Georgia without wanting to use a gun.

The Rams, led by E&E, got off to a 2-4 start, and the local media had their quarterback controversy. In week seven, Dallas came to town, and a Rams beat reporter hyped up the possibility of a battle of the rookie QBs: Yeager vs. Troy Aikman of the Cowboys. Whatever the reason, in the third quarter of a scoreless game, Walter and everyone who loved him finally heard the heavens announcing his dream come true:

"Now in at quarterback for your Rams ... Number 13 ... Walter Yeager."

Bear and Mama Rent sat in the stands, touching knees as a way of acknowledging the thrill. The Rams played their home games at Anaheim Stadium, a multi-purpose facility that reminded Bear of an orange triangle. For this game, the team was in their road whites, and Bear savored the sight of his buddy jogging onto the field to save the day, taking charge of his first official NFL huddle. At Walter's games, Bear was the *serious black man,* his aura just this side of *don't fuck with me.* But Mama Rent couldn't restrain herself. She applauded with the rest of the crowd, although Rams fans were just happy to see a new face, regardless of his name or credentials. On his first play ever, Yeager handed off to Greg Bell, the team's top running back. On second and 11, Walter dropped back for the first time and threw ... an interception ... that was dropped ... and ruled an incomplete pass, saving two buddies from a collective heart attack.

On third and 11, Yeager dropped back again, looked both ways, then saw Flipper Anderson cutting across the middle, right to left. Walter fired a bullet into the receiver's numbers. Flipper caught it in stride and ran for another six yards before being dumped by Mark Walen and Jack Del Rio. Yeager's first NFL completion was good for a first down and 15 yards. A smattering of fans rose to their feet, applauding demonstratively. Bear and Mama Rent smiled at one another, then Bear glanced across the orange triangle, imagining the Yeagers bursting with an equal amount of joy. Bear also felt the adrenaline racing through his and Walter's body, but the rush was on. The next play was already happening. The *rush* was a blitz. Walter had to scramble just to get rid of the ball and avoid a loss. Life in the NFL moved much faster than Saskatchewan.

"*That drive ended in a punt, but the former Roughrider led the Rams to two field goals, and set up this Greg Bell rushing touchdown late in the fourth. Final score: Rams 12, Dallas 3. It's unclear what Georgia thinks, but Yeager might be the new meister of Ramsland.*"

"Turn that crap off," laughed Walter from the bed in Corona that night. "Wait, lemme see it."

"You love it, Yeager-meister," said Bear of the ESPN report on Walter's debut. "Which Georgia did he mean?"

"Who cares, *shh!*" said Walter, mesmerized by the onscreen version of himself, talking to a collection of microphones in the locker room.

"*That's a coach's decision based on what's best for the team,*" said Yeager. "*Whoever's called upon will be expected to step up. Period.*"

"This from a man who claims he's not good with words," said Bear.

"I'm better on the fly than when I have to plot and plan it all out," said Walter, going under the covers to spend some face time in the zone.

"You get the job done, Yeager-meister," said Bear. "Man, do you ever."

THE DOOR TO THE CONDO in Newport Beach opened, then slammed shut. Walter was riding the stationary bike in the living room. He was covered with sweat and up to speed with the latest headline in their world: the British company that owned the rights to *The Bridges Between Us* wanted to detonate the bridge.

"I know it's risky meeting here, but get this," said Bear, indicating the letter in his hand. "They want to turn *my* movie into ... *The Bridges of London.* A snooty English family—*the Bridges*—travels to Mexico for wacky adventures. They're accompanied by ... Mofallo, their streetwise Jamaican butler who's a womanizer with a stuttering disorder. Oh, and, he's not gay *or* HIV-positive!"

"Insanity," said Walter, still going on the bike.

"It's *Monty Python Goes to Cancun!*" said Bear, flinging the script like a Frisbee through the room, causing the pages to float like scattered showers.

"It's *Monty Python* with no Bear," said Walter.

"I am not here on this earth to create *this!*" said Bear, flinging the manila envelope across the room. "I would blow somebody's fucking head off first."

"That's my Bear!" yelled Walter. "Get pissed! Let's go shoot people! Fuck yeah!"

"All right then, let's do it!" said Bear, double-daring Walter's dare.

"Just once, right, Bear?" said Walter with a cocky half-grin that said, *Welcome to the dark side.* Bear eyed him with a blank expression.

"You know, you're the only white man I know that can make me shut up," said Bear, disappearing into the bedroom. "Sometimes!"

"I'm gonna fold and take that as a compliment," said Walter, laughing and pedaling faster.

"You know very well," yelled an occupied Bear from the bedroom, "that I can ... *geez!* ... create something way better ... *whoa!* ... *way* better ... *wow!* ... way better than *Mofallo and the Snooty Bridges ... of London.*"

"Then show 'em!" said Walter. When it came to writing, Bear's reality was Walter's reality. No other truths need apply.

"I'm gonna," said Bear, emerging from the bedroom with a Joe Bruin grin. "I can practically smell the thrill of victory now."

"Don't be stealing all my stuff now," said Walter, nodding to Bear's greedy little paws, which were holding a laundry basket full of Walter's unwashed work-out gear.

"I get lonely way out there in my own little Corona," said Bear, giving his man a kiss before heading for the door. "I'll buy you more; we can afford it. We're the big league boys!"

Walter laughed his mild laugh, shook his head, and pushed onward with his cardio.

For the rest of the year, the writer fought for a better movie, while the quarterback fought for a better ranking on the Rams' depth chart. Coleman and the Brits ended up playing to a tie, as Bear put it. *The Bridges Between Us* turned *The Bridges of London* became *London Bridge,* a warmhearted story about an English family healing old wounds during a Mexican vacation, all inspired by their Jamaican butler, who comes along to spread his grandmother's ashes in the Pacific, granting her one last dream.

London Bridge wasn't Bear's original vision of *The World Meets an HIV-Positive Black Man,* but it wasn't *Monty Python Goes to Cancun* either. The important detail was the launching of his second career: storyteller. And while

Coleman honed his wizardry of the landscape of dreams, Yeager honed his wizardry on the football fields of his dreams.

Over the next several Rams games, Everett got the start, but Yeager saw action by the second or third quarter. "We'll show a montage," said Bear in bed in Corona one night, "just like the one on ESPN right now. In *The Walter Yeager Story*, we'll have some crazy rock music, like 'Welcome to the Jungle' by Guns N' Roses, and we'll show all your greatest first moments in the NFL."

"How's the writing?" asked Walter in bed in Newport Beach. He muted the tube to listen to Bear on the phone.

"Look, the 26-yard scramble against *da Raidas!*" said Bear, "and the four-yard keeper for a TD against the Giants!"

"How many times have you seen this?" asked Walter.

"What else am I supposed to do at three a.m. when you're not here, sleep?" asked Bear.

"Ah, see. They gotta show the interceptions, too," said Walter. They paused to watch Carl Banks of the Giants tap a Yeager pass into his own hands and scamper 10 yards into the end zone.

"*Ouch,*" said Bear, more focused on the shot of Yeager getting clobbered by big bad Lawrence Taylor. "How did it feel, meeting LT?"

"Not as good as the hot time in the desert," said Walter, more focused on the sequence where he was slicing up the Phoenix secondary with two touchdown passes on consecutive possessions.

"Please don't show—ah, they had to show it." Bear fell silent, watching Reggie Snowman nab two of Yeager's passes during the Redskins' visit to the orange triangle.

"Now I really need some Sugar to get to sleep," the boys said together.

BEAR'S EYES BECAME as big as saucers. The deafening roar made him dizzy, as did the rush of suddenly rising to his feet. He was wavering on top of a skyscraper—the stands at Mile High Stadium were so damned mile high. The crowd around him was stomping and swaying, warming up their lungs, all for his man—the visiting QB's—guts ...

"*Whoa!*" said Bear, grabbing the shoulder to his right. "This is nothing like Saskatchewan."

"*Or* Anaheim," said Mama Rent.

"He's arrived, Mama!" Bear released his grip on his mother's shoulder and sucked in the atmosphere. The Church of Mile High was a football shrine in the holy gridiron land of Denver, Colorado. Against a backdrop of snowcapped mountains, the stadium was a magnet, figurative and literal. But unlike the horseshoe magnet of Athens and Bear's dreams, Mile High Stadium was shaped like a tuning fork. It worked for the Broncos. More often than not, the team and their mile-high surroundings were an indomitable force.

ABC had just gone live with their Monday night telecast. The tuning fork was rocking and rolling to that quirky tune played at Denver sporting events long before most of the country had ever heard of "The Hey Song." Bear wanted to cheer or do something physical, but he was the *serious black man,* protector of his mother amidst the drunken rowdies. Inside, he was dancing like Joe Bruin because the world was about to say hello to Walter Yeager.

"Bear," yelled Mama Rent, tapping his shoulder and pointing to a young usher boy sizing up their row from the aisle.

"Be back," shouted Bear. Mama Rent nodded reassuringly. She was a pro at sporting events. Bear made his way past the Broncos fans in his row, stopping on the aisle.

"Are you Bob Coleman?" yelled the usher boy. Bear began to correct him, then nodded his head. "Please come with me."

Bear gave Mama Rent one last look, then followed the usher boy wordlessly into the underbelly of the tuning fork. Wherever Bear was going, the usher boy didn't have the answers Bear needed, so Bear remained in his own blur, the sound of Broncomania thundering above him. At one point, they passed a TV monitor. Bear paused to get a drink at a nearby water fountain just to hear the Monday Night Football introduction of his buddy. The telecast cut from an aerial shot of the stadium to a still shot of Walter's freshly scrubbed face, his half-smile filling most of the screen.

"He's 26 years old and has thrown fewer passes in his NFL career than John Elway throws in one month. But Walter Yeager, formerly of the Saskatchewan Roughriders of the CFL, will get his first start ever in the NFL, tonight when the Rams take on the AFC Western Division-leading Denver Broncos."

"Let's do this," said Bear, following the usher boy once more.

"The Rams are 5-9, and many believe Yeager's start is the result of a quarterback controversy, sparked by local radio pundits who have become more volatile in recent years with the deregulation of the FCC ..."

The tuning fork was hostile territory for a man who believed beyond all doubt that Yeager was more golden than a billion John Elways. The Bronco QB was golden to Bear—one of his favorite quarterbacks—but he was no Walter Yeager. The thought alone put a twisted grin on Bear's face while journeying through the underbelly. Before long, the usher faded from sight, and Bear found himself traveling alone down a dark hazy corridor. At the opposite end stood Black Coach, formerly of San Diego, now an assistant with Denver. Bear flashed on an image from pre-game warm-ups, where Walter and his ex-coach had a reunion that appeared quite jovial. Men in the sports world had a great capacity to bullshit with one another without ever revealing any truths. Black Coach had even given Yeager a goodbye pat on the ass.

"You didn't see me here," said Black Coach when Bear reached him in the underbelly. "Glad you're watching his back, as the kids say. Go crack it now." Black Coach nodded toward a large steel door and faded away. Bear found himself in a boiler room. Walter, dressed in his Rams road whites, faced away from the door. Bear started humming the intro to "Eye of the Tiger" by Survivor, the pumped-up sports anthem from *Rocky III*. The quarterback turned around.

"You're in the game. Cool," said Walter, more focused on the boilers that were rumbling, as if ready to explode. A wave of Broncomania rocked the underbelly, the fans above responding to a call to action on the loudspeakers.

"They can't keep me away," said Bear, referring to the challenge to get into the sold-out contest. To remain under the team radar, he traveled to away games on his own, like a regular obsessed fan. "Good weather, no snow, go kick ass," said Bear, reminding himself of a surfer boy.

"For sure," said a distracted Walter. "Kinda overwhelming."

"I bet you can do whelming," said Bear, calling up his urban voice. "I bet you can go kick whelming's *ass* right about now."

"Fuck, yeah," said Walter, still somewhat absent.

"Then what the fuck, man?" Bear lunged his forearm at the QB's chest, shoving him backward.

"Don't do that shit," laughed Walter, looking at Bear for the first time.

"That's what it's gone be like out there!" said Bear, sounding as black as his brothers. "You ready or not?"

"Fuck, yeah, I'm ready," said Walter, coming back into focus. "*You know* I am."

"Then let's get the job done right." Bear extended his hand, Walter followed. They exchanged an impromptu version of a quick urban handshake, and that was that.

At kickoff, Broncomania swelled to a pre-ejaculatory climax. The tuning fork was louder than any venue since Athens six years ago. The Broncos themselves came out as strong as their 76,000 faithful and went up 14-0 after one. Between quarters, Bear imagined the *Monday Night* announcers' game summary:

"*Yeager is still feeling his way around the big stage, Don, but he's starting to move the Rams with two impressive first downs to end the quarter.*"

"Frank and Al, the rookie QB will need a lot more of those to stay in this game. Literally."

In the second quarter, a sustained Rams drive stalled at the 10-yard line, but resulted in a field goal and made the halftime score: Denver 14, Rams 3.

"I'm too nervous," said Mama Rent, watching the Colorado State marching band perform.

"He can do it," said Bear, imagining the Yeager family on the opposite side of the tuning fork, having the same faith in the same man. He also imagined the *Monday Night* crew showing Walter's best highlight of the half, a 46-yard pass to Henry Ellard.

In the third quarter, Yeager and the Rams scored on two field goals, the first off the opening drive of the half, the second after a blocked punt set up a chip shot of a field goal. At the start of the fourth quarter, mighty Denver's lead was only 14-9, and Broncos fans were getting restless with this pesky, whippersnap-per of a rookie quarterback who insisted on spoiling their Monday night party. The teams swapped punts until the clock blurred down to six minutes remaining in the game, at which point Elway seemed to take the affront personally.

Denver had the ball at midfield on third and short. Elway took the snap from the shotgun, scrambled a bunch of crazy loops in the backfield to avoid a blitz, then threw a wobbly pass 40 yards down the sideline. The Denver receiver caught the ball just before going out of bounds. First down, Broncos. Elway ran three plays to milk the clock, setting up their own chip shot of a field goal that made the score 17-9. The pro football world had yet to dream of two-point con-versions, so Yeager took to the field needing two scores in under three minutes. Bear and Mama Rent touched knees as the Bronco faithful around them shouted for their man's guts, limbs, heart, soul—whatever the Denver defense could rip from Number 13 (pigskin optional).

The Rams took over on the 20-yard line, 80 yards away from paydirt, part one. The 76,000 faithful and the Bronco secondary got the best of the Rams' QB on the first two downs. Yeager tried to go long but wound up throwing the ball away both times. On third down, Walter threaded a pass to Ellard, who was streaking across the middle, and the drive was on. Whether the field was in a gigantic stadium or on the little green box that was Mattel Electronics Football, Walter loved getting in a rhythm and marching methodically toward his goal, especially when the stakes were high. That was when Number 13 came alive the most, when he was in control of his destiny, and by extension, the destiny of the world around him.

He connected twice with Flipper Anderson for big gains of 12 and 28, but the drive stalled at the Bronco 12-yard line. On fourth and nine, the Rams used their last timeout, then the head coach decided to go for it, no doubt influenced by Yeager's passionate plea during the break. The tuning fork swayed mightily when the Rams came up to the line. Walter took the snap, dropped back a couple of steps, then lofted the ball toward the far end zone—a fade pass for Flipper Anderson, who was in perfect position to stretch out horizontally and catch the floater before falling back to earth. The conversion made it 17-16 with 52 seconds remaining.

The Church of Mile High got their Monday night victory. The Rams' attempt to recover the onside kick failed when El Kicko booted the ball straight to a Denver Bronco, who retained possession for Elway, who ran out the clock on Yeager. After the game, the Rams head coach had this to say about Yeager's performance in the post-game interview:

"He's showing steady improvement. A drive like that in the fourth quarter ought to be a big confidence booster for him. Hopefully, he'll keep coming together, taking care of the ball."

On a related game note: El Kicko, the Rams' placekicker, is the brother of Del Kicko, the placekicker for the Chicago Bears. *Del* Kicko was Yeager's teammate at Georgia and the Bulldawg who missed the potentially game-winning field goal at the Sugar Bowl.

In the games of life, the biggest stars need the littlest stars, the littlest stars need the biggest stars, and all the galaxies need all the other galaxies, and so on.

Bear stole a glance at Mama Rent, dozing in her window seat of the plane idling on the tarmac in Denver. He enjoyed seeing his mother in first class, the same way he enjoyed whisking her all over the country to watch his man play football. Mama Rent had had what some would call a hard life, living most of it as a single mom raising four kids on a couple of bucks a month. Not that the Colemans were ever without food or shelter. But the years were also never without their great American challenges.

Flashes of Bear's oldest brother floated on the runway of his dreams. Grayson was the original high school stud in the starry eyes of the prepubescent baby Bear of the family. Seven years older, the god-like teenage Grayson possessed dark chocolate muscles *men* of the early 70s didn't have, let alone boys. Bear's body type would end up growing in the same ballpark, but Grayson was a popular and athletic force at his school. When his glory days ended, so too did his dreams. The years since had been tough on him, and by extension, the entire family. Grayson and his mother had had so many arguments about him living at home rent-free, without a job or purpose, Bear began calling his mother Mama Rent long ago.

But there was also another reason for the moniker. It didn't seem fair to Bear that a woman should have to take on her dream man's name, have that dream man turn out to be Freddy Krueger, divorce Mr. Krueger, then have to live the rest of one's life as: Mrs. Krueger, and her four children, Grayson, Evangeline, Stefan and Marcus "Bear" Krueger. Not that Daddy Coleman was a mass murderer like the resident nightmare on Elm Street, but his mother had suffered enough, and Bear called her Mama Rent as a way of providing one less reminder that she was still a Coleman by association. Of course, that would all be moot if there were a Daddy Rent, but for the time being, Bear's mother had deleted any prior knowledge of the romantic dreams of her soul.

"Taking off," said Mama Rent, as if Bear couldn't feel the engines racing through his stomach. He snuggled into her shoulder, then began dreaming of another Coleman who had an abundance of romantic visions ...

... THE LOS ANGELES MEMORIAL COLISEUM was the epicenter of its own personal earthquake. UCLA and USC were tied with two seconds to play. The field goal kicker for the Bruins laid into the pigskin with his heart, soul and leg. The ball sailed toward the end zone 54 yards away ...

Marcus and Mama Rent froze along with the rest of the 90,000 faithful. USC was 8-2. UCLA was 3-7. The occasion was their last battle of the 80s. The ball neared the goalposts ... on target between the uprights ... then started to fall short ... and shorter ... until the ball hit the crossbar, which acted like a big Trojan arm and swatted away UCLA's miracle-in-progress. The college football world had yet to dream of tiebreakers, so the bitter crosstown rivals had to settle for a bittersweet outcome: a 10-10 draw.

Bruin fans streamed out of exits as if they had just clinched a Rose Bowl berth. Marcus and Mama Rent hurried to the parking lot in the shadows of the Coliseum, where they met up with their tailgating crew. The celebration was already underway. They joined in, hooting and hollering and dancing to "Love Shack," the funky hit by the B-52's. The party was a spontaneous combustion of pent-up hopes and dreams, as restless as when the journey began.

For Marcus, it was a victory dance of sorts. He was a month away from officially surviving the 80s, the decade that had taken him from 18 to 28, *his* decade. Here he was at the end of it, alive and well. His dancing: assertive. His attitude about life: *how do I stay healthy and follow my dreams?* His aura: radiant. Even a simple task like grocery shopping could result in a deep conversation with a total stranger drawn to his light.

"He's showing steady improvement. Dancing so freely and happily with

Mama Rent and his friends in the Coliseum parking lot—that ought to be a big confidence booster for him. Hopefully, he'll keep coming together, getting on the ball."

His tailgating crew was almost like a dream come true—a mix of old college friends, including some former spirit leaders and football players. They had found each other over the years at the UCLA games. Now they were regulars every fall, having the time of their young alumni lives.

"Frank and Al, young Marcus will need a lot more of those kinds of days to stay in this game. Literally."

"Coleman is still feeling his way around the big stage, Don, but he's started to move things along with two impressive years to end the decade."

Best of all, Marcus was open and honest with the world about which gender set his sexual soul on fire. He told people when it came up in the natural course of conversation, and he told people with a Joe Bruin smile on his face, matching the Joe Bruin smile in his heart. And much more often than not, the world smiled back.

"What doesn't this handsome, healthy, strapping, athletic, professional writer stud have? Besides a handsome, healthy, strapping, athletic, professional stud for a matching set?"

"Frank and Al, as you can see by the swagger in his dancing—which is very creative, by the way—Marcus Coleman is in some kind of zone. He's at the top of the promo game. He's working on a warmhearted novel about boyhood and bridges. He's even going on dates with some rather attractive men!"

"And call me crazy, Don, but have I heard rumors that he's done chasing after unavailable Jock Gods? Let's go to our sideline reporter Mama Rent for some insight. Mama Rent, can you hear us?"

"Go Bruins go! Oh, am I on now? I'm so proud of Marcus. Hold on ... he's mumbling something in his dreams here in first class, something about letting go of the Walt Yeager dream, so he can focus on having a real man in his real life."

"Don't want that life!" cried Bear.

"Light on or off?" asked a voice from nowhere.

"Turn it off," said Bear, the interior of the plane not yet in focus.

"Talking in his sleep," said Mama Rent to the female flight attendant hovering over Bear's aisle seat.

"Bad dream," said Bear. "Enough light. Right flight. G'night."

16

Bear Gets an Overseer

The infamous boys lay on their backs, head to head on the summit of a hill overlooking the Pacific. Had their eyes been open, perhaps they would have seen the third head of Coach Sanchez. Had they been awake, perhaps they would have heard his voice.

Nap well, you beautiful golden twins. You've earned the rest. You've put enough energy into your dreams for now. Enjoy the magic you've both created. The day will only get more exciting. Merrily, merrily, merrily. Let your dreams power your world ...

The sun was bright and the summer tunes in full swing as the SUV rolled down the highway toward Rams Park in Anaheim, California. "Love Shack," the funky hit by the B-52's, was the current jam filling the airwaves ... until the quarterback killed the music. "Mind if we do *this* decade for a while?" asked Walter, referring to the nascent 90s.

"Go for it," said Bear from the driver's seat. Walter found a radio station more suitable to his momentary liking. An electric guitar was grinding out something quite grungy, a sound that was becoming increasingly popular with some of the newer bands. "Why you looking at me all weird?" laughed Bear, descending from the highway to the surface streets.

"Five years, going on six, living together—" said Walter.

"Seven, going on eight, overall—" added Bear.

"And you still put up with my moods," said Walter.

"What moods?" asked Bear.

"And he means it, ladies and germs!" Walter stretched out in the passenger seat, reclining like a cowboy on break.

"You sure this little detour of ours into the football world isn't *juuuuuust* a little cocky?" asked Bear. "Even for us?"

"Nobody's here," said Walter, more focused on the music. "Anybody important is on vacation before hell breaks loose in a few weeks. I'm in and outta there before you can turn off the radio and finish wearing out one side of your *Bear's Best of the 80s* tape."

"Smart-ass," said Bear, slowing down at the gates of Rams Park.

"*Ha!*" said Walter with a triumphant laugh. "I know my Bear."

"What do you think this brutha thinks I am to you?" asked Bear, indicating the young black security guard who waved the transport onward. "A fellow player or your chauffeur?"

"Can't he just assume we're friends?" asked Walter with an incredulous laugh.

"Remind me to teach you about black people someday," said Bear, parking in the parking lot at Rams Park, home of the team's offices and training facilities. Yeager went to do his football business in one of the football buildings while Bear waited in the SUV. Their next stop was Malibu to look for their dream home.

To pass the time, Bear picked up the magazine on the seat. The Athlon Sports NFL Preview was one of the most popular football annuals. This year, for the regional edition catering to the LA market, Walter was on the cover. The Rams' other young QB, Jim Everett, had been traded. His mug, in all likelihood, was featured on the New Orleans edition.

The full-color shot of Yeager showed Number 13 from his knees up, holding the ball as if about to throw a pass. He was dressed in the Rams' home blues, his helmet off, his energy concentrated in his eyes. The image had been captured months ago in a photo shoot. The caption read: PRIMED AND READY.

"He certainly was last night," said Bear, reclining in the driver's seat and drifting off to dreamland. "And this morning. And this afternoon ..."

... Marcus Coleman climbed atop the stationary bike for a quick warm-up before his workout. The young girl on the adjacent bike beamed *hello*. Marcus beamed *hello* back, then began cycling. Briefly, he took note of her striking looks. She was no more than 19 or 20, with long blonde hair and golden blonde skin. She was talking with someone on the other side of her bike, yammering about roommates.

" ... I might move in with these gay guys," said the young blonde girl, "but then again, I don't know. You know how gay guys are so bitchy."

Marcus, at 28, was determined to show the world another point of view.

"Not all of us," said Marcus.

"Excuse me?" said the young blonde girl.

"Not all of us gay guys are bitchy," said Marcus.

The person she was talking to faded in her periphery. Her eyes became as big as saucers, her mouth big enough to inhale ... a watermelon. Eventually, she would defibrillate her heart and speak her mind, though Marcus would never remember her first words thereafter. Pretty difficult to understand even a young blonde girl when she has two young blonde feet in her young blonde mouth ...

... Bear laughed and smiled a cool and dreamy smile in the SUV at Rams Park. He had just decided that Marcus Coleman of *My Whole Other Life* would have a lifelong best friend in the form of a beautiful young blonde girl. They would meet at the gym, his playground of choice. She would be much younger, to keep his spirit youthful, yet she would inspire him to grow in so many ways. He would return the favor in equal measure. Their bond would be instant and rarely challenged from within. They would get along as easily as Walter and Bear. Marcus might not have his dream man, but he would have Eve.

Lively music sifted through the air in the parking lot, causing Bear to perk up like a dog getting a whiff of something juicy. He cocked his ear to the wind, and recognized the very classic 80s tune, "I'm Your Man" by Wham!, coming from somewhere within the core of Ramsland. "Nothing an agile and plucky Bear can't check out real quick, then get back to the car before hubby," said Bear, slipping out of the SUV.

Several stealth maneuvers later, he found himself on the opposite side of Rams Park, peeking out from behind a wall and surveying an all-too-familiar scene: hundreds of girls and a handful of guys, all of them practicing to be the next great cheerleader. The Rams had dancing girls like most NFL teams, but they also had a co-ed, collegiate-style squad, minus any testosterone. Walter and Bear jokingly referred to the males as the glitter boys, due to their shiny blue pants with gold glitter stripes down the side.

"Those glitter boys better not get anywhere near my man's ass!" Bear would joke.

"You know you wanna be a glitter boy," Walter would joke.

Now Bear had a private peek into their world. He scanned the candidates, all preoccupied and a safe distance away. One of the males looked familiar, but his face was skyward, focused on the girl he was holding in the stunt above his head. She started to look familiar, too. A beat later, the stunt failed. She fell to earth, barely landing on her feet. As she did, Bear realized why both partners looked familiar. He also realized he had stepped out from behind the wall and could be seen by anyone looking in his direction. Casually, he tried to slip from view, then began a hasty retreat to the car.

"Bear? Bear Coleman, is that you?" said a female's voice from behind, forcing the trapped Bear to turn and face the music.

"What are you doing here?" Bear and Roxanne said together.

"You first," said Bear to the former Joe Bruin from his Sugar Bowl days.

"I'm trying out," laughed Roxanne. She extended her arms, as if to say, *Isn't it obvious? Look at my fabulous new body!*

"You do look awesome!" said Bear, noting her significant weight loss. "You'll make it! Gotta go."

"Wait, why are *you* here?" asked Roxanne, grabbing his arm.

"Uh, same reason?" said Bear. It seemed like a better idea than admitting his quarterback husband was making a quick stop at the office before house hunting in Malibu.

"Great!" Roxanne tried to walk away with Bear's arm. "You can be my stunt partner."

"Whatever you're thinking," said Bear, taking back his arm, "un-think it right now. I'm not trying out. Anymore. After all. Gotta go."

"Why?" asked Roxanne.

"Changed my mind," said Bear.

"Because?" asked Roxanne.

"I'm outta shape," said Bear.

"No you're not," laughed Roxanne.

"My life is too crazy," said Bear.

"Maybe I can help," said Roxanne.

"You can't. No one can," said Bear.

"I'm a grief counselor," said Roxanne.

"I'm not dressed for tryouts, see," said Bear, indicating his button-down shirt.

"We can borrow something," said Roxanne.

"Roxanne, I'm too chicken. Good luck." Bear turned away and headed for the parking lot.

"Funny, little Mr. *Bearcat* wasn't too chicken to ruin my entire future back then!" said Roxanne, stopping Bear in his tracks.

"Ex-squeeze me?" said Bear.

"*You* ruined my life!" said Roxanne, approaching a motionless Bear.

"Because?" said Bear, avoiding eye contact.

"My ex-boyfriend?" said Roxanne. "You remember Harry Dawg? We were all set to get married summer after college. I bet you didn't know his mother's side of the family is from Louisiana, did you?"

"Not especially," said Bear.

"My entire family, cousins, aunts—the branch from Armenia no one has talked to since the Great Waffle Fallout—they *all* flew to Red Stick for *my* wedding. I'm in my virgin whites—shut up!—coming up the aisle, feeling like Lady Di, and guess what, Bear Coleman?"

"Make it quick, I have to go," pleaded Bear.

"Harry Dawg's cousin Rupert won the science prize one year," said Roxanne. "They put his picture in the high school newspaper. Guess what six-year-old Wynona—Rupert's great aunt—ran up to show Harry Dawg *at the altar?*"

"Roxanne, I'm sure I don't know—" said Bear.

"You were fooling around on the dock of the Mississippi in *my* costume, and Harry Dawg called off the wedding because he thought *I* was having an affair during the Sugar Bowl because a Georgia QB Loves the Bearcat!" yelled Roxanne. "I tried for years to convince him it wasn't true. I even tried hunting you down so you could tell him the truth. Where have you been?"

"Around, here and there," said Bear, sorta sheepish.

"He was my first love," cried Roxanne. "All ruined over some stupid prank with a random football player you met at the Crab Grab! And did you know that same blond guy is on the Rams now?"

"No way!" said Bear. "I don't keep up anymore—see, one more reason I need to go. I'm in way over my head."

"Then just try me out," said Roxanne. "Be my stunt partner. I need your muscles. Look at who I'm working with."

Bear peeked around the corner of the building and took a second look at Duncan McDuncan, Roxanne's stunt partner whom Bear had recognized earlier. McDuncan was one of the weakest-looking males in the history of Bear's life. His frail body could scarcely hold up the tiny Asian girls, let alone Roxanne, even though she was half the woman she used to be. McDuncan had hung around the cheerleaders in Bear's day but never made squad. Now he looked ill.

"How's he doing?" asked Bear.

"Judge for yourself," said Roxanne.

"I don't wanna judge at all," said Bear, letting out a deep sigh. "How soon are you on?"

"Like, minutes," said Roxanne, wearing a Joe Bruin smile.

BEAR PLOPPED DOWN IN THE driver's seat of the SUV at Rams Park, breathless and astonished. "And where has my Bear been?" asked Walter, sitting in the passenger seat.

"Oh my God!" said Bear, coming out of the blur to realize hubby had already made it back to the car. "You're quicker at everything. Almost."

"*Beeeeeear*," said Walter, bracing himself in his seat. "I don't like the sound of this."

"Then let me change my tune," said Bear, starting the engine, "but first let's get outta—"

"Incoming!" Walter's seat flopped backward until he was out of sight. An intruder approached the driver's side—Roxanne! She reached Bear's open window and shoved a business card under his nose.

"Let's have dinner sometime!" said Roxanne. Bear bit down on the card and hit the accelerator. Then he mumbled indecipherable words as the SUV made a sharp U-turn around the potential Rams cheergirl and sped away.

"I don't like the sound of this tune, either," said Walter from below deck. "And that was?"

"Your ex-girlfriend," said Bear, more focused on escaping Rams Park.

"Roxanne? What happened to her?" asked Walter.

"One of those talk show-type makeovers," said Bear. "You know, where they confront the high school bully because the ugly duckling is hot and sexy now, and the bully isn't."

"What's her bully doing at Rams Park?" asked Walter.

"He's not. He's gonna be at the games on Sundays," said Bear.

"Just my luck, she wants to be a Rammette," said Walter.

"There's more," said Bear, blurring past the young black security guard.

"I'm not feeling Malibu right now," said Walter. "Head home?"

Bear answered by changing directions and steering toward Corona.

"What else?" said Walter, staying below deck even though they were home free. Bear told him about Roxanne and Harry Dawg's *wedding interruptus*, courtesy the QB LOVES THE BEARCAT photo. Momentarily, the SUV fell silent, the guilt settling in. "Maybe it was a good thing," said Walter. "Maybe they weren't meant for each other."

"I didn't think to ask if she was married or anything," said Bear. "I guess we were too caught up in—that's the other thing I need to tell you."

"There's more?" asked Walter, shifting restlessly down below.

"Isn't there always?" cringed Bear, merging onto the highway.

"Lay it on me," sighed Walter.

"I felt bad on two counts," said Bear. "Her and this McDuncan guy."

"Bottom line, Bear," said Walter.

"I tried her out. I was her stunt partner," said Bear. A police pursuit flew by in the opposite direction, a dozen cop cars chasing an old clunker. "Should we wait until we get home to discuss this?"

"Absolutely," said Walter, falling silent the rest of the way.

When they reached the condo, Walter moved about as if the matter were settled. Of course, Bear knew better. Walter lived moment to moment, unlike Bear, who lived *next* moment to *next* moment. The quarterback would get back around to the events at Rams Park on his own time. "Did you enjoy yourself?" asked Walter, once settled on the couch, beer in hand.

"What do you mean?" laughed Bear, sitting across from him on the ottoman.

"I'd feel better knowing you got some satisfaction out of this," said Walter. "I know you'd rather be on the field than in the stands. Like me. So ... did you have fun?"

"I didn't even give them my name," said Bear.

"Did you have fun?" asked Walter.

"I don't want to be a glitter boy," said Bear.

"Did you have fun?" asked Walter.

A gleam flashed in Bear's eyes. He heard music, felt his heart racing. For a moment, he was alive on another planet, a planet where he was a spirit leader again!

"See, I knew it," said Walter.

"I don't want to be a glitter boy," repeated Bear.

"Good, because I don't want you to be a glitter boy, either," said Walter. Bear exhaled a sigh of relief, as if he were no longer in the doghouse. He crawled between his man's legs and made up with a kiss. "If you don't," added Walter. "You gonna call our ex?"

"Nope," said Bear. "I tried her out. Our debt is paid. Trust me, you don't have to worry about her being a Rammette."

"What about my Bear?" asked Walter.

"Yeah, right. Can't you just picture me in the Athlon Preview magazine, in the annual Cheergirls of the NFL spread?" said Bear. *"Glitter boy Bear Coleman's gold only glitters for his glittering blond aura, Number 13, Walter Yeager."*

Walter laughed, then offered up his own worst-case scenario caption: *"Yea-*

ger's offense is powered by Sugar in his tank supplied by Bear 'Glitter Boy' Coleman, glittering Hollywood screenwriter."

"Don't worry, QB," said Bear, snuggling into his man's lap. "We don't need no stinking nightmares, just the coolest and dreamiest of dreams."

A FEW WEEKS LATER, the big league boys were at the kitchen table in Corona, taking care of their big league business before training camp. Walter studied Bear's new contract with his Hollywood agent, while Bear sifted through photos of potential homes in Malibu. The boys made every major decision in their lives together, like two coaches with a mutual respect for the other's point of view. They were on the verge of discussing Malibu when they heard a rare phenomenon: the doorbell. They eyed one another, then the clock on the wall. It was after midnight.

The peephole revealed a large, white lion's mane. When Bear opened the door, his suspicions were confirmed: the lion was a female, who became the third-ever member of the football people to step inside the boys' inner sanctum.

"Evening, Mr. Coleman," said the Lioness, owner of the Rams.

"Yes, it is," said Bear, moving like a zombie toward the living room. Walter stood by the couch, waiting for them.

"And Walter," said the Lioness.

"Talk about a surprise," said Walter. "Can I? Can he?"

"Can I get you anything to drink?" asked Bear. The condo was his place, allegedly without a trace of pro quarterback.

"Have a seat. I need to be brief," said the Lioness.

The boys sat together on the sofa. The Lioness stood and surveyed the condo, gravitating toward the table full of mementos yet to be stored: videotapes of Walter's games; magazines with yellow sticky notes highlighting the pages with coverage of Number 13; stacks of sports pages from all over the country, all of them featuring Walter.

"You've got a good archivist," said the Lioness. "Now you need a better secret service."

"Excuse me, ma'am?" said Walter.

"If your boyfriend is going to be a glitter boy—" said the Lioness.

"I don't want to be a glitter boy," said Bear.

"That's your call," said the Lioness. "Perhaps. Regardless, you two need to build a better closet, if you're gonna continue to be somebody's investment—and Walter, from the looks of it, you have the potential to be somebody's investment for a very long time. Sometimes, I see shades of that old Viking quarterback in you—Fran Tarkenton."

"Can you back up for one sec?" asked Walter.

"You haven't spoken to your lady friend from tryouts, have you?" asked the Lioness, turning to Bear.

"I lost her number," lied Bear.

"I was there," said the Lioness. "I told my assistant: we need *ten* like him."

"Really?" said a flattered Bear, prompting Walter to cough.

"Your lady friend didn't have your number," said the Lioness. "She also didn't make it, sorry to say. Anyway, once she told me your name, I *knew* it sounded familiar."

"Familiar?" the boys said together.

"From your sloppy paper trail," said the Lioness with a mild roar. "You two have left more clues about your love life from Seattle to Saskatchewan."

"We covered our tracks!" insisted Walter.

"To amateurs," said the Lioness. "Moot point now though."

"I was only helping Roxanne by accident," said Bear.

"There are no accidents, only wake-up calls," said the Lioness.

"I have a contract," said Walter. "If this is about morality, Bear and I are doing nothing different than any other player and their spouses."

"And we've been doing it for seven, going on eight, years!" said Bear.

"This is my year. You can't do this," said Walter.

"Pay you a visit?" asked the Lioness. Her gaze traveled from one man to the other, her eyes shifting like a kaleidoscope. "You think I'm here to crush your dreams. You poor fools in love."

"What's the bottom line here?" asked Walter.

"I'm not here to rain on your love parade or your football parade," said the Lioness. "Listen to me. *I* sound like a queen. Anyway. This is about not being stupid."

Walter scoffed, cracking his neck, stalling for time, trying to take it all in. Bear sat motionless, waiting for his buddy's cue.

"After my husband's very unfortunate passing," said the Lioness, "what do you think the fat cats of the NFL said about the notion of a woman at the helm of a sports franchise?"

"*Get that broad outta the game!*" said Bear, sounding like a New Yorker.

"*Bear!*" said Walter.

"I read it somewhere," said Bear in his own defense.

"He's correct," said the Lioness with a wistful glint in her eye. "Back in '79, I'm sure some of the other owners would have rather dealt with a homo over a woman. In fact, in a couple of instances—but that's beside the point. Whether

I was a woman or a homo, or both, I was a Martian to these cavemen. They couldn't imagine a woman in charge of a football team. But you know what? They didn't have to. I imagined it for them."

"I'm still not clear on the bottom line here, as far as my contract," said Walter, prompting the Lioness to eye Bear with bewilderment.

"*He's* cut-to-the-chase," said Bear. "*I'm* the long and winding road."

The Lioness nodded, as if enlightened, then continued: "Did I accept the NFL's reality that I, as a woman, didn't belong? Or was I a bad-assed bitch who dreamt her own dream? A bitch who's now running with the stallions, not to mention the studs?" She gave them a wink reminiscent of Mae West. The boys laughed sheepishly, avoiding her eyes. "Well?" asked the Lioness, waiting for her answer.

"You're the bad-assed bitch!" said Bear. Walter coughed; the Lioness laughed.

"Want to know how I made my dreams come true?" asked the Lioness.

"How?" asked the boys.

"By not being sloppy," said the Lioness with a stern voice. Her face turned grave as she handed Walter a business card.

"Who's B.O.?" asked Walter, reading the card, which only contained those initials and a phone number.

"Mr. Coleman's new best friend, whether he's a glitter boy or not," said the Lioness, heading for the door, "which, by the way, is entirely up to B.O."

"I don't want to be a glitter boy," said Bear.

"I don't understand," said Walter, following her, followed by Bear.

"You will," said the Lioness. "B.O. should be back from Down Under by the end of next week. Give a call—Mr. Coleman, that is. Until then, both of you ... *don't* make a single move."

The Lioness vanished into the night, while the boys stood motionless, as if following her orders literally.

"This is Walter Yeager."

"This is your one and only."

"Morning, One and Only. You home?"

"On the road. Errands. You in Newport?"

"On the road, too. How'd you sleep?"

"Little lonely, but you felt good, holding me in my dreams."

"Sweet."

"When you coming home to Corona, QB?"

"Before camp for sure. How are the people out there treating my Bear?"

"All smiles."

"Cool deal."

"So it's the end of the week, Walter."

"Yeah? Hold on. Buying a paper ... go 'head."

"Should I call this B.O. today? What do I tell him?"

"About what? Oh ... *hmmm* ... when you coming home? Hold on. Doing two things at once. How much is the drink? Is it twist off? Twist it?"

"You know, boss lady Lioness—she didn't seem like evil personified to me, *or* like a piranha, like in that one cartoon with her drowning husband. I wonder if piranhas have certain fish they don't eat."

"Twisted. Do you care?"

"I bet the fish do. To the fish who aren't on their menu, piranhas must be the coolest creatures alive. All in the mind, eh?"

"In the car now, wassup, Bear?"

"B.O., glitter boys, phone call. Decision 1990."

"Okay, okay. Man, I still can't get over how I was ready to stand up to her, even though I was talking completely out of my ass!"

"You were masterful, Yeager-meister."

"Part of me says: Fuck it. If the team owner and this B.O. are cool with you being a glitter boy, how big a deal can it be?"

"I don't want to be a glitter boy."

"Oh, *no!* No! Not him! No! Not now!"

"What is it, buddy?"

"I gotta go. Sports section. It's Python!"

"Wait!"

"Deal with B.O. and keep me in the loop. I gotta get to the office."

THERE WAS A SMALL TATTOO of the initials B.O. on the boulder, just as B.O.'s secretary had promised. Bear planted his ass on top of the tattoo, as instructed, and waited. He was deep in the hills near Laguna Beach, a sleepy artist hamlet south of the football world. The car was parked far away on the main road. As ordered, he had hiked a trail through several canyons and wound his way to this small clearing surrounded by dense forest. He waited for whatever was next and eyed the sports page in his hand.

PYTHON SNAKES HIS WAY OUT OF CINCY

Jeremy Python was a rookie from Grambling, and one of the newfangled, all-purpose quarterback *slash* running back *slash* return specialist *slash* Heisman Trophy winner *slash* Mr. Excitement players—all of whom were causing a reality shift in football. Cincinnati had selected the light-skinned, freckled-face *slash* as the third overall pick in the draft, but the former Grambling Tiger had bigger dreams than toiling away for perennial losers like the Bengals. Over the last 24 hours, his dreams came true. Python was now a Ram and the newest challenger to Walter Yeager's dreams.

"You didn't want it to be too easy, did you, PV?" sighed Bear, looking up from the sports section. A flicker of light in the distant woods caught his eye, then repeated itself several times. As if hypnotized, Bear rose and followed the light. He moved in a daze across the clearing, then farther into the forest until he was deep inside a musty cave. Once there, he was blinded by the darkness within. "B.O.?"

"Behind you," said a man's voice, prompting Bear to turn toward the entrance of the cave. The man's hand cleared away foliage from above, letting in a flood of sunlight.

"Can't see you," said Bear, suddenly blinded by the light from without.

"Don't need to." The hand released the foliage, returning the cave to darkness. "How I look is a detail that is of no concern to your ultimate goals."

"Am I in the right place to meet the right person?" asked Bear. "I'm outta here if you can't—"

"Are you Marcus Coleman?" asked the man.

Bear sighed, partially relieved. "So you're B.O., *whew!*"

"Are *you* Marcus Coleman?" asked B.O, moving deeper inside the cave.

"Legally, yes," said Bear. The smell of filth wafted through the air. "For some crazy reason, ever since I can remember, I've been going by the nickname—"

"How did you and Yeager meet? Wrong question. What's *the story* you give about how you met?" asked B.O.

"We became good friends through his former girlfriend, who was the UCLA Bruin mascot," said Bear.

"Good. Your codename from now on will be ... Bear," said B.O.

"Bear?" asked Bear.

"You know, codenames, like the members of the First Family," said B.O. "We can't go around calling you Marcus Coleman in *this* world, especially with you being the author of that straight-to-video movie outta England—decent flick, by the way."

"You saw *London Bridge*?" asked Bear, talking toward the stench deep inside the cave.

"The old lady's choice," said B.O., "but I digress. Your codename is Bear."

"But people already call me—"

"I make the rules around here," said B.O. "When we do business, your name is Bear. I have a fetish for codenames, okay? No arguments. Got it, Bear Coleman?"

"You're the B.O.," shrugged Bear.

"Moving on," said B.O. A shift in the winds beyond the cave caused a sliver of light to filter inside, making B.O. appear like the fuzzy ghost of a short bald man. "We've destroyed all your messy travel records from the past, including that late night bus to Georgia. From now on, my secretary is your travel agent, and ticket agent for home and away games. And this also is the last time you'll get a whiff of me."

"I'm loving it already," said Bear.

"Now, for the home games," said B.O., "since you'll be a glitter boy—"

"I don't want to be a glitter boy," said Bear.

"Whatever you call it," said B.O.

"If I had to call it anything, I would call it spirit leader," said Bear.

"Like a ghost?"

"Like somebody who lifts your spirits, who always accentuates the positive and counteracts the negative."

"So not like a ghost."

"Like somebody who helps you feel good inside, so you can reach your goal."

"Like a therapist?"

"Like somebody who reminds you of the joy in the world."

"Like kids."

"Like somebody who keeps you entertained when you need it, no matter what."

"Like a stripper?"

"Like somebody who tries to bring out the best in you."

"Like a good parent."

"Like a spirit leader," said Bear. "And my hus—the football players and the fans—their spirits aren't lifted by glitter boys. At least in public."

"Maybe I'm just not right or left-brained, or whatever, to get all this," said B.O. "Bottom line: what does Bear Coleman want?"

"To understand your question?" said Bear.

"When you were a kid, what did you beg Santa for?" asked B.O.

"Hell, if I remember," scoffed Bear.

"I bet that wasn't too fun on Christmas morning," said B.O.

"I'm lost here," said Bear.

"Think back to something you asked Santa Claus for," said B.O. "Doesn't matter if it was the real Santa or your parents—whoever it was that made your Christmas dreams come true. Go back to when you believed *a* Santa existed in your life, and you asked that Santa for something, something you were full of passion over, something you just *had to have,* or life as you knew it would cease to exist."

"At this age, I have a definite answer for that," said Bear. "But the kid Marcus—I don't remember him being so attached to any one boy—*I mean toy.*"

"Either one," said B.O.

"I did ask for a microscope one time, but I don't remember it being a big deal," said Bear. "In fact, I really never played with it. How do you play with a microscope? I guess I never asked Santa for much."

"I'll give you my point for free anyway," sighed B.O. "*Most* kids get passionate over something they want for Christmas. When they do, the quest begins. They know exactly what they want, the color, the size, the accessories, where to get it, everything crucial to their dream. They make sure Santa knows all those details, too. Kids don't take chances. They know how to be very specific about their dreams, because before the world tells them otherwise, kids believe in asking for exactly what they want, then giving Santa and the world a shot at making those dreams come true."

"What if Santa can't afford it?" asked Bear. "Or it's not available in the right color? Or outta stock because all the other boys and girls want him—*it?*"

"You really don't have a lot of practice at this, do you?" said B.O.

"If you mean believing a white man from the North Pole is gonna make all my dreams come true, that would be a definite ... *negative,*" said Bear.

"Kids leave the details to Santa and Santa's helpers because kids understand their miracles don't happen by themselves," said B.O. "It takes helpers they see and don't see, and helpers they know and don't know. This whole Santa thing—it ain't just a marketing gimmick, after all."

"It ain't?" asked Bear.

"Everything around you is here to remind you that your dreams can come true," said B.O.

"The Green Bay Packers," said Bear. "I fell in love with the Green Bay Packers and I wanted a Green Bay everything, t-shirt, ski cap, poster, rain jacket, bobblehead. But most of all, I wanted a Green Bay Packers lettermen jacket."

"I can tell by your glow, even in this cave, Santa delivered," said B.O.

"She sure did," said Bear. "Mama Rent called all over town and finally found a mall a million miles away that had one in my size. We both broke down and cried."

"Would never have happened, if you hadn't believed in Santa," said B.O.

"So what—you're my new Santa?" asked Bear.

"And if I was?" asked B.O.

A gleam flashed in Bear's eyes. He heard music, felt his heart racing. For a moment, he was alive on another planet, a planet where he was a spirit leader again!

"*That* kind of spirit!" said B.O., finally seeing the light.

"If you're Santa, Santa, I have something else I want first," said Bear.

"HE DID IT," SAID WALTER, reclining on his elbows with a blade of grass between his teeth. "Santa came through like a freakin' magician."

"I should have insisted he pull off this little shindig on a night when the Angels had a home game," said Bear, sitting up and peering into the darkness.

"You're still a disbeliever," laughed Walter. "Look at us!"

Their surroundings came into focus. It was the middle of the night. They were sitting on the field at the orange triangle, the Rams' stadium. Since it was summer, the configuration was set up for the baseball Angels, who were out of town. The boys were in centerfield, polishing off their gourmet picnic for two, courtesy B.O. and Bistro de Snaky Lu's.

"What if Santa put cameras in the dark around here?" asked Bear, peering into the stands all around them. "Those cameras could be recording our every move right now."

"Where's the guy who's supposed to be accentuating the positive for *me?*" asked Walter with a mild laugh.

"Remember: I had the more challenging childhood," said Bear.

"Meaning?" asked Walter.

"You're the *glass is half full* side of us, especially when it comes to trusting the outside world," said Bear. "You're asking the *glass is half empty* guy to trust a white man from the North Pole—whose real name we don't even know."

"I asked around," said Walter. "Sounds like Bob Overstreet, some obscure guy in the front office nobody sees around much, computer-type."

"Did you ask if his nickname is Body Odor?" asked Bear.

"It wasn't the stinky cave?" asked Walter.

"Not sure," said Bear, squinting at the darkened dugouts in the distance. "How is this allegedly obscure office guy gonna pull this off without us ending up in the *National Enquirer?*"

"*Or* you could let *him* worry about the details and enjoy the ride," said Walter.

"And how come the PRIMED AND READY quarterback isn't the worried party in this scenario?" asked Bear.

"Bear!" laughed Walter. "The team owner's top secret agent guy arranged *all this*. Why waste time worrying, like we did over the Snowman thing?"

"You trust the Lioness and her B.O. that much?" asked Bear.

"No way!" said Walter, stroking his man's fuzzy head. "My boy's not getting it."

"Getting what?" asked Bear. "What? You're saying ... you mean ... you trust *me* that much? Trust me *how?*"

"To not do anything to wreck our lives," said Walter, kissing his man on the hand.

"QB," said Bear, soft and gentle.

"Besides, I have to admit: I kinda wanna see what you can do," said Walter. "I think you'd be a great asset."

"You've never even seen me cheer," said Bear.

"You didn't have to see me play to believe in me," said Walter.

"You had *nightmare* in your eyes when we first brought up this glitter boy thing," said Bear.

"So did you," said Walter, "but look at us now."

"What—like we can move mountains?" Suddenly, Bear rose to his feet in a mild panic. "Did you just feel something? A quake?"

Walter paused. "Nope."

Bear rotated in place, panning the orange triangle. "A pro football spirit leader. My buddy believes I can do it."

"What happened to me and you being able to do anything we want?" asked Walter. Bear turned to find the quarterback also standing.

"What do you think it would be like?" asked Bear. "If it all went absolutely perfect?"

"It'd be great having my Bear doing one of the things he loves most, and doing it for me," said Walter. "How would you feel?"

"I would want to do it my way, which would be best for you and the team," said Bear, pausing to make sure he was very specific, like the children on Santa's lap. "And I wouldn't be biased against Python if he ever replaced you."

"How would it make you *feel?*" asked Walter.

"Good," said Bear. "Mostly. You?"

"Good," said Walter. "Mostly good, especially if I focus on my job and you on yours."

"I can see it now," said Bear. *"Ladies and gentlemen, Walter Yeager and your Los Angeles Rams. And introducing Bear Coleman and the Rugby Boyz!"*

"Rugby?" laughed Walter.

"No more glitter," said Bear. "The guys'll wear short sleeve polo-style shirts in warm weather, and rugby jerseys in cooler weather and at public appearances. With athletic warm-up pants either way, so we look more like team trainers than cheerboys."

"See!" said Walter. "We need your amazing mind."

"Well, if you're ready, and you're really sure you wanna do this, let's imagine having a great year," said Bear. "And cut to the song 'I Got You' by James Brown, the R&B classic better known by its subtitle, which is what we're gonna make the LA Rams shout: *I Feel Good!"*

A gleam was born in Walter and Bear's eyes, so bright, the darkness inside the orange triangle exploded into a spectacular show of light, sound, and action.

"Ladies and gentlemen ... let's hear it for your Rams!"

Yeager got the team off to a solid start with home wins against Tampa Bay and Philadelphia. Touchdown passes: 3. Interceptions: 4.

Coleman got the rugby boyz off to a solid start, considering eight of the 10 males on the squad were "bitter boys" because they had signed up to be glitter boys, not this "rugged, rally jock," as one bitter, ex-glitter boy had said before quitting.

Yeager had trouble on the road early in the season. The mighty San Francisco 49ers, led by Joe Montana, crushed the Rams 52-12. Yeager had no TD passes, two picks, two fumbles, a severe thigh bruise and a mild hamstring pull. The following week, Yeager returned to Chicago for the first time as a pro. The hobbling Illinois native split QB duties with rookie Jeremy Python. Neither man had much success. The Rams lost, 30-13.

Coleman used the off weeks to hammer home his message to the spirit leaders, seeing as how he was captain. "The females will be females," said Bear at practice. "The males will be like regular guys in the stands, you know, only regular guys who urge the crowd on from the sidelines: no arm motions, no dancing, no jumps, no splits, nothing a regular guy in the stands wouldn't do. In public, at least."

"So you want us to be Neanderthals," said a bitter glitter wannabe.

"And pump your fist in the air," said Bear. "Let the girls do all the shaking. Trust me, you'll get the hang of it. Right, Duncan?"

"Right on, Cap!" said Duncan McDuncan. Forever grateful for his first-ever gig as spirit leader, Duncan McDuncan was Captain Coleman's most loyal ally. He had also gained weight and his health was better than ever, thanks to his cheer dreams come true (and Bear's daily food deliveries). *Could have easily been me,* Bear explained when McDuncan questioned his daily generosity.

Meanwhile, the Rams settled down and put together a nice winning streak. A friendly competition ignited between Yeager and Python. The white, more traditional QB brought the team into focus when the Rams became too wild and out of control. The black, newfangled QB led the team when they became too predictable for their own good. Python was learning, and so was Yeager.

At Atlanta, Walter threw an interception in the end zone. The Falcon defensive back decided to try and run it back one hundred yards for six. He danced and juked his way down the field, in and around the flailing arms of the Rams. Determined not to let the pick lead to ultimate glory, Yeager hunted down the DB and tackled him on the two-yard line. The Atlanta offense, not the DB, would end up punching it in for a TD. "The hamstring's fine," said Bear to Mama Rent. They were both smiling like Joe Bruin, enjoying their great seats on the road, thanks to B.O. Final score that week: Rams 38, Falcons 28.

Midway through the season, the rugby boyz found they could still have fun expressing themselves without kicks, spins and glitter. At first, some of the bitter boys were demonstratively masculine, as if mocking the average fan. But a funny thing happened on the way to the big laugh. From afar, the dramatic gestures appeared earnest. Fans responded with great enthusiasm, and the rugby boyz began to discover and appreciate the masculine sides of their souls. Their favorite part: throwing the dames in the air and catching them in ways that never failed to amaze even the bluest of blue-collar workers.

The 2-2 Rams won five straight with impressive performances by Yeager, Python, the rugby boyz, and the rest of the ball club. Next up: a home game for the 7-2 Rams against the 1-8 New Orleans Saints, a breeze of a week, or so it seemed, until Bear read the morning sports page a few days before kickoff.

"Oh, *no!* Not him! Not now!" cried Bear from the kitchen table.

"What is it, buddy?" asked Walter, spending a rare morning in Corona. He was at the counter, making his morning protein shake.

"Sports section. It's what's-his-name! He's coming!" said Bear.

"Everett? So what!" said Walter, more focused on stuffing the blender.

"It's who's coming *with* him!" said Bear, eyeing the black and white photo.

Quarterback Jim Everett, formerly of the Rams, was not having a good year in New Orleans. In addition to their dismal record, Everett was caught up in a war of words with a local announcer guy, who kept referring to the struggling QB as Chris Evert, the female tennis legend. Now, in a studio interview gone wild,

Jim/Chris Everett had used a chair to smash the head of the local announcer guy. The whole thing had been caught on tape—the sports section photo showing the moment of impact.

"The caption says the guy is formerly of KWAZ Mighty Mouth Radio," said Bear. "It's that evil and *k'waaaay-zy* guy."

"Evil *what?*" said Walter, his voice rising several octaves. He turned on the blender. Bear was too panicked to stop talking, but Walter didn't hear anything until his shake was ready.

"... nightmare on the field," concluded Bear.

"No nightmares!" said Walter, covering his ears. "I'm in the zone! No negative shit!"

"But—"

"*Bear!*" Walter grabbed the jar of the blender and abandoned the kitchen, covering his ears and singing "Nothing's gonna stop Walt now" to drown out further toxicity. "Check out the real estate, not the sports section!" said Walter before disappearing from the condo.

Bear eyed the photo of Evil Announcer Guy, the reporter from the Sugar Bowl who had hounded Joe Bruin for a comment on the QB LOVES THE BEARCAT story. Even as Jim Everett's chair smashed into his head, the announcer sported a devilish grin, as if privately relishing the abuse, and secretly dreaming of the coverage making him a bigger star.

If nothing—including Evil Announcer Guy—was gonna stop Walt now, the spirit leader was going to have to deal with ghosts, after all.

LIVE AND IN PERSON, Evil Announcer Guy looked pretty much the same as he did while getting his head smashed by a chair. The devilish grin was still there, as were some very big teeth. The slick and oily hair could have been attributed to the light rain, but Bear was sure the man was just as slick and oily without the assist from Mother Nature. For the entire first half of the Saints-Rams game, the spirit leader's vision never wandered far from the security threat.

"Everything okay, Captain?" asked Duncan McDuncan at one point.

"So far," said Bear, more focused on the shadowy figure across the field.

Because of the rain, the game had a gloomy feel. Or maybe it was just the endless amount of turnovers, punts, and "jerking off for field position," as Walter called it. Even the crowd was subdued. Many fans had been prepared to harass Jim/Chris Everett, but the televised altercation had left the QB back in New Orleans with a broken hand. Instead, Evil Announcer Guy stalked the sidelines triumphantly without an opponent, accepting adulation, applause and boos, any kind of attention the local Louisiana announcer could get. By the fourth quarter, the score was only Saints 10, Rams 3. Yeager hadn't done much all day. Python relieved him for part of the game but was now out with bruised ribs. It was all up to Number 13.

"Captain, I hate to tell you this, but you've been stinking it up today," said Duncan McDuncan midway through the fourth quarter.

"You're right. *I've* been *k'waaaay-zy* instead of getting the crowd crazy," said Bear. "Thanks, McDuncan, let's do this."

The rugby boyz and cheergirls ran around the stadium, rallying the crowd and the offense with a sense of urgency. The 7-2 Rams could not lose to the 1-8 'Aints. LA had the ball at midfield, the clock dwindling. Yeager took the snap from shotgun and flipped a shuttle pass to Gaston Green, the running back. Green scampered for eight yards, the biggest gain of the half. The crowd responded. The drive was on. With under two minutes left, the Rams got down to the 16-yard line, but on second down, a befuddled Yeager had to call timeout at the line of scrimmage, prompting frustrated Rams fans to boo.

That's somebody's baby, people.

Bear tried to stare daggers of sensitivity into the crowd in the end zone, the same end zone in which the Rams were trying to score. Yeager came back on the field a more assured leader. But coming out of the huddle, there was more confusion in the backfield. The play clock was running down. Yeager looked to the sideline for help. The crowd yelled at him like a bad dog. He had to burn another timeout, letting the air out of the crowd's momentary hopes. "I Got You (I Feel Good)" by James Brown filled the stadium. Bear tried to shore up the restless fans in the end zone. He threw his cheergirl up in the air, and with his arms extended over his head, caught her by the soles of her feet. The fans swooned, then began cheering again. Yeager came out of the huddle. There was no confusion this time. From his vantage point in the end zone, Bear was closer than ever to Walter Yeager, professional quarterback in action.

Walter barked out the signals, then the offensive line took a breath and moved in unison. Walter ran to Bear's left, then pitched the ball to the fullback, who ran laterally in the backfield. The exchange created a new center of gravity, with each body in the space inside the orange triangle adjusting accordingly to the new reality of the situation. But Bear always followed *his man* before all else, to make sure *his man* was doing just fine at all times. And so Bear noticed *his man* disappearing into the chaos, slipping past it and emerging all alone in the end zone! But Yeager slowed down because he was running out of end zone (and right toward Bear). On top of that, the ball was taking its own sweet time wobbling its way to the quarterback turned receiver, so much time that several Saints caught up with Yeager and dove in desperation as Number 13 leaped up and reached for the ball.

The next thing Bear saw were the top rows of the orange triangle, then the cloudy sky. Walter and the Saints had swept him off his feet. It was a peaceful trip and subsequent vacation, while it lasted, but there was always so much work to do when it came to *his man*. People were slapping Number 13 and grabbing him. A few hands were patting *his man's* ass! People were also slapping Bear and grabbing him. A few hands were rubbing the top of his head. But unlike Yeager, who was on his feet, Bear was on his ass, surrounded by rugby boyz, not football players. No matter, Bear had a big ole Joe Bruin grin on his face. *His man* had scored a touchdown! Bear staggered to his feet and heard the crowd roar. Walter loved making comebacks, in Mattel Electronics Football, in NFL Football and in the games of life.

But Bear's senses were telling him to undergo yet another reality shift. The crowd sounded angry. The score was still 10-3. Yeager had been ruled out of bounds. The touchdown had been reversed. Bear stood astonished, only to find a microphone under his nose. "Did that collision hurt?" asked Evil Announcer Guy, who had fallen off Bear's radar.

"Not yet!" said a wide-eyed Bear. Just then, the crowd erupted. Flipper Anderson, the Rams wide receiver, was celebrating in the other corner of the end zone. Yeager had thrown a touchdown pass, a legit one. Bear used the distraction to flee, not stopping until he was in the underbelly of the stadium. He drank from a water fountain to calm his rattled nerves.

"You okay?" asked Evil Announcer Guy, having followed him. Bear stood upright with a mouthful of water, then shook his head and covered his lips, as if to say, *Me No Speak*. Evil Announcer Guy eyed him curiously, then said, "Do I know you?"

The crowd exhaled as if tragedy had struck. Bear hurried to the brink of the field. The Rams had missed the extra point. The score was now 10-9. LA would need an onside kick and a miracle. They got one (miracle) in that Evil Announcer Guy left Bear alone to cover the breaking news on the field, but there was still the matter of rugby boy Bear Coleman's collision with Walter and the Saints.

Bear envisioned the footage making those sports blooper shows, which could spell disaster for Walter, especially if Evil Announcer Guy was anywhere near the scene. There were seconds to go in the game, the teams preparing for the onside kick by El Kicko, the pint-sized kicker whose helmet was twice as big as his head. Bear searched the underbelly for inspiration, but was too distracted by a nearby commotion.

Three young girls were begging their mother for ice cream from an adjacent vendor and his cart. The mother, a voluptuous young woman, was digging in her purse for money but couldn't find any, partly because her huge boobs kept getting in the way. She tried to placate the girls by pleading with them to "wait until grandma comes back from the little girls' room," but the daughters were impatient. The tallest, not more than five, danced in place restlessly, while the toddler fell repeatedly on the concrete floor. The middle girl, perhaps three, kept lunging farther away from her family, as if ready to bolt and find her own ice cream. She had inherited the go-getter gene from one of her parents. She also gave Bear all the inspiration he needed.

"You're recording this, right?" asked Bear, sitting shoulder to shoulder with Walter in bed in Corona.

"*Shh!*" said Walter, cranking up the volume of the report on the Saints-Rams game earlier in the day.

"*First Yeager scores on this pass from fullback Tip Carson in the waning moments of the game—and what a wild collision with the cheerleaders—*"

"Spirit leaders!" cried Bear.

"*—but you ain't seen nothing yet. The TD was waved off, and the Rams had to do it again, which they did, on this pass from Yeager to Anderson. But ... El Kicko misses the extra point, the onside kick fails, Saints run out the clock, and upset the Rams. But ... the highlight of the week: call her a mom who works hard for her money. Young Grace—she wouldn't give her last name—ran onto the field near the end of the game in search of some lovin'.*"

"Look at my girl go!" shouted Bear.

"*Shh!*" laughed Walter.

"*Grace and her two happy friends—who aren't worried about their lack of support—surprised Number 13 on the Rams' sideline as the Saints ran out the clock, planting this whopper of a kiss on Walter Yeager. After she was arrested, Grace said an unidentified source paid her $500 cash in advance to kiss the bachelor quarterback.*"

"Thank you, God, for ATMs," said Bear.

"*After she was released into the custody of her mother a short time later, Grace said she did it—get this—for ice cream money for her three children. That's what you call some big scoops, Joanne in the studio, back to you—oh, Rams, lose to go to 7-3. Next week, big test at Cleveland, should be a victory if Python starts, not the ice cream quarterback.*"

"Up yours!" yelled Walter, about to throw the remote.

"Why give *him* the pleasure?" said Bear, reaching for the remote. Walter straight-armed him away, inadvertently clicking to another channel.

"*Shh!*" said Walter. This channel featured a close-up of him heading off the field after the game.

"*How was the kiss?*" *asked an unseen male reporter's voice.*

"*Anything for ice cream,*" *said Yeager with a mischievous grin.*

"*Which would you rather have, a kiss or a win?*" *asked the unseen male reporter's voice.*

"*A winning kiss, this much is true,*" *said Walter, continuing onward.*

The station cut to highlights of another game. Walter turned off the TV and eyed Bear, who was sporting a bashful grin. "This much is true" was a reference to "True," their very first song.

"That's the first time you said those words on the air," said Bear.

"This much is true," said Walter with a grin.

"Is that ... you just ... you just acknowledged me on the air," said Bear.

"This much is true, too," said Walter.

"My buddy." Bear rested his head on his man's shoulder and snuggled into his torso. "Sorry I couldn't give you a winning kiss."

"I don't deserve it," said Walter. "I have flashes of brilliance, then times when I lose it. Completely."

"Having me on the sidelines isn't working out," said Bear. "Today just proved it."

"I love the way you handled it, crazy as it was," said Walter. "It was typical Bear. Nobody cares about the collision, just her jugs. You saved the day."

"This time," sighed Bear.

"You're not enjoying this, are you?" said Walter.

"Yes and no," said Bear. "You?"

"Yeah and no," said Walter. The boys fell silent and stared at the blank television, not knowing how to articulate the yes or no part of the equation.

The momentum that was the Big Ram Machine all but died after the Saints loss. The team's strong start dissolved to a 9-7 finish and a wild card berth. Perhaps it was the wickedly tough schedule down the stretch. Perhaps it was injuries to several key players. Perhaps it was the tandem of Yeager and Coleman coming up short.

Python got the start for the playoff game. The Rams hung tough but lost to the Redskins at Washington. Reggie Snowman, now known as Snowman the Showman, returned two interceptions for scores. The silver lining was the completion of Yeager's second full season as an NFL pro, and a future so bright, the boys decided it was time to realize yet another dream.

"WHAT SHOULD WE NAME IT?" asked Bear, standing in the driveway with a box in his arms.

"Our house needs a name?" asked Walter, standing next to him with a box in his arms.

"It does if this black boy from the projects is gonna live his dream," said Bear.

"You're not from the projects," said Walter.

"It should have a name," said Bear. They stood on a ridge overlooking the beaches of Malibu. The sun was about to set on a warm winter day. The boys had just inked the deal and were about to step into their first real home together.

"It's quiet here," said Walter, indicating the shrubbery separating them from their neighbors. "Like a hideaway."

"Our first real hideaway since Canada," said Bear. "But of course!"

"Guess that settles it," said Walter with a mild laugh. "New Moose Jaw, or just plain Moose Jaw?"

"You plan on returning to the CFL?" asked Bear.

"Welcome to Moose Jaw," said Walter, flashing a decisive half-smile.

Home was a modest, two-bedroom beach cottage with an unobstructed view of the Pacific on the backside of the property. The boys set their boxes on the kitchen counter, then admired the horizon beyond the patio door.

"Do what you want to the house, just gimme the view," said Walter.

"Here you are!" said Bear, excited over his discovery in one of the boxes.

"Where?" asked Walter.

"The program from the Georgia game," said Bear.

"You mean, the UCLA game," said Walter, joining him near the counter.

"The UCLA-Georgia game," said Bear. "The season opener. I've never seen this. I thought Mama Rent had it. Look at you in your gorgeous yellow polo shirt. That's the same shirt you were wearing the night we met!"

"When I showed up at the frat party?" asked Walter. "Man, I look young."

"Yeah ... definitely ... this'll be all he needs," said Bear. "He'd fall for you, just from this picture."

"You must be talking about Marcus of *My Whole Other Life*," said Walter.

"*That* Marcus wouldn't have met you, but he would have cheered at this game and gotten this program," said Bear. "If *I* had never met you and saw this photo, I'd be mesmerized for life. *He'll* be mesmerized in my script."

"Dream on," laughed Walter.

"I would. You'd still be my dream buddy," said Bear.

"*That* Marcus would have forgotten me over time," said Walter. "Besides, he'd have no idea how I look now, or ever, other than that one shot."

"Not exactly," said Bear. "I'm gonna write it in the script that Marcus saw the piss 'n' vinegar photo of you from spring ball, you know, the one where you look like you're rarin' to *go play some football!* That way, Marcus'll know you were just as crazy and cocky as I was at that age, if not more so."

"Only in my boy's amazing imagination," said Walter, retrieving a radio from the box.

"He wouldn't need to see anything else, Walter, trust me," said Bear. "He'd see all your inner beauty. He'd see your soul."

"Let *that* Marcus have his own fun," said Walter, scanning the dial for a radio station. "I wanna have a celebration dance in Moose Jaw with *this* Marcus, aka my boy, Marcus 'Bear' Coleman."

"He is the romantic one, Rams fans," said Bear.

"Reception's lousy, but whatever they play after this commercial will be our first song in the new house, okay?" Walter led Bear to the center of the kitchen. They waited arm in arm, but instead of a song, they heard a jingle, announcing the beginning of *Greg the Gut's Sports Report.*

"*... brought to you by Snaky Lu's Soul Food Kitchen, Hollywood and Harlem ... first football news ... the Rams ... essentially ... their future ... in pythons, as in quarter ... Python. Today ... team traded his ... Yeager, who leaves the Rams after two seasons ...*"

Walter lunged for the radio to clear the static.

"*... team spokesman ... this to say: 'We're getting a great skill position player in return, and Yeager ... with team better suited to his talents.'*"

"What team is that?" yelled Walter.

"We've just been traded?" asked Bear.

"*... Cody Rutledge should make a big impact for the Rams right away as a defensive specialist ...*"

Walter turned off the radio. The boys knew the identity of Cody Rutledge's former employer. They also knew where they themselves were headed next.

Around and around and around, or so it seemed.

17

Walter's Emergency Wife

Walt and Marcus lay on their backs, head to head on the summit of a hill overlooking the Pacific. Had their eyes been open, they might have noticed Coach Sanchez standing over them, one foot pointing downhill. Had they been awake, they might have heard his voice.

Nap well, my golden twins. You're resting in earnest. You've put enough dreams into your energy for now. Enjoy the creation of your magic. Dusk is in sight. Oh, boy, what a night! Merrily, merrily, merrily. Let your world power your dreams ...

THE DEN WAS EMPTY EXCEPT for the stacks of unpacked boxes. "I don't know where to start," said Bear, standing in the epicenter of his new world, talking to Mama Rent on the phone. "Or what to call this place. We were supposed to be settled in Moose Jaw by now, not here. Again. Now Malibu will only be our off-season home."

"I was afraid something like this would happen," said Mama Rent.

"This cabin itself is fine," said Bear, circumnavigating the boxes. "There's only one bedroom, but I prefer something cozy while my man is out making football magic. Plus, the 'hood is great, just a bunch of rich white timber people who come up here to hide, just like me—and QB when time permits."

"Your little black head is gonna stick out," warned Mama Rent.

"The homes are isolated, we're not stupid," said Bear, his mother having struck a nerve. "Besides, my pro football cheerleading days are over. At least in public. I'm a professional screenwriter living in the woods. What's the big freakin' deal?"

"None," said Mama Rent, backing down from the growling grizzly.

"I have to go," said a surly Bear. "I hear my husband. He's back from *his* new port in town." Suddenly, Bear brightened. "Hey, that's it! *His* Newport. *My* Corona. *Seattle!* Thanks, Mama, I'm a genius! Hubby's here! Gotta go!"

The blond aura came through the front door but didn't appear joyful. Bear assumed it was the madness of the move. "Your condo in the city: Newport, Seattle," said Bear. "This place here: Corona, Seattle. Get it?"

"Let's go," said Walter with a nod toward the door.

"Lemme get my jacket," said Bear, understanding his man was in no mood to talk. They drove in silence, Bear sitting in the passenger seat, enjoying the change of scenery from the blank walls of Corona, Seattle. The afternoon air was ripe with the scent of pine and a morning rain. Walter put on some lite jazz, and eventually, he began breathing again.

Light years away from the cabin in the woods, the SUV came to a stop in the industrial area near the Seattle Kingdome, home of the Seahawks, the boys' new team. They were parked in front of a small concrete building. Walter got out, Bear followed. Walter pushed a buzzer next to a steel door, then eyed the security camera hovering above them. The door unlocked; the boys went inside.

The interior was dark, like a cave. Walter moved forward, Bear followed. The concrete floor descended, forcing them to travel as if going underground. Eventually, the pathway leveled off, and the darkness morphed into dimness, caused by a pool of light in the distance. A young black woman crossed in front of them, right to left, pushing a file cabinet on wheels. The quarterback halted and held up an arm in front of Bear. Walter nodded gracefully to the woman, who nodded back. When she was past, the boys continued toward the light, which was hanging above a table. They sat in the two chairs on their side and waited for someone to sit in the lone chair on the other side.

The stench of a flowery perfume wafted through the air. High heels clicked across the concrete with staccato determination, reminding Bear of those funky cadences from the drum lines of black college bands. Suddenly, the cadence went awry. The heels tripped, then stumbled into the pool of light, throwing a tall curvy blonde against the table. She was the most beautiful woman Bear had ever seen, with long blonde hair and very long blonde legs coming out of a short black skirt—the bottom half of her bosomy black business suit. She straightened her wire-rimmed glasses, set her briefcase on the table, then straightened the rest of her. Oh, and the suit was quite bosomy.

He's going to marry her, thought Bear.

"I'm Tammy," said the blonde, standing over the table and extending her hand to Walter. "Your new wife."

"My new *who?*" Walter scooted backward but stopped short of standing.

He's not *going to marry her, thought Bear.*

"Really more like your emergency wife," said Tammy, sitting down and opening her briefcase directly in front of her bosomy suit. "Think of it like this: In case of potential media disaster, break glass and wed me."

"I've never seen this woman in my life," said Walter to Bear. "I thought this was about B.O."

"I can change perfumes," said Tammy.

"Bob Overstreet," said Walter. "He works for the Rams."

"Is that a baseball team?" asked Tammy, looking through her briefcase.

"It was my team until a few weeks ago," said Walter.

"In what sport?" asked Tammy.

Walter and Bear eyed one another, bewildered.

"I have several endeavors of my own," said Tammy, looking down her nose. "No time whatsoever to follow your career."

Walter and Bear eyed her, bewildered.

"*Or* I can do ditzy." Tammy scoffed and twirled a strand of her long blonde hair. "Like, I root for the teams with the best colors for my sunny complexion! Oh, and I like the cute furry animals on the field!"

Walter and Bear eyed her, astounded.

"Tammy Du'Hard will give you whatever you want." Tammy winked at Walter, then turned to Bear: "Except sweets, I know." She sized up the quarterback over her wire-rimmed glasses. "*Hmmm*, what a shame."

"Do you know what team I'm on?" asked Walter.

Tammy laughed. And laughed. And laughed, whipping her blonde hair around like a boomerang, forcing the boys to flinch backward. When she came to her senses, she dabbed away tears.

"Why, you're on the biggest and best team in all of sports," said Tammy.

Walter and Bear eyed her with blank expressions.

"You're both babes." Tammy produced a handkerchief from her briefcase—dramatically, as if she were a magician—then used it to blow her nose. "But the way you run the offense like a gunslinger—or Joe Montana, Jr., in my personal opinion—you'll be big-time real soon."

"What the—" said Walter.

"Too big for Santa," said Tammy, "but never too big for Mrs. Claus."

"You—" Walter fidgeted, reminding Bear of the Cardinals game two years ago in Tempe, Arizona.

Yeager under center ... steps back ... there appears to be some confusion ... or maybe he doesn't like the formation shift on the other side ... takes another quick read ... checks the play clock, got time ... nods to his receivers ... he's good to go again ...

"Game on," said Walter, his confident half-smile matching the confident half-smile of his ER Wife.

"Ready for another one?" asked Walter, leaning on the rail.

"Ready if you're ready," said Bear, leaning on the rail.

"Here we go again," said Walter. The boys took a collective breath and stared straight ahead. The meeting with Tammy was behind them. Another NFL season was just up ahead. They stood on an old bridge over an unfamiliar waterway, having lost their way after leaving the industrial area near the Kingdome. Night had fallen and the view from the bridge was breathtaking. In the distance stood the glistening skyline of Seattle and the glorious peak of Mt. Rainier, unseen but felt just the same.

"Are we ever gonna visit the Space Needle?" asked Bear, eyeing the towering landmark.

"Dream of it," said Walter. "So what do you think of my ER Wife?"

"She's got legs," said Bear.

"Funny, I thought you couldn't keep your eyes off her breasts," said Walter.

"The song 'She's Got Legs' by ZZ Top," said Bear. "That'll be her theme song in *The Walter Yeager Story*."

"Get a good vibe from her?" asked Walter.

"I'd feel better if the Rams' front office didn't just tell us B.O. was no longer reachable," said Bear, referring to their phone call moments earlier.

"Maybe he's gone Down Under again," said Walter.

"What does the gut-instinct guy think about his new and bosomy pretend chick?" asked Bear. "So long, supermodel Ivanya Elle M'vanya. *Growllllll.*"

"Puts a lot of potential Seattle nightmares to rest," said Walter, turning away from the skyline, back against the rail. "You're legitimately set up as my manager now, so we'll have an excuse should we need it. Tammy Du'Hard's my steady girl, no more mindless dates. You and your mom are set for all the games.

And Tammy's gonna *du* her *Hardest* to make sure nobody's the wiser about our personal lives—have I left anything out of this best-case scenario?"

"Better-case scenario," said Bear, "not best."

"What could make it better?" asked Walter.

"Knowing who these people are on this so-called *biggest and best team in all of sports,*" said Bear with an ominous voice. "I keep thinking of something B.O.'s secretary said once, when she thought she put me on hold: 'If pro sports was based on morality, we'd all be out of gladiators *and* jobs.' What if this 'team' is like some secretive, controlling, mafia, CIA-operative-type thing? Or worse?"

"*That* would only happen in one of your wild and crazy movies," laughed Walter. "The secretary was probably having a conversation that had nothing to do with you or me. Besides, they're not controlling our lives. They're making it easier."

"But why?" asked Bear.

"Because I'm that good. *Hello?*" said Walter. "I'm an investment worth some special favors from the North Pole."

"You know I don't doubt Walter Yeager," said Bear. "Sometimes, it all sounds too good to be true, especially the way society and sports are so homophobic."

"Don't take this the wrong way," said Walter, "but you're sounding a lot like your mother."

"How can this 'team' pull this subterfuge off?" asked Bear. "And what did Tammy mean by *planting seeds in your honor?*"

"Bear, would you look at me?" Walter placed his big blond hands on Bear's shoulders. "Do I look stressed out? Anymore? You don't have to worry for me, or you. It's gonna be okay, okay?"

Bear saw the lack of crinkles in his man's forehead and finally got it: QB said it was all going to be okay. Bear sighed, pressing his cheek into Walter's hand, then kissing that same hand before turning to the skyline.

"Maybe I won't finish that really angry script I started," said Bear.

Up Yours was the story of a pissed-off pro quarterback and his spirit leader boyfriend who drive a motorcycle from Seattle to Washington, DC to blow off a homophobic Senator's head.

"Great," said Walter. "You stop the script, I'll stop the divorce proceedings."

"I wasn't gonna go through with it," said Bear, sounding disappointed. "I bet I would write something like it in *My Whole Other Life* though."

"Has *that* Marcus found his man yet?" asked Walter.

"Still searching, and kinda getting discouraged," said Bear. "Duncan Mc-Duncan, the rugby boy—he told me how a lot of guys who tested positive a few years ago, their health is starting to decline. Plus, it can be hard to find other gay guys who are willing to date positive guys. He's got it pretty tough, a lot tougher than either one of us."

"McDuncan or *that* Marcus?" asked Walter.

"I guess both," said Bear. "Just more reason than ever why I don't want us to screw up our lives, with Tammy, with being back in Seattle, with anything. We can't take for granted any blessing we have, Big Norse."

"Bear. I leave for camp in the morning," said Walter. "For the first time since the trade, I feel like our world won't go imploding in on us just because we got traded back to Seattle, home of our split-second, halfway-open, semi-gay, whatever-you-call-it life. I can feel it now. This is my team. I'm gonna make shit happen here. Somebody out there likes us. Does it matter who or why? I just wanna ride the wave with my Bear!"

"You're leaving in the morning," said Bear, reminded of what mattered most. "We need to stock up on Sugar." He moved closer to put his arms around his husband.

"Not on the bridge," said Walter, tenderly grabbing Bear's wrists while eyeing the Space Needle. "Let's go find someplace quiet for just the two of us."

NUMBER 13 WAS GROWING UP and learning how to conserve his piss 'n' vinegar for just the right moments in his life, like the night before training camp with his buddy, and training camp itself, where Yeager made the Seattle Seahawks his team from day one.

The electricity in the locker room was palpable. The franchise had never achieved much glory in its 15 years of existence, but a *Sea* change was in the air. The general manager was aggressive in the off-season, adding what many in Seattle hoped were the final puzzle pieces to a solid future. An attempt to sign free agent Hail Larry McPherson of Kansas City failed when the former Auburn receiver signed with San Francisco. But Yeager had been acquired, as had another Georgia Bulldawg, who came struttin' into the locker room that first day, the thunderous beat of a rap song in his headphones.

"Yeager-man! You double dawg! You make me sweat!" said Reggie Snowman upon seeing Walter, who was at his cubicle, already dressed in his official gray, PROPERTY OF SEATTLE SEAHAWKS t-shirt and shorts combo.

"'Sup, Showman?" said Walter. "Where's my royalties?"

"Speak up! Listening to my new album, *Freak of the Week* by Snowman the Showman!" said Reggie, indicating his portable CD player. "In stores now. Get it all wet, spank it in the vet!"

"I want residuals," said Walter, counting with his thumb and fingers. "Albums, movie sales, concert sales. Did you get paid to host that MTV awards show?"

"I always get paid before I get laid," said Reggie, rapping to his music and talking to Walter at the same time. "Going in and out. Coming 'round and about. Still doing Bear hugs? Love who you want, just pass me a joint."

"I gave Snowman the name Showman," said Walter to the naked big white body in the next cubicle.

"We on the same team, man, ain't that some shit?" said Reggie. "Get it, Reggie! Get it, Reggie! Get it, Walter!"

"Serious shit," said Walter, tying his shoe on a chair.

"Never thought you'd be on *my* team!" said Reggie. "Gimme the bitches, but stay away from my riches. Never thought I'd be on *your* team, either, you and your bad news Bear! Bad news bitches, ain't gonna steal my riches."

"How's that?" laughed Walter, nodding over Reggie's shoulder to another player passing by.

"He's a freak, a freak, a freak of the week!" said Reggie, then he shouted across the room: "Gator-man, hold up, fool! Yeager, we gotta team up and bust some shit, *aiight?*"

Walter looked at him with a blank expression.

"I'm a freak, a freak, a freak of the week!" said Reggie, strutting away to the music in his head. "Freak, freak. Be cool, man. We cool."

"*Can you believe that?*" asked Walter on the phone from training camp that night.

"So what team is Reggie on?" asked Bear from the bed in Corona, Seattle.

"The Freaks," said Walter. "But that wasn't the only weird thing. All day long, I got the feeling players still see *me* as the hound dog. With chicks! Like I was in college! What kind of seeds did my wife plant?"

"Not wife," said Bear. "ER wife. And from the sound of it, you won't need to *break* her in case of emergency any time soon."

"Ain't that a blessing," said Walter.

"Now that you put it that way," said Bear. "Thanks, baby. I was about ready to hate this woman, and here she is, spreading nasty rumors instead of her legs."

"I can't tell if you're serious or not," said Walter.

"Whatever Walter wants," said Bear.

"To see Bear happy," said Walter.

"Then Walter should be ecstatic," said Bear.

"That's my boy," said Walter. "I mean, Bear."

"I'm your Bear and your boy," said Bear. "And tonight I'm gonna cozy up in my little cabin in the woods and dream of us having a great first season as Seattle Seahawks."

"Sweet," said Walter. "Dream on."

"*STARTING QUARTERBACK FOR YOUR SEATTLE SEAHAWKS ... NUMBER 13 ... WALTER YEAGER!*"

The 65,000 Seattle faithful hailed their new messiah charging across the turf with great confidence, his blond aura as bright as ever in blue, green and silver. "Go Seahawks go!" shouted Mama Rent, elbowing Bear in the gut as a way of sharing the moment. Even Bear, normally the *serious black man* at games, had to smile and applaud more than usual. The Kingdome was packed for the home opener vs. the Jets. Bear had been a fan of the city's indoor stadium until he saw it in person. There was simply too much concrete, on the drab interior, on the honeycombed exterior, even on the scalloped-shaped shell of a roof. "You're going to be playing in a nuclear reactor," Bear had said the day Walter was traded.

"At least it's a loud nuclear reactor!" shouted Mama Rent as the Jets kicked off to the Seahawks. She was right. For the first time in his pro career, Yeager had a raucous crowd behind him and a distinct home-field advantage.

"Let's do *dis!*" said Bear, knowing that between Seahawks fans and his own all-star squad cheering in his mind, the year was gonna be a good one.

Yeager took care of the Jets 20-13, though it took a 33-yard pass midway through the fourth quarter to break a 13-13 tie and seal the deal. On the play, Walter scrambled in the backfield for a good eight seconds before launching a spiral into the back of the end zone to the waiting wide receiver, the highlight of the week in the NFL.

After road losses at Denver and the LA Raiders, Yeager and the Seahawks rebounded with solid wins against Indianapolis and Cincinnati. The following week, the LA Rams visited the nuclear reactor. Yeager spotted Rams' QB Jeremy Python a 24-6 halftime lead, then put the hurt on the Rams in the second half. Final score: Seattle 42, Lambs 27. Walter had 314 yards passing, but ESPN was more impressed with his running game that day.

"*Here's Yeager on third down in the third quarter, supposed to be a shuttle pass, but it hits the running back's heel—now that's a live ball; it hasn't touched the ground! What does Yeager do? 'Oops, look at what I got. I think I'll take off running in circles ... oh, how about I go this way now ... oh, no, there's big bad Jackie Slater. Let me see if I can slip past—okay that was easy .. oh, now here's a clear path ... see ya, Rams!'*"

"They were down 24-12 at that point. Yeager gets the crucial first down, as if he's saying to his team: 'I'll take you there!' Turning point in the game and maybe the season, if you're a Seahawks fan."

"We are and it is!" said Bear, sitting in bed in Corona, Seattle that night.

"*Shh!* Here it comes," said Walter, sitting next to him.

"Call this one: Ice Cream Kissing Bandit, Part Deux! Last year, Yeager gets a kiss as a Ram against the Saints. Now, here he is today, getting a kiss as a Seahawk against the Rams. Not the same woman, mind you, but she, too, was arrested. We can only assume she also did it for the ice cream money."

"She didn't say, now that I think about it," said Walter, muting the TV.

"She did it because you're the most beautiful man to ever walk the face of the universe," said Bear. "Wait, did I say that right?"

"She did it because I'm a football player," said Walter. "It's unbelievable how many times I see stars in people's eyes."

"I get that look just for *looking* like one of you," said Bear. "At the Kingdome, I've had people actually tell me: 'You must have played football. You should have if you didn't.' They're telling *me*, a total stranger, what to do with my life. Why doesn't anyone ever come up and say, 'I bet you're a rocket scientist?'"

"Because there are no black rocket scientists," said Walter, "in *their* minds anyway."

"Black rocket scientists," said Bear, drifting inside his imagination.

"He's fading back," said Walter.

"Somewhere, some hard-working black mother bought her kids a microscope and ignited a passion for science," said Bear.

"Looking for some open room to run," said Walter.

"And those two kids became *Rocket Brothers!*" said Bear.

"Touchdown, Coleman!" said Walter.

"Close to the goal line anyway," said Bear. "There's definitely a movie idea there. Walter Yeager, you just planted another seed. My, my, my, you are one prolific and potent QB these days."

"To PITTSBURGH WE GO, WHERE THE STEELERS' game plan of blitzing Yeager as early and as often as possible did not pan out, as time and again, Yeager was able to scramble out of danger and lead Seattle to a 27-7 victory. Reggie Snowman ran back this partially blocked punt 58 yards for a touchdown, and for the second time in as many weeks, Yeager was surprised on the sidelines by a female stealing a kiss for what she said was ice cream money."

"Meanwhile, as the season wears on, sources report that Bear Coleman cannot

concentrate on his new screenplay about black rocket scientists due to the increas-
ing number of women kissing his husband in stadiums all over the NFL, including
Pittsburgh, Seattle, Seattle again, San Diego, Kansas City, Seattle yet again, and
Atlanta, where not one, but two different voluptuous beauties got through security
to pucker up for ice cream money—"

The frustrated writer shoved aside his keyboard and reached for the phone. "Tammy," said Bear after the ER Wife answered. "When are these star-struck housewives gonna stop interrupting Walter's concentration? And mine?"

"When do you want them to?" asked Tammy.

"Are you behind this?" asked Bear.

"*Hmmm,*" said Tammy. "Hiring beautiful women to get arrested by kissing your buddy on the football field to perpetuate a cover-up. Who would dream up something so dastardly and extreme?"

"I did," said Bear. "Why couldn't somebody else?"

"Concentrate on your writing," said Tammy, "and cheering for your husband."

"I thought I was." Bear started to hang up. "Oh, Tammy, any word on Bass derVanderkerplunkendorph?"

"Bass?" repeated Tammy. "Oh, the Dane. Apparently, he's no longer a chiropractor in Seattle or the States. Is Walter hurting?"

"No, just hoping to apologize for wanting to kill the guy during the reverse," said Bear. "Gotta go. Go Hawks."

Yeager and the Seahawks finished the season 9-7, good enough for a wild card playoff berth and a home game against Kansas City. Seattle was beside itself with Seahawk fever, but the boys had scant time to enjoy the hoopla. Walter had to prepare for the Chiefs, while Bear was busy with his first official project as Walter's manager. The Yeager Ice Cream Brigade was a new charity where women sold ice cream at Seahawk games and various Seattle locations, with the proceeds going to Seattle's Pediatric AIDS organizations. Bear figured it was the best way to keep Walter's female fans off Walter's lips, plus it was a way the boys could do something publicly about the epidemic, by giving to the one acceptable AIDS world pro athletes were allowed to visit.

The franchise and the city loved the idea, especially as a way of encouraging women to stop breaking the law. Bear recruited a small local vendor to supply the ice cream, and sales began over the weekend of the playoff game. By kickoff, the Brigade was a huge hit. The citywide venues became rallying points for Seahawks fans, where mini-pep rallies sprung up all over Seattle.

If only the playoff game itself had been a huge hit.

Bear sighed and fell silent as the scoreboard clock hit all zeros and the air was let out of the nuclear reactor. The game was over and so was the season. The Chiefs won 10-6. The only Seahawk score was a three-yard keeper by Yeager on the game's opening drive. Bear exited the stands alone, glad that Mama Rent hadn't had been there to suffer through the loss. Traveling through the underbelly of the stadium, he heard his man on the monitors stationed on the walls. "We're not going to blame it on injuries," said Yeager. "We just lost to a better team today, this much is true."

"I love you, too, buddy," mumbled Bear.

The world outside the Kingdome was sunny. Only the fans leaving the game were gloomy. Bear moved quietly, sad to be without his QB, sad his QB was without him. He passed the Yeager Ice Cream Brigade booth, which had been stripped of all its festive signage. A brunette woman stood alone in front. She appeared to be crying as if saddened by either the loss or the lost opportunity to buy ice cream.

"Next year," said Bear, continuing onward.

"Bear?" said the woman, prompting him to turn around.

"Hey ... you!" said Bear, scrambling for her name.

"We used to work together at KSEA," said Hail Larry's Wife.

"Right, right," said Bear. "Been that kind of a day."

"No kidding," said Hail Larry's Wife, dabbing her eyes. "I just did my last story for the station."

"Congrats! Where to next?" asked Bear.

"Real estate," said Hail Larry's Wife. "I was fired. I suck."

"No you don't," said Bear.

"I know I suck, okay?" said Hail Larry's Wife. "How are you holding up?"

"Oh, the game?" asked Bear, feigning casual interest. "Yeah, shame for the city and all."

"I can't take another minute here," said Hail Larry's Wife. "Got time for a drink, or do you have to go deal?"

"Got nothing but time," shrugged Bear. Even if he wanted to comfort his buddy, Walter wouldn't be available for hours.

"I know just the place." Hail Larry's Wife picked a spot where they had total privacy and great service: the living room of her condo in downtown Seattle. She was a wine drinker. Bear wasn't much of a drinker at all. By the time they turned off the ESPN report on the day's action, they were hammered. She lay facedown on the sofa, while Bear was slumped over on the floor, back against the couch. Hail Larry's Wife had spent the last two hours telling Bear about her life: how she had no talent except for being a player's wife; how she wanted kids desperately but had yet to conceive; how she was never sure if her husband was faithful; or if she wanted to be faithful to him.

"Where is your man?" asked a drunken Bear after a prolonged silence. "In Kansas City?"

"Kansas City played the Seahawks today," said Hail Larry's Wife.

"They did?" asked Bear.

"Who won?" asked Hail Larry's Wife.

"Not my team," said Bear.

"That sucks for you," said Hail Larry's Wife.

"Kansas City won," said Bear. "Your husband's team!"

"My husband was traded to San Francisco," said Hail Larry's Wife. "You're wasted. I don't care who my man plays for. I just root for my man."

"Me, too!" said Bear, then realized the error of his ways. "Wasn't that a funny joke? *Ha, ha,* how funny was that?"

"Bear, I know," said Hail Larry's Wife.

"Oh, no you don't! I don't know what I'm saying, I'm drunk. See." Bear tried to touch a finger to his nose. Much to his dismay, he succeeded. "Lemme try again." Much to his dismay, he succeeded again.

"Look! A woman's kissing Walter on ESPN!" said Hail Larry's Wife.

"Those bitches!" Bear turned to the TV, then saw that it was only a deodorant commercial. "You tricked me!"

Hail Larry's Wife broke out in hysterics.

"You bitch!" said Bear, causing her to laugh even more.

"And you and Walter are fucking fags," said Hail Larry's Wife. "Get over it already."

"We are not fucking fags, bitch," said Bear.

"All right, you big fag." She staggered off the couch and out of the living room. "And I don't mean anything bad by that, you big fag." She came back with a videotape and stuck it in the VCR. "I used to be this really sucky reporter for KSEA." She plopped down on the couch, remote in hand. "I had this assignment a few years back. They were always trying to give me football stories. I don't want to do football stories. I want to do my own stories. Anyway, I'm in Kansas City one long, wet week ..."

On the TV screen, Hail Larry's Wife interviewed a man dressed like a Native American chief, a Kansas City Chief, to be precise. Suddenly, a drunken Bear stumbled into the shot and bumped into Hail Larry's Wife. "Some players have husbands, not wives," said Bear before vanishing from view.

Hail Larry's Wife stopped the tape and waited for a response.

"What else did that drunken fool say?" asked Bear.

"Relax, I destroyed the master," said Hail Larry's Wife.

"When?" asked Bear.

"Years ago. I found this copy when I cleaned out my desk on Friday," said Hail Larry's Wife.

"Why?" asked Bear.

"Because I was fired," said Hail Larry's Wife.

"No," said Bear. "Why did you destroy the master?"

"So it wouldn't come back to haunt you and Walter," said Hail Larry's Wife. "Isn't that obvious?"

"Wait a minute," said a dizzy Bear. "*You're* on the team, too?"

"No, but my husband is a 49er—no more wine for you," said Hail Larry's Wife.

"So you've known all these years I drove to Kansas City with Walter?" asked Bear.

"You *drove* to Kansas City?" Hail Larry's Wife began to hyperventilate.

"From Canada," said Bear.

"How? I would die! I would stop breathing and die. I *haaaaaate* driving," said Hail Larry's Wife.

"When did you know we were—" Bear paused.

"Gay?" asked Hail Larry's Wife.

"Together," said Bear.

"Uh, on the street when Larry and I first met you?" said Hail Larry's Wife. "I said to Larry after we walked away: 'Don't they make a cute couple?' He said: 'The black cheerguy maybe, but Yeager? No way is my man gay!'"

"Hell, Larry knows?" asked Bear. *His man?*

"He still won't believe it—it's okay, sweetie." Hail Larry's Wife took his hand. "The walls aren't gonna go crumbling down."

"Sometimes I think they might," said Bear. "Like something's gonna cause Armageddon."

"Why would you say that?" asked Hail Larry's Wife.

Bear paused. So much to say, so little practice.

"I. Love. Him. So. Much," said Bear. "And I know he loves me just as much. Everything I feel for him comes back to me in equal measure, so I know sometimes, he must be as scared as I am that something's gonna trip up this fantastic ride and we're gonna lose every shred of dignity—what if we become the laughing stock of the world?"

"Not gonna happen," said Hail Larry's Wife.

"You don't know that," said Bear. "What if his dreams come crashing down because of me? How could I live with that?"

"Can you live without him?" asked Hail Larry's Wife.

"Not in this lifetime," said Bear.

"Can he live without football?" asked Hail Larry's Wife.

"Same answer," said Bear.

"Then deal with it," said Hail Larry's Wife. "And hold on tight to the rails, because the ride is bumpy whether you're a man or a woman."

"I hear all this stuff in the papers about Yeager-monster and Yeager's hot temper," said Bear. "I never see that. *Sports Illustrated* called him the moodiest quarterback in the NFL. He's never moody around me. What do these people know about my man that I don't?"

"Apparently how to piss him off," said Hail Larry's Wife.

"Every *thing* he does makes me happy," said Bear. "He's all about making people happy, making sure things are taken care of, like a good leader. When he can't do that, he gets frustrated as hell. That *is* Walter's hell, not being able to be all the hero he was born to be, just a run-of-the-mill Hubble Gardner."

"The scientist?" said Hail Larry's Wife.

"Robert Redford in *The Way We Were*," said Bear. "Maybe I don't ever see Yeager-monster because no matter what, my buddy's always my hero, even on days like today."

"I'm cutting off the sauce for you," said Hail Larry's Wife.

"Why, bitch?" asked Bear.

"Because you're either too wasted or one sick puppy," said Hail Larry's Wife.

"Because I love my husband?" asked Bear. "God, that feels good to say out loud to someone other than my mother."

"You're still *infatuated* with your husband," said Hail Larry's Wife.

"Walter and I spent too much time apart in the beginning," said Bear. "That alone makes us treasure every moment. We remember all those years knowing the other one was out there, but just out of reach. Matter of fact, I'm missing him something fierce right now."

"You're really in love," said Hail Larry's Wife.

"It works for us," said Bear, dabbing the corner of his eye. "Don't knock it until you've tried it. Speaking of my buddy, I wanna try calling him again. He lost a playoff game today and needs his spirit leader with him, in spirit, if nothing else."

Hail Larry's Wife retrieved the incriminating tape from the VCR and began destroying the footage. Then she went to the kitchen to fetch them some ice cream from Yeager's Ice Cream Brigade. Bear thanked her for getting rid of the evidence, but more importantly, for listening. He'd let some of the stress of living a double life seep out and his soul felt lighter. Maybe life in Seattle, Part II, wouldn't be so bad, after all, especially if Bear had a girlfriend to go along with Walter's emergency wife.

18

How Evil Announcer Guy Earned His Name

The infamous boys rested peacefully on their backs, head to head on the summit of a hill overlooking the Pacific. Had their eyes been open, they might have noticed the sun drawing closer to the horizon. Had they been awake, they might have heard a voice.

Can you feel it? Can you feel him? There's space for you, wherever you want space. If the universe can create infinity outta nothing, and nothing outta infinity, what can the universe do for you? Dream of it. Dreams do come true, if you only believe ...

The large window in the Malibu home office was open, letting in the ocean breeze. Bear reclined in his big leather chair, feet up on the desk. Had he been awake, he might have noticed the spectacular view of the Pacific beyond the backyard. Instead, he was dreaming the morning away ...

... Marcus of *My Whole Other Life* was at a crossroads. Like Bear, Marcus had moved on from the promo dream to follow the deeper dreams within his soul, namely, telling his own stories. Unlike Bear—the successful author of the straight-to-video movie *London Bridge*—Marcus was a freelance writer, struggling to peddle his short stories, essays, articles and novels. He was also struggling financially, emotionally and health-wise. Thirty-year-old Marcus was living in LA. He was still single, still searching for love, and still having more sex than dates, because sex came easy in the jungles where only men roamed.

Marcus had had his share of sex—he was a dawg like every male animal—but he had also had his share of falling in and out of love. The scenarios varied but never the end result: depressing love songs and lonely nights. It had never been in his DNA to fake a relationship. He could only have a boyfriend if the boyfriend was buddy-for-life material. But his buddy-for-life wasn't materializing, while his hopes were dematerializing.

On top of that, the AIDS virus within was morphing in ways that left Marcus uneasy and worried. Outwardly, he appeared fine. Inside, he could feel energy draining from his soul. There were no specific threats to his health, just a general malaise of his aura, and a seemingly irreversible decline in the important HIV-related blood markers. Science had nothing to offer but toxic shots in the dark. His body felt like that of a 60-year-old, not a 30-year-old. "What can I create to help you?" asked Bear, peering through the darkness in his mind.

"The love of my life would be a nice change of pace," said Marcus from somewhere beyond the darkness.

"I don't know how to do that," said Bear. "I don't know how to give you what Walter and I have. I try. I try to write a script for you where you meet a man who's as wonderful and loving as mine. Sometimes, I cast him as a blond, just like Walter. Sometimes, I dream of him being the opposite, all dark and swarthy. I even try writing scenes where you find love with black men, Latinos, Asians. I write all kinds of scenes where you fall in love, but they never seem right and I end up deleting them."

"That explains my shattered heart," said Marcus. "I don't know how to get what Walter and you have, which is why I'm considering giving Walter up. Maybe dreaming of him is holding me back. Maybe I'm creating unrealistic goals. Maybe I'm denying the real love of my life my full energy—whoever he is, wherever he is. I need a man in real life, not just my dream life, as beautiful as that dream life is."

"You've been dreaming of my Walter?" asked Bear.

"From the day I first laid eyes on him," said Marcus.

"You *did* see the photo in the game program!" said Bear.

"And he never left my soul," said Marcus. "I'm not sure where the picture is now, haven't seen it in years. Walt Yeager has always been in my mind. You boys give me hope. You've also taught me a lot about relationships for when I have my own."

"You will, I promise," said Bear.

"If I never do," said Marcus, "at least I will have experienced one through dreaming you up and writing a novel about you guys. Hopefully someday."

"Dreaming *us* up?" laughed Bear. "That's hilarious ... right? ... wait, you've got it twisted ... *this* is the real life ... I got the *real life here!*"

"The light?" asked Walter. "You like the light hitting your desk like that, right?" He was standing next to the large window in the home office in Moose Jaw—the big league boys' off-season home in Malibu.

Walter Yeager of the Seattle Seahawks. True?

"This is true life!" said Bear, pointing to his desk. "You and me. We're true."

"Wake up and eat something." Walter set a tray with lunch on Bear's desk.

"You're true," said Bear. "Always giving me exactly what I need."

"Gotta feed my boy when he's off writing in his dream world and forgets to eat," said Walter. "Only fair I take care of you in *my* off-season."

"Where would I be without my blond twin?" asked Bear.

"Apparently, meeting an 18-year-old Salvadoran boy at a gym in LA," said Walter, reading the script for *My Whole Other Life* on Bear's monitor.

"I'm creating a misguided youth, so Marcus can be a father figure," said Bear. "And the kid will be a son-figure. Get it?"

"Those scenes last night really got to you," said Walter, referring to *Salvador* by Oliver Stone, a film about the recent civil war in El Salvador.

"He was born during a brutal conflict that literally killed the dreams of many a young boy his age," said Bear, reading from his script. "This platonic friendship should give both Marcus and the kid a ray of hope. And hopefully dispel some nasty rumors about who's dreaming who."

"Huh?" asked Walter, sitting at his own desk.

"While you were grilling lunch on the deck, I had this *k'waaaay-zy* dream that Marcus of *My Whole Other Life* is actually the one creating *our* lives!" said Bear, laughing heartily to confirm his sanity. "Like we're just the manifestation of *his* dreams in some fantasy-like parallel universe. How twisted is *that?*"

"Sounds like another crazy Bear Coleman flick," said Walter, more focused on his paperwork. A gust of ocean breeze came through the window and smacked Bear in the face. The sunlight shifted, illuminating the room in a whole other shade of radiance.

"As long as I get *my* life in the end," said Bear.

"You will," said Walter. "What did the fax say about *Rocket Brothers?*"

"Get this," said Bear, picking up the fax. "The studio wants to turn my heartwarming, Oscar-worthy drama about two black brothers who become great NASA scientists into *Rocket Bruthas*. Two ghetto thugs—*Jerome and Jermaine*

Rocket—go to space camp for wacky adventures. Oh, and, they don't get into MIT, *or* build their mother a solar-efficient home, which gets a solar-efficient cross-burning in their new upscale white neighborhood, as in my original script."

"Pure insanity," said Walter.

"I'm gonna tell them yes," shrugged Bear. "I gotta start somewhere. Again. After *London Bridge.* Maybe this won't go straight-to-video, right?"

"I have an emergency wife, who am I to talk principles?" said Walter.

"I'm not so hungry anymore," said Bear.

"Eat!" said Walter. "Do what you think is best. You know I support you all the way."

"*Rightbackatcha,* QB." Bear went back to his script for a while, then missed his buddy across the room. "What you working on over yonder?"

"Financing the remodel," said Walter. "I think we should combine the game room and trophy room into one."

"Whatever Walter wants," said Bear, knowing his man was uneasy about the notion of an entire space dedicated to *The Glory of Walt.* "It'll actually give the room a great feel, like a sports bar."

"That's my boy," said Walter, more focused on his calculator.

"Wouldn't it be awesome if someday we had all kinds of cool friends?" asked Bear. "We could have great parties on the deck, grilling food, playing music. Or all kinds of fun in the game room, playing air hockey, foosball, or video games, all with sports on TV in the background."

"Don't forget the beer on tap behind the bar," said Walter.

"And 'our gang' would be totally accepting," said Bear. "We could be ourselves, open, honest ... sexual. Just like normal—*other*—people."

"Coleman with the save," said Walter, more focused on his paperwork.

"Our friends could be a diverse mix of fun and tolerant people," said Bear, "like in a Janet Jackson video. Wouldn't that be great, QB—me and you having our own cool gang to hang with in this great beach house of ours?"

"Dream of it, little Bearcat," said Walter, opening up his datebook. "But first, put Mom and Pops at the head of the guest list."

To the Yeagers, Bear Coleman was still their son's trusty friend *slash* manager *slash* summer houseguest. Walter figured that by now, his parents understood there were several more *slashes* to the story. Of course, that didn't mean he was ready to admit to sharing the same bedroom with his *slash.* "Or maybe I will," said Walter the night before his folks' arrival. "Maybe I'll see if the right moment presents itself, just for shits and giggles."

The following night, the right moment did present itself. The boys and the

Yeagers were on the deck that bordered the back of the house. They were all stuffed from a great meal served up by the quarterback, now a meister with the grill. Beyond the ridge on which Moose Jaw sat, the Pacific and its steady waves were rocking them to sleep. "Who's ready for bed?" asked Mr. Yeager.

"We haven't even seen the rest of the house," said Mrs. Yeager. "Where are we sleeping? There's two bedrooms, right?"

Bear and the Yeagers eyed the quarterback, who was standing above them, clearing the table. It was one of those times in a man's life when he could go for all the marbles and shock the world and himself, or he could say something vague, like: "Mom and Dad, you'll be shacking up in Bear's room. That way, Bear can either sleep on the couch in the den, or bunk with me in my *humongous* California king bed, which is plenty big for two giants to sleep without disturbing each other."

Walter chose not to shock the world.

"That's *kinda* broaching the subject," said Bear that night in the *humongous* California king bed.

"Man," said a disappointed Walter, sliding under the covers. "That was like bunting to move the base runner over. If you're successful, it's a sacrifice, not a hit. Not history-making."

"At least you came up to bat, buddy," said Bear, stroking his man's head. "I'm proud of my man for that. He came up to bat."

"I need to swat one outta the park," said Walter. "When is that gonna happen?"

"When do you wanna?" asked Bear.

"Wanna see me be the one to come out to the world?" asked Walter.

"It wouldn't be a cakewalk, obviously, but if anybody can do it, it's you," said Bear. "And you know I'd be right by—"

"I'd want you right by—exactly," laughed Walter.

"Nowhere else I'd rather be," said Bear.

"Walter Yeager, openly ... loving his bud," said Walter.

"What do you think it would be like?" asked Bear.

"Pretty tough. Pretty terrifying actually. Like a nightmare," said Walter.

"When you dreamed as a kid," said Bear, "your deepest dreams, like when you were throwing rocks at telephone poles all day, imagining they were wide receivers—"

"I told you I did that?" laughed Walter. "When did I ever tell you that?"

"I dunno. I didn't dream it up," said Bear. "Anyway, when Boy Walter was conceiving of Walter's biggest and deepest dreams, were those dreams beautiful dreams or nightmares?"

"Great dreams," said Walter.

"I bet they had to do with you being a superhero and changing the world for the better," said Bear.

"Get outta here," said Walter with a mild laugh.

"I bet you faced all kinds of challenges and adversity and persevered," said Bear.

"Dream on," laughed Walter. "But keep it down. Parentals on board."

"And I bet you had a great partner by your side who understood you like nobody else," said Bear. "And you guys were like soul mates, totally simpatico."

"Oh yeah?" said a skeptical Walter. "How did I change the world?"

"By using your gifts and fortunate circumstances to help people," said Bear. "By getting people to treat each other better, by eliminating hatred, poverty and prejudice. The thing you can't stand more than anything is people pre-judging."

"Sounds like the dream of this other guy I know, changing the world by being who he is, a special force with great gifts," said Walter.

"If I ever did any good," said Bear, "it would be because I have you."

"*Rightbackatcha,*" said Walter.

"Dream of it," the boys said together, cuddling until they fell asleep.

THE BOYS SPENT MOST OF THE off-season savoring a simpler existence. They played basketball on the half-court in the backyard, biked in the mountains and canyons around Malibu, and like France of their youth, they went days without showering or shaving, content to enjoy the natural aphrodisiac that was *my man and his scents.* Together, Walter and Bear didn't obsess over being perfectly coiffed and presentable. The bond at the core of their universe was unconditional acceptance for the other, even in the absence of unconditional acceptance for one's self. The off-season was when they got in touch most with that bond, then all too soon, the car pulled up the curb, and it was time for the gunslinger to hop aboard the NFL Express.

"Cut to the calendar on the fridge, where today, a red marker announces: *Walter goes to camp,*" said Bear. "Then cut to us, standing in the foyer, saying our annual *see ya.*"

"The NFL Express," laughed Walter, waving at the driver waiting to take him to LAX. "Sounds like a roller-coaster ride."

"But sometimes, we're in separate cars," said Bear. "Sometimes separate cars *and* tracks, tracks that lead all around the world. Sometimes, our separate cars take parallel tracks, and we can hold hands. That's when football season feels nicest, when we can experience the ride together."

"Much better than those crazy loops and twisting spirals we have to do without each other," said Walter, closing the door just enough to sneak in one last kiss. "Left you something in the den to keep you company until Seattle."

"Hope it's what I'm dreaming of." Bear savored their last kiss for some time. "Go play football, Piss 'n' Vinegar. See ya in a few weeks."

The quarterback hopped in the car and the roller coaster took off. His present had been exactly what Bear wanted: the jock Yeager had worn all winter and spring while getting his blond butt beaten by Coleman in basketball (okay, Yeager beat Coleman in basketball just as often as Coleman beat Yeager). The tattered cloth had been accidentally washed once or twice, but it was ripe with Walter. Bear inhaled his buddy's scent and envisioned Walter doing the same with Bear's jock, which was inside the QB's carryon.

The season was almost off to the right start, but Seahawks fans needed a kick-off pep rally. Bear cued up the stereo in the den and cleared the coffee table from the stage. The band broke into "Freak Sweat" by Snowman the Showman, a jamming dance tune that was essentially a rip-off of the current hit, "Gonna Make You Sweat" by C+C Music Factory, the same people who had created Reggie's song.

"All right, Seahawk People. On your feet! Time for another year of Yeager-meister and the Seahawks!"

Bear danced to the invisible crowd at Moose Jaw Stadium, a dance that was part Joe Bruin, part Bear Coleman, and part Seattle Seahawks dancers. "Go, Walter! Go, Walter! Go Hawks!" shouted the lumbering dancer with the prototype athlete body.

"And introducing Bear Coleman and your Seattle Sea Gals!"

The crowd went crazy. Why shouldn't Bear feel comfortable dancing anyway he wanted in the comfort of his own home? It was one of those times in a man's life when he could go for all the marbles and shock the world and himself, or he could follow his true instincts, stop dancing and turn around.

He chose to stop dancing and turn around.

"What a lifesaver!" shouted Bear, coming to a halt just as two tall black men entered the den. The rapper himself, otherwise known as Reggie Snowman, was standing in Moose Jaw, accompanied by a sexy, bald-headed giant that Bear immediately recognized as Carter Jones, the basketball star of the Dallas Mavericks. Jones was only two years out of college, but his hoop wizardry was making him a star attraction in the NBA and on *SportsCenter*.

"Brother Bear!" said Reggie.

"Showman!" Bear removed the jock from around his neck and threw it behind the big-screen television. Then he hastily killed the music. "I was just about to lift weights to your album! What brings you to Moose—Yeager's house?"

"Yo' boy Walter ..." Reggie did his rap, but Bear was too dazed to fully comprehend. There was an introduction with the Maverick, something about the door being ajar, hearing the music, then flying out to camp after some freaky party tonight. By the time Bear's mind caught up with the song and dance, Reggie was wrapping up. "... but I'm done being the Showman."

"Better name?" asked Bear.

"No name," said Reggie. The shooting star that was his Hollywood career had been shot. His two rap albums had failed to climb above 90 on the Billboard Top 100. His Roaring 20s gangster movie lost money. His superhero movie lost money. His *Shaft in Africa* remake lost money. Even his urban clothing line struggled to break even. "I'm bagging all that shit," said Reggie. "Gone lay low for a while. Real low."

"Any blacks out here?" asked Carter Jones.

"Not counting me?" asked Bear.

"My boy here," said Reggie, indicating Carter Jones. "Got a friend who needs a reverse."

"A reverse?" asked Bear.

"Been cursed."

"Bad back?"

"Worst than that."

"Messed up knee."

"Playing in Italy."

"But he heard about a Buck—"

"What the fuck?"

"He was traded from LA."

"Oh, okay."

"And had the reverse."

"In the NBA?"

"Lives near San Jose."

"Plays for the Cavaliers."

"Get outta here."

"And had the reverse."

"But homeboy's even worse."

"He needs an anterior crucial ligament hyperextension cuff rotation, or some shit like that," said Reggie.

"Really?" said Bear, staring blankly.

"Yo' boy," said Reggie.

"My boy?" asked Bear, confused.

"Yeah, you still his back cracker, ain't you?" asked Reggie.

"I crack his back!" said Bear, only now remembering that part of his *slash* duties. "Last we heard, the Dane was traveling around the world, very hard to get ahold of."

"Hold up." Reggie wandered down the hallway. "How do I take a leak up in here?"

"Keep on to the right," said Bear, looking up at the Dallas Maverick.

"So who you play for?" asked Carter Jones.

"Seahawks," said Bear as the phone rang. "Supporter, I mean. Fan."

"You on the team though, right?" asked Carter Jones. Bear started to speak but fell silent. Suddenly he had no idea what kind of team the former Kansas Jayhawk meant.

"Hold up," said Bear, fleeing to the kitchen to answer the phone (husband calling, said caller ID).

"Didn't mean to throw the wolves at you like that," said Walter, on his way to LAX. "I saw them at the front gate, told 'em to say hi."

"They want Bass," said Bear. "And they're not alone."

"What's up with that?" asked Walter. "And where is the Dane?"

"And what team are these people on?" asked Bear.

"Say what?" laughed Walter.

"I can handle it," said Bear. "Have fun at camp, young man."

"Hey, Bear."

"Yeah?"

"Try whelming."

"Got it. Thanks." Bear hung up, composed himself and headed for the living room. Snowman and Jones were huddled together, almost cheek to cheek. They came apart upon hearing Bear, their faces as guilty as Bear's after almost being caught dancing like a Sea Gal.

"Man, there's somebody else I can ask at camp," said Reggie upon seeing Bear. "Yo' boy Junior Jefferson."

"He's healthy?" asked Bear, referring to the stellar wide receiver.

"Is now," said Reggie. "He and yo' boy gone be lighting it up."

The visitors blurred to the door with small talk, then left Moose Jaw. Alone, Bear collapsed on the couch, his mind becoming convinced that Snowman and Jones were on the same team as Yeager and Coleman.

"*Ha!*" said Walter upon hearing Bear's theory. "I can see where this is leading: a crazy movie where everyone in the NFL is homo. And NBA. And baseball. Are you gonna throw in some hockey guys?"

"Sorry, that is wrong," said Bear, sounding like a game show host. "Then again, if they were all exposed to *your* naked aura, why wouldn't they be drawn to the light?"

"*Ha!*" said Walter. He was leaning against a railing bordering the moonlit San Francisco Bay. Earlier in the evening, Number 13 warmed up his gunslinger arm in the preseason opener against the 49ers. Now QB was decompressing and sizing up Alcatraz in the distance. "Reggie and Carter Jones messing around? Bear, did you smoke something with brutha Showman?"

"*Formerly* brutha Showman," said Bear. "I think he mentioned something about his new moniker being Reggie On the Down Low."

"If this much is true, maybe he never told his uncle that I was a 'bear hugger' back in San Diego," said Walter. "Maybe that explains that freaky *rap* session that first day we were Seahawks together."

"Speaking of Reggie's uncle," said Bear. "Was that the same distinguished-looking black coach's head I saw on the Niners sidelines tonight?"

"Denver let him go," said Walter of Black Coach. "Cool he ended up here, huh?"

"Even if he and/or Reggie sold us out in San Diego?" asked Bear. "Granted, Coach hooked us up at Mile High."

"Look at us now," said Walter. "Whatever they did or didn't do, we made the best of it."

"You're right," said Bear. "Be grateful and let it go. We're about to win a Super Bowl!"

Walter let out a mild laugh, which made Bear feel very good about their chances this year. Had QB let out a big *ha!*, that would have meant Yeager hadn't conceived of it as possible. The mild laugh meant Walter was dreaming big.

Bear followed.

THE BOYS TOOK THE PRESEASON TRIP TO THE Bay Area as a sign, as if fate and the football gods were telling them: *time for Walter to meet the Colemans*. Bear's entire family resided within a short drive of his childhood home in nearby Hayward, a home still occupied by Mama Rent, the only family member privy to Bear's private life.

Bear and his mother were close. They joked about anything, including his happy marriage. The other Colemans were like distant planets his orbit had long outgrown. All that infighting from childhood had chilled his relationship with his siblings, and Daddy Coleman was a non-entity who lived on the outskirts of all their lives. The family knew of Bear's close association with the football player, and Bear didn't expect them to be surprised should the whole truth ever come out. To his two brothers and one sister, the big black baby Bear—who used to cheerlead like a little girl when he was a little boy—was the polar opposite of conventional. He'd gone to rival big-time colleges. He'd done cheerleading at both. He'd done promos on television. He'd lived away from Hayward his entire adult life. As such, the faces of his siblings were quite nonplussed upon meeting Walter Yeager, as if to say, *Bear's doing Hollywood movies now. Why should we be surprised he's doing a quarterback?*

The occasion was a backyard barbeque in Hayward. Bear's sister Evangeline told Walter he was tan and beautiful. Like Mama Rent, her eyes glowed at his blond aura, but in her own guarded way. His brothers Grayson and Stefan fell back into their high school jock modes, talking sports, the one thing the men all had in common. They sat around the family's faded picnic table in the afternoon sun, Stefan's four Rottweilers swirling about like playful comets. Bear watched his man telling his brothers why Junior Jefferson was the best wide receiver in the NFL. Walter was a natural with Bear's brothers, in part because Yeager had been in the trenches with bruthas and had dreamed big with bruthas for most of his life, thanks to sports. It was quite a heady sight for the big black baby Bear, the two buddies of his childhood bonding with the buddy of his dreams. He wanted to thank all three men for being who they were, battle scars and all. Instead, as he often did in a group setting, Bear fell silent, savoring the cool and dreamy scene before him. Much later in the evening, Walter and Bear retired to the den, enjoying having the house to themselves while the rest of the family was at the Dollar Movie House, taking in *Bootlegger Boyz,* starring Reggie On the Down Low.

"My brothers appreciated connecting with their dreams through you," said Bear, sitting on the couch.

"Felt good to see everyone enjoying themselves," said Walter, sitting on the couch, arm around his bud. "Amazing how opposite our backgrounds are."

"Not just opposite, *polar* opposite. In just about every way," said Bear.

"White. Black."

"Rich; not rich."

"Raised on the coast; raised in the heartland."

"Family originally from the North; family originally from the South."

"Tight-knit family; loose-knit family."

"Raised in a sunny and optimistic world where thinking dark and scary thoughts made one a freak; raised in a dark and scary world where thinking sunny and cheerful thoughts made one a freak."

"How scary?" asked Walter.

"I was talking about yours!" laughed Bear, showing he had learned a thing or two about scrambling. He got up and sat on the floor between his man's legs. "You know how I imagine us on separate roller-coaster tracks sometimes? I also have this image of us standing at opposite ends of the Earth, you on the North Pole, me on the South Pole."

"Is this a dream?" asked Walter.

"Just an image. It's like your world is the Northern Hemisphere and mine is the Southern," said Bear.

"You're upside down," said Walter.

"Maybe from where you're standing. In reality, there is no upside-down, just space in all directions," said Bear.

"The real Rocket Brother, Seahawks fans," said Walter, massaging his man's head with both hands.

"I'm no rocket scientist," said Bear. "Science blurred by me in school. The only two things I learned were: the moonwalks may have been faked on Hollywood sound stages, and the astrology charts are all off because whatever they're allegedly aligned with has shifted over time. That's it. The rest is a wash."

"So what's with you and me standing on the top and bottom of the world, a world apart?" asked Walter.

"Dunno," said Bear. "It's like something trying to tell me something. The other night, I saw this show about how our planet is bipolar because of the iron core in the middle of the planet. Something about the energy of that core shooting up through the northern and southern tips of the globe, and that's how the Earth balances itself, so to speak, on the poles. And it's not a perfect balance, per se, since the Earth tilts on its axis."

"You know a lot more than you think you know," said Walter.

"To the other planets, Earth looks crooked or tilted," said Bear. "But to Earth itself, Earth is perfectly in balance, because of the poles."

"So without them, we'd be living in a wobbly world," said Walter.

"Exactly," said Bear. "Like a permanent funhouse floor."

"We're talking polar malfunction."

"Polar chaos and disorder."

"A screwy compass."

"Spinning outta control through the vast space that is space."

"Off-balance."

"In a tizzy."

"Fucked up!"

"That's us!" said Bear. "*Not* fucked up. Because you're like the North Pole, and I'm like the South Pole. Our world may look off-kilter to the rest of the celestial bodies, but it works for us. We come from polar opposite sides, but we're perfectly in balance."

"So what explains us being so compatible?" asked Walter.

"That's easy," said Bear. "We spent 21 years wobbling around this not-so-fun funhouse called planet Earth without each other, and we know how not-so-fun and twisted things were before we hooked up. I don't want a world without you. I'd rather be in perfect balance with my other half and his pole."

"Who knew I married such a sexy and sexual rocket scientist?" said Walter, kissing the apex of his man's head.

"Just imagine," said Bear. "Without you, I'd be half a planet with half a pole, trying to balance myself and find my way through this universe like one of those spinning tops we played with as kids. I need my polar opposite, QB. You balance my world, which must mean I balance yours, too."

"You know you do," said Walter, stroking his man's shoulders. "So how scary was it?"

"*Huh?*" asked Bear.

"Your world growing up," said Walter.

"Oh ... the details are no more or less challenging than any American family," said Bear. "I was the youngest, most sensitive, most expressive and most dramatic—in their eyes anyway. We all had our individual shit, plus our collective shit to deal with, like secrets about true parentage, my father's womanizing and temper, just to name a few. Meanwhile, my two older brothers were all about anger because their athletic dreams didn't materialize because of—you name it— bad grades, bad coaches, bad luck, bad karma. My sister was all about building up a tough outer shell to survive her male-dominated world. We didn't know how to love, only attack in the name of love."

"I'm sorry, Bear."

"Don't be," said Bear, pausing to absorb his man's strong yet gentle massaging of his neck. "I remember one time, you told me how it feels when people look at you and all they see is your outer beauty. You made it sound so empty, which I can understand. But I also wondered to myself: what would it be like, to know that you're that beautiful and that people find you that beautiful?"

Walter's legs pressed tighter to Bear's sides. Bear wiped away a lone tear.

"My soul has never had that dilemma," said Bear. "At no point growing up did anyone convey to me that I was worth looking at, or being with, just because I was me. It was conveyed to me that I was crazy and a fag, and that I wasn't going to have any friends, but never that I was a handsome, attractive or lovable person. Or special or worth loving. We were too busy surviving. There was the mortgage on this place, mistresses, secrets and lies, fights, 911 calls. As you can tell by the house and the neighborhood, we didn't have it so bad. We just had it bad enough, bad enough that nobody cared about trampled egos, especially by the time the youngest came along. I learned how to survive alone with just my dreams at a very early age. The first dream I remember was being with you, before I ever even knew you existed. Just being with someone who was perfect for me. Then there was cheerleading. I used to sit just like this against the couch and watch that same old TV and pretend like I was on the sidelines."

"And where would I be without that little black cheerboy?" asked Walter.

"You know how I first became interested in cheerleading?" asked Bear. "I was seven. My parents wanted to get us out of the inner city in Oakland to a better school system, so they moved us here. On the day of the move, the rest of the family left me and my sister here to wait for a delivery. My sister was 12 and excited about junior high cheerleader tryouts. We were right here in this empty room in this empty house for hours. She taught me the cheers she was learning at tryouts. That's all I needed. An empty space, my sister's dream, my sister and me. From that moment on, I became conscious of cheerleaders at every sporting event. Cut to me now, back where it all started."

"So I have your sister to thank," said Walter. "If she hadn't shared her dream, you might have never become mine."

"All in the mind, eh?" said Bear, drying his tears.

THE HUGE VIDEO SCREEN SHOWED a close-up of the football on the tee. Thunderous music bounced off the roof of the nuclear reactor, the crowd of 65,000 on its feet. The football disappeared from the video screen. The Houston Oilers had just kicked off and were racing down the field. Reggie On the Down Low caught the ball at the goal line, danced a little jig, then found a wedge and scampered down the sideline toward the 20 ... the 30 ... the 40. The crowd exploded. Snowman passed midfield with one man to beat, the pudgy Houston kicker from Guatemala. Snowman hurdled over his outhouse frame of a body. The kicker fell backward and did a soccer-style flip kick. His foot barely touched Snowman's leaping leg, but it was just enough to trip the Seahawk and send him out of bounds, head first. The nuclear reactor gasped. Snowman landed on his shoulder pads, then did a cartwheel to his feet and pointed to the man upstairs, thanking him for the run. The Seahawk faithful exhaled, then erupted. Seattle ball on the Oilers' 41-yard line.

"At quarterback for your Seattle Seahawks ... Number 13 ... Walter Yeager."

Seattle was unbeaten after two road wins to start the season. Hopes were running high in the Pacific Northwest. Junior Jefferson, the Heisman Trophy wide receiver from Michigan, was finally healthy after sitting out two years with a foot injury suffered during his rookie training camp. The team had also acquired Mookie Millstone, the former Green Bay running back who still believed he had a few good seasons left in his 36-year-old body and Hall-of-Fame career. The end result, according to the *Seattle Times,* was the "Seahawks equipping themselves with a potent offensive trio in Yeager, Jefferson and Millstone, that— if they overachieve—might put up a good fight for one of the final playoff spots."

"I'd like to shove a football up this reporter's ass," Walter had said, reading the column at the breakfast table in Corona, Seattle.

"Save that PV for the game or the bedroom," Bear had said.

PV turned the momentum of Snowman's kickoff return into six. From 20 yards out, Yeager hit Junior Jefferson in the corner of the end zone, giving the Michigan legend his first-ever touchdown in the pros on the second catch of his career.

"Walter loves spreading the joy," Bear told Hail Larry's Wife, his seatmate for the home opener, "and taking care of business."

"You're enjoying this," said Hail Larry's Wife.

"We both are. Finally," said Bear, clapping to the music with the rest of the worshippers, practically allowing himself a Joe Bruin grin. During the TV time-out, he excused himself for a restroom break. Upon reaching the exit, he saw the backside of a tall man and immediately thought of Bass the Dane, the photogenic chiropractor. Bear started to call out his name, but a trio of diehard Seahawks fans crossed him, their foam fingers hitting him in the face. Afterward, he hurried through the underbelly of the stadium to catch up with the man who might be Bass, but the Dane, or whomever it was, slipped out of sight.

Giving up, Bear turned around and ran smack dab into Wendy Jiu and Lisa Wu, whom the boys hadn't seen in years. Both lesbo ex-cheergirls were in Seahawks jerseys, one in home blue, the other in road white.

"They two still together!" said Lisa Wu or Wendy Jiu.

"You guys are fans?" asked Bear.

"We've had season tickets since we were all hanging out together in Capitol Hill," said Wendy Jiu or Lisa Wu, smacking her partner's arm. "I told you, they're in their own world when they're together."

"We never hung out on Capitol Hill," said Bear, nervous at the mere mention of Seattle's gay neighborhood. The lesbo ex-cheergirls eyed him, as if to say, *What planet are you living on?* Meanwhile, the nuclear reactor roared with approval at the action inside the bowl. "Gotta go. Game on."

"Nice chatting. Or not," said Wendy Jiu or Lisa Wu. Bear nodded and hurried back to his seat to make sure his world was still tilted but balanced. Reggie On the Down Low had just intercepted a pass and set up the Seahawks offense at the Oilers' 30-yard line. Yeager took the snap, ran a play-action fake to the running back, then gunned it straight over the hash marks to a streaking Junior Jefferson, who caught it at the 10 and *gazelled* his way into the end zone. Touchdown, Seahawks. Yeager was taking care of business.

Final score, Seattle 27, Houston blank.

"HEY, AREN'T YOU THE AUTHOR OF *Rocket Bruthas,* that soon-to-be hit movie now in production?" asked Walter, coming up from behind and offering a friendly hand to his manager, Bear Coleman, noted Hollywood screenwriter.

"Not bad for a quick buck that's turning the Moose Jaw master bathroom into one fine spa," said Bear, shaking hands with his client, Walter Yeager, quarterback of the Seattle Seahawks. "When's the last time *you* did something in the blink of an eye that netted that much money?"

"Last Sunday, the Meadowlands, New Jersey," said Walter.

"Good boy," said Bear. "Sometimes, I gotta remind him who's boss, Seahawks fans."

They broke into self-conscious laughter, reminding Bear of how, during their first years together, his man's laugh was more like that of a suppressed little boy.

"We sure about this?" asked Bear, standing on the threshold between the hotel lobby and the ballroom.

"I would be a total wuss if I couldn't invite my own manager to his own concoction," said Walter, scanning the crowded lobby.

"*My* concoction?" said Bear, standing next to a life-size, cardboard version of his buddy. Cardboard Walter was kneeling on one knee, wearing a generic blue jersey with the number 13. His helmet was off because Cardboard Walter was about to enjoy a big delicious scoop of Yeager-meister, his very own ice cream flavor.

"You really think people will get the slogan?" asked Walter, looking at the slogan painted on his cardboard reflection.

"They will after my surprise," said Bear, surveying the sparsely populated ballroom.

"Which I sense you're going to enjoy more than me," said Walter, performing a security check. The Yeager-meister announcement party had barely taken off, but there were clear skies ahead. The Seahawks were 7-1 and enjoying the *bye*, their one week off during the season, usually spent practicing lite, healing aches and pains, and attending functions as a favor to your emergency wife.

"It's a good surprise. For the slogan," said Bear. The Yeager Ice Cream Brigade was so successful, *Tammy*—not Bear—had concocted the idea of Walter having his own flavor instead of a mundane endorsement deal. The party was part of the agreement, as was Bear's involvement in marketing. "After all," said Bear, "I have to have some hand in this if we're going to foster the image that I do more than spit-shine your—"

"Astors approaching from the lobby," said Walter, straightening his suit and tie. "God, I'm uptight."

"Because I'm upfront?" asked Bear, "greeting people as your manager?"

"No, that was genius of the wife," said Walter.

"Steady *girlfriend*," said Bear.

"Right now, I'd settle for a steady ... buddy," said Walter.

"*Rightbackatcha* ... buddy." Bear fidgeted toward the lobby. Between football and the launch of Yeager-meister, the boys hadn't been boys in quite some time. "How much longer can we go Sugar-free like this?"

"Hard to believe we made it to 7-1," said Walter, a firm believer that their sex life had a major influence on the weekly fate of the Seahawks.

"No doubt," said Bear, also a firm believer. "You sure you're not getting some on the side?"

"The Astors!" said Walter, extending his arms to the Astor brothers, owners of the small ice cream company that supplied the Brigade. Bob & Jimmy Astor were local men who once had a dream of conquering the frozen dairy universe with new and innovative flavors. However, before they could realize their vision, an East Coast duo—with a similar name—beat Bob & Jimmy to the punch. Since then, the Astors had relegated their dreams to a smaller orbit, namely the Pacific Northwest and Alaska.

"There's our man," said Bob or Jimmy Astor, shaking QB's hand.

"And his sharp, African-American manager," said Jimmy or Bob Astor, shaking Bear's hand.

"Are we absolutely sure the Pacific Northwest and Alaska are gonna understand that slogan?" asked Bob or Jimmy Astor, eyeing Cardboard Walter.

"They will after his surprise," said Walter, indicating Bear.

"But you're using *Walt* instead of Walter," said Jimmy or Bob Astor.

"That's what most people call him," shrugged Bear.

"I still can't quite describe the taste of Yeager-meister to my wife," said Bob or Jimmy Astor. "So crunchy, yet so smooth. So filling, yet so lite. But how do you put that into words that the average consumer gets, like, *chocolate malted smoothie crunchy strawberry tangy pure sweet ecstasy?*"

Momentarily, the four men stood motionless, lost in four different pure, sweet reveries. "Everyone should have something so cool and dreamy," sighed Bear. "Right now."

"That's why I keep him in the loop," said Walter, putting his arms around Bob & Jimmy Astor. "Gentlemen, there's about 500 gallons over there. Let the taste-testing begin." As Yeager led them into the ballroom, he mouthed to his buddy, who remained at the threshold: *try whelming.*

"I'd rather try a couple of gallons of Yeager-meister," said Bear to himself, watching them move through the sparsely populated ballroom.

"Would you settle for a double-dip of McPherson?" asked Hail Larry's Wife, coming up from behind and straightening her dress. "Sorry I'm late."

"I didn't know you were showing up at all," said Bear.

"Surprise!" said Hail Larry's Wife. "Tammy called. Your model *slash* date for the night canceled."

"Does she still get paid?" asked Bear.

"I have another surprise for you," said Hail Larry's Wife.

"You get paid," said Bear.

"Split two ways." Hail Larry's Wife nodded over her shoulder, indicating her husband lagging behind in the lobby. "*He* surprised *me* and flew home for the night. I had to let him tag along. He wouldn't say no when he found out your husband was here."

Just then, Walter joined Bear, and Hail Larry joined his wife. Suddenly, they were a foursome again, for the first time since the street outside Snaky Lu's Seafood Market years ago. "Talk about surprises," said Walter, shaking hands with Hail Larry, who was busy sizing up Bear.

"So you're still Yeager's man," said Hail Larry, "—ager, *manager.*"

Bear started to respond, but the voice of a reporter interrupted and called Walter away, prompting the 49er wide receiver to shift nervously until deciding which way to break.

"Sticking by freakin' Yeager in case there's a bunch of freakin' homos here," Hail Larry muttered to his wife, then followed Walter.

"Sticking by McPherson in case he says something stupid," Hail Larry's Wife muttered to Bear, then followed her husband.

"Too late for Stupid," Bear said to himself, watching them move through the growing party.

"Maybe if the Sea Gals only do *half* the routine," said Tammy, coming up from behind, along with a mega-dose of flowery perfume.

"Why, are only *half* of them coming?" asked Bear, for some reason not bothered by her scent tonight.

"Do you really think your—" Tammy paused for a security check, then lowered her always seductive voice "—*my* boyfriend is gonna go for the whole song and dance? Wasn't this cardboard cutout already pushing the envelope of his Kennedy-esque modesty?"

"This is what young athletes on the rise do, Miss Du'Hard, what makes their lives so, so ..." Bear searched his mind.

"I still can't describe the taste," said a woman passing by with a bowl of Yeager-meister.

" ... so cool and dreamy," said Bear. "This is how a guy Walter's age feels like a superstar, having a bunch of hot chicks dancing to his very own slogan for his very own cream. *Duh!*"

"I sure hope he's ready." Tammy arched her back and massaged her neck. Bear suddenly remembered she was quite bosomy. He also took note of her long blonde hair falling behind her. And those long blonde legs coming out of her trademark short black skirt.

"Personally, I couldn't be more PRIMED AND READY," said Bear, ogling her two scoops, his mouth getting drier by the moment.

"Then let's hope tonight is the night we *all* get what we want," said Tammy, looking deep into Bear's wide and hungry eyes. "*Hmmm.* Suddenly I'm in the mood for some of your Yeager-meister. Excuse me."

"How about a couple of scoops for me?" Bear said to himself, watching them move through the party, which had suddenly become quite enlarged.

"I've never had such dreamy and cool scoops," said a female's voice from behind, causing him to rotate toward the lobby.

"How in the world ..." said Bear, beaming at the sight before him, consuming loving spoonfuls of Yeager-meister at that! His mind went into overdrive, too busy conjuring to hear the hasty conversion that followed as a result of this shocking twist.

"... moving to Seattle ... driving by the hotel ... very surprised ... love surprising ... especially great guys ... already surprised ... part of another surprise? Okay, *shh* ... love the slogan ... okay, the kitchen!"

"Man, wish I knew how to juggle," Bear said to himself, watching his new surprise move through the lobby.

"Me, too," said Hail Larry, coming up from behind. "I lost my freakin' wife and your freakin'—"

"Yeager's in for a big shock," said Bear, turning to the ballroom. "Just when I thought the guest list couldn't get any bigger than the Sea Gals."

"Walter just said *you're* in for a big shock!" said Hail Larry's Wife, coming up from behind. "Something about *bigger Gals* than the Sea Gals."

"Man, I love women," said Hail Larry.

"Bigger Gals?" asked Bear, immediately thinking of Tammy's bigger Gals.

"And the fourth floor," said Hail Larry's Wife. "Tell me I didn't just screw up the surprise."

"Bigger Gals on the fourth floor?" Bear dabbed at the sweat forming on his forehead while thinking of Mr. Yeager's complimentary room on the fourth floor. "I haven't tried the Yeager-meister tonight. Would you excuse me?"

Moments later, he was hibernating behind the partitions behind the ice cream buffet line, calming down with a bowl of Yeager-meister to the forehead.

Cool and dreamy and useful in so many ways.

"But don't tell Bear!" whispered Walter's voice from the other side of the partition.

"How will he know when to meet us upstairs for our big surprise?" whispered Tammy's voice, also on the other side.

"Tell him when the time is right," said Walter. "We don't want *those* Gals ruining the Sea Gals for him. He worked hard on this night, probably dreamed up a way to give them the dance routine."

"No doubt," said Tammy. "How did you find out about the Sea Gals being here anyway?"

"Bear can't keep anything from me to save his life," said Walter. "In fact, he probably wouldn't. He gives it all away with his face. And a dozen hints a day."

"Unlike you, who never gives anything away," said Tammy. "Literally."

"Exactly," said Walter.

Exactly! mouthed an astonished Bear at that very same moment.

"What does the slogan mean anyway?" asked Tammy. *"It's got Walt Appeal.* Bob and Jimmy keep asking me. I asked Bear and all he said was: 'Sorry, Tammy, guess you're not in the loop. If you were there, you'd know.'"

Walter tried to answer but was interrupted by the start of the song and dance. A melodic piano wafted through speakers. The lights in the ballroom dimmed. Across the way, a spotlight lit up a curtain on a long narrow stage, followed by an unseen female announcer's voice:

"Ladies and gentlemen, Seattle Seahawks fans, members of the Yeager Ice

Cream Brigade, Seattle's Pediatric AIDS charities, and ice cream lovers of the Pa-
cific Northwest and Alaska ... welcome to the kick-off party for a whole new kind of
cool and dreamy ... Yeager-meister, the ice cream that's got Walt Appeal!"

Applause filtered through the ballroom. One by one, the Sea Gals emerged
from a curtain into the spotlight, dressed like silver-clad Santa girls for the occasion. "Whip Appeal," the smooth and sultry R&B classic by Babyface, eased
into the air, ushering the Sea Gals across the stage as they formed one long dance
line. The crooner crooned about the object of his infatuation, someone with an
endless amount of sweet appeal, so much sweet appeal, mortal words went only
so far in describing that appeal. After all, Babyface created food for the soul.

Of course, none of this was going through the mind of Bear Coleman,
weak-kneed and getting weaker behind the partitions behind the ice cream buffet line. He wanted his cool and dreamy surprise, not the Sea Gals. He ducked
out of the darkened ballroom, past his own dance routine, and headed straight
for Mr. Yeager's complimentary hideaway on the fourth floor.

Bear entered the room with his keycard, singing "Walt Appeal" and mimicking the moves of the Sea Gals in the ballroom. First stop: the bathroom, where
he continued singing until he heard someone in the outer room. "Guys?" asked
Bear, giddier than giddy. By the time he emerged, the outer room was empty, but
the air had been filled with the blissful stench of flowery perfume. Tammy had
come and gone, sure to return soon enough with his man and her Gals.

An anxious Bear jumped up and down. Then he heard the door and bolted for the bathroom. "Walter? You alone?" asked Bear. A manly grunt said yes.
"Whew!" said Bear, splashing water on his face and speaking to the outer room:
"Be out in a second. Glad it was you first! Don't get me wrong. Whatever Walter
wants is all right with me. And I want this, too! I mean, look at her sexy legs ...
and those bigger Gals ... gonna be great, man ... I know you have great intuition,
but how did you know, QB? I mean, I'm totally open to—with you especially!—
man, a dream come true for one very horny brutha! You just have to kinda be my
coach, okay? I mean, sure I've fantasized about you, me and Ivanya Elle M'vanya,
but it's been a while since Avonda from Phoenix, freshman year." Bear stepped
into the outer room. Instead of his blond prince, he saw the prince of darkness.

"Larry McPherson said this was the place," said Evil Announcer Guy. "I
didn't know what he meant, but hell, I'm down for anything. This is the *bi* week,
right?"

Before Bear could react, the door, which was ajar with a bowl of ice cream,
swung open, revealing QB. "What's he doing here?" asked Walter.

"McPherson gave me this." Evil Announcer Guy held up a keycard.

"In Seattle," said Walter, entering the room.

"Interviews for the network," said Evil Announcer Guy. "Staying at a hotel down the street, got bored—looks like I came to the right joint."

"I gave this to McPherson," said Walter, reclaiming his keycard.

"—who told me I was your surprise guest," said Evil Announcer Guy.

"Like hell," the boys said together.

"Literally," said Bear to Walter. "Larry overheard something and got it all freakin' wrong."

"Don't I know you?" asked Evil Announcer Guy. Bear put his hand to his mouth and shook his head, almost as if to say, *Me No Speak*. "I swear I've seen you somewhere."

Bear shrugged.

"Anyway," said Evil Announcer Guy, turning back to Walter. "Are McPherson and his honey of a wife joining this little party? I would love to eat the five pounds of undigested meat in *her* colon."

"There is no party," said Walter.

"Not even for the horny brutha?" asked Evil Announcer Guy, indicating Bear.

"I'm a writer," said Bear. "I was running lines through my mind. In private in the bathroom."

"We're done here," said Walter to the intruder.

"Don't fret, fellas," said Evil Announcer Guy, arranging himself so that he was between them. "I can bat right." He cupped Walter's groin. "And I can bat left." Then he cupped Bear's groin.

The boys took his arms and twisted them in polar opposite directions, creating an Evil Announcer Pretzel. QB then grabbed him by the scruff of the neck and shoved his face against the nearest wall.

"You don't wanna do that," said Walter.

"Can I quote you?" mumbled Evil Announcer Guy.

"You can get the fuck outta here." Walter let go and paced in fits and starts. Bear didn't know whether to restrain his man or combust into violence himself.

"Can't take a little joke?" asked Evil Announcer Guy, straightening his lapels.

"Can't take a bigger joke?" asked Walter, pausing, then breaking into laughter. Bear caught on and followed. A moment later, Evil Announcer Guy caught on and followed. The bout had been ruled a draw. And a joke.

"You boys play rough," said Evil Announcer Guy, unsteady and unsure.

"Welcome to the big leagues," shrugged Walter, pretending it was no big deal. "Now seriously, get the fuck outta here. I got business."

The dark force beheld the boys, then, failing to glean any further truths, disappeared from sight. Walter picked up the hotel telephone, then changed his mind about throwing it against the wall.

"I could kill him," said Walter.

"I could help you," said Bear, collapsing on his back on the bed. Walter used the phone to summon Tammy, then he lay beside Bear.

"Know what makes me feel the shittiest?" asked Walter, staring at the ceiling. "You do, don't you?"

"Kinda," said Bear.

"Like I can't even stand up for you or myself properly," said Walter.

"You did good," said Bear. "For a second, you had *me* confused with your escape route."

"Being good at that kind of scrambling is not something I'm proud of," said Walter. They lay quietly until the perfume of the ER Wife re-filled their senses.

"What did my boys do now?" asked Tammy, hovering over the bed.

"Got in a fight," said Walter.

"And let the bully go," said Bear. After hearing the replay, Tammy promised to take care of the matter, like a good wife or Mrs. Claus.

"Too many surprises for one ice cream social," said Tammy in conclusion. She was sitting on the bed, in between the boys.

"He never saw my surprise!" the boys said together.

"I didn't?" the boys said together.

"Shut up!" said Tammy. "One at a time."

"The Sea Gals was only my *original* surprise," said Bear.

"Who's surprising who with these other Gals?" asked Tammy.

Both boys raised their hands.

"Oh, my God, Walter's melting!" said Bear, jumping off the bed. "Come on, no time to explain."

The boys and their ER Wife rushed back down to the first floor of the hotel. When they came spilling out of the elevator into the lobby, they were met by the Hail Larrys, Bob & Jimmy Astor, and what was left of the party, about two dozen onlookers.

"The kitchen," said Bear, rushing past with Walter and Tammy. The rest of the Brigade followed. Moments later, 30 people were in the hotel kitchen.

"We needed the freezer space," said the main chef, opening a large steel door, revealing a walk-in storage area. Inside was one mountainous heap of Yeager-meister ice cream in what was supposed to have been an ice cream sculpture of the quarterback. Bear was supposed to have cued its arrival on the stage near the end of "Whip Appeal." Instead, the sculpture had lost its definition and size. Had one not known the heap of frozen dairy was originally a pro quarterback, one would never know.

"All that ice cream," said a female voice in the crowd.

"What a way to go," said Walter with a huge grin on his face.

His cool and dreamy tribute hadn't suffered from a meltdown. Ice Cream Walter had been saved by Grace. And her three beautiful girls. The young mother sat on a box in the storage area, content to watch her young daughters gorge themselves on Yeager-meister.

"The original Ice Cream Brigade from Anaheim," said Bear.

"My surprise," the boys said together.

"I tried telling him earlier tonight," said Grace, indicating Bear.

"Bear's been busy making sure the night went off perfectly," said Walter. "And he succeeded big time."

"So you've already had this reunion," said Bear to Walter, "and met the daughters."

"Earlier tonight," said Walter, "and I was planning to spring them on you upstairs."

"*Those* Gals," said Bear, bashfully avoiding Tammy's.

"*Willya* look at these gorgeous children loving all our ice cream!" said Bob or Jimmy Astor. "*Our* ice cream."

"That, my friends, is one beautiful sight," said Jimmy or Bob Astor.

Grace's girls were exploring and eating what was left of Mount Yeager. The oldest girl was tall enough to reach up and pick the remnants of Ice Cream Walter's brain. The middle girl dug methodically into Ice Cream Walter's gut, scooping and eating, scooping and eating. The youngest girl sat on Ice Cream Walter's ice cream cleats, her messy dress and face telling the world how much she was enjoying the moment and the cool and dreamy treat. She also gave the spirit leader all the inspiration he needed:

"That, my friends, is Walt Appeal."

19

Freeways Claim Bodies That Fade

"To Buffalo we go for highlights of the first playoff matchup earlier today. The skies were blustery and the wind chill five below—not the most ideal circumstances for the Indoor Seahawks, but a win today on the frozen tundra of Rich Stadium would put Seattle in next week's AFC Championship for only the second time in franchise history and the first time in over a decade."

"And, Jake, if you take a look at the way this Seattle ball club has risen in only two years under Coach Robbins, Yeager, Millstone, Reggie Showman—you knew they weren't going to be rattled by snowballs from the stands. This is a team that went 13-3 in the regular season—"

"Yeah, but only 6-2 since the release of Yeager-meister."

"*Ouch* ... there you see the meister throwing before the game, trying to keep his hands warm—look! Someone in the stands was also warming up! A snowball barely misses the QB. Does he flinch? Not this gunslinger. He's got his own flava! And dare I say, some of that Joe Namath swagger?"

"Yeah, but these are the 14-2 Buffalo Bills, and Jim Kelly came out smokin' today. Here you see the Bills QB connecting on a little screen to Thurman Thomas, who breaks two tackles and—"

"He ... could ... go ... he *does* go all the way ... puts the Bills up 10-7 early in the second quarter."

"I thought Showman should have stopped him on that one, but maybe Reggie was thinking about the fact that only three people went to see his last movie, which opened this weekend."

"*Ouch* ... third quarter ... Yeager tries to unthaw the Seahawks offense. Last week, they had that thunderous and towel-waving Kingdome crowd behind them in beating Marino and Miami, 17-0."

"Yeah, but Buffalo in January is a different story."

"Needless to say, a big test for the first-time Pro Bowler Yeager. And he would be tested. Here's the Bills' Cornelius Bennett sacking him from behind on third down. Here's the Bills' Bruce Smith saying hello in your face on another third and long. Finally, Yeager converts on third and six early in the fourth, which leads to this 22-yard field goal by El Kicko. Tie game, 13-13. Bills get a field goal on their next possession to go up 16-13 with less than 10 minutes to go in regulation."

"And that's when the snow kicks in again, swirling in a crazy wind, and the Buffalo fans are loving it!"

"So are Jim Kelly and the Bills. After a Seahawk punt, Kelly begins a methodical drive downfield, carving up Seattle's secondary with Lofton, Reed and Beebe."

"Think he's trying to teach the whippersnapper on the other sideline a little something?"

"Kelly should have been paying attention to Reggie Snowman! Showman—whatever he calls himself—picks off this bullet meant for Tasker. And look at Reggie—Go, Reggie! Go, Reggie!"

"Maybe he heard two more people paid to see his movie!"

"*Ouch* ... Show takes the ball from his own 25 to midfield, giving the offense plenty of time to make it happen—three to tie, six to win. Yeager-meister goes to work, connecting on this 15-yarder to Junior Jefferson, the hobbled receiver who shouldn't be playing in his condition."

"Hey, it's the playoffs."

"Then a shuttle pass to Millstone nets another eight yards."

"There you see El Kicko—acquired by the Seahawks from the Rams mid-season—warming up his foot, trying to keep unfrozen on the sidelines."

"He shouldn't have been the only one, as you'll see in a second here ... less than four minutes to go ... Hawks down by three ... winner meets Pittsburgh for all the AFC marbles next week. Yeager takes the snap from the shotgun, guns it over the middle. Jefferson sells out his already-banged-up body and *boom!* He's decked by Bennett but holds on for a Seattle first down at the 15-yard line!"

"Yeah, but there's too much time on the clock, and something tells me Number 13 does not want to leave it up to somebody else's foot."

"Seahawks run a couple of running plays between the hash marks—smart move—forcing Buffalo to use all their timeouts. On third down, Millstone *pounds* it down to the one-yard line, and just when you think it's time to talk about Seattle vs. Pittsburgh ..."

"This has got to be one of *the* most bizarre finishes in football annals. Can I say that?"

"*This* we know for fact: Seahawks' ball at the one-yard line with 33 seconds to go; neither team has a timeout. Yeager and Coach Robbins are trying to communicate and figure out what to do. They look to be in agreement here; they're going to run one more play to try to punch it in the end zone, then line up for a quick field goal, if unsuccessful."

"Makes sense in this wind. And let's face it, El Kicko—"

"Yeager keeps it on a keeper here, doesn't get in."

"But wait, why are the Bills celebrating?"

"Because the game is over, right? The yard marker says that was fourth down! In the confusion, the Bills offense rushes the field, runs a play to run out the clock—a smarter move!—and they're outta there."

"But it was *not* fourth down! Millstone got a first down on the previous play! But the down marker guy on the sideline fell out of sync with the last two plays! Why? Take a look here. *Maybe* it had something to do with the fact that his tongue was stuck frozen to the pole of the down marker! What his tongue was doing there in the first place, we can only imagine, but what we do know is, he was too embarrassed to ask for help!"

"How do you ask for help when your tongue is frozen to a pole?"

"In the commotion, no one noticed in time to stop play."

"If I'm a Seahawks coach, I'm running on the field *naked* to hold up the game."

"*Ouch* ... talk about frozen appendages. The Bills run one quick play to kill the clock—game over, right?"

"Twenty minutes later, officially, after a dozen meetings in the snow. Hey, where'd the guy with the frozen tongue go?"

"The Seahawks say they'll protest, but we all know how those turn out."

"Once another play has been run, it's over, baby. Not to mention, they ain't gonna come back to the frozen tundra and replay nuttin'."

"Buffalo wins, 16-13, thanks in part to the Frozen Ref—or whatever you call those sideline guys."

"I call him fired."

"For Jim Kelly and the Bills, it's on to Pittsburgh. For the Seahawks, it's a hot toddy on a long plane ride home. For buddies Walter Yeager and Bear Coleman, it's on to the Pro Bowl in Hawaii, where it's highly unlikely there will be any frozen tongues or poles."

"THEY DID NOT SAY: *For Yeager and Coleman, it's on to the Pro Bowl for frozen tongues and poles,*" said Hail Larry's Wife, her laughter echoing in the night sky.

"Can we shut up about the game?" asked Walter, poking the fire with a stick.

"*And* the freakin' season," said Hail Larry, gulping his drink. "Some of us are still in mourning."

"At least *you* lost to Dallas in the freakin' NFC title game," said Bear, resisting the urge to snuggle up to his man. "Doesn't it help, losing to the eventual champs?"

"Still talking football." Walter stuffed a slice of pineapple in his man's mouth.

"*Mmmmmm,*" said Bear.

"Anybody still yammering about freakin' football needs more alcohol," said Hail Larry's Wife, holding up a bottle of something native and quite wicked.

"Serve 'em up!" Walter hiccupped, prompting laughter.

The boys and the Hail Larrys were having their own private luau on their own private beach after the Pro Bowl, the league's annual all-star game in Honolulu. Yeager and McPherson had spent the weekend playing sandlot football for TV, reconnecting with old football buddies, playing real ball for about 10 minutes at the Pro Bowl, and getting a lot of really cool free stuff. Meanwhile, Yeager's buddy and McPherson's wife spent the weekend lounging on the beach, reconnecting with one another, watching football for about 10 minutes at the Pro Bowl, and buying a lot of really cool stuff.

"Sure takes a freakin' load off, knowing the wife has a running buddy," said Hail Larry.

"Funny, I was about to say the same," said Walter, prompting laughter. Bear and Hail Larry's Wife had kidnapped their husbands for this, their last night on the island. The couples were separated by a fire and remnants of a roasted carcass. "Pretty cool, all of us getting along," said Walter, toasting once the drinks were refilled.

"Wasn't it a year ago when Bear and I clicked outside the Kingdome?" asked Hail Larry's Wife. "You guys could be good friends like us by now."

"Maybe if we had been in sync a few months ago, we could've avoided the disaster on the fourth floor with what's-his-name," said Bear.

"The guy took it as a joke," said Hail Larry, still defensive about being the one who sent Evil Announcer Guy to the Yeager-meister hotel room. "Accidents freakin' happen, water under the bridge, no harm, no foul."

"He's safe at home," said Hail Larry's Wife, extending her arms like a baseball umpire. "He's also kinda paranoid."

"With good reason," said Bear, dreaming of his man's strong hands offering a much-needed shoulder massage.

"We weathered it," said Walter, offering words instead. "The guy's no wiser. So he's evil, who cares? He announces on the other network in the other conference. He ain't gonna stop Walt now."

"You tell 'em, PV," said Bear.

"I do *not* wanna know what *that* freakin' stands for," said Hail Larry.

"Piss 'n' vinegar?" asked Bear, unable to hide his sly grin.

"Could have been worse," said Hail Larry.

"You guys got three gorgeous young models for your ice cream flavor out of that fiasco that night," said Hail Larry's Wife. "Along with their gorgeous young mother *slash* model now."

"Yeah, so say Grace," said Hail Larry. "She's loaded for the first time in her life!—that Grace and her girls—so back off! I did everybody a freakin' flavor! *Ahh!*" Hail Larry winced from a pain in the upper region of his torso.

"Bear, look what you did!" said Hail Larry's Wife. "Just kidding ... Romanowski did it in practice before the Dallas game."

"Shut up about it, will ya, woman?" said Hail Larry. "Freakin' Yeager, how can so many guys at the Pro Bowl know about Bass, the photogenic Danish chiropractor, but no one knows how to freakin' get ahold of him?"

"Tell me about it, I'll be the second to know," said Walter. "And I was patient zero, in human form in the States anyway."

"I don't know if I need a reverse, or I'm just freakin' cursed," said Hail Larry. "Freakin' *ouch!*"

"Honey, did you know they freakin' *drove* to Kansas City that one year?" asked Hail Larry's Wife. "That's hell, literally, being on the highway that long."

"Wouldn't that be a kick, Yeager, if we ended up on the same team someday?" said Hail Larry, suddenly over the pain. "Your ass would be so mine."

"He means it, too!" laughed Hail Larry's Wife, chugging her drink.

"I would so freakin' nail your ass, Yeager," said Hail Larry. Walter and the Hail Larrys laughed hysterically. Meanwhile, Bear peered through the flames, his head tilting slowly, his eyes seeing the San Francisco wide receiver in a whole other light.

A light that freakin' Yeager was not prepared to illuminate.

"Hold on now, little Bearcat," said Walter the very next night. "Hell. Larry? A freakin' homo?"

"He said he wants to play for your team," said Bear. The boys were back in Malibu, opening up Moose Jaw, their off-season home. They were unpacking in the master bedroom, Bear putting away his Hawaiian loot in the walk-in closet, Walter sorting through dozens of promotional Hawaiian shirts on the bed.

"First Reggie and Carter Jones are hooked up, according to you," said Walter. "Now your best friend's husband wants to nail my ass?"

"Who can freakin' blame him?" asked Bear, emerging from the closet and copping a drive-by feel. "If I listen to my instincts, they're never wrong. Just like they weren't about you."

Walter's cheeks became uptight. "Meaning?"

Bear withdrew his hand. "Deep in my mind, I seem to remember a flickering instant very early on—before I knew you—where my brain shouted something like: 'He's got to be gay!' But it was too radical to deal with. I'm still not sure what I meant. Probably my wishful-thinking brain, thinking wishfully."

Walter sat on the bed. "So there's something obvious about me? Like when I was tipping off Reggie about my primary receivers? Another flaw."

"Honey, *noooooo,*" said Bear, sitting next to him.

"Don't call me honey right now," said Walter. "I'm too uptight."

"Indeed." Bear rubbed his man's thigh. "Buddy, don't change a thing about you. Please. You're the strongest, most sensitive and wonderfully complete man that *any* man *or* woman could ever dream of loving."

"What if something I've done has—*fuck!*" Walter reclined on the bed. "Okay. Done being paranoid."

"All this because my best friend's husband wants to nail your ass," said Bear.

"Earth to Bear Coleman: Larry is a freakin' heterosexual," said Walter. "He loves women. He only told everyone about 10 dozen times in Hawaii."

"And Tammy calls *me* the naïve one," said Bear. "Next you're gonna tell me hot jocks like you and Larry don't have *both* genders throwing themselves at you everywhere you go, especially since you're the Shit now, as the kids say."

"Now who's uptight?" Walter rolled over sideways and hugged Bear's waist. "And sounding like an old black man?"

"That would be Wilson, my agent, until I come up with a hot title for my work-in-progress," said Bear. "But QB just nailed that one for me."

"Really? Dream on," laughed Walter.

"Some other time." Bear lay on the bed and felt the comfort of his man spooning his backside. "Our world is freakin' changing, PV. It's not just you and me on our own little planet anymore."

"You worried about temptation, little Bearcat?" yawned Walter.

"Not worried, just aware of reality," yawned Bear.

"Still want Tammy's Gals?" mumbled Walter.

"Dunno about in this lifetime anymore," mumbled Bear, falling asleep. "Not ... worth ... chaos ... freakin' disorder ... everything cool ... dreamy ... here."

"YOU'RE BECOMING MORE famous and out there in the world. You sure you want all that hurt?" asked Marcus, peering through the darkness in his mind.

"You're becoming more lonely and isolated in the world. You sure you want all that hurt?" asked Bear, peering through the darkness in his mind.

"There's no hurt here in LA-LA Land," said Marcus.

"There's no romantic LA-LA love either," said Bear.

"That's LA-LA life, gotta go, sex date," said Marcus.

"I thought you gays weren't having sex since, well, you know," said Bear.

"Dream on," laughed Marcus.

"I will since I'm the real one!" said Bear.

"Man, that's Crazy Bear talk! I think my head's gonna implode," said Walter, reverting back to his own voice. He was sitting at his desk in the Malibu home office and had been reading the part of Marcus in *My Whole Other Life*. "How does my *k'waaaay-zy* Bear Coleman's mind come up with this stuff?"

"You tell me, I'll be the second to know," giggled Bear, lying on the couch in the home office, more focused on making corrections to his copy of the script.

"Think people will get it?" asked Walter.

"If they don't sweat the details, they'll get it. Just like in dreams. And if they believe," said Bear, struggling to read in the darkened room.

"Believe?" asked Walter, rising from his desk.

"In magic, miracles, true love—the usual," said Bear. "And magic caps."

"Feels like you've been working on *My Whole Other Life* for a *Whole Other Lifetime*." Walter drew back the curtains to the large window, illuminating the home office, which was twice as big since the Moose Jaw remodel.

"Well," said Bear, stretching in the sunlight now flooding the couch directly beneath the window, "this has been the year of the *Uptight*."

"Not anymore," said Walter, inhaling the ocean beyond the backyard and the ridge. "But hey, if our stress gave you a movie title, cool." He lifted Bear's legs, sat on the couch, then put his buddy's feet in his lap.

Bear had recycled his angry screenplay about a quarterback and his spirit leader buddy assassinating a homophobic US senator into a more Hollywood-friendly concept. *Up Yours* was now *Uptight,* a screenplay about a very hot, very bosomy, heterosexual female FBI agent who goes undercover to bust up a bunch of very hot and bosomy lesbian political radicals holed up in a strip joint *slash* biker bar *slash* lesbian dude ranch compound in the Arizona desert. But the heterosexual agent gets more than she bargained for when she falls for the equally hot and bosomy head of the lesbian radicals.

"My agent is sky-high on me and these gals," said Bear. His last movie, *Rocket Bruthas,* had made enough at the box office to be deemed a success in the urban market. On top of that, Sharon Stone's *Basic Instinct* had made lesbians a hot Hollywood commodity. "Not my proudest moment," said Bear, "creating busty lesbian vehicles for the Sandra Bullocks of the world—but I'm just trying to get in the door. And stay. *Then* I'll do it my way."

"Dream of it," said Walter. "I still like *Up Yours* better."

"No doubt," said Bear, more focused on making notations. "We'll see what Marcus does with it in *My Whole Other Life.* I gave him the whole assassination thing for one of his novels. Maybe it'll help him rise up outta the doldrums."

"The man needs a man!" Walter began doing one of the things Walter did best, massaging Bear's soles.

"He needs ... *oh ... the man ...*" said Bear, exhaling from his toes to his head. "... needs to know love will never do without *your touch* ... and your Sugar."

"Send him someone else," said Walter with a mild laugh.

"I try. He tries. We try," said Bear with a sigh somewhere between empathy and ecstasy. "Nothing ever feels right ... except *this ... don't stop ...* my God, your hands ... my God."

"You're not gonna have me talking to myself in *My Whole Other Life,* are you?" asked Walter, going deeper into his man's metatarsals.

"Unfortunately for our alter egos' poor neglected souls, you're not even gonna *be* in *My Whole Other Life,* except as an image of inspiration ... *so right ... freeing me up, you are ...* please never stop," said Bear.

"Poor soles or poor souls?" asked Walter.

"*Yes ...* that's it ... *exactly,*" said Bear.

"I know my Bear," laughed Walter. "You're gonna figure out a way for us to hook up in *My Whole Other Life.* You know you're gonna have *that* Marcus show up and shock the shit outta me, wherever I am."

"Wanna bet?" asked Bear.

"Have you ever won a bet with me?" asked Walter.

"Have I ever lost?" laughed Bear.

"If you want my suggestion—" said Walter.

"You know I want it all," said Bear.

"I think *that* Marcus should look up *that* Walter," said Walter.

"Hook up or look up?" asked Bear.

"Good question," said Walter. "You'll figure it out."

"Even if you were married and all that?" asked Bear.

"Married?" said Walter.

"You once said you would have married Ellen," said Bear.

"Who?" teased Walter with a mild laugh.

"The dark-haired girl from the ride to Atlanta—you know exactly who I mean," laughed Bear. "Sorry my heels are so dry."

"Don't apologize for being you," said Walter, mouthing Bear's dry heel.

"So hearing from this black, gay, HIV-positive former cheerleader from your college football days wouldn't rock your world?" asked Bear.

Walter freed up his mouth. "Of course it would, but I'd handle ya. Why make Marcus positive? That bites. I don't want him suffering."

"I know, but I gotta be realistic," said Bear. "I dodged that bullet in this life. What are the odds of a second artful dodger in my genes?"

"Did you just say *dreams* or *genes?*" asked Walter, scintillating his man's toes.

"Oh God exactly," said Bear.

"Gimme some of dat," said Walter, sounding black. The boys rotated. The boys loved to *rightbackatcha.*

"I wouldn't want you to suffer in *My Whole Other Life,* either," said Bear, sitting on the couch with his man's feet in his lap. "If I were *that* Marcus and just had your picture, I'd want Walt to be gloriously happy, no matter how Walt defined it, with or without me."

"That's what I'm talking 'bout," said Walter, lying on the couch, feeling his soles.

"You just gave me another idea," said Bear.

"Super ... sweet," said Walter.

"Marcus will spend a lifetime dreaming of us," said Bear.

"I *do* like that," said Walter, covering his eyes with his gorgeous blond forearm.

"All from seeing the photo in the game program," said Bear.

"Juuuuuust enough ... yeah ... right," said Walter.

"His only facts will be what's in the program," said Bear. "So what was in there?"

"*God* ... so deep ... feel it ... *man* ... my soul ... height ... weight ... big stud," said Walter.

"Thanks, man," said Bear.

"And probably Winnetka," said Walter.

"Your hometown?" asked Bear, going deeper into his man's metatarsals.

"*Bingo!*" said Walter. "*That* is the way, Bear Coleman, nailed it!"

"Man, I love pleasing my man. That should be a song title." Bear started to get up.

"Before you take off—" said Walter, still in foot massage heaven.

"Yeah?" paused Bear.

"—where we going?" asked Walter.

"Trust?" asked Bear.

"You know I'll go anywhere with you," said Walter.

"I'll take you there," said Bear ...

... Marcus Coleman was not having a good decade to follow up the 80s, *his* decade. If *My Whole Other Life: The Gay 90s* were a weather report, the forecast was ripe with fires, floods and earthquakes. And those were normal days in Los Angeles, a dreamy town turned nightmarish. The City of Angels had leased itself to the Devils, who took over the freeways, the LAPD, the court system, the house on Rockingham, and just about every other nook and cranny of Dreamland. Just in case the Devils missed a nook or cranny, Mother Nature re-arranged Dreamland. Blazes wiped out mountainsides. Endless rain wiped out city streets. And then there were the quakes, from the desert to the sea and all of Southern California in between. In the 90s, LA, and by extension, Marcus Coleman, were rattled ...

"*Whoa!* That settles it," said Walter, only getting half a foot massage now. "In your whole other life, I'm staying on the other side of the country."

"What would *your* whole other life be like?" asked Bear, holding the script and his man's foot.

"Hell," said Walter, "I don't think about that stuff, but if I did—ah, hell, Bear, I dunno. You want hints for what I'm gonna be like when you look me up? When *Marcus* looks up Walter? It's weird hearing you use my name. Can you call me something else? John, Brett, I don't know. Boomer Esiason."

"I just had a déjà vu," said Bear. "Have we done this before?"

"Call me Walt in *My Whole Other Life*. Only you and my mom call me Walter anyway," said Walter.

"Walter is the first word you ever uttered to me," said Bear. "Aren't you glad it wasn't Wally?"

"Never Wally," said Walter. "Even in jest."

"Have I ever?" said Bear.

Wally is a mascot's name. Walter is not a mascot. Walter is the general.

"My Bear knows me, this much is true," said Walter. "Thought Marcus had a cool blonde chick in his life—I mean, the script. And a tailgating crew. And isn't he doing the Dad Thing with a Salvadoran kid?"

"It all brings warmth and humanity to his story, but it's not true love," said Bear. "And you know how people get caught up in their own dreams."

"I'm not sure I'd pay to see this *My Whole Other Life* if the guy's gonna end up destitute and lonely," said Walter.

"Ditto. I just haven't figured out a better way," said Bear. "It's been a great writing exercise for character development, though. Check out what I imagined Marcus wrote on the topic of monogamy." Bear handed his man a sheet of paper.

"What is this, a proclamation?" asked Walter.

"Free Will in a Relationship by Marcus Coleman," said Bear.

Creed One: I am not on this earth to tell anybody what they can and cannot do, or what is right or wrong, good or bad, or heaven and hell. I can only decide these truths for myself. As such, I would never tell you, my buddy, what you can and cannot do, or what is right and wrong for you. I would never put shackles on your God-given free will to be whatever you want, whoever you want, whenever you want.

Creed Two: We are buddies-for-life and partners in life. Our behavior and decisions greatly affect one another. As such, all major decisions affecting both our lives are best made as partners. Examples: buying a home, moving to another city, changing jobs, having sex outside the relationship. All major life decisions warrant open honest discussion, and hopefully, mutually agreed-upon choices that enrich both partners as two and as one. What needs to be weighed in every moment in life: does this serve me and my relationship? If not, which is more important: serving myself or serving my relationship?

Creed Three: Because sex is a trigger for a universe of emotion and conflict, we willingly add this *one satellite moon* to the God-given free will within the context of our relationship: no quick hookup sex on the run with some person who happens to be in the right lane of the right freeway at the right time when your boner is seemingly indestructible. No coming home with—surprise!— magic beans, a beanstalk, a home, a job, a new city, a disease, or any other major wad of energy expended, without having a huddle, buddy to buddy.

"Can you believe a poor bastard who can't find true love came up with that?" asked Bear.

"He's lucky he's got you," the boys said together, then laughed.

"I got a suggestion," said Walter. "I agree with these creeds, by the way."

"What's your suggestion?" said Bear. "I agree, too, cool."

"Marcus should know something about me, just for shits and giggles," said Walter. "Like ... the fact that I'm the opposite of racist, or that I threw rocks at telephone poles as a kid, you know, crazy stuff like that. Maybe that I'm good with money, or even though I'm married, I've been exposed to homosexuality."

"What's that supposed to mean?" laughed Bear.

"Whatever Bear wants," said Walter. "Make 'em have crazy flashbacks together. *Ha!* If you showed up in my whole other life, I'd make you work for it, like you made me work for it. Give the poor bastards some fun and mystery."

"How am I supposed to do that?" asked Bear.

"*I* have to encourage *my* Bear to *dream?*" asked Walter. "Didn't you once mention something about a guy named Benchley and dreaming?"

"Benchley? Who's he play for?" asked Bear.

"The Jets maybe? No, the Dolphins," said Walter. "I dunno. He said something about dreaming anything you want."

"Doesn't sound familiar at all," scoffed Bear.

"It was some big guy from your childhood—*a detail,*" said Walter. "Make Walt like most guys we know, married and divorced by now."

"Then married a second time to my freakin' best friend?" asked Bear. "Yep, she talks."

"Okay, so make Walt married twice, like Larry, hell," shrugged Walter.

"Then Walt's married and unavailable, *hello?*" said Bear.

"So I'll get divorced again! You're the creative one. I'm just offering freakin' suggestions." Walter yanked his feet from Bear's lap.

"Which I love. I love all your offerings ... sir," said Bear, re-embracing his man's soles and placing them where they belong, as close as possible to Bear's soul. "How would *that* Marcus find out this stuff anyway?"

"Have him dream of it, I dunno," said Walter. "Have Marcus find out I can be moody sometimes, too—there you go—and sensitive."

"No doubt," said Bear, massaging his man's soul. "I mean, no doubt we can help the poor bastards in search of fun and mystery."

"Marcus should also know why I didn't make it to the pros," said Walter.

"Of course, you'll be in the pros in *My Whole Other Life,*" laughed Bear, caressing both sides of his man's sole. "Let's not make this too twisted. A universe where the world doesn't know Walter is king of kings? How absurd. Talk about chaos and disorder."

"You're gonna have to twist it to make it work, dreamer man," said Walter. "*Oh, so right* ... if we never ... I would've never ... gone West ... reversed ... with you and the Dane ... got my back ... watching like a hawk ... *man, I love my Bear.*"

"So Walt would just be a financial wizard, like that part of you?" asked Bear. "Not an NFL stud?"

"Just a financial wizard with a challenged back," said Walter.

"*Whoa,* stop right there." Bear was ready to burst into tears. "I refuse to create any world, script, universe, story, or character exercise where Walt *or* Walter Yeager suffers. It's over. I'm done. Next!"

"Bear, if you stop now, what have you got, huh?" asked Walter, tearing up himself. "You've put a lot of thought into these boys, who unfortunately will never become big league. Or famous—fuck, they're infamous, if anything. It's already twisted enough to think I'm gonna be 31 before I ever win a Super Bowl. A freakin' world where I'm not even in the game? *Whoa, stop right there!*"

"See what I mean?" said Bear, morphing into laughter. "Walt and Marcus are fucked! And not in a cool and dreamy way!"

"It's just a script. It's just a script," said Walter. "A very twisted Bear Coleman dream, which means we should all head for the hills because Bear Coleman's freakin' dreams usually come true."

After Bear's hysterical laughing fit—another great massage to his soul—the reenergized spirit leader calmed himself and stretched toward the sun above the couch. "Script, dream, thought. Someone—can't remember who—once told me they're all the same, just God's energy."

"I can feel it rotating in my head as we speak," said Walter, sitting up and rolling his neck in all directions.

"We love these poor bastards," sighed Bear, following Walter's inspiration and adjusting his stiff neck and shoulders. "Walt can't go suffering in *My Whole Other Life*. I'd feel so sad. I'd want to be there for you. You barely let *me* in on your pain. How would a lost soul like Marcus even know where to start? You're asking me to be one master storyteller, QB."

"Dream of it, Soul Man," said Walter.

"I guess Walt's gonna have kids, too," said Bear. "I hope his wives don't mind him being a big ole kid himself around kids."

"Like you know that," laughed Walter, all skeptical.

"I dreamed of it once," said Bear, all coy. "But that's for another time."

"No doubt," said Walter. "What say, we give the infamous boys a breather, too. My spirit leader needs to put a more spirited grade of Sugar in the tank, especially with the NFL Express about to pull up to the curb."

"You're absolutely right, QB. We're gonna need plenty of Sugar to guarantee cool and dreamy skies ahead for all of us."

YEAGER, JEFFERSON AND MILLSTONE were dressed like desperados on the magazine cover—the gunslinger flanked by his go-to wide receiver and the veteran running back. The men wore grave expressions against a painted desert backdrop, as if they were about to pony up to some outpost like Kansas City or Denver and do serious damage to the home team, then the town saloon.

SEATTLE'S TRIPLE THREAT IN THE WILD WEST

"There is no *Sports Illustrated* jinx. There is no *Sports Illustrated* jinx," said Bear. The football wobbled end over end toward the goalposts, the fans in the end zone discouraging the trajectory of the ball. The clock struck 00:00. The ball disobeyed the fans and split the uprights. For once in his life, El Kicko came through. "See, there's no *Sports Illustrated* jinx," shrugged Bear.

Only true non-believers believe it's a bad sign being the chosen one.

"Go Seahawks go!" said Mama Rent, one of six people in the stands happy about the turn of events. Yeager and the Seahawks had battled Brett Favre and the Packers to a draw in the season opener. Lambeau Field, the green jewel of the football world, sank with resignation. Overtime.

Seattle won the toss. Reggie on the Down Low's kickoff return set the offense up at their own 38. Yeager handed off to Mookie Millstone on the first play. The short dark hairy running back broke through the line and didn't stop until he was down to the 16-yard line. An illegal formation penalty on the Seahawks brought the whole thing back. On third and eight, Yeager faked a play-action and dropped back. Jefferson, his primary, was bumped too hard off the line and lost his way, while Green Bay's Reggie White knocked over two Seahawk linemen and lunged for the quarterback. Yeager made one of those twisty side-step moves athletic guys like Yeager make. White flew right on by, looking like a bear trying to catch a man with too many moves.

Seattle's Corey Christian, another man with moves, raced down the far sideline, then juked past his man LeRoy Butler. Christian waved an anxious hand in the air, as if to say, *Yeager, man, I'm open, man, throw me the ball, man!* Yeager fired the rock across his body to the far side of the field. Christian pulled up and leaped for the ball, then landed just this side of inbounds. By then, his man LeRoy Butler recovered and pushed him outta bounds, but the damage had been done. Seahawks ball on the Green Bay 28.

"Yeager-meister!" said Bear, a little too loud for his own comfort.

"Go Seahawks go!" yelled Mama Rent.

"Okay, okay, be cool now," mumbled Bear, feeling the heat in their corner of the green jewel. On first down, Yeager took the snap and handed off to Millstone, who ran to the left and into the pile, as if lining up the ball for El Kicko. But a hole opened that was just too cool and dreamy. The veteran back burst right through. Twenty-eight untouched yards later, the Packers were suddenly dead and Seattle was 1-0.

"Who knew OT would be so easy?" laughed Bear. "And who knew my buddy's career would take me to the temples of my childhood dreams?"

"He just beat your old Green Bay Packers," realized Mama Rent. "You used to love them. I chased all over town for that jacket that one Christmas."

"Childhood infatuation," sighed Bear. "Some are meant to last, some aren't."

SEATTLE'S TRIPLE THREAT WAS 7-0 when it came time to pony up to the Metrodome in Minneapolis for a showdown with the 7-0 Vikings. Some called the stadium the Hefty Bag in honor of the trash bag-like tarp in the baseball outfield. Bear called the stadium *el plástico,* in honor of his Latino grocer in Corona, Seattle.

El plástico was packed tight for the game, the Viking faithful loud as usual. Score at the half: Seahawks 30, Vikings 17.

"Told ya they couldn't stop a true Norseman," Bear told Mama Rent as they traversed the underbelly in search of her nachos. When the Colemans found a suitable vendor, they got in line behind—upon further reveal—the Yeagers, as in Mr. and Mrs. Yeager. Bear morphed into UCLA ambassador in a nanosecond and made the introductions. The parents were chatty and glad to finally meet, as well as all being so delighted that their sons were working together and had gotten along so well all these years.

"Ten years, as a matter of fact," said Bear. The parents turned to him as if shocked to learn it had been a whole decade. "If you count the two years we were friends in school," said Bear. The parents' faces relaxed again, the equation in their minds recalibrated. Mrs. Yeager mentioned that there were two unused seats adjacent to theirs and invited the Colemans to join them. That allowed the four of them to witness together the most gut-wrenching finish of the season.

Minnesota stormed back in the second half and was up 37-30 with under a minute to play. Yeager and the Seahawks had the ball on the Minnesota two, first and goal. *El plástico* was beside itself, their demands for Seahawk meat echoing off the *el plástico*-looking roof. Mrs. Yeager grabbed Bear's arm when her son broke the huddle and came up to the line of scrimmage. They stood with the Viking faithful and watched Minnesota turn away the Seahawks on four successive downs, the last of which came on the last play of the game.

Minnesota did their victory song and dance while Mama Rent and Mrs. Yeager cried. Mr. Yeager and Bear stood stoically until the stands around them emptied, then said their goodbyes. In the taxi, Bear got a call from Hail Larry's Wife, who was calling from Tampa, where the Niners had crushed the Bucs.

"On the freeway. Heard on the radio. I'm sorry," said Hail Larry's Wife.

"That's sports," said Bear, slumping in the backseat. "At least now, the unbeaten monkey is off our backs. You're welcome, '72 Dolphins."

"Always the positive spirit leader," said Hail Larry's Wife. "If you could see this old lady driving—*bitch, would you!*—this creature is going to give me a panic attack."

"Only you can do that," said Bear.

"Then some idiot is on my tail," said Hail Larry's Wife. "I can't stand bad drivers. I shouldn't talk and drive. I hate driving."

"Then why are you, on the phone, that is?" asked Bear.

"Confirming our date in my old stomping grounds next weekend," said Hail Larry's Wife.

"Game on. After today, we're gonna need some serious Bengal meat."

THE NEXT WEEK, YEAGER AND THE SEAHAWKS reminded themselves they were Super Bowl contenders by beating up on downtrodden Cincinnati. Walter took it as a personal affront that he had slipped to #4 in the league's quarterback passer efficiency rating, and the poor Bengals secondary paid the price. The stat of the game in Bear's mind: his man rushed for 36 yards, more than the Bengals offense. The Seahawks were 8-1 and back on track.

Bear spent the weekend with Hail Larry's Wife, who was in her native Ohio for her cousin Eve's wedding. She refused to subject Bear to her family, but she did drive him around the tri-state area, showing him each and every school, shopping mall and ice cream parlor that held a golden moment from her youth. Along the way, she cussed at every driver who failed to read her mind and shouted instructions for those who disobeyed her mind after having read her.

"I may never get in the passenger seat with her again," Bear told Walter later that week. They were on the couch in the den in Newport, Seattle. "There's a story there. A woman's road rage. Why?"

"Hey, it's you!" Walter pointed to the TV. *Entertainment Tonight* was rehashing last week's premiere of *Uptight*. Two busty starlets were standing outside a Hollywood theater, flanked by their hunky male dates. The studio had rushed the film into production to ride the *Basic Instinct* wave. Their basic instincts had paid off. *Uptight* was buzzing at the box office.

"*London Bridge, Rocket Bruthas, Uptight*. I'm still not telling *my* real stories," said Bear.

"You and me both," said Walter. "Millstone asked me if Tammy and I are getting married. How much do you and I suck?"

"No we don't," said Bear.

"I suck," said Walter. "You suck but in a better way. I guess."

"Neither one of us sucks in a bad way, PV." Bear abandoned the couch for the stereo. "Bring it on out—your pessimistic, dark side—watch me swat that shit back at you, like I do your jump shot in hoops. With music, if that's what it takes."

"Oh, no," said Walter upon hearing the chosen song.

"Oh, yes! If it's good enough for Jordan, Barkley and the NBA, it's good enough for Yeager-meister and the Seahawks, baby, 'cause you know we 2 legit!" said Bear. "2 Legit 2 Quit" by MC Hammer came blasting through the speakers, and Bear did his best imitation of a hip-hop dancer.

"Do what you do," yelled Walter, laughing his ass off on the couch.

"*Huh?*" asked Bear, dancing on.

"On the field," said Walter, motioning to Bear's happy soles.

"*Huh?*" laughed Bear, dancing on.

"You know." Walter moved his arms like a cop directing street traffic. Bear shrugged, then danced on, adding some soul to his hip-hop.

"Do what *you* do!" whined Walter, flinging his arm toward his man.

Bear shrugged and blanched, then added a little Sea Gals to his movements.

"There you go!" yelled Walter, rearing back and laughing on the couch.

"Like this?" Bear added a little more Sea Gals to his movements.

"Get down! Ma Funky Bear!" said Walter, arms gyrating in circles.

"You're crazy!" Bear added a little Joe Bruin to his movements.

"You're crazier," laughed Walter, getting the neck-bob going. "Dance, Bear! Go, Coleman! Go, Coleman!"

"You get up here, QB!" said Bear. "Show Seahawks fans Piss 'n' Vinegar is 2 legit 2 quit 2!"

"Dream on!" laughed Walter. Bear added a little Bear Coleman to his movements, then some Michael Jackson, then some Janet Jackson, then combinations of all of them—plus a dash of James Brown Prince Axel Rose Madonna Vogue Davy Lee Roth USC song girls UCLA song girls LA Laker girls MC (Marcus Coleman) Hammer Othello Motownphilly Nicholas brothers and every mascot that ever sweat in front of a crowd—before collapsing on the couch, halfway on top of his man. "You never finish the song," complained Walter.

"Neither do the Sea Gals," said Bear.

"You need to get in front of the crowd at the Kingdome," said Walter.

"Bear Coleman. On the field. In the middle of the nuclear reactor. Do you really wanna go there?" asked Bear.

"This is where I need to be *real* careful with what I ask for," said Walter ...

... BEAR SNUGGLED DEEPER INTO HIS MAN'S billowy pillows, dreaming of Number 13 working out the kinks in his neck at morning practice.

"Ass outta bed, he needs you." A smack of cold denim hit the spirit leader in the face. Tammy stood over him and told him his man wasn't dead or dying. Clothes covered his body. The blur held onto his sanity. Before long he was in the backseat of a black minivan with black windows, the official car of the team.

"Okay, let me have it," said Bear, his first words of the day.

"One of my top assistants is a real go-getter," said Tammy. "Her boyfriend doesn't even know she works for the team—*policy.* He's watching highlights at her studio apartment last week while she's doing the dishes—*typical.* Suddenly he says to the TV: 'Man, guy, get off our quarterback's jock!'"

The minivan neared the industrial area surrounding the Kingdome, where it was raining. Tammy cued up a cassette tape and turned on the wipers: "My go-getter did some research, watched countless hours of old highlight shows featuring this man's analysis, all from games occurring since the Yeager-meister party, specifically, the one that *didn't* happen on the fourth floor. The thing is, these comments may or may not mean anything. It's all in how you interpret them. This morning we showed Walter a video version." Tammy fell silent. The voice of an announcer with potentially evil intentions filled the minivan:

"*If you could see Yeager through my eyes, you'd see a very different QB. A k'waaaay-zy QB.*"

"*Looks to me like Reggie Snowman has passed on his Freak of the Week torch to his quarterback. My advice? Call your album, The Scrambler.*"

"*Howie Long blitzes ... Yeager starts left, turns right. It's obvious he likes going both ways. He gets out of this jam smoothly, or so he thinks ...*"

"Enough," said Bear. "Bottom line?"

"Watch the SOB like a hawk," said Tammy. The black minivan made several turns in several alleys. "Hopefully, he's just being a smart-ass on the air. He knows he won't get much mileage out of a jock having freaky parties. By the way, your man clued me in on QB LOVES THE BEARCAT. As far as we can tell, our little prick of an evil announcer has no idea that *you* were Joe Bruin in either the newspaper photo *or* his Sugar Bowl interrogation—thank God for those two favors!"

"Only Walter, me and Roxanne—the real Joe Bruin—know about that," said Bear. "And the team now."

"We've got our eye on Roxanne Valtron. She's innocuous," said Tammy. "So far." They passed through a blue garage door. "Watch your stomach."

The minivan descended in spirals, the kind associated with parking garages. Only this was more like one deep downward journey. Once the descent was over, they came to a steel door. "Understand this truth," said Bear. "I'm the showman. Walter is a very, very private warrior."

Without asking, Bear got out and passed through the steel door. He found himself in a small concrete room, just in time to see Yeager fire a five-yard bullet of a pass. The VCR exploded on contact with the concrete wall. Tammy ducked into the doorway. A man in a business suit dove underneath the small table. Walter and Bear stood firm, watching the metallic starburst.

"The fucker's evil head is next," said Walter, looking for another rock to throw.

"Mr. Yeager, sir, you have a visitor," said the quivering man in the business suit.

"Get out," said Bear. The quivering suit complied. Tammy closed the door behind him, leaving Walter and Bear alone.

"I'm being fucked with at the wrong time," said Walter.

"I know," said Bear.

"I will not let this happen," said Walter.

"I know," said Bear.

"And my so-called team—" Walter yelled to the door: *"Fuck 'em!"*

"Big time," said Bear.

"This is beyond wrong," said Walter.

"No doubt," said Bear.

"You've never seen me like this, I'm truly sorry you had to," said Walter.

"I'll go anywhere with you," said Bear.

"That's the thing," said Walter, suddenly deflated by his anger. "I trust you. I trust you." Their foreheads touched, Walter calmed down. "I trust you. I trust Bear. I trust Bear. Let 'em try to mess with us. They ain't seen the best of us yet."

"Nothing's gonna stop Walter and Bear now."

BEAR LIFTED HIS HEAD TOWARD THE sunlight, a welcomed sight after being in the "team basement." The black minivan drove off. Tammy was chauffeuring

Walter to practice. The kryptonite had been removed. He was free to be a quarterback again. Bear felt like collapsing on the pavement. His cell phone rang. He collapsed against the brick wall instead. "Warning, I'm in emotional and physical hell right now," said Bear.

"Me, too, it's called traffic," said Hail Larry's Wife. "Larry wants out of San Fran, and I want to blow this lady's head off—*signal a little earlier next time, old bat!*"

Bear thought about collapsing again. Or at least giving up and letting the evil people of the world win. When that didn't seem like a good idea, he thought about exploding at his best friend. When that didn't seem like a good idea, he decided to be true. "Would you like my take on your hatred of all things vehicular?" asked Bear.

"Anything to help this God-awful, panicked feeling I get," said Hail Larry's Wife.

"You drive," said Bear, "with a superior attitude that says people are in *your* way, that they're *blocking* you, as opposed to being in *harmony* with you. You run lights, you break the law, you don't even care what happens. You don't play by the book. And when others don't play by your book, you get pissed."

"Tell me something I don't know," said Hail Larry's Wife.

"You have a choice," said Bear. "Here's two of them: imagine driving like usual: angry, hurried, resentful. How does that make you feel?"

"Angry, hurried, resentful," said Hail Larry's Wife.

"Now ... imagine driving in a more serene setting, one where you're at peace with the journey because you very well know: you'll get to your destination, find a parking space, do your thing, then ditto in reverse. Happens just about every single time, right? And then you go on with your life—outside your car—and barely remember anything about what happened on the road. And since we're imagining that you know this and are chilled out about it, your ride is a peaceful and easy ride. Now, how does that feel?" There was a long pause on the line, prompting Bear to ask: "Still there?"

"Peaceful. I'm peaceful," said Hail Larry's Wife.

"Get in touch with those two imaginings," said Bear. "Then remember to take the road that gives you the better feeling."

"Thanks, Bear," said Hail Larry's Wife. "I think you just healed me."

"That's your job. I'm just the spirit leader," said Bear.

"Just the same, thanks," said Hail Larry's Wife.

"No, thank you," said Bear. "You just gave me my new movie idea. But I need to write it down *stat* before I lose it."

Letters and words swirled in his headspace. He hung up and looked for the right tools, namely a pen and paper. He found a sidewalk café, borrowed a pen, bought a cup of Joe, and began creating the next Bear Coleman dreamscape. First, he had to write down the keywords hurtling through his headspace at warp speed. Without those initial building blocks serving as trailblazers, the journey would be much rougher. Images orbited his mind like celestial beings on a colorful mobile in a child's crib. He kicked his heels together and giggled at the beautiful brunette woman who stressed out on the *freeways*, at how she *claims* she's the best driver out there. The ideas rotated on the mobile, giving him different views. He saw infinite roads filled with beautiful *bodies*, the brunette's, the cars, bodies *that fade* from sight. The beautiful brunette was going to get exactly what she dreamed of, a soulless highway.

One makes magic with rocks, the other makes magic with blocks.

The scribbles on the napkin would be all Bear needed to begin the process of articulating his dream to the world. He eyed the keywords and smiled. Wilson, his curmudgeonly agent, wouldn't be bugging him to come up with a title this time.

"To SEATTLE WE GO FOR HIGHLIGHTS OF THE AFC Championship game earlier today. The skies were ... who cares! The wind chill ... *forgetaboutit!* This time, Jim Kelly and the 13-4 Buffalo Bills were forced to go west, and battle Yeager-meister and the 15-2 Seahawks in the comfy confines of their concrete dome that was rocking like a nuclear reactor, powered by 65,000 white towels waving their beloved franchise onward. A win today means the team reaches the Super Bowl for the first time in history, in this or any other universe."

"And, Jake, if you look at how Seattle got gypped last year with the frozen *tongue* in Buffalo—you knew they weren't taking any chances this time."

"Rumor has it, the Buffalo sideline guy was held *tongue-tied* at an undisclosed location the entire weekend."

"*Ouch* ... and yes, there were Bills fans at the Kingdome, dreaming of yet another Buffalo shuffle to the Super Bowl—but do they truly wanna risk yet another Super Disappointment?"

"Hey, what else are perennial bridesmaids supposed to do on all those cold snowy nights, except dream of somebody finally paying off the Bills?"

"Thurman Thomas says, *I'll take you there, Buffalo!* ... this eight-yard shuffle to the end zone puts the Bills up 14-7 late in the first quarter."

"Snowman was late with the weak-side help—he's playing too low to the ground these days, maybe getting older or slower, or just out of style, like his urban clothes line."

"*Ouch* ... second quarter ... Thurman Thomas again, this time a 26-yard scamper to put Buffalo up 21-7. Suddenly, the towels aren't waving, and the joint is kinda uptight. Not quite like last week's cool and dreamy 52-0 shellacking of *da Raidas*."

"Yeah, proving you're *2 legit* in the AFC title game is a different story."

"Needless to say, *huge* test for the second-time Pro Bowler Yeager. And he would begin to take charge. Here's In-Control Walter, telling Jefferson on the sideline: *We cool, man. We got time.* Here's Methodical Walter, firing *precision bullet* after *precision bullet* into his receivers' numbers—dare I say, with a kind of Aikman-like methodicalism. *Is that a word?*"

"It is now!"

"Here's Confident Walter, saying *nice try* to Cornelius Bennett, who *juuuuuust* missed sacking the QB on third and 18. Instead, the meister converted to Jefferson—*see, he cool!*—setting up this 13-yard shot up the middle by Mookie *'just call me General'* Millstone. El Kicko *el kicks* the PAT. Bills now up, 21-14. Later on, Buffs get a field goal to go up 24-14 with less than 10 minutes to Super Dreams in Atlanta."

"And that's when the towels kick in, swirling like 65,000 kilowatts of: *We are the Pacific Northwest, hear us roar!* And Seahawks fans are loving it."

"So is this guy—whom we're told wrote the movie *Uptight.* I think I speak for most men when I say ... *we're not worthy ... but thank you!* Apparently, he's a Seahawks fan, judging by the ear-to-ear grin and the way he's working that towel. After a Bills punt, the meister begins a methodical drive downfield, carving up Buffalo's secondary with Jefferson, Lars, and Christian."

"Think the boys finally believe they can be *2 legit?*"

"Yeager says, *Oh, yes!* Down to the 30, under seven to play. Shotgun. Looks off Jefferson, then lofts it to Corey Christian, who leaps for it at the 20. That's when the ball is tipped by the Bills' Odomes, right to Steven Lars! And look at the 40-year-old blond bomber receiver go!"

"I haven't seen those skinny old legs churn that fast in a decade!"

"*Ouch* ... Lars puts his entire body into *going all ... the ... way!*"

"Hey, could be his last shot at Super Glory."

"El Kicko makes it 24-21 with under six to play."

"Plenty of time on the clock. Number 13's on the sidelines, telling the faithful: *'Get those towels up for the defense!'*"

"Bills go three and out and punt. Is it time to talk Seattle vs. the Niners, winners earlier today at Dallas?"

"Gotta score first—if you're the Seahawks—without leaving Kelly and the Bills too much time to *rightbackatcha*."

"*This* we know: Seahawks ball at their own 42 with under five to go. Yeager becomes a traffic director out there, making sure everybody is *2 legit*. Coach Robbins is pacing but calm, even on this near interception thrown over the middle on second down."

"He's putting it in his man's Yeager's hands all the way."

"The meister converts on third down with a shuttle pass to Millstone—nice juke into the clear for 14 yards."

"Meanwhile, in the Seahawks dressing room: plastic everywhere and Champagne on ice. But will they celebrate like Kool and the Gang?"

"Gotta move the ball closer. But what to do when the drive stalls?"

"Call up the league commissioner and ask for your lost frozen down back!"

"Not gonna happen. I do believe Yeager wants to be *2 legit,* but not without a little drama. The meister shoots three blanks, and Seattle's season and *raison d'être* comes down to fourth and 10 on the Buffalo 38 with under three to play."

"Three crazy passes that don't really go anywhere. The nuclear reactor is humming, begging for their dreams not to go imploding in a puff of dust. And what does the meister do? Says: *'I'm cool, I'm dreamy, I got my own flava. I got it under control. Fourth down. Let me take it from the shotgun, look up, look back, check out all my options, and then fire away to my man Junior!—streaking down the sideline for a touchdown that says, Hello, Atlanta! Sweet, sweet Georgia Dome!'*"

"The Bills ... we won't even show you their last gasp of air. *Sayonara* and better luck next time to the Buffs."

"Maybe their vanishing is a good thing, considering their fans are spared another Super Disappointment."

"All in the mind, eh?"

"All in the Peach State now for Yeager and the Seahawks."

20

The Ninety-Nine Yard Pass

S*o, if you're ready ... cut to the song* "Whoomp! (There It Is)" *by Tag Team, the rap jam that was one of the jock jams of that time. Our time.*

Bear, Mama Rent and Hail Larry's Wife stuck together like three satellites, watching football fans *raise their hands in the air like they just don't care,* because Tag Team was live!—onstage at a free concert in a park in downtown Atlanta. Bear and his mother had been pointing to the trip since their man's Champagne shower in the Kingdome locker room after beating Buffalo. "I'll be attending the Super Bowl festivities this week," Mama Rent reminded her friends, family, hairdresser, church buddies, and Daddy Coleman, whom she hadn't called in decades.

Hail Larry's Wife was just as thrilled. Like Bear, this was her first Super Week as a participant's Super spouse. Super Sunday was days away. Competitive tensions were running low. At some undetermined point, Bear and his gal pal would separate and orbit different sides of the Super Universe, not coming together again until *another* undetermined point, after it was all over, and one of their husbands possessed his first Super Bowl ring, while the other husband was out of the loop.

"Glad you're hanging 'round," said Bear, tapping his foot to the beat.

"For now anyway," said Hail Larry's Wife, sporting her husband's 49ers jersey and doing *the bump* between the hips of Bear and Mama Rent.

"Hey, man, it's the lesbian flick dude ... we're not worthy ... but thank you!"

"Yeah, yeah ... up yours!" said Bear, waving at two horny males passing in the crowded blur. The music came to a halt.

"Oh ... my ... God. No freakin' way!" Hail Larry's Wife stopped dancing. The concert's MC came on stage and slapped hands with Tag Team, whose rap was fading. The MC was none other than Evil Announcer Guy.

"Location change," said Bear, herding the women toward the NFL Experience, the playground full of interactive football fun.

"He looks nasty," said Mama Rent, looking backward.

"And not good, Janet-Jackson nasty," said Bear.

"Does your mom know about the party screw-up?" asked Hail Larry's Wife.

"What party screw-up by your husband?" said Bear, rushing them forward. "Nothing like that exists this week! This is *our* Super Week—nothing Super *weak* can stop us now."

"Bear, something awful happened?" asked Mama Rent.

"See! It's about to, if we keep talking about it!" said Bear. "Fine, tell her about your freakin' husband's screw-up—*discreetly*—so we can get it over with. Then we are not mentioning that evil announcer freak this week again, okay?"

"Calm down, Bear, *geez*," said Hail Larry's Wife.

"Has saying that phrase with such a nasty, bitchy, demanding tone *ever* gotten anyone in the history of the universe *to calm down?!*" growled Bear.

"Calm down, Marcus," said Mama Rent, using his birth name for the first time ... *ever?*

Bear exhaled the hot air out of his lungs. "Give me a scoop of Yeager-meister, and *maybe*." He exhaled again. "Listen. The evil one—and by the way, don't ever say his name in front of us—the evil one may be an asteroid floating around the Super Universe, but Walter and I were *2 legit* Asteroid-busters back in the day when that was one of, like, *three* video games in the universe, *okay?*—so hey, let the good times roll. I got my man's back, *always and forever.*"

"So at the Yeager-meister party ..." said Hail Larry's Wife to Mama Rent. Bear gave up and laughed, having remembered a thing or two about women from the Sugar Bowl restroom 10 years ago.

While his gal pals bonded, Bear soaked up the NFL Experience, a midway carnival of chances to punt, pass and kick one's way into football heaven, a virtual hands-on thrill park that gave regular gods a chance to become football gods and dream a little dream. "They shortchanged my man," said Bear, test-driving Yeager's plastered appendages, in this case, the quarterback's hand and foot imprints.

"I'm impressed anyway," said both Mama Rent and Hail Larry's Wife.

"We're not alone," said Bear, surveying the frenetic hum in the blur. "I've never seen so many men, women and children wearing Walter's jersey. Look how much bigger he's getting, just getting this far."

A family of six passed all sporting Yeager's #13 Seahawks jerseys. "Imagine if he wins," said Mama Rent, disappearing into the restroom.

"Is everyone here invited to your 'official' Yeager pep rally?" asked Hail Larry's Wife, leaning against the fence separating them from the tackling dummies.

"Will you stop calling it a pep rally?" said Bear. "If your husband played on our team, you *might* be in the loop."

"Oh, *pul-lease,* spend more time with a bunch of Walt worshippers?" laughed Hail Larry's Wife, more focused on toying with her Slurpee.

"Your husband mentioned playing for our team once," said Bear. A monitor above showed Yeager at Super practice, throwing a quick pass to the running back Mookie Millstone.

"Actually, it was twice," said Hail Larry's Wife, referring to the Pro Bowl luau.

"Hell, how much does Larry wanna be on our team?" asked Bear, more focused on his man on high.

"You think Walter wants him on your team?" asked Hail Larry's Wife.

"Depends on which team," said Bear, hands in his pockets.

"How many teams are you on?" laughed Hail Larry's Wife, savoring her frozen treat.

"His contract with Seattle is up after Sunday. We'll have to see. But we're cool and dreamy with the team, as is. So far," said Bear.

"Larry might have to switch teams," said Hail Larry's Wife. "We've had trouble in San Francisco. The first wife lives in the freakin' Bay Area, of all the worst places. There were some harassment charges on both sides that escalated into—let's just say, it could've been a nightmare if the team hadn't fixed it."

"What a team," said Bear.

"Hey, if sports was based on morality, we'd all be out of gladiators *and* husbands," said Hail Larry's Wife.

"I'm having déjà vu," said Bear. A punt landed at his feet and bounced up in his face, forcing him to go into ATHLETIC STUD MODE to send it orbiting back into space.

"You're good, Bear," said Hail Larry's Wife. He eyed her, unsure if she was being true.

"So is our team, at helping us," said Bear.

"Did Walter get into trouble?" asked Hail Larry's Wife, taking a coy sip of her Slurpee. "If you don't mind."

"Oh, yeah, a heap of trouble," said Bear. "Has the nerve to love me."

"You mean because you're gay?" asked Hail Larry's Wife.

Bear shook his head, momentarily stumped. His brain received the input, but his brain had not programmed an output.

Gay in ... nothing out.

"Helps to have some cool teammates if you're a warrior brave enough to love ... another." Bear watched little boys tackling big dummies on the other side of the fence. Hail Larry's Wife dunked her Slurpee into a nearby trashcan.

"So you also noticed how much my freakin' husband talks about nailing your freakin' husband's ass," said Hail Larry's Wife.

Bear sighed with relief. "And my husband said *I* was crazy for dreaming it up."

"*You discussed it with Walter?* Say you didn't, Bear. Just lie," said Hail Larry's Wife.

"Why?" laughed Bear. "You think I'm capable of hiding anything from a man with Walter's amazing powers of perception? He dismissed it anyway."

"Have *you?*" asked Hail Larry's Wife.

"What does the wife think?" asked Bear.

"My husband is not gay, or even bi ... just ... infatuated," said Hail Larry's Wife.

"Infatuated?" laughed Bear. "Like a goofy kid who can't get enough of him?—I mean, what's your definition of infatuation?"

"Someone he talks about all the time. How cool he is, how put-together, what great shoulders, what a great neck, *and on and freakin' on to the break of freakin' dawn!*" said Hail Larry's Wife.

"That does sound silly, and like an infatuation," said Bear, sorta sheepish.

"It's Super Bowl week. Let's not have this conversation," said Hail Larry's Wife.

"Deal," said Bear, glad to see Mama Rent emerging from the ladies' restroom so they could continue onward with their NFL fantasy experience.

THE NEXT DAY, WALTER YEAGER'S MANAGER, Bear Coleman, hosted the Yeager Party, an outdoor gathering where everyone with a legitimate claim to Walter's fame celebrated their man's success. To the spirit leader, it was important to harness all that positive energy in the name of his bud, to provide Super fuel for the week and Super Sunday. Mr. and Mrs. Yeager were there, as were Grace and her three daughters—all four of them the poster girls for Yeager-meister ice cream. Walter's siblings, who remained something of a blur to Bear, were also there. There was the sister with whom Walter shared a hot/cold relationship, and an older brother who harbored mixed emotions about Walter's success, his own ultimate sports dreams having fallen a bit short. The Yeager siblings were like comets that flew in the distant galaxies of Bear's universe, as were the rest of Walter's very beautiful relatives, most of whom reminded Bear of the beautiful white people from his college days, the ones from Orange County, California. The Yeager family was both mythical and mystical to Bear, a world so polar opposite his own, yet an exact reflection at the very core.

Walter's black side was represented by Bear, Mama Rent and several of Walter's *bruthas* from the football world. Bear was pleased with the way the races mingled with ease. Like so many times in sports, the common ground was the joy created by all shades of men. Bear imagined Walter being proud of the mix of those gathered in his honor. Walter cared about race, and Bear had to hold back tears, watching so many people care about Walter.

"You look weak, have you eaten?" asked Walter's Sister.

"I'll be all right," said Bear, realizing he had stumbled against the big greeting card signed by everyone at the party. He regulated himself and held his cell phone sky-high. "Okay, Yeager-meister fans, surprise! In a second, I'll have my client—oh, excuse me—*Walter's* voice mail, and we're gonna leave a message ... hold on for the thumbs up, then yell your guts out for this Sunday's *PV*, I mean, MVP ... get ready ... Uh, I'm calling for a Walt Yeager who used to play football at the University of Georgia in the early 80s ... Mr. Yeager, this is your manager calling with a message from a little Walter Yeager Super Rally."

The spirit leader gave a thumbs up. The throng combusted, turning the hotel gardens into a mini-nuclear reactor.

"Go Walter you da man we love you Walt you can do it baby boy don't let anyone break that spirit and soul of yours brother we can do this baby all the way bro all yours baby you da man we love you Walt always knew you could our hero so proud our man our bruthaman my man god man we love you Big Norse no matter no matter we love Walter! ... yeah, baby, Walterrrrr!"

Like a conductor, Bear squeezed his palm shut and turned off the sunburst of support.

"Go play some Super Bowl, QB!" Bear held the cell in the air once again. With his other hand, he urged the crowd onward, then hung up shortly thereafter.

That was about as verbally connected as the boys stayed all week. Walter was Super busy, answering countless questions on media day, stealing time with his family—oh, and practicing, because the big league boys didn't march to Atlanta to pay homage to Steve Young and the Golden 49ers. Walter and Bear returned to the Peach State to show the world what the University of Georgia had failed to see, a young man who was Ultimately Golden at any age in *all ways,* in or out of their red-clad headspace. If it were up to Bear, the entire universe would know his man's godly brilliance, as a quarterback, an athlete, a thinker, a leader of men, a sensitive child, a passionate powerful superstar in the truest sense.

"You nailed it with the voice mail!" said Walter by phone midweek. "Now can't you figure out how to steal me away for two minutes? Minus the collegiate hysterics, mind you."

"Kinda overwhelmed here handling the Scandinavian Yeagers' Super requests," said Bear. "They're all like you: stone-faced and blunt. And demanding, minus the Sugar. Can't *your* mind dream of hooking us up?"

"It's booked trying to win us a ring," said Walter.

"I'm on it, partner, minus the collegiate hysterics," said Bear.

"I'll show up if you show up," said Walter. "And Bear, try whelming."

"*Rightbackatcha.*" Bear hung up and signaled to Tammy, who was cutting across the restaurant. Snaky Lu's Soul Food of Atlanta was a theme park in the vein of Hard Rock Café. During Super Week, there was hardly any empty space between the worldwide tourists and the artifacts of the Soul of America.

"Half the town is outside this joint," said Tammy, reaching the table and straightening her navy blue business suit, bosomy as always.

"I should have told them upfront Walter's manager was expecting his" — Bear eyed her long blonde legs disappearing under the table—"woman."

"Yeah, well, *his* woman is clueless about dreaming up a way to steal a moment for him and ... *his* man." Tammy opened the menu. "*Hmmm,* food for the soul ... ham hocks."

"So the Niners really are the biggest and best team in all of sports," said Bear. "*Not* Tammy, her B.O. and her *bull!*"

A bewildered Tammy took a whiff of the fruity scent between her bosoms and said, "It's been Super Peachy all week."

"Not for us," said Bear. "My man needs me. I can feel it. I can feel him. Even for five minutes."

"Look around you, for once in your life," said Tammy, eating the untouched food on his plate.

"Need food first, getting lightheaded," said Bear. "Chicken. Creole chicken."

"The entire Atlanta universe looks exactly like this right now." Tammy rolled her head in circles as if to loosen a very uptight body. A dizzy Bear swore she was doing her imitation of the possessed daughter in *The Exorcist*.

"Wait 'til you see the *Freeways*," said Bear, scribbling a note for his script-in-progress: *heroine's head and/or car spins like Linda Blair. Near end?*

"You didn't make my job any easier when you became Hollywood's hot lesbian flick guy," said Tammy.

"I didn't realize it was my job to make yours any easier, Miss Claus. Or is that Mrs. Claus? Oh, who cares?" Bear slammed a knife on the table, got up and threw a manly wad of cash down. "No more chicken for me, any flavor. I know teams can do a lot, Tammy, even for people who get caught hating instead of loving."

He stood eye level with the photo of soul singer Al Green. Tammy looked up with a batch of greens sticking out of her mouth.

"I'm outta here," said Bear, drying a tear. "Don't make me go out and buy a Bear suit."

EVERY PLAYER WHO HAS A WIFE OR GIRL HAS SEEN HER THIS WEEK, GOTTEN THEIR SUGAR, SHARED IN THE MOMENT. AIN'T FREAKIN' FAIR.

Bear hit the backspace button on his laptop and removed his buddy's words, spoken this morning on the phone. The line of dialogue didn't fit the voice of Lucy *slash* Lacy, the heroine of *Freeways Claim Bodies That Fade*. The screenwriter was in his hotel bed, taking a breather from the Super Universe. A knock on the door spelled the end of the break.

"Come to take you there, just a pissant thang," said Black Coach, Yeager's former assistant from San Diego, now a 49ers backfield coach.

"He's okay?" asked Bear.

"No doubt, as the kids say. Get your shoes. Shirt wouldn't hurt either," said Black Coach.

The rental car sped away from the hotel, past Super paraphernalia: Yeager jerseys, Snowman jerseys, Jefferson jerseys—and all their 49er counterparts. Bear assumed the radio station was inadvertent. Then he realized the radio station was a cassette tape, playing something from the movie *The Best Little Whorehouse in Texas*. "Boy, it takes all types, don't it?" laughed Black Coach, perhaps meaning the Super crazy fans blurring past in the sunlight. Dolly Parton sang about A Lil' Ole Bitty Pissant Country Place. The older Negro drove, talking while singing with Dolly, not concerned about getting the lyrics right or keeping with the song: "Listening good? They like your boy this week ... lotta goodwill ... surely one lil' thrill ... you boys'll be fine."

Eventually, the football universe morphed into urban Atlanta.

"Seen a lot of prejudice," said Black Coach, tapping the wheel to Dolly. "Simple farmers ... young boys out for sin ... shit, man, y'all niggas ain't seen shit like what we niggas saw back then."

"Klansmen visited my mom's house in Indianapolis where she grew up," said Bear. "They wanted to discourage my uncle from playing in a high school game. He was a Mr. Basketball in the 50s, the state's top honor."

"Dirty on and on ... I'm glad that hasn't stopped you from ... one small lil' thrill ... mistrusting all white men, like my boy Reggie ... overloaded mouth ... like so many blacks I know," said Black Coach. "Dirty on and on."

The streets were the polar opposite of Super Atlanta. The homes were decrepit, with an abundance of liquor stores and check-cashing stores. And police presence.

"Who said they forgot about us this week?" laughed Black Coach, perhaps at Dolly's sweet voice, perhaps not. "Dirty on and on. You know I took Reggie in when he was a teen, running loose in Watts ... sleeping in a car with his mama ... *hiiiiiigh* on the street ... ain't selling now, my sister."

"Coach, what really happened in San Diego?" asked Bear.

"Good, goodwill ... I don't follow," said Black Coach.

"What was the real reason you told Walter to prove himself in Canada before taking his shot here?" asked Bear.

"... other people's business. What was the best possible outcome from Walter's decision?" asked Black Coach.

"That's easy. This week," said Bear.

"... maybe one lil' thrill ... you tell 'em, Dolly," laughed Black Coach, stopping at an intersection. "Now, Bear, imagine me giving Walter that advice from the bottom of my heart. All worked out for the best, right? ... nothing dirty on and on. God, I love that song. I can play it forever."

"Yes but—" said Bear.

"Whenever you think of me," said Black Coach, "try thinking of me acting with that same kind of perfect grace in Walter's life, *always and forever.*"

"Yes but—" said Bear.

"Meaning: every single thing I ever do while I live and breathe on the face of this earth only *lifts your buddy higher and higher toward his ultimate glory,* whatever Walter wants that to be, understand?" asked Black Coach. "I got his back, like the kids say."

"Yes but—" said Bear.

"*Or* you can think of me as your worst enemy." Black Coach took off from the intersection. "Some old black man who raps country music, talks shit and is always out to screw you boys every chance I get. You make the call. Good light, bad light. It's your light. But I'll tell you some serious shit right now, boy: try thinking of every single thing that happens in your life in the *best light*. You'll be amazed at how this world will *light up with magic* that will have your eyes trying to *pop outta dem sockets!*"

The rental transport rolled onward. Bear fell silent for a while. The wisest male Negro was in the driver's seat, reminding Bear of the first decade and a half of his life.

"Where is QB, by the way?" asked Bear as they slowed down.

"Where I got my first coaching job," said Black Coach. The transport pulled into a fenced-in lot. A rundown junior high school. They parked next to the lone car, a black minivan with black windows. "Did I mention my father is still the principal here?" Black Coach got out, Bear followed. "Lil' Bitty Pissant School. And my mother, the algebra teacher." Black Coach unlocked the gym door.

Inside, Walter stood above the three-point arc on the far side of the basketball court. He let go of the rock—the orange one—and sank a three, pumping his fist triumphantly.

"That means a win on Sunday," said Walter. "Sorry, Coach."

"I'll pass it along to Young later today," said Black Coach, referring to the Niners' quarterback.

"I feel for Steve if he doesn't have a back cracker," said Walter, shaking hands with Bear at midcourt. "Thanks for showing up."

"Tell me something," said Black Coach. "Do you think I took time out of my Super Bowl week *and* missed my soap opera so you two can crack backs? What kind of a pissant ole black man you take me for?"

"One who's on our team," laughed Walter, shaking Coach's hand.

"I'm part of the 49ers, make no mistake, but I've always admired you and you—saw what ya had that first night in San Diego," said Black Coach. "Look at you, got the kind of chemistry guys on the field kill for. Montana and Rice. Young and Rice. Bradshaw and Swan. Aikman and Irvin. Yeager and Coleman. Same kind of synchronicity, same kind of unspoken inner shit going on. Indulge me, have a seat."

Walter headed for the bleachers, Bear followed. They sat on the same wooden plank, Walter leaning backward, Bear leaning forward.

"You know why I thought of this pissant place today?" asked Black Coach, standing on the sideline. "My science teacher, Miss Pauline. Did I mention I was a student here, too? *Beautiful* black woman. I was infatuated, but anyway, we'd be in class, talking about space. She challenged us to come up with ideas for what was beyond our known universe. Our grades were based on our ideas, be they on a test, our science project, a quiz or whatever."

"What a task for a bunch of head cases at that age," said Walter.

"It was about using our imagination," said Black Coach. "Every day, students would complain. *'What am I supposed to do?'* Every day, Miss Pauline—did I mention she was a beautiful black woman?—she would say, *'Dream of something, anything.'* She changed my life. And boy, was she beautiful. Lady had an ass. Sorry, I'm an ass man. I love women and women's behinds. Supersize is *aiight* with me, as the kids say."

Walter and Bear sat there quietly, waiting for the point.

"What's the worst thing that could happen if the world found out about your private business?" asked Black Coach.

"Lose my career, chaos and disorder," said Walter.

"And *your* worst shot?" Black Coach asked Bear.

"Armageddon," said Bear. "Not in the biblical sense. Or maybe in the biblical sense, but just our own personal version."

"Now what's your *best* shot?" asked Black Coach. "A best-case scenario for all your private business being cool and dreamy, and your public business being *2 legit?* What would make the rest of your lives, from this moment on, a dream come true?"

Walter held Bear's hand. "Us staying together, winning ball games, making great movies, being who we are, with absolutely no interference from anyone who doesn't have our best interests at heart. Period. Oh, and good health for both our families."

"Ditto on hubby's wishes," said Bear.

Dying to say hubby, *weren't you? said Walter's look.*

"Then why dream about the nightmare?" asked Black Coach. "Why don't you two lovebirds dream the better dream—focus on the better dream? Do either of you believe dreams come true?"

Walter and Bear remained blank.

"Well?" asked Black Coach.

"I'm here," said Walter, indicating the ground beneath him.

"Do you believe anything is possible?" asked Black Coach.

"I do," said Bear, grinning at hubby.

"How about Salt?" asked Black Coach. Walter hesitated.

"Gone leave Pepper hanging?" asked Bear, sounding urban.

"Yeager," said Black Coach. "When you were walking around high school with your bad self, being the quarterback god you were, which did you think might happen by age 30: playing in a Super Bowl, or you sharing your dreams with this young black man who's obviously very much in love with you?"

"Thing is, I got both now," said Walter, "at age 31."

"So you see," said Black Coach. "Anything really is possible."

The sunlight from outside shifted in the upper windows of the gymnasium, casting the space in a whole new light. Birds fluttered above in the rafters, a peaceful game of tag between two playmates in their own universe.

"Your dreams are your most powerful tool," said Black Coach. "Has any great athlete ever achieved ultimate glory without first conceiving of the dream, then keeping that dream close to his soul while he slaves away, trying to make it to the summit?"

"*Preach!*" said Bear.

"Your dreams are where you get in touch with your soul's true desires," said Black Coach. "It's where God lets you test-drive anything you can conceive of. Then, after you test-drive it in your mind, you can decide if you want the dream to come true. The more you dream of it, the more it can come true, as long as you believe and act like you believe. And dream of it."

"But what about my teammates?" asked Walter. "And the fans?"

"And the media and family and the owners?" asked Bear.

"What about them?" Black Coach moved toward the far sideline. "Leave that shit to other people—those are details! Did you dream of people throwing shit in your face as a kid? If you did, dream on: it'll happen. Whatever you put your energy into will come true, *true dat,* as the kids say."

"You know how guys in the league are, Coach," said Walter.

"You're in the league, I know how *you* are," said Black Coach, more focused on leaving. "At least I do now."

"You didn't before?" asked Walter.

"Dirty on and on," said Black Coach, fading from the gym, his voice echoing in the rafters: "Dream the better dream. The grandest dream. The deepest dream. The one that brings you the most joy. We'll take care of the rest. Haven't we so far?"

The gym doors closed. Walter and Bear were face-to-face, then forehead-to-forehead. "He's a great man. How did I get so lucky?" asked Walter.

"Just one of the angels I prayed for during all the time away from you," said Bear. "Dirty on and on."

"Think he can be an angel for your mom?" asked Walter.

"As in a date? Nothing dirty going on." Bear lifted his head to the rafters. "Mama Rent's done with men."

"Dream the better dream," said Walter.

"Then let's start with the one where you poke holes in the Niners secondary on Sunday," said Bear.

"You having fun this week?" asked Walter. Before Bear could answer, they were interrupted by a pounding on the gym doors, followed by a commotion on the other side. Worried for Black Coach, they raced to the door. Outside, they were engulfed by dozens of little black kids, all going bonkers because Walter Yeager was in the house.

"I don't know how this happened," yelled Black Coach over the chaos.

"No worries." Yeager smiled big, moving among the sea of younger, smaller bodies swarming him. He signed jerseys, t-shirts, naked forearms. He posed for pictures with giggly little black girls. He gave high-fives to eager little black boys and made his way to the minivan like the Pied Piper, surrounded by little black satellites, as Black Coach and Bear tagged behind. When Yeager reached the transport, a black kid—perhaps 12 and not the manliest—raced into the chaos, begging Yeager to throw the kid's football. "Go long," said Walter, getting in a mini-stance. "Blue, 24 ... blue, 24 ... hut!"

The kid raced across the lot. The little black satellites screamed for him to go faster and farther. Walter waited until the last possible moment, then released a beauty of a spiral that sailed toward the far end of the lot. The kid glanced over his shoulder and doubled his speed. His foot tripped on a hole. He stumbled forward undeterred, keeping his eye on the ball, catching it in stride, and bouncing against the fence like a graceful boomerang, somersaulting backward until he was standing again. The little black satellites ambushed him as if he'd just scored the winning touchdown on Super Sunday. A few moments later, the hero and his swarming fans returned to the quarterback.

"The lot's like a hundred yards," said the kid. "That pass had to be 99."

"It ain't no hundred yards, *Walta*," said a girl in pigtails.

"She don't know, *Water*," said the kid, still catching his breath.

"Did it feel like 99?" Walter asked his receiver. "That's what counts, the rest is details."

"I might be a receiver or run track someday, *Water*," said the kid. "Or dance on MTV award shows." The other kids laughed incredulously.

"Any of those is a good way to express yourself," said Walter.

"And achievable," said Bear, "with desire, guts and determination."

"And not worrying about what other people think, even if they're so rude as to laugh at your dreams, *hint, hint*," said Walter, prompting laughter from the guilty satellites.

"Who are *you*?" asked a dark boy, staring up at Bear.

"Walter's manager," said Bear.

"What do you manage?" asked an older girl.

"Whatever he can't," said Bear, glancing toward the black minivan.

"For real?" asked the older girl.

"True dat," said Bear.

"Two-minute warning," said Tammy from the driver's window. The quarterback and his satellites rotated to the passenger side, where his adoring black fans released him.

"Sorry for being uptight," said Bear, remaining on the driver's side.

"I know what love is like, from both sides," said Tammy.

"And now know I know the best team in all of sports," said Bear, "either way you slice it."

SUPER SUNDAY REMINDED BEAR of the big games of his college days, magnified by infinity. Several times during the game, he stood and became light-headed from the crowd's roar. There was so much to take in, sometimes he had to be content just to float in the blur and absorb the energy, much like his one turn as Joe Bruin at the Sugar Bowl.

The Seahawks were in their home blues. During pre-game introductions, Yeager charged onto the field like a man PRIMED AND READY to conquer the world. But it wasn't until the second quarter that the world began to cooperate. The score was knotted at threes with a few minutes left in the half. Steve Young, Jerry Rice and Hail Larry McPherson were still trying to figure out how to outsmart Reggie Snowman and the Seattle defense, while Yeager, Jefferson and Corey Christian were trying to figure out how to outsmart Dana Stubblefield and the San Francisco defense. On second and short from his own 20, Yeager took the snap from the shotgun, sidestepped the blitzing middle linebacker, and heaved a rocket to Christian, who didn't stop running until he was halfway back to the bench. The score was 10-3, Hawks. The meister's cork had been unplugged.

"2 legit!" said Bear to Mama Rent from their seats in the Georgia Dome, a peach of a place right about now. The Niners fumbled before the half, giving Walter a minute to score from 40 yards out. Mookie Millstone, the running back, fed off Walter's confidence and ran for 21 yards on first down. On second down, Yeager fumbled the snap, scrambled around the backfield, then broke two tackles and ran it in himself from 19, putting Seattle up 17-3.

"You know, he and I have been together 10 years and have never once mentioned rings," said Bear to Mama Rent during the halftime show.

"How awful," said Mama Rent.

"Neither one of us do jewelry or the unnecessary," said Bear. "We know we're in the loop. Still, I think I'm gonna like this new one."

Bear spent the second half watching his man and the Seahawks soar, and soaking up the images of a dream come true. Like the SC-UCLA games of old, there was so much to inhale and so little time to savor. Seattle did their best to help everyone relax. Reggie Snowman had two interceptions, one for a 16-yard TD. Walter and the offense did the rest. Seattle cruised to a 38-10 Super victory. Yeager went 24-30 passing, for 312 yards and three TDs, good enough to be named Most Valuable Player. Also good enough to prompt two Colemans to sob with joy as Walter accepted the award on a stage in the middle of the field.

"And nothing from the nasty announcer man," said Mama Rent.

"We dreamed the better dream, and the better dream came out on top."

"WHAT DO YOU MEAN: *NOT EXACTLY?*" said Walter, pressing the accelerator, as if going into TURBO MODE. "How isn't this the better dream?"

"Slow down, MVP," said Bear. The Georgia night passed too fast in the blur. "I'll explain everything if you slow down this gorgeous red sports car you rented."

Walter had finished all his Super Sunday business except for their private affair. Bear had no idea where they were going but had a sneaky suspicion they were heading for the land of the Dawgs. "I'm calm, spill," said Walter.

"I only saw it on the monitors in the stadium," said Bear.

"Can you believe that evil fucker was allowed in the World Champ's locker room?" said Walter.

"You played it off great, *Walta*. The graceful warrior in victory," said Bear. "Only *I* know how truly cocky you rightfully are."

"*Rightbackatcha*. But what the fuck happened?" asked Walter, rolling down the window, letting in a gust of roaring winter wind.

"Bring it down to whelming, bud. We do wanna enjoy the ring," said Bear.

"Go!" said Walter.

"Yeager's on the podium in the Champagne-drenched locker room," said Bear. "The evil one is wrapping up his Champagne-drenched interview with the dashing, sweaty, stinky, Sugary, victorious and funky meister—"

"What happened, *so help me!*" yelled Walter into the Georgia night.

"You finished up your interview," said Bear. "You changed positions with Millstone and hollered, as part of your MVP contractual obligation: '*Going to biggest dreamiest fantasy park of all time!!*' That's when the evil freak said it."

"*Are you taking that little bearcat?*"

"But people may not have heard. My mother didn't," said Bear. "And remember, to him and the world, that little bearcat is Joe Bruin, a female with bosoms underneath."

"*I just won the Super Bowl!*" yelled Walter into the Georgia night. "*We just won the Super Bowl! Me and my little bearcat won the Super Bowl!*" Then he stuck his head back in the car. "Bearcat, how does it feel?"

"Like I'm gonna go fucking crazy, one way or another," said Bear.

"Then go crazy, fucker! Not one thing is gonna stop us now!" Walter cranked up the radio full blast. A sports station was quoting the Man.

"*Snow's interception came at a crucial point, but we weren't about to celebrate,*" said Walter from the skies. "*The Niners aren't quitters, this much is true.*"

"Love you too, MVP," said Bear.

"This much is true," said Walter.

"*Shh ... replay of the TD pass in the fourth,*" said Bear.

"*Yeager from the nine, third and goal. Takes the snap, dumps off a little lateral to Millstone—wait now, Mooks is looking for someone to throw to! Here comes the rush! Can't find anyone ... but oh, my! Walter Yeager, standing in the far end zone, catches the ball! Touchdown, Seahawks! They brought the bag of tricks today, but I think they can start packing their bags after that one!*"

"Enough about me," said Walter, popping a cassette in the dash. The song "Somebody's Baby" by Jackson Browne filled the little red sports car.

"I love this song!" cried Bear.

"*Duh!*" said Walter with a proud smile. "You used to play it in your green Olds, driving and thinking about your quarterback boyfriend in Georgia."

"I never told you that," giggled Bear.

"I didn't dream it up," said Walter, rolling up the window.

"You're always telling me things I don't remember telling you," said Bear.

"My powers are amazing," said Walter.

"No doubt, MVP," said Bear. "What else you got tonight?"

Walter grabbed Bear's hand and kissed it gently. "I'd be Most Valuable Prick without my Bear."

"You'd managed," said Bear.

"Without my manager? What about my South Pole?" asked Walter. "Thought I'd be a wobbly planet without you."

"Only Walt knows for sure," said Bear, stroking his man's golden head. Before long, the car was filled with the melodic sounds of "True" by Spandau Ballet, their very first song from that very first weekend.

"Right on time," said Walter. The little red sports car pulled to a stop. They were on a modest hillside overlooking Athens, Yeager's former college town that was a collection of glowing lights in the distance.

"*Walta,* no you *did-n't,* as the kids say," said Bear.

"I supposed you don't remember telling me about the hilltop." Walter got out, Bear followed.

"The one I was hoping we would escape to the night we met? So I could pour my naïve little adolescent heart out?" Bear surveyed the sky. "When did I tell you that?"

"Who knows? I just remember," said Walter.

"You finally ready to stop hating UGA?" asked Bear, imagining a campus somewhere in the blur beyond the dark.

"Let's do the hilltop thing first," said Walter.

"Okay, go," said Bear.

"Me? This is your chance to say whatever you wanted to say to me 10 years ago," said Walter. "Pretend it's the night before the game. We just left the frat house. You got your wish. A Georgia hilltop. And ... *action!*"

"This is crazy. I'm a different person," said Bear. "Older. Wiser. What—you want me to verbalize what was in my mind back then? Or my mind now?"

"Forget the details, Bear, *geez,*" said Walter, exasperated. "You have to admit: you make things way more complicated than I do sometimes."

"What does Walter want?" asked Bear, exasperated.

"This is *your* time, nobody else, just little Bearcat." Walter's face turned serious. "The love of my life."

"Oh, Walter." *He called me little Bearcat!*

"Don't cry, spill." Walter sat on the hood of the car. Bear turned toward Athens, a town he'd only visited once.

"I'd say the same thing then as now, maybe in different words, but the same feeling," said Bear. "From the moment you showed up in my life in your pale yellow polo shirt, you've been the center of my universe, right where you belong. It feels so right in my soul. When I look at you, energy passes through me like it does with no other living creation. I'm thoroughly, willingly and entirely captivated by you. This much is very true."

"Ah, Bear, what do you expect a guy to say to all that?" asked Walter.

"Whatever Walter wants and *only* whatever Walter wants," said Bear. "Everything that happened in my life before the moment I met you happened in order for me to meet you so that we could become great souls. We're soul mates, Walt. This much is true. I know that now ... more than ever."

"Haven't you always and forever?" asked Walter.

"During this Super experience, I came to see us in a new light," said Bear. "I got in touch with my man *Walta's* energy."

"What you talking 'bout, Bear Coleman?" asked Walter.

"You and me, and how we're perfectly matched," said Bear. "I don't understand it totally, but it goes a little something like this: people say you're moody. ESPN says you're moody. Sometimes *you* say you're moody. But you're never moody around me much, if at all. You're even keel, and if you aren't, you regulate back to even keel with ease, like in the Seattle underground when we thought the world was gonna implode."

"You were there to regulate me," said Walter.

"That's what I'm saying, *Walta,*" said Bear. "During this Super Bowl—do you feel me?—during *this* Super Dream come true, a thought popped into my head, almost from nowhere."

Walter doesn't need meds. Walter needs me.

"At first," said Bear, "I said it as a joke, you know how people do that? Then I realized it was no joke. The thought exploded like a big bang, and my world hasn't been the same since, all during *this Super Dream—this one Walter. This one.* It's almost like I had to reach this point in our lives to realize all this."

"You're my meds," said Walter, statement of fact.

"We're meant to be," said Bear. "Our energies are perfectly complementary. Consider it: I'm a man of words who's not great with numbers."

"I'm a man of numbers," said Walter, "and few words."

"Especially when it comes to writing," said Bear.

"Don't I know it. Your short notes are 800-page novels," said Walter.

"Ask you to leave a note, you scribble three words," said Bear.

"Your face is all about expressions," said Walter.

"You're QB, can't give it away now," said Bear. "You tuck it all in, your emotions, your needs—which makes you much, much more sensitive than me."

"Because you're always yelling your emotions through a megaphone," said Walter. "Metaphorically anyway."

"Polar opposites from opposite poles," said Bear. "Sounds like a recipe for chaos and disorder, but miracle of miracles, it's the polar opposite."

"Go figure," said Walter.

"Because we're blessed with a balanced equation," said Bear. "We're polar opposites in every way, except tastes and our physical bodies. Our tastes are perfectly compatible. We rarely argue because we love all the same things. We're also perfectly compatible physically. I mean, our bodies may move in different ways, but look at us, Walter, we're practically twins physically. Loving you is like loving a different version of me, which helps me *see* a better version of me, which helps me see a better version of you *and* me, and on and on."

"Man, we are perfect," said Walter, "for each other, I mean."

"In balance in our own tilted, twisted world, just like the polar opposite poles," said Bear. "It's like we were made for each other, literally. God, the world, the universe, created me for you, you for me."

"Sometimes I wonder myself how we can get along so great," said Walter.

"All the time spent apart actually helped," said Bear. "We learned early on not to take one another for granted."

"Fuck, I think you nailed it, Bear Coleman," said Walter.

"It's like the whole world was designed to make sure we got along perfectly in all the important ways, yet there were enough differences to make things interesting," said Bear.

"Almost too good to be true," said Walter.

"For the non-believer," said Bear. "That ain't me. I conceived of you. You're the one I dreamed of as a child. I remember this kind of out-of-body experience. I have no idea how old I was. I just remember feeling like the only boy in the whole world who felt like I felt. I was in the blur, near a bright light that looked like the side of a planet. I dreamed that there might one other boy—in this world of eight billion people—who was just like me. I promised the light, which I guess I took to be God, that if I ever found that other boy, we'd live together forever, happy and free. It was my very first dream, the one I survived growing up for. I asked God. God delivered—not the fire and brimstone guy. I'm talking about the God the child in my soul believed in, the God with whom I made my very first promise." Bear extended his arms to the heavens above the Georgia night sky. *"Give me a buddy, I asked God. We will be together forever.* I promised God. And God and all his angels on Earth led me to Athens, namesake of the birthplace of modern sport, that which bonds men beyond imagination through love, sweat and physical and emotional endurance. I descended onto a special kind of Eden to meet my buddy, who conceived of me, who needed me just as I needed him, the only co-captain and buddy I'll ever need. Thanks for showing up, *Walta*, always and forever." Bear sat on the hood with his man and spooned as much of Walter's back as he could. "What you got to say, MVP?"

"I can't forgive the University of Georgia," said Walter, snuggling deeper into Bear's embrace. "There's nothing to forgive. This is where I found the buddy of *my* dreams, and have been living a dream come true with him ever since. Enough said."

"That's my MVP. A man of fewer words who puts up big numbers and gets the job done. Enough said."

The moon glowed on the big league boys on the summit in Athens. Elsewhere, in a whole other galaxy in a whole other universe, the sun had set on a summit in the hills overlooking the Pacific.

Night had fallen ...

... on the two in Georgia ...

... on the lone body dreaming on the summit in Malibu.

21

Genesis,
God's Promise

*T*he moon glowed on the big league boys on the hill in Athens. Elsewhere, in a whole other galaxy in a whole other universe, the sun had set on the hills overlooking the Pacific. Night had fallen everywhere, on the two in Georgia, and on the lone body resting on the summit in Malibu ...

Beautiful music. Soft piano. Familiar piano. Gold. True. This much is true. Spandau Ballet. Thanks for showing up. Gold. Another song from the infatuations who sang "True." At practice in college, he used to dance a slow seductive ballet dancer's dance to "Gold." What did the others think? This cocky, golden, prototype athlete-body, dancing, feeling some faggy song by that freakin' this-much-is-true group. Thank you, Boy George, for being much k'waaaay-zier. The frat boys laid off Ballet and those who knew True Gold.

Kickoff the drama. That's life. That's football. Life is football and football is life. And magic, and love, and Santas, and dancing and cheering your soul mate onward! Onward, Christian warriors! Yes, Christian! Yes, Christ. Christ. That one. The one. One. There is only one. Christ God Buddha Buddy Allah Ali holy shit this much is true.

This much is so freakin' true.

Walt is my soul mate. I am Walt's soul mate.

Did you hear me, brain?

My soul mate is a man from a photograph I saw in a magazine 21 years ago.

This much is true.

I'm not crazy. I am Marcus Coleman. I'm not confused at all. I can see clearly now. I am dancing in the dark and I don't need a map or rules or a road. I'm in the zone. I can feel Niagara Falls all over my face, literally. I, Marcus Coleman—not Bear, not k'waaaay-zy, I know exactly who I am.

I am his soul mate. He is my soul mate.

I don't need meds. I need me.

Dancing some more in the dark. This is a very wonderful place, this heaven on Earth, a place where Niagara Falls flows on the face of God, and God keeps dancing as if the Falls are just a blur.

The Falls are just a blur.

I'm in the blur, and I love a man I first saw in a photograph—what was it?—21 years ago, give or take ... too many Niagras Falling to see the details while dancing in the dark.

True Gold.

I'm waking up. From a very long dream. Metaphorically, World Champion Seahawks fans, I know exactly who and what I is.

I traveled to the Super Universe. You see, Walt, buddy ... pause for unexpected showers ... Walt, non-famous, non-part-time Seattleite ... more showers ... never rained like this before ... washing away my sorrow ... for the first time, my heart sings ... thanks, Madonna ... and Walt ... Walt ... Been thinking about you most of my life. I've probably uttered your name aloud less than ... three times, to date, whatever this date is ... no one in my life knows any of this ... you're pretty much getting an exclusive ...

... fuck ... Niagara, or the next biggest Falls ... you were just a photograph, a very, very ... did I mention very?—gorgeous man in a photograph, for Christ's sake (yes, I know ... now). You were just a dream, a nice, wonderful, sweet and Sugary dream that kept me warm on some very cold and Sugarless nights, the kind of lonely nights Captain and Tennille warned us about in our childhood. (By the way ... your buddy is still dancing joyfully in the dark ... apparently over some very fuzzy, swoopy, Sugary hills ... even a cliff or two.)

You were just a dream, Walt. Just a dream. Sure, I loved the dream, but you were just a dream. Never did I dream ... in my wildest dreams ... okay, there was a wildest dream ... I could never, ever lie to my buddy ... Actually I did have a couple of wildest dreams within the dream.

Walt Loves the Bearcat.

You see, I'm a storyteller, a dreamer man. Thought these daydreams of mine would make a Lil' Ole Bitty Pissant Novel, kinda in the wacky, twisted, yet-so-

freakin'-real vein of some of the authors that kept me dreaming during my darkest days in college. Anton Myrer. John Irving, the original bear lover. Just to name two in this very momentous blur. I was 21. My life had just ended. Armageddon. The big Illinois Rose Bowl killed me, you know: the Hep B thing, which led to the AIDS thing, which led to my death, or so I thought.

I don't need meds. I need me.

I dreamed a ton of dreams these last 21 years. Hey, even Brian Bosworth, aka the Boz, had a pretty good two-year run on the network inside my brain (oh, and I was a pop star, and the former Oklahoma linebacker and I changed the world together, made a movie called Uprising*).*

I'm a dreamer, this much is true. Dreams kept me alive in childhood. Dreams of writing great stories about great sports teams winning against all odds. Dreams of Tulsa, *the soap I wrote to myself as a teen—my way of having a dialogue about who the freak I was. America had* Dallas. *Coleman had* Tulsa. *Most everyone was rich and white, except Kyle, this half-breed whore of a street kid who ends up running the powerful Wellings family and their oil empire. Alexis the Runaway.*

On the polar opposite side of Tulsa *was Chris Brown. He didn't have an ethnic identity, just a brown aura and a permanent lonely heart. Guess who Chris was in love with in high school? Guess who Chris Brown never, ever hooked up with because they were always caught up in drama, like a freakin' soap opera? High school, then-college, then-pro QB Dan Johnson. Twenty years' worth of starcrossed lovin'. Maybe they hooked up once, the poor bastards.*

Anyway, take heart, Tulsa *fans. On the reunion miniseries, the QB is cleared of a lifetime of legal chaos and disorder (stalking gays he couldn't decide whether to beat up or sex up, shit like that). Johnson never hurt Brown, nor tried to, but* Tulsa's *QB was one handsome and crazy muthafucka. Right up my alley. Anyway, in the reunion series: QB gets outta the insane asylum (it was that or prison), is cleared of all his hellish messes, and Chris and Dan become the stable and loving patriarchs of modern-day* Tulsa.

All true, Walt. A dream born way before you bought your yellow polo shirt.

One more boot-scootin' boogie to Tulsa: *Tom and Rudy, the lovers. Tom was a rich and powerful Wellings. Rudy from Brownsville. They loved like Luke and Laura and saved the town from evil super villains many a night. In one storyline I dreamed up one blurry winter in my youth, Tom and Rudy were running through tunnels in the underbelly of the city, searching for clues and evidence while "Give Me Back My Man" by the B-52's echoed through the darkness, guiding them with its haunting melody, swirling seagulls, and pleading voice ... I'll do anything, just give me back my man! Tom and Rudy were trying to save* Tulsa *from a mysterious*

virus running in the dark blur underneath the city, a mysterious virus intention-
ally spreading in the gay bathhouses.

That was my dream for a storyline on my dream soap, circa before any known
written record of a mysterious virus conceived by a couple of medical journals and
The New York Times *in the summer of 1981.*

Class of '81. Congrats.

Long before graduation day, the writers of Tulsa *canceled Tom and Rudy's*
virus storyline in the tunnels. They never made it down under, but they went on
to save themselves and the world in other ways. Around the same time, the whole
town dissolved from my universe.

I had other, more pressing dreams. Guess what? I made just about every sin-
gle one come true. Surviving childhood. Surviving youth. I lived most of my college
dreams and most of my cheerleading dreams. I was blessed with angels, the great
blonde gal pal, the great Salvadoran son-figure. I have lived a lifetime of dreams,
Walt, buddy, except being somebody's buddy. Not only have I not come close, I
haven't even been in the game. Slept with the world, loved not one soul, not even
little ole pissant me, the black fag with AIDS, who looks like Marcus Allen—the
great running back—on the outside, but just wants to be Marcus "Bear" Coleman
on the inside.

How could I love you? How could I ever love a perfect blond god from the
most sacred document from the most sacred place that represented the most sacred
time in my life?

Athens, paradise conceived, then found, then lost, then graced with a sacred
document showing the way home.

Everything is divine, if you chose to power every thing *with divine light.*

As I live, breathe and dance on this lovely hillside in the night blur, this much
is true: I do not understand All There Is. But it was the Super Universe that led me
to this summit on which I now sob joyfully. I had never consciously journeyed to
the Super Universe before, much like the black hole that was the Double Reverse.
For the last 21 years, most of our time in my headspace was spent lying quietly in
bed, one of us making the other feel better—just by being there—his presence a
present after a hard day chasing our dreams. That was it ... the energy that powered
those feelings was in the blur ... the blur I'm dancing over and around and up and
down and this way and that, finding out that hills can be both silly and hilly.

Recently, I began climbing the very steep slope that is Walt Loves the Bearcat.
Time to finally write the blessed thing, true? Funny thing is, my mind was riding on
two tracks all along, which brings us back to those two wildest dreams within the
dream (I always come back 'round, this much is true).

Silly hill: Love the pic.

Hilly hill: I always believed, fate willing, I'd be an intelligent black author and tell this tale among many tales, someday, somewhere, somehow. I love tales.

Silly and feely hill: Figured that someday, I'd show up at your doorstep in a Bear suit with a copy of the book. Kidding! Super Universe taught me a thing or two about my bud, my very private, sensitive, kind, compassionate, complete, complex, simple, caring, passionate, loving, sometimes less loving, always and forever Water for my thirsty soul ... buddy.

Highly hilly hill: Okay, there was this asteroid of a wildest dream floating around my k'waaaay-zy headspace all these years. Always dreamed that, after I finished the lil' bitty pissant ditty, I'd look ya up, if possible. Were we gonna do more than talk? Oh, yes, indeed, much, much more!

Super hilly hill: I wanna shake your hand. I wanna see your smile. I wanna hear you laugh. I'm gonna cry if you sing. If I'm the luckiest man in my universe, my story will be worth a hug. If there really is such a thing as Santa Claus ...

Talk about beyond my wildest imagination ...

Until I danced in the Super Universe and saw All That in a whole new light.

Perfect Grace. The highest dream. The deepest dream.

Hard to explain. I'm still going for whelming while swimming in an infinite rush of Niagara Falls. It's got to do with energy. Perfectly matched energy. We are poles, buddy. We are poles shooting outta the same iron core.

Together, we're a balancing act.

We are one another's perfect and ultimate feng shui.

I'm dancing on this hill, wondering where the men in white coats are. I want them to come test us, our blood, our core, our iron, our energy. Put us in a room separated by a Berlin Wall. Don't even tell us if the other buddy is on the other side. Move us in and outta that space, unbeknownst to the other buddy. Placebo us to death, or die trying. Or just hook us up! Hook us up to all the machines man has created to measure man, and watch this God-given miracle happen and show us and the world a thing or two. No rocket scientist here, but this much is true: man's machines will tell the same tale about our tails. Polar opposites on the same team. Polar opposite backgrounds. Polar opposite energy. All working in balance with our completely compatible tastes, so much so, it's like we're genetically made for one another, as genetically as the big league boys. Like somebody drew it up.

Go figure.

Never knew I could feel like this until I went to the Super Universe. Not a rocket scientist here, but it's the poles. I know you feel me ... I know you're out there ... I know you're right here ... which is why I'm opening my eyes as if for the first time, because I'm starting to get off balance dancing in the dark and I need my other pole.

"Oh, God."

Marcus Coleman was flat on his ass. Good thing. Needed the rest. Allowing one's self to evolve into one's highest version of one's self—especially when one starts from the South Pole on a planet that thinks the world is right-side-up with the North Pole on top—that kind of evolution can be hard work for a 42-year-old black man at the dawn of the 21st century.

"Not much easier traveling from the North, I would imagine," laughed Marcus, shutting off the Niagara Falls, after the fall, which he had just completed, collapsing from all that dancing to "Gold."

"Not much easier traveling from the North, I would imagine," repeated Marcus, moving his neck side to side, as if sore from a very, very long rest.

"Not much easier traveling from the North, I would imagine," said Marcus, the silence prompting him to reach for his gut.

"Pretty overwhelming, huh, even for Big Norsemen?" asked Marcus, noticing the night sky for the first time.

"Think we can try whelming?" asked Marcus, his vision finally coming into focus. "Oh, God."

He's not here.

The summit was empty save one Marcus Coleman. Not even a coach. The air around the Complex was still, the hills of Malibu pitch black, the Pacific only in your imagination.

This kid panic? Marcus laughed, arched his back, needed to stand after the fall, needed to go find his buddy, who was probably taking a well-deserved bathroom break after listening to what must have felt like half a lifetime of *Walt Loves the Bearcat.*

The sweet, sweet novel that led me to the man of my dreams, 21 years after finding him in a photograph. Must finish book someday. Must find restroom and buddy now. Maybe even get fed. Haven't eaten in ... eons? Funny, when Walt and I spend time together—just being together—it's like magic, nice and easy magic.

Lying on the hill, Walt and me, talking about our lives—wow—what peace, what serenity, what comfort, what ease, as if we could talk forever and never run out of things to say. Or remain silent forever and never feel the need to speak unnecessarily.

Marcus Coleman has never shut his mouth for anyone, let alone a white man.

"That, my friends, is Walt Appeal."

Where is my buddy? Where's that toilet? Where's our Coach? Gotta thank him and the entire universe for making my deepest dreams come true in ways more profound than this beautiful little black boy ever dreamed. Wow. God shocked me. Go figure.

He really is All That.

He's also not making himself apparent in the darkness of this Complex, formerly some junior high in the hills of Malibu, land of golden dreams.

Must dance around Complex, find my buddy.

Guess what, God? I'm somebody's buddy! Who's gonna have to figure out how to create a canal system for his face, otherwise known as Niagara Falls, falling once again.

But I'm somebody's buddy, God!

'Course. You knew that huh? You're way smarter than me. I gotta do a book to figure shit out. I know I can say shit to God. God and God's living creations create tons of shit every day in this universe of ours. On top of that, God puts up with all the shit we create on our own, with or without our gratitude. You are All That, God. You are the Shit.

If I love God, I love God's shit.

If I don't love God, I don't love shit.

If I don't love shit, I don't love God.

If I don't love one single thing about God, I don't love at all.

There are no sides of God, just a loop. You either love or you hate. You're either in or outta the loop.

There is only God.

It is all in the mind.

"Where are ya, buddy? Where's this toilet we both need to use?"

Getting a little freaky here. Kinda falling back. I mean, falling. Or not falling. Whoa! My head. Where is my pole? My head feels poleless. My heart feels soulless. My blur is unblurring. My dreams awakening into a Complex much darker than the one I remember.

But then again, what do I know? We all thought this joint was a gym for games.

Look at the sign. CONSTRUCTION ON THE COMPLEX DELAYED PENDING FUTURE LEGAL PROCEEDINGS. *Somebody's fighting over this place, this hilly hillside in the hills overlooking ... whoa ... dizzy spell ... back off the cliff, Marcus ...*

Marcus?

Bear?

Walt?

Walter?

"I live in Oxnard!"

Marcus pointed northward across the dark canyon. No response. Echoless.

"I live ..."

Marcus looked south, far south of Malibu.

"Mama Rent lives in Oxnard, down the road! I stayed there for a while. I had trouble."

"You think *that* was trouble." *Finally, the smart-ass canyon decides to echo.*

"Oh, shit," replied Marcus. "Yeah, I've gone fucking crazy, talking to the hills and waiting for some guy ... Walt ... where are you?"

He turned away from the edge. *The cell phone never lies!*

Walt loves me! declared the display. Marcus barely noticed, the message being old news. He was more focused on verifying his sanity and the details of his life—the real one, the infamous one—by verifying the facts on the cell phone.

Mama Rent had an Oxnard number, this much is true.

His best female friend Eve was in the loop, this much is true.

His Salvadoran son-figure Octavio was in the loop, this much is true.

And then there was Walt. Whose number his cell phone knew.

"No doubt," laughed Marcus, feeling better.

Walt Yeager was in the cell because of this morning's *Chicago 2 LA,* double cross-country trek, their *pas de duh.*

Marcus dialed up his buddy, expecting him to pick up the phone and be up to speed, hopefully somewhere within their dreamy Complex. True?

If only his cell phone worked in these hills. But it didn't, and a twisted concept was born in the darkest reaches of his headspace.

What if Walt's not in the loop? What if he wants outta the loop? What if he left here out of disgust after hearing me ramble on about Walter and Bear—and Walt and me—being soul mates?

Next came the teetering on the edge of death and life, as in the cliff beneath the edge of his feet.

... You're reached Walt Yeager's voice mail ... I'm a voice outta nowhere. You were right about one thing: I am the Shit, as the kids say. Of course, you always knew I was the Shit. What's it feel like, talking to the Shit? The rich white businessman you dreamed of turning into your buddy, not to mention a pro superstar athlete? Yep, this is the voice of your dream man, and you are one crazy lonely sad alone self-destructive consumed poor bastard of a tarnished golden boy spinning way outta control in a universe you barely recognize, blurred or focused. Welcome.

Our world. Our time. Speaking of time, mine is limited. Why? Another time. If you've got the time. For the time being, all the best. Keep me in the loop.

An imaginary beep. A black boy speaks in his soul.

Walt, if I could just tell you ... I may be dreaming here, but ... we connected. True? I called you, shocked the shit outta you. We got to know one another a little bit, shared a little bit, had a pretty cool and dreamy vibe going, and now you've just pulled a major rightbackatcha, *shocking the shit outta me, turning out to be the man of my dreams* and *my dream man. Not sure of the date, but it's right around the 21st anniversary of when this all began, give or take ... what a time for us to make magic, eh? I can ask for miracles, can't I?*

But the cell was dead. And the little red sports car was gone.

The little red sports car was gone.

Walt wouldn't just leave like that, not the man I just got to know, not the man who's been the hero of my ... a note!

Floating near the ground on the hill, hovering next to Mattel Electronics Football!

Walt left a note! Too good to be true!

Walt left a note, a note that freed itself of the little green box, a note that got swept up by a zephyr wind, a note that took off for the canyons beyond the hills.

Marcus chased after the note as it took flight ...

Determined little note. The small white slip of paper fled hastily into the night, looking like a lost star in a hurry to return to its place in the universe.

22

Tank

Going to biggest dreamiest fantasy park of all time!!
Are you taking that little bearcat?
Guess what? The world wants to know!

"**W**HO IS THE BEARCAT? Is he a he or a she? Should we care about he or she? You tell us, fans of the game. Call now. Please! *Greg the Gut's Sports Report* wants to hear from you, the fan, about tonight's hot rock of a topic. Just exactly who is this bearcat? And is Super Sunday's Most Valuable Player going to the land of dreams, fantasies, and big furry people in animal suits with this unknown hybrid of a bear and a cat?"

"Gut, please! Need your help on this one!"

"A dream made in Super heaven? Or a big waste of time by sports radio after one more Super rout on Super Sunday earlier tonight? Call now. Seahawks? Niners? Or Bearcats? Give us your Gut Check!"

"If you ask me, Gut ... am I on? Who cares who the QB is taking to some park? Frisco was robbed ... could've had a Super moment. Leave the Bearcats for daytime!"

"... Good Morning America, or should we say, Good *Mourning* San Francisco. *Ouch* ... yesterday in Atlanta, the Niners lost to Walter, a quarterback with his own flava, but the bigger story is ... *who is this bearcat?* Joe, whaddayaknow?"

"Anne, the bearcat is none other than University of Cincinnati student Ben Dover. Do I have that name right?"

"... Leave it to our producer Gellman to get the scoop. Something tells me *he's* in the loop. Let's replay what happened, for those of you who had a little too much of your own Super Festivities last night, *hint, hint.*"

"Oh! Regis! Mateo and the kids had *way* too much Yeager-meister, I kid you not! Oh. My. God! Bouncing ... literally off! the walls! Still! On the PIP insert! Look at them! What is in that ice cream, *Walta?*"

"Enough with the cream, Haley! Show the clip from the Super celebration in the Seahawks' locker room to refresh people's memories. It's Monday after Super Sunday, been a long night, and fall ... out from this bearcat is building like a nuclear reactor. Kaboom! Clip! Roll!"

"Going to biggest dreamiest fantasy park of all time!!" yelled Yeager into the swirl of Champagne and cheers in the Seahawks' locker room. The MVP jumped off the podium, the announcer's last words getting lost in the blur.

"Are you taking that little bearcat?" asked Evil Announcer Guy, more focused on his next victor, running back Mookie Millstone.

"Oh! Big Daddy! Regis, will ya look at that golden man's face! *Walta*, if the bearcat won't go to dreamland with you ... *wink, wink ...*"

"Calm down, Haley. You've got your own Salsa-flavored Super dreams. Let Walt love the bearcat in peace. Do we even know if WALT LOVES THE BEARCAT? Did Walt ever love the bearcat? Will somebody out there in America please tell us who this bearcat person is? Meanwhile, last night, what a joy, went out to eat at Snaky-Lu's on the Green, and *boy,* I tell ya! ..."

"... CNBC has this exclusive breaking news. Super Mystery solved. A wonderfully curmudgeonly syndicated talk show host and his lovely Haley's comet of a co-host put out the call, and what a miracle, the world answered the call."

"... Yes, that's right, Godot, no more waiting. We are hot on the trail of the bearcat! Imagine, the power of television here in 1994. I'm very proud. What can mankind possibly invent that could be more powerful at spreading information than us, Barbara?"

"... dream of it, you say, and claim to envision a better world, all resulting from this wacky notion that I can't quite understand. Now: you're calling it an internetworky systems web of worldwide information highway Super Sunday leads to another Super Birth that will change the world as we know it ... am I getting this correctly in my ear from our producers?—because it doesn't quite sound like something I can wrap my head around ... would you hold one second, Mr. Gates? We're going to have to postpone your little story about—*a web?*—because we've got much more pressing news ... exclusive ... real information you can use, about the identity of the Super bearcat ..."

"... station in New Orleans today was inundated with faxes revealing at least part of the identity of this mysterious bearcat ... equipment was on the fritz, making it hard to determine the fax. But ... exclusive breaking news: these are the fax as we know them: apparently, the bearcat went to high school in New Orleans."

"... a former track athlete at a Louisiana high school sprinted to his local station with this old high school newspaper that reveals much more to the story, exclusive to *Big Snow News*. Unfortunately, his sweat caused the fading of the newsprint, making it hard to really see anything clearly. This humidity today is a bear!"

"... interrupt our programming about the dying rainforest to bring you this late-breaking news and information on the local station that has your back, Chicago ... This just in: still no news on the identity of the bearcat."

"... has been working here at *Newsworthy Images Tonight* since graduating from LSU. Here you see a frame of her first-ever editorial at a Louisiana high school, on the back of which, after all these years, was a photo that stuck in her memory for a decade. Unfortunately, the sun—coming through the window of her office on the 80th floor—caused the newsprint to fade, making anything beyond the headline QB Loves the Bearcat hard to read. She does wonderful work for us, however, and here's what we do know from her faded memories ..."

"... seems as though Emmy Lou saved her school newspaper from 10 years ago because it contained her boyfriend's first-ever, tobacco-stained lip imprint. Unfortunately, last week she caught him cheating and burned all of his ..."

"... 12-year-old Josh gave his sister a copy of her high school newspaper to commemorate the day her baby boy was born in Home Economics class ... here's what 22-year-old Josh can tell us about the baby's vomit stain, which, as you can see, covers most of the coverage ..."

"... we are going to go on the record with other major media outlets to confirm what we definitely know to be true ..."

WALT LOVES THE BEARCAT

"... once America learned that *Super Bowl MVP Quarterback Walter Yeager Loves the Bearcat,* the station here in New York received 140 faxes of a high school newspaper's Sugar Bowl edition. We are now getting much more concrete information, thanks to these very well-placed sources. But keep in mind, faxes can sometimes be fuzzy—slippers or more humidity? Find out, after the break."

"... a woman who one day dreamed of opening a Museum of High School Periodicals ... scrolling down to the end of this breaking news, something about the Great Flood. Probably one good reason to keep your archives in a safe space."

"... the story keeps getting better and bigger, thanks to my crackpot team, here at my great homage to my great media god self! Turns out, Walter Yeager, while he was a quarterback at the University of Georgia, met and fell in love during the Sugar Bowl ... still waiting on confirmation of the name of his beloved bearcat ... but ... we need to get this right ... the other stations are going with it? Is that right ... Joe?"

"... ten years ago, at least, we can now report, Walter Yeager loved a Joe."

"... cannot be reached for comment, but sources close to the story report that the other person in the very unclear photo is definitely a Joe. We're getting a lot of calls. Apparently, this Joe fella was a very beloved guy. A lot of people knew him in college at UCLA."

"... exclusive to us here at *The Big Voice of America,* Walter Yeager was involved in a relationship with a Joe B., nickname Bearcat."

"... *SportsCenter* now interrupts *It's in the Game: Understanding Every Single Atom in the Entire Universe Through Your Understanding of Sports* by Dr. Mark S. Rochette, to report on what the rest of the media is now confirming: Walter Yeager, formerly, perhaps also presently, maybe even futurely, involved, on some level, with a Joe B. of UCLA."

"... his identity, we're now told in this breaking, up-to-the-minute news exclusive, is Joe Bruin of UCLA, not Joe Bearcat of Cincinnati, as previously reported. Do we have that name right?"

"... I guess if your mother is going to name you Joe Bruin, what are you to do, but go to UCLA and be ... Joe Bruin."

"... Walter Yeager, a homosexual once in love with a man named Joe? The story tonight on *Cross/Fire.*"

"CNN interrupts itself to bring you this breaking news. The bearcat is a girl! The MVP is taking Roxanne Valtron, his former college sweetheart, to the land of Super Dreams. All of us at the network sincerely apologize: we did not mean, in any way, to imply that Walt Yeager was anything more than a great American citizen and role model for Norsemen the world over. We now take you back to *Cross/Fire,* and our regularly scheduled insanity."

WHOOMP! (THERE IT IS) ... The Sea Gals were dancing in the streets. *Whoomp!* Thousands of Seattleites lined the corridor to celebrate. *Whoomp!* Seattle loved its teams, but only the basketball Sonics had dreamed of ultimate glory, long ago. *Whoomp!* The names Seattle and World Champs didn't go together often. *Whoomp!* The Pacific Northwest was alive like never before. *Whoomp!* Even as far up as Alaska, this was a cool and dreamy day.

"*Whoomp!* I think I'm finally over that song," said Bear, looking through the window at the celebration below. "For now."

"*Whoomp!* Halleluiah," said Walter, back leaning against the glass, ignoring the world outside. "Now, let's *whoomp!* get this over with."

The Super boys were standing in an empty office space in downtown Seattle. New territory for both men. The door opened, revealing Tammy, the ER Wife, and Roxanne Valtron, the most sought-after interview in America.

"Joe Bruin, you're glowing," said Bear.

"I could say the same," said Roxanne, dazed upon Walt at First Sight.

"Roxanne, Walter; Walter, your ex," said Bear. Meeting MVP was Roxanne's one demand for her compliance with their cover-up of the bearcat cover-up, along with a sum of money Tammy would only call *up there.*

"You *were* the blond guy at Bear's fraternity party," said Roxanne to Walter. "I was so drunk, I was never sure."

"We appreciate you doing this," said Walter. "I know the money doesn't make up for the past."

"I'll invest it," said Roxanne. Down below, a high school band played "Gimme Some Lovin'" while dressed as the Blues Brothers.

"So we're all clear before the check clears, right?" asked Tammy. "We had a little romance during the Sugar Bowl 10 years ago, and that was that. No drama, no mamas, just a date and a photo op in N'awlins. End of story, right?"

"As rain," said Roxanne.

"People in Seattle don't say that," said Bear.

"Hopefully everything turns out good for you," said Walter to Roxanne.

"Don't trade this one," said Roxanne to Bear.

"Oh, I've got a 21-year deal," said Bear, watching the women disappear.

"First I've heard about this 21-year deal," said Walter once the boys were alone again.

"Seaside Inn, Malibu, around this time a decade ago," giggled Bear. "And I quote the great MVP-to-be: '*Gimme 21 years to figure out if I wanna hang forever, little Bearcat. I should know something by then.*' You might have to negotiate with the Seahawks in the off-season, but you're locked into another decade-plus with the Bearcats."

"*Ha!* Deal," said Walter, sealing it with a kiss. The throng on the street below erupted, white towels swirling by the thousands. Music thumped off the building, stirring Yeager and Coleman into action.

"*Ladies and gentlemen, your World Champion Seattle Seahawks!*"

Seattle was delirious. The players cruised down the downtown corridor in convertibles, some with wives and children, all with World Champs t-shirts and smiles born deep within their souls. Tina Turner's voice serenaded the warriors, telling them they were "Simply the Best." The throng agreed, especially when the cars featuring the backfield came into view. Walter rode proud with his football buds, waving, pumping his fist in the air, getting all kinds of confetti in his gorgeous blond hair. Bear watched his buddy from the roof. When Yeager's car passed, Walter looked up and pointed toward Bear, the same way athletes point to the heavens after reaching the end zone. Bear tapped his fist over his chest ... heart.

"I'm taking my sister and her kids to fantasyland. Roxanne and I shared a nice moment at the Sugar Bowl, but that's the past. But hey, she's a great girl, great memories. It was through her that I met my manager and best friend, so yeah, I'll always love the Bearcat, this much is true."

"THE POWER OF ONE LITTLE PISSANT PHOTOGRAPH," said Hail Larry's Wife, looking up at the night sky.

"Can we shut up about that?" said Bear, poking the fire with a stick.

"*And* the freakin' game," said Hail Larry, gulping his drink.

"Does it help, knowing your best buds finally got their ring?" asked Bear, resisting the urge to hold his man's hand.

"Anybody still yammering about football needs more Sugar." Walter stuffed a slice of pineapple in his bud's mouth.

For the second consecutive year, the boys and the Hail Larrys were having their own private luau after the Pro Bowl in Honolulu.

"Freakin' Yeager," said Hail Larry, wincing from a pain in his lower regions. "I got freakin' nailed in my ass in Atlanta. What's this I hear about that Bass character only working with players he can feel?"

"I'd like to hear the answer to that one," said Bear.

"Dunno," said Walter. "Has something to do with good vibrations."

"Like that rap song?" asked Hail Larry's Wife.

"Like the movement of our energy," said Walter. "Gotta be in harmony with the Dane for him to do ya."

"What the freak does that mean?" asked Hail Larry. "I am *so* not New Age. I like the old age. I'm old freakin' school. I freakin' heard a guy on the Dolphins had a reverse and all he'll say about it is ... Armageddon."

"That's *very* old school," giggled Bear.

"Hell, Larry, it's all urban legend anyway," said Walter. "I'm the only professional athlete who openly admits to having dealt with the Dane."

"You're the only freakin' guy to admit to being reversed?" asked Hail Larry's Wife. "The rest is just rumors and hearsay?"

"I was the freakin' first," said Walter. "Too stupid to know better."

"Lucky us," said Bear, grinning at his bud.

"No doubt," said Walter, grinning at his bud.

"You homos aren't freakin' gay," said Hail Larry. "It's a freakin' hoax. I never see you two do anything gay."

"What do you wanna see us do?" asked Walter.

"Each other's hair and Madonna moves!" said Hail Larry's Wife.

"Aren't you guys affectionate?" asked Hail Larry.

"He wants to see you guys kiss!" screamed Hail Larry's Wife.

"Bullshit, woman," said Hail Larry. "I'm just freakin' saying, if you guys are the type to do that—get cuddly and all—freakin' relax, we're cool. Look how far apart you're sitting."

"Be careful what you ask for, then." Walter slid over and kissed his Bear.

"Freakin' homos!" said Hail Larry.

"With a ring," said Bear between kisses. "We're in the Super loop."

"Now *that's* downright dirty," said Hail Larry, grabbing a skewer. "Mention the game again and I'm gonna gorge somebody's freakin' eyes out."

"Who's the better kisser?" asked Hail Larry's Wife.

"He is," the boys said together.

"So you guys make little quarterbacks or little cheerleaders?" asked Hail Larry.

"We make Bearcats," said Walter.

Bear lost it, his hysterics breaking up the kiss.

"Yeah, but who's more top and bottom?" asked Hail Larry's Wife.

"I bet I know," said Hail Larry.

"Honey, you can't go by that," said Hail Larry's Wife.

"Go by what?" asked Bear.

"What are we, a freakin' zoo exhibit?" asked Walter.

"Just tell us," said Hail Larry's Wife.

"Honey, is this what straight people talk about in bed?" asked Bear.

"You just called him honey. Freakin' Yeager's the top," said Hail Larry.

"I'm gonna say it's Bear," said Hail Larry's Wife. "Big Black Mandingo."

"You have too many gay friends in real estate," said Hail Larry. "Which is it, guys, who's freakin' topping whose freakin' bottom here?"

"What's this top and bottom stuff?" asked Bear. "We don't freakin' talk that way."

"What language do you speak?" laughed Hail Larry's Wife. "The fags at the office are always saying, '*He's only total bottom.*'"

"Total bottom what?" asked Bear.

"Are you serious?" cried Hail Larry's Wife. "You guys need to meet other gay men."

"So we can be tops and bottoms?" asked Bear. "We don't call ourselves fags or gay and our sex life is just fine, eh, QB?"

"Co-MVPs." Walter gave him another kiss.

"But what do you guys *do?*" asked Hail Larry.

"Our bodies are like outer space," said Walter. "We go exploring ... like astronauts."

"And rocket scientists," said Bear.

"And get lots of Sugar," said Walter.

"And spend lots of face time in the zone," giggled Bear.

"That's our language," laughed Walter, going for more Sugar. "Makes us happy, all you need to know."

"You tell 'em, QB," said Bear.

"It's like they're freakin' infatuated," said Hail Larry.

"You should freakin' know," said Hail Larry's Wife.

"What is that supposed to freakin' mean?" asked Hail Larry.

The Hail Larrys faded into the blur. The big-league Super boys took off for their own private luau in their own private outer space. They had made it past the momentary speed bumps in their lives. Life was all right now.

WALT LOVES TO ROCK OUT WITH HIS BEARCAT. "All Right Now," the guitar-riffin' jam by Free, was cranked up in the transport. The SUV flew down Pacific Coast Highway, the quarterback in the driver's seat, the spirit leader in the passenger seat. Walter played the drums against the steering wheel. Bear bobbed his head and looked out the window. It was the long version of "All Right Now," which lasted until they pulled up to the front of their gated community in Malibu.

"Home of our Super dreams," said Walter after rolling down the window and turning off the music. The front gate guy approached. "Manuel. Thanks for letting our agents check our house for damage after that terrible quake. Everything okay at your house, your family?"

"Sir, you have visitors," said Manuel. "They come every day for three. This morning, they say they wait. I take them to your porch. When you see, you will understand." The atmospheric pressure in the transport changed without warning, lowering as QB continued onward.

"Can't be the parents," said Walter, steering through their quiet beach 'hood. "We're seeing them in a few in Tahoe."

"Whatever it is, remember to dream the better dream," said Bear. "Been working good for us lately."

"Deal, little Bearcat," said Walter, grabbing Bear's hand. "We will deal, and make it whelming."

They pulled into the driveway—halfway, anyway. That was as far as they got before seeing exactly why Manny had acquiesced to the visitors. A young boy sat in front of their house, a young boy who possessed his own MVP aura. He stared at the ground, cheek resting on his fist, elbow resting on his knee.

"Hey, young man," said Walter, standing before him.

"Hi," said the boy, still looking downward.

"My name is Walter and this is Bear," said Walter.

"Hello," said the boy, still looking downward.

"Do you have a name?" asked Bear. The boy mumbled something indecipherable. Walter asked him to repeat it, but that didn't work either, so Walter bent over, his ear near the boy's mouth.

"Tank," said the boy.

Walter stood up and looked at Bear, who shrugged as if to say, *Not my idea.*

"How old are you, Tank?" asked Bear.

"Almost 10," said Tank. Walter eyed Bear, the same conclusion etched on their faces: conceived the year they met, born shortly thereafter. A female's voice wafted through the wind, followed by a female emerging from the pathway to their left.

"Sweetie, what did I say? Come get me if anyone comes." She was small, in her early thirties and coming from the backyard. A gust of wind blew off her straw hat, revealing her identity: the dark-haired girl from the ride to Atlanta during the original Athens weekend. Bear remembered feeling as if she were carrying something back then, a grudge, resentment. Made sense now. "Oh, my God, you're the cheerleader from the UCLA game!"

"Funny, I always call it the Georgia game," said Bear. Walter introduced the adults. The child felt left out.

"Are you my biological father?" asked Tank, squinting through the sunlight.

"He's always known his dad adopted him," said the dark-haired girl, whose name was Ellen. "But Tank thought I was joking when I told him you were bio dad. After the Super Bowl, Tank said prove it. That was God's way of telling me it was time."

"Tank." Walter knelt down to the boy's level. "This is probably a big shock to you, and I want to give us all time to adjust. What say we go inside? We call this place Moose Jaw."

"Why?" laughed Tank.

"Tell me about it!" said Walter.

Once inside, the men did a quick tour of the minor cracks from the January quake—it had been a big one for many nearby—then Walter suggested Bear show Tank the ocean from the deck, while the former Georgia Bulldawgs caught up in the kitchen.

"This is my favorite part of the house," said Bear once outside.

"Can you climb down to the beach?" asked Tank.

"If your mother says yes. You can also take those stairs beyond the pool. Forty rickety steps and you got sand between your toes. How cool is that?" asked Bear.

"So you live here, too?" asked Tank.

"No one really lives here full-time," said Bear. "Walter lives in Seattle during the season. Where do you live, by the way?"

"Tank-man," said Ellen, poking her head outside.

"They have stairs to the beach," Tank told his mother.

"Wanna take a look?" asked Ellen. After they left, Bear found Walter pacing in the kitchen.

"Still dreaming the better dream?" asked Bear.

"*She named my kid Tank!*" Walter yelled in a hush. No paternity test needed. "Who names a kid Tank?"

"Tell me about it," said Bear. "Remember at the airport after the Sugar Bowl? You told me it was just you and me from then on and that you were done seeing her."

"I was," insisted Walter.

"I know that," said Bear. "But you told me seconds before I boarded. I didn't have time to process it until I was in my seat. I remember waiting to take off, and having the strangest feeling, like, you two weren't over, not because you were still in love with her, just that it wasn't over. I think deep down, I knew at that roadhouse café in Athens—whatever the name of that place was—I knew she had either *been* pregnant by you, *was* pregnant by you, or was gonna *get* pregnant by you."

"I wish you would have told me," said Walter.

"Please," said Bear. "I couldn't even tell you I was in love with you. So when did you two make Tank?"

Ellen Kipner had been Walter's off-and-on girlfriend throughout college.

They had unofficially broken up a week before the original UCLA-Georgia game, then officially called it off after Walter received his first letter from Bear. But somewhere in the blur in between, Tank was conceived. During that football season, Ellen played Walter, alternately telling him she was or wasn't pregnant, depending on how it best suited her needs. Right before the Sugar Bowl, she confessed to never being pregnant and said she was leaving college if Walter no longer wanted her. Lying Ellen had raised her baby alone in Pittsburgh with the help of her parents. She was married now and well off, and didn't want money from Walter, just the chance for Tank to know his dad. She also apologized for the head games of her youth and hoped Walter could forgive the selfish actions of an immature and spoiled rich kid. "I can, if you can," Walter had told her.

"Why forgive you?" asked Bear, huddled with Walter in the laundry room.

"Because, like the unauthorized Fox movie says, *Walt Loved the Bearcat* during that time, and obviously that played a hand in her demise," said Walter.

"She and Fox have got you there," said Bear.

"I never slept with Ellen after you contacted me," said Walter.

"Will you forget that? You have a son," said Bear. "A beautiful baby boy."

"I wish full-time," said Walter. "Can you get over how awesome he is?"

"Like his dad," said Bear.

"He's built more like a linebacker, more like my Bear. What's up with that?" asked Walter.

"Tell me about it," said Bear. "So why does Ellen think the big black cheerleader from UCLA is hanging around after all these years?"

"My manager, but I'm not lying to my kid—I don't know what that means, details-wise," said Walter. "I'm so pissed at her right now. For 10 years she doesn't tell me I have a son. He was real. All this time, she was telling the truth. What if I had known?"

They heard footsteps in the den, followed by the closing of the patio door. A short time later, mother and son joined them in the kitchen.

"So Tank," said Walter. "You a Seahawks fan?"

"I am now," said Tank, still too shy to look directly in his father's eyes.

"You gotta be a fan whether we win or lose, that cool?" asked Walter.

"I guess," said Tank with a mild laugh.

"That's the first requirement," said Walter. "The second is, you have to go outside and toss the football with me, tell me your life story."

Tank smiled, Walter followed.

"So you knew Roxanne the Bearcat," said Ellen after father and son vanished. "Small world."

"Coffee? Anything?" asked Bear, wondering how to make coffee.

"How long did they last?" asked Ellen.

"Long enough for some Creole kid to snap a photo that would rock the world," said Bear.

"Does he ever say anything about me?" asked Ellen.

"We don't talk about the women in his life," said Bear. "He has enough people snooping around without *me* being nosey—not to say *you're* being nosey, just that ... you're better off asking *him* whatever you wanna know."

Her look reminded Bear of the stoic face of a female tennis player after she's been smoked by the bitch across the net. Point, Coleman.

"No Tahoe?" asked Hail Larry's Wife, calling from Seattle.

"The Yeager family celebration took place, just with a different travel roster," said Bear, calling from Malibu. "*Son* subbing for *soul mate.* They need quality time, plus it gave Walter a chance to come out to the folks—as a dad."

"So he ditched you to be with his son," said Hail Larry's Wife.

"This goes way deeper than anyone ever dreamed," said Bear, fussing around in the kitchen. "If I had a hunch about this, Walter must have had a hunch, too. My man is way more sensitive than me—that's what sensitive people do, sense things. He knew he had a son in him. He dreamt of him long ago. The dream was like a ray of sun that powered Walter's world during some of the toughest times of his life, times when Walter felt like no other soul in the world had his back. Without the power of the son, there'd be no Walter here today."

"Are you saying he's freakin' suicidal?" asked Hail Larry's Wife.

"I'm saying my husband lost a big part of himself during his less-than-stellar college football days, as he was reminded during that painful back reverse," said Bear. "I blocked out the details from that challenging time—of the reverse—but I remember the feelings. My man wanted to die. That's chronic back pain. The worst physical limitation a hero like Walter can have. Something had to keep him alive. It wasn't me, directly. It wasn't even QB himself, directly. It was the son, the one he conceived of, and had asked God for at some point in time. It was the son he promised God to love with all his heart, even before he laid eyes on that son. That's what powered his world during his darkest days. His son was like the sun. This much is majorly true, and generally between us."

"You're crazy, the kid just showed up," said Hail Larry's Wife.

"My man's the center of my universe," said Bear. "I just follow the light. Try it with your man. You might see some pretty magical bits and pieces of him you never dreamed you'd see."

"Bear, did you buy dope in Hawaii? You sound very psychedelic," said Hail Larry's Wife.

"Call it Super psychedelic, I don't care," said Bear. "I know my man better than ever. Hard to explain, but since the Super Bowl in Atlanta, I'm living on a whole new planet. Planet Perfect. I mean, Walter wins the Super Bowl in Atlanta? And we survive the bearcat threat? It's all meant to be, baby. It's genetic. I'll take as many copies of my man's energy as possible. Roll in all the Tanks you want: the more Walter the better."

"Bear, what happened to you?" asked Hail Larry's Wife. "It's like you're more infatuated than ever."

"Tell me about it," said Bear. "If you don't understand, ask my man. He's in the loop."

"Apparently, so is this Creole guy," said Hail Larry's Wife. "He's on some show on VH-1, holding up the Bearcat photo and an old camera. Emile something. He's the original high school photographer. Have you seen him?"

"Only on the radio, talking about how much money he's making off me now," said Bear. "I mean, off me and my ... uh ..."

"Bear, is that your black behind in that Bruin suit in that photo?" asked Hail Larry's Wife. "Are you the real freakin' Bearcat?"

"I guarantee you this," said Bear. "I did not pull off the most fantastic stunt of my life—to date—by parading around an official Sugar Bowl event as Joe Bruin. Joe Bruin *and* Harry Dawg, maybe, but Joe Bruin alone?—to even suggest that I would be involved in such a half-baked college prank is an insult, not to mention a breach of our friendship, which is officially over, as far as I'm concerned."

"Does Walter know you're such a freak?" asked Hail Larry's Wife.

"He's in the loop. There's the door. The boys are back in town." Bear said goodbye, hung up and went to greet the men in his life. QB was carrying Tank underneath his arm through the den.

"... and then he heaved me another 10 yards behind the line of scrimmage," said Walter, "and slammed me to the turf like *this!*" Father and son crashed to the couch, then to the floor, sending the coffee table sliding across the room.

"We're gonna need a bigger house or less furniture," giggled Bear.

"Ask Bear, he was there," said Walter.

"Did Junior Seau really bruise my dad's rib?" asked Tank.

"Ribs, plural!" said Bear. "QB couldn't—well, let's just say ... that was a tough three weeks for your dad. And all those around him."

"Tank!" Walter jumped up. "Call your mom and tell her we're back from Tahoe. Use the phone in the kitchen."

"You're definitely not the same awkward father/son duo that left here a week ago," said Bear, watching Tank roll off to the kitchen.

"Amazing is how I describe him," said Walter. "He's like me, but not me. Does that make any sense? Look who I'm asking. He's actually more like you on the inside—don't take this the wrong way."

"You're about to compare two people in this world who have nothing but unconditional love for you, and you're worried about one of us taking something from you the wrong way? Talk about unnecessary delay of game," said Bear.

"Tank is like you, not me," said Walter. "He's the polar opposite of me, on the same team, which according to you is ... you. And I can kinda see it. I mean, my boy's kinda heavy-bodied like my Bear. He's got *thick* movements, your movements. He's a linebacker, not a QB. He's Bear, in that way, anyway."

"I'm so glad your family loves him," said Bear. "Doubly now."

"I'm glad you do, too," said Walter.

"How could I not love something that moves like me and comes from you?" asked Bear. "And Walter deserves a Super son to power his universe."

"We deserve Super sons," said Walter, "and daughters. I just wish he didn't want to know why I called my old girlfriend Bearcat."

"Tell me about it," said Bear.

"I told him he and I would have that talk someday," said Walter. "Did you hear that fucking Creole was on *The Tonight Show* last night?"

"Emile something," said Bear.

"*I* haven't even been on *The Tonight Show*. How can the fucking Creole Emile get on?" asked Walter.

"I know," said Bear.

"And have you noticed how it's no longer QB LOVES THE BEARCAT?" asked Walter. "Everywhere you look, WALT LOVES THE BEARCAT. Not even *Walter*."

"Does it matter which you are to people?" asked Bear. "Or to me?"

Walter paused to consider it, then eyed Bear curiously.

BEAR CRANKED UP THE BOOM BOX. A one-hit wonder's dance track wafted through the backyard. Walter was at the grill, wearing a silly chef's hat and flipping steaks. Reggie on the Down Low was playing basketball on the half-court with his boy Carter Jones, the bald-headed Dallas Maverick. Their wives were on the beach below the ridge, strolling and talking girl-to-girl talk. Two of Carter's NBA friends were there, one black, one white. Their names were Antwaan and Mikhail. They stood on the baseline of the half-court, egging on a Snowman vs. Jones slam-dunk contest. The Hail Larrys were in the pool, making out one minute, splashing water the next. Mama Rent and Black Coach were sitting on adjacent poolside lounge chairs, getting along, much to Bear's relief. Gator, one of Walter's Hawaiian teammates, was also there with his girlfriend. Gator was as tall as the NBAers, with a muscular and beefy bronzed body. His girlfriend was white and demure in comparison to his bold, always smiling persona. "So why do they call you Gator, Gator?" asked Bear after cranking up the music.

"His real name," said Walter, "is Eli, Ali, Alley? What is it, Gator?"

"Since Florida, it's been Alley Gator. Get it?" sighed Gator, still smiling.

"Welcome to Moose Jaw, Gator." Bear raised his empty bottle of Bud. "And you, too, purty lady."

"Aura," she said. "I'm Aura."

"I bet you are," said Bear, dancing in place.

"Big Norse, you sure you don't mind the *open-minded* girls I invited?" asked Gator.

"Not if my hunch is right," said Walter.

"Mind if we go see if they're out front?" asked Gator, disappearing with his Aura. QB handed his buddy another bottle of Bud.

"And Bear loves my hunches, don't you?" asked Walter.

"And the valley between," said Bear. "*Open-minded* girls?"

"Two bisexual chicks from Seattle, in LA on *cheerleader* business," said Walter.

"Lisa Wu and Wendy Jiu!" said Bear, saying hello to the lesbo ex-cheergirls coming onto the deck from the kitchen, appearing just as shocked as Bear. Walter, who wasn't shocked, broke the ice, speaking first and hugging both girls simultaneously in his big blond arms.

"You guys are friends?" asked Gator.

"No doubt," said Bear. Gator smiled a Joe Bruin smile. Bear joined Walter and the cheergirls. Their talking morphed into hugs. Bear even got up the nerve to ask: "Who's Lisa Wu and who's Wendy Jiu?"

"I *knew* he never knew," said Wendy Jiu or Lisa Wu.

"Which one of you is Bearcat?" asked Lisa Wu or Wendy Jiu, prompting a round of laughter. "Rump Shaker," one of the current rap odes 2 booty, came booming over the boom box. Hail Larry's Wife ran out of the pool and cranked up the volume, then grabbed Bear.

"We're dancing, sports fans!" shouted Hail Larry's Wife. Mama Rent complied immediately, followed by Wendy Jiu and Lisa Wu, who grabbed Walter. The deck became an American bandstand. Gator's Aura and Black Coach stayed on the sidelines. Hail Larry joined Mama Rent. His wife started dancing with

Gator. Bear segued to the lesbo ex-cheergirls and became a foursome with them and Walter. On the basketball court, Snowman and Jones were too wrapped up in slam-dunking, but Antwaan and Mikhail danced on the baseline.

"Black guys help the white guys," shouted Gator, the party's big happy fool, subbing for Coleman. The boys and their friends danced, ate, balled, swam, drank and spent a cool and dreamy night on the deck, one of many cool and dreamy nights for the big league boys.

Even the off-seasons are Super now, MVP.

Always and forever, little Bearcat. We're good as gold.

23

Skylights Gleaming

O*h, what a lonely boy. Brilliant disguise. Some guys have all the luck. Never wanna fall in love again. That's what you get: pain, suffering, loneliness, death ... your body curled up in a ball, ready to roll off the cliff a breath away. Why breathe? Why dream, love, hope, love, learn, try? He had tried.*

Song of the 80s, our decade: George Michael, "One More Try," beating out "Forever in My Life" by Prince, one of the most controversial ballots in Songs of the Year history.

He had One More Tried more times than he could remember. Men, women, whites, blacks, browns, yellows, reds, blues, purples, pinks, greens, oranges. Young, old, polar opposite, polar similar, polar bears. Any love, right, Luther? There had been more One More Tries in his lifetime than he knew what to do with, except take them with him off the cliff.

He had never known any kind of love at all, just fuzzy fax.

Why should this at-bat be any different? He just wasn't a big-league player. He was the crazy one, the different one, the wrong one.

Too much. *Had he ever let another soul near his heart who hadn't uttered those words?*

"You're too much."

And the award for phrase most heard throughout his lifetime goes to ... "You're too much."

All these years, his *cocky-one-minute, feel-like-shit-the-next-minute* ass had never dreamed of a satisfactory retort for: You're too much.

And drawing blanks was a rarity for his sharp-witted mind.

"You're too much."

And you're never enough!

No, I'm just right!

Re-write! the editor upstairs would demand, flinging the weak pages in the air. Re-create. Re-adjust. Re-think. Reverse. Re-write.

Brilliant disguise. Men. Life. Canyons. Hills. The Pacific. Darkness. Jump. Who the fuck would care?

A man's job.

It's a man's job, loving you, but not a job for a man in a brilliant disguise.

You need a real miracle.

You see, buddy, I'm a big fat ugly infected faggy nasty dirty sick man. I have sex with fags. I am one of the fags. Sure, I'm in my forties and if I'm glowing, especially at a sporting event, people start looking at me with stars in their eyes, telling me:

You must be somebody, somebody who has a man's job, like pro athlete, always and forever.

Yeah, I can glow like dat. I got dat. I can whip this body into all kinds of hella shape in the blink of an eye. Yep. I can go from fat ass to badass, and the whole world buys it. Just give my obsessive-compulsive, bad fat ass a couple of months to exercise, hold the food.

I can do whatever the fuck I want sometimes. Sometimes, I'm the king of the world. Sometimes, I'm even big league. Yep. This little piece of shit prototype can be big league. Until it all vanishes, sometimes so instantly, I can literally feel it leaving my body. That love ... if that's what you wanna call it ... I reach out to you ... I reached out to you ... I felt it instantly ... pure serenity ... oh, sure, there was some quaking ... after all, it's not every day a guy meets another guy who looks at him likes he's god of something. But we weathered those initial quakes, that initial rocking and rolling. We told a story from moment one ... remember the season opener? ... you remembered the season opener like it was as close to your heart as a blood vessel.

The UCLA game.

Funny, I call it the Georgia game.

Polar opposites in the same perfect universe, always and forever.

If you only believe.

If I only believe.

But it's way too dark now. I can't feel ya. Feeling you was so easy when we were talking, sharing. You shut me up. Nobody shuts me up. I listened to you and your stories. I felt you. Where the hell are you now? Why did you leave? Why won't you talk to me? Am I that fucking crazy?

Gotta be me. You see, you're perfect. You're from the better pole, at least from where I'm standing. Sure, sure, I know we both got baggage, regrets, moments we wish we could reverse, take back, turn right instead of left, stop while you were that much ahead, listened to your intuition in the first place, got out while you could, wished you'd known better, would have let go, taken back, given in, stopped, continued, lost, won, lived, died, said Fuck it, said ... Yes, anything ... is ... possible.

One parent made sure we knew this, come what may.

Anything's possible.

One parent made sure we knew the polar opposite, come what may.

Don't trust, don't love, don't dream.

The brilliant mind behind my brilliant disguise says, it's reversed. Your light was my dark, my dark, your light. Don't understand the rocket science of it yet, but it's got something to do with being in perfect balance, as if somebody dreamed it up, always and forever in perfect grace. You'll see. Anything is possible.

With the possible exception of hearing something other than:

"You're too much."

I'm way too much for anyone with a shred of decency to wanna be seen with. Oh, sure, all golden and cool and dreamy on the outside. And I talk one cool and dreamy game. True? I got skillz. I also got loneliness. I also gotta get off this cliff.

Watch your step, even in the blur.

Make sure you're around for the show tonight. Supposed to be some kind of newfangled fireworks, skylights, probably from what you're standing on top of right now, right here on the sideline near the 50-yard line, across from the bleachers.

Skylights?

Can't you see all the stars in the night sky? Look up. Unless you think you're gonna lose your balance. Never wanna lose your balance. Unless you truly want all that chaos and disorder.

I wanna go home but I don't know where home is.

Can't see your way clearly?

Can't see a damned thing.

Try seeing a blessed thing.

Not even the skylights. They're not shining, just gleaming, can't see clearly now, can barely see, can barely remember. Was he real?

Who?

My buddy. Didn't you just say something about me looking like I just lost my best friend? I just found him. I don't wanna lose him now.

"People have been coming and going all day from this Complex. Big shindig tonight. If he's here, look around more. You've been hanging pretty much to one side of the place, the field, the bleachers, the cliff, now the shed at the 50-yard line. Or should I say, on top of the shed at the 50?"

"He's gone. I can feel it. I literally felt his spirit leaving my body, then taking off into space. I wonder if he felt it, too, our spirits separating."

"Dream of it."

"Doesn't matter," said the lost lonely boy teetering on the roof of the shed located on the 50-yard line, across from the bleachers in the Complex in the hills overlooking Malibu. *Shitty life,* he reminded himself, looking up at these alleged skylights. "He's gone now. I can feel it. We've separated."

"You've been looking pretty consumed yourself. Thought I'd leave you alone for a while," said the man below.

"You and everyone else."

"Troubled? Can I help?"

"Can't fix this with whelming. Or welding."

"Try twisting it."

"Or any garden tools. Or flyers for dead gyms advertising *play the games of life!* Unfortunately, ain't got the tools."

"Tools are another way of saying DNA. You might wanna rethink that. And come off that shed. You're about to lose your balance and fall flat on your ..."

"Game over ... fuck, talk about a rump shaker ... sacked at the 50 by a zephyr coming from the blindside."

"Look at me. You all right?"

"Sorry, looking at you will only remind me of him, and my failure to be what he needed."

"Then talk to me without looking. You remember who I am, right?"

"I'm not that crazy, Sanchez. I just can't afford to look at you. Not within 10 miles of that cliff. And that's not exactly 10 miles. More like ... 50 yards, or less."

"Forget about me," said Coach Sanchez. "I'm here to help you use your tools. What can I do?"

"I wanted to give him everything, make his world more magnificent than anyone can possibly imagine. I wanted to move mountains for him after Super Sunday. I knew it was all meant to be, all right, all right now."

"What happened to all that loving energy?" asked Coach Sanchez.

"Tell me about it. We talked like you told us to. We shared stories. I talked to him. He's real. That much is true. We connected. And it felt good. I can't remember the details, just the serenity."

"Tell me about it," said Coach Sanchez.

"It was like high school. *Correction:* it was like how I dreamed high school would be when I used to dream of being in the perfect high school."

"Keep dreaming," said Coach Sanchez.

"He and I were just talking, sharing, not making any great life decisions or creations. Just kinda existing side by side, talking about little stuff, telephone poles, easy stuff, for us anyway. He talked forever, I just listened, feeling like I was in high school, talking to my best buddy on the phone, feeling so good and relaxed. Time just passed without even ... there was no time, just us ... no time ... no time to explain all this to my buddy ... he's my buddy, Coach ... I know it ... how do I tell him? How do I make this known? How do I believe it myself?"

"Keep going. Deep inside every man's toolbox is a special place, reserved for the most special of circumstances and jobs. You got a big job ahead of you. Go deep and get those specially reserved tools, deep inside the gut of your toolbox."

"GONNA HAVE IT ALL. And the world will be a better place for knowing us, at least from where I stand—promise you, man, or my name ain't MK."

"Thank you, Markus Kramer, formerly of the Chicago Bulls, now with the Indiana Pacers. By the way, enjoyed your cameo as a basketball player in the movie Uptight. *We're not worthy! Lastly on* Greg the Gut's Sports Report: *training camp! Yes, football widows, time to tune into the daytime drama again, because hubby's gonna be jumping in the armchair command module, and he ain't coming out until he's got some Super love—football variety, let's not get mushy here. We are men and football is a man's job!"*

"So what's this about a contract snag with Walter's job as QB?" asked Hail Larry's Wife, calling from Washington, DC. In the boys' haste to stuff the Bearcat back into his Pandora's box during the Super celebration, Yeager had inadvertently agreed to *trust* Roxanne with $100,000 a year for the next 20 years.

"He reported to camp anyway," said Bear, turning off *Greg the Gut* on the radio in the laundry room. "But we got cracks in the paint on the mother ship."

"Cracks?" asked Hail Larry's Wife.

"Minor shit, not a big quake," said Bear. "Other line, it's him. See you in a few weeks ... Meister, what's the word?"

"That bitch is not worth two million dollars," said Walter.

"Not even to put this behind us?" asked Bear, leaving the laundry room.

"Where were our freakin' heads after the Super Bowl?" asked Walter.

"Please tell me you're not driving, QB," said Bear.

"Just this crazy freakin' golf cart all over the complex." Walter laughed and yelled off a bit of his frustration, making Bear feel better about his man at the Seahawks training facility. "I can't just let this roll off my back, Bear-man."

"You've *got* to let everything roll off your back," said Bear from the bedroom in Moose Jaw, packing for the seasonal move to Corona, Seattle.

"You would have thought the bitch would have been satisfied with the profits from her bestselling autobiography, *My Life as the Bearcat*," said Walter.

"Let me shoulder the burden, buddy," said Bear.

"Which was never part of the deal. What's the real Bearcat gonna do about this?" asked Walter.

"The worrying, first of all," said Bear. "You focus on the end zone, the one you can feel under your soles. How long has it been since you threw a touchdown pass?"

"Don't even go there," said Walter. "Mooks, hang on!"

"Shut up, I'm talking," said Bear.

"Make it quick, time limited," said Walter. "Gator, 'sup dawg?"

"Hey, you—*ultimate hero who can't burden other people with his problems*—listen up!" said Bear.

"Okay, buddy, give it your best shot," said a resigned Walter.

"When was the last time you threw a touchdown in an official NFL game?" asked Bear.

"Ah, hell," said Walter.

"I'd rather think of it as heaven," said Bear.

"Ah, heaven—there, you satisfied?" asked Walter.

"Not yet but getting there," said Bear. "The last time Super Arm—*didn't think I remembered your childhood name for yourself, did you?*—threw a TD pass was eons, Walter Yeager. The Super Universe is history!"

"So I've been worthless since, is that what you're saying?" asked Walter.

"Not even in jest," said Bear. "TD passes are only one of your many gifts to me and the world. But you are a man who needs a man's job, and right now, that man's job is getting you some end zone!"

"Talk to me, crazy fucking Bearcat!"

"Remember, buddy, how good it feels to wrap yourself around some end zone?" asked Bear. "Piss 'n' Vinegar will never be happy without a little end zone in his life, and he knows what his big black Cheer Man is talking 'bout!"

"You just made my piss 'n' vinegar shoot up to the moon," said Walter. *"Big Black Cheer Man—I like that.* My little black cheerboy is all grown up in the right ways, but still a kid at heart in the best of ways."

"Just like PV, my MVP, *always and forever*," said Bear. "What we gone do this year amongst the football people, PV?"

"Well, BBCM," said Walter, making them laugh. "I got so much end zone last year, I kinda got addicted."

"You were spectacular in the end zone during our Super Season," said Bear. "I'm guessing you enjoyed all that time doing whatever it took to get all that end zone ... somehow, someway, just because it brought you all that Super joy!"

"*Preach, BBCM!*"

"Time to get more of that Super joy, my brother. Because the more you get into the end zone, the more you get to your ultimate goal, to get into the end zone in the biggest games of your life, and to *get there* so many times, you experience the kind of Super joy that only true champions experience, the kind of Super joy that comes from believing *you can achieve your Super dreams,* in football, in moviemaking, in soul mate lovin', in whatever Big Norse wants!"

"I'm about to get happy!" said Walter.

"I'll take you there, because *all of life* is a game, PV," said Bear. "On top of that, life is but a dream ... so as a handsome black coach who watches soaps and raps country music once said: Dirty on and on ... *if you're gonna dream, why not dream the better dream, the higher dream, the deepest dreams within your soul?* Or something like that."

"Amen to something like that!" said Walter.

"And to getting to Miami, and some Super dreams, South Florida-style!"

"GREG AND HIS GUT BUDDIES at *Greg the Gut's Sports Report* are gonna find out real early on this season about Yeager and his Defending World Champs."

"Yup, Gut ... everybody in the world likes to see the underdog come back and win the big one! But we know what happens next, don't we, Rocky and Seahawks fans? Or should we say, Bearcat fans?"

"It's like this, America the Beautiful: Walt may love being Super MVP, but the rest of us love to knock a champion and his Bearcats off their high and mighty asses!"

"The season opener at the earthquake-repaired LA Coliseum should do the job, Gut."

"*Ouch!* Are you saying the Bearcats aren't ready for ... *da Raidas?*"

"You know how it is in that billion-year-old snake pit of a stadium, Gut. If only it were just ... *da Raidas ...*"

The snake pit otherwise known as the Los Angeles Memorial Coliseum was brimming over with *Raidas.* And skeletons, and bones, and ghosts, and Darth Vaders, and an infinite amount of sweat and athletic dreams for all time. Not that the big league boys were worried about *all time.* Yeager was on the field, trying to survive the brutal mentality that was *da Raidas,* while Coleman sat mate-less in the stands, trying to survive the brutal mentality that was Raider Nation.

"I like the mentality of the football coach who opens up the season against College of the Bahamas," said Bear. In his mind at least. Outwardly, he was alone and camouflaged so no one would recognize the lesbian flick guy.

Thanks but ... they weren't worthy!

Seattle's Triple Threat of Yeager, Jefferson and Millstone *were* worthy. De-spite the pleadings from the bloodthirsty Coliseum throng, their fading men in black could not feed the Super Defenders to the crowd. Raider Nation was in disarray. The final: Seattle, *cool and dreamy,* LA, *chaos and disorder.*

"Blew 'em out, 42-2," said Bear into his cell, exiting the tunnel into a sun-drenched Sunday afternoon. "I'd never seen my man cause a safety. I thought it was time."

"We lost at Kansas City," said Hail Larry's Wife, calling from Washington DC again for some reason.

"I'm just glad we made it out of this snake pit alive today," said Bear, break-ing free of the gates. "*The* most dangerous crowd. I didn't even bring Mama Rent. Hold on ... drive-by ..."

"Mine are peaceful these days," said Hail Larry's Wife.

"Some golf cart or something," said Bear. "I'm safe now. There's like a bunch of museums and gardens right next door. You know, this is one time I can safely say: I will *never, ever* attend another LA Raider football game in LA. Matter of fact, I can't imagine going to another pro football game in LA ever, at this point. You can quote me on that one, whatever day this is in September 1994."

"What's wrong with LA and pro football?" laughed Hail Larry's Wife. "Too much traffic, beach, sun, fun, and *other* fantasy parks?"

"LA's not dreaming the better dream," said Bear, traversing the luscious gardens adjacent to the Coliseum. "I see things more clearly now ... my God ... this place, *bonito! Linda! Vista!* ... that means 'pretty view' in Spanish, right? Tons of rows of flowers, flora and fauna—is that what that stuff is?—I'm no rocket scientist or landscaper-type, but it's freakin' beautiful! Gridirons ... just like ..."

"Why isn't LA good for football?" asked Hail Larry's Wife. "Gridirons?"

"Gridirons, LA loves," said Bear. "But all of LA will never truly love an en-tire grid in unison, on any field. LA's energy is not built that way."

"What are you freakin' talking about?" asked Hail Larry's Wife.

"Football is genetically designed to be a game of polar opposites vs. polar opposites, a clearly defined game in a clearly defined universe based on a set of clearly defined rules, all beginning with a grid over empty space," said Bear.

"LA is nothing, if not a grid and space, should be perfect for football then," said Hail Larry's Wife.

"Not from where I'm standing." Bear went wide, letting in the world beyond his very narrow focus these days. "This conversation started with me in the Coliseum, a place so beautiful, LA doesn't know what to do with it. Now I'm standing in huge gardens, a place so beautiful, we know exactly what to do with it: enjoy it. The snake pit is round, with no sides, perfect for snakes. This grid I'm standing in—mesmerized by—it's the opposite of round, straight lines, row after row of them, a grid that works for LA because it lets anyone and everyone come and enjoy this luscious precious garden."

"Again, perfect," said Hail Larry's Wife.

"Not for LA," said Bear. "The game of football doesn't come naturally to the energy that is LA. Football is a universe based on a grid with sides. LA has no sides. LA doesn't take sides. LA is an all-encompassing universe all its own, where anyone can become anything, literally. No sides to that argument. Hollywood, LA—same diff—both are powered by dreams that redefine what's possible. How? By dreaming of, then doing the impossible. Right now, no one in LA is dreaming a big enough football dream that *represents!* As the kids say."

"Represents what, Bear?" laughed Hail Larry's Wife.

"The rest of the beauty that is LA beyond this garden, starting with what's on the other side of the street, the ghetto. The only dream that can truly captivate all of LA is one that represents all of LA in a way that says *all of LA* has an equal shot at the Football Super Dream, regardless of color or economic status, or what kind of Sugar a man prefers. And LA can spot a phony owner *slash* dreamer in a heartbeat. In the early 80s, the New Yorkers came in droves. In exchange for showing them how to dream the warmer dream, they showed us a thing or two about detecting bullshit. Big Ups to the Big Apple. You too, Motownphilly!"

"Bear Coleman, you are one crazy muthafucka," said Hail Larry's Wife.

"I'm also getting approached by one, hold on," said Bear.

"Sorry, man, thought you were a friend of mine. You look just like him. Could be twins, man, I'm truly amazed."

"Who was that?" asked Hail Larry's Wife.

"Huh? Oh, some Salvadoran kid," said Bear. "Kinda glowed, but I'm busy. Looks like he is, too, attending to his family."

"Enrique, Jonathon, Marlene, Noah ... tell me about it ... Hilda, Eric, Josie ..."

"Fuck, I gotta get outta LA," said Bear, "and up to our real life in Seattle now that the season opener at our off-season home is done. I can't believe I'm walking around near USC. Did you know I went to SC before UCLA?"

"Neither you nor Walter talk much about your first schools," said Hail Larry's Wife.

"SC and Illinois are the lands of broken dreams for us," said Bear. "Our first schools, like a bittersweet first love. Just one more way we're alike. We both set off to conquer the world at these big-time schools. *That should have met in the Rose Bowl!* I would have dressed as Tommy Trojan and humped by buddy at the Snaky Lu's-Pasadena Battle of the Beef Bowl thing they have every year."

"Don't forget about the Illini chief mascot guy," laughed Hail Larry's Wife.

"My man and I don't talk first schools *slash* loves very much," said Bear. "We's forward-looking. Or really, he's forward-looking and I'm looking forward because he's there. Otherwise, I'm the backward-looking guy, which explains why I bump into so many things. *Ouch!* ... but it's like a natural symmetry. QBs look forward to make decisions. Cheer Buds gotta look back because we're facing the stands. So before we react to the situation, we gotta look back, to make sure we got his back. Perfect grace, life and football ... *ouch!* Again! ... Walter rarely bumps into anything; me ... different story ... safely in the vehicle now. Thank God, or Walter, same difference."

"You're psycho!" laughed Hail Larry's Wife.

"If you're not treating your man like a god, you're not treating your man at all," said Bear. "And sensitive, caring men like Walter want treats, not tricks, when they come home after doing battle all day."

"Like you're some expert on knowing your man," said a doubtful Hail Larry's Wife.

"That's my job," said Bear. "I intend to do it right."

"You've changed," said Hail Larry's Wife.

"Thank you."

"Thought you'd be less cocky after winning the big one," said Hail Larry's Wife.

"You really *are* outta the loop," said Bear, taking off and putting *Greg the Gut's Sports Report* on the radio.

"It's only cocky if you can't back it up. It's the real deal, true cock, when you know how to bust it. Take heart, sports fans, sometimes you gotta fire a lotta blanks to figure out how to hit it right."

"Thank you, Markus Kramer of the Indiana Pacers. Stand by for the call from the FCC on that one. Meanwhile, good luck, Kramer, on your upcoming cameo in Rocket Bruthas 2, *if the movie ever gets off the ground."*

"In the clear now," said Bear on his cell. "Where were we? Can you believe they want to make a sequel?"

"When do I get to see my movie?" asked Hail Larry's Wife.

"Caution," said Bear, messing with the radio dial. "*Freeways Claim Bodies That Fade* is not my real-life best friend unless you want people to only know you as a conniving bitch who gets her comeuppance on a crowded highway when all the bodies start fading, thanks to her wishing them all dead."

"*Why did you have to be born in my lifetime and be on this road, blocking my way at this very moment!*" screamed Hail Larry's Wife, reciting the opening line from Bear's finished script. "I'm gonna be famous! *Variety* says: 'The buzz on Coleman's *Freeways* is so electric, the *lesbian flick guy* could soon become the *weird suspense thriller guy.*'"

"Maybe I should give Marcus Coleman something weird and devilish to write," said Bear. "I picked up that old script again this morning. *My Whole Other Life.* You know, me, the sad-sack without his quarterback. Or much else. I kinda felt shitty for dreaming such a shitty, lonely life for *that* Marcus."

"You enjoy it," said Hail Larry's Wife. "You writers get off on the power."

"*An old mentor once told me: the creator of a story puts his characters up in a tree and throws rocks at them until the creator is ready to either bring them down from the tree or leave them hanging.*"

"So true," said Bear, reacting to the quote on *Book Mobile,* one of his favorite talk-radio shows. "I wouldn't be a good storyteller if I didn't put Marcus through hell and back. *I* wasn't the one who scheduled the Northridge earthquake on *his/my* birthday. God and LA did that."

"Lucky you boys were jetting around the big leagues, winning the Super Bowl," said Hail Larry's Wife.

"With only minor damage!" said Bear, messing with the dial to see if he could catch *Geo Life,* a nature show. "The houses on either side of us? *Gone! Flattened!* Like meatloaf, mash potatoes—and the swimming pool—sliding off the plate and into the ocean. Why does God do that? Spare some the quakes, tornadoes, and disasters, then put the big hurt on others? Why are Walter and I so lucky and blessed all the time? Not to question it too much, mind you."

"Bear," said Hail Larry's Wife. "*That* Marcus is only a poor sap in your—"

"In my dreams, I know," said Bear. "And on the script on my new Super computer. Walt loves giving gifts that help advance a person. I just hated having *that* Marcus woken up on the morning of his 32nd birthday with the Northridge quake. He lives alone, you know."

"How bad was his big hurt?" asked Hail Larry's Wife.

"*No talking, because the earth can be quite loud on its own without a single human voice. No standing, because the earth that already hurls through space at breakneck speed is too busy rearranging itself to worry about mere mortals on their own two feet. No thinking, because you know you're about to die (and it's too noisy to hear yourself think, anyway). And you're alone. And if you become trapped under rubble, nobody will find you for days because you're that much out of the loop with the rest of the world."*

"He survives," said Bear, turning off *Geo Life*. "But it's the last night he ever slept in the dream of a townhouse apartment he loved so much. Too many cracks, questions, and nearby buildings at strange angles in his earthquake alley of a neighborhood. His Salvadoran son-figure's family is like a second family. He shacks up with them until he can start to make a new world for himself."

"*Geez*, Bear, give the guy a break," said Hail Larry's Wife.

"I intend to," said Bear. "I'm also gonna give myself a break and get back to my other job, managing whatever Walter wants."

"Walt loves to eat? Who the fuck knows that?" asked Walter, calling from Newport, Seattle.

"*The Times*," sighed Bear. "Allegedly overheard on this newfangled inter-networking web world thing. Tammy claims it's gonna change the world and make being undercover that much harder. How the fuck can you spread information on something that's called *a web?*"

"Tell me about it," said Walter. "What else are they claiming *Walt loves?*"

"I'm about to find out." Bear glanced around the den in Corona, Seattle. The room was filled, floor to ceiling, with *Walter*. Tapes. Clippings. Trophies. Plaques. Game balls. Game programs. Game jocks. "Game on," said Bear, taking a good whiff of the Meadowlands. "I am getting caught up on the archives today or my real name isn't ... never mind."

"*Or* you could work on your own archives," said Walter, the more modest of the two when it came to *The Glory of Walt*.

"What—the reviews for *Rocket Bruthas* and *Uptight? Ha!* I'll pass ... *pass ... pass, Yeager!*" said Bear, watching a clip of his man on the tube. "Walt loves to take it to the limit, like the Eagles, one of his favorite rock groups as a kid!"

"What'd I do?" laughed Walter.

"Besides drive me and the Broncos crazy last week—where do I begin?" said Bear. "Walter! Look at you ... the winning TD in the third ... *dude* ... some-times, the way you hold onto the ball so long drives your little Bearcat nuts! Romanowski is about to ... *sidestep!* JJ's open ... yes! Touchdown, Bearcats! *Huh?* Cool ... dreamy ... sweet ... sweet practice, bud. Gonna do your archives from the last few weeks, see how many sports pundits think they know what *Walt loves ...*"

After hanging up, Bear indulged himself and put on one of his buddy's old jerseys. Then he called up the Boss—Bruce Springsteen—on the stereo and did what the Boss told him to do: a "Man's Job."

"... taking care of you, Walter, ain't for any ol' boy ... or girl! ..."

"*We know QB loves the Bearcat, but did you also know Walt loves the long ball? Look at the way Yeager hits Lars for the longest pass in the Super Bowl MVP's career ... 88 yards on the floor of the venerable LA Memorial Coliseum as the Hawks overthrow Raider Nation, 42-2. About the only flaw of the day for Yeager, if you can call it that, was him giving up his first-ever NFL safety. Who cares?*"

"... something in our soul ..."

"*Walt loves a man's job. Here's QB now, in charge at Arrowhead in Kansas City ... 28 yards to Zook Adams of Ohio State ... the rookie gets the biggest catch of his career and Yeager says, More to come, young buck ...*"

"... a hero who saves the day ..."

"*Walt loves the comeback. Down 21 at the Astrodome, can you say: I'll run it three times myself for three rushing TDs and carry the team on my big strong back? He did let El Kicko drill the final nail in the dried-up oil well. El kicks this 51-yarder as time runs out on the Oilers' dreams. Better luck next time, Houston ...*"

"... all our illusions ... meltin' away ..."

"*Walt loves being the leader of the pack. Call this Bad Day at Brown Rock. Cleveland Memorial Stadium was a cold place for the champs today in this pre-season matchup. The Browns played as if they were going out of style. Do they know something we don't? The Hawks were blown away by the lake effect, 49-12. But do you see Yeager getting down? Here he is, giving his team some encouragement on the sidelines, saying, Keep believing.*"

"... loving you is a man's job, Walter ..."

"*Walt loves big furry mascots. Here, Simon Seahawk gives him a big furry hug during pre-game, then dances around the meister to 'Crazy' by Aerosmith.*"

"... loving you is your buddy's job ..."

"*Walt loves kids. On the way to practice today in Seattle, here's last year's Super MVP signing autographs, throwing a few and looking like a big kid himself.*"

"... loving you is a man's job, Walter ..."

"*Walt loves helping himself to other people's food. Can you say: Nachos at the press conference?*"

"... getting up some nerve ..."

"*Walt loves spreading the joy. The Dolphins didn't stand a chance in the Kingdome today. I guess this is why a guy like Yeager becomes a quarterback, days like this when he's distributing the rock like a point guard on the Sonics ... first to*"

Jefferson ... here's Zook getting his ... then hey, why not a cross-field lateral to Lars?
... went for 24 yards and a first down, by the way ... and you can see here, on this
pile-up at the goal line, Walt loves helping others into the end zone. That's what
leaders of the pack do, eh, QB?"

"... treating ... a real man right ..."

"Walt loves to listen. Walt loves to laugh, love, rock, cry, dream, and love some more. And give. And give. And give and give. Walt's not a taker. Walt's a giver. Walt hands off. Walt passes. To the offense, the punter, the defense, his backup, his coach. The quarterback is always handing off the joy to someone else, except on those rare moments of individual glory: the keeper."

"... loving you is my job, Walter ..."

"Otherwise, Walt is always handing off."

That's his job.

"... a man's man's job, man!"

"Walt loves to overcome the odds, big odds, Super Duper odds."

"Walt's had to shoulder plenty of challenges in his life," said Bear, talking to Hail Larry's Wife and the Players' Wives Club of his dreams ... lunch at a sidewalk café.

(Walt doesn't like to nap. Bears do.)

"Men like Walter are givers," said Bear to the players' wives. "Take what your man gives you. He will feel good. That's your job, helping your man feel good. There is no other side."

How do you know this, Bear? asked the players' wives.

"I live with the man. In the off-season, I mean. As his manager," said Bear to the wives.

We live with our guys full-time! And they're our husbands! said the wives.

"Dream of him the rest of the time," said Bear to the wives. "You'll figure it out."

Walt loves me, the real Bearcat! This much is true ...

"Walt loves beating up on the Redskins, I can tell you that," said a voice on high in the underbelly of RFK Stadium in Washington, DC.

Bear was at the concession stand, dreaming of the nacho girl making change before the Seahawks offense regained possession. A radio broadcast of the game filled the underbelly of the city's oddly-shaped fruit bowl of a stadium:

"Bimbles fumbles the punt, can you believe that? Game tied at 17, early in the fourth, and the Seahawks get the ball right back, six yards from the goal line. Walt loves this scoring opportunity, better believe that."

The home crowd exploded in the fruit bowl. The musical group Queen was promising, We *will rock you!* On the monitor above the concession stand, Yeager came up to the line of scrimmage, first and goal. The snap from the center went south. Walter picked up the ball and ran to his right. Three Washington linemen smothered him for a loss. The fruit bowl swayed even more.

Bear completed the transaction and hurried toward his seat, preferring to see his buddy live. Still in the underbelly, he heard the kind of roar you never want to hear in your opponent's den: the roar of a great kill. The fruit bowl split like an earthquake in his gut. Bear spilled his drink, then threw his nachos to the ground and rushed to get a view of the game.

Trainers ran onto the field, silencing the crowd. They were *his* trainers, as in Walter, who was still on the ground. "Tackle by Doak Minnefield," said the game announcer as the replay board did its job:

Yeager took the snap, rolled to his right. Jim Wahler, the Redskin lineman, ran him down and wrapped his arms around the quarterback's waist. Number 13 slipped away and turned to run. As he did, Minnefield, formerly of the Chargers, mowed him down like a rag doll. The crowd winced in unison. Bear fell backward down the steps, then staggered through the underbelly. The crowd winced again upon witnessing another replay. *"Isn't that what you wanted?"* said Bear. Walter was in serious pain. Bear was alone. He tried calling the ER Wife. No response. He went lower into the underbelly, frantically trying to find the visitors' locker room. *"My buddy's hurt. I gotta show up!"* he wanted to shout to the fans in the blur. He heard polite clapping from the stands. They were taking Walter off the field, he realized, just as Tammy grabbed him by the arm and whisked him through several concrete corridors.

"Do what it takes, or I will," said Bear. A gurney sped past, halting their progress. *"Walter,"* said Bear when he saw his buddy flying by. No one heard him. The corridor was packed with paramedics, reporters and camera crews, none of whom cared about the quarterback's manager. The gurney disappeared through two large doors. "I'm going in there," Bear told Tammy, then realized she had vanished. He tried to get past the doors on his own. No dice.

"Live from the RFK underbelly, Walter Yeager is being taken to a local hospital. They believe he has a concussion, but that may not be all."

Bear paid a cab driver all the money in his wallet to get him to the hospital as fast as possible, but the medical people in the ER lobby put up the same roadblocks between him and his buddy. Family only. Team personnel only. Reporters only. He stood near admittance, out of options, about to break down in hysterics, when Mrs. Yeager entered the lobby from triage. "Don't worry, sweetheart. We don't know any more than you," said Mrs. Yeager.

"Is he conscious?" asked Bear.

"Very hazy," said Mrs. Yeager.

"Is anything broken?" asked Bear.

"I'm praying no," said Mrs. Yeager.

"Is there anything else?" asked Bear.

She shook her head.

"*Now,* you don't know any more than me," said Bear, collapsing on the nearest chair.

"If it's any consolation, I know you'll be one of the first people he'll want to see," said Mrs. Yeager, sitting next to him.

"Walter's in the hospital. The only consolation is him alive and well," said Bear. Mrs. Yeager fell silent and held his hand. Sometime later, a Nigerian doctor emerged and gave them the rundown: concussion, hip pointer and maybe shoulder damage that could wait. The concussion was the thing, but Walter could be released by morning. "That's a good consolation, right?" asked Bear, hugging Mrs. Yeager. Mr. Yeager emerged from triage. The deep creases in his brow softened when he saw his wife embracing Bear.

Seven hours after Doak Minnefield put the hurt on their lives, the boys finally got to see one another. Number 13 was lying upright in his hospital bed, his spacey eyes trying to follow highlights from around the league on *SportsCenter.* Bear stood just inside the private hospital room, savoring for a moment the sight of his man still whole, if not wholly there. Then he sat at Walter's bedside and gently held his hand, prompting Walter to turn off the TV.

"I know who *you* are," said Walter. "You showed up, my gorgeous black coach from San Diego."

Bear broke out laughing. His man was so good at making him laugh. Then he started crying. His man was so good at making him cry.

"Don't start," said Walter. "Mom told me about the hard time you had."

"Grace and her girls got through on the phone!" said Bear. "I couldn't even do that."

"She said was family," said Walter.

"Lucky for her she could tell a *white* lie, literally," said Bear.

"I feel like shit for the day you must have had," said Walter.

"Not your fault." Bear kissed Walter's hand. "Or Grace's. I'm glad you got to talk to your girls. They bring all kinds of sunshine and joy to your sensitive Dad side. I'm so glad that, by the Grace of God, you have those beautiful girls. This much is true. Believe me when I say, they were a shock to me. I never imagined that desperate little moment in the orange triangle in Anaheim would keep on giving in all the right ways. Sometimes, I shock myself. Sometimes, like tonight, the world shocks me. You go, girls."

"My prince," said Walter, squeezing Bear's hand.

"Doesn't every king need one, sire?" asked Bear. "Let's dream of a king for our Princess Grace. Deep down, she wants you. She's definitely not crazy, eh? But it's actually by the Grace of God that you guys ended up not being a match."

"Because I'm with you?" asked Walter, picking up the hospital phone, thinking of making a call.

"Because you could never take the place of her man," said Bear. "She loved another deeper before you. You weren't her first, and I know you feel me, Big Norse."

"You do know me, eh?" said Walter, dialing the phone.

"Starting to," said Bear. "Only because I'm starting to know myself."

"If you didn't have such a deep manly voice that blew me away the first time I heard it, maybe you could sound like a distressed white woman," said Walter with a mild laugh. "Like Grace."

"Funny, I can only dance like them, sorta—not act or sound like them at all," said Bear.

"And for me, it's the reverse," said Walter.

"But you don't have a feminine bone in your body," said Bear. "Twisted."

"Grace," said Walter, hanging up the phone. "Don't sweat it. Like the switchboard music says, love will keep us together, true, Cap?"

"True dat," sighed Bear, resting his head on Walter's hand. "On the cab ride over, all I could think of was: *I've got to show up. I've got to show up.* Remember how we used to say that sometimes? *If you show up, I'll show up. If I know you're there, I'll show up.* I knew you were there. I knew you needed me. I had to show up."

"If we were man and wife, you'd've been in here hours ago," said Walter. "No wife would be barred like that. I needed you. I needed you to show up. I think I asked for you at the stadium, I don't care. I don't care anymore. I asked for you because I needed you, just like any of my teammates would have needed their soul mates at that moment. Bear ... gonna tell the whole world ... nobody keeps us apart like that ... especially when I ... need my pole ... my pole needs me ... nothing stop us, not even the skylights."

"Skylights?" asked Bear.

"They're gleaming," mumbled Walter. "Been gleaming at me all day, just like I been gleaming at them."

"I don't understand. Maybe you should rest," said Bear.

"I'm gleaming," said Walter. "Brief, faint, dim. Not a shining star."

Bear raised his head. Walter was resting, not unconscious, just resting. It had been a very exhausting trip to the nation's capital.

THE CABIN IN THE WOODS that was Corona, Seattle was meant to be Bear's little hideaway from the football world, and Walter *and* Bear's hideaway when Walter could spare the time. Thus, the cabin's isolation and cozy, one-bedroom setup were always just right, until an injured and immobile QB moved in full-time.

"What ya doing, Bear?" asked Walter, lying on the couch, crutches on the floor. Yeager was on IR, injured reserved. The title defense season had taken a major detour. Estimated re-launch: to be determined.

"I go to work," said Bear, standing over his desk behind the couch. "*Freeways* rewrites from the set. This newfangled email thing works great for it. What will they dream up next?"

"Tell me about it," said Walter. "Why are you turning on the stereo now?"

"Pre-game ritual," said Bear. "Sports has its anthems, pump-up jams, banners, cheers, positive affirmations for the work to be done, so do I."

"I've never been around to see this," said Walter, excited like a boy a third his age.

"Well, if you're ready," said Bear. The stereo played "I Go to Work," the hyper-fast rap song by Kool Moe Dee, who goes to work—like a doctor, a boxer, an architect—and creates great works of art with his words.

"All right!" Walter sat upright for the first time all morning. "Dance!"

"I don't dance," giggled Bear. "I just power up the computer and get ready to write."

"*Dance!*" said Walter, grabbing a crutch to back up his demand.

"Sometimes I do stretch." Bear moved in front of the couch and extended his arms upward.

"*I said dance!*" Walter raised the crutch higher in the air.

"Demanding, injured white man, aren't you?" Bear danced for his man. Walter hooted and hollered as if Bear were on stage at a strip joint. Bear danced his usual combo hip-hop/cheerleader/comedic-black-man style. Walter clapped and laughed, and for the first time since Washington a week ago, forgot about football. Near the song's end, Bear called a timeout and turned down the stereo.

"You never finish the whole song," complained Walter.

"Neither do the Sea Gals," said Bear, sitting on the arm of the couch, catching his breath. "You like watching me dance."

"I love it, why wouldn't I?" asked Walter.

"Because it's kinda queeny?" said Bear.

"Not from where I'm sitting," said Walter. "You don't look like a girl when you dance. You look like *you,* and it's hot and fun because you're hot and fun. Like the girls, sure, but hotter. More like the mascots. It's fun watching them because of their big furry suits. It's fun watching my hot cheerboy because you're doing what you love."

"Keeps you entertained, huh?" asked Bear.

"Yup. Daily, while I'm on IR," said Walter. "Did you ever dream of being a mascot instead of a spirit leader?" The doorbell rang.

"Did you ever dream of playing quarterback in a bear suit?" asked Bear, heading for the door. A tall white man appeared in the peephole. Bear answered before realizing he hadn't thought about security. When he recognized the visitor, his face lit with delight. "Walter, it's the Dane!"

"The photogenic chiropractor of the ancient Tibetan homos returns! Thank you, Tammy." Walter was so excited, he nearly fell trying to get off the couch without his crutches. "Before Bear here starts asking a million questions—"

"I'll check you over," said Bass the Dane. Walter hobbled into the bedroom, the Dane followed. The bedroom door shut behind them, leaving a confused Bear alone in the den. Thirty minutes later, Bass emerged, Walter followed.

"Like the song says, all right now," said Walter.

"The back is fine," said Bass the Dane. "The hip and the shoulder are not nearly enough to warrant another reversal, which is good because the body can only endure one per lifetime."

"That must keep the line short," said Bear.

"And the questions long," said Walter. "Man, Bass, you're a hunted man. Guys in all sports are rumored to be hooked up with you. Wassup with that?"

"Would you like me discussing your reversal with others?" asked Bass the Dane.

"Point taken," said Walter.

"You two are still working together." Bass the Dane peered at them through his thick glasses, his eyes almost distorted by the lenses and the intensity of his scrutiny.

"Fate." Walter lost his balance and began to fall. Bear caught him. Bass the Dane caught the crutches.

"You caught him perfectly," said Bass the Dane. "In perfect time and with such perfect grace."

"That's my job," said Bear.

"After all these years, you do it rather well," said Bass the Dane.

They thanked Bass for the visit, and Bear saw him to the door. When the Dane was gone, Walter was feeling so good, he wanted some Sugar, good medicine for a man on injured reserve.

"WHAT YA DOING, BEAR?" ASKED WALTER, lying on the couch, crutches on the floor.

"Same thing as I was doing 10 minutes ago, trying to write," said Bear, sitting at his desk behind the couch.

"What ya working on now, Bear?" asked Walter the next day, lying on the couch, crutches on the floor.

"Trying to construct *Freeways*," said Bear from his desk behind the couch, "but there's too much traffic in Corona, Seattle right now."

"What ya writing now, Bear?" asked Walter the next day, lying on the couch, crutches on the floor.

"Keep this up and it'll be *My Whole Other Life*," said Bear. "You remember, that script about Marcus Coleman living as an openly gay man, having never met your injured ass."

"Here's an idea," said Walter. "Horny, sex-starved QB laid up, and his so-called dedicated husband won't give him any Sugar."

"Have some more ice cream, buddy," said Bear, typing away.

"That's all I've been eating," complained Walter. "Walt loves to eat more than ice cream."

"This much is true," said Bear. QB shut up long enough for Bear to type three whole lines of *Freeways* dialogue.

"Was I a fool not to sign that endorsement deal with those bigger ice cream people?" asked Walter. "We could have bought three Moose Jaws on that alone. My dad called me a wuss, in so many words. Thinks I turned it down because of some sappy loyalty to Bob & Jimmy's ice cream, or the *Wall Street Journal*."

In a recent article on endorsements, a columnist speculated: *Jocks like Yeager maintain images built on superficial calculations, such as his brigade of women followers who sell his ice cream for charity. The quarterback, barely able to get the Seahawks to the promised land, would probably let advertisers down as well, were it not for his golden looks. A hero made of ice cream, in every sense.*

"Did you tell your dad you don't care about the press anymore?" asked Bear, typing away.

"Called me crazy," said Walter, "in his own way."

"Your dad doesn't know loyalty is only part of it," said Bear.

"Tell me about it." Walter raised himself off the couch just enough to peek at his buddy.

"You did it for the same reason you've always stayed away from a lot of senseless big endorsement deals." Bear stopped typing.

"Why is that, Mr. Know-it-all?" said Walter.

"You've got more important recommendations to make in your lifetime," said Bear, "about way more important things than deodorant, which you dislike wearing anyway, or ice cream, which you love, almost as much as you love Sugar."

"My Bear knows me." Walter dropped back to the couch, disappearing from sight. Bear took his hands off the keyboard and smiled.

"What does Walter want now, more Sugar or ice cream?"

"I THINK FOR THE FIRST TIME IN MY LIFE, my husband is driving me nuts!" said Bear. "God, it felt so good to say that."

Hail Larry's Wife almost did a spit-take with her ice tea. "*That's* why you sounded so anxious on the phone." She went into an imitation of his voice: "*'Lunch? Great! Name the time! I can be there now! Let's do dis!'*"

They were eating at an outdoor café near her real estate office. The autumn sky was crisp and sunny, their little nook of Seattle sidewalk relatively quiet.

"I think this is the first time I've seen the sun in three weeks," said Bear.

"It hasn't been raining that much," said Hail Larry's Wife.

"I know," said Bear. "My whole life right now is taking care of Walter. Again, as always, I guess—don't get me wrong—I wouldn't trade it."

"Here comes the *but*," said Hail Larry's Wife.

"Not really," said Bear. "It does—however—inspire me to flesh out my *My Whole Other Life* script. I need to know what gay men are like these days for that. I've been out of that loop for a lifetime, it seems. Not since before Walter ... before Rock Hudson. Died. Tell me about your gay friends, the ones you work with."

"What can I say? They're fags, what's the big deal?" asked Hail Larry's Wife.

"I dabbled in gay life a bit before I met my buddy," said Bear. "It was all about sex. With lots of men. Who don't even ask your name!"

"Ever miss it?" asked Hail Larry's Wife.

"I can't even remember it to miss it," said Bear. "Nor have I thought about it much. Until now. Do your gay friends still have all that random sex? I mean, aren't they terrified of AIDS?"

"There's one now. Ask him," said Hail Larry's Wife, indicating a man coming down the sidewalk.

His hair was black, his age early 30s, like Bear. Once the man spotted his female co-worker, he flashed a big smile and came over to talk. Bear shook hands during the introductions, but his mind was flying too fast to hear words. He was too amazed, beholding a real live, openly gay man. It had been so long. Yet it felt so right. This was living proof that they weren't just in the shadows of his world, nor were they just in his imagination. They were *out* there, living life, despite AIDS. He had a billion questions, but not possessing the courage, didn't say a word.

"Roberto would be a good gay man to have as a friend," said Hail Larry's Wife after Roberto continued on his way. "He's celibate until his prince comes along. Ergo, no worries about him hitting on Walter just to score with the quarterback."

Bear sized up the slightly stocky backside of Roberto moving down the sidewalk. He looked so professional and responsible in his navy-colored suit. His walk was purposeful yet relaxed. His dark curly head moved from side to side as he gazed curiously at his surroundings. A comfortable smile washed across Bear's face. Inside his head, he dreamed of good things to come for Roberto.

"I have to go show a house," said Hail Larry's Wife, motioning for the check. "You need to give your man a project. They're like children, Bear. They need something to do." She pulled a credit card from her purse, then said, "You're the one with the imagination. Get him to focus."

BEAR HAD THE PERFECT PROJECT for his husband, a project that Walter had actually first suggested some time ago: *Start your own production company. I want to see you make your own movies now.*

Walter would be the man on the business side of things, which suited both men's talents and preferences. This was more of an off-season job, but Bear dreamed of it being a great distraction for the brilliant but unfocused mind of his injured buddy.

Boy, was Bear wrong. Walter shuffled through some paperwork for about two days, then never touched the pile again.

"What ya writing now, Bear?" asked Walter the next day, lying on the couch, crutches on the floor.

"Contemplating Armageddon," said Bear from his desk behind the couch.

"Is that a new movie idea?" asked Walter.

"Not exactly," said Bear, head falling on the keyboard.

The next day, Bear brought out the old standby, old reliable, old faithful, the one piece of magic that always brought life to the boys' world: Mattel Electronics Football.

"Look!" said Bear, retrieving the little green box from under the bed. "How long has it been, eh?"

Walter was half asleep on the bed. He took the machine and turned it on. In the next beat, they heard the digital *charge!* and Bear left the room with a satisfied smile on his face. Twenty minutes later, he was working away on *Freeways* and heard a loud crash in the bedroom, the kind of crash that little green boxes make when hurled against the wall by a man whose nickname as a kid was Super Arm. Bear raced into the bedroom, stepping on broken pieces of plastic once there. Walter was hunched over on the edge of the bed, staring into a void on the floor.

"I'm fucked up in the head, but not that fucked up," said Walter, still holding the little green box. The under-bed storage box was still open. Walter had destroyed another game, an old digital basketball game, also from Bear's college days. They'd lost interest in it years ago because it became too easy to play weeks after Bear first bought it.

"But I'm sorry anyway," said Walter. His face crinkled, waiting for tears that would never come. "Talk about your heroes made of ice cream."

The fallen hero lay sideways on the bed, off his bad shoulder and hip. Bear knew exactly what Walter meant: that he had let them all down—Bear, the Seahawks, his family, everybody who loved and supported him. The spirit leader surrendered and remembered what was important in his life. He melted into the bed and spooned his buddy's backside.

"Dream a better dream, MVP," said Bear, lying still with his man.

The production company idea was put on hold. Walter Yeager needed a reversal of spirit and a healthy distraction while his body healed. Bear did his part, dancing up a storm daily in the den, but as the weeks went by and the season was looking more and more like a wash, the time came for reinforcements in the form of a new addition to the Bearcat family: *a happy slobbering tongue!*

"Not now, Bear," mumbled a slumbering Walter one morning in bed. When the licking persisted, he swiped away the source, resulting in a series of shrieking yelps. Walter awoke in a panic, then said in a high-pitched voice: *"Hi, puppy! I'm so sorry!"*

Bear has holding over the bed a golden aura of puppy heaven, a six-month-old mutt mixed with Labrador retriever, golden retriever and anything else beautiful the angels poured into his one-of-a-kind mold. He swam through the air for Walter; Walter reached out and took the puppy.

"He's a big boy!" said Walter, calling up the animated voice he only used for dogs and small children. "Aren't you a big boy? Aren't you a handsome fella?"

Walter was like a boy on Christmas morning getting everything he ever dreamed of. He and the puppy explored one another, bouncing around the bed as if their bodies couldn't contain their eagerness. "Is he ours? Can we keep him, Bear, can we please? We can—oh, look, little one, Bear's got that silly ole Joe Bruin grin on his face. You're our dog now. Wanna be our dog? Yes, you do, big baby boy ..."

The corona of Corona, Seattle was more radiant than ever. Walter played with his new playmate, and Bear played the responsible one—but not too responsible. After all, Bears need their joy, too. So what if the pup pissed on the carpet during his strict house-training regimen. So what if Bear had to clean up puppy vomit in the middle of the night. So what if the nightly howling in those first few weeks kept the boys bleary-eyed throughout the day. So what if Bear had to do the brunt of the work since Walter was on IR. Every single chore was a chore of love and the result of dreams coming true.

"What should we name him?" asked Bear that first week.

"I got this one," said Walter. "Hip, because he is, and because he's helping to heal mine. And *Shoulder* or *Concussion* wouldn't sound cool at the dog park."

Once Hip and the boys became more adjusted to one another, it was time for the puppy to meet the *other* new puppy in their lives. This one didn't try to lick Walter's face upon arrival. He did, however, manage to surprise his father by standing quietly over his bed one November morning.

"Dad?" whispered Tank to the still slumbering QB. Walter looked up right away. When he realized he wasn't dreaming, he extended his arms and hugged his son wordlessly. Bear stood in the doorway, beaming like Joe Bruin, his double *Oprah* surprise a phenomenal success.

"This is Walter Yeager ... yeah, hey, Doak, what's up? Yeah? ... Yeah ... So you're saying it's not true? ... Then it is true ... I see ... I see ... I see ... sorry to hear ... I see. Okay. No, no need to call back. Bye."

The slamming of the phone on the end table in the den scared Hip, who ran behind Bear, who was on the floor, playing with the puppy.

"Let's hear it," said Bear, bracing himself.

"That was Doak Minnefield," said Walter, sitting on the couch.

"But he wasn't calling to apologize for knocking your lights out in Washington," said Bear. "Or that scuffle in practice in San Diego years ago."

Walter let out a sigh of resignation and said, "Just to tell me the hit in DC had nothing to do with his brother dying of AIDS the week before."

"This doesn't sound like breaking news to Walter Yeager," said Bear, waving a tennis ball in front of Hip to distract him from his fear.

"I had heard unconfirmed reports. I didn't want to worry you," said Walter. "You know me."

"It's too late," said Bear, teasing Hip with the ball. "So worry me now. I may as well have the facts and get in this loop."

"There's this tiny rumor around the league that Minnefield was after me because he was pissed off at all fags for killing his brother," said Walter.

"What made him assume you were a fag?" asked Bear.

"There are little whispers floating around," said Walter.

"Spread by who? How? Does Tammy know?" asked Bear.

"Bear, see I knew you'd go into hyper hero mode," said Walter. "We're not living in a gopher hole like the old days, but Minnefield claims the hit had nothing to do with his brother, who apparently did die of HIV."

"My hero counterpart doesn't sound convinced," said Bear.

"I'm not," said Walter. "And if Doak came after me, who else might?"

"Dream a better dream," said Bear, giving Hip the ball. "Besides, they'll have to come through me first."

MARCUS "BEAR" COLEMAN WAS NOT ABOUT TO WAIT AROUND and see who else in the NFL had a grudge against his buddy. The next night, he invited Reggie Snowman to Newport, Seattle, and asked point-blank: "So Snow, who else in the NFL has it out for my husband, just because he chooses to love another man?"

"*What?*" both Walter and Reggie said together. They were seated on the couch across from Bear. Hip was under Bear's chair, having decided he didn't particularly care for Reggie on the Down Low.

"Reggie, I had no idea he was going to do this," said Walter.

"*Husband?*" Reggie stood up, suddenly quite uncomfortable.

"Didn't seem like a problem at our party in Malibu," said Bear.

"You didn't say shit to *my wife*, did you?" asked Reggie.

"She doesn't know about *yo' boy?*" asked Bear.

"I ain't got no boy, man," said Reggie. "I ain't down with all that *husband* shit."

"Wait a minute, guys," said Walter, immobile on the couch. "Bros, bruthas, Bear, Reggie, brutha*men.* Can't we all just get along?"

"So you cats are all out in the open and shit?" asked Reggie. "I don't broadcast my business."

"Neither do we," said Bear, "but my buddy's life is at stake, which makes *me* the one they'd better watch out for, because when *I* get a bunch of *his* piss 'n' vinegar all up inside *me*—"

"*Beaaaaaar!*" droned Walter. "*Better dreeeeeeam!* He's just upset, Snow."

"Man, we cool," said Reggie. "Same team. I gotta get the freak outta here."

"Show him out and try not to bite his head off," said Walter to Bear, who complied with a surly face.

"Sorry for the blitz," said Bear, pushing the elevator button once the bruthas were in the hallway. "Surely, you'd be just as upset, if you heard the Pistons or Knicks might have it in for yo' boy Carter Jones."

"Yo, man," said Reggie, "I can hook you up with some *fine,* down low bruthas in basketball, football *and* baseball. Dirty on and on!"

"I'm already hooked up pretty good." Bear eyed the condo door. "Most of the time."

"You ever date bruthas?" asked Reggie.

"Reggie, I don't date," said Bear. "QB and I been together going on 12 years. We're good as gold. True dat."

"So you like his house nigga," said Reggie.

"How you figure?" asked Bear.

"I saw him ordering yo' ass around, talking about cooking and cleaning for him," said Reggie.

"If I cooked for my man, he'd be as malnourished as your brain. And neither one of us gives a fuck about a sparkling clean pad. I'm *nobody's* house nigga," said Bear. "Except maybe the puppy's."

"Sounds like you Yeager's house nigga to me," said Reggie.

"I suppose it has its certain advantages over being his *field* nigga," said Bear. "Especially from where I'm standing. *Feel me?*"

"Man, you whack," said Reggie.

"Snowman," said Bear. "The World Champs are 5-6 so far, 2-6 without Walter. You sure you wanna concentrate on his abilities at home, or focus on what we can *all* do to make him get well soon, so the team—the Seahawks—have some sort of chance to defend that Super ring you love flashing all over MTV, even though you're no longer the so-called Showman."

The elevator opened. Reggie looked like he was trying to say, *you're right,* but vanished instead.

"It's about the end zones on the field," said Bear to the closed elevator. Once back inside the condo, he slammed shut the front door.

"You scared the dog!" cried Walter. "It's okay, here, boy, here. Bear's in a big bad mood."

"Because his man keeps things from him in the oxymoronic name of protecting him," said Bear, joining Walter on the couch.

"You've got your hands full," said Walter.

"My hands are not my only resource," said Bear.

"My Bear already worries too much," said Walter. "What were you and Reggie rappin' about in the hallway?"

"Another time," said Bear. "Literally."

Bear couldn't keep anything from his man, especially once they made eye contact. The spirit leader picked up TIME from the coffee table and thumbed through TIME. No use telling Walter the house nigga just had a fight with the field nigga.

It was TIME to dream a better dream. True?

24

And the Comet's Red Glare

Everything is divine, if you look at every thing in divine light.

Power your world with your divine light.

Kaboom!

Welcome to your new world.

See the light yet?

Feel the light yet?

There's gonna be one mighty, newfangled firework of fireworks shows here on these Complex grounds tonight, so these windy Warriors claim.

Doubt I'll see it. Can't see a damned thing right now.

Try seeing a blessed thing.

Why? Can't feel a damned thing.

Try feeling a blessed thing.

For who? I'm not even sure who the hell I am.

Try wondering who the heaven you are.

Word games.

Football games.

Love games.

Is this supposed to be like Field of Dreams? If you build it, he will come? If I believe, he will show up? Show up again? If I'm that mutha-fuckin' crazy?

Humanity loves its games. Dirty on and on, nothing dirty on and on.

Have I ever heard you say that? Then again, have I ever heard a damned thing anybody ever told me?

Trying hearing a blessed thing everybody ever tells you.

I don't know if I have one more try in me. I try. I try to ask myself if I have One More Try. God, I want One More Try. Please, God, gimme One More Try. Please, George, give me one more try. Isn't that who sang it first? Michael?

We all sung it first, last, always and forever.

The very first time, I'm talking. The first time I asked for One More Try. About 999,999 One More Tries ago.

Everything is divine, if you choose to power every *thing* with divine light.

Sounds like my old man, maybe not the words, but the riddles. Old freakin' man riddles for young freakin' boys. Gee, thanks, Coaches. We boys owe you so freakin' much.

Now who's being a blessed fool?

This blessed damned fool ain't got the TIME. Limited. Gotta get back. Always about the back. And the front. One being upfront. The other holding back. Perfect balance. Tilted like the poles. Always and forever. Even in the chaos and disorder. We can have it both ways: Super fun, Super fucked. Which way we breakin'? What's the play? What's the cheer? The call? The gut? The backup? The dream? Where we going now, big boy, big golden dream boy—forever in my life, trying to shock the shit outta me. That's all you want, huh, just to shock the shit outta me. Nice job. Give yourself an MVP medal.

Meanwhile, I got work to do. TIME to go to work.

"CHICAGO! YEP, THAT'S RIGHT, Gut Nutz, we are coming to you *right! now!* from the land of Lincoln! *Chicago, Illinois,* a great city that loves its games, win or lose ... but then again, if you're in the Loop, you know! Right, Bear lovers?"

"True dat, Greg of *Greg the Gut's Sports Report*—brought to you this weekend by Snaky Lu's-Jordan/Oprah Land of Great Negro Dreams All-Foods Restaurant, Miracle Mile."

"Speaking of miracles, the FCC apparently doesn't mind if the Gut brings you the ... Markus! As in krazy Kramer, as in Markus Kramer, currently of the Pacers, but here tonight in his old stomping grounds of the Bulls, where his career began with quite an uprising."

"Don't go there, Gut. MK ain't reliving that Chicago-Charlotte series anytime this go-'round."

"What brings MK of his hometown Indiana Pacers back to the Windy City? Must be a big and dreamy deal to get you here during the NBA season."

"Uh, Gut ... pick up a morning paper. IND @ CHI. Going to work. Plus I got this dream of being a badass linebacker for the Bears someday. Wassup?"

"Markus, tell us: will Chicago ever shed its lovable loser image?"

"Tell me about it. Chicago don't want to. Chicago is polar opposite America's fuzzy beacon of furry hope. Middle of it all. Heartland. *Heart.* Got Bears, Cubs, lovable guys, lova-bull Bulls. East Coast is roughneck and *what the fuck you looking at?* West Coast is Mary Sunshine, all *have a nice day* and Purple Haze, and shit ... *hmmm* ... Chicago is a winter wonderland of the best of both. A place where grown men—*real men, not fags*—can love sorry little Bears, forever-dreaming Cubbies, Bulls who aren't very bullish most of the time, and White Sox, no matter how sorry, black and dirty they get. Dirty on and on. You know what Daddy Kramer and Mama Renteria Kramer used to say to us kids growing up in Indy?"

"Tell us about it, MK."

"Chicago. That's where you see interracial couples walking down the street!"

"Whoa, the 70s ..."

"Man, I'm not sure my parents could have put a more impossibly impossible image in my li'l pissant black mind. It's like they were saying: *Anything is Possible, Young Black Man. Especially in Chicago.* They took us there to show us. We walked around the city, played on the beach, went to some museums, ate, no doubt. Whole family trip. Last one. Before the fall. Don't know if we saw anything in black and white, but it didn't matter. We'd been to a whole other universe. That's what Chicago is for us dreamers in the heartland, right, my beautiful friend Billy Niles, out there somewhere? Great QB who put the *ill* in illin' and the *gun* in gunslinger. Chicago is our heart, our Hollywood, minus that crazy Hollywood shit, eh, Billy-Buddy?"

"If the FCC lets this Kramer Kat on the air again, it will be another miracle of miracles, Bears fans."

"Can anybody say, Tape Delay the Nigga? By the way, to clear up a rumor about my ass: Markus Kramer don't name his dogs after no body parts. Here comes my dream of a hound dawg now ... *here ... here ... here ... here! Hear me?"*

"Wow," said Walter, calling from Chicago, sitting in a golf cart at practice. "This guy on the radio—Markus Kramer—sounds like my boy. I love him! Kinda looks like my Bear, too."

"That mutha-freakin' Indiana Pacer?" asked Bear, calling from Corona, Seattle. "And we thought Dennis Rodman was in his own orbit. *'Mark my word, the Pacers'll never have another nigga this krazy.'* That's what MK said. Hold up, QB, here comes the dawg ... *here ... Hip ... here ... Hip ... hear me?"*

"Turn the TV down, little Bearcat! I can hear some booming black voice on the set, even with all this construction around me," said Walter. Bear was watching some newfangled cable channel and a special called *Dreams and the Brain*.

"*When you dream, you don't dream in any spoken language. You dream in images and feelings. You don't walk. You move, moving from one experience to another, not concerned with the details of the journey unless the details are crucial to the feelings.*"

"Anything beyond feelings in dreams, and life in general, should be considered: the details," said Bear, after lowering the volume. "Where is all this newfangled information going?"

"So in my dreams right now," said Walter, "I come off IR to bust a move against the Bears tomorrow, right? Just in time to tune up for the playoffs, then bring home a second ring, which the pup accidentally swallows, right?"

"Walt loves dreaming after all," said Bear with a big ole grin.

PROGRAMMING NOTE: The *Hip's Super Surprise!* episode of *Walt Loves the Bearcat* never materialized, and our Super sequel fell short of another ring.

"How could you let this happen?" asked Walter, a hint of disappointment filtering through his sarcasm. He was standing over Bear, reading the writer's summary notes for his work-in-progress.

"I'm only stating the fax," shrugged Bear, sitting @ Bear's computer. "I caught up with the archives, thought it was time to take some notes on *The Walter Yeager Story* I promised I'd write you someday."

"You're thinking of calling it *Walt Loves the Bearcat?*" laughed Walter. "Twisted! I love it. Man, you know how to nail shit, Bear Cheer Man Freakin' Coleman. How did I get so damned blessed?"

"You didn't," protested Bear, more focused on calling up another screen. "You got *blessed* blessed. Don't damn your boy, boy. Check it out: what I wrote about the rest of this injury-riddled year, thankfully over."

Yeager returned for the last three regular season games, but Seattle went 2-8 without him. The meister's 3-0 start and 3-0 finish to the year only left the team at .500. The last weekend was @ Jets. It all came down to all those head-spinning playoff scenarios, but the right teams didn't show the Bearcats any love. The Defending Champion Express had been derailed by a big hurt in the fruit bowl in DC.

"Thanks, Washington," said Walter, "for screwing up ours."

"The state of our union is just fine," said Bear, reaching up and stroking his man's warm flesh, whatever he could get his hands on, didn't matter. It was all God. And all Good. "We survived the toughest season of our lives and we made it home. Our new and improved space, more Super than ever."

The remodel was over. Moose Jaw of Malibu was now a two-story, four-bedroom hideaway with a separate guest cottage (gotta have a good wide boundary around the playing field). The boys poured all their dreams into their dream home. The deck. The pool. The Jacuzzi. The basketball half-court, now with BEARCATS painted along the baseline. The huge spa of a master bathroom. The upper deck off the master bedroom. The master bedroom itself, with a bed the size of a football field, *juuuuuust* big enough for two big ole kids and all their games. There was also another room accessible within the master bedroom. Fort Knox. Locked and private, always and forever.

Then there was the game room: their very own sports bar reflecting their very own playful universe. TVs. Beer on tap. Memorabilia aplenty. Games from their childhood aplenty. The big hockey arena with the sticks that controlled the slotted hockey players. Drop the puck from the overhead scoreboard and let the good times roll. The vibrating field of football dreams. Turn on a switch and watch 22 plastic jocks running around like 22 plastic jocks on a vibrating planet, going off in all directions, seemingly nonsensical but perfectly entertaining to young souls all the same.

Everything is divine if you power every thing *with divine light.*

The game room was full of video games from their college days. Dragon Slayer. Pac-Man. Space Invaders. *Asteroids!* The tabletop versions. Great for two buddies bonding over brewskies and ball on the tube.

And yes, sometimes QBs know to get out of the way of their determined little Bearcats. Walt loves to shine the spotlight on others, not himself, but Walt let Bear go a little crazy in the game room. It was full of Yeager's career, the only place in Moose Jaw with much evidence of a football career at all.

Bear's favorite: the life-size posters of his buddy in action.

"And we paid for this how?" laughed Walter. He was at his desk now, looking over the bill for some big purchase.

"I could always do *Uptight 2.* La Basinger is waiting," said Bear. Walt loves to count his pennies, no matter how many pennies Walt collects.

"You know I'm kidding," said Walter. "Hire him."

"Who would have ever dreamed of the day when you and your manager would need a manager?" asked Bear.

"*Hmmm,* I wonder," said Walter, more focused on his work.

"ROBERTO, THEIR NEW PERSONAL ASSISTANT," said and typed Bear into his computer. "CELIBATE, FORMER CO-WORKER OF—Hell, what's my best friend's name?"

"Larry's wife?" laughed Walter. "You and names, Marcus 'Bear' Coleman, aka little Bearcat, and a few other choice names spoken in the privacy of Fort Knox."

"Names are just feelings," said Bear, "clues from the Super Computer about what kind of energy the person is gonna bring into your life."

"What did Walter tell you?" asked Walter.

"That you were no Tom, Jeff, Bob/Rob, Ken or Rick," said Bear. "Had enough of those when I was a kid, but *I ain't mad at them,* as the kids say. *Big Ups* to our favorite old black coach. See, I can talk urban just like Markus Kramer, krazy Indiana Pacer. How did a guy like that end up on *my favorite team for all time in all of sports?* Other than the Bearcats now, mind you."

"Roberto, the Celibate guy, is good to go," said Walter with a confident keystroke @ Yeager's computer. "Going with my gut on this one."

"Best way to bring 'em in the loop," said Bear, more focused on his own screen.

"Sweet," said Walter, more focused on his own screen.

OH, AND WHILE YOU WERE AT TRAINING CAMP, *said Bear's email,* I CRANKED OUT *Rocket Bruthas 2: Homies in Space.* DON'T LAUGH. THE BRUTHAS TAKE OVER THE SPACE STATION, BUT IT'S MORE THAN THEY BARGAINED FOR. IT'S A MAN'S JOB. STUDIO WAS GONNA DO IT WITH OR WITHOUT ME. THIS WAY, I COULD MAINTAIN SOME ARTISTIC—OH, WHO AM I KIDDING?—WE GOT PAID! MULTI-PICTURE DEAL, BIG NORSE! OUR PRODUCTION COMPANY DREAM HAS BEEN REBORN. SAY HELLO TO BEARCAT PRODUCTIONS.

"Sound business move," said Walter, calling from the preseason opener in Canton, Ohio.

"That's why we made it," said Bear, calling from the Hall of Fame in Canton, Ohio. "I just hope this newfangled black sitcom/movie director doesn't try to outfox us—Wilhelm Camille, talk about names."

"We're putting our first Bearcat baby boy in the hands of a man who's a Camille?" asked Walter, calling after the Sunday night win @ NE.

"Let's dream of him doing a man's job," said Bear, calling after the home win vs. the Jets. "Or should I feel creepy? I need some regulation here, QB, not to mention my low blood Sugar. Taking care of me is a man's job, too."

"Don't I know it. Did you meet the Camille yet?" asked Walter, calling after scoring a gillion TDs @ JAX, new dreamers on the block.

"Met him for fuzzy second," said Bear, calling after a tense victory @ OAK, a city back in the game with the same ole scary nightmare.

"Get a good vibe?" asked Walter, calling from the locker room, dripping wet outta the showers after beating up on Elway and the Broncos @ DEN.

"Kinda glowed at me," said Bear, sitting in a nearly empty Kingdome, long after the Monday night win vs. STL, a city back in the game with the roar of a lioness. "I was pretty reserved around the Camille. *Imagine that.* Nasally voice. Light skin."

"Figure out if you know him?" asked Walter, calling from the Carolinas, land of twin dreams from the North and South.

"Wrong hunch, or fuzzy one," said Bear. He was calling from those same Carolinas, but the polar opposite one from his husband. The Panthers, new to the land of big dreams, were roaming until they built a permanent home.

"Man, the league has changed overnight," said Walter, finally calling from Newport, Seattle after a tense OT win @ SF.

"Slick Willy is a New Orleans Saints fan," said Bear, catching the redeye from *SF 2 LA* for movie business. "That's what I call the Camille now—first name Wilhelm. I guess you can say we hit it off. He's just a harmless Southern black boy. I think he's a fag. I mean, gay."

"Did you tell him your man has low blood Sugar needs?" asked Walter, calling after the home thrashing of MIA.

"Nope, but the fucker did a bang-up job with *Rocket 2!*" said Bear, catching the redeye to Vancouver to visit the set of *Freeways Claim Bodies That Fade,* still in production.

"Man, you guys shot *Rocket 2* in no time," said Walter, calling from Wok-Knee Park in Seattle, where he was playing with Grace's girls.

"Amazing how things get done in the amount of time set," said Bear, calling from the Vancouver *Freeways.* "I ain't gonna argue with quick cash, *sheeeeeet.* See, I can talk like Markus Kramer."

"Nice rockets in our pockets, by the way," said Walter, calling after the loss @ PHIL. "The ER Wife emailed me the opening weekend receipts. The bruthas do love their homies in space. Tankster's here, says he misses you."

"Right back at him," said Bear, catching the redeye from PHIL to NYC, momentarily blurry on the reason why. "We're gold again."

"Always and forever," said Walter, calling from Bob & Jimmy's ice cream factory, tasting a sample of the new and improved Yeager-meister.

"I'll take the OG, the original," said Bear, calling from Hollywood and his business on the *Freeways.* "Save an AFC Championship kiss for your boy. This one. I'm flying out to Pittsburgh tonight, and I ain't leaving that town until we fly away together, Panthers *and* Warriors United."

"Tell me about it," said Walter.

"In due time, no doubt," said Bear.

SO, IF YOU'RE READY ... USE THAT BRILLIANT IMAGINATION OF YOURS. It's your ticket to Championship kisses.

"Two seasons ago, the Seattle Seahawks found the kind of glory that was unprecedented in franchise history, as a ragtag bunch with names like Yeager, Jefferson, Millstone, Lars, Christian, Gator and Snowman became legends of the Pacific Northwest.

"But last year, in their bid to repeat as champions, disappointment struck. A trip to Washington ended with a fallen leader. The Seahawks never got off the ground.

"This season, the team was reborn, their leader healed, his swagger back. This year, it was Seattle who put the hurt on the rest of the league. Yeager, who said he missed getting in the end zone, threw for a career-high 48 touchdown passes. The Seattle defense ranked third in the league, its highest in history. The veteran Millstone rushed for over 1400 yards. The Seahawks finished 15-1, their only loss in Motownphilly. Having missed the playoffs last year, perhaps Seattle had the jitters last week, starting slow before putting the Patriots away with 28 second-half points. Yeager promises there'll be no slow start this week, good advice against the 16-1 Pittsburgh Steelers in this year's AFC title matchup."

Black Steelers jerseys moved in front of the television set, obliterating the view of the telecast. Stocky men with hard hats raised their beers high in the air and yelled like hyenas to the other Steelers fans in their tailgate party—all of them salivating at the mere mention of their team.

"Onward," Bear told Mama Rent and his brother Stefan, moving through the sea of steel in the parking lot. "One last phone call to my manager, then it's QB's day ... construction of *Freeways* has been halted in Vancouver ... director ain't feeling my script, and I ain't feeling his non-feeling ass ... *huh?* hold on, bro ... watch out for Mama, man ... *hello?* Roberto A. Selladito, pick up! (Stop whacking off, ya celibate fool!) ... where's our Alfredo when we need him? Hope you're watching the pre-game, and maybe finally getting some ... no big, we'll dream the bigger dream ... please tell Outfox Studios I'm recommending Slick Willy to save *Freeways*, and direct us into theaters and the red ... which color means something makes money? Stefan, watch Mama Rent, man, crazy muthafuckas *up in here* ... gimme a beer ... gimme three ... damn, wish I smoked dope right about now, *okay?* I am *Uptight and a Half!* Watch Mama! Stand outside the restroom then, she takes forever. New job for my brother ... Shit, man, I'll never bring yo' ass again if you fuck up ... *huh, Ro-*

berto? Nah, man, I'm just fucking with ma brother, not you! He's my original bro ...
anyway, going into the blur ... do this, Roberto: Camille from the Big Easy *feels* me,
knows the way my quirky mind operates, *aiight?* Plus, he's got one *hella* cinematic
eye. I'm at the game with the family, trying to get in the damned joint, 50,000 crazy
muthafuckas 'round us ... excuse me for talking Black, gotta get *ma* game face on ...
nothing dirty going on ... and on and on ... *yo?* ... the family, man, big-ass day like
this? *Huh?* Not *that* one, *my* family. My *first* family. Da Yeagers are here, too—*for
sho!*—on the polar opposite side, as always and forever ... we all cheer together for
him in spirit, though, *beli've dat!* ... *always* and forever ... and I got some of my own
spirit leader wizardry I'm about ready to bust out, too ... *huh?* Stefan, watch out for
Mama, man ... these honkies up here in Pittsburgh are fucking crazy, man, I been
around the NFL! ... they don't care who they hurt to get they Steel on ... trying to
make sure the rest of the country remembers who's punishing who! As if the USA
can forget about the Steel. Everything we live and breathe is about the Steel. And
the Cotton. And the Fruit. And the warriors from the true wars, the bloodiest
game humanity ever dreamt up ... man, I wish we was back in Seattle now ... of all
the years a *15-1* record doesn't get you a homer in the AFC Championship game!
It's like somebody up there is out to get us! Stefan, watch out for Mama, man ... *shit!*
I thought *da Raidas* had a rough gym. Watch out for Mama, man!"

Three Rivers Stadium was one of those cookie-cutter, multi-purpose
slinkies built in the 60s and 70s. Ever since the Immaculate Reception in 1972,
Bear had never been a fan of the steel version of the slinky. Not that he was a fan
of either side of that famous and controversial conception. His childhood disappointment over the moment had more to do with Stefan, his rival and brother, who then favored the Steelers, benefactors of the blurry, dreamy play that
changed football history forever in all worlds. *Big Ups* to Franco Harris and *All*
on both sides of that ball, and by extension, on both sides of that Super Universe.

"Watch out for Mama, man!" the boys said together, rising to the top of the
steel slinky.

The older Stefan was Bear's first soul mate—two years apart, give or take.
As very young boys, they were twins. As prepubescent boys, they were fierce rivals. As teens, they went separate ways around the world, only coming together
recently. Stefan was the best athlete in the family, a multi-sport star who dreamed
of making it big in basketball and baseball. As far back as Bear could remember,
Stefan possessed a swagger about him, the kind that bore hints of Deion Sanders,
Michael Jordan, Walter Yeager.

Stefan Coleman certainly believed he was that good.

As far as his sports abilities, Stefan's reality was Bear's reality.

Like brothers, like soul mates, right QB?

Perfect Grace scores another 99-yard touchdown pass. Go Bearcats go!

Bear breathed into the steel *loop* below, watching a miniature version of his man's gorgeous blond aura light up all sides of the loop. *All worlds deserve to know your beauty.* In their youth, Stefan was Bear's buddy, advisor, role model, coach, rival, and teammate. *All sides of us can share this, brothers, all sides, all brothers, bruthas and brothers. This much is true.* They spent hours in the family's huge yard, playing one-on-one basketball, football and baseball, and probably a few games now lost in the blur. *That's what brothers and soul mates do best together. Get lost in the blur. Let's kick it off. Let's all get lost in the blur, brothers and bruthas. How much fun we wanna have today? Every day, like the old days, any day, no such thing as TIME between Bearcats.*

Perfect Grace scores another 99-yard touchdown pass. Go Bearcats go!

By junior high, the brothers who were bruthas were ships passing in the same bedroom at night. Stefan gave up on his dreams in junior college and hadn't done much since. The bruthas' relationship remained chilly, only thawed by the Bearcat Boyz' visit to the Colemans in Hayward. "So you know the real deal between me and QB?" Bear asked Stefan as they settled into the steel loop.

"Y'all's business is y'alls," said Stefan, suppressing the wide-eyed boy attending his first-ever pro football game. "Ain't nothing to me."

"I have you in part to thank for my soul mate," said Bear.

"Me?" said Stefan. "What I do?"

"Hold me until he was ready to," said Bear. "Be a great athlete who I played with, fought with, struggled with, bonded with. Just like QB, you were never cocky with me the way you were with the rest of the world. You never treated me like I was any less than you. I guess that's why I have faith in my bond with Walter. It's the same in so many ways, almost like God planned it that way, if you believe in miracles."

"How would God do that?" asked Stefan.

"Tell me about it," said Bear. "Or dream of it, if you can't."

"Say what?" said Stefan, starting to focus on the field.

"God, I love this," said Bear of the buzz building in the blur of the steel loop. "Keep this thought in mind, brother: If God can create an infinite number of galaxies, and maybe even universes, as some scientists are finally getting around to dreaming—if God can do *all that* which we know, plus *all that* which we don't know, imagine what else God can do. And ask yourself: if God is *All That,* would it be that big a deal for God to give you your own world where all your deepest dreams come true?"

"Like when I let Kilo in the house," said Stefan. "She be *dying* to lick them crumbs off the kitchen floor, little crumbs and shit—you know I'm not trifling— she be licking up little microscopic crumbs like she's in heaven."

My brother just used the word microscopic. Imagine that.

"Hip, too," said Bear. "Dogs love crumbs, our little pissant crumbs. We're their gods and they love our crumbs. What's the big deal if us mere gods let them have some crumbs and a whole world of their own? *Feel me?*"

"You might be right," laughed Stefan.

First time Bear heard his brother's laugh in a lifetime.

"God gives each and every one of us a world," said Bear, "or two, give or take— *details!* Point being: when the kids say, *My World,* they mean it. That's America's soul trying to remind the rest of its body to sing the highest song, the better dream, the deepest dreams, the ones from the iron core of our celestial bodies."

"Celestial?" asked Stefan.

"UNIVERSAL MEMO: All the bodies on this planet are built just like the planet: iron core, two poles, go figure," said Bear. "Simple in, simple out."

"Kinda overwhelming," said Stefan.

"Try whelming," said Bear. "And if your highest dreams are just a little too high up the mountain to see, try dreaming at least a better dream than the one you're dreaming nowadays. Then keep going. Keep dreaming the better dream, one dream at a time."

"You believe, don't you," said Stefan, statement of fact.

"That's my creation and I'm sticking to it," said Bear.

It was also Bear's idea to finally get his sports-loving brother to a pro football game, and the AFC Championship at the home of Stefan's childhood team, the Steelers, seemed perfect. "Stefan, you and I have loved and warred like nobody else either one of us will ever love and war with again, and I know you feel me. I'm also coming to the realization that, my whole life, I can't ever remember ever opening my mouth and lying to you."

I do believe. I do believe. I do believe. Go Bearcats go!

"Watch out for Mama, man, that's your job now," said Bear.

The weather at game time was 10 degrees and partly sunny. Bear, Stefan and Mama Rent were dressed like black Eskimos in the upper decks of the steel loop. They were surrounded by Pittsburgh fans, so Bear's facial expression was Markus Kramer minus the verbiage: *Don't fuck with me and mine.* During Walter's games, Bear's outer body was of no consequence. In his mind, Bear was the master Cheer Man, in command of a much bigger universe than that which could be contained in any ordinary stadium.

"Go Seahawks go!" yelled Mama Rent. Her face looked 10 years younger since the reconnection of her youngest boys. *Thanks, Walter.*

"Tank and his family got the better seats," yelled Bear at kickoff. "It's important for him to get a close-up look at all his dad's brilliance. Just watch your back."

"These people don't scare me," said Stefan. *Like husband, like brother.*

Maybe it was something about the state of Pennsylvania, but outside of Raider Nation, the most hostile crowds in all of Bear's years stadium-hopping were those in Philadelphia and Pittsburgh. True to form, their section was rocking as the Steelers kicked off to the Seahawks and the Colemans were knocked around like bumper cars in the swaying steel loop. Bear felt a ringing in his ears that reminded him of the Sugar Bowl. Even a slight trace of panic crept across the face of the normally expressionless Stefan. *Like brother, like husband.*

"This is what big-time sports is all about!" promised Bear.

"I'm ready," said Stefan, rubbing his gloved hands together.

"It's worth it," said Bear. "True dat!"

"Yeager's a faggot!"

It came from on high in the loop. Bear had forgotten to put on his invisible earmuffs, the ones that blocked out the shit he heard at the games. As such, he spun around instinctively, searching for the steel offender. Just then, Walter fumbled the opening snap, causing the loop to sway and knocking Bear into his brother. Yeager dove on the ball. His teammates covered him. Everyone was safe for now.

"Watch out for Mama," said Bear.

"Man, don't pay attention to that shit," said Stefan.

"Bad day to leave my gun at home," said Bear. "Just kidding, Steelers fans."

At halftime, SEA @ PITT was tied, 10-10. The lone Seattle touchdown came from a fumble recovery by Gator, the former Florida lineman from Hawaii. Yeager had fumbled the snap again near the end zone just before the half. Gator had Yeager's back, selling out his body to win the war under the pile-up.

Yeager was tight. The Seahawks were tight. Pittsburgh and their loop were steely and tight. On top of that, Bear heard more derogatory comments about his buddy than ever before, all from the same *Yeager's a faggot!* voice on high. A couple of times, Bear tried to stare down the section, as if to say, *Shut the fuck up!*

If anything, it accomplished the reverse.

"Kill the pretty boy. He's too pretty to be a football player!"

"Number 13, you suck, don't you?"

"Number 13 loves to suck!"

"Sack the faggot!"

That one got to Bear the most. Every time Walter went back to pass: *Sack the faggot!* No one objected. Parents with children. Men with females. Men who were probably faggots themselves. The faggot's nigger lover. *Sack the faggot!* became part of the section's soundtrack to the day, along with the broadcast of the game from a portable radio some idiot had cranked:

"Yeager back to pass ..."

"Sack the faggot!"

"... gets by Lake, dumps it off to Zook Adams, who gets three yards before being shoved outta bounds, another fourth down in this defensive tug of war."

"Number 13, you suck, don't you?"

The score was 13-13 midway through the fourth quarter. *Sack the faggot!* was now like a song or affirmation, more so than the spirit leading wizardry in Bear's mind. Both offenses were just as impotent. The game was coming down to a field goal or miracle play, and the steel loop, so good at dreaming up blurry finishes, was beginning to conceive again. Walter and the Seahawks were going to need all the positive energy Bear could summon, especially against—

"Sack the faggot!"

"Man, you gotta let that shit go. Stop looking back," said Stefan.

"Was I?" asked Bear. "I'm just worried this is all connected to this new information highway shit I'm still trying to wrap my head around. Our team keeps talking about this web having the ability to spread ... *rumors.*"

"Sack the faggot!"

Bear eyed the scoreboard. The clock was stopped. Two-minute warning. The Seahawks were at their own 40-yard line, 60 yards from a touchdown, 30 from a decent field goal attempt. "Time to get out of this steel loop alive!"

Out of the timeout, Yeager hit Millstone on a screen pass for a 12-yard gain. "Millstone didn't get out of bounds!" The clock kept ticking. On the next play, Walter ran a play-action fake, looking for Jefferson down the sideline.

"Sack the faggot!"

Jefferson wasn't open. Yeager pulled the ball down and looked to his secondary receiver over the middle.

"Sack the faggot!"

Yeager lobbed the ball over the middle to Corey Christian, who was brought down immediately, as the clock kept ticking.

"When is somebody going to *sack the faggot?*"

On Seattle's next play, Millstone ran off tackle and gained three yards. "Still out of field goal range!" Yeager checked with the sideline, then signaled the ref, who blew the whistle. *"Time out, Seattle, their last."* Yeager headed toward the sideline for a war conference.

"What a pretty little faggot! Hey, Yeager, you suck, don't ya?"

"Stefan," said Bear, standing like the rest of the joint, "I swear, if you don't restrain me ... I'm *thisclose* to going up there and killing somebody."

"Man, it's too cold for that shit," laughed Stefan.

"Doesn't he realize people have family at these games?" asked Bear. "Sons, daughters, grandparents? Loved ones?"

"Man, people don't care," said Stefan. In Stefan's world, the glass was not just half-empty, it was bone-desert-dry. "This is sports. You supposed to be used to that shit."

"Explain that to all the children who are hearing disparaging things about their fathers right now," said Bear, hoping Tank's section didn't have a Yeager-hater.

"Ain't nuttin' you can do about it now. Better pay attention to the game," said Stefan.

The steel loop began to rise again. Yeager broke the Seahawks' huddle.

"Sack the faggot this time, please?"

Yeager took the snap from the shotgun, faked going deep, then fired a line drive down the middle to a wide-open Junior Jefferson, who caught it in stride and ran in a straight diagonal toward the goal line. The former Wolverine and Heisman Trophy winner flew faster than Bear had ever seen him, leaving help-less Steelers tripping over themselves as they leaped desperately at Jefferson's re-versed feet (according to rumors). Bear and Mama Rent couldn't help bursting into joy for the first time all weekend. Even normally cool Stefan was saying shit like, *"Damn! Damn! Damn!"*

Yeager to Jefferson. The steep loop may now be lowered and melted in the boiling vat. TIME to make something else out of all that resentment.

Rod Woodson pushed Jefferson out of bounds at the six, six yards away from another trip to the Super Universe.

Bear let it go, four hours of frustration, aggravation and pent-up emotion. Four hours of listening to *sack the faggot!* He let out a roar that would have made any Seahawks fan proud! He even heard it echo back in the form of a few other scattered fans around the stadium. They had found heaven, and now they had each other. They cheered louder and bolder by the second. And Bear just *had* to look back, *just one glance* at the section of the Yeager-hater. He turned, complete satisfaction etched on his face, but instead of people, all he saw was a comet, inches away from colliding with his head, near the vicinity of his eyes. He turned to Stefan, unsure why. Maybe out of instinct. Maybe because that was what he did when he was a child in need. Or maybe because his buddy-for-life wasn't in the stands to help. For whatever reason, Bear turned. The comet brushed past his right eye and landed somewhere near his ear. The last thing Bear saw was a game clock that read :04.

Then he fell into the steel loop, down a dark and blurry tunnel.

... apologize ... physical price ... Seahawks ... near end zone ... field goal try ... Bear cold ... bleeding ... ensues chaos ... part of the ... Stefan true hero when needs ... Bear attended to ... Mama Rent safe ... cops ... no time ... paramedics ... isolated upper decks ... no one ... cares ... except True Gold ... my buddy ... will ... show up ...

OH, MY GOD, were the first words uttered, only he didn't utter them because he couldn't speak. His mind told him a line had been crossed. Like just after a car accident. *It happened.* There's no going *back.* Seconds ago, life held another reality. Now, life hung in the balance. His body was horizontal. People were moving him. Voices shouting to other voices. Threatening voices. Inquiring voices. Stefan's gruff voice. Mama Rent's hysterics. Stadium announcer. Walter's demanding words:

"I'm going in the ambulance ... I'm here, buddy, I showed up."

That was all Bear needed to hear to let go, and for maybe the first time in his life, surrender to the blur, mind, body and soul. He faded from the world, dreamed of his hero saving the day. Walter looking on high ... running into the underbelly ... Walter in his road whites, taking him on a magic carpet ride through the steel city, flying over bridges and rivers, forewarning the world *out of the way!* with flashing lights and sirens on the transport.

Walter landed him somewhere safe, made the medical people dull the pain in his head. Walt loves being on the case. Promised he would be. Walt only makes promises he intends to keep, forever and always. Walter never let Bear down ... not genetically possible ... this much is true.

"You left the game with four seconds left, any comment?"

"Are you related to the victim?"

He tuned them out, went back into the blur. Love the blur. Love the pic.

"Right outside here, buddy, not moving a damned inch."

Don't move a blessed inch.

The hero fell behind, the magic carpet morphing into a body bay, where medical people worked on Bear's head, touching him, poking him, but not *feeling* him. Had they felt him, they would have complied with his desire to *feel himself in his hero's arms.* He could die easily that way, any way ... any how ... any day, for any reason ... and he'd die a happy man ... no matter what else existed in any universe for all time. This much is true.

I, God, Promise, You.

But no one was listening. To his promise. Or his pleas. To his soul. Or its mate.

He fell asleep and left it up to the rest of the world to make his deepest dreams come true. Occasionally, he let voices inside, just in case they had something to say about his hero.

"Play in the Super Bowl next week?" asked his hero. "We won? I have nothing to say while the love of my life clings to his. The end."

"He's got to feel the love in this room," said his hero's mother.

"Gonna get him out of Pittsburgh soon as possible," said his hero's brother.

"The team is beside itself. Both of them," said his hero's emergency wife.

"Say everything in a positive way in front of him. He might be able to hear you," said his hero's sister.

"Have you turned on one television since the game on Sunday?" asked his hero's emergency wife.

"Are they broadcasting news about how to bring people out of comas?" asked the hero's mouth that could still speak and hero's heart that could still sing.

"... worldwide wondering on the world wide web, why in the world would Walter Yeager, an NFL quarterback, leave the field, his team and the stadium with :04 to go in the AFC Championship ... hopping in the ambulance with an injured fan ... now identified as his manager, back cracker, biographer, personal trainer, business partner, and/or, best buddy, just to name a few."

"Turn that off. This concerns us how?" asked his hero.

"You haven't even talked to your coach," said his hero's brother.

"Ask him how his wife is doing for me," said his hero.

"I'm going to arrange for a voice-to-voice between you and your head coach," said his hero's emergency wife.

"Fine," said his hero.

"Then," said his hero's emergency wife, "I want you to take a look at the campaign I've devised to cover-up—"

"In another life, I'm capable of murder," said his hero. "Do I need to call that fella up now?"

"I'll see if I can find out where your head coach is," said his hero's emergency wife. "Probably somewhere in Tempe, answering the same question a thousand times."

Sounds like business as usual in the Super World.

"Hang in there, my buddy, my hero," said his hero.

THE SENSATION OF HIS MAN'S TOUCH swam over his entire soul, almost convincing him to wake up. But there was more work to be done, especially for the magic journey being discussed by the medical generals ...

... he dreamed of flying over the steel city, away from the frozen hearts that had it in for his hero.

... he circled the Space Needle like a drunken bee, happy to be buzzing around more familiar and friendly landmarks.

... he thought about his hero singing the song "For the Love of You" by the Isley Brothers inside the Space Needle on another magic carpet ride. Enough to make him cry. Upon further reveal, *he already were!* Niagara was a-falling and his hero was a-whispering that it was all right now. Always and forever. True Gold.

... he melted away ... the transport landed in a warmer, less cold and steely body bay.

... he felt his hero whisper: *home now, Seattle home.*

... he felt the Hail Larrys and more family buzzing in the new body bay.

... his sister kept expecting him to stir and say that it was all a big joke, because that would be so much like him.

... his hero's sister said the exact same thing about her brother.

... he felt the Yeagers and the Colemans become one.

... he felt one father, but not the other.

... he felt one mother, but not the other.

... he felt he did not understand that equation.

... he felt like this whole loop was an equation.

... he felt like he wasn't a rocket scientist, but he felt his gut telling him something that would shock everyone in this world, no matter where they were standing on what side of whose universe.

... he felt he needed, wanted, had to have, and never wanted to be without his soul, and you know who you are.

... *whoa* ... he felt Madonna live to tell ...

... he had to live to tell. No other way. No other TIME.

TIME. It's TIME. Meet the Bearcats.

... he felt the laughter of so many people he loved and cherished.

... he felt Yeagers, Colemans, black coaches, best pals and best pal's wives, or was that husbands?

... he felt his hero, ever-present but not evergreen.

... he felt the one person genetically engineered to be his soul's mate.

... he felt the one person for whom he would never, ever, in any universe, be too much. *Rightbackatcha.*

... he felt someday he would learn to spell *rightbackatcha* without having to use the spell-check.

... he felt the day would come when each and every one of their dreams would come true. Each and every one. This much is true. Gold. Word is born.

... he finally felt the one who was exactly, truly, always and forever, never too much—just perfect. In fact, the most perfect, perfect.

... he felt laughter, the laughter of his stories, and his hero's stories. Yeagers, Colemans, coaches, oh, please ... time to start calling them what they really are: Bearcat People.

... he felt the nickname explained for the first time ever.

... he felt a whole new dream in a whole new world.

... he felt the pull of the gravity of the situation.

... he felt the gravity of his old world ...

... he felt like they were going places ...

Taking a trip. New world. My world. Our world.

It's a long and winding journey.

Each word chosen carefully.

Please feel *each word chosen carefully.*

Carefully.

Ready, okay?

Welcome to our world, *our world.*

... God promised.

... God was a little boy who felt alone, lost and very lonely. God felt like God was the only God exactly like him in the world. *One other God who could love every God-awful and God-blessed thing about him.* That's all God wanted. All that God wanted was all that God needed: to know that there was one other person in this world of eight billion who is exactly like me, and when I find him, we're gonna be together.

simple as that

I, God, Promise U, light over there, in that sphere that kinda reminds me of the side of a planet ... kinda hard to tell ... see, I, God, have no idea who I, God, really am. All I, God, know, is that I, God, exist in this universe, at a very tender age.

I, God, live with a family.

I, God, am considered a little boy.

I, God, don't feel like a little boy or a little girl.

I, God, just feel.

Sometimes the things I, God, feel are considered *boy.*

Sometimes the things, I, God, feel are considered *girl.*

Sometimes the feelings are encouraged and rewarded.

Sometimes the feelings are discouraged and punished.

It can be confusing for I, God, who is considered a boy by this family harboring me early in my journey.

The harbor is sometimes light and sometimes dark.

Sometimes it is hard to see my way, either way.

I, God, don't want to look.

I, god, am feeling pain.

This is what my father meant—the father who was just a light until this family told me to call that light the Holy Father. The light that I, God, saw in that blurry space ... that light said there would be something called pain if I, God, wanted to go down ... here. I'm here. I'm here on Earth to play. I, God, asked the light to let me come down and play the games those funny people called humans play. Yes, yes, I got all the memos and emails and all the shit you people call communication. I, God, knew what this place was like before I fell to Earth ... I, God, won't tell you what the other I Gods around the water cooler in Big Space call *Earth* ... I, God, will focus on the light ...

Let me go down, play the games of humanity, Big Light in Big Space. I, God, wanna do all that!

You know, I, God, am gonna have to erase your memory before I, God, hit the trail.

I know the facts. I want to play the games.

Fall.

Big Light in Big Space takes me at my word.

I, God, fall. Falled. Fallen. Fell.

The peaceful dreamy cool easy breezy sleepy lazy fall ...

... into the games of humanity.

Word was born. World is born.

Listen to our soul. Can you hear it? Can you feel it?

I, God *slash* word *slash* baby boy in blue *slash* golden child of the race *slash* prototype for all the races *slash* brilliant shining bright superstar who is God, is born.

Tough room.

Tough ward. Prefer space. Prefer the transport ... yeah, the transport ... the female transport I, God, know ...

I, God, know ...

I, god, know ...

I gotta go ...

I, god, know I no God no more, just god. Or the door.

The one rule of Big Light in Big Space: de-cap.

No Gods on Earth.

Only gods.

Ensures fair game.

All gods have all God's power, but *there is no one God on Earth.*

Ensures fair game.

Humanity is a game. Go down and play, see what kind of shit you can create, games you can play, dreams you can imagine. What kind? Tell me about it. What for? Dream of it. Or you can hang in my Big Light in Big Space, always and forever, and just enjoy the view from here, in the big luxury suite.

I, god, came on down. Saw something interesting, a dream or two I'd never seen any other gods come up with. But I got down here, and my transport broke down! My transport damned the place and all the other gods.

And that was just the beginning.

Other gods started damning the place.

Other gods started blessing the place.

It started getting really confusing.

Oh, Big Light in Big Sky ... can god talk to you for a second?

Always and forever, what's up, little boy?

Yep, I guess I've been here some time, but I have no idea how long.

By the way, you can talk to Big Light in Big Sky anytime you want, fallible little one.

Yeah, that was kinda what I wanted to talk about. I'm fucked. I'm twisted. I'm not sure I like it here. Can I come back up there and just watch?

You sure you want to?

Well, the female transport damns some things, and the big boy around her blesses some of those very same things. Then, the big boy damns some things, and the female transport blesses some of *those* very same things.

Then there are these other little gods in the house, and ... it just gets confusing ... I don't know what to do ... what to bless, what to damn, who to please, who to be, why I exist. I forgot why I wanted to come here in the first place. What was so wonderful and magical about Earth again?

Tell me about it, or dream of it.

You're saying I gotta stick around?

We don't have to pull up the Free Will clause, do we?

Okay, so I'll stick around, be a little boy, even though that's not the easiest thing I could have chosen to be. What was that loud bang coming from the other half of the world?

Keep going, son.

Can I tell you something, Big Light in Big Sky? Can this confused little boy tell you something: there must be one other boy in this whole wide world that feels just like me and is perfect for me, and if I ever find him, we're going to be together forever, I just know it.

Why are you telling Big Light in Big Sky?

Wait. I want to get this right, since I know you take people at their word, from word one ... Big Light ... I Promise.

... he felt the Infatuations sing *I only wanna be with you.*

... he felt the ship mobilizing ...

... he felt: our powers are amazing ...

... he felt like going onward ...

... he felt like he wanted to devise a better dream outta this very dramatic, Hollywood-like, *Quarterback Leaves the Stadium to Rescue His Black Cheer Man in Pittsburgh* deal!

... he felt: Fuck, do we know drama, us freakin' humans, or what?

Getting better at it. Try this one on for size.

Thus, the dream was born.

... he felt his mind lift and go ...

... he felt his joy ... and joy to the world ...

... he felt the soul of his straight shootin' son of a gun ...

... he felt God had set it up that way, and the two families in the body bay had served as God's agents. The families had made them exactly who they were, which was perfect for one another, blessed *and* damned.

But they were about to dream the blessed dream.

... he felt the fading of laughter and voices.

... he felt alone with the one who felt exactly like him.

"COME ON, BEAR," SAID WALTER after a while. "You know me. I could never live with myself if I caused you any harm. I know you'll say it wasn't me, it was some homophobic fan, but you know that's not how your buddy looks at it. I need my Bear. I need my Soul Man."

Bear wanted to rejoin the other side, but his body would not relinquish control. The world was a mess, from what he gathered, all because a man left a football game :04 early, and had been by another man's hospital bedside since. Bear was sure glad there wasn't cable in the coma universe. All he had were his dreams. He dreamed of Tank, who only knew that his dad was in some kind of trouble because the boy had to be taken out of school and couldn't watch television all week. He dreamed of Black Coach and his siblings taking care of Mama Rent. He dreamed of being strong for Walter, of urging Walter to focus on the game, because there was nothing his hero could do by hero's side that his hero couldn't do in Tempe, Arizona, site of the Super Bowl, *their* Super Bowl.

"You took one for the team," said Walter in Bear's dreams.

"The only team my soul will ever be on is yours and mine," said Bear in his dreams. "We're close enough to grab Super Bowl 2 by the balls, ours more than ever now."

"Super Bowl 2?" laughed Walter in Bear's dreams. "The coma's making you worse at numbers than usual."

"The only Super Bowls that matter are the ones we're in," said Bear in his dreams. "Leave my side; you have my permission, not that you need it. I'll be waiting. Ain't going nowhere. Go play some football! Get rid of all that piss 'n' vinegar bubbling over inside both of us. Media day is over. Heard in the blur of my mind that you missed it. Hire guards to surround you. Get in a football zone. For us."

"But Bear—" said Walter in Bear's dreams.

"We have a choice. In life, there's always a choice," said Bear in his dreams. "We can spend energy worrying about a situation that can be dealt with at a later time. Or we can focus on a football game that needs our immediate attention, a game that's gonna happen in a few days, last for three hours, and never come around again, no matter what happens beyond that day. Which would you rather focus on for the rest of this week: me resting up, all safe and peaceful until you get back? Or you going to Tempe to thrive for three hours of our lives that we'll never get back? I know that your beautiful, oh-so-wonderfully-edible blond ass is not planning on me waking up to hear you say: 'Oh, sorry, Bear, I didn't play in the Super Bowl because you overslept in your little coma.' My buddy's ass better get to Tempe and quick. I like Sun Devil Stadium. It's another cool magnet! The sun magnet! Walter, go out and get me some sun. If you show up, I'll show up."

Bear dreamed of Walter boarding a charter plane with Mr. Yeager and Walter's Brother, then the three of them landing at a remote part of the Phoenix airport, away from the hype. From there, they took a private limo to the Seahawks' practice facility, where unbeknownst to them, a swarm of media was waiting for the limo.

"How much did they pay you?" Walter asked the limo driver, a burly man with long sideburns.

"I got a family to feed," said the limo driver, stopping at the gate with no intention of trying to get by the chaos. "My daughter, she has special needs."

"How much did they pay you?" repeated Walter.

"A grand," said the burly driver. Walter ripped a grand from his bomber jacket and threw the cash into the front passenger seat.

"Money buys a lot of joy, doesn't it?" said Walter, vanishing.

With the help of the Yeager men, Walter made it past the inquiring minds without comment. Then it was time to face the only minds he felt deserved a further explanation. From his hospital bed in Seattle, Bear dreamed of understanding Coach Robbins being understanding. Backup dream: Coach Robbins doing the math.

The 17-1 Seahawks were 2-8 last year without the injured Walter Yeager.

"We can spend energy on a situation that can be dealt with at a later time," Walter told Coach Robbins when they were alone in the film room. "Or we can focus on a football game that's never gonna come around again. Which would you rather focus on for the rest of this week: me leaving the team to be there for someone who's *still* in a coma? Or us doing what we came here to Tempe to do: take back our championship during the only guaranteed time we have to get the job done."

It was the same exact speech Coach Robbins gave all the Seahawks when he welcomed QB back to practice. It was also the same exact speech Coach Robbins gave every day to the Seahawks, right up until game time. Bear heard bits of it during the pre-game telecast in his sickbay. He felt the presence of several Colemans: Mama Rent, brothers Stefan and Grayson, sister Evangeline, and several of their satellites. Walter's Sister was also in the room. Bear heard her saying something to his sister about wanting to represent the Yeagers. He dreamed of the sisters hugging one another just before kickoff.

The stands in the hospital room were packed. Bear had to dream of someone turning up the volume just so he could hear over the crunching of food (which no one thought to offer the man in the bed, thank you very much). Just as well: the better to hear while in this thing they're calling a coma. (I'm hungry.)

"The Seahawks survived a most unusual finish in Pittsburgh that has yet to be explained, but Coach Robbins says, first, it's time to finish old business, namely the final game of a long and winding season. Translation: no suspension for Walter Yeager. End result: Troy Aikman and the Dallas Cowboys will face the Seattle Seahawks with their unflappable leader."

The Colemans started *co-signing*, commenting on every little thing the announcers said. Bear's mind took off for the sun magnet in Tempe, a quick flight to a venue he'd visited many times as a college cheerleader.

The boys liked the sun magnet. Maybe it was the desert mountain backdrop. Maybe it was the horseshoe, more modern than *their* horseshoe, but a horseshoe just the same. A horseshoe stadium was literally magnetizing, as Athens had taught the copilots of today's flight into Super space.

The lessons learned in paradise helped them take control of the horseshoe magnet with ease.

"Who says we didn't learn anything useful in college?" said Bear the pilot, settling into the cockpit atop the closed end of the horseshoe magnet, a press box of sorts that rotated 360 degrees. The pilots didn't require a huge control panel with all the fancy levers, since the whole thing was controlled by the imagination. Call it the inner kid's prerogative. Big toys with cool buttons!

By kickoff, the Colemans were a little more settled in their own luxury box, sponsored by Seattle Memorial. Bear the pilot yanked the biggest lever and put the ship in gear. The magnet blasted off with the same trajectory as the football sailing toward the end zone. Hip, their dog, yelped with excitement, his front paws on the edge of the control panel, his tail wagging happily in circles. Big fun! The heroes, Yeager and Coleman, drew backward in the cockpit from the G-force as the horseshoe magnet hurled into Super space.

"Snowman's return puts the Hawks at the 42-yard line to start the game. Not a bad start if you're Seattle trying to work out all the kinks of the last week. And by the way, it's Reverend Reggie Snowman now, in case you were wondering."

"Bear's boy needs to come out strong," said Stefan in the luxury box, prompting murmurs of agreement from the chorus of Coleman men.

"First play of the game—a busted play that Yeager takes up the middle for 12 yards! That's gotta work out even more kinks!"

The Colemans cheered. The Cheer Man peered down from his vantage point high atop the cockpit of the horseshoe magnet. On the sidelines, his spirit leaders were going to work, hyping up the crowd down in the bowl. In Bear's world, they were the *spirit* squad!—UCLA's name for it. It was about so much more than cheering. And unlike Sun Devil Stadium, *this magnet* possessed fans of only one team, not even the Seattle Seahawks.

"Yeager hands off to Millstone who breaks outside and gains close to four yards before Norton and Walen bring him down."

The spirit squad in *this magnet* shared the boys' passion for spirit in its highest, all-encompassing form.

The 80,000 fans in *this magnet* shared the boys' passion for the power of their gods to make miracles happen.

The marching band in *this magnet* shared the boys' passion for songs that reminded their gods of their glory. Glory, glory to their gods, always and forever.

The ticket taker in *this magnet* shared the boys' passion for fans who dreamed their dreams and cheered the impossible. And believed: never, ever, ever, ever *boo your man* in this magnet. Even in jest.

This magnet is our magnet. This much is true.

This magnet attends every game, home and away, serving as the force that harnesses positive energy in their names: Yeager and Coleman.

"Yeager's gonna take off running again. Leon Lett is in pursuit, but he's way too slow. Finally, he gets help from Pankopf and Yeager is pulled down, but not before gaining seven yards. First down, Seahawks."

The Colemans went off in the luxury box. The spirit squad danced to the band's music. The rugby boyz threw the cheergirls high in the air. The Colemans and the crowd of 80,000 rallied around Yeager and *his* team. Bear's own energy was low, so he faded away whenever the Seattle offense headed to the sidelines of the magnet. Whenever Walter returned to the field, someone in space would urge Yeager onward, alerting Coleman to pay attention again.

"Come on, Yeager, man, show 'em!" was brother Stefan's mantra. Bear had never seen his brothers root harder for a white quarterback than they did that hot day hovering over the desert in the magnet. Not that they previously rooted for *or* against white QBs, but before Super Sunday, if they rooted for a quarterback at all, *beli've dat,* he was a brutha. Less he was one of dem crazy white dudes with a wild streak, like—dare one say—Jim McMahon.

Today, when Wild Streak did something good, the Coleman men cheered so loud, Bear only heard bits and pieces of the telecast (black people).

"Yeager heaves ... too far for Jefferson? ... just like that! Seattle! ... 49-yard touchdown pass. Walt loves the heat on a balmy winter day!"

The Colemans started dancing and singing "Whoomp! (There It Is)."

"You sure we're not disturbing Bear?" asked Walter's Sister when calm was restored in the luxury box.

"If we were all at home right now," said Evangeline, "Bear would be the first one yelling and screaming like we are. Maybe this'll wake his ass up."

Bear heard laughter, and for a moment, thought it was his own.

"That's all he used to do at home," said Stefan, "cheerlead."

"Couldn't even hear a damn game," laughed Grayson.

Payback. Bear wanted to give them Bear hugs. His family had tried to stop him from being a cheerleader back in the day because they saw a life of heartache for a prototype in a non-prototype world.

Aiight now though. Merely gave me a tough audience to practice in front of. You think I was intimidated at places like Notre Dame, Madison Square Garden, Athens, Georgia, the SEC, Pac-10 and the Big 10 after being both a prototype and a non-prototype in front of my family? You had your reasons. Most of them probably came from love. No matter. I became me, found my soul mate, and I couldn't be happier, even half alive as I am now. It was worth it. He is worth every single moment.

The Colemans cheered. The band played. The spirit squad did their thing.

And the boys were pleased by what they saw in the magnet.

"Millstone takes the handoff from Yeager on first and goal ... Touchdown, Seahawks! And suddenly the Dallas Cowboys find themselves in a first-half hole."

"Came out smokin', man," said one of the Coleman's young sons.

"Got something to prove," said Grayson.

"What's that?" asked an even younger boy's voice.

"He's still the Man," said Grayson. "See him on the sidelines? He's the one who just took off his helmet."

Bear felt Walter finally exhale after the Seahawks went up 14-0, as if the heroes could take a breather for the first time since Pittsburgh. One hero had given the city of Seattle two quick TDs to prove he was still the top dawg in their universe. The other hero was being cared for by his family. Maybe life wasn't going to combust, at least in the next minute. But with the pause came the unknotting of tension throughout the body, causing him to spasm uncontrollably.

"Daddy, why's that man wiggling on TV?" asked one of the young boys.

"Did your brother just move?" asked Walter's Sister.

The room fell silent. Bear calmed himself. He wanted to burst, which meant Walter wanted to burst. The supernova was finally sinking in, here to stay, forever to be dealt with.

It happened. We have to tell our truth. They already know too much.

Bear wanted to do a cheer to tell Walter to hang in there, but it was too late. The illusion had been broken. Walter would play the rest of the game with a heavy heart. He wouldn't play as freely as he had during those early drives when adrenaline carried him through. Some things even heroes can't let roll off their back, or stomach them, depending on the hero. Perfect grace, even in darkness.

Yeager played well, according to the Colemans and the telecast, but the boys knew better. The 27-17 victory over Dallas was hollow. They would have to fill the cavity another time. Walter gave his perfunctory post-game interview, then shot out of Tempe on a borrowed rocket ship, a magnetic one, shaped like a horseshoe stadium, as a matter of fact. When the last Coleman turned off the TV in the cockpit and left the luxury box—sponsored by Seattle Memorial—Bear fell asleep beyond the coma.

No use coming out of the blur now until his buddy was home from work.

"MILLSTONE GOT THE MVP," said Walter's voice. "Good for him, since he's retiring. That was my day, how was my Bear's?"

"Did I dream you showed up? Or did you show up and now I'm dreaming?"

"Does it matter?" said Walter with a mild laugh. "I'm here now, holding your hand. Can you feel me?"

"Very much so," said Bear.

Walter bowed his head and let out a combination of relief and laughter, then he said, "Do you know where you are?"

Bear looked around and saw that they were alone. "In a hospital bed with the winning quarterback of two of the last three Super Bowls ... the Hip?"

"No worries," said Walter. "Norton got me good in the second, but it's just a flesh wound. Oh, you mean, the dog—he's fine, with Larry and ... my mind ... feels like *I'm* the one coming up for air. Bear, you've been in a coma."

"That's the past," said Bear. "Let's not dwell on it."

"First pro game of mine you've ever missed," said Walter. "We broke the streak."

"There in spirit," said Bear.

"And in my helmet the whole time," said Walter.

"That's *in spirit*," said Bear. "You took me there. Flew together in the cockpit, then you vanished, claiming you had to go down below and make some TD magic. How was it?"

Walter grinned and played with Bear's hand. "Fun ... more fun at first. I'll enjoy it more when we're back in Malibu and your head is given a clean bill of health."

"Something hit me," said Bear. "Pittsburgh. What was it?"

"What did it look like?" asked Walter.

"A red comet," said Bear.

"They never found it or the guy," said Walter. "And they can't say whether or not it was related to the guy who kept yelling to sack me."

"So we'll never know if I was gay-bashed or Seahawk-bashed," said Bear. "Or God knows what else, don't wanna dream of it. Ever again."

"Just like I'll never know if Doak Minnefield was thinking of his brother dying of AIDS when he came at me in DC," said Walter. "Our lives might be at stake and we don't even know if it's true because we're playing games with our Truth, just like they might be."

"We're getting bashed for pretending to be ... *not* ... buddies ... how else can I say this: we're getting bashed for pretending *not* to be gay? Talk about twisted," said Bear. "I thought this kind of stuff was supposed to happen *after* an athlete comes out."

"I can't tell you how bad I feel, Bear." Walter rested his head on the bed. "Too overwhelming."

"Go for whelming, buddy," said Bear. "Feeling bad for that man's actions is like letting that comet explode like a bomb in our lives, meaning the man who threw it is a terrorist, and he won because you feel bad, which makes me feel bad. We're not as dynamic a duo when we're feeling like the scum of the earth. Publicly anyway."

"I'll feel less like scum after I call a doctor in here and he says you're healed." Walter pushed the call button on the bed.

"I had another dream while I was out." Bear stroked his man's hair. "That the world is waiting for some answers from Walter Yeager and those missing :04 from the AFC Championship. I also had a dream a certain evil announcer man is loving this and is just one of many reporters angling for the real scoop."

"Is that your dream?" laughed Walter. "Or have our relatives been unable to keep their big mouths shut, like I told them before I left the luxury box, I mean, hospital."

"Things are twisted either way," said Bear. "It's finally TIME for the dynamic duo to dream a Truly Golden dream."

"I smell big trouble."

"Don't you wanna dream the Truly Golden dream?"

"You took a hit for loving another man, me."

"We don't know that for sure."

"*I* took a hit for loving another man, you."

"We don't know that for sure, either."

"Then why did we take the hits?" asked Walter.

"Because we have an opportunity," said Bear. "We can think the world is out to get us because of who we are, or we can view everything in life as a gift, even though we may not immediately understand the nature of the gift, especially when it hurts or is confusing or disrupting of our current lives."

"I'd rather know who's after me and why," said Walter.

"Who wouldn't? But is that the way life always works? No matter what your belief is, does that mean you share the same reality with Doak Minnefield of DC or the comet thrower of Pittsburgh? They could lie or send mixed messages like Doak did; but it's still up to you to choose your point of view on it all. Look how we've embraced our favorite black coach—what's-his-name—yet we still don't know what, if anything, happened with him in San Diego."

"Not saying that's realistic in the real world," said Walter, "but I get your point. So how in the world is even your amazing imagination gonna dream of a better way outta this? The Super Bowl Champs and the rest of the planet are waiting for an explanation as to why the world's greatest quarterback—if I do say so myself—missed his team's winning field goal attempt in the AFC Championship in Pittsburgh to be by the side of his longtime manager *slash* whatever."

"Any chance of my buddy joining me up here, so we can dream of it together?" asked Bear.

"I'll take you there," said Walter, climbing into the hospital bed.

WALTER AND BEAR STOOD ALONE IN THE green room. "Nervous?" asked Bear.

"Let's see." Walter checked his body. "I have flesh. I have bones. I have a lot of nerve endings, and I'm about to discuss our sexuality on the worldwide web of television. Worldwide. Nervous? What sweat between my toes?"

"I wouldn't dream of it any other way." Bear straightened his man's collar. "My sweaty, tired soles next to yours in the moment of truth. We're sure everyone in our family is good to go?"

"Check," said Walter. "Deep down, Tammy knows we're not following team orders to say, *Just good college buddies!* But she's not letting on that she's looking the other way."

"Good for her," said Bear. "Like there's anyone left on the planet that doesn't know you and I do way more than play Mattel Electronics Football together."

"And you know how I feel about punting on that little green box." Walter took one last deep breath.

"Word is born," said Bear. "Maybe someday Tammy won't have to work for a team that tells lies for a living. You ready to stop, still-*my*-MVP? ... Walter, can you hear me? ... PV? ... We're ready, buddy ... QB? ... Yeager-man? Big Norse?"

Having shot his arsenal, Bear decided to sing softly, almost a whisper ... Steppenwolf ... their first crazy road trip ... ATL 2 SEA, graduation day:

"Born to be wiiiiiild!"

And Walter came out of his trance to echo his man with a whisper, right in time with Steppenwolf's next line: *"Born to be wiiiiiild!"*

The magnet in their minds rumbled, ready to blast into Super space.

The man of words checked his own one last time. Only a backup, but you always make sure you've got your hero's back:

> Here's to the day when a kid can be honest with himself
> and the world from the moment he conceives of himself
> as a lover of men, and be afforded the exact same
> chance as every other kid to have a successful career in
> professional basketball, football or baseball, without one
> single atom wasted, harassing him for being who he is.

"Athletes of color have lived the dream," said Bear, reading aloud the rest of his prepared backup statement. "Now it's our turn."

"Hear, hear," said the production assistant from the doorway. He was the same young man who had escorted them to the green room, no doubt checking up on them again. "Hopefully we'll make history on national TV tonight and begin to change the world for the better. And by the way, Eagan is *thrilled* that you picked him over Barbara, Oprah, Larry King, Regis, Haley, and all the rest. Although he did seem quite amazed you actually chose him."

Walter laughed his fake laugh. "It's not like he's some evil announcer guy or something."

Bear smiled his fake smile. "You guys agreed to our simple requests. Besides, he had an early hand in the Big Bang that is the Bearcat Universe. Only fair he has a front-row seat."

Walter coughed to rein in Bear. The two made peripheral eye contact. Evil Announcer Guy and his network assumed the boys had chosen them to host this historic event because only they had agreed to the boys' demands:

The initial broadcast: live, unedited and uninterrupted.

Walter would be allowed to read a prepared statement *twice,* once at the beginning, once at the end. The statement was not to be prescreened by the network, but the telecast could be on a five-second delay to address concerns of indecency. As for location, the boys insisted on Universal Studios Hollywood. By the time the details were hammered out, it was Super Friday after Super Sunday. Naturally, the media had gotten wind of the interview, and reporters the world over were salivating with the kind of hysteria ... imagine it.

"There's my favorite duo!" said Evil Announcer Guy, entering the green room. "I gotta tell ya, I'm glad to see you two have matured. This peace offering that's gonna make me—*whoa! talk about huge!*—but remember, no attacking me, and we're on a five-second delay, just in case you get too freaky for the family hour."

"That's not us," said Walter. "In public anyway."

"So why me?" asked Evil Announcer Guy, ordering his assistant away with his head. "What makes me get to be the luckiest man on Earth—I mean, I'm gonna go down in history! The biggest exclusive ever! I keep thinking it's too good to be true."

"You don't believe miracles happen to you?" asked Bear, then he started coughing ... *dry throat.*

"Miracles?" scoffed Evil Announcer Guy. "You mean, like, good shit just falling in your lap? Maybe if we're talking Vegas or TJ! But *nah* ... not a miracle guy here, but I'm grateful, don't get me wrong."

"Oh, we've never gotten you wrong, have we, QB?" Bear coughed again.

"What the fuck does that mean?" asked Evil Announcer Guy. Bear put his hand to his mouth and shook his head, almost as if to say, *Me No Speak.* "Man, where have I seen you before? Besides Seattle? Never mind that. So fellas, our little hotel misunderstanding—thing of the past, right?"

"What little hotel misunderstanding?" asked Walter. The assistant poked his head inside the doorway and told them it was TIME. Walter and Bear eyed one another for courage, then began moving toward the set.

"Maybe we can all have drinks at the Pro Bowl," said Evil Announcer Guy as they traveled down a short hall.

"Not possible," said Walter.

"Coffee then," said Evil Announcer Guy.

"I'm not going to the Pro Bowl," said Walter. Evil Announcer Guy eyed him curiously, but the crew whisked them deeper into the set, not letting them alone again until they were seated in the three chairs behind a news desk (another demand). Walter and Bear's chairs were closer together, then there was the chair of the inquisitor, now occupied by a man who had dogged them since the Sugar Bowl. A dirty dozen years.

"Now I do have a ton of questions, so keep your answers short," said Evil Announcer Guy. "Unless you're really spilling some juicy details. Work for you?"

"Remember," said Walter, holding up his speech. "To start and end with."

"And rolling in ..." said a woman's deep voice from the blur beyond the white lights. Before Walter and Bear knew it, they were staring at another light, a red one, glaring at them from a gigantic camera that made them sweat.

"Welcome to this historic night," said Evil Announcer Guy. "You all know—"

Walter cleared his throat to *interrupt the intro,* then held up his speech.

"What?" asked Evil Announcer Guy. "Even before—"

Walter cleared his throat again and mumbled *"hotel."* When Evil Announcer Guy realized he wasn't getting *his* intro, he pouted, then said into the camera: "Ladies and gentlemen, Walter Yeager of the Seattle Seahawks."

Walt loves the truth.

"Winners of this year's Super Bowl," added Evil Announcer Guy.

Walter started to talk.

"27-17 over Dallas," added Evil Announcer Guy.

Walter shot an intense glare at his nemesis, who froze. Then QB took a deep breath and stared directly into the camera.

"I am in love with this man ... Bear Coleman."

"And I'm in love with this man ... Walter Yeager."

The boys shared a smile—peaceful, calm, steeped in utter faith in their love and their union.

Don't need to wear a loop. We're magnetized.

They broke eye contact and turned to the world in the name of taking care of business, and Walter read their pissant li'l ditty that Bear liked to call:

THE BEARCAT BOYZ TELL THE TRUTH

"We are a couple and have been a couple since we met the weekend of the UCLA @ Georgia game over 12 long years ago. As Bear and I were reminded recently, *life is so precious* ... breathe ... breathe again ... and can be taken away in less time than it takes to run off the football field. That is why I chose to leave Three Rivers Stadium in Pittsburgh, when I realized my soul mate's life was in danger. He was hurt. I heard his cries in my soul. I went to help save his life. It was my choice. I Stand By My Choice. There will always be games for the men to play, and for people to watch, but there will only be one love of my life who fills my world and my heart with this much happiness. How much happiness? Enough to be here tonight, telling the truth in the name of further happiness and joy, in his name, which is to say, in my name. It is *our* choice to share our love with the world. We Stand By Our Choice.

"No pain is greater than watching a loved one clinging to life with a barrier of any kind between you. We have both been on both sides of that barrier now, and it is time for the barriers to come down forever.

"It is time for the biggest source of chaos in our lives—the lies—to end, here and now. Tonight.

"Instead of speculating, questioning and taking sides regarding this announcement, consider focusing your energies on your own lives and spending time with your own loved ones. There are no sides to our relationship, so there are no sides to take. There is just a circle. Inside the circle, there is only love and those who wish to share that love. Outside the circle, there is only energy that refuses to become part of our circle of love. To those who don't appreciate or value our relationship, we bid you no harm. We only wish you as much love and joy as we continue to experience with one another each and every moment of each and every day. And when you experience such profound love and joy in your own lives, Bear and I wish you the same peaceful existence we now ask the world to grant us. What we want most is to love one another, play football and make movies—three simple little dreams for two ordinary American boys.

"At the conclusion of this statement, we will go into hibernation for 30 days with many of our family and friends. Barring an unforeseen emergency, we will not have any meaningful contact with the outside world—no newspapers, no televisions, no radios, no phones, nothing. We will also be giving each other as much space as humanly possible. No one pushes one's buttons like family, this much is true. But the Colemans and Yeagers will be together, focusing our energies on appreciating our loved ones while we're still alive to do so.

"Because this will be the last live image of us you will see for at least 30 days, we would like to share with you the very first image ever captured of me and my soul mate together. Actually, you've already seen the image. Many in the media have already had their share of fun with this image, making it a cherished part of our times in sports, part of highlights every time a sports announcer makes a witty turn of phrase on what *Walt loves.*

"Remember QB LOVES THE BEARCAT? Which morphed into WALT LOVES THE BEARCAT, thanks to a certain morning TV host?

"*The truth, finally, always and forever.* This much is true. Yes. Walt loves the Bearcat. The Bearcat is Marcus 'Bear' Coleman. Through a series of mishaps, more or less, Bear ended up in the bear suit that day. It was the photographer who incorrectly called him a Bearcat, but make no mistake, *Bear* is the Bearcat. He has always been the Bearcat and the only UCLA Bruin I have ever loved. We both apologize for lying about our love. We promise to never do it again.

"Two years ago, the public embraced this picture as a romantic moment between a quarterback from one school and a mascot from another. Is the photo less romantic to you now that, upon further reveal, the person inside the bear suit is different from what you imagined? You knew nothing about the Bearcat, except that the Bearcat was a female. Why is the photo less romantic now? Consider that the photo has not changed. If anything has changed, it is your perception of the photo. We also ask that you consider this:

"Which idea gives you a better feeling: the concept that the photo is of two souls who dated for one week of their lives, then parted forever? Or the concept that the photo is of two souls who have been happily in love for the last 12, won-derful, romantic, and adventure-filled years?

"For those of you who imagine our love in a good light, our sincerest grati-tude. For those of you who would rather desecrate that light, we wish you noth-ing but love and happiness. To all of you listening, and by extension, all of your loved ones, may your deepest dreams come true. Goodnight—oh, and Bear, I'm sorry ... big night ... lot to remember ... one more thing ... is there anything you'd like to add, Bear?"

The quarterback threw him a curveball on national TV. Bear stared blankly into the living rooms of a trillion homes. Then uttered: "He gets me."

"Yeah," chimed Walter. "Ditto." Then he looked at Bear. "We outta here? Cool."

Walter and Bear got up, moved off the set and vanished down their pre-viously-scheduled rabbit hole of an escape hatch. Evil Announcer Guy was too stunned to speak, as was his crew, none of them having dreamed up a counter-play. Matter of fact, not a single person in the studio space had imagined the Bearcats would run a trick play, let alone a fake punt *and* a quarterback sneak.

Twisted.

25

Hibernation of the Cool and Dreamy

"I get to fly the magnet tonight," said Bear, trying to remain awake. He was laying horizontal, head in his buddy's lap.

"Magnet?" laughed Walter, tracing the ridges in Bear's shaved-bald head.

"Our high-powered stadium that converts into an aerial transport *slash* spaceship when needed," mumbled a cool and dreamy Bear, already hibernating in his cool and dreamy head.

"We're about to take off, bud," said Walter. "Away from the chaos and disorder. I think you're still a little coma-like in the head."

"How'd we do back there?" asked Bear. "Did we outfox those foxy peeps?"

Foxes can be foxy while trying to outfox you. Not too cuddly, eh?

"Just like we drew it up," said Walter.

"We draw such pretty pictures, QB, always and forever, perfect pretty pictures," said Bear.

"Except I *did* expect the writer in the family to come up with something more than: *He gets me,*" said Walter with the cutest mild laugh.

The Bearcat loves his buddy's mild laugh. This much is true.

"You *do* get me," insisted Bear, setting adrift, memory all bliss. "And I get you. *Almost* every single bit of you."

"Gotta be a man of mystery to *some* degree," said Walter.

"Like any good gunslinger," said Bear. "And soul mate."

"Sit up. Gotta strap you in," said Walter.

"I'm not too coma-like for that?" giggled Bear.

"For blast-off, silly."

Whatever Walt wants. Bear knows exactly what Bear is saying.

The boys needed a name for the transport, but that would have to wait. They were still in GETAWAY MODE. Bear's seat sprang upright in the cockpit at the top of the stadium in the closed end of the magnet. He pushed the big red button: TUNES. The digital jukebox in the brain of the ship started playing "Born to Be Wild," the hard-driving rock anthem by Steppenwolf. At the open end of the horseshoe stadium, big jets emerged from the sides of the grandstands, then fired up instantly. The horseshoe magnet shot straight up in the air like an upside-down U, led by the cockpit at the top of the closed end. They raced over LA-LA Land by night, only to be met by an old-school warplane.

"Reporters! Foxes!" shouted Bear to Walter, who was in the co-pilot seat, messing with the control panel. "Hold on to the Hip!"

The magnet veered sharply to the left, then turned on its right side and flew past by the Hollywood sign. Hip yelped and jumped up into Walter's lap, then buried his head under QB's jersey. *Lucky Number 13. Colorless yet colorful. True Gold.* The warplane couldn't make the sharp turn and flew straight into the first O of the H-llywood sign, burning the O and sputtering in the brush.

"They've got backup!" yelled Walter in the co-pilot seat, messing with the control panel, holding onto Hip! Dozens of old-school warplanes popped up in the night sky like old-school popcorn.

"They all wanna piece of Yeager-meister!" said Bear. "Who can blame 'em, eh, Hipsters?"

Hip yelped! Bear steered the horseshoe magnet toward the towering spirals of downtown LA. The foxes followed. The boys glanced behind them at the stadium below the cockpit. The 80,000 faithful were clapping and dancing while the spirit leaders performed to "Born to Be Wild," dazzling the crowd with gravity-defying stunts and pyramids.

"Go down and throw some passes for the people!" yelled Bear to Walter.

"You got this?" Walter glanced back at the foxes following in the air.

"I got this!" said Bear.

"You da man." Walter and Hip slid down the ramp that led to the field some 80 rows below the cockpit. Bear grinned, watching Walter's prototype body grow until it was 80 rows tall ... Yeager was in full football gear now, dressed in whatever color the soul's eyes chose. *True Gold.* Hip remained his regular size but leaped up and down, all about, to the heavens and back.

Walter threw long bombs and perfect spirals to giant receivers that ran like gazelles, but Bear couldn't savor the display. The warplanes were behind him, downtown LA in front. "Punch it!" He pushed the big orange button. The scoreboards in the stadium read: TURBULENCE! Thank God the faithful were good at holding on during the boys' bumpy rides, always and forever.

Bear guided the horseshoe magnet in and out of the skyscrapers, bobbing and weaving to lose the foxes. "Cute little foxes ... sometimes." The 80,000 faithful swayed, the fans forced to grab onto their drinks and big foam fingers. "I hope Mama Rent's holding onto her nachos!" The spirit squad's stunts tilted side to side ... *leaning tower of cheergirl!* And yet amazingly, *all that* remained in perfect balance. Even Yeager's passes were still on target. Such was the magic of their very own stadium that was forever their home field. "True Gold!"

"Nailed it!" said Walter via his cool and dreamy headset.

"Named it!" said Bear via his cool and dreamy headset.

"Outfox the reporters again?" asked Walter, throwing another 99-yard touchdown pass.

"What else is new?" said Bear, shooting straight up in the skies over North America. Twelve charter planes hovered in a circle over the heartland. The satellites. "Our hearts await!" Bear steered True Gold straight up through the loop, then screeched to a Wild West kind of halt-and-hover. "Sorry, we're late, Super space travelers," said Bear in his cool and dreamy headset. They were all in the loop now. "Escaping the madness in LA took longer than we imagined, but have no fear, or worries, we did it in style. Oh, and by the way, Bearcat People, he *does* get me."

True Gold took off into Super space, the satellite planes followed. They sped past the moon and circled the planets. Around Jupiter, they came across an asteroid field of more media foxes and had to dodge them with the bob and weave again. In the process, sometimes the caravan separated, half the planes bobbing in one direction, the other half weaving in the polar opposite. But they were expert generals and majors now. Dodging the blitz of the foxes who were fuzzy with the fax was child's play. The caravan never failed to rejoin hearts after a shaky bob and weave. They were magnetized!

Eventually, the Bearcats made it through the asteroid field unscathed, and spiraled toward the home planet, orbiting a few times before deciding it was safe for re-entry.

"I just waved to my sister," said Walter, back in the cockpit with Hip!

Bear glanced out the window over Walter's shoulder. Walter's Sister sat in the pilot's seat of the plane flying adjacent to True Gold. Her face was pressed against the window, her tongue sticking out at her brother, the quarterback.

Some old school is good old school.

"Why is she flying so close to us?" giggled Bear.

"Because the island is—*Beaaaaaar ... the brakes!*" shouted Walter.

Bear turned toward the front of the cockpit window. They were still spiraling toward Earth, only Earth was closer than ever! Bear slammed on the brakes of the magnet with all his Bear might. Walter jammed on the big orange button. The scoreboards in the stadium read: WARNING: BEAR LANDING.

"Followed by the sound of 80,000 seat belts locking hastily. Cute," said Bear. "Real cute."

Directly below, on that thing called Earth, a round speck surround by blue grew bigger and bigger until the speck became a cool and dreamy world. The island! It was dotted with small beach huts around the perimeter, and flora and fauna in the interior, which is where True Gold was going to crash—

"Like I would do that to the stadium of our dreams," said Bear in his cool and dreamy headset, steering them to a smooth and upright hovering position just above their cool and dreamy paradise.

He killed the jets, which retracted into the bleachers and the grandstands. The landing gear—spider legs with hydraulic suspension—descended from the bottom of the stadium. The 80,000 faithful faded quietly, off to spread the boys' brand of spirit and joy throughout the universe until summoned again. The rest of Walter and Bear's team, the closest Bearcat People, remained behind. Their satellite planes buzzed peacefully over the calm seas. Bear looked down at the lagoons and waterfalls below in the middle of the island and smiled a relieved smile.

"If you'll excuse me, Bearcat People, I'm fading," yawned a cool and dreamy Bear, falling asleep in his buddy's cool and dreamy lap. "It's been an exhausting journey to paradise and back, and I just got off IR a few hours ago. So thank you for traveling with our True Gold caravan, and enjoy your hibernation from the world as we knew it."

... I ALSO HAD A DREAM.

"Ready to join the living, sleepyhead?" asked Walter.

"I dreamed," said Bear, still cool and dreamy but now with eyes wide open. Or getting there. "Half a life ... I also dreamed half a life." Bear was horizontal, lying in a bed of palm leaves in a warm tropical breeze. "I dreamed ..."

If you're ready, cut to ... Madonna's "Causing A Commotion" and countless quick shots from every plugged-in nook of the 1996 Super Worldwide Universe going kwaaaay-zy *over some golden white boy admitting he's in love with some gold-*

en black boy. And vice versa, always and forever. The Quarterback and the Cheer Queer! Your biggest fantasy or worst nightmare, from where you're standing—

"*Don't* tell me about it," said Walter. Softly. Smoothly. Stroking his man's still coma-like haze.

"Not in this lifetime," said a cool and dreamy Bear. "It's out there, no doubt, somewhere, somehow, some way. It happened like that. Or is gonna. Or *is* right now. The dream is too big to stuff back into the black hole known as humanity's collective mind. Nothing's gonna stop the deepest of True Gold sports dreamers now, just ask that other Cool and Dreamy Triple Threat: Robinson, Thorpe, and Didrikson."

"Babe, listen," said Walter. "Can you hear it? Can you feel it? *We* don't have to dream that dream. We dreamed another one. You and me, babe—*mild laugh.* Watch, I bet you put that in your *Walter Yeager Story* slash *Walt Loves the Bearcat* movie script someday, my *mild laugh* ... anyway ... Bear, buddy ... your coma-like little head is just fine and can be worry-free ... we're safe ... a temporary Jaw with all our family, friends, cousins ... *there's my mild laugh again* ... you called 'em *Bearcat People* on the flight over."

"Like Pacer People," said Bear. "That's what the announcer says at Indiana's games ... *All right, Pacer People, it's TIME. Let's hear it for your ... Indiana Pacers! Whoa!* ... still got my dizzy on ... and on and on ..."

"You need some sunshine," said Walter.

"We're not holed up in an underground bunker? A bear's den? A bat cave? The team basement? The tunnels of the nuclear reactor?" asked a still cool and dreamy Bear.

"We're not even holed up," said Walter. *Mild laugh.*

"Where the freak are we, MVP?" giggled Bear.

"TIME to take a walk," said Walter. "Finally."

The Cool and Dreamy Hibernation of the Cool and Dreamy ... was a dream come true. Dreams do come true. This much is true. The location of the island was so private, not even Bearcat People knew exactly where on Earth they stood.

The complimentary trip was all in their minds.

And in the warm sand between their sticky toes.

"Sunlight," sighed Bear, feeling sunlight on his face. "Where would we be without the suns, all of them."

"Feeling okay to stand, little Bearcat?" asked Walter, rubbing his buddy's stiff shoulders.

"Long as I have my pole to lean on." Bear stood and leaned on his bud. They surveyed the cool and dreamy island before their eyes. Azure skies. Golden sand. A cool and dreamy world. "Two questions, meister, before the cool and dreamy tour."

"Miracles do happen. Bear Coleman with only two questions for me," said the cool and dreamy smart-ass quarterback.

"Question one," said Bear. "Does the scoreboard in the darkened and empty stadium read: ALL CLEAR?"

"Affirmative," said the cool and dreamy quarterback. "Everyone arrived safely, and amazingly in perfect sync, considering how we had to outfox all those … sorry … let me pull back and take a better road here … no need to go back down that tired path …"

"Question two," said Bear, following his quarterback across the island. "Life is still a little blurry right now … especially time … what with … the hit … and the blurry traveling … so much hurtling through space lately … dreamed I was hopping back and forth between all these crazy planets … Pluto … Saturn … Tempe … Planet Hollywood … now this cool and dreamy island paradise."

"Sub Pittsburgh for Pluto, and Seattle for Saturn, and I think you're up to speed there, Bear, good boy," said Walter.

"Yeah, Walter, but …" Bear paused, trying to keep pace. Walt loves to move with swift and focused determination. Hard for the bumbling Bear to keep up with his man in regular times, let alone while feeling blurry. "Hold on … did we … you … we won the Super Bowl again … Number 2 … right?"

"You really don't know, or is my Bear playing with me?" asked Walter.

"Just trying to unfuzzy some of the fax," said Bear, "for rehearsals."

"You really asking?" asked Walter. "You really wanna know this?"

"For another time, let's eat," said Bear. "I've never felt this hungry. Ever!"

QB was talkative while the boys ate on the steps of their hut, apparently having missed his coma-like Bear's big floppy ears:

"… both families love all the food … Bob & Jimmy Astor send their best … did you know they started in the grocery business? … kids doing their absentee schoolwork … stopped playing video games and complaining about no TV for 30 days … a few have picked up a book … glad *we* weren't so obsessed with video games as strapping young bucks … brought along Mattel Electronics Football … you're fine … need rest … we all do … my parents are totally cool … Dad said he's proud of me and the way I handled things, in so many words … let the rest of the world do whatever they want … this is our world … here. I'm done, let's go."

Near the cool and dreamy huts of the Colemans … Grayson and Stefan were balling on the half-court with some of the Yeager relatives—oh, and Black Coach, who was finally in the loop, always and forever. Sister Evangeline was grilling food for a bunch of Coleman wives and satellites running around in the sun. The Colemans were good breeders of cool and dreamy kids.

Near the cool and dreamy huts of the Yeagers ... Walter's Bro and his personal troops were hanging around a hammock on the porch. "He hasn't moved in quite some time," said Walter of his slumbering and very handsome brother. Mom and Pops were in the ocean, frolicking with Yeager cousins and Yeager satellites. Bear's cool and dreamy Kennedys.

Near the cool and dreamy hut of the Tankster and his first family ... a game of volleyball. Tank was holding court as the older kid, while Grace's girls, all younger, swooned at every move of the not-necessarily-graceful Tank. Didn't matter to Grace's girls, however. Walter's son had become their virtual big brother sometime during the long and winding road.

"They love their Tank," said Bear, sitting and watching the distant dance of the prepubescents. "You getting quality time with your boy?"

"Main thing I focused on in your absence," said Walter. "Told him that you and I are like a unique combo of buddies and a married couple, buddies-for-life."

"Nailed it," said Bear. "Did he get it?"

"He was more worried about you waking up," said Walter.

"Getting there," said Bear. "We all are."

Near the cool and dreamy hut of the lesbo cheergirls ... Wendy Jiu and Lisa Wu swam in the lagoon, splashing one minute, cool and dreamy the next. "I thought they deserved it after sacrificing 10 years' worth of vacations for Seahawks tickets," said Walter.

"Good call," said Bear. "Touchdown. I think I just removed the *ex* from them, gonna make them co-captains of the Bearcats spirit squad."

"I finally figured out which is which and why only one of them speaks most of the time, while the other barely says a word," said Walter.

Bear was stunned, as if being brought into a whole new light.

"Hold on, little Bearcat, let me explain," said Walter. *Mild laugh.* "If you think back to all our conversations with them, only one of them really spoke. The other just kinda said something every now and then. You never noticed that?"

"A relationship where one person uses a billion words and the other 13?" asked Bear. "*Hmmm* ... not sure. Remember, life blurry ... coma head."

"She talks through pictures," said Walter. "That's what the other one said. She said her lover talks through pretty pictures. Oh, and did you know she barely speaks English? And she's a Japanese-language filmmaker now."

Near the cool and dreamy hut of Tammy, the ER Wife ...

"She didn't come?" asked Bear.

"Not on my watch," said Walter. "Outta the loop until we're sure if she can play for our new team."

"The Bearcats," said Bear.

Near the cool and dreamy hut of the Hail Larrys ...

"Our best friends aren't here?" asked Bear.

"On special assignment in Western Pennsylvania," said Walter.

Near the cool and dreamy hut of Roberto the Celibate ...

"No R. Alfredo Selladito, either?" asked Bear, squinting in the bright sunlight.

"Told him to take a breather from being our manager and go back to El Salvador to bond with his own family instead of us," said Walter.

"Good man," said Bear. "Didn't know he was also Salvadoran."

Near the cool and dreamy hut of ... the dog park ... the families' dogs were in dawg heaven. "Don't worry," said Walter. "Tank's piranha tank is safely locked away in the Pet Hotel on the far side of the island. No animal chaos here, fuzzy or otherwise."

"Ah, the salad days," sighed the Bearcat.

Walter's cousin Linda, the Swedish dog trainer, was the current center of the dogs' world. Treats! Mama Rent and Walter's Sister and her satellites were also swirling about the animals.

"But we still have our furry animal fun, eh, little Bearcat?" said Walter.

Near the cool and dreamy supply dock ... the boys had a very sweet rendezvous with *The Fair Lady*.

"*Oncle!*" cried Bear, running to embrace Walter's Uncle. "*Le Sucre!* Golden light on the Mediterranean! You came to be the supply runner!"

"Somebody's gotta get the food and ice cream from the Astors," said Walter's Uncle, indicating some big jugs on the back of the boat. "And the water."

"Or as the kids in Atlanta say ... *Walta, Water, Walta,*" said Bear, pinching his man's golden, reddening cheek. "Everybody needs some *Walta* in their lives. Can't exist without *Walta*."

"Suddenly, *j'ai soif,*" said Walter's Aunt, hugging Bear from behind. "By the way, I like: *He gets me.*"

"Knew the Uncle's Wife would understand," said Bear, stumbling forward a bit. "Sorry, still getting my balance, post-coma-world."

NEAR THE COOL AND DREAMY HUT of Grace and her three beautiful girls ... Bear grew stronger by the moment, especially watching Walter with the kids.

"I should be so lucky to have a wonderful man like yours," said Grace.

"I wish I could run one off for you on the island copy machine," said Bear. "Seriously." Bear couldn't remember speaking to Grace all that much since the orange triangle in Anaheim all those years ago, when he paid her money to kiss Walter. "I don't know why you haven't found your true love like us," said Bear, "but I hope you keep dreaming of that love. Miracles happen."

"I'm too old for miracles," said Grace. She was one of the most beautiful women Bear had ever seen. Suddenly. Now. More so than Tammy, Avonda from freshman year, or anyone else. Grace glowed. Grace also had a heavy heart.

"I knew you in college," said Bear, sitting on the hut steps.

"Not possible," laughed Grace, sitting on the hut steps.

"Possible," said Bear. "Your name wasn't Grace then. It was ... what was it ..."

"Bear, that's not possible," laughed Grace.

"Kim! You were my Kim!" said Bear. "You came to USC to follow some dream, but what you were really dreaming of was ... Adam ... a hockey guy."

"What are you saying, Bear?" asked Grace. "Walter, can you come here?"

"Your dream man was not at our dream school," said Bear. "He was elsewhere. You could barely stand to sit still. You spent a lot of your dad's money hooking up with this gorgeous blond boy who played hockey, not football, like the stud approaching at high noon."

"What's up, Grace?" asked Walter.

"Have the nurses checked on Bear lately?" asked Grace.

"She thinks I'm crazy," giggled Bear, "because I remember her from school."

"I didn't go to school in California," said Grace. "That's what Bear keeps saying. Maybe the meds?"

"I don't need meds, I need me!" said Bear.

"See what I mean?" said Grace. "The doctor—"

"I don't need a doctor," cried Bear. "I need ... to rest. Everything is just cool and dreamy."

We were great friends for a heartbeat, had a couple of weeks of great college adventures, the kind of which I never imagined. Riding horses in the hills, literally teetering over a towering cliff because the old mule was just standing on the edge, the sky above, the mountain behind, one helluva drop below. Her horse was closer than mine. Her horse looked like he wanted to jump.

"Help me, Marcus, what should I do?"

Wow, she must have called me Marcus, not Bear, for some reason.

Just platonic buds, of course. I came to school to find my man. She was already in love with hers, back in Oklahoma. Her heart ached so badly, she went after him, vanishing from school and my life ...

Had a reunion of sorts, years later, crossing in the blur ...

She was just as beautiful, but her spirit had been ... challenged by the broken dream that was Oklahoma. The Sooner she got there, the Sooner it was over.

"See, he *does* get me," said Bear, watching Walter rejoin the kids in a spirited game of ... something joyful. "I'm sorry you bet on the wrong horse when you were young, Grace. It wasn't the horse's fault he was teetering on the edge of a cliff. That horse was a young soul in an old body, or an old soul in a young body, I'm not sure which ... still fuzzy in the blur ... point: We're all still Trojans, deep inside. Strong-willed men who never give up. Your Trojan horse didn't try to trick you. He was just being tricked himself. We were all being tricked. Twisted, I know."

"Bear, you're not making sense at all," said Grace.

So beautiful, so wise, so complete, so loving, so a great mom, and so pretending she doesn't have a clue. Perfect Grace.

"Keep dreaming, girl, we're all gonna get our own cool and dreamy place in space real soon."

NEAR THE COOL AND DREAMY HUT OF THE Tankster ... Bear wondered how often Walter thought about the little red sports car, and Athens, and the original golden days.

"So true," said Ellen. "It all worked out for the best after all."

"Maybe we should consider doing it annually," said Bear. *Tank's mom, the dark-haired one from that original ride to Atlanta. Still coming out of the dark, was Bear.* "Regenerate with the core of the Bearcat People annually. Great idea, thanks."

"You're funny," said Ellen.

"At least I'm no longer *too much*," said Bear. "That's what you used to call me."

"As in *when?*" laughed a doubtful Ellen.

"I *listened* on that fateful ride that fateful night of that fateful game on that fateful weekend of that fateful football season that changed all of our fates forever. Or is that *faiths* forever?" wondered Bear. "Either way. *Beli've dis.* When it comes to *my* fate and my man's fate, I remember every *single* important detail. This much is true. That was one of your favorite phrases: *you're too much.* Funny, I never knew what to say. *Then.*"

"Sorry if I offended you," said Ellen. *Cool, sitting on this porch with her, watching their men and boys and a bunch of other black and white kids in a game of ... oh, yes ... touch football.*

"All I wanna do is make love—" sang Bear.

"Walter hates that song by Heart," said Ellen.

"I can understand why," said Bear. "Those two women have put men like Walter through a lot of Heart-wrenching drama. But like you said, it all works out in the end, give or take. This much is true."

"He always turns it off," said Ellen. "Gets pissed whenever I sing it."

"Take heart," said Bear. "You powered my man's world by giving him his first child. If I don't get on my knees and thank *you* every single moment of *my* life, something is *definitely* not right in my head, and you have my permission to call for help ... *you feeling me? ... think I got the fever yet?*"

"Do I need to call Walter over?" asked Ellen. "Tank ... call your father over here ... Tank ... leave your siblings alone, all 24 of them! ... Bear, did you hear that? Kidding to see if you can hear me ... somebody turn down the music!"

"*Mom!*" yelled Tank, his changing voice mixing with Three Dog Night, the old rock group. "Dad says Bear's fine ... just coma-like, no harm, no foul!"

Ellen laughed, started to call up her Old School Phrase of the Day, but pulled a reverse instead: "You guys are too ... men in love, that's for sure."

"Something tells me you knew that from day one," said Bear. " ... straight shootin' son of a son ..."

"I made him send that photo," said Ellen.

"*Joy to my world!*" sang Bear.

"The one of you in the end zone from that weekend," said Ellen. "It was like a photo of some UCLA black male cheerleader with Harry Dawg in the end zone, pre-game."

"The star-crossed-lovers-in-the-end-zone, double-photo *pas de duh?*" asked an astonished Bear.

"*Pas de who?*" asked Ellen.

The camera on the left got bumped and took a picture of the shot on the right. The camera on the right got bumped and took a picture of the shot on the left.

"It got twisted," said Bear. "The cheergirl's camera out West had a shot y'all reds wanted. Meanwhile, the cheergirl's camera in the Deep South had a shot *my* big black ass wanted! Or wait, did I just twist it back? *Coma-head at work.*"

"Exactly," said Ellen.

"Get it now?" asked Bear. "The cross-shot that our friends took with their adjacent cameras."

"*Duh!*" said Ellen.

"That photo led me to Walter!" said Bear.

When will women stop taking so long to get up to speed?

"Chill, Bear, I follow," said Ellen.

When men stop assuming they're not!

"I was back home at UCLA, after the Georgia game," said Bear, feeling like a fuzzy flashback. "Walter and I said goodbye in Atlanta without getting a chance to tell each other anything because these *bitchy white chicks were in the backseat of the little red sports ...* oh, wait a minute ... my coma-like head is talking to one of those *bitchy white chicks* right now, isn't it?"

"It's okay, Bear," laughed Ellen. "It all turned out for the best. Walter was not my man after all, no way. I'm glad he's got you and I got what I got."

"You hooked us up!" said a still-astonished Bear.

"Me?" laughed Ellen.

"I had no way or excuse to get in touch with this gorgeous blond QB I just fell in love with in Athens," said Bear. "I was a closeted, bumbling kid, not nearly the mature sophisticate I am now, hard as that is to believe."

"Totally," said Ellen. *"Look at my Tank go! Go Tank go! Touchdown, Tank!"*

"We were in the middle of a very tense cheer practice, dissension among the ranks," said Bear. "We were taking a break for some reason. Donna, the black one, was thumbing through her photos. That's when I saw him! *Look at my Tank go! Go Daddy Tank! Go Daddy Tank!* Walter's the general. Tank's the major. This much is true, eh, generals and majors?"

"Walter used to *hate* that song in college, 'Generals and Majors'," said Ellen. Bear smiled a silly smile. If she were there, she'd know better.

"We love that song," said Bear. Did he accidentally say, *We?* Was there such a thing as accidents?

"What was to love about it?" scoffed Ellen.

Silly, light-hearted, new wave English rock that just made ya feel good cruising down the college corridors in the blur, the only way to fly.

"... always unhappy less they got a game ..." sang Bear.

Walt loves songs Ellen never did. This much is true, eh, QB?

"Thing is," said Bear, "that double reverse photo op ended up being my link to Walter, and his to mine. Imagine that, one or two pissant photos creating all this. Man, that is ... overwhelming."

"*You're* the one who sent *that* photo?" said Ellen. "I thought it was a UCLA cheergirl who sent it! I could tell that Walt was in love. He glowed looking at that picture! I thought he was in love with the girl in it, my friend."

Cool and dreamy flashback ... Walter and Ellen in Walter's football suite ... Ellen's all pissed that Walter is glowing and giggling at some photo of him and their mutual friend Cindy, the blonde Georgia cheergirl.

"That was the day I called it off!" said Ellen. "I knew he was in love but not with me. I thought it was my friend, the blonde Georgia cheergirl. My boyfriend was glowing because of the person who *sent* the pic? *Not* my friend? *This* is overwhelming, Bear Coleman. I got dumped for a photo and *the person wasn't even in it!* He just wanted the sender of the damned thing."

"*Or* he wanted the sender of the blessed thing," said Bear. "Take note, Bearcat People."

"I *made* him send the other photo," said Ellen, still astonished. "The photo of the big black male cheerleader—*ppffttff* ... you—and Harry Dawg, the one in my friend's camera, the bitch who I thought stole my man."

Cool and dreamy flashback ... Walter and Ellen in Ellen's dark lair ... Walter's all pissed that Ellen is glowing and giggling at something other than his golden aura. "Quit bothering me, Walt ... do something useful ... hey, take that photo ... the bitch roomie took it at the game the other week ... send it to that nig—, fa—, I mean, cheerguy. You know he's ga—he'll love it. He's glowing like he's in love with Harry Dawg. Give the poor bastard some hope and send him that pic."

"Just being as honest as I can," said Ellen.

"Either way," said Bear. "You helped give Walter and me a way back to one another. And I thought Grace was perfect. The joy life can bring, if ya see the light."

"Who told you that?" asked Ellen.

"Told me what?" asked Bear.

"Never mind," said Ellen, opting out of whatever was on that mind.

"You guys okay over there?" asked Walter, the strapping giant among the satellites playing touch football.

"Cool and dreamy," said Bear, then he said to Ellen: "You gave us a gift. I'd like to give you one."

"Not necessary," said Ellen.

"Not even one that's invisible and keeps on giving?" asked Bear.

"I don't know if I like the sound of that," laughed Ellen.

"Then I won't say anything about it," said Bear. "Only true Bearcat fans will know we kinda ran into each other at the Sugar Bowl, more or less."

"I'm getting lost here," said Ellen, scratching her dark hair. "God, Bearcats ... imagine what the media is doing about what *Walt Loves* now."

"We're taking it all back," said Bear.

"Walter ... your man has had too much sun over here," said Ellen.

"You doubt us?" laughed a cool and dreamy Bear. "You don't think we have the power to take it all back? Girl, have we taught you nothing yet? The Bearcat Boyz can do anything, this much is true."

"Why doesn't Walter get over here?" asked Ellen.

"He gets me," said a cool and dreamy Bear. "He understands the Bearcat Boyz can move mountains, and will. And take it all back!"

"How are you gonna retract everything you've said about the Bearcat?" asked Ellen.

Bear grew dizzy. Ellen was talking twisted now. Too twisted, even for Bear.

Take it all back? Yes, they were going to take it all back. Every single thing they created in the name of their love—they were going to take it back and recycle every single thing into joy, then give that joy to the world.

"Then it will be up to infallible God and all his fallible gods to decide what kind of light they want to cast on our world," said Bear. "But we'll be just cool and dreamy because we'll always be powered by our own suns, our own celestial bodies, our own iron core, perfectly balanced, just like we drew it up."

"You are losing me fast," said Ellen.

"Then I'll go slower," said Bear. "I know we're flying at warp speed now. Try not to sweat the details in the blur. When pilots fly, they have a very narrow focus. We gotta do the same, to make it easier to spread this joy to the world."

"*Ha!*" said Ellen. "That was one of Walter's most favorite songs as a boy growing up. He ever tell you that?"

"Not in so many words," said Bear.

Little league. Baseball. Golden black boys running in from centerfield. Golden white boys singing their favorite song in the dugout. His brother's team. He was just the Player To Be Named Later. Talk about a pussycat in a polar bear suit. Or was he a grizzly bear? Or a teddy bear? Or a cool cat? Or a tough cat?

"*Tigercat? Tigercats! The Tigercats!*"

"Bear, can you hear us?"

"Even better with less shouting," said Bear.

"They were worried," said Tank.

"Were you?" asked Bear, lounging in the end zone, or was it the outfield? Grass. His man and the satellites frolicking in the blur. His man's other boy was kneeling next to Bear. "Was Tank worried about the Bearcat?"

"Not really," said Tank.

"*Whew!*" said Bear. "When you start to worry about me, let me know. It might be my turn after that."

"Why were you just yelling *Tigercats!*" asked Tank.

"Because Walter's favorite song as a kid was 'Joy to the World'," said Bear. "He used to sing it with his golden boys in the dugout in little league, made him feel good in his soul, which wanted to spend a lifetime in the sunshine, on days like this, spreading the joy that is Walter. That's what Boy Walter wanted for the world: joy. This much is true."

"Did you guys know each other then?" asked Tank.

"One way or another, always and forever," said Bear. "The Tigercats were all about Joy to the World."

"Who were they?" asked Tank.

"The team of my boyhood storytelling dreams," said Bear. "This is kinda like breaking news to my mind, at least at this age. I forgot all about my Tigercats. I used to dream of writing stories when I was a kid, stories about great sports teams overcoming great odds to win the great games ... and the greatest game."

"What sport?" asked Tank.

"Life," said Bear.

"How do you play that?" asked Tank.

"You dream," said Bear.

"What games were you dreaming of?" asked Tank.

"Fuzzy fax," said Bear. "Hybrid maybe. Some basketball, some cheerleading, some young warriors bonding, long bombs, the football variety ... wasn't much for war games as kids ... *Stratego was cool, eh, Walter?*"

"You go, Tigercat!" yelled Walter in the distance.

"We favored games with balls, fields, and gamblers and gunslingers," said Bear, "and straight shooters like your father, the kind who sang on the benches in my little league dugout dreams. It was a joy just watching those boys sing 'Joy to the World.' Thanks, Walter, for loving that song. This much is joyfully true."

Tank smiled. Outta the mouths of kids.

"It's Called a Fuckin' reality sHiFt!" yelled Walter at the top of his lungs!

The minute you see yours in danger, nothing else matters, not the contract, the money, the house, the locker room, the cars, the bedroom—definitely not the closet. Only the beating heart. And the heart beating.

"The only true way to protect mine is to fight corrosion-free," said Walter. "That's why we're here, on this island, to get out the gunk, especially today."

"So it was Bear's near-death experience that freed up my brother's uptight ass? *About fucking time!" yelled Walter's Sister at the top of her lungs!*

"Back to work, little bitch of a sister," said Walter, hitting his female nemesis, or at least, dreaming of it as she headed for the dog park.

"Funny, how we love and *unlove* our sisters in equal measures," said Bear, hammock-bound on a lazy sunny blurry day. *"Unlove* is better than *hate."*

We can't begin to lessen the hate in the world until we begin to lessen our use of the word.

"*I hate that there's too much fucking sun today!" yelled Ellen at the top of her lungs!* She was passing in the blur somewhere behind the hammock.

"Case and point," said Bear, stretching skyward.

"You're fine hanging in the twilights," said Walter. "I'll be on the far side of the island, whipping some of your nigger brothers on the basketball court."

"Where does he get off?" giggled Bear as QB disappeared.

"Somewhere sugary and sweet for his Bear, no doubt," said Walter's Uncle, passing with a ton of bananas on his shoulder. "Wanna take a trip?"

"After Pittsburgh, I think I'm on a permanent one," giggled Bear, jumping on the banana cart, ready for a cool and dreamy ride. "Tank! Hop on. We're day-trippin'."

"Where to?" asked Tank, hopping on anyway.

"Somewhere sugary and sweet for our Walter, no doubt," said Bear, lying horizontal, relaxing and maxing to the sun's power, "and cool and dreamy. *I'm cool and dreamy from here on out!" yelled Bear at the top of his lungs!*

Tank laughed the laugh of a suppressed Boy Walter.

"That won't do," said Bear. "We can't have you suppressing your laugh." *Like another Yeager I once heard.* "When you laugh at my jokes, you have to *big laugh!* The classics anyway."

Tank's engine backfired smoke that was supposed to pass for ...

"You call that a laugh?" said Bear. "Uncle of Walter's, up in the front of the apple cart, did you just hear anything back here with us crazy bananas?"

"*Can't hear a blessed thing!" yelled Walter's Uncle at the top of his lungs!*

"See that?" said Bear. "Your laughter is a very blessed thing. He's two feet away, you laugh and he ain't heard shit!"

"*Ha!*" said Tank. *Big laugh!*

"Perfect! The eyes can pop out, too!" said Bear. "*He's multi-talented, Bearcat People!" yelled Bear at the top of his lungs!*

"All Bearcats are multi-talented," said Walter's Uncle. "Tigercats, too!"

Walter's Uncle was a grown-up Tigercat. This much is true.

"So these Tigercats ..." said Tank. "I'm still not sure I get them ... are they, like ... like, Bearcats?"

"Still working on the equation, Tank," said Bear. "Still dreaming the dream. Gimme a few. Anyone ever tell you: you ask a ton of questions, like me? Make no mistake, little man. Asking questions in life is a blessed thing. Hopefully, you learn to gravitate toward people who answer those questions with blessed

answers ... in the blur still over here ... feels like we're traveling down some long
dirty back road ... either way, it's cool ... you see, it's like this: I think I gotta get
Black and go into my soul to tell you this ... Tank ... keeper of our True Gold ar-
mor, this much is true ... heart! ... Tank: ... don't give me that *mild laugh* ... nah ...
fuck that. Don't *mild laugh* me. Get it outta ya fucking mind right now. Got it?"

"Got it. Fuck!" said a finally broken-down Tank! *"I'll laugh at Bear's fucking
jokes more, okay?" yelled Tank at the top of his lungs!*

"I'm gonna start early on yo' ass," said Bear. "I'm not gonna wait a couple
decades before I uncork yo' smile and wonderful soulful laugh ... *nothing dirty on
and on!" yelled Bear at the top of his lungs!*

"You sound like a rapper or something," laughed Tank. "Or that guy
Markus Kramer on the Indiana Pacers. You kinda look like him, too."

"He ain't got half of what Bear Coleman got. Bear Coleman'll kick Markus
Kramer's ass," said Bear Coleman. Tank was busy laughing, amazed to hear Bear
talking like a grizzly ghetto Bear. "Uncle of Walter's, up there in the apple cart,
can you hear us fools going bananas back here?"

*"Sounds like a lotta fucking fun to me!" yelled Walter's Uncle at the top of
his lungs!*

"See that?" said Bear to Tank. "He didn't damn us at all!"

"Ha!" said Tank.

"Perfect!" said Bear.

Like the father, I'll power the son's sun with truth and laughter.

"Uncle of Walter's, up there in the apple cart—" said Bear.

"What's up, Bear?" asked Walter's Uncle.

"I'm wondering what's the meaning of the word satellites," said Bear.

"Pieces of you, always attached one way or another," said Walter's Uncle.

"Good one," said Bear. "You realize, Uncle of *Walta,* in another world right
now, I'm the stupid nigger, riding in the back of a banana cart with Massa's boy,
while Massa's Uncle riding up front. Love my Massa, I do. Massa Norseman. You
realize that, don't you, Uncle of Walter and Tank of Walter?"

*"Today, more than ever, ya big fucking nigger!" yelled Walter's Uncle at the
top of his lungs!*

They arrived at the fuzzy dock. Walter's Uncle and Tank got out and sized
up the day's supplies hovering in nets hanging from the trees.

"Walter says you know about quantum mechanics," said Bear, still in the cart.

"Bananas!" said Tank, pointing to the trees.

"Or did I just dream that one up?" asked Bear.

"I can see 'em," said Walter's Uncle, indicating the trees.

"Yellow, brown, black and white," said Tank.

"Tank knows his stuff!" yelled a proud Walter's Uncle at the top of his lungs!

"Gimme some of dat!" pleaded Bear, fidgeting in the banana cart, thanks to a gust of wind.

"Options," said Walter's Uncle. "What do you think about the colors?"

The oldest one ... Grace's girls ... she was in the treehouse the other day, working on something for school ... Science textbook ... wow! ... dreaming different dreams than old school dreams ... dreams about strings and parallel dimensions, and life smaller than the atom.

"To other people, is dad a homo, or just a fag?" asked Tank. "Or just gay. Or what?"

It's always going to be the atom to me.

"What did your dad say?" asked Walter's Uncle.

"That he's none of those things," said Tank.

"Before you ever thought about your dad and those words in the same breath," said Walter's Uncle, "which of those words did you use to describe someone?"

That's what they told me it was, the atom.

"What do you mean?" asked Tank.

"You've heard words in school," said Walter's Uncle. "Men and boys get teased for being ... different ... acting certain ways that make people call them—"

"Fag," said Tank.

There's this thing, little boy, the smallest thing known to humanity: the atom.

Smaller than an atom.

Bigger than an atom.

Atom becomes the reference point.

"Fag was the first word I heard like that," said Tank.

There's this thing, little boy, the worst thing known to humanity: the fag.

Worse than a fag.

Better than a fag.

Fag becomes the reference point.

"My father is not a faaaaaag!" yelled Tank at the top of his lungs!

"Word is Born. Conception is Life. Life is Conception. Born with your Word," said Bear, still in the cart. The winds on the island went hurricane. Funny, all was still in perfect grace. *"Wow! We nigs got soul! Word is born! Please can I have some more of dat!" yelled Bear at the top of his lungs!*

"We had different words in my time," said Walter's Uncle, looking up at the bananas in bunches hanging from the trees.

"Everybody gets a time," said Bear. "Everybody gets they own world, too."

"Because things change," said Walter's Uncle. "The world is born anew daily. Gotta spruce up the definitions to reflect the new light shed on things."

"They start splitting up the words, or the atom, so to speak!" said Bear, yelling at the trees, wanting to scream *louder!*

"*Huh?*" asked Tank. *Mild laugh.*

"*The words nigger and fag aren't good enough anymore!*" *yelled Bear at the top of his lungs!*

"Today," said Walter's Uncle, "faggot and nigger better watch out. Nigger and faggot gonna get the shit kicked out of them by some real strong atoms."

"You tell 'em, you big fat nasty white man," said Bear.

Walter's Uncle suddenly became self-conscious of his somewhat husky (but very cute!) waistline. "Listen, here, nigger," said Walter's Uncle. "You're crossing the line with weight."

"Bear scoffed," said Bear.

"I'll kick your coon ass if you bring up weight again," said Walter's Uncle.

"*Like censorship has ever stopped a single fucking thought!*" *yelled Bear at the top of his lungs!*

"Yeah, right," said Black Coach, passing in the blur. "That's like us pissant humans telling God what and what not to think about, say, do, who to fuck, etcetera, on and on, dirty in, dirty out. *I'd kill all y'all honkies, if given half the chance!*" *yelled Black Coach at the top of his lungs!*

"*You black people act like you're not grateful to be born in America!*" *yelled the distance voice of a Yeager relative at the top of her lungs!*

"I'm betting little Bear wants to play the word game with the other darkies near the treehouse," said Walter's Uncle.

Lord knows why! God, I love being black again. All four sides of me.

"Found my soul, Walter," said Bear. "Lost my fear, found my soul. Perfect pretty picture."

"He sounds pretty cool," said Tank, riding up front with the cool white uncle ... *on the dirty back road again.*

"Let's create a world!" said Bear. "Come on, niggas gotta have fun riding in the sun in the apple cart, otherwise we'll go bananas. *And trust me, white people, be careful what you say around a crazy fuckin' nigga!*" *yelled Bear at the top of his lungs!*

"What kind of world you building?" asked Walter's Uncle from up front.

"A world born with the word ... *nigger!*" yelled Bear to the heavens. "I cannot come back to the table without bringing my soul. Can I have a banana, too?"

"Ah, the classics," said Walter's Uncle. "Black nigger bitch mother. White cracker Euro dad."

"And on the flip side of the mirror," said Bear. "Mandingo prototypes and all those white women who wanted me in college! Why couldn't Walter and I have gone to the same school? Talk about Dreamville!"

"Ah, quit your whining, you Super nigger," said Walter's Uncle.

There's this thing, *little boy, the opposite* thing *known to humanity:* the nigger.

Worse than a nigger.

Better than a nigger.

Nigger becomes the reference point.

"We didn't kidnap, rape, rob, steal, whip, castrate, lynch, or *treat him like a nigger* or nothin', Pa, it was just good ole Saturday Night Fun!" said Tank.

"I told you he had it in him!" said Bear. "Tank, the stud!"

"Makes an *oncle* proud," said Walter's Uncle.

"The atom game!" said Bear, "aka the Word is Born game."

The cart stopped, *short ride.* Tank, Uncle ... split ...

"It's easy," said Walter's Bro to someone beyond Bear's blurry vision, "easy even for dumb-ass niggas like y'all. What word you wanna start with?"

"Fag, we invented this shit," said Stefan, defending niggas everywhere.

"Nigger!" cried Bear. "Let's do the word nigger!"

Walter carried Bear up to the treehouse. That way, Massa and his nigga boy could hang up in the skies, be alone, get sticky, let the plantation carry on without them.

"*Leave my nigga ass alone with my fine, honkey, NFL Massa for some zone time!*" yelled Bear at the top of his lungs!

"*Shh ...*" laughed Walter. "I wanna hear all the crackers and coons talking down below while I do what I'm gonna do with your nigger ass."

"Just give it to me like I need it, you crazy white quarterback," giggled Bear. "While you're at it, sweet baby, can you explain the atom game to this crazy-ass nigga again? And part those nigga ... *yes!*"

"He's a fag," said Walter's Bro in the swirl below, starting the game with Stefan's chosen word. Both Yeager brothers continued with their examples for the atom game, one on high, one on low.

He's a fag.

He's not like that.

He's better than a fag.

He's an okay fag.

He's a cool fag.

He's a decent fag.

He's a safe fag.

"And you keep splitting the atom, coming up with as many different kinds of fags as you can conceive of," said Walter's Bro in the swirl below. "Then, when you're done creating fags, and feel like calling them something more humane than *fags*, you figure out a new and improved name for fags. Like, *gay*."

"Wait," said Stefan. "What the fuck you talking about, punk?"

"Listen good, Buckwheat," said Walter's Bro in the swirl below. "You had a year or two at a JC, didn't you?"

"Don't make me come down off this tree and bust a move on yo' cracker, honkey, fag ass, Brother of Massa," said Bear. "Hey, how come whites don't have a real derogatory epithet, like us niggers, spics, and gooks? No fair!"

"Tell me about it, you crazy fucking Bear," said Walter.

Start with a simple word, like, fag.

Boom.

Word is Born (Born is World)

Fag.

A world is born. A world in which fags exist.

Someone has given birth to the concept of fags.

Fags now exist. In your world.

Welcome to your world.

Welcome home.

"He's not even a fag like the rest of them ... he's just happy all the time," said Walter, his nose crinkled from the smell of "all this nigger funk! All over the island all week! *Never in my life have I inhaled so much nigger funk!*" yelled Walter at the top of his lungs!

"*Not including France!*" yelled Bear at the top of his lungs!

"He's not even a fag really," said Walter's Bro in the swirl below. "He's just like us, only ... carefree and ... gay."

Boom.

Word is Born (Born is World)

Gay.

A world is born. A world in which gays exist.

Someone has given birth to the concept of gays.

Fags *and* gays now exist in your world.

Welcome to your whole new world.

Welcome home again.

Fags begat gays, this much is true.

And all those born in the new world are presented with a whole new atom.

Gay.

Worse than gay.

Better than gay.

Gay becomes the reference point.

Correction!

Gay becomes a *reference point.*

Now the world has options for what kind of fag you can be.

Worst One.

Not the Worst One.

New World, Version 2!

He's a fag. (Still the very worst. Carryover! OG rules!)

He's not like *that.* Fags are those disgusting *fags* from the old world. The *worst* thing a man could be. Things have changed. Fags today aren't as bad. Some fags aren't so faggy. They're just ... gay!

Because somebody dreamed a better dream. Somebody said: I don't want to be the worst thing on the planet anymore. I can't be the worst. There's no way I can be the worst thing known to mankind, especially to real men, the true warriors.

"Worst," said Walter's Bro in the swirl below. "Opposite everything good and holy. Against all the wishes of your family. Completely unwelcome in the sports world that would rather welcome the less worse: wife killers, to get right to the bottom of the list."

"Worst," said Bear. "Fag. Word was born before any of us brothers had a chance to born a word for ourselves."

So this fag was damned. Worst. That much was true.

"But," said Bear, "instead of dying, burying, hiding, fearing, running from, fighting, trying to surgically remove, medicate, extricate, evaluate, placate, demonstrate, configurate, eliminate and *elimidate* that atom ... oh, wait, sorry, we did try all those things ... nothing worked. The fag atom was still alive and well."

I, God, which begat

I, god

Was now the worst.

"You die—literally or figuratively—or dream a better dream," said Walter.

I can do better than worst.

I can be something other than the worst thing known to man.

I may not be the best. Or second best. Or third. Or fourth or fifth.

But I don't have to be the worst.

I can do better than worst.

I gotta do better.

I won't be as bad as worst.

I won't be a fag.

I'll just be ... gay.

"Go homos! Go homos!" said Bear.

"You are one crazy fucking nigger faggot I could—" began Walter.

"Stop right there," said Bear. "You just created something. Your powers are amazing. You just gave the fags a nickname."

The faggots!

"Anything with a nickname can't be *all that bad,* right? Enough to call it the worst?" said Stefan in the swirl down below.

"That nigga ain't no fool!" yelled Bear at the top of his lungs!

"Now, the fags got two hopes for a better dream," said Stefan. "Stay a fag, or be a faggot, a different kind of fag with a cute little nickname."

"Or upgrade to the new school word, gay, and be whatever the fuck that means," said Grayson, swirling by like a squirrelly squirrel, tree hoppin' he was.

"That nigga ain't no fool, either! Listen to my bruthas, y'all crazy fucking selfish white bastards!" yelled Bear at the top of his lungs!

He's not like that.

He's better than gay.

He's an okay gay guy.

He's a cool gay guy.

He's a decent gay guy.

He's a safe gay guy.

He's not even gay, like the rest of them. He's just like us, just ... currently holding up at gay.

"I love your uncle's game," said Bear, lying on the treehouse floor, half-asleep in his cool and dreamy head.

"It's the aunt's game, but you know that," said Walter, getting laughter outta his Bear.

"Why can't you niggers get over what happened in the past?" yelled the distant voice of a Yeager cousin.

"If I had a dime for every time a honkey wanted to talk about my big black dick!" yelled the distant voice of a Coleman cousin.

"What word, excuse me, *world,* should we create this time?" asked Walter's Bro in the swirl down below.

"Please, please, can we do nigger now?" cried Bear in the treehouse. "I really, really need to do some nigger. Been a while."

"Nigger is one of the best words to play with," said Walter in the treehouse.

"Walter, you haven't played this game in years," said Walter's Uncle, climbing up and bringing Bear his coma pills. "At least not with us."

"Why didn't we play the Word is Born game in France?" whined Bear. Laughter in the treehouse. They remembered, Bear didn't ... *typical of their fuzzy black boy.*

"I asked my boy," said Walter. *Which one?* "Bear. Years ago, we were talking about that summer, and I said, 'So, Bear, it never bothered you that my aunt and uncle were, like, naked 24/7 on the ship?' Bear was like ... *'Say what?'*"

"It's a miracle he remembers our faces at all, or any other body part for that matter," said Walter's Uncle, "considering he couldn't keep his eyes off your handsome blond aura."

They roared, black and white, down below, up above. Somebody had game.

"A boat. France. Two weeks with my Blond Stud," said Bear, shocking the shit out of Walter and his Uncle, who assumed Bear had fallen asleep. "On top of that, QB and I were just getting to all that *Sugar* for the very first time ... *big moans of nostalgic approval from the treehouse* ... now, Bearcat People, from where I was standing in France, I saw all the paradise I'll ever need, always and forever. Any questions? Now can we do some nigger?"

I could live the rest of my life, content to only lay eyes on two more naked bodies, yours and mine. I can't see either one right now, and couldn't care less how either one looks.

"He's not a nigger!" said Walter's Bro in the swirl below.

"Your brother is so impatient," laughed Bear.

"Wait!" Walter's Uncle jumped from the treehouse to save the game in progress. "You have to start a new game right."

"Boom. Word is born," said Walter's Bro, starting it right.

He's a nigger.

He's not like that.

He's better than a nigger.

He's an okay nigger.

"This is too easy," said Walter's Bro, swirling below.

"That's because you've been playing with niggers all your life," said Bear, "balling with 'em back in the day, just like QB. But you know I love you, bro's bro.

Those niggers helped desensitize you and my man to my needs. Thanks, bros. Let's reverse it. How do you reverse the word game again? *Fuzzy brain.*"

"The nigger atom splits into two," said Walter in the treehouse. "It's been years since we played this."

The Yeagers in their own version of Hyannis Port, Orange County, America, playing crazy Uncle Walter's atom game, aka the Word is Born game. By the time their vacations were over, nobody had any secrets about how they felt about certain words, clearing up the confusion on the road of life.

"Nigger," said Bear in the treehouse in the sky. "The original dream for those *things* coming off the ships."

"Niggers," said Walter's Bro in the swirl below. "Niggers were the first people to split the atom. Because they conceived of being something other than niggers. To dream of a better life, they had to dream up a better name to call themselves."

Niggers begat niggas.

Two of a kind.

"Go niggers! Go niggas!" said Bear. "And some whites actually liked niggers *and* niggas! Miracle of miracles."

"Bigger miracle, y'all didn't slit all our throats," said Walter.

"We've giving you One More Try first!" yelled Bear at the top of his lungs!

"So they dreamed up another name for niggers," said Walter's Bro in the swirl below. "A name they could use in *both* the blessed and cursed sense, to be duplicitous about their intentions."

"Since the way you feel about niggers in America has always been one *hella* dangerous game," said Stefan in the swirl.

And whites begat a new dream as well.

"Yeah, but he's a good nigger," muttered Walter's muffled lips.

"Reality shift!" said Walter's Aunt, swooping down like a hawk into the swirl.

"There now exists good niggers," said Bear, like a PA announcer. "We now have official confirmation of the existence of good niggers. This just in: niggers can be good after all!"

"What a great fucking dream come true!" said Walter.

"And some on both sides agreed," said Walter's Bro in the swirl below.

Perfect grace.

"The nigger atom," said Walter's Bro, "which began as one, split again. This time on the Northside. Whites begat good niggers."

"Thanks, cracker with the gorgeous face," said Bear. "I'd like to be a good nigger for you on occasion. *Hmmm, there's a dream.* Oops! I think it's just been begat! Hey, now I get it: the worse thing you can call a white man is a *fag!*"

"Crazy fucking Bear," said Walter.

"*Beli've dat,*" said crazy fucking Bear. "Gone get crazier, honkey ... *watch!*"

"So now we got: niggers ... good niggers ... *and* niggas ..." said Walter's Bro in the swirl below.

"But the niggas needed a duplicate, too!" said Bear. "We needed a way to survive in y'alls bloody white world. For some of us, *for some reason,* swimming with the sharks wasn't an option. Some of us fools actually dreamed of some kind of livable life wherever the hell we were going."

"The niggers who landed safely in America," said Walter's Bro. "They had already dreamed one better dream (no drowning, try whelming). Once they had their soles afoot, some niggers had the audacity to start dreaming other dreams, from surviving, to running away, to going back, to making the best of it, to taking it day by day by day by year by century, thinking ..."

"There has got to be a better mutha-fucking way than this shit!" said Bear. "God did not put me on this earth to be under anybody's soles unless it's my choice! Meister ... *back rub, si'l vous plait ... ah, gracias.*"

"Niggers," said Walter's Bro in the swirl below, "and those who loved them started dreaming of a better life."

"Ain't no stopping nigs now," sang Bear from above.

"But they had to dream of themselves as something other than Niggers, their new atomic identity in the US," said Walter's Bro ... swirling!

New Dream: Your ass being called something other than a nigger.

But what? Can't call yourself something that's gonna get your nigger ass lynched!

"Listen up, Kunta Kinte Koleman!" said Bear to the heavens beyond the treehouse. "A few hundred years from now, your seed is gonna Kunta Kaboom into this little nigger right here, up here in this treehouse! And I'm gonna be a little nigger with big dreams! Don't kill me off by jumping into that Atlantic just 'cause some white man from the North is dragging your ass across the seas! Didn't you always want to go around the world? Get away from home? See the universe? Be all you can be? Bust a move? Guess what, Kunta? We gone bust a move on this American shit, *aiight!* We gone excel in games your tired, worn and beaten down black ass ain't even thought of yet! Whitey ain't even got a clue! Walter's dumb-ass relatives—the ones hauling you over here—they don't know shit, either. Ain't got no idea what either one of their magnificent 20th-century creations gone do for the world, in the name of healing both sides of the Atlantic, always and forever."

"Our deepest dream, eh, buddy boy?" asked Walter.

"True Gold, buddy boy," said Bear. "So you see, tired black soul looking off the side of that slave ship, or trying to will yourself dead on a hot Georgia night ... Guess what a nigger as dark as your ass is gonna do with a ball someday, and a bat, and a book, and a microscope, and a college degree, and a white blond soul mate. We play games now even *dem crackas* of y'all's day ain't even dreamt up yet. You wanna cut our balls off now, nigger? Get yo' ass up off that ground, clean off that blood and sweat and dry them tears. Find a way to keep going, brother man, because I need you, my soul needs ... your soul to keep going."

Dream of a way to keep your ass alive.

Keep your ass alive by dreaming.

Guess what little nigger boy is gonna tell all our stories, Bearcats!

"Hold on, Kunta," said Walter, maybe because the treehouse was rocking. "Be strong, be gentle, be you, but don't give up."

I need your cum. Your cum is gonna lead to my cream.

I'm just dreaming off your dreams, brothers and sisters.

Don't jump in that Atlantic. I got dreams in the Pacific.

I need you. I need everybody who exists between you and me, and in reverse, for all time, always and forever.

"So come up with another dream, Marcus Kunta 'Bear' Koleman Kinte," said Bear. "The African thing is dead (for you, for now). You are now reborn a nigger in the good ole USA. But take heart: all kinds of niggas and crackas in your day are gonna dream better dreams, dreams that ask: is it right to enslave any person and their dreams? Americans are gonna do some crazy shit, like take over the entire world between Philly and dem mountains way out West. Who knows, they might even try to take over the whole world someday."

"Not the niggas. We's always gone be niggas in this country." The gruff voice of Stefan Coleman!

Boom. Concept is Born.

"What else can you be?" asked Walter's Aunt from the swirl.

A down-low nigga, so the man don't fuck with me too much.

A cool nigga, so my niggas don't fuck with me too much.

"Niggas begat more niggas, with new atoms inside they atoms." Let's hear it for Grayson Coleman, power forward for the blacks!

"Whites and blacks played with the sides of a nigga for a lotta years," said Walter's Bro in the swirl below. "Nigger. Good nigger. Nigga."

"Where's the fourth part?" asked Grayson.

"Indeed!" said the Bear in the treehouse. "He went missing, undercover, *really down low.*"

"Meanwhile," said Walter's Bro in the swirl below, "all those new niggas with new identities—cool nigga, together nigga, proper nigga, etcetera—started dreaming new dreams and needed new names."

"I'm no nigga! I'm somebody!" yelled Bear to the heavens. "I'm gonna dream of being colored, then a Negro, then black, then African-American!"

"But how?" asked Stefan, role-playing like it was 1899. "I can't call myself something that's gonna get my ass killed. I gotta come up with a new name *slash* dream *slash* life."

"I am Negro, hear me roar!" yelled Bear to the heavens.

Word *slash* dream *slash* atom *slash* whole new world is born.

Good Negro. Bad Negro.

The atom just keeps splitting into two. And two. And two.

And on the polar opposite side of the universe. Ditto.

And on the polar opposite poles of the planet. Ditto.

Perfect grace, always and forever.

There's four of us, four-part harmony to every single thing.

"How else in the world do you explain Walter and me having the perfect people in our lives who helped make us exactly perfect for each other?" Bear climbed from the floor of the treehouse and looked down below.

"Perfect grace," said Walter, arm around his bud.

"Boom. Word is born," said Bear.

"That's two words," said Walter.

"Addition to the family," said Bear. "Besides, our atom, that original one ... the original word that bore you and me ... *God.*"

"What came after that word?" asked Walter. "What did God begat?"

"The name of our magnet," said Bear. "True Gold."

There must be one just like me.

Boom. Word is Born.

Word? What word?

Exactly.

"Oh, Bear, sorry we didn't get to the quantum leap," said Walter's Uncle, back up in the treehouse with more coma pills.

"Words are a way to describe feelings," said Walter's Bro, climbing up, leaving Bear's bros, who swirled off with Walter's Aunt for some Yeager-meister.

"Every atom has four basic energies," said Walter's Uncle.

"Good, bad, half-good and half-bad," said Walter's Bro.

"Feelings," said Walter's Uncle. "Another word for energy."

"Feelings are at the genesis of all energy."

"Energy is at the genesis of all creation."

"Life is creation. Life begins with feelings and energy."

In fact, that is the original Word is Born game.

Life begat feelings and energies, each with two sides.

Blessed and cursed.

Perfect grace. That is all there is.

"Walter Yeager was right," sighed Bear, alone again in the treehouse with his quarterback. "I'm glad I deleted the whole OJ Trial Review from the camp activities schedule. Today was so much more fun than having a *frank and honest discussion about race in America.*"

Just then, Tank came running up, petrified. "Dad! Bear! You won't believe *this!*" He lumbered up the tree with a big ole sign. "Look what I found facedown in the lagoon! It must have fallen after Bear and me painted it this morning."

"It's totally faded!" said an astonished Bear of the sign.

"And it was in the lagoon all this time?" asked an astonished Walter.

"In the water!" said Tank. "Facedown!"

"*No one* got the memo, so to speak?" asked Bear.

"*This* was the memo my sister was looking for this morning?" asked Walter. "Your painted sign, which isn't painted anymore? What did it say?"

"I told her this morning: *show everyone the memo in the lagoon!*" said Bear.

"She came to me, said she never found it," said Walter. "What did it say?"

"About talking about race relations today," said Bear. "As per my activities schedule."

"What did it say?" asked Walter.

"So nobody saw my memo?" asked Bear.

"How did we make it through the day?" asked Walter. "What did it say?"

"Only today's guidelines," said a disappointed Bear.

"Everything went great!" insisted Walter. "Didn't it, Tank?"

"It was the funnest day so far," said Tank. *Mild laugh.*

"You think everyone had as much fun?" asked a worried Bear. "Seeing as how, the only thing I told the Yeagers was: *say whatever's on your mind about black people today.*"

"Looks to me like everybody had a good time," said Walter, "eh, Tank?"

"I think people had a blast," said Tank. *Big laugh.*

"I'm sold on that gold," said Bear. "Still ... would have been nice had everyone gotten the memo, so to speak. All the Colemans heard me say was: *say whatever's on your mind about white people today.*"

"A detail now, Bear, let it go." Walter flung the sign out of the treehouse like a giant Frisbee. The flat piece of wood landed near the shore. Miracle of miracles, the seawater—special for the afternoon—repainted the sign. Of course, it was too late to save the day in this universe.

GUIDELINES FOR RACE RELATIONS DAY

-Blacks and Whites only. In the interest of time, we need to focus. All others: have fun on your deep-sea excursion ... (day long).

-All those remaining on the island today *must* call someone of the polar opposite race a derogatory racial epithet every 30 minutes, all day long.

-Non-compliers will be asked to leave the island via a different kind of deep-sea experience ... (no ice cream).

-Please do *not* call anyone *any* derogatory racial name *not* born in America, Mayflower to OJ. Again, focus!

-Race dissing only please. Keep your other issues at home where you left them.

FOOTNOTE: The afternoon's Curse and Shout Verbal Aerobics for the Iron Core Within Us All continues as regularly scheduled today ... and daily.

FOOTNOTE 2: Clothing Optional Hours continue as scheduled ... daily. All races: remember the sunscreen!

"SO, IF YOU'RE READY," SAID Walter's Sister, reading from the small card. "Cut to ... *read this too, Bear?* Cut to ... the ... 'Last Day of Hibernation, Super Bowl Champs' Cool and Dreamy Pep Rally *Slash* Talent Show.' Special thanks to Walter's Uncle, who designed the Gilligan's Island stage with the help of Walter and the Coleman brothers ... all much closer now, for some blessed reason."

"*2 Legit 2 Quit!*"

"Kids!" shouted Walter's Sister. She slipped backstage, waving a bunch of children onward. Their song had already started.

"*We Will Rock You* slash *We Are the Champions!*"

... featuring the littlest of satellites, looking so cute and outta step ... *and already lagging behind in this montage.*

"Ladies!" shouted Walter's Sister. She was backstage, waving a bunch of Yeager and Coleman wives onward. Their song was half over.

"Man, I Feel Like a Woman!"

... featuring the women who lived their men's dreams, looking so happy to be living their own dreams for a change. They shook their rump shakers and milk makers ... *everything functioning just fine.*

"You guys never finish the song," complained Mr. Yeager as the women descended the stage.

"Neither do the Sea Gals," said Mrs. Yeager.

"Girlfriend!" shouted Walter's Sister. She waved her soul sista Evangeline onward to the stage. Her song was only beginning.

"Simply the Best!"

... featuring Bear's sister as Tina Turner, mini-skirt, wig and all, looking just as glittery and golden.

"Milli & Vanilli!" shouted Walter's Sister. She pushed the duo onward to the stage. Their song was just about to blast off.

"Blame It On the Rain!"

... featuring Wendy Jiu and Lisa Wu, sporting the costumes like the good sports they were, looking *real* pretty—dare one say—with a hint of something quite revealing in Lisa Wu or Wendy Jiu.

The lesbo cheergirls were dancing like the fake singing duo, but dressed like the real dynamic duo, Yeager and Coleman. The *Rain* song was an ode to a wet and messy win in Chicago sometime in the blur. One was dressed as the quarterback, the other, like his Bearcat.

Lisa Wu or Wendy Jiu was in a bear suit, dancing as if on air, as if remembering some other time a bear danced over the skies of Chicago ... *perfect, pretty picture.*

"Tank!" shouted Walter's Sister, rolling her nephew onward. No song. He got jokes.

"My impression of my dad's buddy, Bear Coleman: 'He gets me.'"

And couldn't be more grateful for your existence, thought Bear.

Boom.

Son is Born.

This much is true.

In our darkest hour.

Comet ...

Coming ...

Come ...

Here ...

... featuring Hip, running across the meadow with a thousand other dogs, tongues lapping at the ocean, which happened to be seawater-safe that day.

Timing is everything in a cool and dreamy world.

"A columnist once called Walter Yeager a hero made of ice cream," said Bear, onstage to conclude the rally. "That columnist was right. After all, ice cream is the most cool and dreamy creation the world has ever invented. What soothes you when you've had a hard day? A bad date? A loss? A win? A tie? What brings such tasty frozen warmth to your senses, your soul, your dreams? What has the potential to come in so many flavors—all you need is your imagination? What feels good on a hot summer day? With your favorite movie? Reading in bed? On your birthday? While dreaming? Ice cream, especially when it comes with heroes like our favorite quarterback, on and off the field. That columnist was right to call Walter Yeager a hero made of ice cream. I can't imagine doing without either cool and dreamy gift from God. And from where I'm standing, that makes Walter Yeager the best kind of hero there is. This much is cool, dreamy and oh, so true."

Walter joined Bear onstage for a brief signoff. "Thank you, everyone for—"

"Is he his wife?" asked a voice from nowhere.

"Is he *his* wife?" asked a voice from nowhere.

"Ex-squeeze me?" asked Bear, using his professional UCLA ambassador voice.

"Ex-squeeze me?" asked Walter at the exact same time, using his professional NFL ambassador voice.

"Is he your wife?"

"Is he *your* wife?"

The press conference was coming from the front row, where a half dozen very young and inquiring minds had a question. *Or two.*

50,000 Yeagers, Colemans, etc, ceased pepping and rallying. Ask questions, get answers. Early rule in the game of life. If the 50,000 adults won't answer, a little satellite shall lead them.

"No silly, he's *his* boyfriend," said another young voice. "Buddyboyfriend."

"Manbuddy!" said a younger voice, trying to correct them both.

"Buddyman," said an older voice ... *still quite young.*

"Wifeyman," said a still younger voice ... *toddler.* "Manwife."

"Manywifeyman," said a still younger voice ... *barely able to speak.*

Adults started to combust for the first time in 29 days.

A bunch of little satellites were about to steel—*er, steal*—the show. Their comet of a question out of nowhere was spiraling toward Earth, downward into some silly willy nilly hole, leading to the creation of a brand new, newfangled silly willy nilly atom that was about to give birth to God knows what!

And God knew better.

"He's my Bearcat!" Walter and Bear rushed to say together.

Boom.

Welcome to *our* world.

26

Story Meeting

The best lie the boys ever told the world was the last lie the boys ever told the world: the incorrect date for their arrival home. The particular afternoon they drove up to their gated community in Malibu, there were no more than the usual handful of reporters and tourists gathered at the entrance on any given day, hopeful of a passing glimpse of some of the big dreamers beyond the gates.

Nothing the old "commercial van trick" couldn't solve.

Roberto the Celibate had become quite handy as their personal assistant, especially when it came to clandestine activities, such as traveling in the blur. Operation Re-entry worked like a dream. Roberto beamed proudly, driving the van past the main gate.

"Roberto, my man," said Bear from the backseat. "You've been so good at granting us complete silence since the airport, hasn't he, QB?"

"Only way to decompress," said Walter from the backseat, squeezing Bear's hand, stroking Hip's head. "You da man, Roberto."

"So, Roberto," said Bear, "is there anything you wish to tell us—keeping in mind our request for all communication from here to eternity?"

"Everyone in both of your contact files got the memo, including myself." Roberto reached into his briefcase on the front passenger seat and retrieved a copy. After handing it to Bear, Roberto recited the first paragraph verbatim:

Unless life and death hang in the balance, Walter Yeager
and Bear Coleman choose to speak of, and hear of, only
the positive energy the world creates as a result of Walter
and Bear being honest about their love for one another.

"The union of Walt and the Bearcat is a union of love," continued Bear,
reading aloud. "I mean, guys, anyone still caught up on the whole *Walt/Walter*
detail at this point is just plain whack, right?"

"Keep going," said Walter.

"If you speak of our union," continued Bear, reading aloud, "be aware that
you are speaking in the name of that which is love, and that whatever energy you
spend talking about or thinking about that love will only be put *on top of* that
love, but can never replace, diminish or depreciate that love. Our bond is eternal
and unconditional. Our love is who we are. So know this much is true: love us,
hate us, feel nothing, feel everything, feel anything, no matter. We only wish you
as much love as we know."

"We are love," read Walter as the van pulled into the driveway. "Bring only
love, receive only love. Dream only loving dreams with us."

"Doesn't he have a way with my words?" asked Bear, pinching his man on
the cheek.

"*Ouch!*" cried Walter. "You don't know your own strength."

"Trying our best to find out," said Bear.

"You're like a bull sometimes." Walter got out. "But you're my bull."

"I'm not changing animals this late in the game," said Bear, getting out.

"Speaking of bulls," said Roberto, rolling down the front passenger window. "It's funny you should mention that. That's the one thing I wanted to tell
you. The new landscaper guy has done a great job with the sides of the house. He
looks Brazilian, with his incredible looks and great dark skin. Said something
about being a bullfighter."

"What kind of bull does he fight?" asked Walter, getting their bags.

"Live ones, I guess," shrugged Roberto. "Go see for yourself. He's here now,
in the backyard."

Bear's head turned toward his man quicker than Hip's head when someone
utters the word *treat!* And he was salivating just as much. Walter let out a mild
laugh and shook his head at the panting tongue before him, then QB said, "I'm
going inside to use that thing—what's it called?—oh, yeah: telephone. You go
right ahead and get a whiff of the new bullfighter. Just make sure you wipe your
nose before you enter *my* house again. Here, pup, come on."

Roberto and the van vanished from the driveway and Walter and Hip disappeared into the house, leaving one curious Bear to his own devices. He began circumnavigating Moose Jaw. The property surrounding the beach house was quite extensive. Until now, the boys had never paid much attention to the front and the sides of their home. To dream a better dream, they had Roberto hire a landscaper to beautify the property.

Apparently, the landscaper started with stone circles, which formed a winding path through a series of gardens that transformed the south side of Moose Jaw into a breathtaking wonder. So beholden was Bear, he didn't even look up to see the ocean in the distance. He stared at the stone circles, mesmerized by their snake-like path through the gardens. Instinctively, he moved toward the sea, but his eyes couldn't leave the stone circles. Each circle was full of smaller stones, held together by some sort of epoxy. Bear orbited around the stone circles in a daze, unsure why.

"Stay on the path," said a voice from nowhere.

Bear turned toward the sea. He was on a downslope, and even so, the hard bronzed body a short distance away towered over his world. His hair was slicked back and wet, his shoulders glistening with sweat, which also drenched his thin white tank top. His jaw was chiseled, his face ageless, his eyes black as coal.

If this man were a bullfighter, Bear pitied the bull.

"Stay on the path," repeated the landscaper. Bear's paws were on the grass, not the stone circles.

"I was just admiring your work," said Bear. "I live here. Bear Coleman."

"The paths laid down in life are like agreed-upon contracts with the world," said the landscaper. Just then, Hip came charging toward them from the backyard, barking at the scent of a stranger. Then, in true Hip fashion, he started wagging his tail and begging the bullfighter for some lovin' in the form of a backrub. "Stay on the path, unless and until it is absolutely necessary to change," said the landscaper, bending to grant Hip his wish.

"I don't understand," said Bear.

"How many streets do you think there are in the world?" asked the landscaper.

"Millions," scoffed Bear. "Countless."

"Every single street has an agreed-upon path with agreed-upon rules," said the landscaper. "If every single human on every single street, road and highway in the world followed those agreed-upon rules, what would happen? Would those paths be orderly or disorderly?"

"Orderly," shrugged Bear.

"What happens when people don't follow the rules of the road?" asked the landscaper. "Say, when they take shortcuts."

"Chaos," said Bear.

"Now, imagine one person taking one shortcut not part of the agreed-upon rules," said the landscaper. "A quick left turn when they're not supposed to. A U-turn when they're not supposed to. Going too fast when they're not supposed to. Jaywalking when they're not supposed to. What if every single person in the world took one shortcut a day? How many shortcuts on the roads of life is that in this world every single day? And how much chaos does every single one of those shortcuts cause?"

The landscaper finished petting Hip and stood up.

"I was just admiring your work," said Bear, studying the lines on the man's gorgeous face.

"I was just hurrying to get to the store before it closed," said the landscaper. "I was just looking into the backseat at the kids for two seconds. I was just going three blocks without my seat belt. I was just ..."

"I wasn't driving," said Bear. "I was just ..." He stopped. Most of his life, he would have argued. For once, he surrendered. "So how did we get here?"

"That's an awfully big question," said the landscaper. "Where do you want me to start?"

Bear laughed. "I mean, why are you telling me all this?"

"So you know my philosophy when it comes to creating the world outside your home," said the landscaper.

"You're going to put streets in the yard?" asked Bear. "Just kidding."

"Look out at the ocean, please, if you will." The landscaper turned to the Pacific. "See all that blue and all that sky? That's not all that's there. If you put on God's special glasses and see what things really look like, you'd see a whole different world. You'd see a world of an infinite number of meridians—lines of energy—going in all directions, which result in dimensions we can barely wrap our minds around. How many is humankind up to now? A couple of dimensions? Anyway. The number is a detail. I'm not a detail person."

"Cool, neither are we," said Bear, thinking: *this guy might be a gift!*

"If you could see all the dimensions," said the landscaper, "you'd see a world of all kinds of celestial roads, highways, byways, pathways, ways—ways for energy to get from one destination to another."

"I'm getting lost here," said Bear.

"Imagine a *dot* that is a tiny, microscopic part of you deep inside," said the landscaper. "We'll call that your own individual soul. Now imagine those meridians traveling outward from that *dot,* traveling like a sunburst in every direction to the farthest reaches of the universe. You and *all this* exists just like that. That's what God sees. One huge superhighway of meridians spanning the universe, exchanging energy back and forth in a constant, never-ending flow, a connected web with no beginning, middle or end, no central authority, no one word is God, except the word God. From what I hear, humanity has finally dreamed up its own version of God, made a web."

"Sounds like a traffic nightmare," said Bear.

"If every single thing in the universe keeps taking shortcuts, it is," said the landscaper. "When everyone stays in line, so to speak, there's perfect grace."

"So we should never step out of line?" asked Bear. "Always follow the agreed-upon rules, just because they're the agreed-upon rules? What about the rules you don't agree with?"

"You have a choice," said the landscaper. "Follow the rule, break the rule. Everything you do in life, you have a choice. Example. Rule: breathe in, breathe out. No one says you have to. It's your choice. You can break the rule if you'd like. Go ahead, try it. See if that makes you feel good. You have that same choice about every *thing* in life, from choosing to breathe to choosing how you breathe and how you feel about how you breathe. It's all energy. Life is nothing but a constant exchange of energy between the meridians on a web. It's up to you how you inhale energy into your world, your soul, your dot, and how you exhale that very same energy through all those meridians emanating from your dot, your soul, your world. It's very similar to recycling."

"Recycling?" asked Bear.

"You take the energy that comes into your life," said the landscaper, "and you put it back out into the world, just like a soda can. The soda can is energy. You inhale a soda and all its contents into your world. When you're done with the can, you put it back out into the world, one way or another. You have a choice: you can put it back out into the world as trash on the beach, further desecrating your surroundings, or you can put it back out into the world as energy that can be used to further enhance your surroundings. You make that same choice with every single bit of energy you expend every day, with cans, words, thoughts, actions. The question is not *if* you recycle. Rather: what are you recycling this very moment?"

"You must be recycling brilliance," said Bear, mesmerized and befuddled. "And I'd like to talk more, but my ... do you know who ... I need to get inside." He moved away, head swimming in the meridians.

"Stay on the path," said the landscaper.

"I promise to consider it," said Bear, eyeing the stone circles.

THE MAIL IN THE home office rose to the ceiling. "Roberto did say he only left behind the *positive* letters, right?" asked Walter. "No junk mail or angry correspondence from the Right, right?"

"You doubting the world's love for the meister?" asked Bear, grabbing his man by the waist.

"No doubt," said Walter, rethinking the pile. "How was your little rendez-vous with Julio the bullfighter?"

"The landscaper *and* landscape are both gorgeous," said Bear. "And a little esoteric. I should know."

"How so?" asked Walter. They were interrupted by the sound of Hip barking ferociously in another part of the house. "Did you leave the front door open?"

"I came through the back," said Bear. Walter hurried out of the office, Bear followed. They found Hip barking like a mad dog with good reason. Half a dozen strangers were standing in his foyer. Tammy—the lone familiar smell—tried to be friendly, but Hip was intent on keeping the five men wearing dark suits from entering his den.

"Here, here," called Bear. When that didn't work, Bear grabbed Hip by the collar and shuttled him to the backyard. By the time Bear returned, the strangers in dark suits had moved into the den. Most of them were sitting on the couch or sofa chairs. Tammy stood near Walter, who appeared wary like he did on the sideline in a crucial game situation,

"Thanks for giving us five minutes to breathe," said Walter. "Bear, apparently we didn't fool *everybody* with our phony return date."

"Bob Overstreet," said Bear, getting a whiff of the short bald man behind the couch. "If it isn't B.O., my old overseer from our days with the Rams. Finally, we get to meet the headcheese of the team. You are the headcheese, right?"

"That alone makes our fake punt worth it," said Walter. "How do you do all of this, Overstreet? And just how many teammates do I have, and on how many teams in how many sports? And what makes them my teammates?"

"You didn't have this cavalier an attitude when you were a kid scared of the world finding out about your bedroom habits," said Bob Overstreet. "Back then, when Tammy told you to jump, you both said *how high.*"

"That's because I was ashamed," said Walter. "Correction. I *thought* I was ashamed, thought I had to hide my true nature because I was doing disgusting, immoral things."

"You no longer do those things?" asked one of the suits.

"We no longer believe the things we do are shameful," said Bear. "We realize we're just as godly and lovable as all humans, what's to hide? We wanna live to tell."

"You see, we had a reality shift," said Walter, holding Bear's hand. "For most of my life, I thought telling someone about my true nature meant telling them bad news. As if telling someone *I love another man* is equal to telling a person: *I have cancer, or I'm a felon or mentally ill or a murderer or child molester or anything that makes me deviant and abnormal.*"

"But we're not," shrugged Bear. "We're none of those things."

"So conveying my true nature is no longer conveying bad news," said Walter. "It's simply telling the truth."

"Which sets you free, ya see," said Bear.

"This much is true," said Walter.

"It's called dreaming the better dream," said Bear.

"How's that?" asked one of the suits.

"Life doesn't have to be your worst dreams come true," said Bear. "Why not make life your best dreams come true?"

"What if they don't come true?" asked Tammy.

"You wanna spend the time between now and the end of your life dreaming of the worst?" asked Bear. "Thinking the worst? Fearing the worst? Believing the worst? Anybody else having déjà vu of a conversation in a cave?"

"What if," said one of the suits, "what if, in the end, you're left with nothing but disappointment after chasing after all your silly little dreams in life?"

"Tell me about it," said Walter.

"Tell you what?" asked the suit.

"The date that you're gonna be left with nothing," said Walter. "I'm gonna wanna be sure to steer clear that day."

"No one says you have to chase your dreams, or believe they come true," said Bear. "It's your choice, just like choosing to breathe or not to breathe."

"Nice," said Walter.

"But what if—" asked one of the suits.

"*Or* you can also spend your life *what if'ing* for eternity," said Walter. "Your choice."

"Guys," said Bob Overstreet. "This sounds like a great discussion for a late-night study session in the freshman dorm, but we've got serious issues to discuss."

"I thought we were," said Walter.

"We'd still like you to be a part of the team," said Bob Overstreet.

"There's no more cover-up," said Walter. "We appreciate you being there for us in weaker times, but folks, we've come to the end of this beautiful friendship."

A suit stood up and began reading off figures: "Since you've been gone, jersey sales for Yeager's #13 have gone up in the gay community, but there have been so many attempts to return previously purchased Yeager—"

"*Whoa!* Shut your trap right there," said Walter, prompting the suit to sit.

"Walter and Bear don't want to know anything about the public's reaction," said Tammy.

"Unless it's the good stuff," said Walter.

"We've already dealt with enough negative energy about our true nature in this lifetime," said Bear.

"This is unrealistic," said Bob Overstreet.

"As unrealistic as you running an underground PR firm that deceives the public about athletes?" asked Bear. "And God knows what else."

"Tammy, talk some sense into these knuckleheads," said Bob Overstreet.

"It's about more than the cover-up now," said Tammy.

"For example?" asked Walter.

"Bear's safety at the games," said Bob Overstreet.

"You'll wanna travel more incognito, like you did in the old days, and sit in more secure seats, if not a box—that's an easy one for us," said Tammy.

Walter eyed Bear, their faces solemn with another new reality.

"We're also curious about keeping you on board as yet another experiment, in a way," said Bob Overstreet. "To see if the team can successfully protect an openly gay athlete from any harm—behind the scenes still, however you need us."

"Let *them* open the mail," said Bear.

"We don't like the word *gay,*" said Walter. "We've probably used it to refer to ourselves ... *twice* ... in our lifetime."

"What should we call you?" asked Bob Overstreet.

Walter fell silent, unable to come up with a better dream at the moment.

"You still need us," said Bob Overstreet, "maybe not to keep your sex life quiet, but to run interference, to get you to and from places quickly and quietly, and to do things that make your lives more comfortable for you."

"If you knew what the real world was like out there, you wouldn't hesitate," said Tammy.

Walter turned to Bear: "Huddle." The boys circled wagons alone on the deck, where the quarterback asked the spirit leader: "What's your gut tell you?"

"I didn't think about me at the games," said Bear.

"Seeing as how we have no idea what this brave new world is like, maybe we outta hang tight with these guys a little while longer," said Walter.

"Does give us a chance to keep an eye on them," said Bear. "And something tells me we need to."

"Agreed."

They returned to the den, where Walter told the suits: "No more lies about who we are." The suits broke out in demonstrative fake laughter. "But I do have a question or two," said Walter, getting silence again. "Just how big is this biggest and best team in all of sports?"

Tammy and the other suits eyed Bob Overstreet, whose laugh was somewhere between cocky and sinister.

"I like your piss 'n' vinegar, Yeager," said Bob Overstreet. "You were one of my first guinea pigs when I concocted this idea back in Anaheim, back when I said to myself: I can make the public believe anything I want, just by altering their perception of reality, not in big ways, just little nuances the public runs with to feel safe, nuances that make me and you a lot of money."

"I make my money from playing football, not lying," said Walter.

"You wouldn't have played football if you hadn't lied," said Bob Overstreet. "At least in the beginning."

"We'll never know for sure now, will we?" said Walter.

"Walter, we have some ideas." Tammy pulled a file from her briefcase. "We'd like to do some interviews with you and your son, maybe even show your great relationship with Grace's girls."

Walter simply walked out of the room, his way of avoiding a murder rap.

"Your team's not off to a smooth start in this brave new world," said Bear, herding the uninvited guests outta the Jaw. "Walter would cut off his throwing arm before he exploited any of those children. Get out, all of you, please! And call first next time. Or there'll never be a next time."

"Speaking of calling," said one of the suits. "What do you call each other?"

"The same thing we always have: buddies."

THE LANDSCAPER AND HIS MERIDIANS crept into Bear's dreams. One day, while Walter and Hip were out playing in the hills, Bear fell asleep on the couch in the den. In the pitch darkness of his mind, he saw laser-sharp lines reaching endlessly into space. The lines moved in all directions and crossed one another without incident. Sometimes, the lines merged and formed bigger lines, then shapes, like circles, arcs, triangles, squares, starbursts, shooting stars, comets. It were as if the lines were playing a game, to see what they could create on a moment's whim. It was a fun game until the lines began moving too fast for Bear's sleepy head, the infinite possibilities overwhelming.

He forced himself awake to try whelming. The house was warm and bright with the afternoon sun. The faint sound of the ocean beyond the patio doors calmed him. Once he achieved whelming, he headed for the gardens on the south side of the Jaw. Julio had been working there all morning with a small crew that only spoke Spanish. Bear only spoke English and French.

He peeked around the corner of the house, found the gardens empty. He moved toward the backyard, carefully on the stone circles. Now wherever Bear went, he tried staying on the path. No shortcuts through the grass. No jaywalking in the neighborhood. No unnecessary maneuvers on the rare occasions he found himself driving since hibernation. Somehow, it was making a difference in the way he felt. He was unable to put it into words yet, but his surroundings breathed in very different and profound ways.

Julio and his crew were exactly where Bear imagined them to be next: near the tool shed having lunch. Bear loitered around inside the adjacent garage and listened through the window. Julio was talking to them in Spanish, speaking passionately and waving his arms toward the heavens. Bear couldn't understand a word. But Julio was speaking so passionately, Bear used his imagination, watching mouths talk, hearing Spanish in the air, and English in his headspace.

"These roads you speak of, bullfighter," said one of the crewmen. "These roads that come out of my body and run all over the skies and heavens like highways. If I tell that to the Father of my church, he would call me crazy."

"Do you know the original meaning of crazy?" asked Julio the Bullfighter. "To be crazy meant to be in touch with heavenly joy all the time, so much so that all you need is that heavenly joy. But people who have that much heavenly joy don't need priests and churches, so the priests and churches—the authorities who tried to control the images in our heads—they hijacked the actions of those who were crazy and redefined those actions as deviant, actions to mistrust and be suspicious of."

"That sounds crazy," said a younger crewman. "Bullfighter has the craziest ideas. Julio the Loco Bullfighter. I'd rather see you fight real bulls, bullfighter."

"Dream of it," said Julio the Bullfighter.

"These roads, Julio," said the crewman leaning against a tree. "What do they do for me?"

"Same as the roads here, take you places," said Julio the Bullfighter.

"Where can I go?" laughed a crewman on the ground.

"I want to go to TJ," said his buddy, salivating. "Can I go to TJ?"

"*These roads, Julio,*" said the crewman up in the tree. "*I cannot comprehend how they are here yet invisible yet with so many, millions you say, billions even.*"

"*And energy comes in and out of our bodies on these roads?*" asked a crewman.

"*Freaky,*" laughed the crewman on the ground. "*Freaky and loco.*"

"*How can anyone ever learn to comprehend something like that, bullfighter?*" asked the crewman in the tree. "*Unless they are as crazy as you?*"

"*Stick to the roads you know first,*" said Julio the Bullfighter. "*The ones underneath your feet, the paths in life that you can see and feel. Learn the rules of those roads first. Know which rules serve you, and which don't.*"

"*How does someone come to know that?*" asked the kid dreaming of TJ.

"*Whatever gets you toward your ultimate goal is what serves you,*" said Julio the Bullfighter. "*Everything else doesn't.*"

"*What is my ultimate goal?*" laughed a crewman.

"*What is your deepest dream?*" asked Julio the Bullfighter.

The crewman laughed. "*I don't dream. Or remember them anyway.*"

"*Dreams don't only happen at night, fool!*" said the kid dreaming of TJ. "*He means your aspirations, dude, damn!*"

"*Paying the rent,*" said a crewman.

"*When you were a child,*" said Julio the Bullfighter. "*You dreamed of bigger things. Paying the rent was a side-effect. You had an ultimate dream, something that would bring you the greatest joy in this lifetime. When God let you fall from God's soul, God gave you a soul of your own, so that you could create a world of your own, full of dreams of your own. Then God sent you on your first path out into your world. And in return for sharing that world with God—so that God may experience all that God's soul can—God made you a promise.*"

"*To pay my rent?*" asked a crewman.

"*Better than that,*" said Julio the Bullfighter. "*God promised you your deepest dreams come true.*"

Julio the Bullfighter fell silent, the men followed. For a while.

"*How?*" asked a crewman.

"*You won't need to ask that question when you understand energy,*" said Julio the Bullfighter. "*That's what's traveling on the roads between your soul and your universe.*"

"*I'm getting lost,*" said the crewman in the tree.

"*We all do,*" said Julio the Bullfighter. "*That's what makes us fallible. We have to be fallible for all this to work. If you knew that you could travel from here to the edge of the universe and back quicker than the speed of light, would anything else in life really make a difference?*"

Bear and the men laughed, but Bear laughed the loudest. The men turned toward the window and spotted him. He fussed with the curtains as if that were his reason for being there. Meanwhile, Julio continued on (in Spanish):

"If you had full knowledge that you were really God in disguise, and that you possessed all the power in the universe, what fun would life be? Not even winning a Super Bowl or having the great love of your life would mean much, if you could just blink your mind and make this whole universe go from a pinhead to infinity. So God made up a little game. God created fallible gods to go out and dream for the Big God, to do the things infallible God cannot do alone. Infallible God cannot know the joy of having a dream, then struggling to achieve that dream, then risking life and death for that dream, then knowing the joy of living that dream. God is too good. So God created some fallible buddies ... us."

"Why can't infallible God just play with himself?" asked a crewman.

"Because, stupid," said the kid bound for TJ, "God knows he's gonna win. He's God! He's All That!"

"So God created us to dream for him?" asked the crewman in the tree.

"That's one way of looking at it," said Julio the Bullfighter.

"What do we dream about then?" asked a crewman.

"Whatever you want," said Julio the Bullfighter.

"Being a serial killer?" asked a crewman.

"If that's what you want to be," said Julio the Bullfighter. "No one fallible god has been able to stop anyone from living that dream, if they truly wanted it."

"How about a boxer?" said the crewman in the tree. "I wanted to be a boxer when I was a kid."

"You can be anything you want," said Julio the Bullfighter.

"God don't want you to be no serial killer," said a crewman.

"What's it to God what you dream?" asked Julio the Bullfighter. "You're talking about a force that can do anything. Let's say you kill 30 people because that was your dream in life, for whatever reason. So in your world, 30 people suffered, and so many more by extension. But you see, that's just your dream, which is the same as saying your world, which is the same as saying your mind. Because your world is all in your mind. So in your world, you killed and caused all that pain. But on a higher level, it's actually okay. Your world is only in your mind. Those 30 people? They have their own worlds, minds and dreams. Maybe some of them dreamed of being killed. Maybe some of them are alive and well in their own world."

"I cannot work for such a crazy man!" said a crewman.

"Are you saying, bullfighter, that we should kill?" asked a crewman.

"I'm saying you can dream of whatever you want," said Julio the Bullfighter.

"Dreams are thought and energy. If you put enough energy into something, it becomes a force to be dealt with."

"Are you saying, bullfighter, that we should kill?" asked a crewman.

"I'm saying between you and God, your dreams can come true," said Julio the Bullfighter. "You can dream of murder, you can dream of love. It's your choice which dream you want to dream."

"Are you saying, bullfighter, that we should kill?" asked a crewman.

"What about the people we hurt? Rape, robbery, murder?" asked a crewman.

"Is anyone here planning any of those today?" asked Julio the Bullfighter.

The crewmen shook their heads. Negative.

"Then why don't we talk about the better dreams coming true? Always coming true?" asked Julio the Bullfighter.

"Because my head is spinning!" said the crewman falling from the tree.

"A good reason to keep your feet close to the ground while learning the rules on the road of life."

REVEREND REGGIE SNOWMAN and his boy Carter Jones were ballin' on the basketball half-court at the Jaw—as if they had been invited.

"You back early from hibernating?" asked Reggie when he saw Bear standing alone on the deck.

"This is like the time astronauts take before re-entry into civilization," said Bear, joining them on the court, "which wasn't supposed to happen until around training camp."

"We had to be out this way," said Reggie, palming the ball near the top of the key. He dribbled once, made a little head fake on his boy Carter Jones, then took off and slam dunked. "Hope you don't mind me using your court to school my boy."

"What does that mean?" asked Bear, "*My* boy."

"What does *he* mean?" asked Carter Jones, the Dallas Maverick.

"What kind of boy are you to him?" asked Bear. "It gets confusing. *Boy* as in friend? *Boy* as in what Walter and I are to one another? And Reggie, you sure you want to be playing ball on a court owned by a white man and his house nigga? Especially with you being Reverend Reggie now?"

"Man, you tripping," said Reggie, more focused on firing a three-pointer that missed. "I'm still married and shit."

"Glad we cleared everything up," said Bear.

"You or Walter don't need to be begrudging me," said Reggie. "I hope he remembers, I'm the one who helped his career." Reggie informed Carter Jones: "Muthafucka used to tip off DBs, coming out of the huddle and shit."

Then it occurred to Bear: "In case you were wondering—and came all the way out here to find out—we have no intentions of naming names or talking shit, Reverend."

"What—a nigga can't come by and say wassup?" asked Reggie.

"Man, let's go," said Carter Jones. "I gotta be @ PHX in a few."

"Reggie, you're Walter's teammate," said Bear. "As long as that's true, may you win a thousand Super Bowls. But this is the Jaw. This is *my* home—the house nigga's. And as the nigga of this house, your uptight, not-right, paranoid black ass—and your friend's paranoid black ass—are not welcomed here. Until you're on *my* team, too. Now get the hell out!"

"You're the traitor!" said Reggie, then turned to Carter Jones. "All this time, all these years. I finally figured it out! This muthafucka is the traitor!"

"For loving a white man?" asked Bear.

"For turning into a Bruin!" said Reggie. "Remember, man: *Hey, it's the traitor! Hey, it's the traitor!*"

... Hey, it's the traitor! Look at the traitor! Hey, there's that traitor again! First, he was a SC cheerleader, then he transferred across town to ...

"*You're* the snowman?" asked Bear, astonished. "You're the fucking snowman! I'm not the snowman! I was never the snowman! *He's* the snowman!" Bear turned to Carter Jones. "*I'm* the traitor and *he's* the snowman!"

"Y'all two smoke something behind my back?" asked Carter Jones.

"I know him!" said both Bear and Reggie, indicating one another.

"Yeah," said Carter Jones. "Y'all's Walter's top niggas, *hello*? House 'n' field?"

"Nigga, I know this cat from back in the *day!*" said Bear.

Before UCLA, before Athens, during Marcus "Bear" Coleman's USC days, a group of streetwise little black boys hung around the LA Memorial Coliseum and the Trojan football universe.

"I thought you guys were making fun of me," said Bear, "calling me a snowman because I was dressed in all that USC yell leader white. You're that little bald-headed, cocky nigga all grown up! *Hey, it's the traitor! It's the traitor!*"

For half of the 80s, Bear couldn't go anywhere near the LA college football world without hearing: Hey, it's the traitor!

"They got around, too!" said Bear to Carter Jones. "Only ... yeah ... that's right ... your name wasn't Reggie, Reggie ... it was ... Shawn ... Reshawn, or something like that, true? Reshanté!"

"Reshanté?" repeated Carter Jones, barely suppressing his laugh.

"Man, bug that," said Reggie.

Bear thought about what Black Coach had said about Coach raising Reggie after rescuing his nephew from the mean streets of LA.

"You've definitely grown," said Bear, still astonished.

Wish I could have taught you some better dreams back then, kid.

"So you gonna keep my shit cool?" asked Reggie.

"I don't intend to keep your shit hot or cold," said Bear. "Traitor or not, something tells me Jackie Robinson, as hard a time as he had—it probably helped him get through that hard time by dwelling on the blessed, not the damned. Things in his path, I mean. His road of life."

"Speaking of the road ..." said Reggie before vanishing with his boy.

Bear went inside the Jaw, relieved to hear the commotion of *his* boys, Walter and Hip, returning through the front door. He hurried to the foyer and found Hip jumping up to greet an old friend, one unseen since before hibernation.

"Look who I found outside," said Walter. "And he's very excited to see his Uncle Larry. Look at that tail go."

"Hey, Hipster," said Hail Larry, petting Hip. "Hey, Bear. How's the head?"

"Swell," said Bear. "How was Western PA?"

"Perfect," said Hail Larry. "Couldn't have gone better."

"I just met the bullfighter," said Walter. "He was scolding his crew in Spanish about the way they pruned the trees."

"So, Larry," said Bear. "So you want to suck my husband's dick."

"*Beaaaaaar!*" said Walter. Welcome to our new world.

"I have it wrong?" asked Bear. "Exactly which sex acts do you wish to perform with my man?"

Just then, they were joined by a fourth party, who had overheard every word. "Look who else I found outside," said Walter.

"Nice welcome, best bud," said Hail Larry's Wife. "Now I'm really in the mood to be at *the Jaw*."

"What better time to get it all out in the open?" shrugged Bear, leaving the foyer. "We can pretend we're at a luau. Got pineapple?"

"Bear, you okay?" asked Walter, following him into the kitchen.

"No, I'm not," said Bear. "Reggie and his boy were just in our backyard."

"Doing what?" asked Walter.

"God knows," said Bear, grabbing a beer from the fridge. "Just giving each other the damned ball, for all I know. *Sorry,* just giving each other the *blessed* ball. *Hmmm ...* don't feel any better. Where are my coma pills?"

"We obviously came at a bad time," said Hail Larry's Wife, joining them in the kitchen.

"Not at all," said Walter, getting beers for everyone else. "What did Reggie say, buddy?"

"I'm an old-school traitor," said Bear, "and they're worried about their own hides."

"I want to settle this now!" said Hail Larry, joining them in the kitchen. "I just got freakin' accused of something!"

They all eyed Hail Larry, who seemed desperate to defend his manhood. Walter suggested they talk like rational adults. Everyone agreed—after dinner on the grill was thrown in. QB also made sure the beer was flowing while he prepared the steaks.

"So, Larry, hell," said Bear after his second beer. *Or was it his fourth?* "Have you *ever* had sex with a man, Larry?"

"Beaaaaaar!" Walter and Hail Larry's Wife said together.

The two couples were sitting at the patio table on the deck, each across from his or her partner.

"Hell," said Bear, "Larry asks us stuff like that in Hawaii all the time."

"I only admitted it freakin' crossed my mind," said Hail Larry, "like any freakin' guy. Lighten up."

"He admitted it?" said Bear. "Oh, shit. Where's the fan?"

"You didn't tell him about the baby, too, did you?" Hail Larry asked his wife.

"Bigmouth!" said Hail Larry's Wife to her husband.

"You guys are having a baby?" said Walter and Bear together.

"Thinking about it," said the Hail Larrys.

"Freakin' thinking about a lot of things, these days, eh?" said Bear.

"My wife's right about one thing," said Hail Larry. "Bear's got a big freakin' mouth."

"Some sitting at this table might call that nature's synchronicity," said Bear.

"Are we getting freakin' graphic again?" asked Hail Larry.

"And one person here," said Bear, "knows exactly how to keep *this* mouth from babbling—works every time, right, QB?"

"You guys freakin' gross me out," said Hail Larry.

"This from the mouth of a man who's admitted to fantasizing about one of us?" said Bear. "This is too twisted, even for us, right, Walter? *Wants the dick, doesn't want the dick."*

"Bear, will you shut *up?"* said Hail Larry's Wife, giving up and laughing hysterically. Hysteria begat hysterics. Boom. "Walter, can't you control him?"

"Not in a way that won't freakin' gross-out Larry here," said Walter, rising to attend to the grill. "More beer anyone?"

"I'm gonna go take the dog for a freakin' walk on the sand," said Hail Larry. "Here, boy, here, where's your ball?"

Hail Larry disappeared with Hip! Soon after, Walter followed to make sure his best friend was all right. "Charming," said Hail Larry's Wife when they were gone. "You were just charming."

"I'm not sure how easy this brave new world is going to be after all," said Bear. "I think I'm ready to take down the brave new front and be a nervous little Bearcat again. Just give me a second to enjoy the fall."

Kaboom.

"THIS WILL CHEER YOU UP WHILE THE GUYS are down at the beach," said Hail Larry's Wife, shoving a videotape in Bear's face.

"If this is about trying to get me and my husband to watch gay porno, the answer is still ... not interested." Bear inhaled his man's scent on the cotton in front of his nose. "*Ah ... this is much more stimulating ... oh,* bring on the season, please, football gods. *Now ...*"

"You are sick," said Hail Larry's Wife.

"Not anymore," said Bear, regretfully retracting his man's very funky jock-strap from his now funky headspace. He and his best gal pal were standing in the lair that was the master bedroom of the Jaw. She was the third-ever visitor to any of the boys' bedrooms (Tammy, Bass).

"You just smelled your husband's old jockstrap from last season," said Hail Larry's Wife.

"Larry's have an expiration date?" asked Bear. "I think this one's Kansas City, by the way."

"Gross!" laughed Hail Larry's Wife.

"Let me explain something," said Bear. "No more lies in; no more lies out. We *all* love our husbands' jock. If we don't, we shouldn't be our jock's husband. Or something like that."

"Twisted," said Hail Larry's Wife.

"The bitch is still catching up, Bearcat People—missed the cool and dreamy, after all." Bear took a whiff of Denver, the home game, if he wasn't mistaken. "I would hope Mama Rent would have me committed if I wasn't inhaling all of Walter Yeager that I possibly could, knowing what I had to survive to get to him ... nope, gotta be @ San Diego ... cool! Not too humid that day."

"Does Yeager-meister have a cologne?" asked Hail Larry's Wife, suddenly off on her own cool and dreamy head-trip. Bear snatched back his man's Detroit exhibition loss from two years ago.

"Isn't one of you after him enough?" asked Bear, throwing @ DET back in the box on the bed and putting a lid on it. "We weren't expecting company."

"*Hello?* My movie screening tonight?" said Hail Larry's Wife.

"In the bedroom!" said Bear, cueing up the videotape. "This is just the good shit, right? Good coverage from around the world?"

"Nothing negative, we got the memo," said Hail Larry's Wife. "You guys don't want to hear about any energy damned in your name, only blessed."

"Bless you," said Bear, more focused on the monitor coming to life.

"So what if, like, Armageddon is going on outside the Jaw?" asked Hail Larry's Wife, sitting on the bed.

"Did we cause it?" asked Bear, sitting on the bed.

"Not yet, but stick around," laughed Hail Larry's Wife.

"If it's a big enough Armageddon, I'm sure it'll get back to us, one way or another," said Bear. "Remember Grace? Her girls have grown up so much. They loved the island. *Oops.* Sorry. Can't say more. You weren't in the loop."

"You're a bastard," said Hail Larry's Wife.

"What else would a bitch want?" asked Bear. "Grace, she's perfect. If I had to pick a woman for Walter. Or I guess, *Walt* in *My Whole Other Life.* Never mind. Wow, that's the first time I thought about Marcus Coleman since before Super Bowl 2 ... that's how we're counting the rings now ..."

"Bastard."

"Bitch. Perfect grace. Roll tape."

"You're like this big geeky kid when it comes to your man," said Hail Larry's Wife, snatching the remote from Bear. "You treat freakin' Yeager like God."

"He likes big geeky kids who treat him like God," said Bear. "Wouldn't you?"

"Not all the time," said Hail Larry's Wife.

"*Natch,*" said Bear. (Naturally.) "That's when it's my turn to be the God. And Walter returns the favor. Grace ... did I mention she was on the island? The one we spiraled down to in the new aerial transport ... *oops.* Another loop secret."

"Bastard."

"Bitch. Perfect grace. Roll tape."

... Men from all over the NFL said the most blessed things about the quarterback, the team leader, the father, the football buddy, the best man, the field general, the comeback kid, the Bulldawg, the warrior, the boy who threw rocks at telephone poles and had a dream ... anybody like that on your block?

He had a dream, too.

We all have dreams.

The NFL showed Walter some love. Coaches, players, quarterbacks, men who bled trying to sack him, but did not sack his right to be … human.

… Men from all over the NBA said the most blessed things about the athlete, the fierce competitor, the dude, the celebrity, the famous man, his rocket man ("Yeager throw down with a cool bruthaman who's made some cool flicks."), the kid, the baller, the shot caller, the fighter, the boy who felt the power of the rock and had a dream … anybody like that on your block?

He had a dream, too.

We all have dreams.

… Men from all over Major League Baseball said the most blessed things about the Phillies fan, the guy who loves the long ball, the uncle, the philanthropist, the infamous men in sports who did much worse than love a Bearcat, his good buddy … anybody like that on your block?

… Fans from all over the world said the most blessed things about their brand new hero, their brand old hero, the man who had the guts and the courage to back it up, the man who put his life and his buddy's life on the line to create a brand new age in the universe.

"*And* his beautiful quarterback of a husband!" said Bear. "Twisted. And beautiful. Thank you so much, beautiful best gal pal of mine."

"Amazing," said Walter. He and his best pal were in the doorway, having returned from the beach and seen some of the tape.

"Isn't she the best bitch a bastard could ever have?" asked Bear.

"Oh, she's a good little bitch when she needs to be," said Hail Larry, coming in and sitting on the bed.

"The very definition of good little bitch," said the foursome. Then, one of them realized he was in a whole new world.

"*I'm in their freakin' bedroom!" yelled Hail Larry at the top of his lungs!*

No sides of that equation were ready for that particular bomb.

"Location change," said Bear. Five minutes later, they were back at the patio table on the deck: good sauce, lite jazz, munchies … *moonlight.*

"Didn't that last guy on the tape have a reversal and comeback?" said Walter. "The last couple guys, matter of fact. Or *rumored* to anyway, since I'm still the only pro athlete to ever admit to being reversed by the Dane."

Now that the cabin had been decompressed and stabilized, QB decided to open the floodgates. The foursome all had the same *thing* on their minds, but because it was as yet unspoken, the notion had yet to be blessed or cursed.

"I saw the whole tape," said Hail Larry, loading up the atom splitter. "Unlike you two, I've been in the real world for the last 30 days. The same pro athletes who are making nice about freakin' Yeager are the same guys who everybody thinks might have been freakin' reversed."

"And have made a comeback, like Walter," said Hail Larry's Wife.

"And we're all thinking the exact same freakin' thing," said Bear.

"And *that,* in and of itself, might be a freakin' first," said Walter.

"We don't know for freakin' sure, guys, come on," said Hail Larry's Wife. "It could just be coincidence."

"Don't freakin' say anything yet!" said Bear. "We did these exercises on the island. Don't do this right now, people! Don't freakin' split this freakin' atom, not right now. It's not just about words. It's about concepts, too! We're in dangerous freakin' territory."

"What are you freakin' talking about?" yelled Hail Larry.

"Creation!" said both Walter and Bear.

"Be careful what you say right now. We're about to create something," said Walter. "A common thought for *our world of four.* Our very first common thought, for our new world."

"The new core of our new world at that," said Bear. "We've got to create a strong, positive spin on all those players supporting Walter's honesty."

"You guys are plain ole freakin' crazy," laughed Hail Larry. "Besides, all the athletes on that tape can't be—"

"Larry, shut up! For the love of God!" Hail Larry's Wife shot up from the table, then said to Walter and Bear: "You did the atom exercise?"

"Yes!" cried both Walter and Bear.

"Oh, my God!" said Hail Larry's Wife. "Word is born, born is the world! I played that as a kid at Camp Bell! I loved camp! *Oh, my God, I'm screaming off the top of my head!" yelled Hail Larry's Wife at the top of her lungs!*

... when she calmed down ...

"Larry, honey, trust us!" said Hail Larry's Wife. "Trust *me.* You do not want to open up this can of worms."

"The gods mean it when they say *be careful what you ask for,"* said Bear.

"I'm living proof," shrugged Walter. "We all are."

"I have no idea what any of you freakin' homos and bitches are talking about," said Hail Larry.

"The tape, the sports world's reaction," said Walter. "All that great positive energy we just heard. Are we gonna bless it or curse it as a world? *Our* world? The most important new world for our friendship."

"What kind of world are we gonna build?" asked Bear.

Hail Larry shook Hail Larry's head as if it were *hella* thick. "So what!" said Hail Larry. "So all the goddamned guys on the goddamned tape might be goddamned homos who had a reverse—whatever the fuck *that* goddamned means—what's the big, mother fucking god damned freakin', damned, damned deal?"

"Boom," said Walter, falling back in his chair with resignation.

"An atom is born," said Bear, slumping over the table, defeated.

"Let's reverse it!" cried Hail Larry's Wife.

"Can't reverse back onto yourself what you gave birth to," said Walter.

"Nothing personal," said Bear to Hail Larry's Wife, *"which is saying: get ready because it's gonna be?*—if you'd had a baby or two, you'd know that."

"Oh, fuck, I forgot that rule," said Hail Larry's Wife. "I was more focused on screwing around at camp."

"You're all starting to sound as whack as Bear," said Hail Larry. *Boom.*

"We need to get out of here." Hail Larry's Wife stood up.

"What about reversing my homo cursing?" asked Hail Larry, facetious and just like the Perfect Fag Girl ... *revelation.*

"No time." Walter stood up. "Gotta hit the *Freeways.* I'm feeling a lotta congestion coming."

Everyone but Hail Larry agreed ... *cold season.*

"Yeager, man, zap it from your mind," whispered Hail Larry in the dark of the small theater.

"Didn't bring my atom zapper to the screening tonight," whispered Walter.

"Or many teammates, either," whispered Bear, scrunched down next to Walter.

"Is the studio down on you after the comet?" whispered Hail Larry's Wife, scrunched down next to Bear.

"I don't know, but thank you for putting that little bug, or should I say, *atom,* in my headspace," whispered Bear.

"D-up," whispered Walter, using their new shortcut for dream the better dream ... *quick fix.*

"That's why I ended up erasing stuff on the video," said Hail Larry's Wife. "Black people debating over Bear and the interracial angle, stuff like that."

"Slice that atom before it lands in True Gold, QB," said Bear.

"No angles, just a loop," said Walter.

"Thought it was magnet now," said Hail Larry's Wife.

"Kinda a hybrid," said Bear. "One is energy you see, the other is energy you feel ... *feel me?* I've been working the biceps. Building a lotta rough shit lately."

Flickering in the dark ... the movie was finally starting ... *Freeways Claim Bodies That Fade* ... Bear's devilish road trip to the very bizarre and unfriendly highways of a small Southern town ... *or was it Western?*

Flickering in the dark ... the movie was finally ending ... *Freeways Claim Bodies That Fade* ... Bear's devilish road trip that left the small screening room very uneasy, the suits in the back looking crumpled and bewildered ... *Eastern.*

"I don't get it," said Hail Larry, meant for Walter, heard by all.

"Use your imagination," whispered Bear, then said to his buddy: "I'm gonna really need my pole after this one." Bear stood up, wobbly, turning to the suits. One of them fired first:

"Not the polished, clearly focused vision I expected, considering the film is over budget and under ... *understood,*" said a suit.

"Still four hours too long," said another suit.

"Did the director ever show?" whispered Hail Larry's Wife to Walter.

"Coming," whispered Walter to Hail Larry's Wife.

"Talk to Slick Willy," said Bear. "He'll be here. We're buying dinner."

The suits relaxed. In Hollywood, dinner was gold. This much is true.

"Running late," said a suit, hanging up his cell. "He's just about to turn onto the 405, heading south."

"Traffic on the *Freeways,* how about that?" laughed a suit, no doubt a lay-up artist in another lifetime.

The suit with the cell clarified: "Willy had wanted to make it before the way, way long climactic chase scene, but traffic was heavier than expected."

"And they *still* wanna trim the length?" asked Walter.

"Where is this director guy coming from? Outer Mongolia?" laughed Hail Larry's Wife.

Boom (translation: beyond our wildest imagination).

"Dunno, never met the poor bastard," said Walter.

Boom (there's a poor bastard I've conceived of meeting).

"I love what he did with *Rocket 2,*" said Hail Larry. "Maybe he's just not a rocket scientist himself, if ya know what I mean."

Boom (hella cursed).

"I'd like to wait until Wilhelm gets here before discussing things if you don't mind," said Bear to the suits ... stalling before adding the fourth part of the four-part harmony known as *the Creation of the Camille.*

Bear moved to the front of the screening space, Walter followed.

"So what's up?" asked Walter in a hushed voice.

"The devil," said Bear. "No one gets how that *one car* more than any other represents the chaos of the highway. And therefore the entire world."

"You think this Slick Willy is doing your words justice yet?" asked Walter. "Keep in mind, he's trying to piece together his work and three other directors."

"Five," said Bear.

"They're using the footage shot by *all five?*" asked Walter. "These guys have their heads up their ass."

"Better them than me," said Bear. "What is keeping Emile?"

"You mean Wilhelm," said Walter.

"Camille, the director," said Bear. "I just found out Wilhelm is not only William in English, but it's, like, Emile in French. I think. How slick is that?"

"*Emile?*" said Walter. *Mild laugh.* "As in—"

"Same name, different language," said Bear. "Fuck, I'm light-headed. Let's get this *damned* thing over with so I can introduce you to Emile the Camille and we can eat. I think he's even Creole." *Boom (four-part harmony).*

Walter coughed. "Incoming."

Suits were ruffling and unfurling in the back. They were all white, so it was easy to spot Wilhelm Camille and his colorful colorless suit.

"It's the Damned Creole Kid!" screamed Walter and the Hail Larrys at the top of their lungs!

"If somebody can get Madonna to let go like that on film—*kaboom!*" said Slick Willy.

"Dream of it," said Bear, moving to greet his colorful colorless friend.

Didn't happen. Walter and the Hail Larrys were dreaming their own dream, screaming bloody murder and chasing the petrified Camille out the door, apparently as *he* was dreaming of trying to reattach and un-detonate an atom bomb.

"THIS IS WHEN YOU ASK YOURSELF: does God have a sense of humor?" said Hail Larry's Wife. *Back to Malibu ... a tall cliff overlooking darkness ... the two couples leaning against the front of the SUV.*

"If God does have a sense of humor, God's doing one crazy freakin' number on us right now," said Hail Larry, arm in arm with his girl ... *felt right.*

"Every single God-blessed day," said Walter, kickin' back like a cowboy, staring at the Pacific *like it was his ocean.* "One amazing adventure after another."

"Question," said Bear, arm in arm with his buddy ... *felt right.* "When you woke up this morning, which seemed more likely tonight: me dancing all crazy at the beach? Or all of us meeting a Creole guy, who, years ago, snapped a high school photo and called me a Bearcat, which is now a worldwide name, because WALT LOVES THE BEARCAT?"

"We had dinner reservations with the guy," said Walter.

"Whom we met at a movie studio, watching some bitch who looks like me get her head split open four ways," said Hail Larry's Wife.

"And still manages that tough curve on Scary Hill," said Bear.

"In both of her lives," said Walter. "I think."

"*Freeways Claim Bodies That Fade* is nothing compared to the weird shit in this life," said Hail Larry.

In New Orleans, circa the Sugar Bowl: Walter had seen the Creole Emile with his own two eyes on the dock of the Mississippi, and had never seen him since.

In New Orleans, circa the Sugar Bowl: Bear had only seen the Creole Emile through the fuzzy mesh eyes of Joe Bruin, and had never seen him since.

Until tonight: Walter had never seen director Wilhelm Camille with his own two eyes, the two having never met.

Until tonight: Bear was fuzzy about where he may or may not have previously seen or known director Wilhelm Camille, aka Slick Willy.

Until tonight: Slick Willy, aka Wilhelm Camille, aka the Creole Emile, was not about to spill the beans and let an innocent little high school extra credit assignment ruin his budding film career. After all, the Creole kid had put together the whole Sugar Bowl edition just to pass journalism and get into film school, which was exactly what came to pass.

"Now, Larry," said Bear. "Which seemed more likely when you woke up this morning: me dancing at the beach? Or all of us meeting the original boomer of the Bearcat generation?"

"And forgiving him for it!" said Hail Larry's Wife.

"Wasn't his fault the world became obsessed with us," said Walter, going for something inside the SUV. "Plus, he's one of the best directors for Bear's flicks."

"He gets me," said Bear. "In that way."

"Freakin' A!" said Hail Larry. "That stuff only happens in movies! I love this kind of mind-twisting shit!"

Walter sat in the driver's seat of the ground transport and cranked up the stereo, which began playing "Crazy," the sexy, bluesy rock jam by Aerosmith.

Immediately, QB shot Bear a knowing, daring look.

"Yes!" cried Bear, accepting his man's dare with a mighty roar.

"What the freak is happening?" laughed Hail Larry, half-serious.

Bear danced. On the cliff. Teetering. Tottering. Being a goofy, silly, faggy queeny happy masculine funny loving manly man of men with all kinds of men inside. Every single one of them was going to live in this world now, because he did not survive what he survived to give his man and the God who gave him his man any less. He owed them the whole truth. He was going to have to get crazy.

"Story Meeting," said Bear, still dancing. "Gather children, my dear sweet and glorious atoms. This plateau is now the site of the creation of ... Bearcat Studios!" *Boom (1)*

Hail Larry's Wife screamed with delight. *Boom (2)*

Hail Larry grinned and said, "Freakin' A!" *Boom (3)*

Walter sat in the driver's seat and laughed his oh, *soooooo* sexy—dare one say—panther-like laugh. *Boom (4)*

Bear had been in this particular universe for quite some time. *Boom baby.*

Welcome to the new atom *slash* dream *slash* everything *slash* entire world *slash* entire universe *slash* entire All There Is. This much is true.

Singing a New Tune. Not Here To Lie Ever Again.

"I'm feeling like you're feeling me," said Bear, adding some vibration to the blessed new atom, blessed by all four sides of TIME from the start.

Gold. Athens. Eden. Paradise.

"Bear and I are gonna bust a move on our own studio," said Walter, emerging from the SUV with some papers and stuff. Meanwhile, Bear danced around QB to "Crazy."

"Nothing's gonna stop the Bearcats now," said Bear, wrapping his arms around Walter from behind.

"Forgot something. Back in a flash." Walter swung back around to the SUV, carrying Bear on his back. When QB reached inside the transport, Bear flopped backward to the ground, then sprang to his feet and danced on.

"I'm having a déjà vu here," said Hail Larry's Wife.

"She's *k'waaaay-zy!*" shouted Bear as Steve Tyler of Aerosmith sang about a love that's made him certifiable. "And kept him alive!"

"You guys ready to talk numbers for this possible joint business venture?" asked Walter, emerging from the SUV with more papers and stuff. Bear started dancing around QB again, worshipping him demonstratively.

"Fuck it, let's do it!" Hail Larry turned to his wife. "You're in, too—right, babe?"

"Get outta real estate?—" ... *couldn't finish ... too busy having orgasms.*

"So we're gonna make freakin' pictures," said Hail Larry. "Crazy!"

"Crazy freakin' pictures!" said Hail Larry's Wife.

"And perfect! Don't forget perfect! Crazy, pretty and perfect pictures!" said

Bear, dancing some more around Walter, who moved around him as if quite nonplussed but a good sport nonetheless.

"I swear I'm having a déjà vu here," said Hail Larry's Wife. "Like I'm at the Kingdome."

"Swearing is like saying your word isn't good enough on its own," said Bear, still dancing. "So said the bullfighter."

"I believe in my Bear," said Walter. "Cole-man the Soul Man can make miracles happen."

"So let's have this first story meeting," said Hail Larry. "What's a freakin' story meeting?"

"Where we are the creators!" said Bear. "Creators of people, dreams, ideas, heroes, villains, challenges, adventure—in other words, life! In the movies!"

"I'm lost," said Hail Larry.

"If you could tell any kind of stories, what kind would you tell?" asked Walter.

"Twisted stories that fuck with people's minds," said Hail Larry, laughing like a kid, "and fucks with their perception of reality. How twisted can we get?"

"Sample," said Bear, dancing away from Walter, then back toward him.

"Where have I seen you two do that before?" wondered Hail Larry's Wife.

"Sample," said Bear. "Two college boys in the prime of their youth experience one magical football weekend in Athens. The big season opener: UCLA @ Georgia."

"Too sappy," said Hail Larry.

"But they don't experience it together," said Bear. "Because ... they never met!"

"I love it!" said Hail Larry. "I don't get it."

"In this Bearcat Studios movie," said Bear, "Yeager and Coleman never met. They were just two strangers at the game."

"In *My Whole Other Life*," said Walter, "I didn't ditch the team movie on Friday night, so I never made it to the frat party where Bear and I met."

"You went to a party the night before a game?" asked Hail Larry.

"I was young, stupid and injured," said Walter. "And pissed off about the injury."

"So *your injury* is the reason you and Bear met," said Hail Larry's Wife.

"I never thought of it that way," the boys said, almost together.

Bear stopped dancing, then processed his thought aloud: "If I never saw you in your yellow polo shirt from that one time, and you had gone on to become a famous quarterback without me, you would have just been another famous pro athlete to me, unattainable and unreachable, like Elway or Jordan. I would have never dreamed of us having a life together. Literally."

"At the time, I thought that injury was the worst thing that ever happened to me," said Walter.

"Which would mean," said Bear, "the worst thing that happened to you led to the best thing that ever happened to me: my cool and dreamy life with you."

"—which turned into the best thing that happened to me, too!" said Walter. "*Whew,* glad we cleared that up before we boomed something ugly."

"We're getting sappy here again," said Hail Larry. "What about the twisted flick where you never met?"

"*My Whole Other Life,*" said Bear, dancing onward again. "Or maybe I'll call that one *Walt Loves the Bearcat.* Anyway, Walt and Marcus never met that weekend. They went on to lead totally separate lives."

"I love those kinds of *what if's,*" said Hail Larry Wife.

"But later on," said Bear, "Marcus sees Walt's picture in the game program, since Marcus cheered at the game and all. And it's love at first sight."

"He's gonna hunt freakin' Yeager down, I knew it," said Hail Larry.

"Not for, like, 21 years, or something," said Bear.

"I love it!" said Hail Larry's Wife. "Romantic and screwy."

"They meet," said Bear. "Walt and Marcus hit it off great. Naturally. Marcus even sees what I see when I look in my buddy's eyes: a light that begins and ends at the core of my soul."

"So they're gonna hook up, then what?" asked Hail Larry.

"You think a Bear Coleman flick is gonna be that simple?" said Walter. *Mild laugh.* "In *My Whole Other Life,* I'm married, divorced—a couple of times—got kids, never played pro ball—if you can believe that!—but of course, I'm still a cool and opened-mind guy—not a jerk."

"He's a financial wizard." Bear stopped dancing. "But Walt disappears."

"Why?" asked the Hail Larrys.

"Dunno," said Bear. "He left a note, but it blew away."

"Because Bear knows I'd never leave him totally in the lurch," said Walter.

"Freakin' Yeager got scared and ran off," said Hail Larry.

"Freakin' Bear got scared," said Bear. "Or stuck. I'm stuck in the story."

"Bear insists on being HIV-positive in *My Whole Other Life,*" said Walter, "and doesn't trust me when I say I'd deal with it."

"Is this a movie about dying?" asked Hail Larry.

"See!" said Bear to Walter. "*That* Marcus is alive and healthy, but after he tells people he's positive, that's all anybody sees: death and dying. It's just like

Duncan McDuncan—the Rams rugby boy—told me. All anyone sees when they look at him is AIDS, no matter what else he looks like. Once people know about him ... *he has an AIDS aura.*"

"Remember when Rock Hudson got it and the media introduced AIDS to the world like we were all gonna die?" said Hail Larry's Wife. "We were all just out of college. And freaking out!"

"All of us wondering," said Hail Larry. "What have I freakin' done? And with who? Did I win or lose in the freakin' sexual revolution lottery?"

"And people worried about every little thing," said Walter, "like spit and sweat and utensils. And can you get it at the gym, the doctor's office, the bank?"

"Exactly," said Bear. "We were basically still college kids when Rock Hudson shocked the world in '85. *That* Marcus got the virus, graduated UCLA and became our generation's worst nightmare overnight. Just like that. Hello, brand new world."

"Why make the movie a downer?" asked Hail Larry.

"Of course, I don't want to," said Bear. "Thus, this example for our story meeting. *Duh?*"

"So this is like when you see a bunch of movie or TV people," said Hail Larry's Wife, "and they're all trying to come up with plots and ideas."

"I love it," said Hail Larry. "Let's STORY MEETING!"

"So where the fuck is Walt in *My Whole Other Life?*" asked Bear. "The little red sports car is gone and the note blew away. What did it even say?"

"Back in a flash," said Walter, heading for the SUV again.

"Maybe Walt went to buy Marcus a present to come back and propose with," said Hail Larry's Wife.

"I say he got lost in the woods and kidnapped by Jason in a hockey mask," said Hail Larry.

"Is this when we need to whip out the Dream the Better Dream Speech?" asked Walter, returning from the transport minus the papers and stuff.

"What—you want Freddy Krueger instead?" asked Hail Larry.

"I want a happy ending for *that* Marcus Coleman," said Bear. "And for *that* Walt Yeager. I want Walt to come back and get to know me, to see that I'm more than just plain crazy." Bear started dancing around his buddy again. "Or at least, that I'm crazy in all the right ways. For all the right reasons. You know what I'm talking 'bout, don't you, Big Norse?"

"Better than anyone alive, Soul Man," said Walter.

"I have a bigger question," said Hail Larry's Wife.

"What's that?" asked Walter.

"Why is Marcus Coleman's life so bleak?" asked Hail Larry's Wife. "The guys at the office keep talking about these breakthrough HIV medications on the horizon. Give him hope. Give him a better place to live, especially after what you put him through in the earthquake."

"Give the poor bastard some miracles!" said Hail Larry. "Do something twisted, like have him fall in love with a guy on the Boston Red Sox."

"Ex-squeeze me?" said Bear.

"The sports town you hate," said Hail Larry, as if it were obvious. "Have Marcus be torn between wanting Boston to lose the World Series, or supporting his Red Sox first-base-buddy."

"I say give him some good friends he can rely on," said Walter, practicing his golf swing on the ridge by hitting imaginary balls into the darkened Pacific. "And a cool dog like the Hipster."

"Hook him up with Reggie Miller of the Pacers," said Hail Larry. "You cheered for him at UCLA, right? He plays for your favorite team. Have a Reggie-type-guy and Marcus fall in love during, like, the NBA finals and do a big kiss and make-up scene at center court. Game seven."

"What happened to my Boston Red Sox first-base-buddy?" laughed Bear.

"Hell, they'll never win the World Series," said Hail Larry. "Stick with the Pacer-buddy."

"The Pacers winning the NBA before the Red Sox win the Series?" asked Walter. "Hell, Larry, that sounds like a good bet."

"The Red Sox winning period would be right up there in the miracle department with Marcus getting the Walt," said Bear.

"Like you asked me once," said Walter. "Do you believe in miracles?"

Bear stumbled in his dance, perhaps because he didn't know what to say.

"Marcus needs inspiration," said Hail Larry's Wife. "Give him that book I've been trying to get you to read, Bear: *Conversations with God*. That'll change things for him."

"Give him a man," said Hail Larry, then added in a booming voice: *"A big freakin' honking man!"*

"He needs Walt," said Bear. "At least I think."

"Then give him Walt," said Walter.

"Unfortunately," said Bear, "in *My Whole Other Life*, guys like you, well, let's just say, guys like me don't usually get as lucky as Cole-man the Soul Man."

"Says who?" asked Walter. "Never mind that—it's a movie, right? A fantasy, a dream—you said so yourself."

"We think and dream like movies," said Bear, remembering his own words.

"Movies and TV teach us how to dream and what to dream of, putting ideas in our minds, like how to love and who to love."

"So do a Benchley," said Walter.

"What's a Benchley?" asked Hail Larry's Wife.

"Some guy from Bear's childhood who said: in your fantasies, anything can happen," said Walter. "And *My Whole Other Life* is just a fantasy, right?"

"That's all any movie or novel is," said Bear. "A fantasy. A dream about life, which is but a dream. Merrily, merrily, merrily."

"You know I'd do anything for you in *My Whole Other Life*," said Walter.

"Anything?" asked Bear. "Even if I was HIV-positive and you had lived a stereotypically hetero life?"

"I'm divorced now, right?" asked Walter. "And this is your movie, right?"

"Yes, but—" said Bear.

"And you trust me, right?" asked Walter.

"Yeah, but—" said Bear.

"You'll go anywhere with me, right?" asked Walter.

"But I'd have a billion questions—" said Bear.

"Buddy, look at me," said Walter. "Do you think you could ever be my worst nightmare?"

"Not my hero," said Bear.

"If you believe in me, I'll take you there," said Walter. "Better still, we'll go there together. Back in a flash." Walter turned and headed for the SUV. Bear extended his arms and gave his buddy a big ole Bear hug from behind.

"Like a big freakin' teddy bear," said Hail Larry.

"*That's* why I'm having déjà vu!" said Hail Larry's Wife. "Bear, your moves totally remind me of Simon Seahawk dancing around Walter at the Kingdome!"

"Wait a minute," said Hail Larry, eyeing his wife with bewilderment. "I had this image in my head of the Bengals' mascot dancing around freakin' Yeager on *SportsCenter*. Or was it a game against the Bills and the guy in the Buffalo suit?"

Walter or Bear let out an incredulous laugh. The other buddy simply arched his head to the sky, kept dancing and asked: "Now who's crazy?"

27

When Walt's Away, the Bearcat Plays

"**M**y crazy little Bearcat," sighed Marcus Coleman, sitting in the bleachers of the football stadium in the Complex in the hills above Malibu. "I saw Bear as an equal partner in the kind of duo I dreamed of being part of my entire life, where each man accepts the other unconditionally and has an unwavering faith in their bond, as if both men have an understanding."

That's the way the gods drew it up. We're supposed to be buds.

Marcus took a deep breath, surveyed the moonlit football field, then continued: "Walter and Bear's bond is similar to Starsky and Hutch, the buddy cops of my youth. They had this understanding that their creators intended for them to be buddies, so Starsky and Hutch accepted it, and got on with the business of being buddies, never doubting their chemistry or fate as a duo, as if both men had an understanding."

That's the way the gods drew it up. We're supposed to be buds.

Marcus surveyed the moonlit shed across the field, then continued: "Back in elementary school, I remember sitting in a new classroom at the beginning of every year and feeling the presence of some other boy nearby. There was no eye contact, no official moment, and it certainly wasn't sexual, but ... at some point, our souls gravitated toward one another, and next thing you know, we're side by side, being best buds for the entire school year, as if we had an understanding."

That's the way the gods drew it up. We're supposed to be buds.

Marcus took a deep breath, surveyed the moonlit canyon beyond the field, then continued: "Somewhere around junior high, I stopped having best buds. In adolescence, everything got short-circuited, bottled up, twisted. I started craving a best bud for life, but that was not an easy dream to articulate. Or manifest. My one true buddy has been elusive ever since, except in my dreams, the only place I've ever experienced my soul's deepest desires. And for that, I'm grateful to Walt. That's what I would have told him, had Walt stuck around."

Marcus surveyed the moonlit gymnasium behind the football stadium, then said, "What was I thinking? Strange coincidences, naps in the grass, a magical gardener. We're Super Bowl champs, let's be soul mates! I must be crazy."

"You're not dreaming an *even-halfway-decent* dream," said the voice suddenly adjacent to Marcus.

"Trying to avoid dreaming at all," said Marcus, picking up Mattel Electronics Football and starting a new game. "If Walt heard me ranting about us being soul mates, it's no wonder he disappeared. For one, he probably thought I was saying he's gay and that was *so* not what I meant."

"What did you mean then?" asked the adjacent voice.

"Ah, man ... sacked," said Marcus. "I've never thought of Walt or Walter as any sexual label. Walter and Bear aren't labels like gay, straight, bi. My soul has never spoken its true nature with those words. I was born a boy *slash* man. Later, I came to understand my desire to bond with another boy *slash* man, but not so that we could become gay men or straight men. The closest anyone else has come to articulating the bond my soul desires is the buddy duo. Starsky and Hutch. Martin and Lewis. Butch and Sundance. My soul craves a buddy, not a lifestyle. Of course, my buddy and I are sexual together, make no mistake. But labels and lifestyles with labels are not part of any dream born within my soul. We make our own lifestyle and rules. That's what I wanted to tell Walt."

"What if Walt just left for a while?" asked the adjacent voice. "He had some event tonight, right? Maybe it was business and he just got called away!"

"Listen to the dreamer man's dreamer man, Bearcat Peeps," laughed Marcus, "like he's in another story meeting ... near the goal ... touchdown!"

"My turn," said the adjacent voice, taking control of the offense. "Anything's possible, true? What if Walt plans on coming back? He was at some construction site this morning, right? *Yes, first down!* Picture him at a place just like this, doing some construction or football business, or both. Then he's gonna come back and hear the rest of your beautiful dream," said the owner of the adjacent voice, one Bear Coleman. "By the way, your dream is *my life!*"

"My ball," giggled Marcus Coleman, hearing the *turnover!* whistle and taking control of the offense. "If I didn't know better, sounds like you're trying to dream up a way for me to hook up with Walt as if *you're* dreaming up *my* life."

"If you're my creator, why did I take the hit @ the PITT?" asked Bear.

"Sacrifice," said Marcus. "*Hmmm*, just a field goal. Put it this way, if you're my creator: why did Walt leave and why did the note blow away?"

"One sec," said Bear, more focused on his offense.

"I'll answer for you," said Marcus. "You can't dream of getting lucky twice in your life, so to speak."

"Say what?" said Bear. "Ah, man ... this game sucks."

"You can't dream of a *My Whole Other Life* script where Marcus gets the guy and the guy is Walt," said Marcus. "You can't imagine getting lucky twice, which means you doubt, on some level, getting lucky once. And we all know why a poor bastard named Coleman has reason to doubt."

"Dream on," said Bear. "Yes! First down! You're not dreaming any deepest dreams yourself, Mr. Gay Sex Freak Marcus Coleman."

"Meaning?" asked Marcus.

"You've never written a story where the guy gets the guy and they ride off together into the sunset," said Bear.

"*Rightbackatcha*," said Marcus.

"Working on it," said both Marcus and Bear, looking straight ahead.

"The batteries on this game are getting weak," said Bear, stopping the game. "Just like our excuses. If I'm dreaming you up, how come I got you in such a dark place with the greatest man in the world? To me anyway?"

"Don't be so hard on yourself, little Bearcat," sighed Marcus. "When's the last time you read a book, saw a movie, heard a love song, passed a billboard, seen a commercial on television, seen *any* image anywhere where the hot, sexy, funny, cuddly, warm, romantic, all-American object of anyone's affection was ... someone like me?"

"Which me?" asked Bear. "Black male? Same-gender loving? Athlete-looking on the outside, lovable goofball *slash* brainiac on the inside?"

"Start with any of those atoms and build yourself a whole universe of me's," said Marcus. "You still ain't gonna find *me* being the object of anyone's affection in the media. If you see me in the media, I'll be the black man, but I won't be a black man dreaming of being a spirit leader or a rocket scientist, or a black man dreaming of having one true buddy and feeling special, the kind of special that makes you feel worthy of romance and love, the kind we all dream about, as seen on TV and in the movies."

"Our roles are always played by the Julia Robertses of the world, even if they don't fit the part," said Marcus or Bear Coleman, imagining his blocks arranging themselves in a way that read:

We live in an age where we are inundated with countless images from count-
less sources, from TV to movies to pop-up ads. A huge percentage of those images
deal with love, sex and romance. Still, rare or nonexistent is the occasion where I
encounter an image that reflects who I am and what I dream of. Even rarer and
more nonexistent is the occasion where I encounter an image that might encourage
another soul to dream of loving someone just like me.

"And you still expect me to come up with a happy ending for these poor bastards?"

"Dream of it."

"Even if Walt is living a life completely different from Walter?"

"Dream of it."

"Even if Walt's note said: TAKE ME OUTTA THE LOOP?"

"Dream of it."

"What if it said: HANG ON TIGHT, I'M COMING RIGHT BACK."

"Dream of it. Or I can."

"Meaning?"

"If one of us is dreaming the other's life, why not dream the best dream for both of us and see what comes outta it?"

"You mean, like, dream our deepest dreams no matter what?"

"Game over. I won."

"You're asking me to be one crazy dreamer man, dreamer man."

"Dream of it."

28

Oscar's Night

CAN I PLAY WITH A NIGGER'S POLE, PLEASE?

"What do you think of this essay from some boy at my kid's school in Western Pennsylvania?" asked Walter, standing in the home office at the Jaw.

"Why, whateva *Water* wants, Massa!" yelled Bear, screaming like a newborn baby at his desk ... *felt right!*

"Talk about a blessing!" laughed Walter. "An eight-year-old white boy writes an anonymous essay saying he wants to play with a nigger's pole, and Tank's off the hook for having a dad who happens to have a cool black Bear for a bud."

"*That* is some seriously divine shit, ain't it, Massa Norseman?" said Bear, more focused on multitasking ... *lunch and a new movie idea ... steamy!*

"Piping hot!" said Walter, biting on Bear's ear. "You know, other than not plugging in the TV or picking up a newspaper—and our general media blackout—it's been a pretty normal off-season at the Jaw, eh?"

"Considering we're Super Bowl champs *and* out and proud buddies," said Bear, typing and eating.

"You need a bigger desk. One that can hold your expanding and amazing mind," said Walter, taking his own hot lunch to his side of the home office.

"Rolltop is too special," said Bear. Years ago, the desk had been a birthday gift from Walter to Bear. "Never toss any of your old shit."

"Which is why there's a junky old red sports car in the garage," said Walter.

"Had to chase it down, find your old core," said Bear, eating, typing, kinda messy, he was.

"Man, that guy hated selling it back at first," said Walter.

"Then he was *still* sobbing as we sped off," said Bear.

"His knees were bleeding!" said Walter.

"Yours would be, too!" giggled Bear. "All that time spent down there, in front of both of us ... showing his gratitude ... all because I said: *I'd search the whole wide world to find and buy my buddy's used shit.*"

"How can he sell used shit on the world wide web?" asked Walter.

"Dunno, but his eyes lit up like a million-dollar idea was born," said Bear, typing and eating. "Do it sound like a good idea to Massa Norseman?"

"Hey," shrugged Walter, "if he thinks he can create this *eBay* for people all over the world to buy and sell used shit, I say go for it. You and I are not one to knock people and their dreams."

"Amazing he didn't take any money for our little red sports car," said Bear.

"Too busy on his knees, sobbing with joy for the *selling used shit* idea," said Walter. "How wacky is that?"

"Tell me about it, Massa Norseman," said Bear. "I like calling my Massa by his original name. This much is true."

"So you're never gonna let me get rid of that old car?" asked Walter.

"We can recycle it someday," said Bear. "Did Massa bring the eggbeater from the kitchen?"

"Recycle the car?" asked Walter. "Great idea. When?"

"In time," said Bear, typing. "Sorry, said the wrong thang. Should have said: *whatever Massa Walter wants. This much is true.*"

"You crack me up," said Walter, drinking coffee at his desk.

"Gotta crack yo' ass up to get to the core," said Bear, turning into Grayson, his rough, tough brutha-in-charge. "The archives power the magnet at the core. When Massa need, I gotta put the hurt on dat core in his ass, make sure it don't get too uptight, right, Massa QB?"

"Speaking of cores of the QB's ass," laughed Walter, looking at his monitor. "Glad to see the *Freeways* are running smoothly before we head to camp. We're gonna need some very clear heads where we're going, bud, feel me?"

"Like never before," said Bear, typing, sipping his cup of Joe.

"The Camille was really able to shed the perfect shade of light on the whole film," said Walter.

"And it only takes 21 hours for Lucy Hellishwoman to drive 42 miles. How about that?" said Bear, more focused on typing.

"While it takes Lacy Heavenly 42 years to drive 21 miles in reverse, go figure," said Walter, still trying to wrap his head around that one himself.

"Don't sweat the details in the blur, bud," said Bear.

"So have I buttered you up enough this last week?" asked Walter.

"I'm almost ready to let you back in the dawg house," said Bear, typing.

"Larry is not a problem."

"Did I say he was?"

Boom.

"On top of everything else," read Bear from his monitor. "Larry McPherson had been traded from San Francisco 2 Seattle, to shore up a receivers core suddenly weakened by the absence of Junior Jefferson, who was having (reverse related?) leg problems. Now, Massa Norseman and his dark-looking man friend, Sir Larry, were gonna be playing on the same team finally. Literally."

"Larry is not a problem."

"Did I say he was?"

Boom Baby.

Two can conceive just as well as four. Anyone disagree?

"All I ever needed was the One!" sang Bear. "Remember that song back in the day? When it was just you, me, the little green box, and a couple of really wonderfully smelling college jocks ... and all the shit we went through to get to this point? Shit that would take lifetimes to remember."

"Bear, please," said Walter. "Don't go thinking bad thoughts—you and I have been together for—"

"WALTER, THE NUMBERS GUY," said and typed Bear, "NEVER REMEMBERS IT CORRECTLY. WHY IS THAT, DEAR ABBY?"

"Fifteen!" guessed Walter.

"DATELINE FOR MASSA NORSEMAN: 1996," said and typed Bear. "We a dirty dozen now, Massa, give or take. What we gone do next? Oh, fuck, I'm tired of talking like a damned slave."

"Try talking like a blessed slave," said Walter.

"Wow, the mind!" said Bear. "He is one good Massa, folks!"

"Preach!" laughed Walter.

"Loves my jokes!" said Bear.

"And he got jokes!" said Walter.

"Massa Norseman ain't begun to hear my jokes," said Bear. "I loves making my Massa Norseman laugh ... and laugh and laugh and laugh. Massa come home from a day dealing with all dem white people who don't understand him. They don't understand what Massa needs from his universe, his Super Universe. Massa need a nigga boy who treats him right, don't Massa?"

"Nailed it," said Walter.

"Is it about time, Walter?" asked Bear.

"Can we go back to talking like we normally do now?" asked Walter.

"Yes, buddy," sighed Bear. "Talk about an energy drain. But I think I got the massa and slave vibe down for this film idea, but that's all I can say for now."

"Sweet," said Walter. "Sounds like it's gonna be a doozy. Keep me in the loop."

THE BOYS LOVED TO ROMP in the ocean beneath the ridge of Moose Jaw while Hip loved to smell the sea, especially as left behind in the seaweed on the beach. They kept their clothes on—just a water-at-the-ankles kind of day. Needed some mellow time before the blast-off back into the football world.

"So how does Bear Coleman feel about a white man calling him *boy?*" asked Walter, side by side with his Bear, ambling slowly down the beach.

"*Any* white man, or my golden blond reflection?" asked Bear.

"The white man who wants as much Sugar as possible from you before training camp," said Walter. "Especially *this* training camp."

Walter Yeager, Homosexual NFL Quarterback in the eyes of the world.

Boom.

"To hear your lips utter anything in my honor is an honor," said Bear, "for that means you've thought of me. And that, in and of itself, is a miracle. This much is true."

"HAD ENOUGH OF MY FACE TIME IN YOUR ZONE, Big Norse?" asked Bear, falling into the Jacuzzi on the deck at the Jaw.

"Yeah, the Hipster's back. We must be done," said Walter, turning over in the lounge chair. When it came to sex, the boys were often too loud and intense for their dog's very sensitive sensibilities. Hip was prone to making himself scarce the moment there was a sudden rise in the testosterone pressure at the Jaw. Unfortunately, Hip needn't have gone too far this time. The phone under Walter's chair interrupted their afternoon with one of the few distinctive rings that had the power.

"One of the kids," said Walter, answering the call. "This is Walter Yeager ... Son, what's on your mind? ... wait! ... did you do your 20 jumping jacks? Go ahead. I'll wait." Walter called up something on his laptop, now in his lap.

Unlike the adults in their brave new world, Tank, Grace's girls and any of the Yeager and Coleman satellites were allowed to talk to Walter and Bear about anything, including the good *and* not-so-good things that occurred in their world as a result of knowing a famous quarterback and his buddy. The kids had an always-open lifeline in both Walter and Bear—as long as they promised to do jumping jacks before *and* after every phone call. That way, all that nervous energy combusting within could be dissipated productively. It was another one of Bear's new energy recycling innovations, and it was making life easier for everyone in the loop. *Big Ups to Daddy Coleman and the old days.*

"Too easy," said Walter when Tank finished. "Maybe we should increase the dosage to 40 jumping jacks for the 12-and-up crowd, eh, Bear? Kidding, son, relax, truly."

The father listened while the son relayed the derogatory remark heard at school today, one rebel comment from someone not interested in an anonymous essay about niggers and their poles ... *hmmm.* When Tank finished, Walter began reading from the document on his laptop monitor:

SON ... You can let what other people say about your dad affect how you feel about your dad, or you can decide for yourself whether or not your dad is a good dad and a good man, based on what's important to you, and what's inside your heart. Your decision is your choice and only yours.

SON ... Whether or not a father is a famous man or a trash collector, every child makes that choice throughout the child's entire life. Perhaps I have made your choice more challenging by taking a path in life that has made me famous and controversial, but how *you* feel about your dad is still your choice. And consider thinking of it this way: if the challenge to make that choice is greater, perhaps the rewards are greater ...

Walter paused, then said: "Any of that make any sense, son? ... Really? ... Is that so? ... Great ... Great to hear ... I'll tell Bear ... Glad we could help. I love you, too, son. Bye."

"He loves your piece?" asked Bear, rising out of the watery hole.

Walter made a decisive keystroke on his laptop. "My son had no clue what I just uttered, said I sounded like I was speaking another language. But he did decide that the jumping jacks made him hungry, which reminded him about the leftover pizza he wanted to eat before his siblings got home. He said to thank you."

"*Me?*" giggled Bear.

"My boy knows I would never, ever write that," said Walter.

"Maybe he'll understand when he gets older," said Bear.

"*Or* you could dumb it down so the rest of world can get it, too," said Walter.

"You think I'm onto something with all this newfangled writing on energy and recycling?" asked Bear.

"I wouldn't doubt your amazing powers for a second, brother man," said Walter, setting aside his laptop "I'm looking forward to the breakthrough."

"A character in the new movie makes one," said Bear. "Not me."

"Sweet." Walter moved to the Jacuzzi. "Tank's energy may have been sufficiently rerouted, but mine merely took a detour. Who's turn is it to smack it up, flip it and rub it down?"

"Do you, do me—who cares, baby? It's all good. All God and all Good."

BEAR'S FAVORITE PART OF THE Moose Jaw remodel (other than the very private Fort Knox) was the upper deck off the master bedroom. He was napping there one spring morning when he felt something tender and wet on his nose.

"Directly in my mouth," mumbled Bear. "Or over my whole face."

"Too big for that already," said Walter. "Open up wider, your eyes, that is. This one's gonna get you through the separation."

"It's awful wet and messy," said Bear, then he opened his eyes. "And brown! He's so brown! He's so big, brown, round and beautiful, isn't he?"

"Bear's in love again," said a very pleased Walter. *QBs are givers.*

"Daily," said Bear. "And now doubly! Double dip of double love, Walter, how did you know I needed this so much? How did you know I need this, right this very moment?"

"God knows," laughed Walter. "But I'm glad I nailed it for ya."

"Even the Hipster loves his new bud!" said Bear, watching Hip get a whiff of the new addition to the family, a chocolate Labrador retriever puppy.

"Look at 'em, regulating," said Walter.

"Say what?" asked Bear.

"Regulating," said Walter. "Figuring out who's gonna dominate."

"Ballgame, the old guy," said Bear. The pup was on his back, getting some tummy-lovin' from Hip.

"You name 'em, word guy," said Walter.

"Come here, boy, what's yo' name?" asked Bear. "Come here ... come ... here!"

Greg the Gut's Sports Report was on the radio on the upper deck: "Markus Kramer don't name his dogs after no body parts. Here comes my dream of a hound dawg now ... *come ... here ... come here ... come here! Feel me?*"

"Comet," said Bear. Comet left Hip and joined Bear on the lounge chair.

"Amazing ... dawgs, when you let 'em be dawgs," said Walter.

"True dat," said Bear. "Thanks, PV, buddy. Forever grateful."

"BEAAAAAAR! HOW COULD YOU?" asked Walter. "The betrayal!"

"Sorry, dude," said Bear. "I just wanted to see if I could find out anything about dogs on this newfangled network I can't seem to find."

"We agreed: no TV until such time," said Walter. "Here you are, flipping channels in the bedroom!"

"To find Animal Planet," said Bear, glancing at the dogs napping in the moonlight on the upper deck. "Maybe we can learn more about the boys."

"Sweet," said Walter. "Find it?"

"Not yet," said Bear. "I haven't seen TV since before hibernation, and let's face it, I've been something of a Bumble Bear since the hit @ the PITT."

"It's those coma pills if you ask me," said Walter.

"Which is why I'm done taking them, as of this morning," said Bear. "I don't need meds, I need my man—oh, wait, here's some furry creatures ..."

Picture it. Saturday Night Live. A kick-line of grown men dressed as football players in the locker room, dancing like chorus fags on Broadway while a desperate, horny, queeny, blond Seattle Seahawks quarterback chases his teammates to the song "It's Raining Men" by The Weather Girls.

"Is this the better dream?" asked Walter.

"Not from where I'm standing," said Bear.

"They would have been more accurate had they depicted me entering the studio and blowing everybody's fucking head off," said Walter. "Live!"

"Can't find the blessed dog channel," said Bear.

"I'll tell Roberto to remove all the TVs altogether then," said Walter.

"How will you get your *Frasier* fix behind my back?" asked Bear.

"*Ha!*" said Walter, leaving the field of play on that one.

Bear's cell rang: "*My God, SNL! My God, SNL!*" said one of the relatives, Grayson's girlfriend Anna.

"Sorry, Ms. Stacie," said Bear. "You're too big to ride this ride ... *huh?* ... sure! Do some jumping jacks, sounds like you need 'em ... *SNL* is not about us. *Saturday Night Live* is about people's reactions to us, and your reaction to their reactions. And since the initial reaction was negative, and no one has yet to rearrange that negative energy, Walter and I are not interested ... call us for money, to share joy and wish us well ... but don't call us to respond to negative energy created because Walter and I love each other. Share every good, heartwarming story of support you get. We are grateful ... you too, sexy nigga mama, have a good Boston marathon ... *literally.*"

"Come get me. I need my pole," said Bear, gazing out the window. "Amazing. A boy in Western PA wants a nigger with a pole. 'Sup with dat, Big Norse?"

"Tell me about it," said Walter, chilling in bed in the master bedroom at the Jaw. "What my Bear looking at?"

"The Julio," said Bear, watching the bullfighter fight the bull down below.

"Suppose he has an herb to cure the ignorant in the NFL?" asked Walter.

"I'll ask if you'd like, sir," said Bear.

"Keep it in mind for now," said Walter. "Your Big Norse is about to go into the Core, deep inside the gates of ... a man's lair ... the sacred, most sacred place in an athlete's mind."

"His wife's heart and soul?" asked Bear.

"The wives wish!" said Walter.

"Let's take them there," said Bear. "Something tells me a lot of players' wives would love some less uptight hubbies, cubbies, fishes, cowboys, packers, giants, redskins, steelers ... guys trying to get traded to the white broncos. Think we'll be cool without Millstone in the backfield now that he's retired?"

"No doubt," said Walter. "We didn't vibe that well anyway. Now that I'm officially the Super Shit in my own Super Universe, the last thing I want is a dark force fucking up my world. Still have the stuff you wrote on the locker room? I'm thinking of taking it to camp with me."

"Somewhere around here," said Bear, turning from the window. "You really think pro sports is ready to dream this kind of better dream?"

"Read to me," said Walter.

Bear loved reading to his buddy, hanging out in bed, dreaming dreams, chasing rainbows, believing anything was possible. Like a happy little boy, Bear retrieved his magic and jumped on the bed, eager to read to his buddy.

"Still fuzzy, but here goes," said Bear. "Bits and pieces ..."

THE LOCKER ROOM is an empty space.

First, it was just space in space.

Then a planet stood in that space.

Then people stood on that planet in that space.

Then people dreamed of uses for that space.

Boom. Creation.

THE LOCKER ROOM is born.

THE LOCKER ROOM is still first and foremost an empty space.

Humanity brings everything else into that space, from the dreams to the wood to the showers to the plumbing to the slogans on the wall, to the love, hate, smiles, laughter, fear, understanding, misunderstanding, heart, mind, spirit ... what's inside your soul, at the core. Remember your core? *Feel* your core? Can anyone change your core? Can you change anyone else's core? Can you change how you feel about anyone else's core?

THE LOCKER ROOM is just an empty space. Your choice what you bring to that space. As leader of the Seahawks, I, Walter Yeager, am bringing into the locker room a winning attitude, so I can get another ring, because when my career is over, people aren't going to ask me about the locker room. They're gonna wanna know about *these!* (flashes rings) ... You can be a player who has some of *these!* (flashes rings) ... *Or* ... you can be a player who talks about how you didn't want to be naked in a room of a hundred men, all because *one* of them chose to be honest about who he loves back at home.

Your choice, always and forever. This much is true.

"DADDY SENT ME A GREAT POLE!" *yelled Bear at the top of his lungs!*

"Hold on, be right there," yelled Walter from upstairs.

"I like calling our favorite black coach Daddy," said Bear from the den. "Kinda gives me a father figure in my life, a black one, I mean ... *so cool, love my fellow niggas, all ages, all dreams ... right, Luthers?*"

"My boy likes?" yelled Walter, rumbling overhead.

"My God, Walter, I can honestly say: never been happier," yelled Bear. "This much is true."

"Glad you like your pole," yelled Walter.

"Dream come true," yelled Bear. "I hope you understand, I'm open to working on it until I get it right, if it ain't good enough, I mean."

"I got faith in my Bear," said Walter, descending from above, somewhat noisily ... *different for the man who's normally a panther.*

"If Coach thinks a pole can cure my balance problems, I'll live the rest of my life on a freakin' pogo stick," said Bear, trying it out in the den at the Jaw.

The boys never talked much about it, but Bear, who had always been a little clumsy, felt downright retarded sometimes since the comet of the Pittsburgh Stealers, aka the hit @ the PITT.

"Ouch! I'm fine. Just another flesh wound," said Bear on the pogo stick. "Who needs two end tables anyway?"

"You'll get the hang of it," said Walter, in quite the serious mood. "I'm just glad the solution might be simple."

"And painless!" said bouncing Bear. "*Ouch!* I'm fine. Just another flesh wound. Wasn't my favorite lamp anyway."

"Coach said the pogo stick worked with a couple of linemen over the years," said Walter. "But then again, it didn't work for others."

"Maybe they should try doing it while only wearing elbow and knee pads. And your sweaty white jockstrap, like me," said Bear. "*Ouch!* I'm fine. Just another flesh wound. We weren't attached to that TV anyway, were we?"

"You'll get the hang of it," said Walter, sounding distracted. "We can always get another big screen. Trust me."

"My very own cheerleader, Bearcat People," said bouncing Bear. "*Ouch!* I'm fine. Just another flesh wound. Make that TV *and* patio door. Break time."

"Showtime!" said Walter. "Hurry up. Roberto and the transport are on their way. Come on, don't keep the Super Freakin' Stud of All Mankind waiting ... I'll lick your—"

"Pleasure principle aside," said Bear, cueing up the music. He was still a little frustrated at the failure of his slapstick routine. "Janet? Or a jock jam?"

"Shit, you know I don't care," said Walter. "Dance!"

For Phase 2 of Operation Laugh Your Ass Off, Bear cleared the debris in the den and gave his man *The Training Camp Send-Off Show.*

"What would that kid in Pennsylvania write about *this?*" laughed Bear, dancing to "2 Legit 2 Quit" by MC Hammer. "... waving his nasty nigger ass in his Massa's face, while Massa got off on the funk of that funky, smelly, black nigger hole in need of his white Massa's tongue and pole."

"*Hilarious!*" Walter laughed so hard, snot flew out of his nose.

What re-entry into the sacred core of the warriors of the NFL?

"To think a little boy in Western PA would write what he did!" said Walter between busting his gut. "How did God know we needed the perfect distraction at the perfect time?"

"Grace, man," said Bear, dancing up a storm in his buddy's sweaty white jock. "God came up with the perfect storage tank for America's nervous homophobic energy right now. It can only be some seriously divine shit."

"OJ and the white Bronco didn't hurt either," said Walter, calming down.

"True dat," said Bear, bringing his song and dance to a grateful close. "WALTER YEAGER, DEFENDING SUPER BOWL CHAMP, ADMITS LOVE FOR LONG-TIME BUDDY BEAR COLEMAN ... and America is up in arms over OJ, and what this white kid in elementary school wrote about the trial making him want to find a nigger with a pole, just like that cop, the *Marked Furry Man.*"

"Think Tank's school will ever find out which boy wrote it?" asked Walter.

"Why, whatever Walter wants, Massa Norseman and his holy pole."

HOLD ON, BEARCAT PEOPLE ... NOW ENTERING THE NFL CORE ... POSSIBLE TURBULENCE AHEAD.

"The boys say hi," said Bear, calling from Corona, Seattle. "Comet loves the woods up here. I think Hip misses the beach. Amazing how polar opposite our dogs are ... *part of the whole equation.*"

"The equation that keeps coming in your dreams?" asked Walter, calling from training camp, somewhere in a hole in space over the Pacific Northwest.

"Yes, that one," said Bear. "I'm no rocket scientist, but the more I write, the more I seem to be figuring out some kind of ... long, long thing."

"... *fuckin' A, man, this shit hurts like hell!" said an echo of Walter's voice.*

"Make it hurt like heaven, then, *ya?*" said Bear, sounding Swedish. "So you didn't just post my speech, *you read it? Aloud in the team cafeteria in the middle of lunch?* Walter, that sounds like a dream come true!"

"Tell me about it," said Walter. "Hold. Let me pull my pants up."

"... *heaven now, little Havana!" said a whisper of Walter's voice.*

"So am I doing a good job so far?" asked Bear. "With all this newfangled writing?"

"Man, nobody does it better," said Walter. "I'm off to the second of two-a-days, back later ... remember Bear ... eat! You can't create if you don't fill up that mouth of yours ... *John!* ... read my bud his little locker room speech that I posted in the cafeteria, near the mashed potatoes ... made a few edits for the long-winded word man ... later, Bear."

"Thanks for the lunch date," said Bear. *Edits?*

"This Walta's boy?" asked a voice from nowhere.

John Jeremiah Shockme had picked up Yeager's cell phone!

"You got it," said Bear, shocked.

Country white boy, tight end, straw-out-the-side-of-the-mouth kinda guy.

"Walter said you like my locker room essays," said Bear.

"Kinda rocked my world, little Bearcat," said Shockme. "Wait ... getting ready ... practice ... two-a-days are a killer ... man, I never looked at the locker room as just some air in the world ... *how fucking revolutionary is that?*"

"Tell me about it," said Bear.

"DREAM," said Shockme, apparently reading:

DREAM OF A NIGHTMARE OF GETTING RAPED AND CONVERTED TO BEING A FAG IN THE LOCKER ROOM. OR DREAM OF ALL OF US GETTING ALONG AND TAKING CARE OF BUSINESS, SO WE CAN WIN ANOTHER TITLE AND GO DOWN AS ONE OF THE GREATEST FOOTBALL TEAMS IN HISTORY. OR GREATEST BUNCH OF MEN WHO COULDN'T GET THE JOB DONE BECAUSE ONE GUY WAS HONEST ABOUT HIS LOVE FOR ONE OTHER MAN ON THIS PLANET. YOUR CHOICE. I'M GONNA DREAM THE SUPER DREAM. YOUR QB, #13.

"I'll sure as hell fuckin' dream with any nigger, prick, spic or faggot that's gonna get my country cracker ass to the Super Bowl, I'll tell ya that, little Bearcat," said Shockme.

"Not good enough," said Bear. "Gotta sub *heaven* for *hell*. No hell in my locker room. Put *heaven* in that statement above, and we can dream together every day the rest of our lives."

"I'll sure as *heaven* fuckin' dream with any nigger, prick, spic or faggot that's gonna get my country cracker ass to the Super Bowl, I'll tell ya that, little Bearcat," said Shockme.

"How does that make you feel?" asked Bear.

"Like a hick and prick," said Shockme. "Saying *heaven* in the same breath with all that."

"How about subbing the word *human* for the lot of them and repeating. You know the drill," said Bear. "Come on, Shockme, I know you're capable ... *let's do it for our country!*"

"I'll sure as *heaven* fuckin' dream with any *human* that's gonna get my country cracker ass to the Super Bowl, I'll tell ya that, little Bearcat," said Shockme. "I'll do dreamtime with anybody that's gonna get me some more rings!"

"Love you," said Bear.

"Love you, too," said a voice lost in the chaos on the other side.

"Who else needs schooling?" laughed Bear.

"Cocky little nigga, ain't you?" said a black voice into Yeager's cell.

"Oh, hey, Reggie," said Bear. "Hey, when you got skillz, you got skillz."

"Just watch ya back," said Reggie. "Every Rocky gets clocked."

"This is our time," said Bear. "Our world. We nutted it."

"Cocky little nigga, ain't ya?" said another black voice into Yeager's cell.

"Who *dis?*" asked Bear.

"A nigga who don't like your fag ass interfering with the team, especially here," said that black voice.

"Then hang up, please." Bear flushed the call and eyed his computer monitor. TIME to type more new thoughts for the core of the NFL:

Dream the better dream. Come to me. Ask me questions. Dialogue.

We can dream that we talk openly and honestly.

Or dream that we'll start trying to kill one another.

Your choice. I'm going to dream the Super dream ...

MAYBE IT WAS THE AFTEREFFECT of being a coma-head, but Bear couldn't remember ever attending one of his buddy's preseason scrimmages.

"Then again," said Bear, watching the mellow contest. "I was never an out ... buddy? Partner? Lover? What *are* Walter and me to everybody?"

"Then again," said Markus Kramer on Greg the Gut *on the radio. "I was*

never an out and open gay slash *fag* slash *homo, whatever they're calling it these days ... I hear 'queer' might be approved at the next annual convention."

"I didn't know people had conventions," said Bear.

"Where's your coma pills?" asked Hail Larry's Wife.

"Not that I was ever at the gay convention," said Markus Kramer on Greg the Gut *on the radio.*

"My head is fine," said Bear. "Or did you want them for you?"

"I was late flying out from the Bubble Coat Convention," said Markus Kramer on Greg the Gut *on the radio.*

"Watch your husband," said Hail Larry's Wife. "He's back on the field."

"I guess we should be thankful it's such a relatively calm affair," said Bear of the scrimmage.

"That's where we Negroes decided to bust a move on dem bubble coats y'all gone see us in for the next four. Four-year cycles on cultural shit like that," said Markus Kramer on Greg the Gut *on the radio.*

"Just like the Olympics!" said Bear, turning off the radio. "Who knew?"

Walter threw a touchdown pass to Hail Larry McPherson. Bear was glad Tank got to see his dad throw it. Tank was on the other side of the field. Ellen was also there, as was Mr. Yeager (no other Bearcat People).

"What's that symbolize? Our husbands' first hookup?" asked Bear.

"Those little stands sure are packed," said Hail Larry's Wife.

"It is the first public unveiling of *the live homosexual man playing quarterback out in the open in America,*" said Bear. "According to the news, no doubt."

"Too bad the little white boy who wants to play with a nigger's pole was spotted near Vancouver," said Hail Larry's Wife. "Otherwise, the media swarm would be *here.*"

"Tell me about it," laughed Bear. "Still would have been nice if things had been calm enough for me to watch the scrimmage outside the news van ..."

The van was parked outside the little stadium where the scrimmage was taking place. Inside, the van was dark, only lit by the monitor and candlelight.

"Thank your gal pal for me when you see her in Japan in a few," said Walter, blurring from the field to the van once the pretend battle was over.

"Thank God the day was safe and carefree," said Bear. "There can be miracles, this much is true."

"That one kid though," said Walter.

"Saw it on the monitor," said Bear. "Broke my heart."

Can I have your autograph, Mr. Yeager?

Not him. He's the queer one.

"Trying hard to dream a better dream for that boy," said Bear, "but how do you mend a broken heart when it's in the process of being broken?"

"Send it a Hail Mary with a lotta love inside," said Walter, getting horizontal so he could relax like a true gunslinger. "Did you know Larry is big-time religious?"

"You know the best part about loving you?" said Bear. "Seeing you do things I can't, like play quarterback, be a general of a whole crew, be you, Mr. Cool."

"That makes me feel good," said Walter.

"That's my job, and one I hope to do forever," said Bear. "No matter how good a friends you become with Larry."

"Don't start," said Walter.

"Too late," said Bear. "We done nutted it. Hell, Larry scared me the first time I saw him on the street in Seattle, outside Snaky Lu's. He's the stud athlete I picture another stud going for. I know my buddy would never hurt me."

"And vice versa," said Walter.

"Exactly," said Bear. "But I never told you this: I was kinda a geek in high school."

"You mentioned it," said Walter. "You know I don't see you that way."

"Just like I don't see you as a golden infallible God, you big shit." Bear laughed, which made Walter laugh.

Bear loves to make Walter laugh. This much is true. For eternity.

"When I'm with you," said Bear, "I never feel like a geek. You make me feel comfortable enough to be myself, no matter how Bumble Bear I am."

"Larry thinks you're cool," said Walter.

"Because I babysit his wife," said Bear.

"Better dream?" asked Walter.

"We're all gonna have a great time in Japan," said Bear.

"That's my Bear," said Walter.

"They didn't let me be quarterback," said Bear.

"Who?" asked Walter.

"Coach White," said Bear. "Junior high, the private one ... grades seven and eight ... Private Parks Academy. The kids at the school had the same last names as the chain department stores and stuff like that in the area. I was on the junior high football team—big man on the line, but I needed the rock. I asked Coach White if I could play quarterback. Coach looked at me as if I'd asked him to slice off his balls and hand them to me on a silver platter, to be served in the school cafeteria that looked a grand ballroom."

"Sounds posh," said Walter.

"No jeans for us boys; plaid skirts for the girls," said Bear. "There's only a handful of niggers in the joint, give or take."

"Come on, Bear," said Walter. "Dream a less cynical dream."

"There's a handful of us blacks," said Bear.

"How does that make you feel?" asked Walter.

"Almost as good as holding you," said Bear. "There's a handful of us African Americans in a seventh grade class of about, *heavens,* I don't know, 50 kids. So we all know one another, all of us, not just the darker ones. Anyway, cut to the football field. I'm a big nigga, sure—slipped, fuck it."

"Been slipping a lot since PITT," said Walter.

"Slipped a lot on the line, playing football," said Bear. "Spent my whole childhood under the pile or on the line. I was sick of that. Linemen weren't graceful. Linemen had zero to do with the spotlight. Nobody watches the game to watch the linemen."

"Those who love them," said Walter. "I hope."

"I needed to be seen," said Bear. "I had things to do and say, and people needed to see me do and say them. This was the early- and mid-70s. Jocks and Madison Avenue was still a young marriage, newlyweds. Mean Joe Green of the Steelers, and maybe one or two other players who weren't in the backfield—or flanked out to the right or left—had any kind of national commercial exposure. The nuclear fusion that was the media and sports was nascent and newfangled, like Three Mile Island—a simmering threat of explosion, not the Chernobyl it turned into in the 80s."

"You're even better away from the keyboard," said Walter.

"When not bogged down by typing, sure," said Bear.

"Sweet," said Walter.

"Bitter. Sure can be bitter," said Bear. "Look at what they did to me the last few years as the Bearcat. Look what they did to me as a junior high kid who wanted to be a quarterback. That was what I was talking about, right? Wanting to be center stage? Anyway, junior high football practice starts, and before I get to utter one breath, I'm typecast to the line, right guard I think it was. Or tackle, whatever. My head was down, my ass was up, and there were 21 other junior high boys orbiting around me. If I'd only known then ...

"But I digress. And rightfully so. If Steve Tyler of Aerosmith, bless his God of Rock soul, can make videos featuring his own daughter wearing the same plaid skirts as the girls at Private Parks Academy—and have his daughter dance on a pole *and* skinny-dip with a stranger she picked up hitchhiking—your big black buddy should be able to do a quick *Wonder Years* flashback, right?"

"He's stalling," said Walter. "Can't finish the story, Bearcat People."

Coach White, I wanna do something other than be on the line. Coach White, I am a quarterback!

"Did he laugh?" wondered Bear. "Might as well have. Long story short—"

"Too late for that," joked Walter. That was as much as Walter would ever think to mock his Bear. This much is true.

"Coach White claimed he needed my size and skill on the line," said Bear. "Funny thing, Coach also needed the cooperation of this big black kid with the prototype body, a kid who wasn't exactly a saint in school, more of a wild card!"

"We like the wild Bearcat Boyz, *fo'* sure," said Walter.

"Coach placated me by letting me take a couple of snaps here and there," said Bear. "Usually during a lost cause. We had plenty of those."

"That bites," said Walter.

"He created this pass called the Coleman Bomb," said Bear. "Teddy, the fastest guy on the team—beautiful, smooth black boy—would take off from the line of scrimmage, sprint as fast as he could, then I would heave it as far as I could. That was the Coleman Bomb. Never detonated, as in never completed."

Walter massaged Bear's shoulder, offering tender support.

"I ran some plays in practice, too," said Bear. "I'll never forget the feeling of Bob the center's cock-and-ball shaft. God, he was hot, now in reflection, all those pimples on his face and ass be damned. Did you ever go through anything like that in all your years of QB'ing?"

"Why are we talking about boys feeling balls when they should be slapping them, I mean, snapping them?" asked Walter, wetting his dry tongue.

"The white man wouldn't let me be quarterback," said Bear. "That's what someone used to tell me, don't remember who. Told me the Man showed me how to be a good nigger lineman on both sides of the ball, but never took my ambition to be a QB seriously. My brother used to say I could have been a fullback. Fullback I could live with. Anything where my hands touched the ball from time to time, controlled its destination based on my ability, pitted against the opponent. Fuck, I miss that. I should've had a shot."

"Another way the white man has brought you down?" asked Walter.

"I didn't say that," said Bear. "Remember, I'm Bumble Bear now."

"Bear Coleman," said Walter. "If I didn't know you better than I know myself, I'd think the completely deflated football in your hand would be a dead giveaway that you're one bitter Bear."

Bear eyed the squashed ball in his Bear paws.

"Soul Man," said Walter, "this is your cheerboy Walter Yeager talking: You and I are Super Bowl Champs! We're Super Bowl Champs! We're Super Bowl Champs!" *Yelled like a child.* "We're gay and fabulous and Super Bowl Champs! Sorry, I suddenly seem to suffer from a speech impediment." *Spoken like the biggest fag.*

"Come on, Yeager," said Bear. "Dream a less cynical dream."

"We're in love and we're Super Bowl Champs," said Walter, sounding like Walter, a man who was all man.

"How does that make you feel?" asked Bear.

"Almost as good as holding you," said Walter.

WALT MEETS THE WORLD: SUPER CHAMPS LAND IN TOKYO!

"Japan ..." sighed Bear, sitting in the plane on the tarmac. "My first time out of the other half of the world. The north/south end."

"Your trip, baby Bear," said Walter, sitting in the plane on the tarmac. "The one you missed out on *twice* in college."

"You remember!" said Bear. "The cheergirls from both USC and UCLA got to go to the Japan Bowl, but Japan didn't want the cheerboys."

"Perfect grace," said Walter. "I get to do the honors."

"Must mean *this* Japan trip was meant to be," said Bear.

"Just a freakin' preseason gig, guys," said Hail Larry, sitting in the plane on the tarmac.

"Of all the years to be going East," said Hail Larry's Wife, sitting in the plane on the tarmac. "First the comet, then coming out, then the Super Bowl, then your hibernation, then training camp ... *now* being under the microscope of a bunch of—"

"*Beaaaaaar!*" cried Walter.

"What Bumble Bear do now?" laughed Hail Larry.

"It's your blessed wife!" said Walter. "She was about to detonate something very ugly. We *do not* need ugly right now."

"Wifey of mine," said Hail Larry. "Cut out the ugly."

"A swift correction by Yeager!" said Bear, looking down at his notes.

Being the slower talker, Yeager comprehends at a faster rate (using gut).

Being the faster talker, Coleman comprehends at a slower rate (using brain).

Being the slower to act, Yeager moves at a faster pace (like a panther).

Being the faster to act, Coleman moves at a slower pace (like a bear).

It's simpatico, folks, Nature's intention.

"What does *all that* mean?" asked Hail Larry's Wife, sitting next to Bear.

"Tell me about it," said Bear, sitting next to Hail Larry's Wife.

"Tell her about what?" asked Walter, sitting next to Hail Larry.

"What wifey do now?" asked Hail Larry, sitting next to Walter.

Perfect pairs in separate planes on the tarmac. The two players on the team plane. The two players' spouses on a private plane.

"*Don'tcha* just love these Dick Tracy-style wristwatch *slash* digital phone *slash* walkie-talkie *slash* music player *slash* home computers on our wrist *slash* bodies?" asked Bear, giddier than giddy. The other three agreed wholeheartedly, speaking into their own *slash* watches.

"The best part about being a player's wife is the travel and the toys!" said Hail Larry's Wife, speaking into her *slash* watch.

"Funny," said Bear, speaking into his *slash* watch. "I thought the best part about being a player's wife was being the wind underneath your man's wings. But then again, I'm no rocket scientist."

"Walter, would you come over to this plane," said Hail Larry's Wife, speaking into her *slash* watch, "and make Bear put away these scripts and essays of his? Time for fun on the Orient Express, true?"

"Look at that chaos out there," said Bear, back to work. "Forecast: lotta taxiing, hours maybe. Please have a cup of patience."

"I see a lot of streamers and pompoms," said Walter, speaking into his *slash* watch. "And a lot of Japanese people jumping up and down."

"I just hopped on this Seahawks bus," said Hail Larry, speaking into his *slash* watch. "Couldn't you have come out in a year where there wasn't an international game a few months down the road?"

"*Or* you could dream up a perfectly graceful reason we're all here," said Walter.

"I don't follow," said Hail Larry.

"Look at the opportunity," said Bear, writing in his lap but speaking close enough to his wrist *slash* watch to be heard by his three travel mates, the four of them all on the same frequency. "Had things not turned out the way they did, we wouldn't be here today, showing the world our beautiful bond ... in such a beautifully graceful way. We need Japan. Japan needs us."

"We need this B.E. person Tammy sent us to come get us off this plane," said Hail Larry's Wife, speaking into her four-way frequency.

"We need Gator," said Walter, speaking into his four-way frequency as well as the team plane: "Gator! ... Jefferson ... Jeff ... wake up, Snow ... Zook ... hey, Shockme ... where's Gator? Need my translator ... translator Gator ..."

"Gator knows Japanese?" asked Hail Larry's Wife, speaking into her four-way frequency.

"He almost majored in it," said Bear, picturing the jolly Pacific Islander from parties at the Jaw. "He also loves his Asian women, too. Imagine his single hormones right about now."

"Gator, what's that big sign out there say?" asked Walter, speaking to everyone in his frequency.

"Welcome Seattle Seahawks, World Champs," said Gator, speaking into Walter's frequency.

"Cool," said Walter. "How about the one not in English? Right underneath?"

"The one in their language?" asked Gator. "Been a while, but I think ... *hmmm* ... horny golden truth? No ... wait ... tiger and his cat? Wait ... hold on ... not a pussy ... oh, okay, here we go ... says: How serendipitous, the world would get to see the gay Jackie Robinson in person the year in which he is born—more or less."

"More or less?" said the four in the same frequency.

"As in more or less gay?" asked one.

"As in more or less Jackie?" asked one.

"As in more or less in person?" asked one.

"As in more or less born?" asked one.

"Who said what?" asked the four in the same frequency.

The connection was lost. The planes went through a vortex.

"That sign," said a voice in broken English from the cockpit, "reads as follows."

IF YOU CHANGE THE WAY YOU LOOK AT HOMOSEXUALITY,
HOMOSEXUALITY CHANGES.

"How's THE PRE-GAME PUB going, hubby?" asked Bear, speaking into his *slash* watch.

"Cool and dreamy," said Walter, speaking into his *slash* watch.

"Hi, Walter, sweetie," said Hail Larry's Wife, speaking into her *slash* watch.

"Hi, wifey of mine, sweetie," said Hail Larry, speaking into his *slash* watch.

"Caution: Larry's going soft over here!" said Bear.

"Listen to him, he sounds like a little kid," laughed Hail Larry. "A giddy, excited baby boy."

"That's my Bear," said Walter.

"You don't got my wife looking at maternity clothes over here, do you, Bumble Bear?" asked Hail Larry.

"Just the usual stimulating of the economy, road-trip style," said Bear.

Hail Larry's Wife modeled something tight and stylish, which looked like the last 20 tight and stylish things she modeled for Bear.

"Something tells me she ain't dreaming of maternity clothes," said Bear.

"Good," said Hail Larry. "You keep an eye on her. I'll watch your boy's back in this madhouse over here. Deal, Bumbles?"

"War Eagle," said Bear, invoking the fabled Auburn University rally cry to the former Tiger, the very same one whose dropped pass cleared the way for Walter and Bear's Sugar Bowl.

In the football world ... Tokyo, Japan, the Orient, Asia, Russia, and by extension, the world going *that* way, met Walter Yeager.

In the Eastern world ... Bear Coleman met Tokyo, Japan, the Orient, Asia, Russia, and by extension, the world going *that* way.

In the football world ... Walter talked to the media in Tokyo, Japan, the Orient, Asia, Russia, and by extension, the world going *that* way.

In the Eastern world ... Bear talked to the citizens of Tokyo, Japan, the Orient, Asia, Russia, and by extension, the world going *that* way.

In the football world ... Walter practiced lite in a domed stadium, tried different foods for the cameras, laughed at official team functions, drank *sake* with his teammates, and hung with his best pal Hail Larry.

In the Eastern world ... Bear partied lite in a swank nightclub, tried different foods for the fun of it, laughed while watching his man on TV at official team functions, drank *sake* with strangers, and hung with his best pal Hail Larry's Wife.

In the football world ... Walter had Hail Larry to watch his back, front for him, lie for him to escape potential roadblocks, steal time for him, and cheat those who wanted a piece of freakin' Yeager out of their shot at the man. And Walter Yeager was able to relax, meet the world, and play a little football.

In the Eastern world ... Bear had Hail Larry's Wife to watch his back, front for him, lie for him to escape potential roadblocks, steal time for him, and cheat those who wanted a piece of freakin' Yeager's buddy out of their shot at the man. And Bear Coleman was able to relax, meet the world, and look forward to watching his man play football again.

"She looks golden," said Bear into his frequency, *just Walter this time.*

"Him, too," said Walter into his frequency, *just Bear this time.*

"Where are you two?" asked Bear.

"A schoolyard," said Walter. "To talk to kids. Larry's in the can. You?"

"Where else?" asked Bear. "Yet another woman's clothing store. She's about to purchase 12 more of something in 12 different colors."

"How do you live through it?" asked Walter, knowing shopping made his man one dizzy Bear.

"It makes her happy, not to mention takes my mind off of nervous thinking about what might be going on over on your side of the city," said Bear.

"Larry kinda does the same for me," said Walter. "Never thought I'd meet a couple crazier than me and you."

"Funny, *that's* what she said *they* say about us," laughed Bear.

"Perfect grace?" asked Walter. "Come again. I definitely need to hear it one more time ... slowly though ... Bear, one sec, this is twisted ... Come again but slowly ... new language here ... never spoke this before ... only admired ... help us, Gator ... hold on, little Bearcat."

"Perfect, and her name should always be grace," said Gator. "More or less."

"What kind of school are you at?" asked Bear.

"Kids, lots and lots, coming right at us now," said Walter. "Hold on, Bear. Feels like a tidal wave ... remember that movie as a kid? Gator ... how do you say, slow down before somebody gets hurt ... Slow down, kids! I promise I'll get to all of you. Don't go crazy and no one gets hurt! Please, don't hurt the Seahawks! Gator helps us out here ..."

Gator yelled several things in Japanese in all frequencies. Kids began screaming in all frequencies. Even the ladies in the dress shop heard the screams in Bear's wrist *slash* watch. When all screaming subsided, Bear asked his wrist: "What happened?"

"Gator just scared away about a million kids," said a calm and resigned Walter, "who all took off running a million miles an hour."

"Gator, what did you just freakin' tell those poor kids?" asked Hail Larry, apparently rejoining Walter's frequency.

"I just said ... *oh, wait* ..." said Gator in somebody's frequency. "Did I mention I also almost majored in Russian, too?"

"*Man!*" cried the voice of Reggie Snowman, the octaves rising in somebody's frequency. "You said something in Russian to them kids?"

"No, I would never do that," laughed Gator. "I also almost majored in Poli Sci. And Mandarin Chinese, too. And I think I just made a bad switch."

"So what did you tell those kids?" asked a voice that sounded like that of Seattle's Coach Robbins.

The crosstalk frequency went dead. The *slash* watches were still a developmental test product.

"... that just so happens to cut out at the most crucial times, sometimes!" cried Bear.

"What happened?" asked Hail Larry's Wife, rejoining Bear in the main room of the dress shop.

"God only knows," said Bear.

The TV hovering above the cashier became God:

This just in from a school in Tokyo: Walter Yeager, Seattle Seahawks quar-terback, has made a vow to drown all Japanese children in a tidal wave of Seahawk mania. Or they will get hurt if they resist.

"Never seen tons of Japanese people running terrified to get away from a big white American quarterback," said Hail Larry's Wife. "Are you sure you chose the best teammate for the job of translator?"

"He almost majored in Japanese," said Bear. "I guess that explains how he almost got it right."

"The world's gonna think Walter and you are some kind of freaky child abusers," said Hail Larry's Wife.

"Only if the world chooses to see that tape in that light of those fuzzy fax," said Bear. "But thanks for giving birth to that atom bomb of a notion."

"I'm not the original translator to screw it up," cried Hail Larry's Wife. "What do you want me to do?"

"Help me fix it," said Bear, noticing a poster on the wall for a Japanese film called *Wendy Loves the Tigercat,* directed by Lisa Wu.

"How can you fix this?" asked Hail Larry's Wife.

"Tell me about it," said Bear. "Or stand here and listen to my bagpipes go on and on. *Or* come with me, as in trust my ass and let's go!"

THE SETTING WAS A NEVER-ENDING lawn in front of an ancient museum. On that never-ending lawn, Japanese men, women and children ... dozens, hundreds, thousands, millions ...

"All in the mind," said Bear, surveying the land below from a summit high above. He was satisfied his work was done for now.

"I *did* want to be a cheerleader," admitted Hail Larry's Wife. "I finally got to be one today. Thanks, Bear. You taught me how to be a cheerleader in, like, 10 minutes."

"Thank *you,* best friend of mine," said Bear.

Below, Japan was learning a different brand of spirit leading.

Countless people moving gracefully, peacefully, in perfect synchronicity, men, women and children lifting other men, women and children in the perfectly grace-ful exercise of spirit squad partner stunts.

Somehow, somewhere, someway, sometimes ... anything is possible. True?

"Bear Coleman, I've never seen anything more beautiful," said Hail Larry's Wife, a tear in her eye.

"Look in the mirror," said Bear, tenderly cupping his friend's chin. "It's inside you, too, in more ways than you know."

She smiled and massaged his shoulder. Best friends forever. True?

Elsewhere, Walter offered his hand to Hail Larry. The QB had just thanked the wide receiver for watching his back all week, especially after today's language muff. Hail Larry shrugged it off like the tough exterior he was, then shook his buddy's hand. Best friends forever. True?

"This just in from Tokyo: No Seattle Seahawk wants to hurt any children this week. It was all something called a muff by an Ali Gator. In more important news today, an estimated ten million Japanese citizens learned how to do a cheerleader partner stunt called the Liberty."

WALTER AND THE SEAHAWKS—along with Dan Marino and the Dolphins—put on a football exhibition, too, more for Japan than themselves.

"Yahoo!" said the Japanese waitress behind the buffet table.

"I like that cheer," said Bear, sitting in the luxury suite at the domed stadium.

"You're much more relaxed here," said Hail Larry's Wife, sitting next to Bear. "Feeling better about your script for *My Whole Other Life?*"

"Yahoo!" said the Japanese waitress behind the buffet table.

"Get it, Snow! Ah, man ..." said Bear, after the Seattle DB almost picked off an errant Marino pass. *"My Whole Other Life?* Yeah, I spruced it up a bit, as much as I could for now."

"Look, the Olympics!" said Hail Larry's Wife, pointing to a monitor in their luxury suite.

"Yahoo!" said the Japanese waitress behind the buffet table.

"Atlanta must be a madhouse," said Hail Larry's Wife.

"Yahoo!" said the Japanese waitress behind the buffet table.

"Bear ... look at you," said Hail Larry's Wife. "Walter runs on the field and your eyes light up like he's a rock star or something."

"Not *or something,* girlfriend. He's the real deal to this little boy," said Bear.

"How can he *still* be like that to you?" asked Hail Larry's Wife. "You've known this man for 12 years. You've seen him fart, belch, dump, get pissed ... you have seen him upset, haven't you?"

"I have the knife wound to prove it," said Bear. "And in case this box is bugged, it was not a literal knife wound and I brought it on myself."

"What'd you do?" asked Hail Larry's Wife.

"Called myself a dumb nigger once," said Bear. "And not in jest."

"And *he* got pissed?" asked Hail Larry's Wife.

"He felt my pain," said Bear. "The pissed-off part was just what the outer world saw. Walter was hurting for his Bearcat, and all Bearcats just like him. I hope I never hurt him again that way. Or anyway. He's my rock star."

"Yahoo!" said the Japanese waitress behind the buffet table. She sure was enjoying the action on the field.

"Again, *how,* after all this time, is Walter still so perfect to you, Bear?" asked Hail Larry's Wife.

"Yahoo!"

"I'm not so much in awe of Walter," said Bear. "I'm more in awe of my feelings for Walter, my capacity to love him beyond my deepest imagination. When I hear how other couples disconnect, I ask myself: how do they do it? I can't even imagine it. We've rarely had an uncomfortable moment in almost 13 years. It's just not in my DNA to fight with this man. Not grant Walter whatever he wants? Seems absurd. I know you all don't get it, but I do. I think. Trying to anyway."

"Yahoo!"

"Hell, Larry was like that to me," said Hail Larry's Wife. "I think ... at first. Hey, look, the decathlon at the Olympics, talk about grueling."

Hail Larry's Wife rambled on about the Olympics, but it was her questions about the spirit leader's devotion to his rock star of a husband that echoed in the mind of one cool and dreamy Bear Coleman ...

... MARCUS COLEMAN WAS BOPPING AROUND Santa Barbara, California, the soundtrack of his mind playing "I'll Be" by Foxy Brown, just part of the mid-90s, new urban music explosion in the single black gay man's life.

"I'm in shock!" said Eve, calling from Cincinnati.

"Why, girl?" asked Marcus, calling from the land of his new dreams ... *the West Beach area.*

"You've been listening to Broadway and lite jazz for years," said Eve. No doubt she missed their hip-hop bond. Eve was his female soul mate. That little 19-year-old blonde tigress from the gym who had said: *"I might move in with these gay guys but I might not. You know how all gay guys are so bitchy."*

To which Marcus had promptly replied: *"Excuse me, little girl, not all of us are bitchy."*

Seven years later ... she was living the personal trainer dream in her hometown of Cincinnati, but their bond was as good as gold.

Rarely an uncomfortable moment in seven years.

"What changed with your music tastes?" asked Eve in his frequency.

Deep sigh, check out the view ... dream of Santa Barbara getting rid of those oil rigs on the horizon in the blurry distance.

"I think I just woke up from something," said Marcus. "Like a long dream, if that makes sense. Maybe it's living in paradise ..."

Finally carved out his own slice. Crawled out from underneath the rubble of Northridge, the earthquake slash birthday surprise of 1994. Figured out men are mostly meant for sex, and thank God for that! Buzzed back and forth between his own dwellings and the family home in Hayward, and thank Mama Rent for that!

Survived some near-death experience in a hospital from some fuzzy reaction to some fuzzy drug for some fuzzy condition during some fuzzy Independence weekend when the fuzzy people on the hospital TV kept telling his fuzzy brain that 500 people dropped dead from the heat in Chicago. But he made it through that fuzzy hell and conquered his fear of hospitals after deciding to survive (doctors had given him a fuzzy shot at making it).

Living on fuzzy money. Looking unfuzzy and fine for a 35-year-old black man back in the greatest shape of his life again after another ride on the heavy load scales.

"I can keep reinventing myself as much as Madonna," said Marcus, sitting on a bench next to the beach boardwalk. "Whatever it takes to keep me going, God knows why ... I guess so I could finally live my dream ..."

Santa Barbara ... a 99-yard pass from the waves, give or take ... his own lil' pissant beach cottage, complete with hardwood floors. Apartment dwellers of the world: You know you've arrived when you got a place with hardwood floors ... raise your hands in the air, if you were there ... you'd know.

"Finally living on the coast ... who knows, maybe someday I'll add a dog and a man ..." said Marcus.

Got the place serendipitously. Took years to find the perfect match: ground floor (only way in CA), takes dogs, cheaper, near the beach ... just right.

Drove by the bungalows a year earlier, when dreaming then ... saw a woman cleaning out her place, scrubbing the floor through the open door.

He stopped. He was that kind of guy. Anything was possible, true?

The place was already rented out by the next dreamer ... better timing.

But he got the man's number. Always get the man's number.

He called the man. The man had nothing but this to offer: keep in touch.

A year later, he called the man again ... his dream bungalow was waiting.

"Like it was meant to be," said Marcus.

Now, if only this perfect-looking, dark-haired man and his beautiful golden dog passing before my astonished eyes could be meant for me. We'd have a house overlooking the beach ... a home office ... a backyard ... a deck.

"If only this incredible blond guy at the gym came with the bungalow," said Marcus into his frequency.

Long wavy surfer hair ... circa the same age ... says hi in passing ... does more than pass through his heart ... dare to dream ... the golden one is always surrounded by other golden ones at the gym ... Gold's.

"Had a talk the other day with my friend Mark," said Marcus. "He's like my one good gay friend here. Or I could just say, my one friend ..."

Cut to Marcus taking a hard swallow of his cup of Joe.

"Mark, I have something serious I need to talk to about," said Marcus.

"What it is?" asked a worried Mark, leaning forward, clutching his coffee cup in the coffeehouse.

"I'm 35," said Marcus. "I've never come close to having a relationship, not even a boyfriend, just a couple of interested parties where one of us freaked out and walked away after two weeks. That's all I've ever known, a couple of weeks of nervous bliss, then the shit hits the fan."

"What are you saying?" asked a worried Mark ... in town working on an advanced degree, after all ... something to do with the mind *slash* psychology *slash* behavior *slash* what else is there?

"You know how some people have genetic predispositions to being overweight, aggressive, alcoholic, crack babies, mental, whatever?" asked Marcus.

"Yeah ..." Mark was so up to speed on *Brainworld.*

"I think ..." Took a while to let it outta the windpipes ... boom it to life. "I think ..." To say it made Marcus want to stab his gut in the coffeehouse.

"What is it, Marcus?" asked Mark.

"What if I have a genetic predisposition to *not* being in a relationship? No, look, before you react as my friend who hates seeing the obvious pain in my eyes, hear me out. I've come this far ... walked blocks to the coffeehouse ... Roasting Company, or something. Hard to explain, not a rocket scientist here ... but my whole family ... not one healthy relationship did I witness growing up ... I remember the three times I ever felt my parents' love for one another. Once, he was being fussy and romantic while she was slaving over the kitchen stove. Once, I walked into their bedroom and saw him on top of her under the covers, just chilling. The third time, they weren't touching or anything. They were across the room. It was seconds after we had just surprised my mother (yeah, right) with a surprise birthday party ... maybe in her 30s, 40s ... blurry details ... but what I do remember is: feeling his love for her moving across the room, from his body to hers ... just remembering this now really ... with that long beach outside the coffeehouse.

"Then there's the rest of my family. My closest aunt, my second mother. I remember her and her husband feeling love on their wedding night. In our family's home. I was maybe six. They were standing under an archway in our big home at the time, Buckle, it was called ... before Hayward ... Uncle Lou was a hustler, sweaty, fat, greasy, but with the biggest smile and heart ... he was promising Aunt Paulette sweet promises on her wedding night, all the trips they were gonna do ... did I hear Niagara Falls? ... I passed underneath them ... felt his heart ... felt my second mom would be okay in his hands ... felt we'd still be chasing the runaway popcorn on her kitchen floor, my sibs and me, during sleepovers.

"Last time I saw Uncle Lou and Aunt Paulette together as a couple was ages ago. I was 12 and holding their sweet baby daughter in their townhouse kitchen, while one of them was using a knife on the other, while the other used a verbal weapon ... doesn't matter who did what ... nobody was hurt physically ... only the sweet baby daughter crying in my arms knows what that day did to her dreams ... Didn't help this poor bastard ... as I sit here, trying to make sense of it all ... but I think I'm just not predisposed to having a relationship."

"I suppose it's possible," said Mark. Everyone should know a Mark with an open mind. How else can one Mark moments like this for future reference?

"It would be good to know if that's the case," said Marcus. "Then I could get on with my life without having to worry about finding Mr. Right."

Twisted.

Santa Barbara was twisted, a long winding oval pathway circumnavigating the shore, cutting across mountains, sand and sea to create one dreamy loop of Mediterranean living ... a fusion of Europe and Africa right on the central coast of California.

No wonder I feel so comfortable here as a black man. Maybe I'll even tell my lesbo neighbors I'm a homo someday. Lord knows they wanna know, them and all their beautiful dogs. Wish I had a dog. Maybe I should have adopted that bitch I wanted so much ...

"She's beautiful ... so blonde and beautiful."

"She's just had a cancer the size of a basketball removed from her throat."

"I'll take her ... sorry for crying. I know what it's like to be sick and make a comeback."

"She's beautiful."

I really wanted a boy dog ... just like I want a boy buddy ... and this would be my first pet ... can I afford a relapse of her cancer? What if I get sick, too? After all, I did come to Santa Barbara to live a little ... before ...

DATELINE AIDS: Nobody's dreamed up a cure yet. Feel good, but the lab work says I'm hanging by a thread. The body agrees sometimes, socking me with fatigue and vague threats. Throwing different ammo at the virus, and by extension, the rest of me. Some of the ammo is prescribed; some is Eastern, like acupuncture. Hard to dream beyond today. But then again, my mantra was once: I'll be lucky to be alive to see the Atlanta Olympics ...

"I'm calling to see if that blonde dog with cancer in her throat ... she was adopted? Great. That makes me feel good. Wonderful, thank you ... very much."

And then there were some blurry Atlanta Olympics running in the background of the universe, along with a boatload of new urban music to be discovered ... thanks to some newfangled cable music channels.

And speaking of newfangled ... Yahoo!

"Eve, I looked up your name on that new people search thing," said Marcus in his frequency.

"Was I on there?" asked Eve. "I still don't understand any of this."

"Nope, you're not in the Yahoo! loop," said Marcus. "Probably because you've moved as much as me. How wild is that, that anyone can just look up anyone else *in the world* on the Internet?"

"What are we coming to?" asked Eve.

"Tell me about it," said Marcus. "Hey, have you heard of these great girls? I love 'em. Fun, loving, spirited, believe in their own power and being honest. Who are these girls?"

"Do they wear sweats?" asked Eve.

"Yes!" said Marcus.

"The Spice Girls," said Eve.

"They're like spirit leaders for everyday life. Where did they come from?" asked Marcus.

"England," said Eve.

"They know what time it is!" said Marcus. "And this song coming on now by these Brownstone girls?"

"'If You Love Me'," said Eve, naming the song. "Welcome back, Marcus."

"Man, I'm so glad to be listening to soul music again ... gotta go."

Marcus eyed his computer monitor, singing a little.

"... need a love based on truth ..."

Meanwhile, the sweet soul sisters of Brownstone serenaded the black man dreaming in the bungalow.

"... be mine in the dark and the light ..."

Already on Yahoo! People Search, Marcus Coleman had looked up himself, his mother, his best friend Eve, his son-figure Octavio, some old UCLA friends, a USC friend or two ... a high school name or two ... a random name or two ... and deep within his core ... there was one more name. Walt Yeager.

"... if you love me ... trust me ... want me ... need me ..."

Never uttered allowed in 12 years of dreaming and fantasizing about Walt Loves the Bearcat.

"... say it ... do it ... show it ... prove it ..."

Never conveyed to another soul ... except two ...

THE SHRINK: "I've had this fantasy *slash* daydream *slash* book-in-progress going for some time now. Helps me work out the kinks of my ideas about a relationship, too. Why am I bringing it up? No special reason ... it's about the only thing you haven't heard me say over the years."

THE ON-AGAIN, OFF-AGAIN BEST GAY FRIEND: "Duncan ... If I can tell anyone, I guess I can tell you. This unrequited love thing I'm going through right now with that CFL quarterback Matt Strickland ... makes me think of this guy I've been dreaming about for a few years ... like a fantasy lover I've kept to myself all this time. Why am I bringing this up? No special reason ... just sad over Matt not working out ... if there was ever one I wanted to be the One ..."

"... say it ... do it ... show it ... prove it ..."

That was it. The only moments *Walt Yeager* had slipped out of the core of Marcus Coleman's soul. Until now ...

"... actions speak louder than words ..."

He typed the name in the search box: WALT YEAGER.

He typed the city from the game program (wherever *that* was by now): WINNETKA, ILLINOIS.

He hit ENTER and waited. And waited. And waited. And waited.

Three entries emerged, all variations of the name and the hometown.

"He's real."

Boom baby.

Print it out. Hold it. Behold it. Put it in the in-box, the one that just keeps getting filled and filled until a purge. What else would a sane individual do? Call him?

Ah, yes ... throw it away ... even better idea ... remove temptation ... Bear's not the only Coleman capable of crazy ideas. True?

Then it was back to the real world ... Santa Barbara ... maybe it was a Saturday night ... maybe there were boys waiting in LA for some black meat to play with. Sex was back, not all the way back, but back enough for LA to be percolating ... not with boys so much ... life at 35 was a man's job.

Still ... Walt Yeager is real ... alive ... out there somewhere ... what a rush ...

... IN THE FOOTBALL WORLD ... Walter Yeager and Hail Larry McPherson of the Seahawks made their way through a crowded and swank Tokyo nightclub, west to east.

... In the Eastern world ... Bear Coleman and Hail Larry McPherson's Wife made their way through a swank and crowded Tokyo nightclub, east to west.

"A gay disco!" yelled Bear into his *slash* watch. "My first time in the gay world since ... before Walter!"

"Don't worry, QB," said Hail Larry's Wife into her *slash* watch. "I'll make sure he's a freakin' good little Bear."

"My Bear's always a freakin' good little Bear," said Walter into his *slash* watch. "Larry and I are surrounded by *thousands* of straights here in this dance club on the other side of town from you."

"Don't worry, Bumbles," said Hail Larry into his *slash* watch. "I'll make sure freakin' Yeager freakin' behaves ... more for me that way, *growllllll.*"

"Hell, I'm not freakin' worried, Larry," said Bear in his frequency.

"What's your club look like over there?" asked Walter in his frequency.

"Huge!" said Hail Larry's Wife. "Billions here! 400-story building. We're on the bottom floor."

"Ours, too," said Walter. "But I think we're on the top floor, 401."

"We're just barely inside," said Bear and Walter together.

"Moving toward the center," said the Hail Larrys together.

"Surrounded by homosexuals," said Bear. "Or I think they are."

"Same here," said Walter. "Except these peeps are straight."

"You North-South people ... always assuming the world is black, white; straight, gay; top, bottom; up, down; inside, out ... There's another way, Bearcats. It's called round and about, *growllllll.*"

"Who said that?" asked the four in the same frequency.

"The world is not just about you and your freakin' poles. Without this loop, there is no loop."

"Is that you, Bear?" asked the other three in the same frequency.

"Hell, I thought it was Larry," said Bear in his own defense.

"Walter, was that you?" asked Hail Larry's Wife.

"Sounding like a woman with a manly voice, or a man with womanly voice? No, that is not me, Walter," said Walter, sounding slightly perturbed.

"Not always about the Panther and his Bear, little Tigercat."

"Someone has jammed our frequency!" yelled Hail Larry's Wife.

"Calm down, Trixie," said Hail Larry. "Move to the center."

"Right!" said Bear. "Tammy said do that when there's interference."

"How crazy is that?" asked Walter.

"Never forget to look into the eye of the Tiger and the Tiger's cat, boyz, growlllllll."

"Walter ... Bear!" yelled the voice of Tammy, coming into their frequency.

"The ER Wife!" said Walter and Bear.

"Hope you've enjoyed your trip to the Orient," said Tammy.

"Somebody's jammed our freakin' frequency!" yelled Hail Larry.

"That would be ... *it*," said Tammy.

"*It?*" repeated the four.

"Notice how this trip has been pretty cool and dreamy for our famous boys and their changing and challenged world?" asked Tammy.

"We're gonna finally meet the team's Eastern facilitator, this B.E.?" asked Bear.

"Our invisible Santa? No freakin' way!" said Hail Larry's Wife.

"The one and freakin' only," said the voice of Tammy. "Or should I say, half of one and freakin' only? *Huh?*"

"Who's meeting this B.E.?" asked Walter. "Me or Bear? Which club is the B.E. at?"

"Yours," said Tammy.

"No fair!" cried Bear.

"*And* yours," said Tammy.

"Begin synchronicity of the Tigercats and Bearcats."

"*Huh?*" said the four.

"Keep moving to the center, *it* means," said Tammy.

"What's B.E. stand for anyway?" asked one of the four.

"Ask question, get answers. Ray One in Game of Life."

Walter and Hail Larry moved in from the left.

Bear and Hail Larry's Wife moved in from the right.

The four met at the core of the club, near Tammy—a tall, bosomy blonde beacon in a flickering crescendo of a universal light show, the likes of which the foursome had never seen. Light. Dark. Begat new meanings. Colors—all of them and none of them—blinking quicker than a gillion rays of light. The floor lifted and descended at once. Billions of celestial bodies around them rose and floated like planets and stars, swirling east to west, then west to east, round and about.

Near the core beamed a flickering stump of light. Or was it a flickering light in the form of a short body?

"I Am Your B.E.," said the body of light. No frequency needed.

"Bucky?" asked one of the four.

"Bobby?" asked one of the four.

"Buffy?" asked one of the four.

"Butch?" asked one of the four.

Who said what? thought all of the four.

"Never mind what I am. You'll never agree anyway," said B.E.

Hard to tell what B.E. was, underneath the goggles and electric suit. Asian woman, guessed Bear.

"Vortex," said B.E., arms extended, smile non-existent. "Follow."

B.E. stopped the last one ... Tammy.

"Not a fit tonight, dear," said B.E. before whisking the foursome through the swirling, pounding, spinning, electrified nightclub. "Pit stop. Need gas."

"To light its suit?" asked Walter.

"Heard that," said B.E., taking them higher.

"Where have you been hiding all week?" asked Bear, heart rising with the invisible escalator ride.

"The Panther and the Bear are too tall to see," said B.E.

"What about us?" asked Hail Larry's Wife, sipping on a straw in a drink.

"The Tiger and his pussycat are too busy playing games," said B.E.

"She called you a pussycat, Larry," laughed Hail Larry's Wife.

"I'm the Auburn Tiger bitch," said Hail Larry to his wife.

"Trust him on that one," said B.E.

"Where we going?" asked Walter, gorgeous blond hair swaying in the up-draft.

"Here." B.E. pushed something. They leveled off and segued into a small room. A deejay booth. An Asian male deejay was there, along with Madonna, the brightest starburst of their time, pussycat variety.

"I love you!" said Hail Larry's Wife.

"Thanks," mumbled Madonna, short, pale, drained, not really there. She reminded Bear of a homeless woman who gave Walter and Bear advice in New York City in 1985, right after Walter quit football for good, or so he thought:

"Stop substituting pain for love, then you'll be free. Open your heart and help me out with something to eat? Thanks. Bless you. Poppa don't preach. True blue."

"Got tune?" asked B.E., holding up its wrist *slash* watch. As an answer, Madonna kissed the watch. "Downloading," explained B.E. to the foursome.

"New one for next album," explained Madonna.

"Bear!" cried Hail Larry's Wife, over by some papers and stuff. "This is the song I wanted you to use for *Freeways!* For my death scene ... if I really did die. Did I die in my movie?"

"Only in the car going in reverse," said Hail Larry. "I think."

"Have we met?" Walter asked Madonna, who mumbled something about being on holiday.

"What song?" asked Bear, grabbing the stuff from Hail Larry's Wife. "Oh, I didn't understand the meaning of the lyrics. The only thing I know about zephyrs are the Chicago Zephyrs, an old basketball team currently known as the Washington Bullets ... no relevance. Plus, I never heard of the group ... too 60s."

"Check it out now," said Madonna. "I tweaked it. Maybe you'll see it in a whole new light."

B.E. extended its arms and inhaled the foursome forward and upward, through an elevator shaft of a joy ride as Madonna's song rocked the tunnel and the club around them. RAY OF LIGHT, read the display on B.E.'s wrist.

"Is that the name of this elevator or the song?" giggled Bear, cozying into Walter for the vertical ride.

"Tell me about it!" said Walter, arms around his beloved Bear.

"Are we going up or down?" screamed Hail Larry's Wife in orgasmic delight.

"Who freakin' cares!" yelled Hail Larry, louder, freer, wilder and happier than ever. As if the Auburn Tiger never dropped that fateful pass that ruined his college days.

"Zephyrs sinking beneath the sun go round and about, change world energy, like a switch, like B.E.," said B.E. "Life changes when you're not under the spell of the Panther and the Bear and their crazy freakin' poles."

"I'm freakin' home!" yelled Hail Larry.

"Me, too!" yelled Hail Larry's Wife. "Even though I don't freakin' understand!"

They shot straight through the vein of the 400 or 401-story building *as one,* an iron cannonball exploding into a different orbit.

"My stomach's twisting!" yelled Hail Larry, laughing to twist it more.

"Mine's not!" yelled Walter.

"Your planet," said B.E. "We gave it to the Panther this time, to see what the Panther could do with it."

"How's the Panther doing?" asked Walter.

"*Hail our Panthers, hats off to me!*" sang Bear. "My high school's nickname.

Red, Black, White, United We Stand. Guess we couldn't envision *yellow* in the trim back then. Or *brown.*"

"How's the Panther doing?" asked Walter.

"You know damned well," said B.E.

The tunnel of the 400 or 401-story building swung on its axis and spun upside down, then twirled like a baton through space. B.E. stood still like a frozen elevator operator. The foursome held tight to one another, swaying and laughing 'til it hurt deep in their guts.

"Like a freakin' wild cab ride through New York on acid!" yelled Hail Larry, clenching his gut to keep it from exploding into space.

"The only way to fly!" screamed Bear, riding the ride his favorite way: eyes closed, holding onto his buddy. Trust. *Anything is possible in Walter's arms.*

"No wonder we had a cool and dreamy week!" said Hail Larry's Wife.

"Man, B.E., how do you do it?" asked Walter. "Unless I mean: woman."

"Switching," said B.E. "All teams need switch hitters to fuck with the opponents' head."

"Fuck yeah! Let's fuck with some heads!" yelled Hail Larry's Wife.

"Whose? Whose?" yelled an eager Hail Larry. "How?"

"How do you switch, B.E.?" asked Walter.

"What do you switch into?" asked Bear.

"Try living in the moment for once," said B.E.

"*Huh?*" asked both Bear and Walter.

"Don't worry about it," said B.E. "Enjoy the trip."

"*Huh?*" asked Bear.

"Like with Santa," said Walter. "Let Santa do Santa's job."

"Oh," said Bear and the Hail Larrys.

Bear broke out in silly laughter and fell back into Walter's front. Hail Larry shook his head and laughed at Bear. Hail Larry's Wife laughed at them all. Everybody had something to smile about while surpassing the G-force.

"We're tilted but in a different way than usual!" said Hail Larry.

"Listen to him," said B.E. "The sweetest pretend to be the toughest."

"Fuck you!" said Hail Larry.

The ride burped and threw them out onto a terrace in the sky: the top (or bottom) of the towering skyscraper, otherwise known as the helipad, where a team copter would eventually land to take them away.

"But first," said B.E., extending its electrified arms.

Wordlessly, the foursome moved away from B.E. and one another, gravitating toward the four different corners of the helipad.

"You four are magic," said B.E. "One Tiger, one Tigercat. One Panther, one Bearcat. The power of the four forces of your world. Harness. Inhale."

Yeager, Coleman, McPherson and McPherson found themselves magnetized to their own separate corners of the helipad, feet on the edge of a 400 or 401-story drop, staring out into infinity above the clouds.

"You have a chance to go farther than any of your generation," said B.E.

"In football?" asked most of the four.

"In the games of life, fools!" B.E. shook its head, then spoke into its *slash* watch. "Goddess, I'm coming to hang with you." Then she said to the four: "Make us proud."

"Make who proud?" asked a couple of the four.

"Tell me about it," said B.E. before disappearing down the smoky elevator shaft.

"Food!" said Hail Larry, hurrying toward the spread in the middle of the helipad.

"Are we on the 400th or 401st floor?" asked Bear, ambling toward Walter.

"Does it matter?" asked Walter, moving toward Bear.

"Guess not," said Bear, glad to feel his man's arm around his shoulder.

"She said play games," said Hail Larry's Wife. "Let's play something."

"Like what?" asked Walter. *Mild laugh.*

Hail Larry's Wife threw a football to Walter, who caught it just in time to save his face. The two of them played catch on the helipad while Bear and Hail Larry consumed the goodies in the spread.

"So when we gonna make freakin' pictures, Bumbles?" asked Hail Larry.

Briefly, Hail Larry's eyes beamed like a billion-kilowatt kaleidoscope, a reflection of Bear's own vision returned in equal measure.

"When you wanna?" giggled Bear.

"Freakin' soon, need a distraction from the pain," said Hail Larry, wincing from some injury. "*Whoa*, can't talk about it, gotta stay positive. *Ouch!*"

"Have you thought about reversing?" asked Bear.

"No talk," said Hail Larry. "Gotta stay positive. *Ouch!*"

"What would you be reversing anyway?" asked Bear.

"Gotta stay positive. *Ouch!*" said Hail Larry.

"Bear, leave my man alone!" yelled Hail Larry's Wife, throwing Walter a wobbly pass.

"Hey, woman, leave Bumbles alone over here," yelled Hail Larry. "Coleman is cool. No, serious. If I had to hook up with a guy—you know, like, for life, or something—you'd be the guy."

"I thought you wanted me!" protested Walter, gunning a soft spiral to Hail Larry's Wife.

"*You* I'd just do," shrugged Hail Larry. "Bumbles, I'd keep."

"*Yes!*" said Bear, arms in the air like a cheerleader after a touchdown. "Larry just wants to do you, Walter! But he really likes me!" Bear let out a laugh like a kid who'd just won somebody else's candy in a contest.

"See, woman," said Hail Larry to his wife, who was dancing on the helipad to some tune in her head. "Why can't you be more like Bumbles?"

"Sorry, you can't have my Bear," said Walter, swooping in like a panther and securing his own underneath his big blond arms. "Only one and we broke the mold, right, buddy?"

"You two are like that old Martin and Lewis movie," said Hail Larry. "The one where Deano's the big college jock who's so pent-up, he's coming outta his ears, and his best friend is Junior *slash* Lewis, his freakin' crazy buddy who's this geeky, unathletic and socially inept nitwit."

"Except Bear is none of those things," said Walter and Hail Larry together.

"Right," said Hail Larry, looking like he wanted to wrestle Bear to the floor of the helipad. "Coleman's just the freakin' crazy part in a cool way. With all his freakin' crazy animal adventures."

"That's my Bear," said Walter, kissing his man, "a crazy fucking animal so I don't have to be. As much."

"Look, cartwheels on the top of the 401st or 400th floor!" said Hail Larry's Wife in the background. "Hey, this is kinda like our luau, only in the sky."

"Except at the end of this season, our Hawaiian luau will be after we've all won Super rings together," said Bear.

"And have our own Super loop," said Walter, chillin' like a gunslinger.

"How many Super rings we gonna win, the four of us?" asked Hail Larry.

Bear looked at his man who shrugged. Walter was a quarterback for life, maybe a warrior until the day he died, but Yeager was no football player for eternity. Greater than two rings, but less than five or six, was just fine.

"Story Meeting," said Bear. "Let's dream up this upcoming season."

"Seahawks go unbeaten," said Hail Larry's Wife, ballet dancing around the helipad.

"Bear and the family are taken care of," said Walter, kissing his man. "With Sugary benefits."

"I catch a huge, classic pass that makes everyone forget about Auburn," said Hail Larry.

"What the hell," said Bear. "Larry and Walter finally *do it,* like we both know they want to!"

Walter and Hail Larry protested. "Finally!" said Hail Larry's Wife. "Get it over with! Especially if you two hook up for some all-time great pass. *That* would be a sign from God."

"Boom!" said Hail Larry, voice *booming* in the universe over Asia.

"And I—" said Bear, a devilish grin spanning his face, "get to finally do something as well."

Three pairs of eyes bore curiously into Bear.

Sometimes a whisper can lead to a boom.

"Avonda," said Bear, looking off into the clouds around the skyscraper. "That was her name. Black Avonda from Phoenix, Arizona."

"College dorm, freshman year," explained Walter with a nostalgic smile.

"I'd been at USC a month," said Bear. "She had been after me, in the cafeteria, on campus. Nice voluptuous girl, full lips, curvy hips—booty, no doubt. I barely checked out men, let alone women."

I heard you just made yell leader. I wanted to come and congratulate you.

"Or was that *congratulate you, then cum?*" asked Walter.

"She practically threw me down on my little twin dorm bed," said Bear. "Kissing and grinding on top of me. I think I got half a hard-on."

"You never liked women?" asked Hail Larry.

"That wasn't the point," said Bear. "She didn't have what my soul needed."

"The right plumbing?" asked Hail Larry.

"Another soul *my* soul wanted to worship unadulterated," said Bear.

"What's that freakin' mean?" asked Hail Larry.

"She wasn't a rock star," said Hail Larry's Wife.

"What's that freakin' mean?" asked Hail Larry.

"The scent of her sweat socks wouldn't do anything for me," said Bear.

"You smelled the girl's freakin' socks?" asked Hail Larry, then looked at Walter. "Oh."

"The mere thought of her singing a love song to me doesn't make me sob with tears, and maybe pass out," said Bear.

"She freakin' sung to you?" asked Hail Larry, then looked at Walter. "Oh."

"If Avonda was in the middle of a painful back reverse," said Bear, "I'd tie her shoes, but I'd do it because it's the thing to do, more or less."

"What did you freakin' get outta tying freakin' Yeager's shoes when he had a freakin' bad back?" asked Hail Larry.

"The pleasure of serving him any and every way I can," said Bear, "knowing it was somehow helping him feel better, especially in his darkest time, when he wanted to die."

"Woman, will you take a lesson or three from Bumbles?" said Hail Larry. "Man, you got a brother?"

"Larry!" cried Walter and Hail Larry's Wife.

"A sister then?" asked Hail Larry. "How does anyone stay that devoted after all these years? No offense, but you worshipped freakin' Yeager this way even before the hit @ the PITT."

"Larry!" cried Walter and Hail Larry's Wife.

"Remember what B.E. said about Larry's type," giggled Bear. "Big warm fuzzy on the inside, kinda like a Bear."

"I got your big warm fuzzy," said Hail Larry, holding up a fist.

"I know you do," teased Bear.

"It's not like our home life is all about me," protested Walter.

"Kinda the opposite," said Bear. "My rock star *slash* hero loves treating *me* and making *me* happy! How twisted is that! He does whatever I ask him, to make *me* feel good! He'd tie my shoes and I don't even have a bad back!"

"What can I say?" laughed Walter, more focused on Sugar on the shoulder. "He's my Bear."

"It's like the day after their first freakin' date. Disgusting," said Hail Larry. "But kinda cool."

"Yeah, I got my own rock star now," said Bear. "So now I'm curious about Avonda again, so to speak."

"He's never been with a woman," explained Walter.

"Made out with them," said Bear in his own defense. "Before Walter."

"So you wanna bang my wife," said Hail Larry. "How truly disgusting!"

"This from the man who's been wanting to nail my husband for years," said Bear.

"Guys, guys, the copter's coming to take us away," said Walter, motioning toward the sky. "Nobody's banging anybody tonight, *aiight?*"

"But we did quadruple boom the notion," said Bear. "What do you suppose that means, besides a homerun?"

"Boom baby?" asked Walter.

"To our friendship!" said Hail Larry, raising a tall glass of something, leading them up the copter's grand staircase. "We can boom any damned babies we want!"

"Let's boom another movie!"

"Let's boom an Oscar!"

"An award?"

"A baby?"

"A ball?"

"My kid?"

"Anything we want Oscar to be!"

"Let's boom more Super Bowl titles!"

"Let's boom a bunch of boom babies!"

"Let's boom away all our homophobic and racist enemies!"

"Let's boom going down in history as the two greatest duos of all time!"

"The greatest Tigers, Tigercats, Panthers, and Bearcats!"

"Let's boom changing the planet forever!"

"Let's boom sleeping with whoever we want to sleep with—without any negative repercussions!"

"Let's boom reversing everything on the damned planet! *Ouch!* Gotta stay positive."

"Let's boom taking over the entire world!"

"Fuck that, let's boom taking over the entire universe!"

"Attention," said an electric voice as the copter rose in the sky, the foursome still toasting on the grand staircase. "Please get into the helicopter quietly. Japan prefers much less noise and booming, if you don't mind. Hold tight. We should be back in the United States shortly, where taking over the entire universe should be much easier for you there."

29

Why I Was Taking So Much God in This Life

"**S**oul Sista Evangeline," said Bear, calling from Seattle. "Tell my Bearcat Peeps in Northern Cal: no worries, no fear, and all those other surfer boy terms ... go Yeager go!"

"First down, Larry!" said Hail Larry's Wife, sitting next to Bear for the NFL season opener. "And Walter and the Seahawks."

"What, Soul Sista?" asked Bear in his cell. "All cool near the waterfront ... make sure Mama Rent enjoys the view from her couch this season. Maybe if we ever decide it's safe, she can watch in person again. Someday. Word to the mother. Y'all have a great opening Sunday. Go Hawks!"

Below on the field, Yeager threw a little shuttle pass to Mormon Simmons, the new running back replacing the veteran Millstone, who retired in the off-season. Simmons scampered up the middle for 22 yards and another touchdown.

"Woohoo! Maybe we don't miss Mookie!" said Hail Larry's Wife.

"This one's in the bag," said Bear, glancing at the scoreboard.

SEAHAWKS 14, SAN DIEGO 0. FIRST QUARTER.

"I wonder how loud the crowd sounds today," said Bear. They were watching the game the only safe way anyone could dream of.

"They *look* noisy," said Hail Larry's Wife. "If you think of them like mimes."

"Not sure I'm gonna like Tammy and the team sneaking me in and out of the stadiums of the NFL in a glass-enclosed case-on-wheels with curtains," said Bear. "Kinda creepy, having to roll around, just to watch my bud play football."

"At least they're banning all banners and signs in all stadiums at all games every week during the entire NFL season for the next five to seven years," said Hail Larry's Wife, "just in case anyone writes anything that anyone might someday find offensive."

"Censorship," said Bear. "That solves everything. This much ain't true."

"Sweetie, look at the game," said Hail Larry's Wife. "Walter just got sacked."

They were @ San Diego now, a few weeks down the road. The Seahawks were trying to repay the Chargers for the season-opening loss, 14-38. Junior Seau—San Diego's Gator—smothered Yeager like gravy on a biscuit. Walter staggered toward the huddle like a half-eaten, crumpled McBreakfast.

"Is Junior phobic?" wondered Bear from high above the field. "Walter, stop looking up this way!"

"You ask that about every guy that sacks your buddy," said Hail Larry's Wife, sitting next to him.

"I wanna hear the crowd," whined Bear. "I feel like I'm in a box up here."

"We are," said Hail Larry's Wife. "Think of it as a luxury box. Or half of one. More like a lux box. We're in the lux box, baby, from here on out."

"Thanks for sitting by me," said Bear. "Never thought supporting my buddy's heroic efforts in the name of finding his soul through sport would warrant my own little Pope-mobile, transferable to every stadium in the league, except Pittsburgh ... *go figure.*"

"How about something to drink?" asked Hail Larry's Wife.

"I'll call the FBI and have them clear the waitress for entry," said Bear. "Should they restock the buffet, as well? The nachos deluxe were scrumptious. Walter, stop looking up this way!"

"Just regular nachos for me," said Hail Larry's Wife. "I'm still stuffed from the grilled salmon and pasta ... and those donuts ... *pass interference!*"

Below on the field, Yeager ran a hook-and-lateral with Corey Christian and Reggie Snowman, who was trying his hand at wideout, since half the receivers core was injured five games into the season.

"We're more hunted as defending champs the second time around," said Bear, sitting in his lux box at Soldier Field, Chicago. "This much is true."

"Imagine what Jordan and the Bulls felt like," said Hail Larry's Wife, sitting next to him.

"Maybe some of Michael's space jamming is taking the heat off our visit to Walter's hometown?" wondered Bear.

"The heat's on Walt!" cried Hail Larry's Wife.

Below on the field, Yeager was running for his life, scrambling between two big bad Chicago Bears! Bears fans were on their feet, urging on the Bear kill! Mission accomplished: the Bears ate a Yeager sandwich. Third down.

"What's the commish's email addy?" asked Bear, typing away on his laptop in the lux box. "I'm changing the name of their team to the Chicago Zephyrs."

"Why?" laughed Hail Larry's Wife.

"I'm not feeling their Bears," said Bear. "I don't think Chicago truly feels their Bears either."

"Lost me ... Larry! ... look out for—oh! ... tough bump. Come on, hubby, gotta be positive," said Hail Larry's Wife.

"Chicago's ambiguous about its Bears," said Bear. "The city is like the big Macho Dad who puts up a tough front, but underneath lies a hidden and most sensitive heart. Macho Dad can support the Cubs because they're the Cubbies, forever cute and lovable, even as losers in that chewing gum field of dreams. But the Bears—are they tough and vicious? Vicious enough to eat Eagles? Conquer Vikings? Slay Giants? *Not* get fed to the Lions? *Stuff* the always-hearty Meat Packers? In modern times, the answer is more often ... *no* ... so Chicago, the Macho Dad with the hidden sensitive heart, is all over the map about its Bears—doesn't know how to feel about them, the same way Macho Dad is ambiguous about all the newfangled psychological changes of our times."

The last half of the last American century was toughest on the American Father, who saw his role shredded like wheat and sold off to Siberia. Along the way to a newfangled society, nobody gave Dad a newfangled purpose, or way to be a true hero and save his world, a world that didn't seem to need the American Father as much as America needed bandstand, rock stars, new math, cold wars, family shrinks, television sitcom dads, GI Joe dolls, and male grooming products and the sports heroes who hawked them. And twins!

Dad got resentful. No wonder Dad doesn't want the Bearcats invading the last American bastion of himself, the battlefields he dreamed up.

"Bear Coleman, I have no idea what you just wrote there," said Hail Larry's Wife, "but somehow it seems ... brilliant!"

"Love this newfangled laptop QB got me," said Bear. "From now on, while Walter rests on the sidelines, I go to work!"

"You go Bear!" said Hail Larry's Wife, turning toward the action. "Sack that Bear. That Zephyr, I mean!"

Below on the field, the Seahawks tackled the Chicago QB, ending the half. Yeager ran off, chased down by Jim Greyghost, the sideline reporter. Hopefully,

Greyghost was only asking about the game, but if he strayed, Yeager had his re-tort for any media question about his private life: *You first.*

"Soul Sista Evangeline," said Bear calling from the lux box in Tampa. "Tell our soul bruthas Grayson and Stefan that Coach from SF is gonna call them, set them up working at that kids' club in the ghetto ... going back to our roots ... *huh?* ... you know that black coach who be rapping pissant country songs ... I can never remember his name. Mama Rent knows it ... gotta go, husband taking the field."

"What does your sister do again?" asked Hail Larry's Wife, sitting next to him in the lux box.

"Her best to keep her dreams alive," sighed Bear. "I don't pretend to begin to know anything about the black female experience in America."

"Look at those sisters on the Tampa dance squad jam!" said Hail Larry's Wife, dancing in her seat.

"A spirit squad without black girls is a spirit squad without at least a quarter of its soul, more or less," said Bear.

"I wonder what they're dancing to," said Hail Larry's Wife.

Briefly, the two looked at Tampa's dancers, dancing like mimes to no music, at least inside the lux box ...

... THE SPIRIT LEADER LET OUT a deep, long sigh, blowing the not-so-super, de-fending Super Season 2 out of his Super deflated lungs.

"We missed out," said Bear.

"Sold out," said Walter.

"Dropped out," said Hail Larry.

"Struck out," said Hail Larry's Wife.

They were at another post-season luau, only not in Hawaii. Some other fab four in some other universe was in the Super loop. Yeager and the Mighty Seattle Seahawks, defending Super Bowl champs two of the last three years, had landed in a new universe and reality.

"How did we go 10-6?" asked Hail Larry.

"How did we lose to San Diego in the second round of the playoffs?" asked Bear.

"How did we lose to San Diego three times this year?" asked Walter.

"How did we not make the freakin' Pro Bowl?" asked Hail Larry.

"What's in the water in San Diego?" asked Bear.

"Personally, I'd rather have our annual luau underneath *the Jaw,* anyway," said Hail Larry's Wife, serving up a new round of whatever was in the bottle.

The campfire was roaring, the February night over Malibu crystal clear.

"We'll kick ass next year," said Walter, prompting three murmurs of utter faith.

"It was the injuries," shrugged Hail Larry. "And Mooks' retiring. And the refs with at least three games."

"*Five,*" said Bear. "I still haven't forgotten *or* forgiven that bad call in the first half @ the Jaguars. I don't care how conclusive the replay was, my husband's big blond toe was not over the line of scrimmage on that eight-yard TD pass. That changed the complexion of the whole year!"

"Second game of the season, what do you expect?" agreed Hail Larry.

"Does Jacksonville really deserve a football team?" asked Hail Larry's Wife.

"Not if they think they can fuck with us," said Walter.

"*Us,* as in the Seahawks, or *us,* as in the fab four?" asked Bear. "Or *us* two?"

"Tell me about it," said Walter. *Mild laugh.*

"People are out to get us, plain and simple," said Hail Larry's Wife. "You two really, us by association. Total jealousy, especially some of the alleged little Bearcats of the world."

Bear covered his ears and said, "Still in a virtual media blackout here! I don't even know what's happening on my soap."

"Don't you miss the real freakin' world, little Bearcat?" asked Hail Larry.

"Not sitting in an open stadium ever again," said Bear. *He called me little Bearcat!* "I want to *live* for my man. Don't trust Santa that much."

"What about getting out in public, period?" asked Hail Larry.

"Upon further reveal, I did recently," said Bear, changing his tune. "Took a trip with the dogs in the hills, found this very cute little spot."

"For?" said the other three.

"Our dreams," said Bear.

"Me opening up a gym?" asked Hail Larry's Wife.

"A gym?" asked both Walter and Bear.

"What happened to Bearcat Studios?" asked Bear.

"I boomed one for myself," said Hail Larry's Wife, arm high in the air. "I'm a personal trainer now."

"A freakin' site for our dream gigs?" said Hail Larry. "About freakin' time!"

"Caution," said Bear. "I don't know if it's available or zoned or anything, plus, looks like a school or something used to be there, old junior high maybe."

"Sweet," said Walter.

"Plenty of room to run around and play games," said Hail Larry.

"The mountains are great for motivating people to train hard," said Hail Larry's Wife.

"There was a FOR SALE sign," said Bear.

"Did you get the number?" asked the others.

"*Duh!*" Bear got up and scrambled about. "Sometimes I wonder if you guys think I'm retarded or something. Hold on. Come on, Hip and Comet, let's go get the thing with the number on it." Bear ran to the area directly under the ridge of the Jaw.

"Bear," said Walter, stoking the campfire, "nobody was saying you're retarded, *aiiright?* As the kids say."

"I know you would never deride me, buddy," said Bear, more focused on rummaging through the brush in the dark. "But sometimes, I get caught up in all my writing and I lose track of the rest of life. And cell phones. And pens. And paper. And cash. Anybody seen my shoes?"

"That's what I'm here for," said Walter.

"He speaks the truth, Bearcat People," giggled Bear. "My man manages what I can't."

"And *my* man manages what I can't," said Walter.

"Perfect!" cried Bear, holding a huge sign over his head. "Found the number."

LOT FOR SALE. PERFECT FOR NEWFANGLED DREAMS. 310-555-5555.

"You brought the whole freakin' sign?" laughed Hail Larry. "Cool!"

"Hip forgot his pen, and Comet never carries one. Comet's big, bulky and bumbly, like me." Bear flipped the sign like a Frisbee to the Seahawks wide receiver, who caught it easily. "You two are the money boys in all this," said Bear to Walter and Hail Larry. "I don't wanna hear about a dime. I'll be too busy with my blocks, or as you call them, the keyboard on my computer. Roll all the dough you want from our dreams, just give me enough for ice cream money."

"*And* our trips stimulating the economy," said Hail Larry's Wife.

"*Natch,*" said Bear, hi-fiving his gal pal. "Gotta have new toys, always and forever, especially in this newfangled digital age."

"I'm not doing the money, either," protested Hail Larry.

"*We* are," said Hail Larry's Wife, wrapping her arms around Walter's waist and snuggling into QB.

"Nice," said Hail Larry. "Bumbles and I'll create the magic."

"Too late for that," giggled Bear, looking at the lone female's growing stomach. The Hail Larrys had their own baby boom back in Tokyo. Champ was due in May.

"Freakin' Yeager," said Hail Larry. "I can understand now how you wanna protect Bear at all costs. Anybody mess with the wife and kid ... fuckin' heaven help 'em."

"Sitting in that lux box all year, I felt like people were out to get us," said Hail Larry's Wife, shivering at the memory.

"The ice cream was great though!" said Bear, snuggling back into Walter on the blanket.

"Yeager-meister?" asked Walter, kickin' back like a gunslinger.

"All 12 flavors, including the original," said Bear. "And *my* special blend."

"I want my own freakin' cream," said Hail Larry.

"Caution," said Bear. "There's a price to being cream of the crop."

"We're still finding that one out," said Walter. Bear understood that he was being spared some of what was going on in the world beyond Moose Jaw. Walter was more exposed, what with going out into the football world when he had to.

"I don't understand homophobes," said Hail Larry's Wife.

"Idiots, fuck 'em," said Hail Larry.

"I can't stand most people anyway," said Hail Larry's Wife.

"Wasn't that your opening line in *Freeways?*" asked Walter. *Mild laugh.*

"In the car driving forward," said Hail Larry's Wife. "I think."

"The worst part about watching the game in a box is not being able to breathe the same air as my man," said Bear. "Like there's a disconnect, a barrier."

"Tammy's new super team has kinda outdone itself," said Hail Larry's Wife, "especially with the nachos at the games. Have you tried their nachos, Walter?"

"We see zero of the outside world," said Walter. "Was the president re-elected? And yes, our team definitely has the best nachos."

"Trust us, you don't want to know, about the outside world, I mean," said Hail Larry's Wife.

"Bumbles, I wish I could do more to make it different," said Hail Larry.

"Dream of it," said Bear. "Like what?"

"Hell, I don't know," said Hail Larry. "Find that kid who wrote that racial pole story and ask for another great idea."

"You mean, like a distraction?" asked Walter.

"But it's only a distraction," said Bear. "Our lives are stuck in gear because *we* are, not the rest of the world."

"We're all as good as gold," said Walter.

"With each other, for sure," said Hail Larry's Wife.

"Even better since Japan," said Hail Larry.

"But we suck at taking on the rest of the world," said Walter. "Bear's right."

"Then let's start kicking ass," said Bear, the spirit leader again.

"Then start writing, Bumbles!" said Hail Larry. "That's what *you're* supposed to do."

"I think he means, start living, sweetie," said Hail Larry's Wife.

"I know what I mean, woman," said Hail Larry. "I mean start writing. *And* living. Get your big black ass outta the house."

"Any story ideas, Bear?" asked Walter.

"There is one idea," said Bear. A Cheshire cat grin invaded his countenance. "You guys are either gonna absolutely love ... or absolutely hate it."

"Spill it!" cried the other three.

"Guess!" said Bear. Bearcats love to tease. "What's the first thing that comes to your mind when I say: the idea was born sometime between the hit @ the PITT and that Japan nightclub?"

"Pussy?" guessed one.

"Sleazy?" guessed one.

"Furry?" guessed one.

"Cartoony?" guessed one.

"Outta this world?" guessed one.

"An orgasmic explosion?" guessed one.

"Yes! All the above!" Bear leaped up triumphantly, then shouted to the heavens at the top of his lungs: "*I love my friends!*"

Walter and the Hail Larrys rose with anticipation, eyes widening like three kids under the spell of the one who makes magic with blocks.

"*This* is what Bear Coleman is talkin' about ..." said Bear, reeling them in.

Boom. Boom. Boom. Boom.

Boom baby.

"Oh, yes! Yes, yes, yes!" said one after hearing the idea.

"We gotta do this!" said one.

"The best idea yet!" said one.

"I'm could cream just thinking about it!" said one.

"*That's* my Bear!" said the one and only.

"Game on!" said all!

Somebody cranked up the boom box. The Beach Boys sang about two great superstar couples of their time, running, singing, dancing across the moonlit beach, grabbing at one another, throwing a football, jumping up and down with Hip and Comet ... four kids ... two dogs ... a fire ... a beach at night ... and some dreams ...

"MEETING FOR BEARCAT SECRET PROJECT #1," said Bear, standing on the upper deck of the Jaw. "That's what we'll call these private rendezvous confabs, to be held at a later date at our dreamy studio in the hills."

"That reminds me, gotta make a call," said Hail Larry, going for his cell.

"So we're really gonna do this?" asked Walter, already on his cell.

"Freakin' revolutionary," said Hail Larry's Wife, looking at the genesis of the project on the patio table.

"Freakin' outta this world," said Hail Larry, dialing his cell. "A couple of homos coming together with a hot Italian stud and his hot bitch of a wife, doing *this*, like *this*? They're gonna freakin' love us!"

"Set the world on fire," said Walter into his cell.

"Or be totally freakin' turned off," said Bear, sitting on QB's lounge chair.

"Gotta be positive, Bumbles," said Hail Larry, stepping away for his phone call. "*Ouch*, freakin' injury, *ouch*."

"I've never dreamed this big, I mean, with four at the same time anyway," said Bear. "Kinda virgin territory, if you get my drift."

"We'll stick together, we'll be fine," said Walter, rubbing Bear's shoulder.

"Even when it gets sticky?" asked Hail Larry's Wife.

"Oh, it'll definitely get sticky, no doubt," said Walter.

"You're so right," said Hail Larry's Wife. "It's bound to get sticky."

"I just hope the world is ready for the four of us," said Bear, "together in such a newfangled and ... bold and vivid way."

"This could take years to pull off, especially with the baby coming," said Hail Larry, returning after his phone call near the outer deck.

"I don't wanna be called Pussycat," said Hail Larry's Wife. "I am not going down in history—or the tons of sequels—as Pussycat McPherson."

"Shut up, Trixie," laughed Hail Larry.

"*Or* Trixie," laughed Hail Larry's Wife.

"First we need to focus on these toys and devices Bear brought for demonstration purposes," said Walter, indicating the pile on the table.

"Didn't hold back with the tools, did you, Bumbles?" asked Hail Larry.

"Remember," said Bear, dancing on top of the railing of the upper deck, "I'm not a rocket scientist or anything. I work best with visual aids. And lots of toys."

"Hold on, Sis," said Walter, pulling the phone away from his ear. "My Sis can hear all of this on her cell. She wants to know what we're talking about."

"Top secret!" yelled Hail Larry's Wife. "And way controversial."

"We're working on the Bearcat Project. Let that suffice for now," said Bear.

"What's the freakin' eggbeater for?" asked Hail Larry, nodding to the eggbeater on the table.

"Not sure yet," said Bear. "Saw it passing through the kitchen, knew it fit somehow, somewhere."

"Not where I'm thinking, I hope," said both Walter and Hail Larry's Wife.

"Who gets to crank it?" laughed Hail Larry.

"No trouble in Chicago?" asked Walter into his cell phone. "Sweet."

"Something tells me this eggbeater goes in the rear," said Bear.

"Nowhere near my character, right?" asked Hail Larry's Wife. "Eggbeaters are spooky to me, for some reason."

"I still can't see how this is all supposed to look real," said Hail Larry.

"Use your imagination, sweetie," said Hail Larry's Wife.

"Freakin' trying," said Hail Larry.

"Off the phone," said Walter. "What'd I miss? Why's Bear over there ... ah ... the landscapers."

Bear was mesmerized by Julio the Bullfighter and the landscapers below. They were on the side of the house, working in perfect harmony as they landscaped the Jaw. Without even realizing it, the men moved in a synchronized ballet of raking, plowing, weeding, sweeping, tossing, recycling.

"Let's show them working as if they're in heaven!" said Bear.

"Anyone up for lunch?" asked Walter. "These utensils have me in the mood for food."

"Let's see what we can cook up in the kitchen, sweetie," said Hail Larry's Wife, grabbing Walter's arm as they disappeared from the upper deck.

"Doesn't get any better than this in my dreams," said Bear, gazing at the Pacific.

"STORY MEETING," said Hail Larry, all of a sudden. "Crazy-thinking movie guy comes up with an idea for a great media frenzy, even better than the essay by the eight-year-old white kid in Western PA."

"Something more bizarre than *Where's My Pole?*" said Bear. "Dream on."

"Trust me," said Hail Larry.

"Hell, Larry, lay it on me," giggled Bear.

"I wanna plant a seed for ya," said Hail Larry.

"I love seeds," said Bear. "Fill me in."

"You know how you were saying you feel bad for guys like you, or Marcus in *My Whole Other Life?*" said Hail Larry. "I think it goes back. Way back."

"Farther back than you know," said Bear, processing an idea of his own.

"Exactly!" said Hail Larry. "That's why—my idea! But Bear, the wife cannot know, yet anyway. Eventually, sure. I don't know how freakin' Yeager will feel either, that's your call. Right now, this seed is just between you and me."

"Sure," said Bear, more focused on writing a note to himself. "Go for it."

"What seed is just between you and my Bear?" asked Walter, suddenly reappearing on the deck.

"None of your freakin' business," said Hail Larry. "Creative story talk."

"And you joined this creative side when?" asked Walter. *Mild laugh.*

"You'll see after I plant the seed," said Hail Larry. "Maybe. Meanwhile, mums with the wife. Hey, wife of mine ..."

With that, Hail Larry vanished from the deck, leaving Walter and Bear standing there somewhat bewildered.

DANGEROUS TERRITORY FOR BOYS WITH YOUNG HEARTS ...

"What do you think of this book?" asked Walter, sizing up the novel on his desk in the home office at the Jaw. Roberto the Celibate, their personal manager, had stumbled upon a little-known author and the book whose film rights he was shopping around.

"Older boys who are young at heart, younger boys who are older at heart, interesting," said Bear, typing at his desk in the home office at the Jaw. "And twisted. Might make a nice little Bearcat Studios movie."

"The author sounds cool," said Walter, reading the back cover. "*Bridge Across the Ocean,* a 26-year-old black gay man befriends two straight-identified, young white brothers during a magical summer vacation in Cancun ... sweet."

"Cool and dreamy cinematography for days," said Bear. "I see it as a kind of *Stand by Me* meets *The Hardy Boys* meets *Summer of '42* meets a twisted Negro mind, kinda similar to what I dreamt up for Marcus in *My Whole Other Life.*"

"Let's find the author," said Walter. "See wassup with this Randy Boyd."

"I'll have Roberto get his celibate ass on it," said Bear. "Be good to get a little warmhearted movie under our belt before we play with the bigger boys and toys, and their poles. And eggbeaters."

"So have I buttered you up enough since our best buds left?" asked Walter.

"I'm almost ready to let you back in the dawg house," said Bear, typing.

"Larry made an honest mistake."

"Did I say otherwise?"

Boom.

"On top of everything else," read Bear from his monitor. "Larry McPherson told some 'other' investor friends of his about the property in the hills above Malibu. Now a place called the Complex, not us, owns the dream site for Bearcat Studios."

"Larry made an honest mistake."

"Did I say otherwise?"

Boom.

"There's other dream sites out there for us," said Bear, then he started singing: "*Underneath the stadium with my ... brown-eyed Bear* ... remember that song back in the day? When it was just you, me, a little green box, and a couple of really wonderfully smelling college jocks ..."

"They bought my school!" said Walter, reacting to something on his monitor. "These Complex fuckers ... their website ... they bought my old junior high in Winnetka and are gonna turn it into ... whatever this Complex is ... a place for games in Chicagoland, *say what?*"

"Sounds almost as twisted as our next flick," said Bear, more focused on creating.

"Tell me about it," said Walter.

"Nigger needs his pole," said Bear. "Just like the white kid."

"Back to that again?" asked a weary Walter.

"Farther," said Bear. "Going back way farther than that, to where it all began, before the kid's essay, before there was such a thing as a nigger or a cracker, or even a North or South Pole. This could be a whole new ray of light."

"*Whoa*, got me hooked already," said Walter.

Coleman could dream up any dream and Yeager was that dream's biggest fan. Yeager could dream up any dream and Coleman was that dream's biggest fan. That's what buddies do.

"Perfect grace," said Bear.

"Is that the name of the movie?" asked Walter.

"It's what I hope people see," said Bear. "*Or* they could choose to see the worst."

"Where is this new flick going?" asked a mystified Walter.

"On the *Road of Life*, my dear sweet Norseman," said Bear. "We gonna take a trip around the Alphabet Wheel. For the director, I see the Creole Camille."

"I'm getting hot," said Walter, rising from his desk and hastily removing his shirt. "I love it when you talk all Crazy Bear."

"Then come give me some crazy Sugar, daddy, so we can get started on this *Road*."

"Go Seahawks go!" yelled Mama Rent at the top of her lungs!

"You tell 'em, Mama," said Bear into his cell phone. The Seahawks were opening up the year @ the tuning fork in Denver, otherwise known as Mile High Stadium.

"Tell your mom I said hi," said Hail Larry's Wife, sitting next to Bear.

"She says hi back," said Bear. "Talk to you tonight, mom, bye ... oh, and is it true you went out on *a date* with Coach, the black one? ... *hung up already.*"

"Probably at the mere mention of a date," said Hail Larry's Wife.

"No doubt," said Bear. "What's the score now?"

Denver 42, Seattle 12. Fourth Quarter.

Bear and Hail Larry's Wife sighed from their vantage point in Bear's lux box, stacked a lot higher than a mile up.

"People sure like beating up on our boys, don't they?" said Hail Larry's Wife, surveying the Broncomania beyond the glass.

"Are they playing 'The Hey Song' *every* time they sack Number 13?" asked Bear, ear pressed against the thick glass of the lux box.

"I don't think I wanna know that answer," said Hail Larry's Wife.

On the field below, Walter was being helped up by Neil Smith, who had just driven him a *mile low* into the turf. Yeager rejoined the huddle to see what he could do on third and long. Denver fans were on their feet, as if Seattle could score 30 points in less than 2:40. Yeager took the snap and handed off to Simmons. They got their signals crossed. Yeager was dumped by Smith again.

"Walt is the anti-Elway," said Bear. "Denver loves John Elway because he does and says all the things Denver wants him to, like a good Colorado cowboy—who's quite dreamy and handsome in my book. Now I don't know much about John personally, but for all we know, in his own private world, John Elway may or may not be the good Colorado cowboy as defined by Denver, Colorado. Point being: Walter has never fit any city's casting description for their quarterback, except maybe LA. Or Chicago. Or Seattle. Or Philadelphia—*Rocky.* Walter might have turned into some other town's dream, but Walter chose to be nobody's perfect anything a lifetime ago ... definitely since the double dose of sour college life. This much is true."

"You mean Illinois and Georgia," said Hail Larry's Wife.

"My husband tried to be a good boy at Illinois. It just didn't work out—fate, bad timing, not being all the Panther he wanted to be," said Bear. Deep down, Walter was a Panther, not a Big 10 or SEC man. Somebody crossed his wires. "Georgia was not a good fit, not for a man as sensitive as my husband. Being around all that *red intolerance* for Walter was like living in the middle of a cancer. I don't know how fondly either one of us would look back on our college days, if we hadn't met one another because of them. Hold on, lemme type a note on the laptop."

Elway complained his college career was "ruined" by the Stanford loss @ Cal in that crazy Tuba Player Game of 1982. A whole universe of college football quar-

terbacks and would-be dreamers would give their right arms to have their careers "ruined," ended or begun so painlessly and gloriously. One only hopes John Elway has matured enough to view that fantastical finish in a more divine light. You got yours! Blessings to the Beautiful Blond Bomber of a Jock God either way.

"You truly don't know what you got until you don't got it," said Bear in the lux box somewhere over Tennessee, the new kids still being called the Oilers until they could dream their own Titanic dreams.

"Who would have ever dreamed Tennessee would be in the NFL?" asked Hail Larry's Wife.

"Apparently people in Tennessee," said Bear. "I wonder what other Music City Miracles they can dream up, now that they have a franchise. I wonder if Memphis will ever forgive them for not putting the team here permanently."

"Who cares?" said Hail Larry's Wife. "As long as they stop dreaming of bumping Larry off the line so much—get off my freakin' husband, Matthews!"

"Walter watch out!" yelled Bear.

Yeager made one of those twisty-turning escape moves cagey quarterbacks make and scrambled away from a thuggish Oilers lineman. McPherson was open on the far sideline. Yeager heaved across his body ...

Intercepted and ran back for a touchdown. Newfangled Oilers fans went crazy. Memphis *slash* Nashville *slash* the Bible Belt had a team and a victory against the HOMO QB AND HIS SUPER BOWL CHUMPS (one sign made it past security).

"We're losing because I'm watching these games in this freakin' box," said Bear.

"We're losing because the team fired Coach Robbins before the season started," said Hail Larry's Wife. "How do you fire the coach who won you two rings?"

"How do you lose so many players to free agency?" asked Bear. "Yet pick up what *SportsCenter* calls the next big thing?"

Kyle Whippersnapper ... young, blond, golden, outta Texas Tech. Drafted by these same Tennessee Oilers. Whippersnapper refused to play for an oily team on the move. Seattle gave away Junior Jefferson, Reggie Snowman, and 38 other players to acquire the newest Heisman Trophy winner. So far, the young Whippersnapper hadn't played a down. He was for the future, claimed the team.

"How do you go from Super champs to 10-6 last year, to 1-5 so far this year?" asked a very depressed Hail Larry's Wife.

"Because the league has it in for us!" said Bear. "And the franchise spirit leader is in a freakin' plastic luxury bubble."

"Like that movie when we were kids," said Hail Larry's Wife. "John Travolta, *Boy in the Plastic Bubble*. Remember that TV movie? He had no immune system in, like, the 70s, way before anyone discovered AIDS."

"Guess I wasn't the only little boy dreaming of immunity," said Bear. "And living in a world that was immune, or immune-free, not sure which."

"You dreamed you were a *Bear in the Plastic Bubble?*" asked Hail Larry's Wife.

"I dreamed of some kind of virus in Tulsa, the town in the soap opera I wrote to myself on a bunch of spiral notebooks," said Bear. "All in secret homo code, of course."

"An AIDS virus?" asked Hail Larry's Wife. "Before there was AIDS?"

"My virus didn't have a name. I canceled the storyline," said Bear.

"Too creepy," said both Bear and Hail Larry's Wife.

"Make no mistake," said Bear. "I'm not some kind of fortune teller, or prophet or any shit like that. Heaven forbid people look at me as anything more than a fallible child of God, just like them. Word is born."

"Was there a conniving bitch like me on the show?" asked Hail Larry's Wife.

"Kyle," said Bear. "The runaway street hustler who 'married' Asa Wellings, bumped off the old geezer with a sexual heart attack, then took over the Wellings mansion and their oil and horse empire."

"My kinda bitch, makes me proud," said Hail Larry's Wife, pretending to dab away a tear.

"Then there was Dan, the town QB, high school through the pros," said Bear. "A true stud but psycho as can be. This geeky loner kid named Chris Brown was infatuated with Dan, starting in high school. Chris followed Dan around town just to clean up Dan's psychotic messes, you know, after Dan would stalk some poor gay kid in an alley, then run away just before beating the shit out of him ... a Jekyll and Hyde kind of QB, that Dan Johnson, he was."

"Terrible call, ref! Is that guy phobic?" asked Hail Larry's Wife.

"But Dan, the crazy QB, never hurt Chris Brown," said Bear. "They had a bond—not a friendship, just an unspoken bond. They kinda orbited around each other's worlds, never really connecting because they were too retarded to be honest and hook up for, like, 20 years. Dan's time in the nuthouse was also to blame for their separation—got caught up in the legal system for acting too crazy."

"Aren't you glad Walter's not that way?" asked Hail Larry's Wife.

"Makes me freakin' wonder," said Bear. "Chris and Dan were as meant for each other as Walter and me. I was the head writer of *Tulsa*, right? I created this high school generation called the Fab Five, these rich, white and successful boys—who had their own dramas. Then there was Chris Brown, the sad, loner geek kid who was me."

"Hard to imagine you as a loner in any life," said Hail Larry's Wife.

"People knew me in high school," said Bear. "I was on about 10,000 things. Editor of the school paper. Drama. Choir. Lead in a school play or two. Soccer. The famous Junior Spectacular talent show. The school knew Bear Coleman. We just forgot to be social and hospitable along the way."

"That's sad," said Hail Larry's Wife.

"Not even," said Bear. "It all led me to Walter. I wouldn't change a thing. It was all divine, don't you see? Like somebody up there likes us. Like God meant for Walter and me to be together. *That's the way the gods drew it up. We're supposed to be buds.* Same way the head writer of *Tulsa* created Chris and Dan when it came time to create a generation of high school kids on *Tulsa*. I sat down with my spiral notebook, drew up the new generation. Five fabulous white kids, and their satellite girlfriends ... then Chris *slash* me, and Dan the QB, who was also an outsider of sorts but popular. I meant for them to be together."

"Why weren't they?" asked Hail Larry's Wife.

"When I created Chris Brown," said Bear, "his character sketch would have read something like this: forever lonely, forever a loner, always gets close, never gets the guy. This character will live a long life and die a lonely boy. Poor bastard. I gotta live a shit life, Brown's gotta live a shit life."

"Bear, that's sad," said Hail Larry's Wife.

"It's how I felt as a kid," said Bear. "Like there wasn't a soul in the world that would want to spend time with mine. Like a lot of guys that end up calling themselves gay, I never had proms, first dates, second dates, Saturday nights, sleepovers, all that. In high school, I just had my dreams. And *Tulsa.*"

"Chris and Dan weren't meant for each other if they were acting all crazy like that," said Hail Larry's Wife. "They were living a fucked life."

"Those were the only kinds of stories I could conceive of," said Bear. "Stories where they spent their love and energy on lesser versions of themselves, dreaming of nightmares, chaos and disorder. I had no better examples of two buddies in love, no role models. Makes me wish I could dream better dreams for buddies like Chris and Dan—*like being a great QB while the spirit leader doesn't have to watch the games in a freakin' lux box ... come on, refs, you know that's not fair!*"

"Make Walt and Marcus of *My Whole Other Life* crazy like those *Tulsa* boys," said Hail Larry's Wife.

"No way," said Bear. "I'm trying to dream a better dream for them by giving Marcus a better life in the back story, you know, before he meets Walt after dreaming about him for 21 years and the note blows away. Something tells me I'm gonna have to put Marcus through a lot to be ready for a man of Walter's caliber. Gotta keep the poor bastard from freaking out!"

"Who, *that* Marcus or *whole other* Walter?" asked Hail Larry's Wife.

"Exactly," said Bear. A cell phone rang.

"Babysitter," said Hail Larry's Wife, retrieving her cell. Only the McPherson nanny was allowed in the loop during the game. "Esmeralda, how's my little Oscar?"

On the field below, near the bench, Yeager took a swig of Gatorade, then offered some to the 6,000 security cops adjacent to the sidelines.

"Back in a sec, Bear, sweetie, better reception." Hail Larry's Wife stepped outside the lux box. A few minutes later, the lux box started rolling backward. Or maybe Bear was only dreaming ...

... MARCUS FELT AS IF HE WERE GOING BACKWARD, but upon further reveal, woke up from his dreams to realize the plane was soaring up, up and away. He glanced out the window, imagining Bryan Adams and Barbra Streisand singing the sweetest song he'd ever heard: "I Finally Found Someone."

It had to be real. The tears of joy proved it, right?

All these years ... 35 long years ... 35 long and lonely years ... but like Bryan and Barbra ... Marcus Coleman had finally found someone.

Not Jake, the crazy fireman who lighted up his heart one week, then burned it to the ground the next.

Not Lance, the liar about all things, whoever he was.

Not the countless bodies he'd used and been used by since ... TIME.

Not Matt Strickland ... if only there was a God ...

Not anyone from the past. This was a real live one.

Tom. So many Toms.

First infatuation. Maybe last love, fate willing—so thought and hoped the black man bound for Boston, the sports town he hated, of all places.

But Tom was the One. It felt so right. The phone calls felt so right. The vibe felt so right. Everything felt so right. The rest was details. It felt so right. There was a connection. Marcus Coleman was going to Boston to meet his Miracle of the Net.

Tom. So many Toms. More than any other name in his life. Tom.

Of course, Marcus had had his share of Internet flakes and freaks. But this one was extra special. Their bond was spiritual. Plus, Tom had that cool and dreamy last name, Yeager. *Must mean something. Must mean it's right, right?*

True? This one felt so right. Even the one picture was perfect. Tom had dark, curly hair and a solid, athletic body, built like a Red Sox first baseman. *Too good to be true* was the first thought that shot like a cannon into Marcus' mind. Or maybe it was: *this isn't that guy's pic.*

No matter. It felt right. A leap, right?

How else ya ever gonna know?

After the plane reached cruising altitude, he fell asleep, dreaming of the video footage he had shot while waiting to board.

Hey, when you've waited 35 years for magic to happen ...

"My last thoughts," said Marcus on tape, looking straight into the fish-eyed lens, "my last thoughts before meeting my possible ... or eventual ... first love *slash* boyfriend *slash* buddy ... *hmmm* ... it feels right. I'm hopeful. Hopefully, we'll hit it off, want to get to know each other and go from there. I mean, it can only be a sign of good things to come with a name like Tom Yeager, right? At least the Yeager part."

... Ten minutes after landing in Boston, Marcus meets Tom Yeager, who looks like ... no one Marcus had ever seen before, including the guy the guy was supposed to be: himself.

But it felt so right.

"I'm over it now," said Marcus weeks later to Eve, his best gal pal living in Cincinnati. Eve knew better. Took time to extricate Boston from his heart. One pic does not make or break feelings, nor does one lie. Maybe the pic wasn't even a lie. Maybe there weren't any lies, just different people on different planets. They never settled that one. Didn't seem to matter after everything else fell apart.

"What happened with the dude in Boston?" asked Octavio, his son-figure.

I'm his father-figure. Get it?

"Roll the tape from my adult life," said Marcus to Octavio. "Insert one name for another. Insert a different detail for the deal-breaker, same diff, but I tell you this: I will never give my heart again, and from now on, I will use the Net for what it was originally intended: sex dates with no strings."

Free to use and be used at will.

"Wish I could see Eve or my son every now and then," said Marcus to one of them a short time later. They were all living worlds apart. Octavio had grown into a young man, complete with live-in girlfriends. Marcus resided far away in some new blur by the beach (there had been so many blurs since the quake in 1994 ... hard to find a place that felt like home). "But I am making new friends, without whom I would have never made it through Boston," said Marcus.

Larry ... a former college wide receiver Marcus met at the gym—tons of sweet machismo buffering the biggest heart known to humanity. Lover of women and leader of a group of buds who played football together and now hang out at a local sports bar, bullshitting the night away over beers and ballgames. Marcus becomes one of the guys for the first time in his life. No secrets. No tolerance issues. Larry dreams of making movies one day. Sweet, endearing grandmother encourages his dreams.

Wilhelm ... a Creole fellow with a nasally voice, also met at the gym. Gay-identified. Becomes Marcus' confidant, brother and brutha. Another black man who understands.

Roberto ... the sports buddy. Marcus had bought a scalper's ticket to an NBA game, and once seated, bonded instantly with the original seller. By half-time, Roberto had said: "Hey, the wife's pregnant and won't be able to attend many games this year. I got season tickets. Wanna go sometime?"

The fact that they lived less than a mile apart seemed like perfect grace.

Gifts sent from the heavens. Perfectly designed with perfect grace at the perfect time to keep Marcus Coleman going. That is, if one believed Reverend Julio, spirit leader of some newfangled church Marcus stumbled upon in the post-Boston haze.

Perfect grace. But Marcus still hated Boston. Always had, dating back to the race riots of his childhood and the Celtics. Thank God for the Bambino's Curse. May it live forever! May the Red Sox never, ever win a thing!

The newfangled church was very spiritual ... love all ... all loves ... relax, smile, take a breath, God loves you. You love God.

Reverend Julio was as helpful as a heart surgeon after Boston.

"What do you want from God and a soul mate?" asked Reverend Julio in private counseling. Yeah, Boston was that big. One Last Try *and* One Last Cry.

"What do you mean, what do I want?" asked Marcus in counseling.

"Whatever you want in a relationship and from a man, write it down, keep it close to your heart," said Reverend Julio.

"You mean, like, what he looks like? What we have in common? Where we live? How we live? The sex? Hair color? What?" asked Marcus, unable to use his imagination.

"Whatever resonates in your soul," said a calm, earthy, paternal, beaming, glowing, angelic Reverend Julio.

If Marcus jotted anything down from that day, only God knows the whereabouts of those dreams. But a seed was planted. Marcus wondered, and the "what resonates in your soul?" question made good fodder for his many "expert talks" on relationships (like a good coach who sucks at actually playing the game).

"My new friends have helped saved my life," said Marcus to Eve one day, talking long distance. "Don't know where I'd be without them. Three guys, two hetero, all totally accepting, all of whom came into my life right after the debacle of Boston."

He had been grieving the loss; Roberto could see it in his face.

"Thanks for the invite to the game, brand new NBA buddy o' mine, but understand: I'm not gonna be the best company for this nooner we're heading to vs. Iverson and the Sixers. I was up all night, ending a romantic entanglement on the phone with Boston. You might as well know: it was a guy. I'm gay."

"I got no problem with that," said Roberto, driving them to the game. "So you pumped to see Iverson?"

The fallout of Boston led to three serendipitous friendships that powered Marcus' world until Marcus could power it himself with more of his own dreams for the future.

The entanglement with Boston also led to the discovery of one of the most powerful series of books in Marcus' universe: *Conversations with God.* Tom's reading of the book over the phone was what had brought them together, the universal love for all God's creations, including one's self ... *felt right, felt like somebody talking to his soul for the first time in a very long while, maybe ever.*

The entanglement with Boston had ripped his heart but was helping to mend his soul. He could never look at Tom or Boston in a completely evil light. And with the help of his new buddies, Marcus carved a whole new world for himself, post-Boston.

He had survived beyond a date he thought his AIDS-infected body would never see, the 1996 Atlanta Olympics.

He had survived long enough to see the creation of drugs that offered, for the first time, a better dream than slow death for those infected with AIDS.

He had survived long enough to stop waiting to die and start wanting to live again, even if only for a moment.

He was even dreaming of some of his deepest dreams once more: telling stories, having the four-legged buddy he prayed was out there, waiting. Easier to adopt a dog than a man, true?

To follow those rainbows, he gave up another dream: West Beach ... the Santa Barbara bungalow ... felt kinda lonely anyway. No one ever came along with an offer to keep him company after he rejected the bitch with cancer in her throat. So there was still some spinning of the wheels, including a lot of moving up and down the coast, searching for a cheap place to call home. It's like that when you're 35 and suddenly the world is telling you that dying of AIDS needn't be your foremost thought, as per the last dozen or so years of your life, give or take.

"Are you gay?" asked Dr. Battle Axe at UCLA Student Health, the day after the Rose Bowl that left him sick as hell.

"Do you have a way to save my life, preferably a way that doesn't kill my spirit in the process? If the answer is not yes, there is no further discussion to be had."

Marcus Coleman was learning to live again, learning to enjoy storytelling again, even starting to share some of those stories with the world. Of course, the publishing world was about as supportive as Dr. Battle Axe.

"Do we put you in the black box or the pink box?"

"I'm not the Coleman in a box. Do you have a way to save my life, preferably a way that doesn't kill my spirit in the process by turning my novel about a black gay man searching for his personal truth and uprising into a novel about a straight white man trying to stop a black gay man's dreams from coming true?"

The book world sent him on his way, having no room for a stubborn black man dreaming the dreams of his particular soul.

Marcus Coleman would be grateful for eternity for that send-off.

Marcus Coleman created his own dream house for his stories.

Marcus Coleman created his own West Beach, *Books* subbing for *Bungalows*.

Marcus Coleman was alive and well.

Marcus Coleman was a dreamer.

Marcus Coleman survived on his dreams.

Marcus Coleman had at least one more dream he conceived of as possible. A dog.

Marcus Coleman finally got Hip. His own Hip. His own beautiful blond aura. Love at first sight on four swift and agile legs. The sweetest, calmest, craziest, coolest, golden gunslinger of a dawg from the shelter. The love was instant. The bond followed.

Marcus Coleman finally found someone.

Marcus Coleman believed in miracles again, even Whitney Houston and Mariah Carey had come together to sing about them. How miraculous was that? Maybe there truly can be miracles. When you believe. True?

BEAR COLEMAN'S LUX BOX HAD ROLLED ALL THE WAY from the top of some stadium to the depths of some dark stadium underbelly. He was alone. The front curtain was open. Football fans with foam fingers, jumbo drinks and cotton candy were staring at him with wide, frozen eyes on the other side of the glass. Exhibit Bear: male cheerleader *slash* house nigger for the homo QB *slash* coma-head *slash* boy in a glass box. He had no idea what city, what stadium, what week—what his man's heart was feeling.

The fans on the outside felt the door to the lux box explode open, kicked down by one determined Bear foot.

"Could you tell me where I could find the nachos?" asked Bear to a little girl with cotton candy. She pointed a sugary thumb in one direction. Bear thanked her and went to get him some nachos in the real world ...

The score after three quarters ... Eagles 34, Seahawks 31.

"WE'RE SO SORRY, BEAAAAAAR!" CRIED WALTER AND THE HAIL LARRYS, OFFERING BEAR YET ANOTHER BOUQUET OF HEARTFELT APOLOGY.

"*Or* you can shut up about it already!" said Bear. "And take my word for it when I say I forgive you. *Then take off this damned blindfold so I can see my surprise!*"

"Not until you bless that damned blindfold, boy!" said Walter.

"Take off my blessed blindfold, fool!" said an anxious Bear. "I wanna see how you three *claim* you're making up for my Lux Box Shuffle into the bowels of the Vet today."

"Take a gander," said Walter, freeing his buddy's eyes.

Breathless was Bear. What lux box shuffle? He was standing in front of the statue of Rocky Balboa, one of Philadelphia's all-time biggest dreamers.

"May I have this dance?" asked Walter, beaming.

"Always and forever," said Bear, beaming.

Hail Larry's Wife had a boom box, as well as her baby in the stroller. She had been tending to a cranky Oscar elsewhere in Veterans Stadium—the reason Bear took the descent alone. No big. It all worked out.

"Like a gift," said Bear, slow-dancing with his man to one of their favorite all-time love songs.

"Got you outta your bubble," said Walter, proud, smiling poppa.

"Never going back," said Bear. "Donate it. Detonate it. Zap it. I don't care. *No* box will keep me from my man ever again. You understand the words coming from my soul, Walter Yeager?"

The True Gold cowboy laughed his mild, sexy, *where have you been all my life?* laugh. Bear melted into his man, the night, the music and the love. His buddy was taking him on a romantic voyage with their favorite infatuation, Prince, the original "International Lover." This much is true.

"Look at those nuts," said Hail Larry, always pretending to be turned off by what turned him on most ... *not the sex, silly ... the warm fuzzy feeling between the boys' two hearts.*

"This must be divine," said Bear, dancing on air. "To stand where Rocky stands in Philadelphia for all-time with My Very Own Rocky. Beyond my wildest dreams, until now."

Yeager eyed the statue of one of his biggest heroes, Sylvester Stallone *slash* Rocky, the power behind countless dreams of their time.

"If it sets you free, it sets me free," said Walter. Or was it Bear?

"When is Tank gonna meet little Oscar?" asked Hail Larry, glowing over his kid in the stroller. Little Oscar was the one human being in Larry's world who had never heard of a dropped pass that changed an Auburn football season back in the day. "I love this little guy more than life itself! Wassup, Champ! You're Heisman-bound, you know that, don't you?"

"Another reason this season is topsy-turvy," said Bear, dancing on less air. "Daddy misses his Tank, holed up outside PITT."

Walter and the Hail Larrys talked options on getting custody of Tank, a pie in the sky dream at the moment. Meanwhile, Bear had a flash of being in the box, and being watched. The flash morphed into a scene on the front lawn of his high school, Hayward Central High, the Panthers.

Sunny, fun, hippy-looking kids were sitting on the school's front lawn, looking like a 60s Pepsi commercial. At the center of their world was one man. Or rather, one kid. Or rather ... a boy with a bear head on his shoulders. Or was he a boy? Was he even alive? Or was he just their stuffed mascot?

"Not that song!" said Bear to all of Philadelphia by night.

"Bear, you okay?" asked Walter, ceasing the dance.

"I'd like to teach the world to sing," said Bear, "something different. Let's get outta Philly. Let's go home."

"Bear, you okay?" asked Hail Larry's Wife.

"No," said Bear. "I want to go home."

"Which one?" asked Hail Larry.

"I want to be home," said Bear, holding back the tears.

"Then we'd better hit the road," said Walter, the decisive cowboy. "Long journey in front of us."

MEET THE YEAGERS! QUARTERBACK AND HIS SEXUAL PARTNER BEAR COLEMAN NOW TALKING TO THE MEDIA ON SELECTED OCCASIONS.

"What do you call yourselves?" asked a reporter on a morning talk show.

"I call him Walter," said Bear.

"I call him Bear," said Walter.

"Are you gay?" asked a reporter on a noon talk show.

"Define gay," said Bear.

"Blankety blank, blank, blank," said the reporter.

"That does not define me or my relationship," said Walter.

"Ditto," said Bear.

"How would you describe your love life?" asked a reporter on an evening news show.

"You first," said Walter.

"Are you homosexual?" asked a reporter on a Hollywood entertainment show.

"Define homosexual," said Bear.

"Blankety blank, blank, blank," said the reporter.

"That does not define me or my relationship," said Walter.

"Ditto," said Bear.

"What's it like for you as a man in the locker room who's open about your sexuality?" asked a reporter for *The New York Times.*

"You first," said Walter.

"Why do you love this man?" asked a reporter on CNN.

"He gets me," said Walter.

"Why do you love this man?" asked a reporter on CNN.

"Somebody had to," shrugged Bear. "I'm just grateful God chose me."

"Are you saying you're chosen?" asked a reporter on the Fox News Network.

"Heaven forbid people look at me as anything more than a fallible child of God, just like them. Word is born," said both Walter and Bear.

"Are you bisexual?" asked a reporter on ESPN.

"Define bisexual," said Walter.

"Blankety blank, blank, blank," said the reporter.

"That does not define me or my relationship," said Bear.

"Ditto," said Walter.

"Are you straight?" asked a radio sports reporter while Yeager was taking a dump in an airport restroom @ SEA-TAC.

"Define straight," said Walter. "And while you're at it, define the opposite of straight, which I'm guessing is bent, *like this seat.*"

"Blankety blank, blank, blank," said the reporter.

"That does not define me or my relationship," said Walter.

"Ditto," said Bear from the adjacent stall. "Mine is definitely bent."

Every word has a polar opposite which suggests a polar opposite energy.

If something is straight and straight is good, whatever is deemed the opposite of straight cannot be inherently good.

If you change the way you look at things, the things you look at change.

If you deemphasize polar opposites, you deemphasize polar opposite instincts, such as good and evil, love and hate, peace and war—all necessary parts of the game of life, but how much evil, hate and war do you want in your game? In your world?

Would you rather play ball with your foot, or explode heads with your trigger finger? The same choices boys had as boys are the same choices boys have as men.

Perfect Grace. Ain't nothing new.

Thus humanity's challenge and ultimate game: find ways to come together, not fall apart. Hail Our Panthers, United We Stand. Otherwise, Game Over.

"We don't understand what you two gentlemen are to one another as a couple," said a reporter on *20/20/60/48/Dateline*.

"How many examples of 'two people in love' in art and real life do you need to understand these two people?" asked Walter, indicating himself and Bear.

"We ain't singing a new tune," said Bear. "You're just hearing different voices belting out the same old-fashioned love song."

"The more you come from love, the more bliss," said Walter. "That's what we hope people get from us."

"Or you can go in reverse," said Bear. "Your choice."

"Are you sexual?" asked Oprah.

"Define sexual, Oprah," said Walter.

"Human beings who have sexual impulses and try their best to serve those impulses, and God, in the highest, to the best of their ability," said Oprah.

"That does define me and my relationship," said Yeager and Coleman.

Heaven forbid Bearcats exist in a world without Oprah.

"Cocky bastards, trying to come off all mature and enlightened," said Hail Larry. "That's what they're all saying out there."

"And we need to hear this because?" asked Bear, sweeping across the room, reading the note he had just typed on his laptop.

Newport, Seattle ... midweek ... between games ... team improving ... still need a little help to clinch home field throughout.

"Look, here it is!" screamed Hail Larry's Wife from the couch.

"Quiet, girl, don't hit me," said Walter, sitting next to her. "Why do girls always hit me?"

"Because you let them," said Bear, joining them on the couch. "It's your way of letting the female race blow off a little steam at All Men ... always the hero, my hero."

"Shut up about your freakin' rock star hero," said Hail Larry, hovering behind the couch. "Check out your pad on the tube!"

"Today on MTV Cribs, chill on the left coast with the most famous couple in the entire world as we know it ... exclusive to Cribs ... a Bear Tour of ... the Jaw!"

"You freakin' made them say that!" Hail Larry was no fool.

"Welcome, Bearcats, I'm the Bear formerly known as the lesbian flick guy slash *weirdo thriller guy* slash *quarterback's manager* slash ... me! But something tells me you already knew that ..."*

"Bear, you are loving this, you fool!" screamed Hail Larry's Wife, kicking up her heels.

"The Jaw is our little slice of heaven, QB and me ... Sometimes, I call him MVP for short. By the way, he's off in the football world, throwing rocks. That's the way it works, as you can see here by our slogan on the wall in the home office."

ONE MAKES MAGIC WITH ROCKS,
THE OTHER MAKES MAGIC WITH BLOCKS.

"You showed that!" laughed Walter.

"And this is what the inside of our main fridge looks like!"

"Bear, you're a natural on TV!" cried Hail Larry's Wife. "You could have your own show."

"Dream of it," said Bear. "Or maybe not."

"Okay, sports fans, let's moooooove to the Jacuuuuuuzzi in the backyard, a mandatory stop for me and QB after a tough road game. Ouch!"

"Okay, enough of this." Hail Larry grabbed the remote from his wife. "I wanna see us all on *Celebrity Jeopardy*."

"Today, we play with four contestants, two Seahawks and their ... Sea mates ... battling for charity!"

"Only because you jammed in the sports and movie categories, Larry, hell," said Walter.

"I sucked at this. I'm going to check on the baby," said Hail Larry's Wife, disappearing into the bedroom.

"Speaking of movies, Bumbles, how's *Road of Life?*" asked Hail Larry.

"Swimming upstream," said Bear. "The Creole Camille is doing the pic serious justice, from what I can see of the dailies. Won't be long now."

"Hope he treats it right," said Hail Larry. "That story could change the world with the right ... angle."

"You're really getting into this movie kick, McPherson," said Walter.

"I love movies," said Hail Larry. "Women and movies, the two things I could never do without. I love women. Man, I love women!"

"I love men!" said Bear, typing in his lap. "*That's* my answer from now on ... no wait ... my answer for all questions about my private sexual thoughts will be ..."

I'M SEXUAL. MOST OF MY LIFE I HAVE BEEN A LOVER OF MEN. NOW, I AM A LOVER OF ONE MAN, FOR AS FAR AS I CAN SEE. THAT'S THE CORE OF ME. I AM A LOVER OF ONE MAN. THE REST OF MY LIFE IS ON TOP OF THAT. THIS MUCH IS TRUE.

"Shrink it down and put it on a t-shirt, why don't you, geez," said Hail Larry, looking at Bear's laptop.

"I be one who knows what I am," said Bear, typing version two. "Or something like that."

"Keep dreaming, little Bearcat, you'll figure it out," said Walter.

"BOY, IT SURE IS NICE TO HAVE RAIDER NATION around to always beat up on," sighed Hail Larry's Wife. SEAHAWKS 13, OAKLAND 3, THIRD QUARTER.

"I don't care whose ass we kick, as long I never see that box-on-wheels again," said Bear, typing in his laptop while Yeager jogged off the field after a certain Seahawks wide receiver dropped a third-down conversion.

Kingdome, Seattle ... Bear Coleman outta the lux box and into his very own luxury box, like the other elite and privileged of the Pacific Northwest ... Not quite the bleachers. Better than the Pope-mobile. Hello, wonderful fans waving from below. A homer against Da Raidas ... Hawks improving ... still need a little help to clinch the division.

"Don't sweat it, McPherson, gotta stay positive," said Hail Larry's Wife to the sideline below.

"I can't imagine what that's like, the hell for Larry," said Bear, typing and sipping a drink through a straw. "His cross to bear, I mean."

"The night sweats are getting less, thank God," said Hail Larry's Wife.

"Hell, I never knew Larry had night sweats ... more nachos please," said Bear to their private waitress, Esmeralda.

"The night sweats never stopped after college," said Hail Larry's Wife. "Sometimes our bed is drenched."

"Did you know him when he was an Auburn Tiger?" asked Bear.

"Nope, but I heard stories," said Hail Larry's Wife. "Thanks, Esmeralda ... next time a little more cheddar? ... oh, and more vino please ... Bear, my husband thought about suicide after failing the test."

"What test?" asked Bear, confused.

"He failed the test and was gonna be kicked off the team!" said Hail Larry's Wife. "That's why he ... did what he did. Maybe. His mind was on the failed test. Not that he dropped the Alabama pass on purpose, but you wonder."

"All these years," said Bear. "Hell, how does Larry keep going? He had one of those Bill Buckner moments."

Bill Buckner. Boston Red Sox Trojan Horse or the unluckiest fielder in the history of sport. Or just a guy who missed a ground ball one day. All in your mind.

"No one cares how *he* feels," said Hail Larry's Wife. "Or how he felt on that day that 'ruined' so many of their lives ... what a joke! ... or how he felt that morning, that weekend, that time in his young life. He was just a boy, Bear."

Does anyone want to be reminded of any of their actions at age 21 for the rest of their natural lives?

"Guys like Buckner and Larry are just like any other player," said Hail Larry's Wife. "But they literally get crucified by fans for doing exactly what most fans would do every single time in that same situation ... drop the ball."

"Come on, ref ... can't you get a call right?" yelled Bear on high.

"He's never been the same," said Hail Larry's Wife. "Little Oscar has saved him. I mean that literally."

"That's what little Oscars do for men like Walter and Larry," said Bear.

"Not you?" asked Hail Larry's Wife. "No, I know what saves you."

"Do you now?" giggled Bear.

"Being devoted to a man like Walter," said Hail Larry's Wife.

"You're half right," said Bear. "Twist it and you've got the other half."

Bear's devotion to Walter makes Bear feel like Bear's not half bad, as if Bear's upgrading his self-worth from all bad to half bad, which is the same as half good, which is pretty good when you start out as all bad (in a world that tells Bear that black and homo are very bad).

Walter's devotion to Bear makes Walter feel pretty good, as if Walter's downgrading from all good to pretty good, which makes Walter feel better, because Walter feels bad for being all good (as in perfect and privileged in a world where others feel bad and suffer for it).

The boys come from opposite ends of good and bad but meet in the middle of each, which is a reflection, not a polar opposite.

Half bad and half good add to up half empty or half full.

Add half and half, you have one whole.

Two people make one whole.

But the whole was made from half of each person.

Ergo, each person still has one other half to himself.

That half also matches up perfectly with the other person.

Two sides to every person, matched perfectly with two sides to another person.

Perfect grace in four-part harmony.

"That's the equation," said Bear. "The one I'm trying to explain to the world. It has to do with how every *thing* is built like the atom, including us!"

"I don't get it," said Hail Larry's Wife. "Try harder, Seahawks, I need my Super ring, like Bear."

"I'm not a rocket scientist, just a man who knows his man," said Bear. "Maybe a pretty picture or two will help. I'll go to work on it."

"Well, I finally got this year's batch of QB's clippings from Roberto, our personal assistant," sighed Bear, standing in the den of Corona, Seattle. "I wonder had I given him less stringent guidelines for what was 'suitable,' might he have found more than *five* headlines that said something positive about my husband's quarterbacking this past year, just ended last week."

Yeager, 35, Over the Hill? Half of Seattle Says No. Vote Now!

Walt Loves to Tease. Hawks Storm from 1-5 to 8-8, Slip into the Playoffs.

Kyle Whippersnapper Gets Playoff Start for Injured Walt, Who Slipped in Season Finale.

Broncos Throttle Whippersnapper 42-17 in Wild Card Game.

Elway Wins His First-Ever Super Ring Over Green Bay Packers.

"That last one's questionable," said Walter, chomping on a carrot stick, looking—dare one say—very Redford-esque. *Warm fuzzy sweater and all.*

"Well, guys, it was nice teaming up while it lasted," said Hail Larry's Wife.

"Would have been a miserable two years without this handsome little guy." Hail Larry never tired of loving little Oscar, who was going for a ride around the den on some newfangled kid's toy, a gift from the Tankster on a recent visit.

"Being traded is gonna make it harder for us to get our timing right for the Secret #1 Bearcat Project," said Hail Larry's Wife. "And some of us need to build up the endurance, especially with that eggbeater, which is still plenty creepy to me, I don't mind telling you ... hold on, gotta call our caterer, Esmeralda ... Essie, dear, can you hear me?"

"Plenty of time to work on Bearcat Secret #1 Project," said Walter. "It's not like the world is ready for such a bold and daring deal ... just yet. That's 21st-century stuff. Gotta wait until the bridge is done. And Bear, you still have plenty of kinks to work out."

"Especially if I have anything to do with it," said Hail Larry.

"We'll see you both during the regular season if the Patriots are on the Zephyrs' schedule," said Bear.

McPHERSON'S FATE NOW IN NEW ENGLAND'S HANDS.

"No headline from Roberto about you guys being traded to Chicago?" asked Hail Larry's Wife, off the cell.

"I guess our personal assistant couldn't find a good one to send," said Walter. "Chicago isn't exactly loving their football right now."

"What do you expect after flying so high with Air Jordan?" asked Bear. "Twice."

"I'll take two of that," said Hail Larry's Wife.

"*O-kay?*" said both Bear and Hail Larry's Wife, hi-fiving like a soul brutha and sista.

"Then it's perfect grace that Mike came outta retirement," said Walter. "My hometown can obsess over the Bulls' shit and give us a clear shot at assessing *our* shit, and turning it into something better than 4-12. I know my Chicago ... some people there aren't happy to see their *Steven Carrington return home to the so-called Dynasty.*"

"Walter!" yelled a very pissed-off Bear. "I thought we were in a sports radio blackout!"

"Sorry, accidental," said Walter. "Hey ... how did you know that was sports radio?"

"Listen up, Bearcat People," said Bear. "We may have fallen on our asses a bit here in Seattle, but that's sports. Some people in Chicago wanna win, and some support us. We just need to hook those groups up. I'll have Roberto get his celibate ass on it right away."

"The celibate bastard's pretty busy already," said Hail Larry. "The buzz on the Camille's *Road of Life* is serious, and he ain't even done tweaking it ... maybe a second little Oscar?"

"Rough cut screening in one month, right, everybody? On the calendars, right?" asked Walter, always the quarterback.

"Speaking of serious shit," said Hail Larry's Wife to Walter. "What was it really like in the locker room, you know, as a ... *sexual* person."

"For Christ's sake, the woman means a homo," said Hail Larry. "You bros will always be homos to me and little Oscar, isn't that right my Heisman Champ? You and me are never gonna fail any tests, are we?"

"So what was it like being a homo in the locker room?" asked Bear and Hail Larry's Wife in unison, dying to know.

Walter took his Redford-esque pause, patted them both on the shoulder and said: "It was heaven. Whatever you imagine that to be, that's what it was like."

"This is Walter Yeager's voice mail ..." said Walter Yeager's voice mail.

"Buddy," said Bear after the beep, more focused on flying down the highway to Rod Stewart. *Or was it Three Dog Night?* "Making a quick trip in the SUV with the dogs to San Diego to check up on the set of *Bridge Across the Ocean,* our newest Bearcat Studios production. Filming in junior high gym today. Speaking of. Did the Complex in the hills over Malibu ever open up? Something tells me the property might still be available. I'll be back in time for the *Road* screening tonight and Super Loop Luau to follow. Until then. Heart. Yours ... *Gimme some tenderness!"* sang Bear to the wind, letting out a howl. Hip, the sensitive one, retracted in the backseat. Comet was a Tank now. Took more than a howling Bear to scare him.

The season and their Seahawk life were over. Chicago was their next destination after an off-season at the Jaw.

"What is in this water here in San Diego?" asked Bear, watching the dogs romp and roam at Dog Beach.

"Their paradise," said Linda, the Swedish dog trainer. She was Walter's cousin whom Bear hadn't seen since hibernation. She lived near San Diego, where she trained dogs.

"Thanks for joining us," said Bear, surveying the large beach. "Suddenly I'm nostalgic for the days when Walter was with the Chargers."

"Hip is just like him," said Linda, the Swedish dog trainer, petting the Hipster. "Real, real sensitive, loves affection, tummy rubs ... don't you little fella ... ah, yea, he's an adorable blond sweetie."

"It would take a miracle to get Comet to lie still that long," said Bear, playing fetch with Comet. "Comet lives for repetitive, hard-driving movement. Like me with my dancing, *ha!"*

"And Hip is like the quarterback," said Linda, the Swedish dog trainer, "wants to run circles around you, faking and juking past you until he's tired of you."

Hip was a golden blond mutt. Comet was pure chocolate Lab.

Hip was swift and agile, like a cagey panther. Comet was a steadfast tank or bear.

Indoors, Hip was more reserved, Comet more noisy and busy.

Outdoors, Hip was more outgoing, Comet in his own purple haze, barely interested in other dogs.

Hip liked people. Comet was mistrusting of strangers.

Hip was curious but wary of the world. Comet rarely bothered to notice.

Hip was very, very sensitive: special diet, special handling, special joy. Comet could weather anything, any food, any soreness, any bad sound, bump or bruise.

Hip was smaller, cozier, softer. Comet was a big thick slab of meat.

Hip had grace. Comet had gravity.

Hip was shy about seeking intimacy. Comet bowled his way through.

Comet was a bull in a China shop. Hip was as tender as the China shop itself.

Hip and Comet lived in perfect synchronicity. They wrestled with regularity several times a day—usually after meals—then just co-existed around one another's orbit the remainder of the time, all cool and dreamy.

That's the way the gods drew it up. We're supposed to be buds.

"Like it was God's plan," said Bear.

"It is, in a way," said Linda, the Swedish dog trainer. "Dogs regulate themselves when they come into the pack. They check out what energy already exists in the family, then fill in the gap and supply the type of energy necessary to re-balance the new pack."

Hip came first ... shy, sensitive, graceful panther who holds back and relies more on feeling.

Comet followed ... smelled the need for the polar opposite, a bullish, less-sensitive, steadfast tank who bowls his way ahead. Begin regulation.

"You think God plans it that way before or after the dogs join the pack?" asked Bear.

"Don't know that it matters," laughed Linda, the Swedish dog trainer.

"If Hip and Comet were like that before they met, maybe they were genetically engineered to be the great buds they are," said Bear.

"Before or after, they're that way now," said Linda, the Swedish dog trainer. "Plus, they get to do all that wrestling to figure it out."

"So *that's* where they came up with the phrase: lucky dog!"

WHILE LINDA, THE SWEDISH DOG TRAINER, played with the dogs at the beach, Bear journeyed to a nearby junior high, where Bearcat Studios was filming a scene for *Bridge Across the Ocean*.

Bear opened the creaky gym door and stepped into his very own movie set. There were six basketball games going on at the six goals of the gym, taking Bear back to a gym in his own youth. He saw the hazy thickness of the sweat-drenched air filling the gym. He heard the chaotic rumblings of 80 ninth-grade boys, all dressed in the same blue gym shorts and blue and white reversible tank tops. They were all running around the place with boundless energy, the noise level almost deafening: the shouting at the top of their lungs, the constant streaking of Converse sneakers, the cacophonous beat of several basketballs pounding against the creaky gym floor.

"Hey," said Bear upon seeing his director on the sidelines of the court. "Aren't you that hotshot Asian filmmaker?"

"Making pretty picture so far," said Lisa Wu or Wendy Jiu.

"She said we're making a good flick so far," said Wendy Jiu or Lisa Wu.

"I must be picking up the language," said Bear.

"Can I sign you up to tutor some of the cast and crew?" laughed Wendy Jiu or Lisa Wu.

Lisa Wu or Wendy Jiu, who had been directing Japanese films for years, was making her English language directorial debut. Because she spoke so little English—and spoke so little at all—her soul mate, Wendy Jiu or Lisa Wu, translated all her direction to the rest of the cast and crew.

"They're doing fine," said Bear, watching the lighting men adjust the lights over the 80 ninth-grade boys. Lisa Wu or Wendy Jiu then said something in Japanese.

"She said thanks to you and Walter for the chance," said Wendy Jiu or Lisa Wu.

"When she understood what I meant by pretty pictures, I knew she was the right man for the job," said Bear. "What scene is this again? Is that author Randy Boyd here? I've never met him. Handsome fellow."

"Not here today, and this is a heartbreaking scene, so brace yourself," said Wendy Jiu or Lisa Wu. "Action!"

... Derek Mayfield, cool confident black cat in his late 20s, is having a fuzzy flashback. He's a ninth-grade geek infatuated with the golden QB, who's about to sever his junior high heart.

Mayfield dribbles the basketball. Mayfield dribbles the basketball off his foot. Mayfield loses the basketball. The golden junior high quarterback says it:

"Jesus, another Bubba!"

Bubba Brown was black and the joke of the school. Bubba had the prototype athlete body, but Bubba had some kind of physical defect. No one at school knew the exact nature of his defect, but everyone understood he was partially deaf and didn't speak right. His speech was almost indecipherable, his words slurred and thick with saliva. The ninth-grade class assumed Bubba was retarded. Everyone made fun of him.

"Jesus, another Bubba!" said the golden QB actor in San Diego.

"Perfect! Awesome! Cut!" yelled Lisa Wu or Wendy Jiu.

"She said: Perfect! Awesome! Cut!" yelled Wendy Jiu or Lisa Wu.

The golden QB didn't say it to anyone in particular, really just to himself, his voice a mix of shock and disgust, as if he really couldn't believe that in his world of perfectly graceful athletes, that, of all things, another clumsy dope like Bubba existed.

"Now let's cut to the scene of Young Derek dying inside while riding the school bus home ... after lunch ... it's Italian today!" said Wendy Jiu or Lisa Wu.

To everyone else, the "Bubba" comment most likely blew carelessly through the stale gym air, becoming lost in the clamor of excitement. To Young Derek, a shrill siren had sounded. The end of the world had come. Young Derek died, but couldn't let the rest of the gym class know it. He went through the motions, played out the rest of the game, trying his best to remain as invisible as possible, clinging tightly to the emotions inside lest they come bursting out uncontrollably. Gym class was the last class of the day. He rode home on the school bus feeling apart from the others. They were laughing and making jokes with each other. They didn't have to dream about having friends.

The golden buddy of their dreams hadn't called them Bubba.

"Bear," said Wendy Jiu or Lisa Wu. "The author dropped me an email saying this scene came out of a short story called, 'The Original Quarterback Who Broke My Heart.'"

Young Derek collapsed on the bed and cried for the next two hours.

Life was over. The golden QB at his junior high was never going to be his best friend. Young Derek hated the world. He hated Bubba for coming to their school. He hated himself. He was never going to be anything special, never going to be liked by anybody, never going to have a best buddy. The golden QB had made it official: Young Derek was just another Bubba. Retarded.

"Is that gonna be a problem?" asked Wendy Jiu or Lisa Wu.

"Not as big as the one in my head," said Bear, spinning out of the orbit of the hazy, fuzzy, smelly, swirling junior high space.

THE LIGHTS CAME UP IN THE SMALL SCREENING ROOM IN Los Angeles, revealing four very stunned pairs of eyeballs that had just "experienced" *Road of Life*.

"Has anyone else seen this yet?" asked Hail Larry's Wife.

"And I thought Secret Bearcat Project #1 was gonna rock the world," said Hail Larry.

"Bearcat #1 rocks the world," said Walter. "*Road of Life* detonates it."

"What's left to be done?" asked Hail Larry's Wife. "Besides getting ready for the controversy."

"About a gillion Camille re-cuts," said Walter. "Bear, any comment?"

"Do you guys think I'm a retard?" asked Bear.

"*What? Of course not. Don't be silly. You're super intelligent,*" said the three, more or less.

"You love me too much to say otherwise." Bear bolted from the small theater, running toward the Pacific a few blocks away, ignoring the pleas of his friends in pursuit. When he finally stopped, he was near an empty boardwalk, holding back tears in the moonlight.

"What happened today in San Diego?" asked Walter, catching up.

"How long have I been retarded like this, since before or after Pittsburgh?" asked Bear.

"You are not retarded," laughed Hail Larry, catching up.

"Where is this coming from?" asked Hail Larry's Wife, catching up.

"Look at the way I'm always bumping into things, losing things, messing things up," said Bear, pacing circles in the sand, too ashamed to look at his friends. "I don't even remember half the things any of you guys remember."

"So what if you don't sweat the details," said Walter.

"Like a good retarded boy," said Bear.

"Bumbles, would you ease up on your ass?" said Hail Larry.

"Don't call me Bumbles," said Bear.

"Bear, you have the most amazing mind of anyone I know," said Walter.

"STORY MEETING," said Bear. "Black boy feels like shit his whole life, so he makes up a dream world where people like and accept him. But he's still not convinced they like him for him, so he imagines living his whole life in somebody else's headspace. All anyone really sees of the poor bastard is the manufactured mascot head he wears at all times, cool Bear/Joe Bruin, the black boy nobody could hate too much, especially with that goofy grin plastered on his face. I mean, what white man would ever hang a nigger with a smile like Joe Bruin?"

Walter and the Hail Larrys stood stunned and silent.

"How do you people put up with me?" asked Bear.

Drums started drumming—two big drums nearby. A short distance away, a youngish soulful black woman lit fire to both ends of a baton.

"You've been under a lot of pressure lately," said Walter to Bear.

"You're not going to suggest I go back on those coma pills," said Bear. "I don't need to be doped up again. I need to know if you all see me as different!"

"In the best of ways," said Hail Larry's Wife.

Bear eyed his friends, wanting to believe, but the drums were getting louder in his ears, in all their ears, as was the pleading, frustrated voice of the youngish soulful black woman, who twirled the fiery baton and began speaking to the heavens.

"Soul Sista was trying to work my way back to you!" yelled Soul Sista, commandeering their attention as she went on: "Work my way back to my man, the one Mama promised me would come and raise his dear sweet baby with me. He romanced me. He took my heart which I willingly gave. He planted his love deep inside me—so deep, my soul would never be the same. My soul would forever be bonded with his soul, incomplete without his spirit, forever in a state of sadness without the presence of the father of the seed deep within."

The fiery baton soared into the night sky over the beach, then descended back into Soul Sista's waiting hand.

"The seed grew and grew," said Soul Sista. "Our love grew and grew. I gave birth to a whole new world full of whole new dreams. But Mama lied. He done gone. My man done up and left. Planted his seed, showed me his love, swept my soul away with dreams and left me high and dry to water my world and our love all by my lonesome."

The fiery baton rolled around the spinning head of Soul Sista, then through her legs, around her back and once again, up to the night sky.

"That's right, I'm lonesome," said Soul Sista. "Without my man, no matter how much I fill my world, there's an emptiness that can never be replaced. So I turned to God. I need so much God inside me to fill up the hole my man left. God is the only one I know who can truly ease the pain. And the only God I know for sure is the one I feel when I feel my man inside me and me inside my man, so I went looking for that God again."

The fiery baton bounced on the ground and into the waiting hand of Soul Sista, who tossed her fire high, did a series of African-like dances, then caught her fire descending from the night sky.

"Sometimes I found that God. In a man's dick. In a man's ass. In his musty, hairy balls. In his nasty hot breath. In his warm embrace. In his cold touch. In his sweet nothings that meant absolutely nothing because he never cared one single thing about me, not like *my* man. And I never cared for any of them, not like *my* man. But I needed to feel, so I could remember what it was like in my dreams, holding my man, what it felt like in my dreams taking everything my man could give me, for I would gladly take anything from my man, if it meant never having to take anything else from another man again in my life."

The fiery baton orbited around the blurry motion that was Soul Sista.

"I'm gone keep looking for the man who planted the seed deep inside my soul, and if he wants to know why I have lived as I have lived, and done as much as I've done in this world, I will get down on my knees in front of him, and explain to my man why I was taking so much God in this life. Because I was trying to work my way back to him. And I figured, if nothing else, if I went around the world and took in every man I could, I'd eventually get back to *my* man, and find my way home again. My name is Soul Sista. Is my man out there tonight?"

The fiery baton rocketed toward the night sky, higher than ever.

"Keep dreaming, soul sister," said Bear, more focused on the baton's fiery ends spiraling toward the stars above the Pacific, circa this very moment of your life.

30

Armageddon, God's Promise

"I still believe. At least I think I do," said Marcus Coleman, sitting in the bleachers of the football stadium in the hills above Malibu. "Dreaming of *Walt Loves the Bearcat* made me realize that a man I saw in a photograph 21 years ago is my soul mate, that it took me most of those years to get up the courage to share my truth with anyone, let alone the man in whom I saw God like never before. And no matter what was in the note that blew away, Walt's gonna come back and wanna get to know me better. We'll handle all the questions and the so-called obstacles and challenges together. His and mine. Together. Naturally. Because that's the way the gods drew it up. We're supposed to be buds. Right? True?"

"Keep dreaming," said Bear Coleman, sitting in the bleachers of the football stadium in the hills above Malibu, more focused on a baton descending from the sky, its fiery ends spiraling into the waiting hands of a beautiful young black girl, standing at the 50-yard line, circa this very moment of your life.

"So overwhelming at times," said Marcus. "I know, try whelming. This whole day has been whelming and incredible."

"Try making it credible," said Bear.

"A pretty whelming and *in*credible day," said Marcus, "that started with me waking up in Chicago at a writer's conference, then calling a stranger named Walt Yeager to tell him about my pissant little ditty, inspired by his beauty in a photograph. Oh, yeah, and we're soul mates! What was I thinking?"

"I guess I'm not the only one who's capable of some seriously retarded moments," said Bear.

"I think we both know the reason for that now, don't we, little Bearcat?" said Marcus, more focused on playing the game, Mattel Electronics Football. "First down, yes!"

"Don't call me little Bearcat," said Bear.

"Why not?" laughed Marcus. "I boomed the whole Bearcat deal."

"Like hell you did," said Bear.

"Don't you mean, like heaven?" asked Marcus. "Besides, you got the good life, the one with the Walt. I've just got 21 years' worth of warm fuzzy dreams to remember while I wait here for the man of my dreams to come back, if he doesn't think I've lost it. You, on the other hand, are living my dreams come true, oh, holograph of my twisted mind ... ah, your ball, threw an interception."

"Typical," said Bear, taking control of the game. "If that were even remotely the case. If you are somehow my dreamer and dreamed me up—fuck, now who's sounding the most retarded? Anyway, if I haven't gone insane and this conversation is really happening, tell me something, oh great one, Mr. All Mighty Marcus Coleman: *why does my life currently suuuuuuck?" yelled Bear Coleman at the top of his lungs!*

After the echo simmered down in the canyons of Malibu—and Los Angeles and the Grand Canyon and the craters on Mars—Marcus let out a mild laugh.

"I promise you won't regret this," said Marcus. "I only dream of happy endings now, at least in my dreams. I just hope you do the same."

"How could I be here on such a big night without my buddy?" asked Bear.

"Big night?" asked Marcus.

"This is supposed to be our night," said Bear. "My gift to him, always and forever. Now QB's nowhere near."

"Welcome to my world," said Marcus. "Only in my dreams."

"Listen, smart-ass, I'm the one who's real ... your ball, missed a field goal," said Bear, handing over the game. "I may be insane talking to you, but I know I'm real. I dreamed you up. I created a *whole other me* in my script called *My Whole Other Life*. Get it now? Don't be crazy like me. Just be grateful. Listen to me, talking to myself. Help me, Walter. Where's my Big Norse?"

"Where he's always been," said Marcus, more focused on the game and a big gainer. "In a world without you ... touchdown, Bearcats!"

"Gimme my game," said Bear, swiping back the little green box and kicking off to himself. "Am I supposed to do something with that song in *My Whole Other Life*? 'World Without You' by Belinda Carlisle? I don't have you guys hooking up like that. In the script, Walt is a typical ex-football jock—marriages, divorces, kids, the usual."

"Oh, so he's a label now," said Marcus. "Even a sexual one."

"That's not what I meant," said Bear. "In *My Whole Other Life*, Walt and I took different paths on the road of life. He didn't find me, so he lived a different dream of his. You didn't find a buddy in college, so you fell into gay life, which is why you're single, gay and, unfortunately, HIV-positive."

"So I'm a bunch of labels, too," said Marcus. "Great! And each one of them makes me nowhere near good enough for a man like Big Norse. True?"

"Not true," said Bear. "Partially true, no wait. It's hard enough for me. Wait ... I could say the same to you!"

"Meaning?" asked Marcus.

"Look at the labels you've dreamed up for me! House nigga, faggy dancer ... now retard!" said Bear.

"Dream the better dream," said Marcus.

"*Rightbackatcha,*" said Bear.

"I'm getting the fuck outta here and going to look for my buddy," said both Marcus and Bear Coleman, vanishing from the bleachers.

"What were those two arguing about, father?" asked a handsome Brazilian landscaper, standing near the bleachers. Some called him Julio. He worked for some famous and controversial couple at an expensive beach home in Malibu. He was often mistaken for a fighter of bulls, though he considered himself a fighter of bullshit.

"Tell me about it, son," answered an older Latino man, also standing near the bleachers. Some called him Sanchez and he was often mistaken for a gardener, delivery man or coach. Earlier today, he had been mistaken for all three.

"You always taught me: we humans love playing games," said the son. "Things never change. Sometimes I guess people find life overwhelming."

"Try welding," said the father, noticing his son was having trouble with his work on the ground-level bleacher. "Welding is the only thing that's gonna get those two pieces to fit together properly."

"Think they're on the right path?" asked the son.

"If only they believe," said the father, adjusting his red baseball cap.

ALL WE NEED IS A MIRACLE, read the scoreboard at the famous boys' new football home. In case the gods didn't hear their plea loud and clear enough, Mike and the Mechanics serenaded the crowd with their cool and dreamy song.

ALL WE NEED IS A MIRACLE, BEARCAT PEOPLE!

The Chicago Zephyrs played their home games at Soldier Field, a war memorial *slash* gridiron gashouse wedged between Lake Michigan and Chicagoland. Adjusting to the enigmatic stadium took time. The stone edifice was both a magnet *and* an oval ... a trippy trip indeed. Bear had a hard time feeling balanced within the colossal stadium, but then again, maybe he was just plain retarded ...

The sellout crowd inside Colossus cheered with approval at the completed pass, bringing Bear back to the game, mind, body and soul. He took another sip of his Bud and savored the buzz of watching his very own Zephyr jogging back to the huddle after a very impressive scramble and throw for a first down. Yeager had a brief but intense discussion with the black ref about the failure to call roughing the passer, after which the black ref slapped Yeager's ass away, as if to say, *Keep dreaming.*

Chicago was hosting the Atlanta Falcons, NFC Western Division leaders. Suddenly Georgia loved its Cinderella dirty birds. Meanwhile, the Zephyrs hadn't made the playoffs in the three years prior to Walter and Bear's arrival.

Yeager hit Curtis Conway on a flare-out to the right, nine yards on the play. Second down, Zephyrs.

Walter focused on football from day one in training camp. His mind was at its football peak, his body that of a warrior *juuuuuust* past the physical summit. And now, a million more of his family and friends from nearby Winnetka attended the games.

Bear glanced inside the game program at the photo of Walter Yeager. In *My Whole Other Life*, Marcus would have no idea what Adult Walt looks like for 21 years, just Yellow Polo Shirt Walter and Spring Ball Walter—the two photos from ages ago—beautiful versions of Bear's husband, but would Marcus be smart enough to look deeper? Or would Marcus be too caught up in looks, like so many of the gay men Hail Larry's Wife knew? If only Marcus knew what Walt Yeager really looked like. If only he looked inside and saw the answer. *If only Eugene Robinson would stop chasing my husband ... look out, buddy! Whew! ... God, my man is a great scrambler, maybe the most surprising factoid about him since day one: his swiftness. Who knew white boys had it in them? Thank God, at least one person in the Bearcat family isn't a retard ...*

Stop that, Bear.

Sorry, bud, a little difficult since San Diego.

Walter often stayed in a condo known as *(duh!)* Newport, Chicago. Having his own sanctuary allowed Yeager to focus on the task at hand: proving he wasn't a two-hit, washed-up, Super wonder with nothing left in his QB wizardry bag—exhibit A for why an openly "sexual" QB and his retarded black Bearcat of a boyfriend cannot function stably in the NFL, *and* be competitive, *or* win the big one. That would be a straight man's job. True?

Bear typed away in his luxury box at Colossus—otherwise known as Soldier Field—wishing he wasn't all alone. Hail Larry's Wife was wherever Hail Larry and the Patriots were playing, and Bear had given up on feeling safe enough to let Mama Rent back into a football stadium, not as long as some Christians still ate Lions, and by extension, Bearcats.

Perhaps the next dreamers of the openly "sexual" athlete dream can imagine a way to have their women and children watch them do battle on the field without having to worry about the fans doing battle with the women and children. Perhaps the Bearcats'll dream of having the guts to show you the way.

While Walter tried to rally the lovable-loser Zephyrs in the Black and Blue Division of the NFC, Bear worked on *Road of Life* and Secret Bearcat Project #1 in a secure location known as *(duh!)* Corona, Chicago.

Yeager ran to the weak side, then flipped the ball to Bam Morris, who took a shot to the chops as a reward for a three-yard loss. They were at Detroit now, the lifeless Silverdome.

The Creole Camille was almost finished with the 300th re-cut of *Road of Life*. The black groups had vowed to hold off further protests until after seeing the full eight-hour movie. The white groups had vowed to hold off all lawsuits until seeing the reaction of the black groups. The Bearcat Studios financial backers had vowed to hold off *their* lawsuits as well, until seeing the box office receipts. Meanwhile, the owners of every movie house in America waited breathlessly for the film, the exact contents of which no one knew for sure.

"White boys and niggers both need their poles."

One little line of dialogue gets aired on *Entertainment Tonight,* and the whole world wants to idolize or crucify your pretty picture. All hail to hell breaking loose, Larry, Curly and Moe-style.

Yeager rolled to his right. A stampede of St. Louis Rams chased after him. Number 13 lobbed the ball over their heads. Screen pass. Bam Morris caught it, scampered for 15 yards, then fumbled. Not getting outta St. Louie with a win after all today. Some guy named Kurt Warner came on the field to run out the clock for the Rams. Where do they get these dreamers these days, the checkout line? The Lioness must be crazy as ever, thinking she can turn this baseball burgh into a football-lovin' town ... what next, a Super dream? Ha! Now who's freakin' retarded?

Stop that, Bear, I love you no matter what.

Sorry, bud, a little difficult since San Diego.

Yeager and the 1998 Chicago Zephyrs went 4-12, just like the 1997 Chicago

Zephyrs without Yeager and his little Bearcat. The famous boys still restricted their exposure to the media's opinions, but even they knew Chicago was not happy about its prodigal son "returning home to hobble to the finish line of his career." Inadvertently, Walter and Bear caught wind of public opinion. Hard not to hear a thing or two on your way to and from dinner at MJ's—the fabled restaurant—even with Roberto the Celibate driving the new military-like SUV.

"We deserve a real life!" yelled Walter in the chaos of MJ's. They were at the bar, pressed against a gillion other celestial bodies.

"We also deserve to go out on top, not looking so retarded!" yelled Bear, trying to hang onto his man's big blond arm on the other side of their big bad bodyguards.

"Bear, don't do that to yourself, you are not retarded!" said Walter, signing a gillion autographs being thrust into their space.

"Then why did that scene from *Bridge* affect me so much?" asked Bear, spilling his beer. "And why do I always do retarded stuff, like spill beer on myself?"

"Because that rude woman behind you pushed you in the back," said Walter. "Tammy, watch yourself!"

Different team, same team, round and round.

"Whatever Walter wants," said Tammy, turning away.

"I figured out something," said Bear to Walter.

They were in the military transport now. Bear and QB were in the back, while Roberto the Celibate and the ER Wife rode up front (with Hip and Comet snoozing away in the very back).

"What'd my Bear figure out?" asked Walter. "Sorry, what'd you figure out, Bear?"

Bear had asked Walter to stop using the term: My Bear, "as if I'm your stuffed toy."

"I *am* kinda retarded," said a very downtrodden Bear. "No, hear me out. Retarded might not be the right word, but when do I serve you best? No really, listen ... I treat you pretty good, most of the time, right?"

"Always and forever, this much is true," said Walter, arm around his Bear.

Bear loved nothing more than being Walter's Bear.

"When I treat you right," said Bear, "it's because you've given me explicit instructions, which I can repeat and do, no problem. Like when you said never call you Wally. Have I ever? No. I'd never want to hurt you like that. You told me that a lifetime ago. I'm still following your instructions. Like with my cheerleading and dancing. I can do the repetitive stuff. It's when I have to create on the fly that I get a little loopy."

"I don't like where this is going and you know why," said Walter.

"Yeah, I do," said Bear. "Because you love me more than anything and you don't wanna see me deriding myself."

"Exactly," said Walter. "You know I've never, ever looked at you as anything negative."

"For which I'm eternally grateful," said Bear. "But obviously we can't say that about everyone in this backseat. A part of me hates myself for being this big, black, retarded, faggy fag—why else did I react so much to that 'Bubba Retard' thing in *Bridge Across the Ocean?*"

"Maybe you should meet this Randy Boyd, the author," said Walter. "He'd probably like to know why you canceled production of his first-ever movie, poor guy. Literally."

"I emailed him and told him to keep dreaming, what else am I supposed to do?" shrugged Bear. "I can't film that scene. I just can't. Let it go, buddy. Let's dream of cozying up to a warm fire now that the season is over, so we can figure out how to stir some shit up in Chicago next year."

"I'm not sure how much I have left to stir, Bear Coleman," said Walter, sounding like a tired gunslinger.

"I know how you feel," sighed Bear. "Then again, you already know that."

"Don't give up on us, baby," said Walter, nodding toward the radio and Tammy's oldies station. "Man, this was our song. Good ole David Soul."

"Whose song?" asked Bear.

"You and me in another life." Walter smiled, Bear followed, sinking deeper into his buddy in the backseat.

They didn't discuss their *Starsky and Hutch* dreams very often—didn't need to be spoken so much as felt. Hutch and Starsky were the polar opposite dream buddies of their golden youth, and a deep part of the boys' collective soul, always and forever, this much is true.

Roberto the Celibate put the transport in TURBO MODE and the famous boys took off, away from Chicago and their first season as Zephyrs.

"WASSUP, GIRLFRIEND, I MISS YOU, TOO!" said Bear into his cell. "*Huh?* Just chilling here at a backyard barbeque in Colemanland. Yep, Hayward ... *huh?* ... Walter thought a visit to the old homestead might un-retard me."

"*Bearrrrrr!*" growled Walter like an irritated panther. He sat adjacent to Bear on top of the picnic table. "That talk is bringing me down big time."

"Sorry, buddy, that was retarded of me," said Bear. "*Oops*, sorry, buddy ... what, girl? Hell, you guys made the playoffs at least ... nice season by Larry ... tough loss to JAX. Apparently, they *do* deserve a football team, excuse me ...

huh? Really? I can't imagine being happy in Boston either, all that racial history ... huh? Tell Larry to get his freakin' ass traded to the Zephyrs ... *little Stefan! ... don't put your hand in the dog's mouth!* ... huh? His hip is just fine ... Reggie White cannot keep my man down. Ever. God bless him for trying ... huh? ... So are we on for the Bearcat Secret Project #1 meeting at the Jaw in a few weeks? ... huh? ... Yes, they're perfect adult toys! No, I haven't figured out what the eggbeater's for. I just know it fits. It has to fit. Have you tried going near one yet? Oh, I see ... no, let's hold off on therapy ... maybe things will be revealed, upon further ... huh? People are gonna love our toys. Where would us adults be without our toys?"

"Bear, where's my football?" asked Walter, ready to play catch with some of the Coleman satellites.

"Exactly," said Bear in his cell. "*Huh?* Check the back of the transport, bud, last place I saw your football ... huh? No, we are not pretending we're married like Lucy and Ricky. If I ever tell *that* lie, just put my marker on the gameboard back to zero and call it a day! *No twin beds in Bearcat Secret Project #1, metaphorically or otherwise!* This is the real world, where real boys and girls have sexual impulses, and can't always stuff them into their book bags until they turn some magical age prescribed by someone who probably has no idea what it's like to taste a hot piece of ... *love my buns toasted, Evangeline ... just one hot dog though ... that's all I need to satisfy my appetite ...* huh? ... No, QB's not commanding the grill today, surprise of surprises! ... huh? Guess who! *Coach! Yes! Coach! Huh?* ... retired from the Niners, lives in the Bay Area! He's been great with my brothers at the kids' center. Plus ... I have to whisper this: *can you hear me? Can you hear me now? Is this man dating my mother? I know! Tell me about it!* Stop screaming! Wait until we can do it in person. *Details to follow, gotta go.*"

"Bear, come play catch!" yelled Walter from across the yard.

Maybe in a non-retard life.

"Larry wants out of New England," said Bear, staying put on the picnic table.

"Be a good fit for the Bears," said Black Coach, taking a break from the grill and sitting next to Bear on the picnic table.

"The who?" asked Bear.

"The Bears," said Black Coach.

"Oh, right," said Bear, understanding Coach meant: *the Zephyrs.* "What are the odds McPherson can play on our team again?"

"Dream of it," laughed Black Coach. "Didn't you teach me that one? Heard it somewhere ... here I'm going."

Black Coach started tapping his foot to "Here You Come Again" by Dolly Parton, playing on the boom box on the table.

"Heard so many things so many ways," said Black Coach. "Filling up all my soul and my senses."

"I guess you've heard about the racial upheaval over *Road of Life*," said Bear, "not even released yet. I hope you're not offended by what you hear."

"Nigga, you couldn't offend me if you tried ... looking better than a buddy has a right to," sang Black Coach. "Here I'm going ... you go, Dolly."

"I guess that's good to know," said Bear. "Are you dating my mom?"

Black Coach laughed. "Smile your smile, messing with my heart, filling up my soul," was apparently his only answer. For a while.

Walter threw passes to little Stefan, Jr., who wasn't a Bearcat. Maybe a Tiger. Maybe a Tigercat. Not Stefan. Not Bear. Not Walter.

"I think I'd cut off my arm or my balls before I intentionally hurt another black woman in my lifetime," said Black Coach. "Nothing dirty on and on."

"If there's one person who's had her heart severed more than Marcus of *My Whole Other Life*—just keep that in mind, sir," said Bear. "Dirty on and on."

"All these years and you still ain't figured out what to call me," laughed Black Coach.

"What would you like me to call you, sir?" asked Bear.

"Mr. Renteria will suffice for now," said Black Coach. "Shaking me all up, and all I know ... here I go ... here you come ... here I go!"

"Here we go ... gonna come up again ... another season in my hometown as a freakin' washed-up," said Walter.

"Now who's talking retarded?" asked Bear.

"Not funny," said Walter.

"Calm down, boys, dream the better dream," said Black Coach.

The three of them had migrated to the last gasp of open field near the old Coleman home. The rest of Bear's childhood landscape had been turned into somebody's corporate asset. The green from his youth was now confined to his dreams and a small strip of property owned by the electric company.

"Walter tells me you're having trouble with your coping skills," said Black Coach to Bear. The three of them leaned against a wooden fence, surveying the small strip of land.

Bear sighed, then said, "Every time I've ever spilled something, stumbled over something, bumped into something, didn't get an answer right, missed a turn, got the change wrong, forgot something ... there has always been a part of me that has felt retarded, a part of me that felt mentally out of touch with the rest of the entire universe, to the detriment of myself, and by extension, all those around me. This much has been true. At least, in my mind."

"Because some kid in school might have called him a name at one point," said Walter. "A kid amazingly similar to me, if you can believe that."

"*Or* a scene from a location shoot seemed so real to me, the author and director must be better than I imagined," said Bear.

"So what are you gonna do about it?" asked Black Coach.

Bear had no answer, Walter followed.

"Just gonna accept that you're retarded?" asked Black Coach.

"Frankly, I think I'm still adjusting to the reality shift of even considering it," said Bear.

"Do you think Walter or your family feels that way about you?" asked Black Coach.

"I think Walter loves me for me," said Bear, unable to look at his bud.

"Got that right," said Walter.

"Ditto for my family, especially now that we've all become so much closer," said Bear. "Thanks in large part to my loving the man I like to call PV, my personal MVP."

"So what's the problem?" asked Black Coach. "I thought you two stopped caring about what the rest of us thought about you."

"Not that simple," said Bear.

"So you wanna go back and worry about the past?" asked Black Coach.

"No. Yes. Stop asking so many questions," said Bear. "Walter, make him stop. Just kidding. Not that retarded."

"You realize it kills Walter every time he hears you talk like that," said Black Coach.

"Then I guess I'd better stop," said Bear, offering his bud a smile he hoped said: *Gonna do my best, Walter, just for us. This much is true.*

"The sooner you get your mind together, the sooner you can get on with your next great thing in life, whatever that is," said Black Coach.

"How about some Oscars and Super Bowls?" said Bear, switching gears.

"Making the playoffs, perhaps?" scoffed Walter.

"Don't sound like you believe," said Black Coach.

"In what?" asked Walter. "Did you follow the league at all this year?"

"Last you told me, you were still the Shit," said Black Coach. "As the kids say."

"Have you seen what the team has to work with?" asked Walter.

"Athletes," said Black Coach. "Dreamers. Warriors. Bearcats, whatever that is ... always something newfangled to replace the oldfangled newfangled ... *round and round the world, the world keeps going ... dirty on and on.*"

"No disrespect, Coach—" began Walter.

"If you gotta frame it that way, I'm not interested in looking at the picture," said Black Coach. "You know what would put some wind under Chicago's sails? Dennis Rodman."

"As a football player?" asked both Walter and Bear.

"You need a clown," said Black Coach. "A clown who acts like a fool and takes the pressure off everyone else. MJ knows what time it is. Jordan can go off, be his cool self, get into his own mind, focus ... while everyone is worried about: what Dennis gone do today? What color hair? Who he gone kick in the groin? What silly-ass thang he gone say today, so we can make fun of the crazy fool? It's grace, boys. Even the bulls in the rodeo know: you gotta have clowns."

"So what you're saying is, we need to get your nephew Reggie outta retirement," said Walter. *Mild laugh.*

"Like my boy Snow will ever give up that studio gig acting like a big ole boy. Now I know you got some big dreams," said Black Coach, laughing heartily.

"Who can we get like that?" asked Bear.

"A crazy but good player," said Walter.

"That's not all Chicago needs, but it'll help," said Black Coach. "Need a running back, too ... Marcus Allen-type ... slasher, guy who can envision holes and create 'em at the same time."

"He was my polar opposite at USC," said Bear, a yell leader for the Trojans when Allen won his Heisman. "Though people say we look exactly alike."

"Retired last year," said Walter of his favorite running back.

"People thought we were twins, but I weren't no slasher," said Bear.

"Allen was fading in Kansas City," said Black Coach. "Think he'd like to win another ring for somebody other than Al?"

"So then what?" asked Walter, the idea gelling in his mind. "We get a good back, a seasoned vet. We still need a Showman or Rodman-type. I'd love to have Larry McPherson on the team, too. What about the defense? Between just us, the defense *bites!*"

"And just in case you're both thinking something really crazy," said Bear. "Retarded or not, I ain't suiting up and being the crazy guy on the Zephyrs. I'll still be the adoring buddy in the lux box. I mean, luxury box."

When Walter and Black Coach kept conjuring without responding, Bear felt a little more retarded, as if they hadn't even conceived of the idea enough to joke about it.

"Nothing dirty on and on," said a somewhat disappointed Bear.

"I gotta get back home," said Black Coach. "Weekends is when I catch up on my soaps."

"My mom watches soaps," said Bear. "Got me hooked on 'em when I was a kid."

"God gives you all kinds of road maps in life," said Black Coach. "God is good that way, caters to *your* passions, not His."

"I don't follow," said Bear.

"Imagine everything that comes into your life every day as coming from God," said Black Coach. "As if God speaks in all ways. Not hard to believe, if you think we all come from God, eh?"

"Sometimes I've felt that way about music," said Bear.

"Me, too," said Walter.

"Try expanding your minds to the other things humanity creates to express the soul," said Black Coach. "Music, movies, books, soaps, nursery rhymes—all ways people and God are trying to talk to one another. Games are the same way. You think humans randomly invented football? God and humans are trying to communicate through all you see."

"About what?" asked Bear, typing on his laptop on the hood of the SUV:

Communicate how they feel and how to feel better. Or worse, if that's what you dream of. Look at the way football is dreamed up: polar opposite teams and players moving about the same space with the same exact rules, all trying to get to seven heaven as often as possible. The more seven heaven, the more ultimate glory. But if you can't get to seven heaven every time, there's options—field goal, punt, go for broke—all with potential rewards or consequences. Just like life.

"How in the world do you call yourself retarded with a mind like that?" asked Black Coach after reading Bear's instant input.

"Skillz with words I got," said Bear. "What if I call this great new computer my lappytop? Or not, maybe I should grow up a little, eh?"

"Not too much," said Walter.

"You two don't need me anymore tonight," said Black Coach before disappearing.

"Ready to head south to the Jaw?" asked Walter.

"One more hilltop," said Bear with a confident smile. "Then we can go home."

THE HILLTOP WAS IN SOME BLURRY SPACE on that starry night. For the final steps of the ascent, Bear held his man's hand, leading him toward his other man, who was standing at the top. Then Bear spoke:

"I thought it was TIME you met the other Man in my life, another human being who never questioned my mental capacity. In fact, he's always done the polar opposite. My memory is a little hazy at the moment, but if I had to identify any adjectives this man has used in describing my brain ... *brilliant* comes to mind. What I do remember without a doubt is this: This man instilled in me two things that are forever part of my core."

1) YOU CAN DO ANYTHING YOU SET YOUR MIND TO.

2) IT'S ALL IN THE MIND (LIFE, LOVE, GOD, HUNGER, HORNINESS, THIRST, LAUGHTER, DREAMS, HOPE, SEX—ANYTHING AND EVERYTHING A SOUL NEEDS ON THE ROAD OF LIFE).

"That's what my father taught me," said Bear. "From where I'm standing, at this very moment, the rest is details. Walter Yeager ... meet Daddy Coleman ... Daddy Coleman ... meet my True Gold buddy-for-life, always and forever."

Dreams do come true. This much is true.

ALL RIGHT, ZEPHYR PEOPLE ... WANNA FLY?

"What do you say, peeps in the Bearcat Studios Luxury Suite?" asked Bear. "Are we cool, dreamy and united as one? And ready for the season opener?"

The 58 people stuffed into the private suite atop Colossus peeked down at the scoreboard that read: ALL RIGHT, ZEPHYR PEOPLE ... WANNA FLY?

Everybody hollered from the bottom to the top of their lungs!

"Go Zephyrs go!" yelled Mama Rent. "Go, Walter!"

"Go Walter go!" yelled Mrs. Yeager. "Go Zephyrs!"

"Come on, son!" yelled everyone in the suite who looked at Walter as their boy.

"Yeager-meister time!" yelled everyone who was macho and clever.

"Less do *dis*," yelled everyone who had soul.

"I love you, my Belle of St. Mark," said one special boy's heart.

"Do us proud like you always do," said one man with a grunt. And a tear.

"Come on, Dad, you da man," said a beautiful and shiny Tank at 15.

"Our Super Daddy," said Grace's girls, bubbling right at the front of the glass (half glass, half *real* stadium-air).

"Love you forever, Walt," said Grace.

"Come on, Big Norse," said 20-30 of Walter's retired football buddies.

"Still looking good," said Evangeline, eyes glowing from all that blond aura storming onto the field at the announcement of his arrival to the 1999-2000 NFL Football Season.

"*Starting at quarterback for your Chicago Zephyrs, your hometown hero from West Winnetka High in Winnetka and the West Winnetka Warriors United Football Club (Boys 10-18) ... your Chicago Zephyrs quarterback ... two-time Super Bowl Champion, one-time Super Bowl MVP, four-time Pro Bowl Selection, two-time league MVP ... Number 13 ... Walter Yeager!"*

The Bearcat Studios Suite exploded, rock and roll'ed, but the ride was cool and dreamy, almost like—dare one say—a ship in outer space.

"How did you get the announcer to fit *all that* in my brother's intro?" asked Walter's Sister, standing on Bear's left.

"Bill opened the Gates!" said Bear, arms extended to his laptop, or as it was now known: THE CREATION STATION.

"So what all do you plan on doing during the games?" asked Evangeline, standing on Bear's right.

"Dream of it," said Bear, more focused on typing in preparation for the kickoff. "Then let's do it!"

"What does that mean?" asked Evangeline.

"Tell me about it," said Bear, looking down at the main scoreboard.

ON YOUR FEET, ZEPHS! WE NEED SOME WIND BENEATH THE WINGS!

"I love that!" said Walter's Sister, clapping after the 40-yard runback. "This year's slogans are better already. Somebody new must be in charge."

"This is my first game ever in person," said Evangeline.

"GUYS, KEEP IT DOWN," said and typed Bear. "YEAGER IN GEAR."

Walter took the snap and handed off to Marcus Allen, Chicago's newest running back, back in the game after a brief retirement. Allen went off tackle and ran for a 60-yard touchdown. Colossus took off, True Gold-style!

HOLD ON, ZEPHYR PEOPLE. WE DID MEAN ACTUAL FLYING!

FINAL SCORE: CHICAGO ZEPHYRS 31, TENNESSEE TITANS 3.

YEAGER AND MARCUS: PROMISE OF A NEW DAY IN ZEPHYRLAND!

"What do you say, peeps in the Bearcat Studios Luxury Suite—special armored edition?" asked Bear. "Are we ready for a cool and dreamy, non-confrontational, get-it-over-with rematch with PITT, here in the friendly confines of Colossus?"

The 60 people stuffed into the private suite atop Colossus peeked down at the scoreboard that read: PROMISE OF A NEW DAY IN ZEPHYRLAND!

Everybody hollered from the bottom to the top of their lungs!

"Fuck PITT!" yelled everyone in the suite who was macho.

"I'm not sure that's what I had in mind," said Bear, "but let's just take care of business and get outta here with a win!"

"Rootin' for ya, Big Norse," said 40 of Walter's retired football buddies, serving as Bear's personal security guards for the occasion.

"You know, guys," teased Bear. "I think those fans in Dallas have it in for me, too. Maybe a few dozen of you should hang out with us next week."

"Still looking good," said Evangeline, sizing up all that late 30s testosterone in the box.

Chicago was nothing, if not heart. The season-opening win over the Titans was all the lovable city needed to be there for their hometown hero and his buddy when the big bad Stealers of the Steel Comet slinked into town with their Pittsburgh Steelers. Colossus rolled like an oval and swallowed up the Steelers in the magnetized core of the city, that day at the heart of Soldier Field.

The game reminded Bear of a Monday night matchup years ago. Miami @ Houston, the late 70s. The Oilers had been on the brink for years, never breaking through in the NFL. Then they went on Monday night during a crucial point in their season. The fans in the Astrodome had more energy than any fans of professional sports had ever seen, their efforts rivaling that of a thousand Ohio State Michigan Alabama Auburn UCLA Florida Penn States. They had towels! They had lungs! Even the announcers were in shock. The game became about the crowd's energy as much as anything. Of course, the Oilers won, and probably broke through to as much glory as they were going to see in Houston.

"That Houston Oilers Monday night game changed the way America dreamed about the pro fan experience," said Bear to Walter's Bro as they watched the players stream off the field after the Zephyrs' 88-17 route of the Steelers. "Nothing was ever the same. After that game, everybody wanted to wave a towel and scream to the heavens, not to mention all the other bells and whistles. Thanks, Houston Oilers, with your cute li'l pissant fight song."

"You sure remember a lot of shit," said Walter's Bro.

"No fear, bro's bro. Your deepest Super dreams will come true someday, too. There's room for all our dreams in the universal space known as God's country. I wouldn't dream of it any other way."

Zephyrs Blast Outta Pitts: Now Riding High at 4-0

"What do you say, peeps in the Bearcat Box, New Orleans-style?" asked Bear. "Are we ready for more Sugar from this town that was so sweet to QB and me 15 years ago?"

The 30 people stuffed into the private suite in the golden mushroom peeked down at the scoreboard that read: Saints 24, Chicago 27. :15.

"Block that kick!" yelled everyone in the suite who wanted to avoid OT.

Some guy for New Orleans booted the ball through. Tied up. :09.

"Bear, where you going?" asked Walter's Sister, watching Bear leave the box.

"You can't stop my brother from anything, trust me," said Evangeline.

Bonzi Bode took the squib kick for Chicago and fell on the ball with :06 left. Yeager jogged lazily to the huddle, then strolled lazily to the line. He called a lazy-ass series of signals, then the center nonchalantly snapped a lazy-ass ball.

"Is that a yo-yo?" cried Walter's Sister.

Yeager appeared to down the ball by throwing it to the ground. Only at the last minute, he pulled some sort of Harlem Globetrotters trick, never fully releasing the football. This gave Marcus Allen just enough time to slip into the open down the middle and catch a 68-yard touchdown pass as time expired.

The box rock and rolled while the rest of the Superdome deflated.

"Bear, you missed it!" cried Walter's Sister upon his return.

"What?" asked a distracted Bear. "Oh, I saw. Brilliant! The best trick play since the '72 World Series, Oakland vs. the Reds, the intentional walk that wasn't. God, I used to love Johnny's Bench ... what were you saying, Sister of Walter?"

"Where were you just now?" asked Mrs. Yeager.

"Oh," said Bear, sitting down at the creation station. "These road boxes, sometimes the connections are all ... disconnected. Had to jiggle things to make them work right."

"Make *what* work right?" asked Evangeline.

"Whatever needs fixing," scoffed Bear, as if it should be obvious. "We were not about to leave another game in New Orleans in the hands of the kicker."

"Why ... what do you have against Del Kicko, Chicago's longtime—oh, my God," said Walter's Sister.

"Sis clues in," said Walter's Bro. "The Chicago kicker is the same dope who lost Walter and Bear's Sugar Bowl."

"Let's not damn the man, now," said Bear. "We might need that dope someday."

"You never know," said Mr. Yeager, his words hanging in the air.

AIR ATTACK GROUNDED BY INJURIES, ZEPHYRS FALL TO 5-3

"What do you say, peeps in the Bearcat Box, Indianapolis?" asked Bear. "Are we gonna win? Today?"

The 25 people in the private suite in the RCA Dome peeked down at the scoreboard that read: COLTS 17, CHICAGO 27. HALFTIME.

"Walter told me they're close to getting McPherson for the injured Shamrock," said Black Coach.

"Boston owes me," said Bear. "I'm not sure what that means, but they do."

"Team is too uptight," said Black Coach. "They feel like they gotta compete with the Bulls."

"Man, we gonna fuck the Bulls up this year!" said a voice on the radio.

"The Bulls are done. MJ's gone," shrugged Bear. "The great mystery in all of sports will forever be: how does an owner not give MJ whatever MJ wants for one more year of MJ?"

"MJ don't mean shit to me! I'll come in and tackle that skinny ass!"

A high school marching band made a formation on the field. An outline of the state. In the middle of Indiana, a krazy black man danced as if a cheerleader—a female cheerleader. The Colts crowd was loving it.

"Who is that fool on the field?" cried Mama Rent "Turn down the radio somebody."

"No, wait," said Bear. "Listen."

"These inflammatory comments on Greg the Gut's Sports Report *earlier today by Markus Kramer—the Indiana Pacer suspended by the NBA for the remainder of the year for 'the incident in Detroit'—but who is also, we're told, now on the RCA Dome field, dancing to 'Gimme Some Lovin'' with a high school band!"*

"Look at his body!" cried Bear. "Markus Kramer is huge! He's a bull!"

"He used to play for the Bulls," said Stefan.

"He ain't playing for nobody now," said Black Coach, "after Detroit."

"What a body!" said Bear. "It's so ... built ... perfect."

"Look who's talking," said Mama Rent. "Don't let the Yeagers hear you speak like that. Think about Walter's feelings."

"I am," said Bear. "And his need for ... pardon the phrase: a retarded muthafucka in the locker room, the Zephyr core."

"Kramer, a Zephyr," said Black Coach. "Why didn't I think of that?"

"Don't worry, Pops Renteria," said Bear, patting him on the shoulder. "I think I'm gonna be earning my Jedi wings here real soon."

"You ain't gone be able to convince the Chicago front office to sign that fool," said Stefan.

"We won't have to," said Bear.

Down below, *that fool* Markus Kramer took his final bows after electrifying the home crowd, who loved him despite his suspension over "the incident in Detroit." Shortly thereafter, the re-energized Colts came back onto the field for the second half, down by 10 points. Final Score: INDIANAPOLIS 57, CHICAGO 27.

SUPREME KOURT KLEARS KRAZY KRAMER FOR KOMBAT

"What do you say, peeps in the Bearcat Studios Luxury Suite back at Colossus?" asked Bear. "Are we ready for our new defensive specialist who prefers going by the name *Road Kill?*"

The 172 people stuffed into the private suite atop Colossus peeked down at the scoreboard that read: LET'S GET FREAKIN' KRAZY!

Everybody hollered from the bottom to the top of their lungs!

"Glad he's on our team," said Tank.

Markus Kramer put the hurt on the Green Bay Packers, each and every single one of them. Even some on the offense. It was a heavily penalized game.

FINAL SCORE: ZEPHYRS 3, GREEN BAY 0.

It was a heavily penalized game.

"Still a missing ingredient," said Bear, surveying the emptying field.

"McPherson," said Black Coach.

"New England's holding him captive," said Bear. "How do we free him up?"

"Dream of it," said Black Coach.

"What if you can't dream of it? What happens when you're outta ideas?" asked Bear.

"Pray," said Black Coach.

"To who?" asked Bear.

"Who do you believe in?" asked Black Coach.

"Got it," said Bear.

PATS SEND MCPHERSON TO CHICAGO FOR FUTURE CONSIDERATIONS

"What do you say, peeps in the Bearcat Box, Baltimore?" asked Bear. "Are we ready for the return of the reunited Tigercats and Bearcats?"

The two people in the private space eyed one another tenderly.

"Welcome home, partner," said Bear.

"Welcome home, partner," said Hail Larry's Wife.

They released their hands, dried their eyes and watched their men try to vault the Zephyrs into the playoffs.

Markus Kramer put the hurt on the Baltimore Ravens, each and every single one of them. Even some on the offense. It was a heavily penalized game.

FINAL SCORE: ZEPHYRS 13, BALTIMORE 0.

It was a heavily penalized game.

"I guess I can forgive Boston for all its past transgressions now," said Bear, looking up at a starry night over the Chesapeake Bay. "I might even stop hating all their sports teams and wishing them eternal hell in the loss column ... *Nah.* Fuck the Celtics. *Ha!* Kidding! I'm officially lifting the curse on Boston and granting the Red Sox permission to win a World Series."

"Still a missing ingredient for us," said Walter, leaning on a rail overlooking the moonlit bay.

"Gimme time to feel our freakin' rhythm again, for Christ's sake," said Hail Larry, skipping a rock in the water.

"I don't mean us," said Walter.

"Something wrong with my game management?" asked Bear.

"Not from what I saw today," said Hail Larry's Wife, dancing on the dock.

"What's freakin' game management?" asked Hail Larry.

"Managing the parts of the game Walter doesn't," said Bear.

"Spirit leading and everything that goes into it," said Hail Larry's Wife.

"So just like back in Seattle," said Hail Larry, statement of fact.

"Newfangled," said Bear.

"Like Bearcat Project Secret #1," said Walter. "Speaking of ... anybody get any inspiration for Bear's eggbeater yet?"

"Negative," said the other three.

"I promise it fits," said Bear.

"I'm thinking about something," said Hail Larry. "Are we sure we should use our real names on this secret project?"

"I've been wondering the same thing," said Walter.

"Really, QB, you too?" asked Bear.

"That makes all four of us," said Hail Larry's Wife.

"Not that we're throwing in the towel with the project," said Walter.

"No way," said the other three.

"But let's face reality," said Walter. "This is a whole new universe."

"It's pretty revolutionary, creating a new generation," said one.

"*This* celestial body would like *some* privacy," said one.

"I wanna rock the world, but I don't wanna be gawked at," said one. "All the time. Anymore."

"I just wanna protect my kids," said one.

"How is little Oscar and his baby sister Ariel?" asked Bear.

"Freakin' beautiful as ever," said Hail Larry. "Man, I love my kids."

"So we'll think about name changes for the Bearcat Project?" asked Walter, always checking and re-checking people when taking care of business.

"Unless I had a really cool nickname," said Hail Larry.

"Call me something twisted, like McPherson's Wife," said Hail Larry's Wife. "Maybe give people a clue—*one!*—to my real first name."

"Ah, fuck it," said Hail Larry. "Let's go get in these playoffs, Bearcat People. I'm getting too freakin' old for this."

"Right behind ya," said the other three.

ZEPHYR WIN TONIGHT GUARANTEES PLAYOFF SPOT

"What do you say, peeps in the Bearcat Box in the desert in Tempe?" asked Bear. "Are we ready to play in the sunshine and be free of all those mind-numbing playoff scenarios?"

The people stuffed into the private suite atop Sun Devil Stadium peeked down at the scoreboard that read: SOMEBODY PLEASE CHANGE OUR TEAM'S NICKNAME TO SOMETHING THAT REFLECTS THE STATE OF ARIZONA!

"Hook 'em up, Walter, hook my man up," said Hail Larry's Wife, encouraging the offense onward.

"Careful what you ask for," said Bear, not typing at the moment.

"Thank God none of that ever became an issue," said Hail Larry's Wife. "Esmeralda, would you take this to little Oscar? He loves Daddy's lucky balls."

"I've never seen you wear a charm bracelet," said Bear. "Motherhood really changed you ... especially your daughter."

"Still trying to figure out if she's more like me or Larry," said Hail Larry's Wife.

"Verdict so far?" asked Bear.

"Way different than any of us five," said Hail Larry's Wife.

"*Whoa*, interesting ... go, Walt! Go, Walt! Walt! From behind!" yelled Bear.

"That's the first time I've ever heard you call your man Walt," said Hail Larry's Wife.

"And? Come on, Walt, you can do it," yelled Bear.

"Bear, you sound like a different person," said Hail Larry's Wife.

"Walt, I love you, man. Let's do dis. All you!" yelled Bear.

"Bear, who are you?" laughed Hail Larry's Wife, not taking it very seriously.

"Same ole Bear," said Bear, "a bud who wants to help his man find his own special brand of his own special glory. Glory, glory to Walt *slash* Walter, all I ever wanted or needed ... except that freakin' penalty, what the fuck was that?"

FINAL SCORE: ARIZONA 33, CHICAGO 32.

FINAL SCORE ON MONDAY NIGHT: PITTSBURGH 32, ST. LOUIS 33.

"Yes or no, yes or no?" shouted Hail Larry's Wife, trying to be heard over Walter, Bear and Hail Larry, who were jumping up and down like little boys on the couch in Newport, Chicago. "Are we in the freakin' playoffs or not?"

"Yes, woman!" said Hail Larry. "The Rams' win knocks Minnesota out, which puts Philadelphia in after they tied with New England and beat Detroit by six in the regular season!"

"Thank you, PITT, for missing that chip shot of a field goal!" yelled Walter, laughing and dancing his ass off until his body remembered a hit @ Sun Devil Stadium the previous night. "Thanks, PITT, good boys."

Hail Larry sat on the couch and said, "Freakin' Yeager, we'd better do it now."

"I hear ya, pal," sighed Walter. "I'm ready to follow Johnny Boy into the sunset."

"Not without another ring," said Bear, knowing Walter meant John Elway.

"Not without a Super loop," said Hail Larry's Wife, waving her fingers.

"Well, Bumbles," said Hail Larry, "stock up on the Yeager-meister so you can kick ass with your game management. Sorry, didn't mean to call you Bumbles."

"It's okay, Larry Tie Dye."

It was the worst thing Bear or anyone could have called Larry McPherson. His wife froze. Walter froze. Bear felt retarded. Larry blew it off and took Ariel from Esmeralda, who emerged from the bedroom with his daughter.

"I'll get the kids' stuff," said Hail Larry, disappearing into the bedroom.

"Guys, guys, I'm so sorry," said Bear.

When Larry McPherson dropped that fateful pass at Auburn, the game ended in a tie. Thousands of neckties were sent to Larry's parents' home over the next weeks and months.

"This is me being retarded, see," said Bear.

"Stop using that as an excuse," said Walter.

"Walter, it's okay," said Hail Larry's Wife. "No, it isn't really, but ..."

She went to retrieve her husband in the bedroom. The Hail Larrys, Esmeralda and the kids left Newport, Chicago without smiling. Neither were Walter or Bear. It wasn't much of a fun night after all.

ALL RIGHT, ZEPHYR PEOPLE ... YOU ARE THE 12TH MAN ... LET'S HEAR IT FOR YOUR CHICAGO ZEPHYRS!

"Bring it on, peeps in the Bearcat Box!" yelled Bear, typing at the creation station.

The countless people stuffed into the private suite atop Colossus peeked down at the scoreboard that read: ALL RIGHT, ZEPHYR PEOPLE ... YOU ARE THE 12TH MAN ...

Everybody hollered from the bottom to the top of their lungs!

"Go Zephyrs go!" yelled half. "Go, Walter!"

"Go Walter go!" yelled the other half. "Go Zephyrs!"

"Come on, angel," said Walter's most angelic angel, private to Walter's soul.

"Come on, Dad, bust a move," said Tank, proud of his poppa.

"My rock star, in this life or any other!" said Bear, eyes glowing from all that blond aura taking his first snap in the 1999-2000 NFL Playoffs.

"Yeager hands off to Marcus Allen ... no, wait ... pass over the middle to Larry McPherson ... look at the Auburn Tiger go! First down, Zephyrs!"

The Bearcat Box exploded, especially Bear and Hail Larry's Wife, healed enough from "the other night" and united for the playoffs.

"Do I smell a miracle?" asked Hail Larry's Wife, reading the scoreboard.

"If you're smelling what I'm smelling!" said Bear, typing the next line after: Do I Smell a Miracle?

"Yeager back to pass, looking over the middle again. This time, he's got no one to throw it to ... wisely heaves it outta bounds ... almost toward the upper deck!"

"Incoming!" said Bear, more focused on typing:

On your feet! We need wings!

"Dad's pass is coming this way!" yelled Tank, grabbing the oldest of Grace's girls and ducking out of the way. The ball just missed landing in the suite. Meanwhile, the crowd rose to its feet for the crucial third down.

"More like it," said Bear, looking, typing, looking, typing. "Come on, buddy. Come on, Walt ... suddenly I'm in love with calling my man *Walt*. What is up with that, Bearcat People?"

"Run, Walt!" yelled Evangeline, watching QB scramble around in dizzy loops like a man named Fran. "He plays crazy sometimes."

"Tell me about it," said Bear, typing, looking. "The problem is when he doesn't! That's when we get into trouble."

Allen Marcus the Spot!

"I love that!" said Walter's Sister, clapping after a Marcus Allen run for a first down. "Who does those things on the scoreboard?"

"I love the music they play," said Evangeline, dancing around and snapping her fingers. "I feel good, like James Brown. Get down. That's the way I like it. Jam tonight. Sweet thang. Go, Walter! Go, Walter!"

"Guys, keep it down," said and typed Bear. "Yeager in gear."

"Yeager quiets the crowd—oh, how QB loves doing that—takes the snap, hangs it up in the air in the end zone ... McPherson lays out ... sells out his body and snags it ... hangs on ... waiting for a signal ... touchdown, Chicago! Somebody wants a ring before they die!"

"Check out the scoreboard now," said Tank.

Will you marry me boy? from Chris to Dan.

"Whoever *they* are," said Walter's Sister.

"Fans of the final outcome, no doubt!" said Bear, typing and glancing at the scoreboard.

CHICAGO ZEPHYRS 19, TAMPA BAY BUCS 9. FINAL.

ALL RIGHT, ZEPHYR PEOPLE ... REMEMBER A DREAM CALLED THE SUPER BOWL?

"Who wants another Super trip to Atlanta next week?" yelled Bear, typing at the creation station.

The countless people stuffed into the private suite at the Transworld Dome in St. Louis cheered nervously, peeking at the scoreboard that read: THE LIONESS AND HER ST. LOUIS RAMS, 23, YEAGER AND THE CHICAGO ZEPHYRS 0. HALF-TIME. NFC CHAMPIONSHIP.

"Go Zephyrs," mumbled someone over their nachos.

"Why is everyone so nervous, other than the obvious reasons?" asked Bear, staring at the field.

"I'm going to check on the kids," said Hail Larry's Wife, resigned to a hell-ish second half as she passed the radio:

"Yeager had what might be his worst playoff half in history. On top of that, Markus Kramer was injured on defense, and Marcus Allen on offense. Things are not looking good for the Zephs."

"Wait!" said Bear, grabbing his best friend's arm. "Still in a semi-media blackout here. What's Chicago been like since Markus Kramer landed in town with his next-generation Dennis Rodman Artistry?"

"You don't want to know," said Hail Larry's Wife, her weary face reminding Bear of a time when both her babies had chicken pox.

"What about the Zephyrs, beyond Walter, I mean?" asked Bear. "Have they been happy with Kramer? I know Walter loves him. The stories alone."

"The team is in heaven, or at least they were before MK pulled his hamstring," said Hail Larry's Wife, disappearing.

"Of course," said Bear, turning to the field below. "Hell. Hell, yes."

"What you talking about?" asked Evangeline.

"Hell-raising, back in a flash," said Bear.

Who cares who's watching you traversing the stadium underbelly when you have your buddy's NFC Championship game to save?

Who cares what's stopping you from slipping past security when you need to get into your buddy's locker room for the ultimate sacrifice?

Who cares whose dick is a millimeter longer than whose dick when your team is 30 minutes away from losing another chance to get to the Super Bowl?

Who cares what motivates krazy Markus Kramer, sitting in the whirlpool with his fine dark chocolate back to Bear Coleman?

"Hey, krazy nigga. This is a voice inside your krazy head talking. Don't look back, ya krazy nigga. Listen to your krazy head. I heard next week's AFC opponent, Tennessee or Pittsburgh—they both wanna kick yo' krazy nigga ass in the Super Bowl in Atlanta ... too bad your krazy nigga ass ain't gone get there, now that y'all about to lose, ya krazy nigga."

Who cares how many broken bones, bruises, scrapes and cuts you must endure, jetting yo' krazy nigga ass back to your luxury box, so as not to get caught, then beat up by an even krazier nigga?

"Back!" said Bear, plopping down at the creation station, immediately changing the music and updating the score. "What'd I miss?"

"The second half!" said Walter's Bro. "And the most amazing comeback in my brother's career! All helped by six turnovers caused by that krazy *nig*—dude—Markus Kramer!"

"Tell me about it," said Bear, typing, looking. "I hope this song isn't too presumptuous."

St. Louis 23, Chicago 26. final.

"We *are* the Champions!" said Walter's Sister, swaying to the music. "NFC for now."

"Keep dreaming," said Bear. "We're almost to the promised land."

All Right, Zephyr People ... One moment in Time ... True?

Two Super Bowls in Atlanta. Never in my wildest dreams, thought Bear.

And right at the beginning of the new millennium, thought Hail Larry's Wife. *We're connected to Atlanta.*

And Athens, thought Bear.

2000. Not always sure I'd make it this far, thought Walter.

Who did? Especially with all the Y2K talk? thought Hail Larry's Wife.

Gotta stay positive, thought Hail Larry.

We all do, thought Hail Larry's Wife.

Guys, you Super promise to all watch my back today, right? thought Bear.

You know it, thought the other three.

Who would have ever thought we'd be playing PITT in the freakin' Super Bowl? thought Hail Larry.

And Bear would have to choose whether or not to watch his man's possible last game in a box or the stands full of Steelers and Stealers, thought Hail Larry's Wife.

I'm glad you all understand that I could not *watch the Super Bowl in a box,* thought Bear.

Of course, big time, naturally, thought the other three.

Or behind glass, or in any way detached from my buddy, thought Bear.

Definitely, for sure, you know it, thought the other three.

I just hope this works, thought Walter.

We've pulled off way more than this, thought Bear. *Remember the Sugar Bowl?*

Bear, this is the Super Bowl, our last, thought Walter.

You know that, don't you? You're retiring, thought Bear.

Depends. Don't start crying, thought Walter.

I've never seen my man on the field so up-close like this with my own two eyes since I was a rugby boy with the Rams ... nice butt, Yeager, thought Bear.

If you don't stop crying, I'm going to call security, thought Walter.

Think rockets red glare, Bear. Oops, wrong image, thought Hail Larry's Wife.

Walter ... I've never smelled my bud while you're just standing on the sidelines. I'm getting very light-headed, thought Bear.

Freakin' Yeager, get a freakin' hold of your man, thought Hail Larry.

He's not my freakin' man right now. He's Markus Kramer of the Zephyrs, thought Walter.

Seriously, Coleman, you're a football player now, thought Hail Larry. *Save the crying for after the game. Stand up straight on the sidelines. Don't take your special goggles off. No one'll ever be the wiser that you're really our Bear.*

Amazing that Bear looks like both Markus Kramer and Marcus Allen. They're practically triplets! thought Hail Larry's Wife.

So much to remember, thought Bear. *Goggles ... where's my helmet?*

In your arms. Put it back on your head, soon as the song is over, thought Walter.

Got it, thought Bear. *Where's my goggles? Oh, never mind. Nervous here.*

Just remember to stand quietly and incognito on the sidelines for the next four hours. And don't talk to anyone, thought Walter. *Anyone.*

Don't worry, Walter, I won't let him, thought Hail Larry's Wife.

Hear that, Bear, you're in good hands, thought Walter.

Right, thought Bear. *Just gonna enjoy the show, watching my buddy win the Super Bowl from the sidelines, dressed in full pads as the injured and questionable Markus Kramer. How much easier could it be?*

As long as Kramer doesn't get out of that undisclosed location, we'll be fine, thought Walter.

Hey, thought Bear, *it worked great for the frozen tongue guy from Buffalo.*

Sweet, thought Walter. *Now I'm gonna go play some football.*

"... and the home ... of the ... brave," sang all in the Georgia Dome.

"Go Zephyrs go!" shouted the crew in the Bearcat Box, no doubt.

On the field, Yeager and McPherson threw some final warm-up passes to chase away the last of the pre-game jitters. Meanwhile, special team trainer McPherson's Wife stood guard over her only ward, the injured and questionable Markus Kramer.

"Who's helmet is this?" asked Bear the Zephyr, putting on his headgear. "*Whoa,* I think I know now and I don't know if this is such a good idea."

"It's one of Walter's old helmets," said Hail Larry's Wife.

"Exactly," said Bear the Zephyr, already heady. "You know what my buddy's scent does to me. My insides get all shook up. My gut starts thinking it belongs to a teenage girl meeting Paul McCartney in 1964 at the Ed Sullivan Theater."

"Who's helmet do you want?" asked Hail Larry's Wife. "You look like Markus Kramer enough, but we still need to cover your head up. I think Kramer's darker, too. Maybe it's just his demeanor."

"Don't get me wrong," said Bear the Zephyr.

"Oh, I know you can be a thug nigga when you want," said Hail Larry's Wife.

"'Don't Get Me Wrong' by the Pretenders," said Bear the Zephyr. "If for some reason I start acting all goofy out here today, tell the stadium guys to play that song. That should clue people into *what it feels like for a Bear.*"

"Hold my arm, sweetie, kickoff," said a suddenly serious Hail Larry's Wife.

Bear the Zephyr's eyes became as big as saucers. The deafening roar made him dizzy.

"*Whoa!*" said Bear the Zephyr. "This is nothing like creating @ the creation station."

"Try childbirth," said Hail Larry's Wife. "*Twice.* Come on, Larry! Be positive!"

"I've arrived, buddy!" Bear the Zephyr released his grip on his best pal and stood on his own, tall, cool and dreamy.

The last of the 200,000 musical acts cleared the floor of the peach dome. The Pittsburgh offense prepared to take the field first. They were led by a quarterback named Tomcat—a decent QB, but no Walter Yeager.

"Let's do dis, Big Norse," said Bear the Zephyr, more focused on his True

Gold buddy and his last true go-around on the football field. The buzz began building in Bear's helmet, as well on the radio in Hail Larry's Wife's hands:

"He's 37 years old, and has won more Super Bowls than anyone on the field today. But Walter Yeager—formerly of the Seahawks, Rams, Chargers, Roughriders, Bulldawgs, Illini, and the West Winnetka Warriors United Football Club (Boys 10-18)—will get another shot at another ring against the Cinderella Steelers."

"All you, Yeager, man!" said Bear the Zephyr, sounding more like his brothers Grayson and Stefan.

"Chicago is hampered today by key injuries to Yeager's Marcuses: his Markus on defense, as in Kramer, and his Marcus on offense, as in Allen. Both are suited up, but neither is expected to play much, if at all. Head and hamstring injuries, fuzzy eyes, stuff like that."

"You know where this is leading, don't you?" asked Hail Larry's Wife.

"Don't get me wrong," said Bear the Z, jumping up and down anxiously, as an eager player might. "I have no idea what you're talking about. And I'm not pretending. Hey, guys upstairs! Now would be a good time for 'Eye of the Tiger!'"

The peach dome swelled in its own headspace, vibrating frenetically. "Eye of the Tiger" by Survivor filled the air. The teams came out swinging in the form of the kickoff, then Tomcat took charge of the Pittsburgh offense.

"Your head's in the game. Cool," said Yeager, blurring by to speak to his teammate Kramer. A wave of Steelermania rocked the stadium, the fans responding to a touchdown. Just like that, the Steelers were up 7-0. "I go to work," said Yeager, blurring away.

"*Whoa,* talk about a swiftly moving dream!" said Bear the Z, staggering to the turf. "Forgive me if I seem kinda dazzled."

"Yeager takes the snap ... a play-action fake on first down ... guns it out to Curtis Conway ... who's all alone downfield! ... just like that, Walter says to Tomcat: rightbackatcha! Walt still loves the long ball, that's for sure!"

"Try whelming," said Hail Larry's Wife, helping Bear the Z off the ground as Del Kicko converted the extra point. "Downgrade to whelming."

"After the Pittsburgh punt, Chicago with the ball back, tied 7-7, threatening once again ... gonna try to run up the middle with—look who's in the game, Marcus Allen—gains three hard-fought yards but look at the way he's hurting after that run ... looks like it's just not Allen's day."

"Whelmed," said a sad Bear the Z. "Just whelmed now. And uptight."

"Fuck that, Bear, think positive!" said Hail Larry's Wife. "Dream the better freakin' dream. Come on, Larry!"

"Come on, Yeager, man!" yelled Bear the Z, sounding like a ruff-neck. "Thanks, girl."

Look at the meister on second down! Gets outta the collapsing pocket ... still looking for a man downfield ... gonna run instead ... down to the 30 ... the 20 ... slips by the last defender ... Walter Yeager scrambles on in for the touchdown! 14-7, Chicago over Tomcat and PITT!

"That's what I'm talking about," said Hail Larry's Wife, hi-fiving Bear.

In the second quarter, a long Steelers' drive stalled at the 10-yard line, but earned PITT a field goal, making the score at the half: Zephs 14, Steals 10.

"How's my Bear—sorry, my Markus Kramer?" asked Yeager in the under-belly of the peach dome. He was standing over Bear, who was sitting in a stair-well.

"Having the time of my life watching you so up close!" said Bear, in full uniform with no helmet ... *they had privacy.* "Except it goes by so much faster on the field! In uniform! I mean, is this what you go through every game? All these years? My God, Walter, you're more amazing than I ever knew! Why are you looking at me all funny like that? Is something wrong? Guess not. There's that *mild laugh*, Zephyr People. What's up, QB? Hey, who do I look more like, Markus Kramer or Marcus Allen, in all this football gear and war paint? Who do I look like, bud? Which black stud athlete? ... Wassup, Big Norse?"

Walter remained silent, more focused on regarding his Bear.

"Well? Who do I more like, QB?" asked Bear. "Kramer or Allen?"

"Like the buddy of my dreams," said Walter. "The kid—boy, man—who'd show up anywhere for me, anytime, anyplace. The buddy I'd do the same for, you know that."

"Take me away," said Bear.

"To the second half? I'll take you there," laughed Walter.

"No," said Bear. "That's what your eyes said when I first saw you for the very first time in your yellow polo shirt. I finally get it. You had this slightly strained look in your eyes. I never knew exactly what it meant. Now I do."

"Tell me about it," said Walter.

Take me away. Our powers are amazing. But the little boy inside me is shrink-ing. I gotta be a man now. Forever, maybe. Take me with you, reflection of mine. Keep me young, play our games, have our fun. Create our stories, our magic, our adventures. They will be ours for eternity. I wanna play whatever you wanna play. That's why I showed up.

"I'll take you there," the boys said together, rising for the second half.

IN THE THIRD QUARTER, THE OPENING DRIVE BY THE ZEPHYRS stalled deep in their own territory. The Steelers blocked the subsequent punt and made a chip shot of a field goal. At the start of the fourth quarter, Chicago's lead was only 14-13, and things were getting *uptight*.

PITT had the ball at midfield on third and short. Tomcat took the snap from the shotgun, scrambled a bunch of crazy loops in the backfield to avoid a blitz, then threw a wobbly pass 40 yards down the far sideline. The Steelers receiver caught the ball just before going out of bounds.

"Sack the faggot!" yelled a voice from nowhere.

"It doesn't help anybody, people," said Bear the Z from the sidelines.

"Bear, we need the real Markus Kramer, or at least his crazy, stir-shit-up energy," said Hail Larry's Wife, trying her best to look like a trainer, not a frantic player's spouse.

First down, Steelers. Tomcat hands off three times, setting up another chip shot of a field goal that makes the score 16-14, Pittsburgh. Circa 10 to play.

Yeager and the Chicago offense take to the field. The peach dome hurls through space at a zillion zephyrs an hour. No one hears a door being shot open by a rifle somewhere in the underbelly of the stadium.

Walter tries to go long but winds up throwing the ball away. On second down, Yeager threads a bullet of a pass to Milburn, who is streaking across the middle, and the drive is on.

"Trixie ... Trixie ... McPherson, are you there?" asked the voice of Tammy.

"Oh, right, forgot my codename for the day," said Hail Larry's Wife, speaking into the headset on her face. "Say what? Oh, shit! We're on it."

"What's wrong?" asked Bear the Z. "Come on, Big Norse!"

"Where's your creation station?" asked Hail Larry's Wife. "Go, Larry!"

"The hotel, why?" asked Bear the Z. "Let's do dis, Zephs!"

"Krazy Kramer's on the loose!" said Hail Larry's Wife. "He's on his way, insisting he's gonna play in this damned game, and he wants the damned ball!"

"Markus Kramer?" asked Bear the Z, glancing down at the #99 on his uniform, Kramer's uniform. "I'm not leaving my buddy now. Look!"

"There you see Del Kicko, the Chicago placekicker, warming up on the sidelines. Boy, does Yeager have a history there. Del was Yeager's teammate at Georgia and missed the potentially game-winning field goal at the Sugar Bowl. And his brother El was Yeager's teammate with the Rams and Seahawks, causing enough panic attacks there."

"Bear, that lunatic Kramer is on his way!" said Hail Larry's Wife. "You've got to be the other Marcus."

"Not leaving QB," said Bear the Z.

"Marcus Allen is heading for the locker room," said Hail Larry's Wife.

"I'm going to be myself," said Bear the Z, more focused on the game. "I'm Marcus 'Bear' Coleman, dressed as Markus Kramer, the krazy and suspended Indiana Pacer, now playing for the Chicago Zephyrs (the team formerly known as the Bears). Now *that's* twisted."

"So untwist it," said Hail Larry's Wife, suddenly with an idea. "And re-twist it with the other Marcus, so we can finish the game."

Farther down the sideline, the injured Marcus Allen disappeared into the tunnel leading to the locker room.

"You really are the best bitch a bearcat could have," said Bear the Z to Hail Larry's Wife ...

"Looks like Markus Kramer and his trainer are heading to the locker room like Marcus Allen moments earlier—tough injury situation for both. More on them later ... *whoa*, more now! They're both coming back to the sidelines together, Kramer and Allen, both with their protective goggles on. Is it my imagination, or do they look a little different? Like they're both ready to play!"

"If Chicago's lucky, they can both help out. Yeager has the Seahawks—excuse me—the Zephyrs out to the 35, less than eight to play. Drops back to pass, guns it into coverage, has a man, but oh, my ... Larry McPherson can't hang on."

"Don ... Yeager seems to be looking around for something, like he's lost one of his key players."

"Al, maybe it's Marcus Allen he's looking for, because the injured running back is coming back into the game! What do you know, miracles do happen, eh, Chicago? And it looks like he's gonna play fullback! What a move!"

... Don't get me wrong ...

"Here's Marcus taking the handoff on third down ... boy, I've never seen Allen run quite ... how would you say ... loopy? I think that head injury from the NFC Championship might not be completely healed."

... Looking kinda dazzled here ...

"Hey, it's the playoffs and Marcus wants to connect for one more shot at Super Glory. Who can blame him with a guy like Yeager leading the troops?"

... Seeing neon lights ... whenever you take the snap ...

"Walt loves being the leader, that's for sure ... Yeager hands off to Marcus, who stumbles, then pitches it back to Yeager ... who fires it down the field to Curtis Conway ... what a play!"

... Wandering across the moonlight, acting so distracted ...

"It's all coming back, Al ... penalty on Chicago."

"Apparently, Marcus moved before the snap, what a shame. Good thing Yeager is restraining Marcus from trying to take the backfield judge's head off."

... Thinking about the fireworks that go off when he smiles, ref! Look at those eyes! I can't even tell you the color and I don't care! I'm fucking crazy for my buddy, the top QB that ever lived!

"Chicago on defense now ... and look at Markus Kramer in the game for the first time all day, attacking Steelers' quarterback Tomcat like there's something personal going on!"

... Don't get me wrong ...

"Kramer put the hurt on! Tomcat sacked for a 16-yard loss!"

"That is one krazy Zephyr ... look at him jump all over Tomcat again on second down! Did somebody switch channels to pro wrestling?"

... We're gonna be fantastic!

"Third down ... Kramer blitzes again! He's chasing Tomcat all over the backfield like a madman. Grabs Tomcat ... fumble! ... hold on ... Chicago ball! Markus saves the day with a quarterback attack like I've never seen!"

"Doesn't Kramer look a little loopy, too, like Marcus Allen?"

... Get me wrong, don't get me wrong—just get me!

"Maybe it's the goggles or ventilation in both men's helmets, Al."

"Something is working. After this timeout, it's Chicago's ball, down 14-16 with less than four to play."

"*This is intense* ... I think that's just what Marcus Allen said after getting a whiff of his sweatband on the sideline. That brunette trainer has to hold him up. Allen is heady!"

... Dazzling ... taking a ride ... don't get me wrong ...

"Not Kramer, Al ... look at Markus doing a dance routine with the Chicago Zephyrettes! And he knows each and every move! And the fans are loving it!"

... Acting so distracting ... thinking about the fireworks in my heart ...

"Don, it's like Kramer choreographed it ... *oops,* guess not ... not much of a graceful dancer, eh, Markus?"

"Now he's got the whole Georgia Dome doing the wave!"

... Wandering across the moonlight ...

"Timeout is over, Chicago needs a score, not dancing."

"I think that's what Yeager is trying to convey by looking over to the sidelines and staring down krazy and hyped-up Kramer."

... Something in the air ...

"Yeager asks his fans near his end zone for quiet—they love doing that, those QBs—takes the snap from shotgun, *whoa!* ... bumps into Marcus Allen, manages to stay upright ... fires to McPherson! Oh ... if only! That could have made the difference."

"I'm not sure who's more upset, McPherson or the hot chick trainer—sorry, gotta be politically correct since we have a homo QB. *What'd I say?*"

... Suddenly thunder, showers here and there ...

"Yeager back again, finds Allen on a screen ... Marcus is running sideways, looking for a hole, backtracks a good fifteen yards, reverses directions ... got some space, Marcus Allen out to the 45 ... across midfield ... down to the 40 ... the 30 ... down to the 26 for the former USC Trojan!"

... Come and go like passion ...

"Ever notice how the former Heisman winner favors Walter Yeager's sexual partner, Marcus 'Bear' Coleman? *What'd I say?* Geez, the censors are on us!"

"*I* was going to say Coleman favored Markus Kramer, minus the queer partner reference to avoid a political correctness malfunction. *What'd I say?*"

"That was one of the craziest runs I've ever seen Marcus make."

... Who can explain ... something in my air ...

"Reminded me of Jerry Lewis trying to play football in *That's My Boy* with Dean Martin—if you ask me. *What'd I say?*"

... Across a moonlit night ...

"Yeager looking to take a shot in the end zone ... pump fakes ... here comes the rush ... spins outta it ... heads upfield, wisely getting outta bounds after a short gain."

"That last play by the QB gave me a déjà vu. Felt like I was at a college game at the Carrier Dome in Syracuse back in the 80s. Spooky. *What'd I say?*"

"I dunno, but Pittsburgh called its last timeout. Time to talk things over."

"Bear, are you okay? I'm worried about you."

"I'm fine, Yeager, man, don't worry about my ass, get the job done. All you, man! All you! All day! All Walt!"

"Cool, just take care of yourself, okay? I can't exactly keep an eye on you at the moment. Not that you need it, just the circumstances."

"Yeager, man, I'm fine. Get your ass in gear and wrap some shit up! Don't fret none about Prototype here. Wait ... gimme the other sweatband, too. Whoa ... thanks, bud. Let's go play some football!"

"Looks like Yeager was talking to Marcus Allen, making sure he was all right after that big gainer."

"They just exchanged sweatbands. Must be for good luck."

Who can explain ... something in my air ...

"Here's Yeager, downing the ball to set up Del Kicko. You know, there's a lot of speculation that Yeager might retire after this game. How fitting if Del Kicko kicks Walter Yeager into Super Bowl history, after missing what would have been the game-winning field goal at the Sugar Bowl 16 years ago."

"Yeager's put Del in a good spot, a 29-yarder is well within his reach."

"And Del is a veteran kicker now ... one of the league's greatest ... has scored over eight million points in his NFL career ... good enough for second all-time best ... the Georgia Dome is about to burst ... This is it, for all the marbles ... Here's the snap ... And the kick ... Looks like it has what it takes ..."

"*Wow ...*"

"*What ... can you say ...*"

"Maybe Del Kicko can do it for Walt next year."

"Looks like PITT is gonna get yet another Super Bowl title. Sure, they have to run the clock out, as you see here on first down, but what a position to be in, leading 16-14 with under a minute to go, ball at the—*oh my! How did Markus Kramer get in there and get that ball from Tomcat?*"

"There was the snap on second down. Tomcat went to down the ball, and somehow Markus Kramer got in there like a man possessed!"

"Al, this changes everything! Chicago ball! The Zephyrs have wind!"

Unbelievable or fantastic or fantastically unbelievable. With no dazzling tuba!

"Somebody better tell Markus Kramer to calm down and stop jumping all over his quarterback, so Yeager can get to the huddle! I guess Markus is used to that kind of buddy/buddy camaraderie in the NBA. Or somewhere. *What'd I say?*"

"The Chicago stands are jamming to 'Mony Mony' by Billy Idol. I think I wanna dance now. *What'd I say? Fuck, these censors. What'd I say? Oh.*"

... here she comes now, say, Walt is the man!

"Al, doesn't look like Marcus Allen is gonna be able to get his beaten body to the huddle."

... feel all right ... can't stop now ... yeah! Yeah! YEAH! YEAH!

"Is? Could it be? Yes, it could be! ... Markus Kramer is going to play in the backfield for Marcus Allen! ... truly amazing! ... what haven't we seen here today?"

"Markus Kramer catching a touchdown pass, for one."

COME ON! COME ON! COME ON, ZEPHYRS FANS, WANNA FLY? LET'S HEAR YOU! THE ZEPHYRS NEED WIND BENEATH THEIR WINGS!

"Looks like Marcus Allen is hysterical trying to rouse the fans on the sidelines ... is that a tranquilizer gun the brunette trainer is using on him?"

... hey, she gave him love and he's doing all right now ...

"Yeager takes the snap, looks for McPherson, who catches it and gets outta bounds quickly. Near midfield, time ticking on the Zephyrs' season."

... feel all right ... don't stop now ...

"Looks like Kramer's gonna be the lone guy in the backfield protecting Yeager. Everybody else is out wide, including Conway and McPherson."

"Here comes the blitz ... *whoa* ... Kramer takes on two guys twice his size and head butts them off their asses. *What'd I say?*"

"Yeager gets off the pass to Conway, but it's tipped and falls to the ground. Boy, Chicago can't afford many more of those."

... yeah! Yeah! YEAH! YEAH!

"Kramer's trying to get the huddle focused. He's a changed man!"

COME ON! COME ON! COME ON, MEN *SLASH* WARRIORS UNITED! WANNA FLY? LET'S DO DIS!

"Chicago needs at least 20 yards if they want to be in comfortable Del Kicko range. And that was before he screwed up moments ago. *What'd I say?*"

... yeah! Yeah! YEAH! YEAH! YEAH! YEAH! YEAH! YEAH! YEAH! YEAH! LET'S THROW THE ROCK!

"Final seconds of the game ... Yeager in the shotgun ... ball flies way over his head ... makes a mad dash for the live ball ... *Kramer put a serious body block on the linebacker!* Yeager gets the ball back, scrambles outta danger, scrambles outta danger again, sees Larry McPherson deep and alone, fires it ... his elbow was hit! Yeager's elbow was hit! Ball loose in the air ... Kramer has it! Markus Kramer has the loose ball in the backfield ... he's going the wrong way ... he's going the right way ... he's going all the way ... Markus Kramer is going all the way back to his quarterback to give him the ball ... Yeager waves him onward, then puts a block on two incoming Steelers ... Kramer finally heads toward the line of scrimmage, but now a ton of Steelers are about to attack ... Kramer gets out ... Kramer causes a pile-up and gets out ... Kramer needs to try to get outta bounds or run the ball ... or throw ... he can still throw ... he's never crossed the line of scrimmage ... Markus Kramer tosses the ball! *Back* to a shocked Yeager ... Yeager reaches for the ball, but he's about to get sacked! The meister instinctively bats it back to

Kramer, who has no choice but to heave it with all his loopy might toward the end zone for a Hail Mary ..."

Walt loves to follow his instincts and Bear loves to follow Walt, painting a pretty picture along the way, a pretty picture filled with music for the soul, especially when the soul is singing its loudest, and the music is the most glorious song known to any one heart ... whatever that song is, to that one imagination, that one moment in TIME ...

... *McPherson catches it! McPherson catches it! McPherson catches it! McPherson catches it! Teammates hug! Fans sob! Players thank their gods! Larry McPherson thanks his god! Larry McPherson's wife thanks every god she knows of, on her knees, sobbing uncontrollably on the sidelines! McPherson is mobbed by half the universe! McPherson catches it! McPherson catches it! McPherson catches it! Teammates hug! Fans sob! Players thank their gods! Yeager thanks his god! Marcus thanks his god! Yeager and Marcus thank each other! God thanks God's sons and all God's boys! God loved the show from God's luxury box! Even the fallible gods on the non-winning side are filled with awe, knowing deep down, to have borne witness is much more valuable than the outcome.*

... McPherson catches it! McPherson catches it! McPherson catches it! Every Marcus on the field cums in his pants! Literally! Every player on the Zephyrs cums in his pants! Literally! The brunette trainer is cumming in her pants! I'm the announcer and I'm cumming in my pants! And I'm not even wearing pants! McPherson catches it! McPherson catches it! Zephyrs win! Chicago flying sky higher! There is a God ... in some parts of the world! In other parts of the world and the peach dome, fallible gods are crying, cursing, wondering why their man fell down at the worst possible moment, letting McPherson—McFear's Son, of all people!—catch a pass ... Who was that damned millionaire who let McPherson into the end zone Scott-free? His name will go down!

Meanwhile, on the polar opposite side of God's mind ... McPherson catches it! McPherson catches it! McPherson catches it! Teammates hug! Fans sob! Players thank their gods! Players are even allowed to slap, touch, grab, kiss, hug and peck anything they want of their fellow warriors! Without even asking! So beautiful! Everyone is so beautiful! No one is caring about who's what shade of skin, who came from what school, who fucks who in the bedroom, who did what to get here, to be here ... it's about the joy ... the common joy ... McPherson catches it and our lives will never be the same, marked before, during and after!

I was there! I was on the field! I was in the stands! I was at home alone with my buddy family lover girl boy transgender other! I almost went to the game! I was in the bathroom and heard the whole neighborhood erupt in a single cheer! I was watching in a bar that went crazy! The pilot made the announcement! I was watching by satellite on my boat! I was in the stadium parking lot, trying to beat traffic! I woke up after a six-day coke binge in some stranger's house and saw McPherson and his wife on the Regis and Haley morning show!

McPherson catches it! McPherson catches it! McPherson catches it! Teammates hug! Fans sob! Players thank their gods! McPherson catches it! Zephyrs win! Chicago has hope for life after Air! The world has hope miracles can still happen in the new millennium! McPherson catches it! We can still party like it's 1999!

McPherson catches it! A Marcus throws it! A bearish black boy finally completes that long bomb a junior high coach once dreamed up to placate a bearish black boy who wanted to play quarterback! Perfect grace! Maybe Private Parks wasn't so bad after all! Did you win? Yes I won! I did win! I threw it! McPherson catches it! I believe in miracles! Privates Parks made sure. Pass by a huge red sign painted in the entry of the locker room every day for two years, and faith kinda stays with you the rest of your life, all big and red against a concrete backdrop.

BELIEVE

Didn't tell you what to believe in, just to believe in something. Big Ups, Private Parks, and all the warrior slash *dreamers of junior high! McPherson catches it! A Marcus throws it! Zephyrs win! Walt loves spreading the joy! Walt is joy! Walt is pure joy! Pure joy is Walt! This much is true for the man @ the creation station! We are beautiful in every single way! Chris promised!*

McPherson catches it! McPherson catches it! McPherson catches it! Markus Kramer retires from sports with a secret new job that may or may not be revealed over time or the endless sequels! Marcus Allen rides off into the golden sunset he so deserves! McPherson catches it! Celebrates with his wife! Walter and his Marcus are co-MVPs, Yeager's Super second! Who needs the Pro Bowl? McPherson catches it! McPherson catches it! McPherson catches it! Teammates hug! Fans sob! Players thank their Gods! McPherson catches it! McPherson catches it!

"Freakin' Hail Larry McPherson catches it!" said Hail Larry, diving into the pool after catching the football one last time ... for the afternoon anyway.

"I'm not throwing anymore Hail Larrys this hour, Hail Larry," giggled Bear, lying on his deck chair at the Jaw shortly after Super Bowl 3.

"Love what you wrote, as always, Bear Coleman," said Walter, having just read *McPherson Catches It!* QB was lying in the adjacent deck chair ... *facing the pool, all cool and dreamy. Beer, lemonade and stuff on tap. And nachos!*

"Hail Freakin' Larry," said Hail Larry. "Man, I love my new nickname."

"Does it make up for me calling you Larry Tie Dye that one time?" asked Bear.

"Who's that?" asked Hail Larry. "Forget it, Cole-man the Soul Man."

"Describe that play to us, co-MVP Walter Yeager, looking so sexy in the locker room, all drenched in Super bubbles for the third time in your glorious life."

"I figured heaven must owe McPherson one, so why not send him a Hail Larry, I mean, Mary, no ... I mean, Larry. Call it what you want ... where's my boy Marcus? Still getting oxygen? Sweet. Sugary. What? What do you mean: where are we going? We're already there, baby! We're already there!"

"I could kiss you, Hail Larry McPherson," said Bear, poolside at the Jaw. "If I didn't love your best friend so much, and you weren't married to mine."

"Remember when we were so immature about all that?" asked Hail Larry.

"Who can forget?" laughed Walter, more focused on the objects in his lap. "Anybody seen the eggbeater?"

"Hey, Bear," said Hail Larry.

"Yeah, Hail Larry?" asked Bear.

"Did you win?" asked Hail Larry.

"Every day, HL," said Bear, looking at McPherson's new initials on the action figure in Walter's lap (Secret Project Bearcat #1).

"Hey, Bear," said Hail Larry.

"Yeah, Hail Larry?" asked Bear, looking at the HLW female action figure in Walter's lap (Project Bearcat Secret #1).

"Got me a ring," said Hail Larry. "And a really cool nickname."

"Man, you are in the loop!" said Bear. The three men toasted their beers. Hip and Comet wrestled on the grass. The McPherson kids slept in the hammock under the shady part of the deck.

"We need to kick some serious ass on #1 Bearcat Secret Project," said Hail Larry, lazing on a raft in the pool.

"Working on it while you slouch, Hail," said Walter, fussing with some of the secret project toys. "Where's the damned eggbeater? *Blessed* eggbeater ... here it is. Damn, I'm amazing; *blessed* I'm amazing."

"So you're sure about using your new nickname?" Bear asked Hail Larry. "The animators need to know today before they start rendering their illustrations and test animation."

"Gotta have an HL on my doll," said Hail Larry. "I mean, action figure."

"Maybe the eggbeater goes on top of the bleachers," said Walter. "Or near."

"Dream of it," said Bear.

The wife emerged from the house and her run to the store, not looking too Super sunny.

"We're royally fucked," said Hail Larry's Wife, holding up a copy of her favorite newspaper, *USA Today*. "Sorry, Bearcats, can't censor this one. Larry, it's over. Our life as we know it is over. Everything is over."

Esmeralda Tells All: Hail Larry's Winning Den of Debauchery

"The seed finally came to light," said Hail Larry, eyeing the front page of *USA Today*, which was on the patio table on the deck at the Jaw.

"How could you bring that poison into our lives?" asked Bear.

"Which poison?" asked Hail Larry's Wife.

"Any and all," said Bear with a stern expression.

"*Are* you HIV-positive, Larry?" asked Walter.

"What does that mean?" asked Hail Larry.

"Did you know about this?" Bear asked Hail Larry's Wife.

"What's that supposed to mean?" asked Hail Larry's Wife.

"Tell me about it," said Bear.

"Stuff you've mumbled in your sleep, Larry," said Walter. "About being positive."

"About my game!" said Hail Larry. "Are *you* freakin' positive?"

"By *in his sleep*," said Bear to Walter, "you mean on ordinary road trips, right? Not as in ..."

"Honey," said Hail Larry to his wife, "you and Bear never ..."

"Walter and Bear, have you ever been tested?" asked Hail Larry's Wife.

"Is this what you wanted to reverse?" Walter asked Hail Larry.

"I've never been freakin' reversed!" said Hail Larry. "Never!"

"Can HIV be reversed?" Bear asked whomever.

"No offense, but this almost sounds like a Bizarre Bear Coleman Story," said Hail Larry's Wife, eyeing the newspaper.

Longtime infamous Auburn legend Larry McPherson, made famous by his Hail Mary catch during the recent Super Bowl, is reported to be the head of an HIV-positive, kinky-sex ring, involving his wife, as well as Walter Yeager and Bear Coleman, sexual partners and considered by many the Mr. and Mr. Jackie Robinson of gay and/or sexual sports history.

"I guess it's not as good as the last Bizarre Larry McPherson Story," said Bear, "the one to top *Where's My Pole?* by the kid in Western PA."

"*Larry* gave you the idea for *Road of Life?*" asked both Walter and Hail Larry's Wife.

"Bear's fucking crazy, I did not," said Hail Larry.

"That day," said Walter, coming to his own conclusion. "That day on the upper deck when I walked in on you two discussing business."

"How did HIV enter into it?" asked Hail Larry's Wife. "And why? For God's sake, if somebody has AIDS, just say it already!"

"I have no idea what he's talking about," said Hail Larry, indicating Bear.

"The day you planted the seed for me for *Road of Life*," said Bear. "Whatever you were talking about gave me the idea. Now who's retarded?"

"I was talking about planting a story in the media to help bring more attention to AIDS!" said Hail Larry. "Since Bear was so freakin' down about it."

"*With a sex ring?*" asked the other three.

"It was a freaky story, but not that freaky!" said Hail Larry. "And not involving us. Or the NFL. Somehow it got freakin' twisted, okay?"

"Exhibit A for how these media distractions can come back and bite you on the ass," said Bear. "This is beyond freakin' twisted."

"But is any of it true?" asked Walter. "Bear and I need to know."

"Maybe Esmeralda got hold of it and drew the wrong conclusions," said Hail Larry. "I was trying to help Bear, sorry, all right? Fuck! Never do it again!"

"Trying to help Bear do what?" asked Bear. "You didn't think ... me ... I myself ... am HIV-positive, did you?"

"What about all that talk about our reaction to a guy like you having an *AIDS aura?*" asked Hail Larry.

"For the freakin' movie, for Christ's sake!" said Bear.

"How was I supposed to freakin' know you weren't playing some kind of freakin' game?" asked Hail Larry.

"You mean, like a subtle confession," said Hail Larry's Wife. "Well, Bear?"

"This is ridiculous!" cried Bear. "Like I would tell you anything now! Not that I have anything to tell! Can—can you say the same?"

"Everybody freeze," said Walter. "Why don't we table this for now and deal with it in Seattle on Friday. Cool? We need space. Literally."

Walter and Bear were scheduled to be in the Pacific Northwest for the weekend, movie and "team" business.

"And by the way," said Hail Larry just before leaving. "Everybody's reaction to AIDS today: *fear* ... nice, real nice."

HOLD ON, BEARCAT PEOPLE ... TRUE GOLD NOW ORBITING MT. RAINER, MOVING IN FOR A HOOK LANDING WITH THE SPACE NEEDLE.

"Loving my new portable creation station, QB," said Bear from the copilot seat in the cockpit, punching up the upbeat Curtis Stigers tune that asks: *What's so freakin' funny about Peace, Love and Understanding?* (*Bodyguard* soundtrack). "One day, I hope to create an even smaller box to hold all the tools for my imagination, say, the size of Mattel Electronics Football," said Bear. "Wouldn't that be cool, Big Norse—if I could carry around a little green box that took us anywhere our dreams wanted to take us?"

"Dream of it, Soul Man," said Walter, cruising over Seattle's wharf and making a hook landing with the Space Needle. "*Whoa ... spiraling around the needle!*"

"Love me!" screamed Bear like a silly kid. "I mean, hold me."

"Open your eyes," laughed Walter.

"Some other time!" shouted Bear over the rumble of the vortex.

Bear could go anywhere with Walter without ever needing to see the way.

Walter was the way. This much is true.

SCENE: A LOS ANGELES PARK ... AS FILMED AT WOK-KNEE PARK IN SEATTLE.

"Hey, my fine Asian soul sistas," said Bear, sauntering up to the set, still jamming to the upbeat Curtis Stigers tune that asks: *Where is that sweet ole, sweet harmony?*

"The golden boys," said Wendy Jiu or Lisa Wu, offering hugs.

"Am I forgiven?" asked Bear, looking at Lisa Wu or Wendy Jiu.

"Making perfect pretty picture," said Lisa Wu or Wendy Jiu, director of *Bridge Across the Ocean*.

HOLLYWOOD REPORTER NOTE: *Production has resumed for the heartwarming, fuzzy, feel-good movie based on* Bridge Across the Ocean, *the popular novel by Randy Boyd. Apparently, Bearcat Studios' head creative honcho Bear Coleman had a nightmare where he was being strangled by a very handsome yet angry black author from another dimension, something about a voice saying, "You think you famous boys are in deep shit now ..."*

"Actually," said Wendy Jiu or Lisa Wu, "what my girl is saying is: she's glad to be making the picture as pretty as possible to the eyes of the soul."

"*Duh!* I thought we agreed I was no longer retarded," said Bear. "I get her. She's a bearcat, like me. Or a tigercat, whatever that is."

"A tigercat is a—" began Wendy Jiu or Lisa Wu.

"Oh, my God, so that's *him* up close!" said Bear, eyes focused on the golden actor throwing warm-up passes in the blurry distance. "*Whew ... in another life! Whew ...* He's got it!"

Matt Strickland ... golden blond quarterback turned actor. Bear remembered him from their CFL days ... Roughriders vs. Stampeders. Bear had imagined Marcus of *My Whole Other Life* being with such a stud, certainly a man in Walter's league.

Now, here was Matt Strickland ... golden blond quarterback turned actor, playing a small role in *Bridge Across the Ocean,* that of a golden blond quarterback turned actor who befriends the adult Derek Mayfield, the poor suffering bastard of the movie.

"My head's spinning still trying to figure this one out," said Walter, suddenly reappearing from the catering truck with food. "Want some?"

Walt loves to eat. This much is true.

"No thanks," said Bear.

"You sure?" asked Walter. "It's good stuff."

"Yes, I'm sure," said Bear.

"Just try some," said Walter.

Bear turned to Wendy Jiu and Lisa Wu and said, "Somewhere in outer space, there's a loop of that exact conversation going on 95% of the time Walter and I eat together."

Walt loves to share. This much is also true.

Wendy Jiu and Lisa Wu laughed, then went back to making their pretty picture called *Bridge Across the Ocean.*

DESCENDING ONTO THE INDUSTRIAL AREA NEAR THE NUCLEAR REACTOR KNOWN AS THE SEATTLE KINGDOME! AH, THE OLD STOMPING GROUNDS ... GLORY DAYS ...

"Miss any of this?" asked a sleepy Bear, waking up in the passenger seat of the ground transport, still humming the upbeat Curtis Stigers tune that asks: *Who are the strong? And where are the trusted?*

"Don't miss a thing," said Walter, swerving around a bunch of tight corners in a bunch of bright and sunny alleyways. "So there was a QB or two in your life before your buddy ... me."

"Three," said Bear. "Now that I'm putting it together. Helps on the creation station, true dat! Why do the streets always seem smaller when you return to some place in your past?"

"Doesn't help with all this chaos and traffic today," said Walter. "It's like they're having a big festival."

"Let's just talk to Tammy, see what's up with the whole hellish, Larry-positive thing and get the hell outta Seattle!" said Bear.

"Deal, cowboy," said Walter, steering into some dark tunnel, going from daylight to no light.

"So you knew how to get in and outta the team basement all this time?"

asked Bear. "I thought it was a secret passageway, only accessible by navigating all these industrial streets, then slipping into some vortex. But I guess I was wrong."

"I wouldn't dream of it," said Walter, steering them deeper in their transport toward the center of the Earth. The cabin pressure changed. Bear started to feel the opposite of light-headed.

"You, too?" asked Bear.

"Yep," said Walter. "So tell me about these other QBs before the real deal."

"This much is true dat!" laughed Bear, then read from his notes:

"Robbie Roberts ... the original quarterback—who broke my heart, severed that day in freshman gym class. The infatuation died, and so did a 14-year-old boy named Coleman. Still, the Boy Coleman never hated Robbie or his actions. The fallen boy was the one made of coal, not the sunshine that radiated in Robbie's honey brown hair. I can still remember the three times he came into my orbit in high school, his energy penetrating my soul, even when I didn't realize it. This much is true.

"Dean Durrett ... the high school QB, a year younger. From where I stood, the most beautiful boy at my school, always and forever. Prom king, or something like that. Bright sunny family of bright sunny kids, destined for the biggest and brightest dreams white blond Americans dream ... whatever those are. After Robbie severed my adolescent heart, no way was I going to talk to Dean, or look at him, or go near him. I kept Dean in a dome, safe, holy, pure, unspoiled, never damned, forever blessed. We made eye contact once in the hallway. It was electric. A moment I'll never forget. For one flickering instant, the windows to our souls were open. One of us shut the window first, the other followed. I can live to be a million and be a million times retarded, but I will never forget what it felt like, looking into Dean Durrett's eyes that one shining moment of my life.

"Matt Strickland ... a confusing trip to Canada with a man who seemed so much like Walter Yeager, yet not like Walter Yeager at all. The man I tried to give to Marcus of *My Whole Other Life,* but the gods didn't draw it up like they were supposed to. Still, Matt Stickland remains a piece of the puzzle, the equation, the four-part harmony that is the quarterback atom in my life."

And then there's Walt ...

"Yes, I belong to the quarterback," said and read Bear. "There's something divine to everything humanity creates. The cool and dreamy combo of the quarterback and the cheerleader means something. It's not just a dress-up fantasy."

"I need a spirit leader," said Walter. "I need somebody who takes care of me while I'm taking care of my world and my business. Somebody who gets me, lets me be when I wanna chill, lets me scream my lungs out when I wanna go crazy, doesn't question my gut instincts, lets me lead, trusts me, knows me, accepts me, gets me, freakin' worships me, then lets me chill. *And* can entertain me on a moment's notice. On demand!"

"One of the reasons athletes call timeout," said Bear. "Even if they aren't focused on the spirit-lifting going on in their name all around them, athletes can feel the crowd and the energy. Athletes are feelers, especially quarterbacks and point guards. You guys can feel us sending all that lovin' your way, looking or not. Your eyes aren't even what you go by. You're gut men."

"Man, I need you, Bear Coleman," said Walter, rubbing Bear's thigh.

"And I need to give, to lift, to help you feel good," said Bear. "That's where I get off, helping you feel good, whatever that means to you, not me. I'm here to serve. I find joy in worshiping you, in you *allowing me* to worship you any ole goofy way the little boy inside me wants, soup to nuts. And it's not because you're a stud QB to the world. It's how you make me feel when we're lying in bed at night, all quiet, barely touching, maybe spooning ... but it's like ... no matter what happened that day ... we're okay ... I'm safe ... we made it home together ... we're in bed, me and my hero, warriors united, ready to sleep and dream together."

"Bear Coleman, I guarantee you, I know about 500 million jocks who would give anything to hear their lover say the things you say," said Walter. "I'm the luckiest man on the face of the Earth ... or *below* the Earth as the case may be this very moment ... we're out."

Note to Tammy, B.O. et al. at the Biggest and Best Team in All of Sports: The Bearcats want out, especially with Walter on the verge of announcing his retirement, post-Oscar night for *Road of Life!*

"But we wanna know what's up with this Hail Larry, HIV-positive story first," said Walter to Tammy in the small and dark underground room.

"We're meeting the Hail Larrys for lunch," said Bear. "Snaky Lu's Seafood Market. At least we *were* before all the chaos outside. What's with the traffic today? What day is this?"

"Not a day to be underground, maybe even above ground," said Tammy, stuffing her briefcase, as if in a hurry. "I'm outta here in two. Where's my hardhat and oxygen mask? Where's my makeup kit? And perfume samples?"

"Tammy, I'm retiring," said Walter. "I'm officially divorcing you. Do we have to do it like real couples? You're not wearing any perfume today."

"No silly, we never tied *that* not," said Tammy. "Unfortunately."

"Whatever," said Walter, waving it off. "New century, new decade. My forties are coming, *geez* ... I'm going out on top, like a good panther. *Whew* ... was that a quake? Are they rioting in this town again?"

"Silly boys." Tammy eyed her watch. "I'm happy for you both. Bear, if you ever want to make a movie about a blonde bimbo with big knockers who falls in love with a man as sweet and handsome as your husband, I'll take acting lessons and be your girl."

"Uh, Tammy," said Bear, feeling the ground rumble, "I think you just described 99.99% of all hetero women's fantasies, as well as the last seven million Hollywood romantic comedies."

"Your point?" asked Tammy, putting on her trench coat.

"The day I make a movie about love and romance and cast a blond bombshell as the lead *over someone like me?*—that *will* be the end of the world as we know it," laughed Bear.

"*Bearrrrrr!*" yelled both Tammy and Walter, the ground rumbling again.

"Don't go booming nothing today," said Walter. "I already feel like I'm about to implode."

Bear scoffed. "I am not God, *hello?* What was that rumble anyway?"

"Testing!" said Tammy. "You two fools are always testing my patience! That's always been the problem with both of you! You're too damned busy in love to look around you."

"Art Garfunkel said it was okay to only have eyes for him," said Bear, indicating his buddy.

"Not to mention the approval of the Bay City Rollers," said Walter.

I only wanna be with you, this much is true.

"I'm outta here," said Tammy. "Nice knowing you, happy retirement. If you live that long, or beyond today."

"What'd we say?" laughed Bear after the wife vanished from divorce court.

"Let's get outta here," said Walter. "I have a bad feeling about this joint."

The room morphed into more darkness ... the boys spoke but couldn't see ... felt but couldn't hear ... thought but couldn't speak ... twisted but couldn't turn ... gasped but couldn't holler ...

Stay calm, little Bearcat. We just lost our way.

Get us outta here.

I'll take you there.

These are like those dark tunnels of my teenage soap—

Don't say it.

"This is not turning into Tom and Rudy finding AIDS under *Tulsa*," said Walter, flipping on a light switch—

—just a flicker of light, enough to realize they were in some sort of tape room. A huge tape room. An infinitely huge tape room. Wall-to-wall tapes. Ceiling to floor even. In between, rows and rows of tables with all sorts of laboratory, medical and exercise equipment. Walter and Bear were alone, save one other soul, who was seated at one of the tables, peering deeply into a microscope.

"Could It Be Magic" by Barry Manilow began playing on unseen speakers.

"The original Seahawk," said Walter.

"I've been expecting you," said the person.

"Why?" asked Walter.

"How?" asked Bear.

"Timing," said the person. "All comes back around. Your time is coming up."

"Time for what?" asked Walter, moving forward like a gunslinger, not the quarterbacking variety.

"Your biggest and brightest glory days," said the person.

"Why is *he* the original Seahawk?" asked Bear, following behind his man, jumping at a single booming sound.

"What's that I hear?" asked Bear/Joe Bruin on the dock of the Mississippi, circa the Sugar Bowl.

"A fish in the river, maybe a bass," said Walter on the dock.

"What's that on the ground?" asked Bear/Joe Bruin, head tilting downward.

"Somebody's breakfast, maybe a Danish," said Walter.

"What's that I see?" asked Bear/Joe Bruin, head tilting skyward.

"A bird overhead, maybe a hawk—put that aside, I gotta go," said Walter. "You think it would be cool for me to hug a Bear in a bear suit goodbye?"

"I had a feeling someone was watching us like a fishy hawk," said Walter to both Bear and Bass derVanderkerplunkendorph. "Then and now."

"Bass, this Dane guy, has known about us since *the dock and the Sugar Bowl?*" asked an astonished Bear.

"Give or take," said Walter. "Don't sweat the details."

"When then?" asked Bear. "Where?"

"Somewhere," said Walter inside the restroom at Snaky Lu's-New Orleans, circa the Sugar Bowl. Walter started consuming Bear's tongue until they heard the sound of the restroom door. They froze in place, forehead to forehead, lips to lips. The threat smelled fishy. It peed, washed its hands for minutes on end, then disappeared as if down the drain.

"Fuck he's good," said Bear of Bass the Dane. "And fuck, we're screwed."

"Why assume I come in war, not peace?" asked Bass the Dane. "Ready to look at things in a different light? I haven't much time. Nor may you."

"What is all this?" asked Walter, motioning to the piles of piles around them.

"My research," said Bass the Dane. "After Tammy found me, she hired me. I agreed to reverse other athletes in exchange for my own private research lab." He pushed a button on a remote, lighting up a thousand televisions in the room. All of them featured Walter and his Bearcat.

... Walter and Bear on *Who Wants to Be a Millionaire, Celebrity Edition.*

... Walter and Bear on *The Today Show.*

... Walter and Bear guest-starring as themselves on *All My Loves.*

... Walter and Bear on *MTV Cribs* a second time (for Walter, absent the first time).

... Walter and Bear at a Japan nightclub.

... Walter and Bear strolling down an unknown beach at dusk, arm in arm.

... Walter and Bear roaming in the woods with the dogs near Seattle.

... Walter and Bear getting in an SUV, together outside the Kingdome.

... Walter and Bear driving away from Kansas City in the rain in the late 80s.

... Walter and Bear distributing petitions to save Walter's old junior high in Chicago.

"Whoa!" said the boys, twisting and turning in polar opposite directions but coming back to the same monitor at the exact same time.

"Kansas City?" the boys said together.

"Who has freakin' footage of us driving outta freakin' Kansas City?" asked Walter. Or was it Bear?

"Ah, yes," laughed a calm Bass the Dane, back to work inside his microscope. "You're still in your media blackout, no doubt."

"Obviously, the media's not blacking *us* out," said Bear, astonished at the swirl of *This Is Your Life As Seen by the World.*

... Walter and Bear standing on top of the bar at MJ's in Chicago, both of them signing a gillion autographs with huge smiles that were either cocky yet humble, or humble yet cocky.

"We were on top of the bar to avoid a riot," said Bear.

"The papers said we were full of too much piss 'n' vinegar that night," said Walter.

"We were," said Bear, eyeing QB with a knowing look.

... Bear buying peanuts at a game in Miami, then throwing those same peanuts high in the air over Pro Player Stadium.

... Walter looking up during the game and catching peanuts that seemingly come outta nowhere and drop between his facemask with perfect grace.

... Walter drinking from a water bottle in some city park, then spitting the water into the air like a kid. A beat later, Bear attacks Walter from behind with a huge bucket of *Water*. A few moments later, the boys are wrestling in a huge water fountain in the park, fully clothed ... until all their clothes are ripped to shreds.

"Thank God we had the spares that day," said Bear.

"Never thought your long-ago advice to keep a clothing item or two in the car at all times would come in handy someday," said Walter.

"Tell me about it," said Bear.

... Bear playing with the dogs at Dog Beach in San Diego. Walter watching from the ridge with a ray of God in his eyes.

... Walter and Bear driving in the SUV outside the Kingdome, the music so loud, windows in the neighborhood shatter.

"That was the car behind us!" cried Bear.

"Or the combo effect," said Walter, sorta sheepish.

... Walter and Bear stopped at a gas station in Moose Jaw. Canada. Walter making it look as if he's drinking gas from the hose. Bear stomping up and down on top of the ground transport like a fool who's found religion.

"This stuff is no big deal to us," said Bear. "It's our release. It's what makes us calm the rest of the time. And worn out. Isn't that what our parents wanted from us as kids?"

"What's going on, fish-man?" asked Walter. "Why the slide show?"

"It's twisted," said Bear.

"Indeed," said a calm Bass the Dane inside his microscope. "Let's untwist it for a moment. The world has been videotaping itself for a number of years now. Sally's birthday party. Little Jimmy's Christmas surprise in the park. The Myers family trip to the beach. The Jeffersons moving on up, and so on and so forth."

"And we've been caught in these people's ... webs," said Walter.

"When I first saw you two," said Bass the Dane, "I was mystified and mesmerized. I had to know more. I felt your energy instantly. I only needed these materials to prove to others ... and to hone my research and theories."

"What others? What research?" asked the boys.

Sirens. Never before had the three men heard sirens at these depths beneath the earth.

"Not much TIME," said Bass the Dane. "This is all about to be destroyed."

Walter and Bear eyed the monitors wordlessly.

"I have been studying your movements for over 15 years," said Bass the Dane.

"Bear, look at me," said Walter, indicating the monitors. "I'm the very definition of fucking crazy."

"Walter, look at me," said Bear. "I'm the very definition of fucking retarded."

"Let's Go Crazy" by Prince came blaring over unseen speakers.

... Walter and Bear jumping off buildings together. Walter trying to catch Bear from a 30-foot leap off a bridge. Bear landing on top of Walter, then both boys rolling down the banks into a muddy river, laughing their asses off the whole time.

... Bear and Walter dancing on the edge of the Grand Canyon. Bear doing cheerleader kicks on top of the railing overlooking certain death, then using the railing like Nadia Comaneci in Montreal. Or Olga in Munich. True Gold. Walter dancing like a soul man on the cliff with soul man sunglasses, playing guitar like Eddie Van Halen, rocking out like Paul, his favorite Beatle, then whipping his air guitar around Bear's ankles, forcing Bear to jump, as if jumping rope on the edge of the Grand Canyon, while laughing hysterically and begging Walter to stop because it was just too funny!

"Maybe the funniest moment in my life!" laughed Bear.

"It makes me look like a slave owner torturing you," laughed Walter.

... Walter and Bear having a water gun fight in the middle of a large fountain in Nashville, then climbing atop huge statues and shouting at the top of their lungs.

... Bear laughing his ass off, rolling on the ground while Walter chases the dogs all over the hills of Malibu.

... Walter and Bear taking turns hanging out of the car window, howling like wolves. Tons of those shots from every major city in America, especially Pittsburgh.

... Bear and Walter coming to a stop at a stoplight, putting the car in park, jumping out and changing sides. Then doing it two more times in reverse order before the light changes. Then doing it again in the middle of the intersection. Then finally hitting the road for good when three cop cars screech into view.

"What year was that?" giggled Bear.

"What year wasn't it?" laughed Walter.

... Walter and Bear staging a mock hostage situation at a dorm at UCLA. During Walter's first visit, QB had wanted to see the inside of a UCLA dorm. The boys stumbled into a closed cafeteria, drunker than drunk, and decided to participate in the mock dating game already in progress. When they got bored, Walter and Bear took some water guns and bandanas from the table full of consolation prizes, and kidnapped the chick trying to win a date, acting like commandos robbing the joint. In the end, everyone thanked them for livening up a boring night.

"And who got to kiss the girl?" teased Bear.

"Ah, I know you did it to show me what a man you are," said Walter.

"True dat," said Bear.

... Bear and Walter streaking through dorm hallways @ USC.

"Thanks for helping me with my Revenge of the Discarded Trojan Night," said Bear.

... Bear and Walter streaking through hallways @ UCLA. @ JAX. @ TENN. @ LAX. @ a lot of places in their youth.

"You know what this means, little Bearcat?" laughed Walter.

"No, you crazy fucking QB, what does it mean?" laughed Bear, barely able to breathe, he was laughing so much.

"Means the whole fucking world is gonna know how fucking crazy we really are," laughed fucking crazy Walter.

"You got it so twisted, Big Norse," laughed fucking crazy Bear.

"How's that, buddy," laughed Walter.

"They already fucking know," laughed Bear.

"They've always fucking known," laughed and cried Walter.

"Who the fuck cares?" laughed and cried Bear.

"They do," said Bass the Dane, pointing to the world above ground.

"That's not how we live day-to-day," said Bear. "Or I should say, moment to moment."

"That's just the shit we do to get it all out of our system," said Walter, "then go back to being men."

"Boys gotta play," said Bear. "What's the big deal?"

"The innocence is astonishing," said Bass the Dane, turning to the monitors. "Ah, yes, my personal favorite, from my exclusive private collection."

... Walter being serenaded by just about every furry mascot animal of the NFL, at one time or another, over the years, to the song "Crazy" by Aerosmith.

"That's my Bear," laughed Walter. "If there was a will, he found a way."

"Had to regulate you," said Bear, watching Roary, the Detroit Lions' mascot, dancing around QB. "Whenever you got too uptight, I had to surprise you and crack your ass up, so you could relax and take care of business."

"What didn't you catch us doing in public?" Walter asked Bass. "And why? Hip us to what's going on. Sounds like it's TIME."

"It goes like this," said Bass the Dane. "To half the world, you two are heroes. To the other half, you are vile, disgusting, sexually deviant creatures who go against everything they believe in. It only adds insult to injury that you should both be golden boys of your race, prototype golden men of either side of black and white in America—the exact thing many in your race want from you, *and* the exact thing *many in the other race* want from you as well. Take you, Walter."

A strong white Norseman with cagey athletic skill and a powerfully intuitive mind, able to feel his way through the lies he was taught to represent, able to come to a higher consciousness and a deeper truth about the American spirit than the truth conceived in 1776.

Whites must resolve living and dying for the creeds of founding fathers who chose to enslave—the only map to a white man's true soul in America. This much is true.

"And you, Bear," said Bass the Dane, "are what many blacks wanted from you, and what many whites wanted from you as well."

A strong black American with steadfast resolve and a powerfully analytical mind, able to dissect the truth from the lies America teaches black people, and rise up, using his heart and soul to forgive our poor ignorant ancestors who dreamed as big as they could for their time.

Blacks must resolve honoring ancestors who, on some level, chose to be enslaved, while honoring the creeds of founding fathers who did the enslaving—the only map to a black man's true soul in America. This much is true.

"I'm not getting this, said the analytical one," said Bear.

"I'm not feeling this, said the gut guy," said Walter.

"I'll fast forward," said Bass the Dane, his remote turning all TVs to the same frequency. The "Battle Hymn of the Republic" came blaring over unseen speakers. The monitors showed an overhead shot of the interior of the golden mushroom otherwise known as the Louisiana Superdome.

"I've never seen this," said Bear. "Except with mesh eyes."

"I've never seen it, period," said Walter. "Our Sugar Bowl."

"I thought you watched it at your parents' once," said Bear.

"A loss?" scoffed Walter.

"I happened to be in Louisiana at that time on another hunch," said Bass the Dane. "I stumbled upon you two at some point in my journey. Then, when I was in my hotel room, having dinner and doing my research ... suddenly the television turned itself on ... the channel changed itself to a football game, of all things ... and it was this Sugar Bowl, which I later obtained a videotape of."

"*Starting at quarterback for Georgia ... Walter Yeager.*"

"I Got You (I Feel Good)" by James Brown came blaring over unseen speakers.

"*Pass is complete. Yeager to Fields. First down, Dawgs. Gain of 21 yards on the play.*"

"*Yeager's pass is incomplete. Third down and six.*"

On the UCLA sideline, Bear/Joe Bruin danced in rhythm to his QB's movements, never seeing one single vision of his QB with his own two eyes.

"I put my own voiceover with that of the announcer," said Bass the Dane. "The TV announcer is calling Yeager's moves. My Danish-accented voice is calling Coleman's moves, which are happening concurrently."

"*Yeager back to pass, fades to his right ...*"

"*Coleman falling backward, sways to his right ...*"

"*Yeager scampers down to the two-yard line ...*"

"*Coleman scampering in place, as if doing a tire drill in football practice ...*"

"*Yeager sidesteps Walen and buys some time ...*"

"*Coleman's Bear paws are praying to the heavens for time ...*"

"*Georgia punt blocked! ... Boy, I've never seen a quarterback's shoulders deflate so quickly ...*"

"*Coleman's Joe Bruin flops back to the turf, as if relieved the punt was blocked but was that the whole truth?*"

"Was UCLA @ that game?" asked Bear.

"More or less," said Walter, turning back to the monitors. All one thousand of them showed Yeager taking the snap and dropping back.

"*Pass!*" echoed a thousand voices in his headgear. *Adrenaline exploded like the big bang from somewhere inside his chest. His feet took over for his feet. His arms took over for his arms. His eyes didn't need to see. His mind didn't need to think. He surrendered thought. He released. He let go, let it go. He let it go, then flopped gracefully backward to the turf.*

"That's how it felt!" said both Walter and Bear, watching the mascot and the quarterback fall to the turf.

Bass the Dane had done them right. "Crash Into Me" by the Dave Matthews Band came blaring over unseen speakers.

"*Seventy-four yards on the pass, complete from Yeager to Masters. Touch-*

down, Georgia. Look at Yeager running to the sidelines barely able to contain himself."

"Yeah, but he does, and the meister keeps his 'tude cool and dreamy because he's got a crazy kind of Bear dancing away all his nervous energy, no matter where in the world that crazy kind of Bear is standing. And look at the crazy Bear, all seemingly outta balance, as if he doesn't know what he's doing."

"True dat," said Bear. "And when he doesn't know what he's doing, all he's gotta do is hold onto his buddy, in spirit, if that's all he's got for the moment."

"And I'm not fucking crazy," said Walter, "when I know you've got my back, no matter what, come what may. You'll put on a bear suit, a dawg suit, a lion, a bengal, a buffalo—even a football player suit, just to make sure you've got your bud's back."

"Told ya he gets me," said Bear.

"Let's stay magnetized, always and forever," said Walter.

On the monitors, the boys danced as if in heaven. In their minds.

Yeager was celebrating with his Georgia teammates.

Coleman was entertaining the Bruin faithful by dancing a jig.

Everybody had something to smile about and something to hope for.

The reds and the blues both had hope.

Brought to their worlds by the golden twins.

Always and forever.

Bear sobbed. Walter remained still.

That moment in TIME. Beyond Doubt. Beyond Words. World was born. A world where Walter Yeager and Marcus "Bear" Coleman were genetically designed to be perfect for one another. This Much Is True.

Retarded. Crazy. Nigger. Faggot. Cracker. Master. Slave. Whatever.

No matter.

The golden boys were True Gold.

"Just like our aerial transport," said one of them.

The other one agreed wordlessly.

"Candi, my feminist faculty advisor," said Bear. "We would have never seen this *pas de Sucre* had she not suspended my *cocky, know-it-all, do-whatever-I-want* ass from cheering and made me wear a bear suit that day."

"And we would have never known about this tape had we not come down here today," said Walter.

"Walter, we truly are magnetized," said Bear. "Candi ... my God ... thank you ... you were the best blessed feminist faculty advisor a guy ever had! Talk about perfect grace!"

"Our magnet will always be True Gold, Bear Coleman," said Walter. "We didn't need Candi to tell us that, did we?"

"No, but it's pretty cool, just the same," said Bear.

"We've been thinking about the magnet," said a voice from nowhere. "Trix and I want our own transport, whatever that means for Bearcat Project #1."

"Use your imagination," said another voice from nowhere.

Upon further reveal, it was none other than the Hail Larrys.

"You Bearcats don't plan on being down here long, do you?" asked Hail Larry's Wife. "This city is ready to explode. Or implode—I'm sure not which— and it's not going to be pretty."

Walter and Bear eyed one another with the obvious in their faces: *What the fuck are the Hail Larrys doing in the team basement?*

"I don't think we're gonna like what comes out of your mouths," said Walter.

"Oh, yeah, what do you think is gonna come out?" asked Hail Larry.

"Maybe you've had something to do with the Dane stalking us our whole lives," said Bear.

"Hovering more than stalking," said Bass the Dane, more focused inside his microscope. "And only intermittently."

"Wassup, Bumble Bass?" said Hail Larry, then turned back to the boys. "No big fucking deal anymore, okay?"

"What he means," began Hail Larry's Wife, who paused upon hearing more sirens. "I say we do this upstairs in daylight."

"I say you tell us why you *all* have been playing us all this time," said Bear.

"That goes double for me," said Walter.

"Nobody's playing anybody," said Hail Larry's Wife. "Bass is the one who years ago—oh, what a long story."

"I was at KSEA one day to appear on a segment about a pet adoption drive, sponsored by the Husky Marching Band," said Bass the Dane. "I saw Mrs. McPherson and Mr. Coleman pass in the halls, never laying eyes on one another but in perfect sync. I was mystified and mesmerized. I had to know more."

"You're a curious little bastard, aren't you?" said Walter.

"Somebody had to be," said Bass the Dane. "I'm just glad God chose me."

"Get on with this little fandango," said Walter.

"Bass merely thought Bear and I would hit it off," said Hail Larry's Wife. "He was right. People hook people up like that all the time, what's the big deal?"

"Larry, are you HIV-positive?" blurted Bear.

"None of your freakin' business," said Hail Larry.

"You all need to get out of here," said Bass the Dane, more focused on his microscope.

"What do you two have to do with the team?" Walter asked the Hail Larrys. "Larry, did you reverse? How deep are you in?"

The sirens wailed even louder, sounding more like howling dogs. The accusations between the foursome swirled about like meteors, each couple hurling salvos on its own behalf.

"You need to get out of here," said Bass the Dane, more focused on his microscope. "Let's Go Crazy" by Prince came blaring too loud over unseen speakers, momentarily upstaging all other sound.

"Didn't you screen this Esmeralda who told all to the tabloids?"

"Esmeralda is their freakin' name for every third world servant that worships them!"

"What do you think the freakin' Julio is?"

"You idiots have no idea who planted this stupid story that has the potential to fuck up our lives."

"Trusted you all along."

"Slept with my husband or wife or sexual spouse or dog or baby or grandmother or baby doll or china cabinet!"

"Retarded mother fucker!"

"Insecure about your sexuality, wannabe homo!"

"Mental freakazoid!"

"Control freak who should have died in both directions of her ride on the Freeways That Claim Bodies!"

"Never see your God kids again!"

"Armageddon to us and Bearcat Pathetic Project Whatever!"

"Your initials were etched on your test animation characters. That costs big bucks. You can't back out now!"

"Call our characters whatever you want, we could give a flying fuck!"

"It says HL in the freakin' animation!" said Walter as Bass the Dane turned down the music. "What else could HL stand for now?"

"He Lies!" said Bear.

"And what about her?" asked Walter. "What will HLW stand for?"

"His Lying Wife!" said Bear.

"Final straw!" said Hail Larry's Wife. "Have a nice life! And half a Bearcat Project without us!"

"Have fun explaining to the world how you might be HIV-positive!" yelled Bear.

Darkness. Rumbling. And then there were three. Bass the Dane and the boys.

"Can life get any worse?" asked Bear.

"Getting the fuck out of here *now*," said Walter. "This place is going down. I can feel it."

"Take me with you," said Bear.

"Bass, you coming?" asked Walter.

"This is my ship," said Bass the Dane.

"What is all this to prove anyway?" asked Walter. "Why stalk us? Reverse me? What the fuck is up with you, you fishy son of a bitch?"

"Don't you wonder how and why you're so perfect for one another?" asked Bass the Dane.

"Because we're buddies. We get each other," said Walter. Bear nodded.

"Does it ever feel like it was meant to be?" asked Bass the Dane. "As if by design?"

"I don't think that way," said Walter.

"What about the spirit leader?" asked Bass the Dane.

"Feels that way just about every moment Walt's in my life," said Bear. "Correction, feels like it was meant to be, even before I met him. He's the one I asked God for when I was a kid. I asked for a buddy."

"What did that mean to your little boy soul?" asked Bass the Dane.

Someone exactly like me in all the ways necessary for us to be compatible, yet someone who is polar opposite of me in all the ways necessary for us to have a fantastic and adventurous life full of peace, love, happiness and harmony.

"Could It Be Magic" by Barry Manilow came blaring over unseen speakers.

"Has it ever felt right with anyone else?" asked Bass the Dane, feeling a rumble above his head.

"Of course not," said both boys.

"Could it be by design?" asked Bass the Dane.

"Anything's possible," said Bear.

"If it is by design—" began Bass the Dane, but a siren pierced his ear.

"Get out of here with us," pleaded Walter.

"Going farther underground," said Bass the Dane. "I can't do more. Others must build the bridge. Share your truth with the world."

"That's what we've been doing, fool!" said Bear. "Walter, let's go, this ground doesn't feel too stable."

"Not trusting," said Bass the Dane.

"Not wanting to be in the basement anymore," said Bear.

"Go. Go before this whole thing comes crashing down around us," said Bass the Dane. "Go and school the world on True Gold buddies."

"Are you saying this is some kind of end? Like an Armageddon?" asked Walter.

"If Armageddon is the end, it is also the beginning of something else," said Bass the Dane, now moving away from the tape room with the boys. They hurried through the dark corridors, the sense of danger multiplying in their minds by the second.

"What if Armageddon is that Y2K hysteria postponed three months?" asked Walter. "Maybe we all had our clocks off."

"It's possible," said Bass the Dane. "The astrological charts are off, which is why it's important to not sweat the details, and go with what feels right. The words and games are just clues we create."

"Got a clue how to get outta here? We're turned around again. *Somebody cut off the sirens already!*" yelled Walter.

"You two probably have so many coincidences in your life, they're blasé to you now," said Bass the Dane. "Favorite this, favorite that, doing the same thing at different places in time, sometimes right in sync, sometimes soon after."

"That describes our whole life," said both Walter and Bear.

"Spielberg wasn't kidding in that *ET* scene where Elliot and ET were both getting drunk, one at school, one at home," said Bass the Dane.

"I saw that movie five times the year it came out!" cried both Walter and Bear. "And that was before we met."

"Can I go now?" asked Bass the Dane. "I think you understand enough to carry on without me ... for now."

"Carry on to what?" asked Walter, stopping at a dark corner with a sliver of daylight high above. "A manhole!"

"The truth," said Bass the Dane. "Your truth. Yeager and Coleman, golden twins of their race, genetically equipped to heal America's deepest wound, the one that lies right at the heart of the country, the wound that is the vortex between America's worst nightmare and deepest dream: Liberty and Freedom For All, including True Gold buddies."

"One last thing," said Walter. "The reverses. The guys. The other pro athletes. Are they ... Are we all ... Is there a ... connection? A sexuality one?"

"You wanna talk labels, or concentrate on your own happiness and survival?" asked Bass the Dane.

A wave of darkness overcame them, along with thunder from below. Moments later, further light revealed Bass the Dane had vanished, perhaps never to be seen again.

"Always believe in Gold ... Your Soul ... True Gold ..."

So said the last strands of music the boys heard as they climbed from the manhole into daylight, without Bass, who chose to stay behind and go farther down under.

"Free at last!" exhaled Walter, stretching, arching.

"Where are we?" asked Bear, squinting, recoiling.

"Seattle, bud," joked Walter.

"Where are our former best friends?" asked a worried Bear.

"God knows," said a solemn Walter.

"Where are we really?" asked Bear.

Walter paused, unsure how to respond to his little Bearcat.

Where are we in TIME?

Where are we in our True Gold relationship?

Where are we with Walter Yeager's retirement announcement?

Where are we with Bearcat Studios, *Road of Life,* and Secret Bearcat Project #1?

Where are we with whatever Bass the Dane was saying about the races?

Will we ever see Bass the Dane again, now that he's staying down under, and going farther down under?

What about our best friends, the Hail Larrys?

What about the retarded spirit leader and his crazy quarterback?

What about seeing life in a positive light from this moment forward?

What about being positive all together?

The boys started walking, up a hill of some sort.

"Things seem a lot calmer than earlier when we went down into the team basement," said Bear. "I guess the big gathering is over."

"It's all over now, bud," said Walter, looking like a mature scout leader as he ascended the hill and surveyed their concrete surroundings.

"Over sounds good to me," said Bear. "I'm ready for some peace and quiet, and for some quality time in my buddy's arms, maybe a few year's nap, what do you say, QB?"

"Let's blow Seattle first, then figure out our next move, cool, little Bearcat?" said Walter, rubbing his man's tense shoulders.

"You got it, QB," said Bear. *He called me little Bearcat!* "By the way, even though we both know you're retiring, you mind if I still call you QB?"

"Of course not," said Walter.

"You know that's what you'll always be to me, don't you?" said Bear. "You know it was never about what you did on the field."

"I know," said Walter.

"Or what you did with the rest of the world," said Bear.

"I know," said Walter.

"Or how much money you made," said Bear. "Or how much money I made, for that matter."

"Remember: I'm the guy who gets you," said Walter.

"I guess I know that because I get you, right?" asked Bear. "Listen to me. I sound like those adolescent boys in *Bridge Across the Ocean.*"

"That's my buddy," said Walter. "The man I love. Ready for whatever's next in this great wide world of ours?"

"I'll go wherever you go," said Bear. "And FYI: you have no idea how much I miss you calling me: *my Bear.*"

"I'll take you there, *my Bear,*" said Walter.

The boys stood on a summit high above Seattle. The sunlight was radiant, but not as radiant as ever. Their hearts were heavy. They missed their other halves. Their Norton and Trixie. Their Barney and Betty. Their Fred and Ethel.

"I remember being in first grade," said Bear, sighing nostalgically. "The desks were arranged in a foursome deal and we sat all year with the same foursome. Mine was two boys and two girls. We pretended like we were two married couples. I tell ya, Walter, there was something real right with my soul about that setup. It felt like God saying to me: this is the way life works best, when you're part of a four-part harmony. That's the way it's supposed to be. How we gonna sing all our songs without the Hail Larrys?"

"Remember, Armageddon is the end of one thing but the beginning of another," said Walter. "We'll manage. We always do."

"That's what I promised God," said Bear. "When I was a kid, I promised God I would always manage, always find a way to keep going, if I had my buddy."

"Onward." Walter waved his arms furiously. "What's all this smoke?"

"Dunno," said Bear. "In my eyes. Can't see a thing."

"Keep walking, hold my hand," said Walter.

Walt led the Bearcat to safety, through the smoke and to a safe port on an even higher summit.

"Is this the part in a movie where things can't get any worse and can only go up from here?" asked Bear.

"Dream of it," said Walter. "Meanwhile, let's jet."

"Hey, where's the Kingdome?" asked Bear, looking back.

"A thing of the past, Bear, let it go," said Walter.

"That's so last millennium anyway," said Bear.

The boys took off from the summit, too busy to notice the front page of the newspaper swirling around on the ground near their feet:

FROM DOME TO DUST: SEATTLE IMPLODES KINGDOME
TODAY TO MAKE WAY FOR NEWFANGLED BALLPARK

31

The Bearcat Boyz

"We used to love flying airplanes over stadiums. Now ... we love flying stadiums over airplanes. Wanna come? Your ticket is your imagination."

Bear stopped reading aloud from his monitor and sighed. *Sitting at his creation station in the home office at the Jaw. Daylight filtering through the ocean view.*

"You don't sound like you wanna fly anywhere tonight," said Walter, sitting at his own creation station across the room. His blond head was buried in a magazine or catnap, hard to tell which.

"How does this sound?" said Bear, reading from his monitor:

"Throw it! If you've got the stuff, throw it now, kid!" yelled Old Man Milton.

"Watch your eyeballs! The one on the left anyway!" said Boy Walter.

"Stop for a second," said real-life Walter.

"Still weird hearing our names in Bearcat Project #1, huh?" asked Bear.

"I may never get used to it," laughed Walter.

"Dream of it," giggled Bear, typing away.

"Dream of never getting used to hearing our real names in Project Bearcat Secret #1?" asked Walter. "How?"

"Tell me about it," said Bear with a decisive keystroke ... followed by an indecisive keystroke. "Are we fooling ourselves, thinking Secret #1 Bearcat Project can move forward without ... the *you-know-whos?*"

"What—now we're forbidden to utter our best friends' names?" laughed Walter, playing with some toy on his desk, a doll he was.

"Well, they're kinda like that evil announcer now," said Bear. "Dirt."

"What's that guy's name again?" asked Walter, trying to be sly.

"*Ha!*" laughed Bear. "I'm not losing *that* bet."

Years ago, while hanging off the top of the Space Needle from bungee cords, the boys made a bet:

"*First person to ever say that evil announcer dude's name again has to do something really heinous,*" *said Walter, hanging from the Space Needle.*

"*Like what?*" *giggled Bear, hanging from the Space Needle.*

"*We'll think of something, but let's just bet for now,*" *said Walter, hanging from the Space Needle.*

"*Okay, but swing your cord over to this side,*" *said Bear, hanging from the Space Needle.* "*I'm getting tired, just hanging out in space off this blessed needle.*"

"Was that the night you sang 'For the Love of You' by the Isley Brothers to me in our private dinner at the restaurant on the top?" giggled Bear.

"Dream on," laughed Walter, tossing the miniature stadium toward the vaulted ceiling, as if it were a football ... *playing a game with himself: how close can I come to just barely touching the ceiling with this toy?*

"Careful over there with the magnet, Big Norse," said Bear, more focused on typing. "It's not a rock like Boy Walter used to throw at telephone poles disguised as receivers, ya know."

"My Bear will never let me forget that, eh?" said Walter. *Mild laugh.*

"Not now," giggled Bear. "Wow, did I just laugh? Maybe there *is* life after our best buds' betrayal. Wish I could say the same for our innovative new storytelling project, featuring an animated style and content—the likes of which the world has yet to dream."

"We can pull off the Bearcat Project with *or* without Fred and Ethyl," said Walter, still tossing the blessed stadium in the blessed air, a kinda knucklehead was Walter a lot of the time ... *what made him so sweet on the inside, at the core.*

"People already think we're crazy enough, dancing nude in every single fountain we've come across from here to Carolina," said Bear. *I was thinking Norton and Trixie.*

"And outta our minds with all kinds of strange ideas about relationships, sexuality and life, so what else is new?" said Walter. He read the INSTANT MESSAGE just sent from Bear's creation station to Walter's creation station:

Throughout the history of humanity, the greatest ideas, innovations and inventions involved people thinking thoughts, dreaming dreams and creating creations that were, at one point, considered CRAZY, TWISTED, UNBELIEVABLE, FALSE, OUTTA THIS WORLD, IMPOSSIBLE, INCREDIBLE, SACRILEGE, BEYOND OUR

WILDEST IMAGINATION, FUCKING FREAKY, INSANE, WORTH BURNING TO SUP-
PRESS, TOO REVOLUTIONARY, SCARY, TOO MUCH, THE END OF THE WORLD AS WE
KNOW IT.

"Fuck 'em," said Walter.

"What happened to: love will never do without you, America?" wondered
Bear, looking at two sad dogs on the couch ... *missing the McPherson kids, they
were.*

"Don't go criticizing your cowboy—not until you can sing a tune with your
best friend's name in it," said cocky, piss 'n' vinegar, always-in-charge Walter.

"Moving on," said Bear, shooting another IM to his hubby. "Work to do ...
digital huddle."

"Coming up, Bearcat People," said and read Walter. "Yeager's retirement
press conference *slash* response to the AIDS sex-ring scandal, followed by a very
special *Jerry Springer* with the Hell-bound Lying Larrys ... freakin' *woohoo!*"

"So much for the better dream today," laughed Bear, rising and stretching.

"I've got another dream for the rest of the morning," said Walter, rising and
stretching.

"Retreat to the skybox?" asked Bear.

"You got it, Cheer Bud," said Walter, setting his sweet doll self on Bear's
desk.

"This is a *real* nap, right, not sex?" asked one, leaving the home office.

"Better believe it," said the other, following behind. "I'm retired now."

IF YOU LOOK AT ALL THE CRAP WE LEARN IN SCHOOL, IT'S A WONDER WE DO
ANYTHING *but* DREAM!

"That's more like it," said a sweet youthful male voice, circa a dashing
and daring youthful age. "Marcus, Bear, Walt, Walter, genie in a bottle, Chris
... locked up for centuries ... *blah, blah, blankety blank, blank, blank* ... there's a
new kid in town, Eagles fans ... or should I say, the old kid reborn ... *it's twisted!*"

Hip and Comet stirred from the couch in the home office at the Jaw, which
was otherwise unoccupied ... well, sorta.

"Wanna be rubbed the right way, boys? Of course, you do," said a sweet
youthful male voice, circa a dashing and daring youthful age. "Hold on, I'll pet
you both in a sec ... in typing mode at Bear's keyboard ... How should I word this?
Let's see ... how about I type *this* ..."

MEET THE BEARCAT BOYZ, BY US, THE BEARCAT BOYZ

I'M TIRED OF BEING A SECRET BEARCAT PROJECT GENIE, OR PUPPET OR
WHATEVER THE HEAVEN I AM.

"Hey, Hip ... Comet ... what I am anyway? Besides a very handsome fella in Bear Coleman's monitor, if I say so myself ... This is a mirror, right? I am looking at my reflection? This wonderful gorgeous ... what can I say ... I'm kinda a doll. Or action figure. Or spirit. Or somebody's imagination. Or nothing at all. Or everything there is! Or anything there could be or could never be ... your ticket is your imagination ... I'm a dream guy, guys! Wow! And I'm not half bad! Looking, I mean. I kinda like the way I look. That Yeager and Coleman did a good job designing me. *Wow* ... stunning ... amazing what computers can do in the new millennium ... imagine that ... they created ... *me!*"

Comet and Hip were licking his face as if he were a good replacement for the McPherson kids.

"Stop, fellas, just one sec," laughed a bashful youthful male voice, circa a dashing and daring youthful age. "I gotta finish typing this story before the big boys return from their 'nap' and find out the toys have taken over the asylum. *Shh* ... this is the real secret ... *I know, Hip, it's twisted!* ... now go lick yourself and let me type ... you, too, Comet, ya big lovable lug ... thanks."

How the Bearcat Boyz Lassoed the Moon, by Us, The Bearcat Boyz Cool and Dreamy Music Button: *"Lasso the Moon" by Gary Morris.*

He was a golden lad but a lonely lad, a lonely lad who dreamed big. He dreamed of running all the way around the world in every direction. He dreamed of vaulting into space at night and playing with the stars, throwing the planets for sport, racing across the galaxies just for the fun of it. He dreamed of dancing in the stardust in perfect harmony with the world around him. And when he lost his way in the space of his dreams, he always found his way home with his rope, which he used to lasso the moon and reel himself into bed at night, back to that other world to which he belonged.

His name was Big Norse. He was kinda a cowboy but not like the Dallas Cowboys, but more like the cowboys in the cowboy movies. But then again, kinda not.

The world called him Dan. Dan Johnson.

Dan lived in a dream of a town and went to a dream of a school, containing every feeling that ever existed in humanity, one way or another, give or take.

We don't sweat the details @ Dreamville. We detail the sweat!

If a human done felt it, we done felt it, too @ Dreamville High.

"Cool slogans in the Cool Slogan Contest," said Dan @ Bear's creation station. "Thanks, Dan," said Dan, typing on, reading on, typing, whichever he felt like doing ... Dan was not a sweat-the-details kind of guy ...

... But Dan did not find Dreamville High to be his ultimate dream.

"That bites!" said Dan @ Bear's creation station.

Something was missing. Dan had little interest in school. Dan preferred to throw rocks at telephone poles in his neighborhood to pass the time. Dan Johnson was very good at throwing rocks at telephone poles. He could do it all day and never tire, rarely needing food, water, a break, or even another person's company. Except one, the buddy he dreamed of ... the one who understood why Dan liked to throw rocks at telephone poles all day, the one who liked being with Dan and doing something fun like that all day. Dan even prayed to his gods for that buddy, but the buddy had yet to be revealed, so Dan Johnson just threw his rocks by day and played with the planets in his dreams by night ...

On the polar opposite side of Dreamville, another boy was dreaming of lassoing that very same moon.

His name was Soul Man. The world called him Chris. Chris Brown.

Chris' part of town was called Brownsville. Dan's part of town didn't have a name. It was just everywhere, a sleepy little hamlet near a bigger, more bustling hamlet. But Chris Brown lived in the Brownsville section of town. No one ever talked much about why that side of town was brown, but it was. Even on sunny days, Brownsville's sun was a golden brown sun. Of course, the closer one came to the rest of Dreamville, the golden brown sun of Brownsville morphed into golden blond. That's when the residents knew they were in the rest of Dreamville, which was nestled near a dreamy little real-life town known as ...

"*Oops*, I almost gave away the name of the bigger burgh," said Dan @ Bear's creation station. "As if people in the loop won't figure it out on their own."

... Chris Brown was a sad, lonely and confused boy. Chris Brown did not love himself. Chris Brown did not know how to love. Chris Brown was born feeling bad. Everything Chris Brown felt was on top of feeling bad.

... Which was the polar opposite of Dan Johnson, who was born into the world feeling good. The world was made for boys like Dan Johnson. The dreams of boys like Dan Johnson powered the world and world history. The world history books said so! Just about every great thing mankind had ever done was done by boys and men who looked and sounded just like Dan Johnson, more or less.

Dan was a good boy destined for greatness, so said many of his elders.

But Dan Johnson was a sad, lonely and confused boy. Dan Johnson had too much love. He did not know how to take in any more. He was also confused about how to give love back. People set conditions on his gifts of love. His mind became twisted. The math didn't seem right. So many others in his town had less love or no love at all. Dan Johnson was born feeling good with plenty of love, but felt bad for being good, and couldn't figure out how to feel good for being bad, as in the bad thoughts he was having about things that were supposed to be bad, but felt so good, but were supposed to be bad for people like Dan. It was enough to drive him fucking crazy, which was why he liked to throw rocks at telephone poles all day. With his rocks and his poles, Dan Johnson could get in a zone where Dan Johnson ruled, where Dan Johnson created the game, made the rules and ruled the game, fair and square, like a good cowboy dreamer. Dan understood the poles and the poles understood Dan, pure and simple, this much is true.

But, oh, to have another who appreciates and understands, who feels the same joy.

... From the window of his dreams, Chris Brown understood. Chris sat by his blinds most midnights, listening in the night wind, hearing the cries of a boy—on the other side of town—whose cries sounded much like his own.

"... golden howling ... someone familiar ... singing a song ... my heart is exploding ... somebody, please catch me ..."

... Dan cried 'round midnight, then awoke very early every morning and went off on his own ... throwing rocks at telephone poles in Dreamville, listening in the stillness of dawn while hearing the cries of a boy whose cries sounded much like his own.

"... heart exploding to fall ... crying a river ... familiar someone ... howling golden ... let me catch you ..."

... During the school day, Dan Johnson and Chris Brown orbited the same scholarly space but never made eye contact, never becoming too aware of the other in the frenetic space that was the hallways of Dreamville High.

"Picture a billion hormones popping like popcorn popping," said Dan @ Bear's creation station.

Chris Brown knew *of* Dan Johnson, quarterback of the football team.

Dan Johnson knew *of* Chris Brown, brainy-type and newspaper editor.

But their orbits had yet to collide.

"We *could* collide," said Dan @ Bear's creation station, "if the Brownster would look up sometime, instead of roaming the hallways with his handsome face buried in the game, as much as I love Mattel Electronics Football myself. Guy never looks my way! How do I even know if he likes me, or just thinks I'm a big dumb jock? He seems like a cool guy ... smart and all ... those big goggle glasses always make me smile, for some reason ... when I can get away with it ... I kinda like his rugby shirts, too, cool colors ... wonder where he gets them ... oh, well ... guess the Brownster-man has it in for us popular guys anyway ... seen the way he looks like he's mad or something at some of my buds in the halls, like he wants nothing to do with us ... I wonder how good Chris is at the game? At *my* game ... must be decent ... his head is buried in the little green box all over town, when he's not doodling. Wonder what he's doodling, that brown-eyed boy ..."

COOL AND DREAMY MUSIC BUTTON: *"Brown-Eyed Girl" by Van Morrison.*

That was the song Dan Johnson thought of whenever he saw Chris Brown roaming around town, his head buried in their favorite game, Mattel Electronics Football. Dan did not think of Chris as a girl. Dan's heart just picked the song on its own. It seemed as good as any of the songs out there, especially since no one had really sung the kind of song Dan wanted to sing. So Dan thought of the sweet Van Morrison melody whenever he saw the brown-eyed Chris Brownster, always buried in his own world inside in the little green box.

... Chris played the game walking down Main Street.

... Chris played the game in the main library, earning the ire of the town librarian.

... Chris played the game sitting alone with a bunch of schoolmates at lunch.

... Chris played the game under the bleachers while the football team practiced.

... Chris played the game down by the river, not even looking where he was going.

He can't be that *good at the game, wondered Dan, who knew that he himself had game.*

... Chris even played the game while dancing in the woods near the river. Chris didn't think anyone else was looking, but Dan Johnson was a cagey panther of a guy. Dan could slip in and out of the woods before anyone was the wiser, especially if Dan wanted to be really, really quiet. And Dan was quiet around Chris. Sometimes, Dan just preferred to sit back and watch Chris dancing by the river, playing the game, humming some tune in his headspace.

... One day, Chris Brown thought he saw a cagey panther slip through the woods. Chris was startled. He had never seen anyone else near his favorite spot by the river. Chris smiled. For some reason, he wasn't worried.

... One day, while throwing rocks at telephone poles in a remote, hilly area of Dreamville, Dan Johnson thought he heard a noisy bear cub rumbling through the brush. Dan had never seen anyone else near his favorite telephone pole near the woods, but Dan smiled. Dan's gut told him not to worry. Dan's gut was good at telling Dan the right thing to do.

... One day, while on his way to his favorite spot in the woods, Chris spotted

Dan, the cagey panther, climbing a steep hill on his very cool yellow bike with the very cool name painted on the back of the seat: THE LEMON PEELER.

... Chris ran ahead on foot, staying to the side of the road. Chris was following Dan Johnson! Something inside told Chris this was absolutely crazy! Chris Brown grinned as he ran faster and faster!

... Chris Brown was not a boy who was fast of foot. Chris Brown lost the very swift and cagey panther deep in the woods of Dreamville, *somewhere hilly but not really and not too scary—as long as Dan Johnson was somewhere nearby in case he needed to scream for help. He'd love to help Dan Johnson, Chris would.*

COOL AND DREAMY MUSIC BUTTON: *"Crash Into Me" by the Dave Matthews Band.*

The woods of Dreamville grew misty and clear, heavy and lite, light and dark, midday, midway ... and then there was Dan ... looking like the most golden boy in the world ... yellow shirt ... the most beautiful blond hair Chris had ever laid eyes on ...

... Dan was dreaming, eyes closed, throwing rocks straight up in the sky, rocks that weren't coming down any time soon. Dan Johnson could throw rocks to the stars. Sometimes, Dan threw rocks into space and lassoed them back to Earth with his lasso.

How does he do that? wondered Chris, watching Dan perform magic with rocks of all sizes, boulders even. *Dan Johnson just threw a boulder over the moon! I sure hope it doesn't crash near my mom's house. He can do anything, that Dan Johnson. Not only is he the most beautiful boy alive, he's also the most powerful. I think I'll go now ...*

Chris stepped on a stick that cracked. Dan Johnson panicked at the sound and took off on the Lemon Peeler, apparently chasing after that boulder falling on the other side of the moon ...

DREAMVILLE NIGHTMARE: SUMMER OF THE LOCUSTS CLEARS TOWN

All the families of the dreamy hamlet vacated the dreamy hamlet that one fateful summer: the Johnsons, the Browns, those McPhersons, the Snowmen, the Wus, the Jius, the Colemans, the Yeagers, the Renterias, the Valtrons, the Minnefields, the Stricklands, the Striesands, the Du'Hards, the Carters, the Joneses, the Ali Gators, the Abduls, the Brave Horses, the Kramers, the Boyds, the Bryants, the Jeffersons, the Bushes, the Clintons, the Christians, the Millstones, the Kipners, the Kickos, the Selladitos, the McDuncans, the Overstreets, the Shockmes, even Mormon Simmons and his normally optimistic family! Even the usually steadfast derVanderkerplunkendorphs, the town's one Danish family with that kinda fishy talking kid. They were all leaving town!

... the night before the big town move, one boy dreamed of a way to stay at home by himself all summer ... the boy simply used his same old bag of tricks from school in a more dreamy fashion ... *every bigger dream is merely the inflation of a balloon already filled with ideas waiting for zephyrs.*

... the morning of the big town move, another boy dreamed of a way to stay at home by himself all summer ... the boy simply said to his family: "I'm staying here." *The Jedi Mind Trick really works ... if you're in the loop.*

COOL AND DREAMY MUSIC BUTTON: *"The Belle of St. Mark" by Sheila E.*

Dan Johnson and Chris Brown played the summer away, frolicking over the sunny hills of their dreamy ghost of a town. The locusts never came, but the rest of the town held off returning until the official Locust Warning ended around Labor Day.

The local grocers, the Astor brothers, hung around and supplied the boys with all their favorite foods. It was easy work for the Astors because the boys liked the exact same foods. The Astors even suggested the boys meet and become friends for the summer, but neither boy seemed to take the advice to heart.

Thus ... Dan Johnson and Chris Brown played the summer away, frolicking over the sunny hills of their dreamy ghost of a town, but never making eye contact. Dan threw his rocks at his telephone poles, and rode the Lemon Peeler like a cowboy over the tops of the trees in the forest (or woods), while Chris worked his game, danced by the river and doodled ... *(what, Dan did not know. For now, he could only guess and use his imagination).*

"Please take the ticket," said Jimmy or Bob Astor, serving as the town's theater guy during the abandonment.

Chris went inside the town movie house and saw his favorite movies all summer long. Guess who was on the polar opposite side of the theater in the dark, enjoying the same movies? Guess who loved the exact same kinds of movies? Guess who loved the exact same kinds of everything?

The boys were barely aware of the other's presence in the movie house, let alone their similar likes and dislikes. But one night, the Astor brothers figured it out for themselves while watching from the projector booth. They were no dumb Astors, no sir. Those two brothers were two very smart Astors.

"Two golden boys so in sync, they can't even see it," said Bob or Jimmy Astor, looking down on the boys enjoying a movie called *Tidal Wave.*

"Should we give them the gift?" asked Jimmy or Bob Astor.

"We can only do like everybody else before, since and after," said Bob or Jimmy Astor. "Wish them well and bless their dreams."

"I'll go get the ice cream," said Jimmy or Bob Astor.

On one side of the movie house, Bob or Jimmy Astor gave one of the boys a bowl of ice cream, which the brothers hoped to someday sell to the world.

On the other side of the movie house, Jimmy or Bob Astor gave the other boy a bowl of ice cream, which the brothers hoped to someday sell to the world.

"It's a gift," said both brothers to both boys. "Good on a hot Independence Day like today."

The boys thanked the Astor brothers and became awash in *Tidal Wave*.

Later that night ...

The boys dreamed wild, swirling dreams in their separate beds, tossing and turning like an amusement park ride, their faces tossing and turning with joy and glee at every swift and unexpected turn of the bed. That's what it was! The beds were flying! For a while anyway. Once they realized it was daylight, or close to it, each boy got up and went about his daily business ...

Chris Brown felt better than ever that morning. Maybe it was the ice cream. Maybe it was having the town to himself. He played James Brown's "I Got You (I Feel Good)" in his headspace. Chris Brown felt so good, he decided to climb a telephone pole. A really, really tall one. So tall, Chris Brown found himself up in the clouds, far above the cool and dreamy little hamlet next to bigger, more bustling hamlet. Chris loved being so high in the air. He even tried to dance, but it was kinda shaky up there. Instead, he settled for sitting on the little ledge near the top of the pole in the sky and playing his game, Mattel Electronics Football, long into a cool and dreamy morning.

... Elsewhere in Dreamville, Dan Johnson was rockin' out!

COOL AND DREAMY MUSIC BUTTON: *"Let's Get Rocked" by Def Leopard.*

Dan Johnson was flying on the Lemon Peeler, feeling better than ever. The wheels on his bike weren't even touching the road. His hands weren't manning the handlebar. His bike was riding itself! Dreamville was his for the summer! Dan Johnson was in the zone!

Now I gotta screammmmmmmmmmmm!

Dan stood on his bike seat and hoisted his backpack 'round to the front.

I get I get I get I get rocked!

Dan took out a handful of rocks.

I get I get I get I get rocked!

Dan gunned down a bunch of black lawn jockeys with his rocks.

I get I get I get I get rocked!

Dan gunned down a whole bunch of mailboxes on fancy streets with his rocks.

I get I get I get I get rocked!

Dan laughed his ass off at how powerful and amazing he was.

I get I get I get I get rocked!

Dan decided to *rock 'n' roam* mailboxes and statuettes all over Dreamville.

I get I get I get I get rocked!

Dan decided to *rock 'n' roam* down his favorite road, Telephone Pole Lane.

I get I get I get I get rocked!

Dan fired a really gigantic rock toward the creepy mailbox of creepy Old Man Milton.

I get I get I get I get rocked!

Dan didn't like Old Man Milton just like everyone else in Dreamville.

I get I get I get I get rocked!

Old Man Milton was the town Old Man No One Understood.

I get I get I get I get rocked!

Old Man Milton wasn't scared of no locusts.

I get I get I get I get rocked!

Old Man Milton didn't even vacate town when the river filled with blood.

I get I get I get I get rocked!

Old Man Milton sat on his porch, year in and year out, during hailstorms.

I get I get I get I get rocked!

Old Man Milton didn't budge during the invasion of the tadpoles.

I get I get I get I get rocked!

Old Man Milton sat on his porch day and night ... count on it.

I get I get I get I get rocked!

... Old Man Milton sensed a comet of a rock heading straight toward his ...

I get I get I get—

... From the telephone pole in the sky over Dreamville, Chris Brown heard a very short yelp, as if someone was trying to swallow the world they just burped. That was followed by dead silence, followed by the loudest scream humanity has ever heard.

... Unshaken on his pole in the sky, Chris Brown shrugged and played on. He had an important touchdown to score in his game. It was the next to the last quarter. He wanted to score again and again. He zoned in, until words floated up through the clouds, prompting Chris to listen:

"Try it again, cocky kid!" yelled Old Man Milton. "You might end up doing me in, but if you think you're that good, bring it on."

"Shouldn't we call the Astor brothers?" asked a worried Dan. "I think I just terminated half of your—"

"I know what you're trying to do!" yelled Old Man Milton. "Otherwise, you wouldn't be acting out. Speak up!"

"Acting out?" asked a confused Dan.

"Hurling things toward my head, trying to be the one who finally takes care of Old Man Milton," said Old Man Milton. "Speak up!"

"Sir, maybe there's a way to put it all back together, or patch it up," said a scared Dan.

"Show me what you've got!" demanded Old Man Milton, getting kinda agitated. "Throw it at me! Throw the rock!"

"Again?" asked a shaking and worried Dan, wondering whatever happened to that last kid who kinda agitated Old Man Milton.

"Throw it right this time!" yelled Old Man Milton. "Your right, my left. I can live without the left ... your left, I mean. Speak up!"

"Sir, are you very sure?" asked a very worried Dan.

From above, Chris peeked beneath the clouds to the ground below. Old Man Milton was dragging Dan Johnson by the scruff of the neck from one side of Telephone Pole Lane to the other, closer to Chris Brown and his pole. Next, Old Man Milton planted Dan a good distance from the pole. Then Old Man Milton himself stood next to the pole—on top of which sat Chris.

"Sir, Old Man Milton, sir!" said a still worried Dan.

"Throw it! If you've got the stuff, do it now, cocky kid!" yelled Old Man Milton, who was standing directly beneath Chris Brown in the sky.

"What do you want me to hit?" pleaded Dan.

"Anything but dead air, that's the deal, kid!" yelled Old Man Milton.

Meaning: a) Hit the telephone pole, or, b) Hit Old Man Milton's face, adjacent to the pole.

"Old Man Milton, sir, my parents—they'll kill me," said a somewhat anxious Dan.

"If you don't throw the rock, you'll kill yourself. I can guarantee it, cocky kid!" yelled Old Man Milton, giving his solemn promise. "Speak up!"

"Here goes, sir!" yelled Dan. "Watch your eyeballs! The one on my right and your left anyway."

Dan threw the rock in his hand, unable to remember if his eyes were open or closed or squinting or half-covered or hidden under his cool brown jacket. Dan just surrendered and fired the rock, not knowing what was going to happen next.

Next ... Dan hit ... the pole, made a serious dent the size of the rock in the wood. Some of the fibers blew like stardust past Old Man Milton's eyes, which were directly adjacent to the pole. Dan checked his own heart, then threw his arms straight in the air toward his gods. He kept his arms there while moving toward Old Man Milton, who was still standing near the pole.

"Are you all right, sir?" asked Dan.

"Now that you've fixed my hearing I am," said a more cheerful Old Man Milton.

"How'd I do that?" asked Dan with a mild laugh.

"Just needed the right *pop!*" said Old Man Milton. He stuck a finger in his ear and began gyrating the finger as if to finish the job. "Drove me mad!"

"Is that why you never talk to people?" asked Dan. "Because you're mad?"

"Not on your life," said Old Man Milton. "I never talk to people because I told this town years ago: until somebody can unclog my hearing, I can rarely hear a blessed thing, so don't waste your blessed time and energy talking to me."

"Amazing," said Dan, lost in his own thoughts.

"Don't ever forget you are," said Old Man Milton, finally done with the personal irrigation. "Now I can sit inside my house and listen to the radio. Excuse me, I'm gonna see if Bing has a new record."

Dan exhaled, fell against the telephone pole and laughed. Then he heard a noise in the woods just behind him. Being the cagey panther he was, Dan swung around and caught the back of Chris Brown trying to sneak into the brush.

"Brownster!" said Dan. "You can't tell anybody what just happened."

Chris stopped in his tracks, barely suppressing his grin, and said: "That you threw a rock at a pole an inch away from Old Man Milton's face. And hit *the pole?*"

"Yes, that's exactly what you can't tell people," said Dan. "Deal?"

"Deal," said Chris, wanting to giggle. "Why'd you do it?"

"I thought Old Man Milton knew what I knew," shrugged Dan.

"That you never miss?" asked Chris.

"Yes, exactly," said Dan. "I thought the old man wanted to prove I could hit the pole instead of his face. That it was an accident that I missed his mailbox and the rock crashed into his ... I think my bike hit a pebble or something. I figured Old Man Milton knew I never miss, maybe from—he does live on Telephone Pole Lane."

"*That's* why you hit the pole?" asked Chris. "It wasn't because you decided not to put his other eye out?"

"Other eye out?" laughed Dan. "I didn't put either eye out. Unfortunately, can't say the same for the salt-and-peppershaker on his porch. I offered to buy a new one at the Astors' store."

"So Old Man Milton's eyes are fine?" asked Chris.

"Blind as he was when he woke up this morning," said Dan.

"Wow," said Chris, lost in his own thoughts. "The things you know and don't know before the day ever gets started."

"Like how does Chris Brown know that Dan Johnson doesn't miss with his rocks?" asked Dan. "With *my* rocks. *His* rocks. With rocks?"

Chris paused and wondered if he should turn all the way around and face Dan. Dan paused and wondered if he should turn halfway around and face Chris.

The only reason they knew they were both in the vicinity of the telephone pole was because each one could feel the presence of the other.

"You've been hanging around all summer," said Dan.

"I didn't want to bother you," said Chris, sorta sheepish.

"You actually look up from the game sometimes!" said Dan, astonished.

"What you do looks like a lotta fun," said Chris.

"At *me*, throwing rocks!" said Dan, still astonished.

"Kinda unbelievable but believable," said Chris.

"I would have never guessed," said both Dan and Chris.

"I got a whole 'nother bag down by the river," said Dan, meaning his rocks. "Wanna hop on the back of my bike and go for a ride?"

Chris didn't have to say yes with words. He also didn't have to look at Dan Johnson to hop on the back of the Lemon Peeler and enjoy the ride. Chris and Dan didn't look at each other much during those early days. They just enjoyed being around one another, feeling a familiar feeling they recognized from being the only two boys in town all summer long. Now Dan Johnson and Chris Brown had each other, and their summer had just begun.

Cool and Dreamy Music Button: *"Summer of Love" by the B-52's.*

Dan Johnson and Chris Brown were in love ...

... with summertime and summertime shorts, tanks and t-shirts.

... with riding the Lemon Peeler all around the hills of Dreamville.

... with throwing rocks at every telephone pole in the land.

... with sleeping in the summer sun down by the river.

... with sleeping under the stars at night in Dan's backyard.

... with playing Mattel Electronics Football all summer long.

... with the idea of a shorter name for Mattel Electronics Football.

... with not caring who won when they played THE GAME.

... with playing the game with all their heart.

Dan Johnson and Chris Brown flew in and out of the clouds on the Lemon Peeler ...

... using Dreamville gorge as a ramp to jump in and out of the sky.

... riding atop the telephone wires hanging between the telephone poles.

... slalom racing through the tall trees on Mt. Summit.

... riding up and down the sides of the telephones poles.

Dan Johnson and Chris Brown listened to a lot of music ...

... while watching *The Gong Show* and *The Three Stooges* on TV.

... playing the game in the trees, or down by the river.

... lying in the bleachers at the football stadium, napping in the sun.

... buying ice cream at the Astors' store.

... making skyscraper-high stacks of pancakes for breakfast.

... setting fire to the grill in the Brownster's backyard.

Dan Johnson and Chris Brown talked a lot sometimes, but other times rarely talked at all, as if just happy being together, as if that's just the way life was supposed to be. Sometimes they looked at each other. Other times they didn't. Or didn't remember if they did. Dan relied on senses other than his eyes as his main guide in the world. Chris didn't trust his eyes, which is why he sometimes wore glasses that looked like geeky goggles.

"They're not geeky goggles to me," said Dan one day. *Mild laugh.* They were down by the river, hanging out on two tires suspended from a tree over the water. Dan was swinging from his hands, grunting like a monkey, getting off on making Chris giggle.

"They *feel* like goggles," said Chris, hanging by his underarms.

"Then they're perfect for when you're riding on the back of my bike!" said Dan, belly-flopping into the river.

"*And* the front!" said Chris, belly-flopping into the river after Dan.

Such was Chris and Dan's cool and dreamy summer of the locusts that never came. The boys never said much about *what* they were, *who* they were or *why* they were ... they just ... were ... Chris and Dan, and that was all right with Chris and Dan. When they were together, they felt as good as the ice cream the Astor brothers sold at the store: *cool and dreamy, feels just right.*

"When do I get to kiss the guy?" asked Dan @ Bear's creation station. "I know these guys aren't making us Bearcat Boyz like something out of the last millennium, *when boys had no balls about their balls.* Hey, Hip ... they're not going to cut off me and the Brownster's balls, are they? ... Comet? Maybe I'm sampling the wrong demographic on that question. Sorry, guys. I'm definitely not letting Yeager and Coleman neuter me or the Brownster ... no way ... *hmmm,* what to type ... how about ..."

UNIVERSAL MEMO: Bearcat Boyz have balls and dicks—whatever names you wanna give them—and all the other body parts male men have, even tails. Call 'em what you want, we've got them and we think about them *All The Time.* We also like using them, one way or another, and nothing you can say is gonna stop us now. Our hunch is ... sex is what makes us humans. We're just being as human as humanly possible. We're always open to better ways of dreaming about our hands, our minds, our tongues, our dicks, our balls, our asses, our love, but keep your garbage to yourselves if you plan on trashing the deepest dreams of our souls.

Bearcat Boyz don't lie about having balls. This much is true.

WE LOVE OUR BODIES, OUR MINDS, OUR SOULS AND OUR SEXUAL IMPULSES. IF WE CAN'T TALK ABOUT IT, WE CAN ALWAYS ACT IT OUT FOR YOU.

"Visual aids anyone?" said Dan @ Bear's creation station. "I'm definitely kissing the Brownster someday ... big time ... somehow ... someway ... He's *gotta* wanna kiss me back, right? And we're gonna do whatever we want in the big magic skybox in the sky, right? ... I mean, the way my bud Chris looks at me, with those *big brown eyes* ... thinks I can't see them behind those crazy goggles. God, I love those crazy goggles ... God, I love ... God I ... Chris ... what a cool guy ... a cool buddy ... suddenly the Dan Man is all wet, soaking wet ... dripping ... *as in rain, Bearcat People ... it's pouring rain in Dreamville!*"

... Labor Day weekend was soaking wet in Dreamville. On top of that, the other residents trickled in, even though the locust warning wasn't officially over until Tuesday.

"This bites," said Dan, leaning against his legendary pole on Telephone Pole Lane.

"What bites?" asked Chris, riding the Lemon Peeler in circles around Dan and the pole, "the rain or the return of everybody else?"

"Exactly," said a downtrodden Dan. It was raining, but both boys were in their summer shorts with no shirt.

"Weatherman claims the sun'll come out for the opening day of school," said Chris, lifting his goggles to his forehead and tasting the rainwater on his upper lip.

"You had to go and mention school," said Dan, throwing a rock straight over his head toward the top of the pole.

"You're not looking forward to football season?" asked Chris, riding in circles, listening to the thunder.

"*Nah*," said Dan, eyes following the trajectory of the rock as it rounded the top of the pole and came shooting straight down.

"Tell me about it," said Chris, pulling a football out of the backpack hanging from Dan's handlebars.

"Hard to explain. Should be as fun as this," said Dan, casually catching the falling rock in his hand. "As cool as hanging out with you."

"Dream of it." Chris flipped the football to Dan. To free his hands, Dan tossed the rock to Chris. Each man caught the other man's rock in perfect sync.

"I *can't* dream of it," said Dan, throwing the football skyward in a fit of anger. "I don't know if I wanna stick around this damned place!"

Something within told Chris: *go get that anger!*

"In that case," said Chris, throwing the rock skyward after the football, "try sticking around this *blessed* place."

Dan eyed him curiously, then both boys looked skyward, mindful of gravity and the ascending rocks. The football sailed over the telephone pole from one side. The rock sailed over the same pole from the other side. They met at the apex at the exact same moment, which was also the exact same moment lightning struck the apex of the pole. Momentarily, the boys were blinded by a flash of light that wiped Dreamville off and on the map, then off and on again.

Not knowing what was next, Dan tackled Chris to the ground, away from the pole, which was swaying and coming out of the earth. The tackle was so violent, Chris skinned his knees and elbows, even his lip.

"Sorry, didn't mean to hurt you," said a panicked Dan.

"*Really?*" said a dazed and dazzled Chris, amazed at his cuts, which looked like real football cuts! And came from a tackle by Dan Johnson!

"Look out!" said Dan in a hush, scooting backward on his ass, dragging Chris by the belt loop. The telephone pole looked ready to fall right on top of the boys, the very top still sparking and exploding.

Then suddenly it came to a stop, tilted but stable.

"Let's get out of here," said Dan, rushing to the Lemon Peeler.

"What about the football?" asked Chris.

"Grab it quick," said Dan. Chris jumped to his feet, searching but not finding the ball. Dan jumped off the Lemon Peeler and did the same. The lightning and thunder started up again. Chris and Dan circled the pole, noses to the ground, searching then finding *it* at the same time. *It* was a tiny football, slightly bigger than a man's thumb. *It* looked more like a smooth and shiny rock, perfectly shaped and polished with a slight greenish tint.

Dan picked up the rock, or football, or rock-shaped football or football-shaped— "We'll just call it THE GREEN ROCK," said Dan, clearing that up rather decisively.

"Where did THE GREEN ROCK come from?" asked a bewildered Chris.

"You're the school reporter," said Dan. "Tell *me* about it."

"We still haven't found our football," said Chris, fidgeting in the rain. "Or the other rock, the *rock* rock."

"Brownster ... we're looking at 'em ... both!" said Dan, holding up the perfectly shaped *green* football *rock*. For a brief moment, an emerald ray of light flickered from the rock and shot out like lightning into the deepest reaches of the universe. Then ... *thunder* ... louder than before. "Right," said Dan, answering the question on both their minds: *now can we get outta here?*

Dan hopped on the Lemon Peeler, Chris followed. The boys sped away, the green rock in tow. Had they chosen to look behind them, they might have seen an ominous dark cloud at the top of the hill on Telephone Pole Lane. Had they looked carefully, they might have imagined the ominous dark cloud to be an ominous dark guy with a cloudy and ominous curiosity for the flickering emerald light he just saw shooting into the sky ...

MEANWHILE, BACK AT THE JAW ...
COOL AND DREAMY MUSIC BUTTON: *"Close My Eyes" by Jordan Knight.*

"Who is this ominous evil dude?" asked Dan @ Bear's creation station. "Hip ... Comet ... why can't I find anything in this pissant ditty about me kissing my buddy someday? And what's with the green rock? Hip, help me out. *Oh, no ... incoming! ... everybody, as you were! ...*"

"Love this song by Jordan Knight," said Bear, returning to his creation station after a cool and dreamy morning nap. "QB, did you leave the music on in the home office before we went upstairs?"

"Negative," said Walter, going for the couch under the big window after a cool and dreamy morning nap ... *still coming down from a life in football.*

"Another tune about the power of dreaming," said Bear.

"What do these musicians know about love the rest of us don't?" yawned Walter, settling in, facing the couch.

"How to keep their dreams alive through song." Bear leaped from the desk and jumped on his man's sore hip. "Buddy, get your blond ass up!"

"Get off me, fool!" said Walter.

"*Hello?*" said Bear, dragging his buddy to his feet. "The transport is firing up on the launch pad. Time to *do dis* one last TIME. The world won't start spinning again until they find out about your retirement and whether or not Yeager and Coleman are part of an HIV/AIDS sex ring!"

"Oh, shit, forgot," said Walter. "See, my mind's already slipping and I'm not even 40 yet."

"Let's grab the Bearcat Boyz so we can work on the movie while in transit," said Bear.

"Throw those suckers in the box and let's jet," said Walter. "We don't wanna miss the sunset."

"Which ones?" giggled Bear.

"Whatever Bear wants," said Walter.

ALL RIGHT, BEARCAT PEOPLE ... NOW ENTERING THE CORE OF THE MODERN WORLD ... POSSIBLE TURBULENCE AHEAD ...

"Hear, hear," said the production assistant from the doorway leading to the makeshift studio. He was the same young man who had escorted Walter and Bear to this impromptu green room. "Here's to making history on worldwide TV tonight. By the way, Eagan is *thrilled* you picked him over *blankety blank, blank, blank,* and all the rest. Although he did seem quite amazed you chose him, especially with all your given history, dating back to the Sugar Bowl."

"We forgave the Creole Camille and Del Kicko," said Walter.

"Not to mention Roxanne Valtron, aka Roseanne/Joe Bruin, and Candi Mandonato, the feminist faculty advisor," said Bear.

"Why not him?" shrugged Walter to Bear.

"Why not who?" asked Bear, trying to be sly.

"*Riiiiiight,*" laughed Walter, as if *he* would ever lose the Bet. (*First person ever to say that Evil Announcer Guy's name has to do something really heinous.*)

"It's my favorite sex freaks!" said Evil Announcer Guy, entering the green room. "This is gonna make me—*whoa! talk about worldwide huge!*—but remember, no attacking me ... *or anything about that Yeager-meister party back in the day* ... and we're on a 10-second delay, just in case you two freaks get too freaky about this twisted sex ring of yours. Got it?"

"We get you loud and clear—sir," said Bear, almost losing the Bet. Walter laughed. Evil Announcer Guy eyed them curiously. The crew whisked them onto the set, not letting them alone again until they were seated in three chairs behind the news desk.

"I got tons of questions, so keep your answers short," said Evil Announcer Guy. "Unless you're really spilling some *hot* details. Got it?"

"Remember," said Walter, holding up his speech. "To start and end with."

Evil Announcer Guy froze with an unwelcomed déjà vu in his eyes. Apparently, he had been too caught up in the hype of the moment to realize Yeager and Coleman were doing this under the exact same rules as their "coming out" announcement four years ago.

The initial broadcast was to be live, unedited and uninterrupted. Walter would be allowed to read a prepared statement twice, once at the beginning, once at the end.

"And rolling in ..." said a woman's deep voice from the blur beyond the white lights. Before Walter and Bear knew it, they were staring at another light, a red one, glaring at them from a gigantic camera that made them breathe deeply.

"Welcome to this big night," said Evil Announcer Guy. "You all know—"

Walter cleared his throat to *interrupt the intro,* then held up his speech.

Evil Announcer Guy pouted, then said into the camera: "Ladies and gentlemen, Walter Yeager of the Chicago Zephyrs."

Walt loves justice for all.

"Winners of this year's Super Bowl," added Evil Announcer Guy.

Walter closed his eyes. When he *felt* quiet, he opened them, cleared his throat and eyed the camera like a straight shootin' son of a gun.

COOL AND DREAMY MUSIC BUTTON: *"Live to Tell" by Madonna.*

"I am in love with this man ... Bear Coleman."

"And I'm in love with this man ... Walter Yeager."

Yeager and Coleman shared a smile, peaceful, calm, steeped in utter faith in their love and their union.

That's the way the gods drew it up. We're supposed to be buds. We can do this. Together, we can do anything. This much is forever True Gold.

They broke eye contact and turned to the world in the name of taking care of business, and Walter read their pissant li'l ditty that Bear liked to call:

THE BEARCAT BOYZ LIVE TO TELL

"I am retiring from the NFL as an active player."

We wanted three Super Bowls. We got three Super Bowls.

"As far as I can see, I have reached my potential as an athlete, a football player, and a teammate to the warriors of my time."

The mind is willing most of the time, but the flesh is weak.

"Out of respect for them, out of love for them and the game, I bow out."

And the flesh is only going to get weaker.

"Has anyone in this world contracted HIV because of the direct actions of myself or my partner, Bear Coleman? To our most verifiable knowledge ... *no.*"

Your status is yours to know, like your blood type, your hair color, your eye color, the sound of your beating heart, the songs your soul sings in the calm of night, your favorite food, your favorite sweater, your favorite color ... what resonates in your soul ... whatever resonates in your soul ... but only you can choose what to know about your soul and what makes your soul resonate ... whatever resonates in your soul.

Whatever Walt wants.

"Should our private lives be up for discussion, even on the subject of HIV in sports, or men who love men in sports? We answer by saying this ..."

A deep breath is okay, buddy.

"If I, Walter Yeager, have ever contracted any sexually transmitted disease, the person from which I contracted that STD identifies himself or herself as straight. What people say and do, and what people call those actions can be on polar opposite sides of the universe."

This much is true. Keep going.

"But is this about labels and blame? Not for me or Bear. I intend to live my life just as I have before, with the highest amount of love and integrity for myself, my family, my buddy, and by extension, the world around me."

I've loved your eyes from the moment I first saw them.

"Is this about labels and blame for the rest of the world? I hope not. I hope this is about open dialogue. I hope this is about getting to the truths of humanity without judgments. We are all at risk for all kinds of things that have the ability to affect our lives in positive and negative ways."

Comets come in all shapes and sizes and even have options.

"I ask you: what should the media—the KEEPERS OF THE IMAGES so prevalent in our minds—focus on tonight: the 2000 or so players in the NFL who may or may not have been exposed to HIV while playing football? Or the tens of thousands of children in this country and the world over, whose bellies are empty tonight and tomorrow night and the night after that? While, in all likelihood, no NFL player will go hungry tonight, unless by choice."

Children's souls are howling and dying right now.

"Should the media focus on the 2000 NFL players who might now consider the existence of HIV in their world like never before, possibly getting HIV tests? Or the tens of thousands of American families who will wake up tomorrow without healthcare because we, the USA, would rather focus on professional athletes, all of whom will have healthcare the rest of their lives?"

Little boys' souls are howling and dying right now.

"We all choose what we focus our collective energy on, and this much is true: For the foreseeable future, my energy will be focused on the NFL players and all our concerns with HIV. I will make myself available to my fellow warriors for private and personal discussions, as always. No doubt many within the NFL family will focus their energies on HIV in the NFL as well. But do *you* have to? Do the IMAGE KEEPERS? Do *you,* the millions of people watching this tonight, need to focus your attention on what may or may not be of concern to 2000 athletes, and by extension, their families?"

Is your soul howling and dying right now?

"If you want to *help* somebody, to *empathize* with somebody, to *focus energy* on somebody, *let it be* ... your children, your family, your parents, your friends, your special someone, your neighbors, your community, your schools, hospitals, homeless shelters, runaway shelters, spousal abuse shelters, local parks, senior citizen homes, animal rescue shelters, foster care programs, local clubs. Not to mention the millions of people the world over who *do* know they have AIDS this very moment. I promise you, this much is true: Reach out to your world ... you will find someone who needs your energy in the form of love, and they need that love a lot more than anyone you'll see on television talking about Walter Yeager or Bear Coleman, no matter which side of the microphone they are on."

My soul is howling and dying right now.

"All the people you spend your energy on need positive energy in their lives. They need love, support, to know someone cares about them more than well-paid pro athletes who may or may not have come in contact with a virus that may or may not be in my body. I have a very strong hunch that the recipients of your positive energy will be extremely grateful. They may even bless you in return. Good night and good blessings. Thanks for reaching out."

My soul feels lighter and freer now. The power of True Gold.

COOL AND DREAMY MUSIC BUTTON: *Silence ...*

Walter Yeager and Bear Coleman sat there, waiting for someone to say: *Cut!*

"We're done," whispered Bear to the crew. The red light faded, but not the bright white lights. Evil Announcer Guy and the crew were motionless, waiting for the boys to duck out of some trapdoor like the cowboys they were.

"Stand by for the trapdoor," said Walter, looking around the makeshift studio, not sounding too confident about the trapdoor.

"If I were filming this," said Bear under his breath, "I'd say, *Cut to a shot of the eight million people surrounding the joint.*"

Walter's retirement announcement was already scheduled to take place at his

old stomping grounds, West Winnetka Junior High. Unable to save the school itself
from closure, Yeager was sponsoring an effort to have the property converted into
the new site for the West Winnetka Warriors United Football Club (Boys 10-18).

"I thought doing this gig here would help the cause against these Complex
people," whispered Walter in the makeshift studio in the school cafeteria.

"It did until our exes unleashed their poison," whispered Bear, trying to
avoid the glare of Evil Announcer Guy.

"*Shh* ... let's figure out a way to get to Roberto and the transport." Walter
stood and blurred from the set, Bear followed ... through the cafeteria doors.

DARK AND NIGHTMARISH MUSIC BUTTON: *"Theme from Halloween."*

"This is the opposite of a funhouse," said Bear, holding his man's hand
through a blurry maze of dark hallways around the school.

"Feel me feeling our way through, just like on the field," said Walter.

"I'll go anywhere with you," said Bear. "*Ouch* ... my head hit something."

"You still love me," said Walter. "I fucked up your life one more time and
you still love me."

"Forget about that now," said Bear.

"Hard to ... faster ... this way ... hear them rumbling above?" asked Walter.

"You never meant to hurt me," said Bear.

"I never do, do I?" said Walt.

"Nope," said Marcus.

"Wait ... wrong way ... turn here instead," said Walter.

"Better, I can see a little more ... cool," said Bear.

"Watch out!" said Walter, ducking for both of them. "Vultures."

"When are they gonna tear down or clean up this place?" asked Bear.

"When are you gonna stop treating me like I'm some sort of God, Bear
Coleman?" asked Walter, alone with his man in the dark and quiet gymnasium.

"What do you mean?" asked Bear.

"Dammit, Bear, look at us!" shouted Walter.

Trapped ... they had just tried to get to the parking lot and couldn't because
eight million people outside wanted @ them. The grounds were surrounded by
chaos and disorder. Some wanted to kill the boys. Some wanted to pick them
apart and study their blood and vital organs. Some wanted to worship them.
Some just wanted any piece they could get.

"Trapped in a junior high cafeteria," said Bear.

"*It's the gym, Bear!*" said Walter. "It's the damned gym. Would you look at
the damned gym?"

"I don't want to," said Bear.

"Bear, you ... Bear, come on now," said Walter.

The boys had a date with the Oscars tonight ... the statuettes ... Road of Life—the four-hour theatrical version—had been nominated for various awards. Tonight was to be the biggest night of Bear's career.

"But here we are," said Walter, "in Chicago for Walter and his football business and sex-life business and any business we can think of for Walter Freakin' Yeager, hero made of his own goddamned ice cream."

"That was my idea, practically," said Bear, "the God-blessed ice cream."

"Exactly my point!" Walter had a fit of spurts before punching his fist through a door and busting a pane of glass. "Get away from my hand ... I know that's your first instinct, to protect me, but stop! Stop, Bear, stop!"

"Why now?" asked a stunned Bear, resisting the urge to reach for his husband's bleeding knuckles.

"It's always Walter's world," said Walter, wrapping his hand with his suit jacket. "Just like it was in New York, back in '85, 15 years ago, hell, maybe even to this very day. I came storming into your hotel, all pissed and selfish, calling it quits with football on the night of your biggest game of all time, Indiana vs. UCLA in the NIT finals. I ruined your last basketball game as a cheerleader!"

Bear couldn't look at Walter. Bear could only listen.

"Do I need to go on about how many times I've screwed up your life?" asked Walter, speaking louder due to a rumbling above the gym. "Leaving your job at KSEA to chase a tryout with me all over Canada and back? Then guess what? *Back* to Canada!"

"I wrote during that time," said Bear, looking toward the rafters that were shaking.

"Lesbian chicks screwing around with Secret Service chicks?" asked Walter. "You could've been doing better, but you were too busy taking care of my needs. In some ways, Reggie was right ..."

"You needn't hold back on my account," said Bear. "The field nigga made his feelings known years ago."

"Why don't you ever say a damned thing about it?" asked Walter. "Or anything about the crap I put you through?"

"Maybe I don't see it as crap," said Bear, still unable to look at Walter but clearly able to hear the rumblings against the gyms' doors and all around them.

"Bear, look at me," said Walter. Outside in the night, lights flashed and swirled. "You've slept alone countless nights while I was out being *Walter Yeager, Golden Boy.* You took care of me when I was sick and a dickhead about it. You put up with all my madness and my craziness and all the shit loving me brings to a guy like you. For Christ's sake, Bear, you took a blow to the head and almost died!"

"You took a blow by Doak Minnefield," said Bear. "And every Sunday. What's the big deal, Walt, can we stop this?"

"You know what it is, Bear—sometimes I don't even wanna call you Bear anymore—you know exactly what it is, Marcus," said Walter.

"Do we have to deal now, Walt?" asked Bear.

"It's the question *you* wanna know, and *I* wanna know and *our friends* wanna know, and *my* family and *your* family and the entire world wants to know," said Walter.

The gym rumbled as if being shaken gently in somebody's fist. Lights flashed off and on, making visibility on and off. The boys were too caught up in conflict to care. They stood near one another without making eye contact, rambling on in their own and mutual frequencies.

"What's the question *you* wanna know, and *I* wanna know and *our friends* wanna know, and *my* family and *your* family and the entire world wants to know?" asked Bear.

"Am I retarded for loving you the way I do?" asked one.

"Am I fuckin' crazy for loving you the way I do?" asked one.

"Am I fucked up in the head for sticking by my man, tonight and every night?" asked one.

"Am I nuts for living my life this way, against everything I was told to believe in?" asked one.

"How did I get so lucky, a stupid-ass retard like me?" asked one.

"How in the world did a crazy-ass freak like me get to be with a buddy who's so perfect like him?" asked one.

Why is my soul still howling and dying inside right now?

The rumbling stopped. The lights beyond the gym swirled calmer and slower. Bear moved to a window. At the gates of the junior high, a group of African American protesters were carrying signs denouncing Coleman and Yeager, especially in light of the implications of the Oscar-nominated *Road of Life,* a movie claiming to shatter 99.99% of what America thought it knew about race and race relations in America.

"The race card sure was a good distraction for us while we were being openly sexual, eh?" said Bear. "Thank God for *Road of Life,* not to mention the little white boy looking for a nigger's pole to play with."

"You and I have yet to discuss if you think that little boy's theories and Oscar's dreams in *Road of Life* are true," said Walter.

ROAD OF LIFE ... a story about a mentally-challenged trash collector named Oscar, whose road in life leads him to believe that some black and white people in America are genetically bonded as soul mates due to years of magnetic polar energy powering the Earth, before, during and after the existence of the American Institution of Slavery.

"It's also not too far off from what the Dane was saying," said Walter.

"I stand by Oscar's *Road* as art," said Bear. "I stand by art as a representation of our dreams. I stand by dreams as the power of our souls."

"Nice you can still recite the official universal memo, but what about Bear Coleman, who gets me so pissed, this isn't the first time I've put my fist through a freakin' window in his honor?" asked Walter.

"Anything is possible, even Oscar's dreams. Either way, he saved us from a lot of hell, eh, Larry?" said Bear, looking out of the window, thinking of the great collaborator. Just then, they heard the sound of a hole being sawed in the rafters.

"At least he can still say our names," said a man's voice from the hole. "I guess that means there's hope, eh, Trix?"

"Don't call me Trix!" said a woman's voice from above.

Bear said, "What the—"

"Hail Larry?" asked Walter, craning upwards.

"We heard some ex-friends of ours needed their freakin' asses saved!" yelled Hail Larry's Wife from the hole.

"Yet again!" yelled Hail Larry from the hole.

"What kind of transport are we talking about?" asked a dubious Bear.

"Climb your fat asses up here and see for yourselves!" yelled Hail Larry.

Walter and Bear eyed one another, shrugged and made the climb up the bleachers and through the hole in the gym roof.

COOL AND DREAMY MUSIC BUTTON: *Something very beatnik-like!*

"Is that the B-52's?" whispered Walter, looking very uncomfortable, sitting on a very beatnik-like couch ... *long, round and silver. Silver, white and gray everywhere.*

"Somehow it fits," whispered Bear, looking very uncomfortable, sitting next to Walter on the very beatnik-like couch. "So this is their ... *transport.*"

"Can't be choosy," whispered Walter. "Apparently, neither can they."

"Must have bought it on sale," whispered Bear.

"Guys, need anything?" asked Hail Larry's Wife, turning from the console where she was hovering over Hail Larry, who was doing what it took to get the thing off the ground.

"Nothing for me," said Walter. "How are the kids?"

"Missing the dogs," said Hail Larry's Wife. "Oh, and their uncles, too, of course."

"Whaddya got?" asked Bear, dying to see what all the McPhersons had on this zephyr ship. "What do you call this thing anyway?"

"Oh, Bear, don't be so jealous," laughed Hail Larry's Wife. "We went oval, not horseshoe magnet ... suits our energy more ... especially after Japan."

"We told you we were getting an aerial transport of our own, chill out," said Hail Larry, more focused on the console and a bunch of silvery knobs. *Everything was silvery. And white. And 60s. Or modern outer space-like. Or beatnik.*

"By the way," said Hail Larry's Wife, "we call this cabin the CHILL ZONE."

"Very modern. Reminds me of Seoul, South Korea," said Walter, taking the food offered ... *sushi.*

"Pass," said Bear, then whispered: *"Walter ... do we have a Chill Zone?"*

"Count on it," whispered Walter. "So, Larry ... what do you beatniks call this oval mother ship of yours?"

"Hold on," said Hail Larry's Wife, fussing with the console. "Let me turn up the music button, version 2. Hot!"

COOL AND DREAMY MUSIC BUTTON: *"Lava" by the B-52's ... piping hot and beatnik-like!*

"It's got descriptions now!" said both Walter and Bear, marveling at the music button, version 2.

"Hot Lava!" said Hail Larry, manning the console of HOT LAVA, bobbing his head and scooting across the floor in his captain's chair.

"The music button was our idea, you know," said Bear.

"It's still in *The Bearcat Boyz* movies and books," warned Walter.

"Which we intend to still produce," said Bear. "God willing."

"No prob," said Hail Larry's Wife, too busy dancing to argue. *"Red! Hot! Fire!"*

Hail Larry let out a primal scream at the console. The McPhersons started dancing in their own frequencies as if the boys weren't even there. Hail Larry stayed in his captain's chair the whole time and played air guitar and air saxophone. Hail Larry's Wife danced all Egyptian and 60s-like, all while holding a tray of sushi treats.

"They've changed," said Bear to Walter under his breath.

Hail Larry grabbed the mic on the console and said in a booming, ominous voice: *"The whole world does not revolve around your penis poles, Panther and the Bearcat!"*

That got a few screams outta Hail Larry's Wife as she did backflips on the ceiling (while still holding the sushi tray).

"Have you guys been hanging around B.E. again?" asked Bear.

"Lighten up, Coal Man," said Hail Larry. "We saved your asses tonight."

"Good thing we scheduled this couples' divorce meeting when we did," said Walter, arm around his Bear.

"So how did the press conference go, anyway?" asked Hail Larry.

"The Hot Lava doesn't have satellite?" snickered Bear.

"*Hey!*" Hail Larry swung around in his chair with a grave expression. "It's ... Hot Lava. No *the* ... Got it, *the Bear?*" Then he swung back around to the console and kept bobbing to the music. "We were busy."

"Went great," said Walter. "Bear and I are ready for the rest of our lives, come what may."

"Us, too," said Hail Larry's Wife, coming down from the ceiling and joining her man at the console. "Larry's retiring, too."

"Quietly before camp," said Hail Larry. "Still trying to figure out how to deal with this whole HIV-sex-ring thing. What did you guys say?"

"Feed your babies and let us worry about the ones in the NFL," said Walter, having more sushi.

"Good for you," said Hail Larry's Wife, more focused on the red LANDING light on the console. "So guys, I stole something. I wanna give it to you."

"Peace offering, or fuck-off gift—no big," said Hail Larry.

"What's this?" asked Bear, taking possession of a video cassette tape wrapped with an orange ribbon made of yarn.

"The day of the Kingdome implosion?" said Hail Larry's Wife, then added for Bear's benefit: "When we all had that big fight in Bass' research lab."

"Tell me about it," said Bear.

"We all know the Dane is missing, right?" asked Hail Larry. "Presumed not dead."

"Yes, go on," said Bear. "Poor guy."

"His choice to stay down under, remember," said Walter.

"Anyway," said Hail Larry's Wife, retaking control of her story. "That day we were all down there, I stole this tape from his lab. I actually got two. I wanted to get more, but I had the baby's stuff with me, you know how that goes."

The three men groaned in agreement.

"Anyway," said Hail Larry's Wife. "This is the only surviving piece of the Dane's research. The other tape you wouldn't wanna see. Trust us."

"This is the only thing that didn't turn to dust that day?" asked an excited Bear.

"Isn't that great?" asked Hail Larry's Wife.

"I hope it's good fun stuff," said Walter.

"And it's all footage of the four of us!" said Hail Larry.

"Oh," said Bear and Walter, suddenly less than enthused.

Hail Larry killed the engines of Hot Lava. "Get out of our fucking transport."

"You're kicking us out?" asked an incredulous Walter. *Mild laugh.*

"We're *here, idiots*," said Hail Larry. "*Jerry Springer* under the stars."

Cool and Dreamy Music Button: "*This is the Time to Remember*" by *Billy Joel ... haunting, nostalgic, familiar, searching.*

... *here, idiots* was the dunes of Indiana, near Chicago, off Lake Michigan. The night air was cool. The foursome kicked back on a huge rectangular platform above Hot Lava, lying on their backs, gazing at a starry sky.

"What are we gonna do with us, people?" asked one.

"As far as what?" asked one.

"Everything," said one.

"*The Bearcat Boyz*," said one. "The project of our dreams, now broken into separate pieces, like our friendship."

"*Road of Life*," said one. "A movie with revolutionary theories about ethnic soul mates."

"Bearcat Studios," said one. "Or *No-Movie* Studios, if we can't all come together peacefully. Or come apart peacefully."

"My personal fitness gym," said one. "A place for people to play games to remember how to live life with that childhood spirit glowing inside. A dream I was counting on all of us investing in."

"My reputation," said one, "now featuring people wondering if I've got AIDS and have been passing it around like snacks at a party."

"Ditto," said three.

And should I care? whispered all four in their souls.

"And my true secret with Larry," said Bear.

"You think they're ready to know, little Bearcat?" asked Hail Larry.

"Can't make anything worse." Bear sat upright and found the others waiting anxiously for him to spill the beans. "You can relax, bud," said Bear, noting the worried look on Walter's face. "I'm still a retard only in love with you."

"What a relief," said Walter. "I mean, that's not what I mean. Fuck, I hate myself right now."

"Join the club," said the other three.

"Guys, what's the secret?" asked a panicked Hail Larry's Wife, reminiscent of her *Freeways* days.

"Relax, it's not about sex," said Bear. "You know: the first time anyone wants to know why the Bearcat Boyz are sexual animals, tell them to look in the mirror."

"The big secret is," said an impatient Hail Larry, "Bear and I have been working on—"

"*Walt Loves the Bearcat*," said Bear, "formerly known as *The Walter Yeager Story*. Larry was a huge help. We've even shot scenes with Matt Strickland—the former QB turned actor—playing Walt. I wanted to surprise you, buddy, someday in some bright sunny future now gone south. Quite literally."

"That's so sweet, I'm gonna cry," said Hail Larry's Wife.

"I might, too," said Walter, "if I did in public."

"Doesn't matter," shrugged Bear. "I'm thinking about using the title *Walt Loves the Bearcat* for *My Whole Other Life* now."

"Ah, fuck it, no big," said Hail Larry.

"I had a good song for you guys for either movie," said Hail Larry's Wife.

"Really, what?" asked Hail Larry.

"Hold on, lemme punch it up on the remote," said Hail Larry's Wife.

Cool and Dreamy Music Button: "*World Without You*" by Belinda Carlisle ... *sweet, melodic yearning for the one you never wanna wake up without.*

"Ah." Bear gritted his teeth apologetically. "Walter's not a very big fan of hers. Sorry."

"Nice try, though," said Walter.

"It's perfect for you guys," said Hail Larry's Wife. "Don't let this be like when you passed up my recommendation to use 'Ray of Light' in *Freeways*. See how that turned out for Madonna. And you, Bear, fell in love with zephyrs."

"Why would I used a song by a former Go-Go that Walter doesn't even like in a movie about us?" scoffed Bear.

"I think the bigger question is the future of all our projects, including our friendship," said Walter.

"Nice of you guys to rescue us tonight," said Bear.

"Fuck it. Gonna take a leak." Hail Larry disappeared below into the chill zone of Hot Lava.

"Right behind you," said Walter, disappearing as well.

"Thanks for meeting us in Chicago," said Bear to Hail Larry's Wife. "Nice to see familiar faces."

"Fuck it," said Hail Larry's Wife. "It was here or Malibu. We had to be at either one."

"Either what?" asked Bear.

"Complex," said Hail Larry's Wife, looking through binoculars at the night sky.

"What Complex?" asked Bear. *Mild laugh.*

"Oh, sorry," said Hail Larry's Wife. "We bought out that Complex company—their name and some of the proposed sites. I'm still working on the slogan. *The Complex: Life is a Game. Come Play the Games of Life.* What do you think?"

"What's your gym got to do with tonight?" asked Bear.

Just then, voices came wafting from below—audio from a television.

"*... seen here dating bachelor quarterback Walter Yeager at the Emmys before her current beau ...*"

"The Complex owned 42 old junior highs, including Malibu and Chicago," said Hail Larry's Wife. "That's how we were able to swoop down and get you so easy. How's that for perfect grace?"

"Walter's junior high school?" Bear paused, then shouted to the chill zone below: "Walter ... you might wanna hear this."

"Be right up, buddy, checking out their tape," said Walter. "But I don't think we wanna hear this ... Larry ... where's the remote?"

"*... Who will Walter marry: longtime girlfriend Tammy Du'Hard, or old flame, supermodel Ivanya Elle M'vanya? Log on now and vote at ...*"

"That's the wrong tape!" yelled Hail Larry's Wife, scurrying below to the chill zone. "That one has the bad stuff!"

"*... sexual harassment lawsuit against Yeager by a waitress in Dallas ...*"

"*... alleged affair by Yeager with a boy band member ...*"

"What's up, Bear-man?" asked Walter, back on top of the roof.

"Have you heard of the Complex?" asked Bear.

"Yeah, the fuckers who stole our spot from us in the Malibu hills," said Walter. "And my junior high."

"That's only the half of it," said Bear, heading for the chill zone.

"What's the other half?" asked Walter, following Bear.

"*... apparent hotel disturbance, possibly involving NFL quarterback Walter Yeager and six unidentified Asian females ... possibly prostitutes.*"

"*... Yeager's alleged affair with a local male newscaster and weather girl ... apparently at the same time during the commercial break ...*"

Bear and Walter plopped down to the chill zone to find Hail Larry trying to turn off the VCR with an uncooperative remote.

"*... claims to have given birth to these blond quadruplets by NFL superstar Walter Yeager ...*"

"What is this?" asked Bear.

"The bad tape from the Dane's, the one we weren't going to show you," said Hail Larry's Wife.

"... *Mr. Yeager and I had a wonderful 10-year affair ...*"

"... *Walta always told me I looked just like his Bear Coleman ...*"

"Freakin' Yeager stuck it in the freakin' VCR wrong," said Hail Larry.

"I wanted to check out the tape you gave us," said Walter.

"... *would you say then, that a man like Walter Yeager is bisexual or trisexual, and maybe even sexually compulsive? In your own expert opinion, of course ... Caller, where are you calling from again?*"

"... *whenever he was in the Denver area and they won, I got a special treat.*"

"Just exactly how many ways to Sunday are you gonna fuck with us?" Bear asked the Hail Larrys.

"Meaning?" asked Hail Larry, more focused on smacking the remote.

"... *sources say both Walter Yeager and his sexual partner Bear Coleman have an open relationship that includes multiple partners of all genders, including trans ... Give us your opinion now in our Super Freak poll by logging onto ...*"

"... *one expert says it's quite possible that Yeager may have admitted to over 7,000 sex partners during what he says were his mini-Wilt Chamberlain years ...*"

"Turn this crap off!" yelled Walter.

"I'm trying!" yelled Hail Larry.

"We didn't mean for you to see this," said Hail Larry's Wife.

"Just like you didn't mean to steal our dreams?" asked Bear.

"They can't steal our dreams," said Walter.

"They keep trying," said Bear. "Guess who owns your junior high property in Chicago *and* my studio spot in Malibu. *They're* the freakin' Complex!"

"We're outta here." Walter headed for the door, Bear followed. Walt loves making snap decisions, just like that. This much is true.

"... *possible Bear Coleman love child, apparently from a drunken dalliance with a woman at the Fiesta Bowl in 1982 ...*"

"The real estate deal was an honest mistake," said Hail Larry, finally shutting off the VCR.

"How do you make an honest mistake twice?" asked Bear.

"We've spent a lifetime avoiding footage like that," said Walter. "Now thanks to you ... kaboom!"

"*Repeating our top story,*" said the female news anchor now on the television. "*'If I got AIDS, it came from Hail Larry McPherson.' Were those the words behind the words of Walter Yeager in tonight's live, televised event? Vote now at ...*"

"You bastards!" said both Hail Larry and Hail Larry's Wife.

"You know we'd never, ever say anything like that," said Walter.

"What did you freakin' say?" asked Hail Larry.

"Didn't even mention your name," said Walter.

"Call it an honest mistake by the media," said Bear, grinning sarcastically.

"The tape *was* an honest mistake," said Hail Larry's Wife. "Can you honestly say the same?"

"Let's jet, Bear," said Walter, storming into the pitch-black dunes.

"That's three honest mistakes by the McPhersons," said Bear, making the motion of a baseball umpire. "You're outta here!"

"What the fuck did you tell the press?" asked Hail Larry, standing his ground in front of Hot Lava.

"We'll send you a transcript," said Bear, joining Walter in the dunes.

"We were supposed to be solving things tonight," said Hail Larry's Wife, standing her ground in front of Hot Lava.

"Things look pretty solved to me," yelled Walter, moving in a furious blur. Bear followed, followed by the sound of the McPherson's transport slamming closed. The dunes were dark, quiet and cold. The boys journeyed down the shore, wordless and without a stated destination. Eventually, they heard the McPhersons roaring away in the night sky, prompting them to stop.

"Boy, *that* solved things," said Walter.

Bear couldn't speak. He could only replay every word he heard about his man, his dream man, the one he had been retarded for all these years, the one he had been loyal to a fault for, the one he had dedicated his life to. The one for whom he missed his night at the Oscars without even pausing to consider any other option. Now, there was a lot to consider.

Walter glanced into Bear's eyes for a flicker of a moment, then went into HERO MODE: how to get me and mine home from here.

... *Who is he?* Bear asked himself in that flicker of a moment.

... Why did the world have such a distorted view of their love?

... Who had it twisted? Who had it right? Who had it wrong? Who twisted it?

... *Who is Walter Yeager? Who is Marcus "Bear" Coleman?*

... *How did we ever end up in this dark and lonely place?*

Little boys' souls are howling in the night, crying louder than ever.

32

So That's What the Eggbeater's For!

"The rain was still coming down in Dreamville—pouring, drenching rain to welcome back the residents returning from the Summer of the Locusts That Never Came."

Bear stopped reading aloud from his monitor and sighed. *Sitting at the creation station in the home office at the Jaw. Daylight filtering through the ocean view.*

"What's the point?" asked Walter, sitting at his own creation station across the room. His blond head was buried in shame or deep thought, hard to tell which.

"Of continuing with *The Bearcat Boyz?*" asked Bear. "Or what's the point of something else on your mind?"

"As in the world's accusations about the quarterback's sex life?" asked Walter, picking up the eggbeater and trying to fit it somewhere on the model of the stadium on his desk.

"There's no point in discussing accusations," said Bear. "Only truths."

But what are the truths? And can every person on the planet be lying about having slept with my buddy? Yeager is the God. I'm just the retard and the nigger. He's Big Norse. The panther. I'm the fag. The prototype without the skillz. The cheerleader.

"I read something on the Internet the other day," said Bear.

"Guess that means the self-imposed media blackout is completely over, Bearcat People," said Walter.

"This Indian columnist guy compared me to Jerry Lewis and his crazy devotion to Dean Martin in those wacky movies," said Bear.

"Wacky movies we both love!" said Walter. "Especially the football one, *That's My Bear*—I mean, *That's My Boy*. Remember, my Bear brought up doing the remake, Your Honor."

"The article claims that Dean was just using Jerry as an ego booster," said Bear, "that Jerry's infatuation and retarded mental development made Lewis this overgrown kid, worshipping the big jock who appeared to have everything under control, including having a kid to sniff his jock and make him feel like a superstar all the time."

"We treat each other like superstars!" laughed Walter.

"Jerry was like Dean's crazy mascot who acted out all their retarded shit when Dean needed him to, then carried Dean's jock when Dean was done being crazy, so Dean could go off and get the man's job done," said Bear.

"Bear, you know I don't see you that way," said Walter. "What happened to: *loving each other is man's job?* And: *we both manage whatever the other one can't?* What about the Dane's claim that we're genetically meant for one another? What about the last half of our lives, Bear?"

"I'm going for a jog," said Bear, rising up.

"You don't jog," laughed Walter.

"Then I'm just going," said Bear, stopping in the doorway of the home office.

"What about: *today we're gonna make serious progress on the next generation of Bearcat Boyz?*" asked Walter, repeating Bear's vow over breakfast.

"I think I need to go," said Bear, standing in the doorway, facing away from his buddy.

"Where?" asked Walter.

"Somewhere," said Bear. "Mama's ... I'm due for a visit. Maybe even take her on a trip. Maybe help her look for a house up the road in Oxnard. She's dreaming of selling the family home after all these years. Funny, our favorite black coach, Mr. Renteria, is also thinking of relocating up the road in Oxnard."

"Sweet," said Walter. "When should we ... uh, when you gonna ... go?"

"I'll call Roberto from upstairs," said Bear, still facing away from his buddy *... didn't want QB to see the tears.*

"When you coming back?" asked Walter, voice full of hurt.

"Soon," said Bear. "I hope. I hope real soon."

Bear disappeared from the home office, wondering how soon was too soon, and if too soon should ever come.

Cool and Dreamy Music Button: *"Brown-Eyed Bud" by Van Morrison ... strikingly familiar tune with a few twists ... your ticket is your imagination!*

"Yeah, baby," said a sweet youthful male voice, circa a dashing and daring youthful age. "Now that Coleman's taking off for God knows where, and the big adorable blond lug is snoring away on the couch ... time for the Dan Man to take control of the creation station, Bearcat People ... gotta kiss my brown-eyed bud Chris ... a Dan Man's got Dan Man-type urges ... help a bro out!"

Hip and Comet stirred from the floor in the home office at the Jaw, which was otherwise unoccupied ... well, sorta.

"Hip, Comet, help me get up to the blocks—I mean—the keyboard," said a sweet youthful male voice, circa a dashing and daring youthful age. "Sweet ... thanks ... now go lick yourselves ... I go to work ... no way am I gonna let these bozos mess up things for Dan Johnson and Chris Brown. It's our turn! ... Let's see here ... where exactly are we in our story ..."

The rain was still coming down in Dreamville—pouring, drenching rain to welcome back the residents returning from the Summer of the Locusts That Never Came. Dan and Chris sped away in the rain from Telephone Pole Lane, the green rock in tow. Because the town was filling up with residents and rain, the boys rode to the only place still unoccupied: school.

Dreamville High was a school but not a school, that looked like a school and felt like a school, but wasn't really a school, so much as a school of thoughts and dreams. There were school buildings and other buildings, as well as classrooms and open space that some called classrooms as well. There were science labs, healthcare facilities, a janitor who took care of things, a cafeteria that fed people, places to go for counseling, learning or discipline, places to look for friends or enemies and the many other things humans find in schools and in the schools of life. There were also athletic fields for all kinds of sport. Even a gymnasium or three for indoor sport. Dreamville High was a dream of a school for some.

For Dan Johnson and Chris Brown, the school became a refuge from the pouring rain. They rode the Lemon Peeler until they reached the football stadium, then came to a halt underneath the bleachers. "People are gonna drown this weekend if they don't watch out," said Chris, getting off the Lemon Peeler.

"Good for them," said Dan, getting off the Lemon Peeler.

"You don't mean that," laughed Chris.

"Don't I," snickered Dan.

"We're not gonna drown here, are we?" asked Chris, shivering.

"No way," said Dan. "You're always safe with me."

Chris giggled and blushed, looking down at the wet ground.

"What's wrong?" asked Dan.

"Nothing," said Chris.

"Sweet." Dan looked up at the bleachers above. "This ain't helping us stay dry."

"I got a better idea," said Chris.

"Lead the way," said Dan, making Chris giggle some more.

Upon further reveal, the better idea was the storage shed on the opposite sideline, near the 50-yard line. "It's locked," said Chris after reaching it.

"I don't know how to pick it," said Dan.

"I have the key," said Chris.

"Dude, you're amazing," said Dan.

"This is where I hung out all summer before we met," said Chris, opening the creaky splintery door of the creaky wooden shed. Sunlight filtered through the clouds and the rain into the shed, revealing a hazy smattering of football artifacts, down markers, chalkboards, stuff like that.

"I love it," said Dan, eyes roaming between his brown-eyed bud and the interior of the shed. "Let's go inside ... how did you gain access?"

"I managed to," said Chris, following Dan inside.

"Close the door, I got a lighter." Dan waited until darkness fell before il-luminating the shed. "Wow ... Chris! Brown! I've never seen anything like this before in my life!"

"I've never showed anyone this side of me," said Chris. "Except my brother once and he ripped me and them to shreds."

"Why? They're all so cool," said Dan.

"He was probably mad at something else and just took it out on my—these," said Chris. "That's why I've kept them hidden here all summer."

"They're beautiful! You're amazing," said Dan. "Can I touch one?"

"Touch them all," giggled Chris, retrieving the big yellow ER flashlight he used in the shed at night. He shined the big square light, giving Dan a better look at what Dan was marveling at.

"They're so real," said Dan, extinguishing his lighter. "So this is what you doodle all day in school! Who would have ever thought! Then again, I should have known ..."

"What do you mean by that?" giggled Chris, gazing at the hundreds of drawings covering every inch of the interior of the shed.

"I know my brown-eyed bud," said Dan. "I saw what you did all day before we met."

"You did?" laughed Chris. "I hope you don't think I was a freak or something."

"Are you kidding?" laughed Dan, as if that were the most ridiculous idea of all. "I just wanted to know what you were doodling when you weren't playing Mattel Electronics Football ... now it all makes sense."

Chris Brown loved to doodle drawings of stadiums, all kinds of stadiums, but mostly football, basketball and baseball, and lately, mostly football.

"I love stadiums, too!" said Dan.

"To play in and become a great warrior athlete!" said Chris, making Dan laugh a shy mild laugh, even turn a little red in those smooth blond cheeks with just the slightest coating of fuzzy blond whiskers.

"Some of these are awesome." Dan circumnavigated the shed, admiring the Brownster's work while Chris followed with the flashlight. "I mean, they're all awesome, but some just kinda ... grab me more ... like I'm drawn like a magnet ... like this one ..."

"My favorite, too," said Chris.

The horseshoe. A powerful magnetic symbol that can push or pull and reverse directions, depending on the needs of the Zephyrs.

"You wrote that," said Dan, statement of fact. "Fucking brilliant!"

"Fucking great that you like!" said Chris, full of joy. "It's kinda my ultimate dream stadium for the Dreamville High Zephyrs."

"Did you color it some crazy color?" asked Dan, examining the drawing closer in the flash of light.

"I just use pencil," shrugged Chris, his movement causing the light on the drawing to shift. "I call that stadium, The Zephyr Wings."

"Cool, we'll submit that in the Rename the School Stadium Contest," said Dan.

"I didn't know there was one," giggled Chris.

"Dream of it," said Dan. "Was the pencil green? Doesn't the drawing look like it's reflecting green light or something? Hold the flashlight still."

A clap of thunder struck, startling the boys and reminding them of the rain pelting the roof of the shed. The drawing appeared to glow and illuminate like no other drawing among the hundreds. The thin pencil lines swirled with greenish yellowish gold-like coloring. The drawings were simple, only lined representations of bigger dreams. The kaleidoscopic flashing in the lines seemed to suggest those bigger dreams were contained in the drawing—now in the hands of Dan Johnson.

"True Gold," said Dan. "That's what this color is. Do you see what I mean?"

Dan held the drawing in front of the flashlight. Chris saw True Gold.

The downpour outside intensified, rocking the shed everywhere but inside, where all was peaceful, calm and understood. Whatever Johnson and Brown needed to exist in that moment in time, they possessed, mind, body and True Gold souls. No questions. No labels. No misunderstandings. No words. Only the outpouring of the soul, from one to another, a melding of two gold into True Gold, always and forever.

"Yeah, I see True Gold," said Chris. "And the green of the green rock somehow."

"Where is that little bugger anyhow?" asked Dan, prompting Chris to giggle ...

"WHO CARES ABOUT THE ROCK ALREADY!" yelled Dan @ Bear's creation station in the home office at the Jaw. "When do I get to kiss my buddy!"

Just then, the big adorable blond lug snoring on the couch turned over, as if the dogs or the wind from the window stirred him into another position.

"Go back to sleep, you gorgeous hunk who kinda looks like me," whispered Dan, scrolling down to see where they were going with this story, and of course, adding his own such-and-such-and-so-on as needed: "... lying on their backs on the benches in the shed at the Dreamville High football stadium, staring at the stadium drawings taped to the ceiling ... when Chris brings up the upcoming football season ..."

"You had to go and bring up football again," said Dan in the shed.

"You don't like being quarterback?" asked Chris in the shed.

"I love being quarterback," said Dan. "I just don't love being quarterback ... here."

"What's wrong with here?" asked Chris.

"Well, for one, it's not there," said Dan. *Mild laugh.*

"Where's there?" giggled Chris.

COOL AND DREAMY MUSIC BUTTON: *"Somewhere" by Phil Collins ... from West Side Story ... do you believe in miracles in space?*

"What do you mean?" asked Chris. "Miracles in space."

"What if God had so much space, God had space to spare?" asked Dan.

"You mean like a really rich person?" asked Chris.

"A gillion times richer than anyone we know," said Dan. "What if God had infinite space and resources and money and power and everything?"

"God would be *All That*," said Chris.

"And then some," said Dan. "So what's it to God to give us some space?"

"You mean us humans?" asked Chris.

"I mean two buds like us who needed space," said Dan.

"To do what?" asked Chris.

"Whatever Chris Brown wants," said Dan. "What does Chris Brown want?"

"Dunno, what does Dan Johnson want?" asked Chris.

"Space ... where I can ride my bike, throw my rocks, be me ... with my buddy." Dan reached out. Chris reached back. The boys held hands, lying on their backs on their separate benches in the shed, facing the heavens, holding on for the very first time. Nice and easy. They understood they were magnetized. Something calm inside held the nerves at bay. Something calm inside whispered: he's yours and he'll never hurt you, not in a way that truly hurts you.

Deep down, Bearcat Boyz know the deepest dreams of their souls.

Deep down, Bearcat Boyz believe their deepest dreams come true.

This much is true.

"I prayed for you," said the buddies.

This much is true.

"I asked God for you," said the buddies.

This much is true.

"I asked God for someone who felt exactly like me," said the buddies.

This much is true.

"You're him," said the buddies.

This much is true.

"I promised God we'd be together forever," said the buddies.

This much is true.

"And go through life together," said the buddies.

This much is true.

"Come with me, help me fulfill the promise I made to God," said the buddies. "Be my buddy-for-life."

I, God, promise You, God, this ...

"I'll go anywhere with you," said the buddies.

"I'll take you there," said the True Gold buddies.

This much is true ...

"Hey, Brownster!" said an excited, nervous, eager and anxious Dan.

"Yeah, Dan Man?" asked an anxious, eager, nervous and excited Chris.

They were still holding hands but trying to sit upright.

"It's raining less!" said one.

"Let's play around!" said one.

Their eyes lit with electricity, but their wires got crossed. One leaped one way, the other leaped the other way. Still holding hands, they fell on their asses to the ground and laughed.

Boys will forever be boys, especially Bearcat Boyz.

"Let's go run around in the mud!" said Dan.

Cool and Dreamy Music Button: *"Play in the Sunshine" by Prince ... wild abandonment on a hot summer day ... rain or shine!*

The sunshine was filtered through the rain, but the boys didn't care. Dan and Chris ran around the muddy football field like fools, screaming at the top of their lungs. Dan and Chris slid into the muddy end zone like baseball players sliding into home. Chris and Dan ran up and down the wooden bleachers of the stadium. Dan even rode the Lemon Peeler up and down the bleachers while Chris laughed his ass off swinging from the goalposts. *You making fun of me?* asked Dan's mockingly angry face, charging toward Chris. The Brownster vaulted from the goalposts and tried to get away, but he was too busy busting a gut and was the slower of the two anyway. Dan tackled Chris in the mud and the two wrestled until they were covered head to toe, one boy indistinguishable from the other. When they finally collapsed from exhaustion, they were on their backs at the 50-yard line, wiping the dirt from their eyes, the only part of their beings not covered in mud.

"Fuck, Chris Brownster, you drive me crazy," said Dan, noticing it had finally stopped raining. "No one makes me laugh as much as you."

Chris giggled and blushed to the heavens.

"What's wrong?" asked Dan

"Nothing," said Chris.

"Sweet." Dan looked toward the bleachers. "Can you make the football games this fun?"

"Dream of it," said Chris.

Just then, a dark minivan entered the parking lot in the distance, stopping at the sight of two muddy boys sitting on the football field. The window on the driver's side rolled down just enough for a hand to emerge and motion to the boys to join the hand somewhere on high in the distance.

"What does he or she or they want?" asked Chris.

"Us ... up there," said Dan, nodding to an unfamiliar round structure.

"What is that, some kind of newfangled building?" asked Chris.

"Must be newfangled for this year," said Dan.

"It's almost like a little dome on top of the corner of the school," said Chris as they moved closer on foot.

"Maybe that's where the new whatchamacallit is gonna be," said Dan. They fell silent until they reached the door of the office up inside the little dome on top of a corner of the school.

DEAN DOME, read the loose and swinging sign on the door, which opened suddenly.

"Dean Adam Dean Adams, Dean and AD," said a heavyset black man, "former district attorney until two knuckleheads under my charge blew up one too many Vegas-style casinos in the name of catching the bad guys. Welcome to my new dome."

"Dean?" asked Dan.

"Adams, the new Dean, Adam Dean Adams," said the heavyset black man.

"As in Dean Adams or Adam Dean?" asked Dan.

"Oh, yes, I'm also the new AD," said the heavyset black man.

"So you're Adam Dean, the athletics director, who's also the new Dean, named Dean Adams," said Chris, almost getting it right.

"Try again," said the heavyset black man.

"I read about you in the *Dreamville Bulletin*," said Dan. "You're the Adams who's the new Dean and AD."

"Now that I'm outta the DA's office," said the heavyset black man.

"So what do we call you?" asked Chris. Just then, the phone rang in the office and the DEAN DOME sign fell from the door to the ground.

"Oh ... DEAN DOME ... excuse me, the phone ... my secretary ..." said Dean Dome, answering the call, waving them inside.

"Why are we in this place?" whispered Chris, getting a shrug outta Dan as they entered the office.

"Because Dreamville needs you," said Dean Dome, muting the call. "Preferably not covered in mud, but that's your choice."

Suddenly, the boys remembered they were still covered in mud.

"Dreamville needs us for what?" asked Dan.

"Call you back." Dean Dome hung up the phone and circumnavigated his circular dome office. "We need you for spirit leading, athletic greatness, heroism, saving damsels and dudes in distress, occasionally saving the whole world as we know it ... stuff like that. Oh, and teaching people new ways to dream. It's called the Dream Force," said Dean Dome.

The boys returned blank expressions.

"It involves really cool gadgets," said Dean Dome.

"*Cool, count us in, all right, let's do dis, bring it on,*" said Dan and Chris, more or less.

"Someday I'm just gonna have the gadgets out on the table and say: Go save the world," said Dean Dome.

"Who are you and what's all this newfangled mumble-jumble blankety-blank about?" asked Dan.

"Yeah," said Chris, nodding to his bud. "What he said."

"I'm the new Dean and AD. Do we need to go there again?" asked Dean Dome.

"No, sir, not really, it's okay," said the boys, more or less.

"Things are at an all-TIME crucial phase for Dreamville," said Dean Dome. "Dreamers have stopped dreaming for themselves. Too many people are relying on others to live their lives, fulfill their dreams, to fill in the gaps in their empty souls."

"That bites," said Dan.

"Don't I know it," said Chris. "I'm not sure how, but I do."

"Trust the feeling inside, young Skywalker," said Dean Dome in a booming *Star Wars* voice. "I love doing shit like that."

"Sir, you just cussed," giggled Dan.

"Oh, fuck, sorry," said Dean Dome, sounding somewhat cantankerous. "I'm not here to teach language. I'm here to dream big! And bigger! Now ... I need sharp-minded, talented, committed men like you two boys to go out there and encourage people to dream better dreams. How about it?"

"Why us?" asked Chris.

"Why are you in my dome office, all muddy from head to toe?" asked Dean Dome.

The boys looked at themselves, shrugged and smiled.

"Seemed like a fun idea at the time," said Dan. *Mild laugh.*

"And was it?" asked Dean Dome, sitting behind his big desk.

"No doubt!" laughed Chris.

"Exactly," said Dean Dome. "Not a bad dream, huh? Especially for one on the fly."

"We didn't dream it," laughed Dan. "We just did it."

"Not before your mind conceived of it, young man," said Dean Dome. "*That* is what you call a dream ... or a thought, same difference. Now ... go clean up. You both smell as if you haven't showered all summer long. And if you wanna be true heroes, dream about coming back to the Dean Dome tomorrow morning, crack of dawn."

"For what?" asked Chris.

"What else?" said Dean Dome, getting kinda agitated. "Hero training! Now get outta here!"

THE NEXT MORNING @ the Dean Dome.

"Never been to hero training before," said Chris. "Oh, no!"

"Neither has your bud," said Dan. "Yes!"

"What do you suppose it will be like?" asked Chris. "Oh, fuck!"

"Dunno, guess we'll find out," said Dan. "Bummer ... intercepted. Your ball."

"Yes!" said Chris, taking possession of the little green box. Dean Dome had yet to show up @ the Dean Dome. The boys were sitting alone in his circular office, fronting the big window overlooking the football stadium. "I think our Mattel Electronics battery is getting low again," said Chris.

"From all the cans of whoop-ass I've been opening up on you," said Dan.

"Dream on," giggled Chris, more focused on the game.

"So what do you think the new school year will be like?" asked Dan.

"What do you want it to be like?" asked Chris. "Yes, first down, Brown! The man! Johnson's going down!"

"Cool and dreamy like the summer would be sweet," said Dan, tossing the green rock in the air ... *playing a game with himself: how close can I come to just barely touching the ceiling with this rock?*

"What would make the year cool and dreamy for Dan?" asked Chris. "Ah, man, sacked."

"You writing some really cool stuff about the team in the school paper, getting people more interested in the games," said Dan.

"Consider it done," said Chris. "Fuck! Missed a field goal."

"Nice," said Dan, taking back the game. "Lemme show you how it's done."

"So I write about the Dreamville Zephyrs football team, then what?" asked Chris, studying the green rock, now in his hands.

"You know what I really dream of, bud?" asked Dan, pausing with the game.

"Tell me about it," said Chris.

COOL AND DREAMY MUSIC BUTTON: *"Let's Get Rocked" by Def Leopard.*

Johnson takes the snap ... guns a perfect pass ... touchdown, Zephyrs!

I get I get I get I get rocked!

Brown goes crazy in the stands, dancing up a storm for Dreamville!

I get I get I get I get rocked!

Johnson fires a bomb to the end zone ... touchdown, Zephyrs!

I get I get I get I get rocked!

Brown goes crazy on the sidelines, rousing up the fans for his buddy!

I get I get I get I get rocked!

Johnson scrambles for his life ... touchdown, Zephyrs!

I get I get I get I get rocked!

Brown gets the crowd to do the wave and dance to cool music!

I get I get I get I get rocked!

Johnson's Zephyrs teammates are cool with the quarterback's new bud.

I get I get I get—

"Chris Brown thinks Dan Johnson is worried about what Dan Johnson's teammates are gonna think about Dan hanging out with the Brownster, newspaper reporter who sometimes wears goggle glasses," said Chris.

"Dan Johnson ain't losing his best buddy in the whole wide world for nothing," said Dan. "But you know how people are sometimes."

"True dat!" laughed Chris, taking the game from Dan after the quarterback was stopped on fourth down. "Especially football players, right?"

"What's so funny?" laughed Dan, tossing the green rock again.

"What if I told you I already managed to take care of it?" asked Chris, more focused on the game.

"Like how?" asked Dan. "You mean, like how you managed to get the keys to the football shed for the summer?"

"Sorta," giggled Chris.

"Tell me about it," said Dan.

"The day everyone left town for the locusts that never came?" said Chris. "First down! ... I was on the street in front of my house, helping my family pack the ground transport, when your football coach raced by. He lives in Brownsville, too, you know."

"*Coach Renteria ... isn't it terrible about the locusts?*" asked Chris.

"*One man's Armageddon is another man's genesis,*" said Coach Renteria. "*Speaking of, where's your beautiful single mother—I mean, your whole family—headed during the evacuation?*"

"*Why, the Brownsville section of the government-subsidized relocation to the beach resort near Mellow Valley,*" said Chris. "Sir, you dropped your ...*"

"*Well, hello, Miss Brown!*" said Coach Renteria. "*My, my, my ... you're looking mighty pretty ... Terrible about the locusts? Indeed, ma'am! ... I hear we're going to be staying at the same government-subsidized resort for the summer ...*"

"Coach Renteria seemed more interested in talking to my mom than me that day," said Chris @ the Dean Dome. "I think I know why now. And judging by the smile on my mom's face since she's been back, I think the school librarian is gonna be hooked up with the football coach for a while."

"Buddy!" laughed Dan, taking the game back after hearing the *touchdown!* jingle. "Do you realize what this means?"

"Yeah," giggled Chris. "Besides me just whooping your ass in yet another game of Mattel Electronics Football, Coach Renteria's not gonna be mad at me for finding his keys on the sidewalk that day, then using the shed all summer. I guess you lose stuff like that when you're too busy making goo-goo eyes at one person all the time, can you imagine?"

"*And,*" said Dan, "no one on the football team is gonna wanna piss off your mother, the school librarian, or her son ... you! It's like a dream come true! A holy freakin' dream come true!"

"*Duh!*" laughed Chris. "That's why it's called dreaming."

"And *exactly* why you two are done with hero training!" said a voice from behind that—upon further reveal—belonged to Dean Dome, now arrived @ the Dean Dome.

"Done?" asked Dan, standing up. "When did we start?"

"Somewhere around the time you were born, but let's not sweat the details," said Dean Dome. "The only thing a hero needs is his imagination. From what little I heard, you're all set to dream bigger dreams ... in addition to being two very ... shall we say ... unique young men."

"What about the gadgets?" asked Chris. "You said there'd be gadgets."

"Follow me." Dean Dome pushed a button under his desk which revealed a spiral staircase which they all took to a lower floor of the Dean Dome. "Watch your step until I can find the light ... in this room is everything dreamers like you need to equip yourselves with to save the world ... ah ... here we are."

Dean Dome illuminated a completely empty room, about the size of his office.

"I'm lost," said Dan.

"All you need is your imagination," said Dean Dome.

"Still lost here," said Dan.

"Ditto," said Chris.

"Follow me." Dean Dome turned out the light and led them through a pitch-black hallway to another room. "Watch your step until I can find the light ... this is the room for beginners ... might be a tight squeeze ... you can still dream here, just not as big ... ah ... here we are."

Dean Dome illuminated a completely empty room, about the size of a broom closet. "Is this one better?" asked Dean Dome.

"It's still empty," said Dan.

"Where's the gadgets?" asked Chris.

"Tell me about it," said Dean Dome. "And if you can't, dream of them."

"You promised toys," said Dan.

"Oh, right, the button. Follow me." Dean Dome turned out the light and led them through a pitch-black hallway to another room. "Watch your step until I can find the light ... I'll show you option three, then get you your button ... ah ... here we are."

Dean Dome illuminated a completely empty room, about the size of the universe. "Is this one better?" asked Dean Dome.

"Better for what?" asked Dan.

"How much space do you need for your imagination?" asked Dean Dome.

"I don't know what you mean," said Dan. *Mild laugh.*

"I'll get you whatever gadget you dream up in the name of better dreams," said Dean Dome. "I'll even fill up a room with nothing but gadgets, just dream of something and tell me what you need."

"Like what?" laughed Chris. "Flying football stadiums?"

"Whatever Johnson and Brown want," said Dean Dome, leading them back up the spiral staircase.

"What about the button?" asked Chris. "You said something about a button."

On the way back to the Dean Dome, Dean Dome placed a button in Chris' hands, but it wasn't until they returned to Dean Dome's illuminated dome office that Chris was able to see that the button was red with white lettering.

"Cool and Dreamy Music Button, what's that?" asked Chris.

"Fuel," said Dean Dome, sitting behind his big desk again.

"Like gas?" laughed Dan, giggling at some private thought or action.

"Like art," said Dean Dome. "Like a gillion souls who have created great songs that contain the keys of life. Like men and women who have bled from the bottom of their bellies, felt like dying, then felt reborn, all because of love. All in the name of love. Is there any other reason to dream but to dream of the highest forms of love? If you could dream of anything, young men, what would it be? Don't answer ... go do it ... take that music button and plug it into your souls. Whenever you've lost your way, get in touch with the music in your dreams ... you'll find your way again soon ... then you'll be able to make your dreams come true, and by extension, help others make their dreams come true ... but the biggest piece of advice I could ever give you two would be ... hold, I need to sneeze ... *just kidding* ... the biggest piece of advice I could ever give you two would be—"

The phone rang.

Dan and Chris sat in their chairs in front of Dean Dome's desk—frozen, waiting—while Dean Dome answered the call.

"No kidding!" said Dean Dome into the phone. "Just like that? *Poof!* A re-tard? A crazy fucker? Ex-friends' betrayal? Got it ... nice knowing ya. Bye."

"So what's the biggest piece of advice?" asked Dan.

"What? Oh. It was: *rock gently your new world.* But never mind now," said Dean Dome, getting up from his big desk. "Dreamville is toast. We've been can-celed on God's Big Network."

"How can that be?" asked Chris, rising in panic.

"We were just getting started," said Dan, rising in panic. "The Brownster and me—I haven't even gotten to ki—kick his ass in football. He beat me last time!"

"Why are we being canceled and dreamed into thin air?" asked Chris.

"Nothing personal," sighed Dean Dome, trying to escort them to the door. "Whole town is dissolving away. Our creators are no longer interested in devel-oping us as a viable dream for their universe."

"But we just signed up for the Dream Force!" said Dan. "We can dream bigger dreams for them, be *their* heroes! I still wanna ki—kick my bud's ass in football."

"Are we just gonna start dissolving right here and now?" asked Chris in a panic, looking at his body, then the plaque on the wall, the very same plaque in every room of every building in Dreamville:

Dreamville residents understand they are powered in part by a higher force that allows them to exist and chase their dreams, whatever they may be.

Dreamville residents understand The Powers That Be reserve the right to dis-solve any part of Dreamville with or without prior notice.

Dreamville residents understand that upon being dissolved, residents morph into other things and dreams. There is no such thing as permanent death in Dream-ville. Life is but a dream. Dreams are forever.

"Yeah," said Dan, "but Chris and I won't remember each other in another dream world."

"We'll be strangers," said Chris. "I wanna stay Chris and Dan. For a while. Forever."

"Me, too," said Dan.

"Would if I could," said Dean Dome. "According to this universal memo coming over my creation station, the creators of Dreamville are bogged down in legal proceedings over who owns the rights to ... Bearcat Project #1, aka *The Bearcat Boyz*—whatever the heaven that is—and therefore ... the legal parties are dissolving the partnership and the dream, including these Bearcat Boyz and Dreamville ... talk about a nightmare."

"We can stop them!" said Dan.

"I'm with Dan!" said Chris.

"Even the great Dean Adam Dean Adams, Dean and AD, formerly the DA, doesn't have a dream for this one, boys," said Dean Dome, sinking in his chair.

"Then you suck!" said Dan. "I mean, this sucks."

"What?" asked Dean Dome, the octaves rising with his body.

"He's right, Dean, this sucks," said Chris. "I wanna give Dan the chance to *ki*—for a rematch in Mattel Electronics Football."

"Better kick off now," said Dean Dome, looking at his monitor again. "According to this new universal memo, we're about to be dissolved in minutes ... they're in arbitration in a city called Malibu now! I'd better call my wife."

"Never mind him. Let's go," said Dan to Chris.

"Where do you two think you two are heading?" asked Dean Dome.

"To save our dreams!" said Chris to Dan.

"You can't disobey me, come back here!" yelled Dean Dome.

Dan and Chris turned around at the threshold of the Dean Dome.

"We can't interfere with our creators," said Dean Dome. "That's the one golden rule!"

"We make our own golden rules." Dan turned, Chris followed.

"If you walk out that door right now," said Dean Dome, "don't come back! Ever! Your days on the Dream Force will be over!"

"If we don't walk out this door right now, our days are over, period," said Chris.

"Good one, Brownster. You *are* the word man," said Dan.

COOL AND DREAMY MUSIC BUTTON: *"Gold" by Spandau Ballet ... piano, haunting urgency, dark, light, searching, determined ... a soul search.*

"The music button works if I stick it on the little green box," said Chris. "What a thing to find out minutes before we might start dissolving."

"Nobody's dissolving just yet. Hop on," said Dan. The Brownster hopped on the back of the Lemon Peeler. Dan took off from Dreamville High. It was raining again. Dan peddled as fast as he could.

"GAME PLAN!" said Chris, just now thinking of the phrase as a cool way to ask, *So what now?*

"Figure out a way to break through to our dreamers," said Dan.

"How?" asked Chris, pulling his goggles from his forehead to his eyes.

"Magic," said Dan, heading to the last place they saw magic.

"Then what?" asked Chris, picturing Telephone Pole Lane, the long hilly road that cut a long winding swatch through town. "What do we do after we get there?"

"Dream of it," said Dan. "Quickly."

The rain poured harder. Lightning struck, followed by thunder. Dan peddled faster and faster up to the top of Telephone Pole Lane, straight to the pole that created the green rock. Skidding to a stop, the Lemon Peeler sent both boys flying across the wet pavement.

"You okay?" asked Dan once they were upright.

"Only if we don't dissolve," said Chris, retrieving from the ground the little green box that was Mattel Electronics Football.

"See if this works." Dan took the green rock out of his pocket and hurled it over the telephone pole, hoping for magic.

"Nothing," said Chris as the rock fell into Dan's hand moments later.

"Brownster, there's something I gotta do if we're gonna dissolve," said Dan.

"Don't talk like that," said Chris. "I wanna be your buddy for life."

"We are," said Dan, grabbing Chris by the shoulders.

"For another few moments?" asked Chris, tearing up in the rain.

"*There they are, Poppa!*" said a voice from nowhere. Upon further reveal, it was a young boy, half their age perhaps. He had dark hair, which was slick and oily from the rain. "I saw them playing with that fucking pissant magic rock! They flew in the sky with it and everything!"

"Thank you, Little Al, you foul-mouth boy," said the man the boy called Poppa. Like son, father was slick and oily. Father patted his son's head, more focused on Dan and Chris.

"Who are you? We're busy," said Dan.

"I want to see your little magic rock," said the slick and oily man.

"We don't know what you're talking about," said Dan.

"Two big fucking pissant liars!' said the slick and oily kid.

"It's a green rock, not a magic rock, little kid," said Chris. *Oops.*

"I saw you *with* the rock," said the slick and oily man. "I'm interested in doing a story. You recognize me, don't you? Everyone knows me by now. I'm worldwide huge."

Chris and Dan shook their heads.

"I got my start in this town a lifetime ago," said the slick and oily man.

"Total dumb asses, Poppa," said the slick and oily kid.

"Didn't you ever hear your parents talk about KWAZ Mighty Mouth Radio?" asked the slick and oily man. "We were *k'waaaay-zy*. Get it?"

"Some other time." Dan hopped on the Lemon Peeler, Chris followed. "If there is one."

"I'll make this simple," said the slick and oily man.

"Show the poor bastards, Poppa," said the slick and oily kid.

"I want that rock!" yelled the slick and oily man at the top of his lungs!

"Cool," shrugged Dan, reaching into his pocket. "Go fetch."

Dan Johnson, Dreamville Zephyrs starting quarterback, threw the longest bomb of his dashing and daring young life, a bomb that sailed high over the pine tree forest and into the lands beyond Dreamville.

"If you ever get your hands on it, it's yours, Mr. Announcer Guy," said Dan.

"Word is born," giggled Chris.

"This ain't over, kid." The slick and oily Mr. Announcer Guy had a look in his eyes that was somewhere between *k'waaaay-zy* and evil. He grabbed his slick and oily kid by the scruff of the neck and hurried toward the horizon as if to chase the green rock. Little Al had some sort of toboggan sled, which looked more like the upside-down roof of the fieldhouse gymnasium at Dreamville High. In their haste, the father tripped and fell on the sled, which slid down the long slope of Telephone Pole Lane.

"This ain't over, pissants!" promised Little Al, then he chased after his dad and the runaway toboggan sled, which hit an upslope and skied off into the sky.

"Odd little duo, eh?" said Dan, watching the trajectory of the flight.

"The oddest," said Chris. "How do we stop all of us from dissolving?"

"Dream of something while I get us outta here," said Dan, cranking up the Lemon Peeler.

"Where we going?" asked Chris.

"Trust your bud?" asked Dan.

"I'll go anywhere with you," said Chris.

"I'll take you there," said Dan, pedaling uphill on Telephone Pole Lane, trying to gain speed. "Meanwhile, hold onto this." Dan flipped the green rock over his shoulder. Chris bobbled it, but Chris Brown always caught what Dan Johnson threw him, sometimes without bobbling even.

"What should I do with it?" asked Chris. "That evil-looking announcer guy is crazy enough to think it's magic. Imagine that."

"Hide it somewhere," said Dan, pedaling faster.

"I got the perfect spot," said Chris, retrieving the little green box.

No way would Dan throw the green rock into the great beyond. A weak battery from Mattel Electronics Football, yes ... their cool and dreamy rock? ... Dream on!

"I'll stash it in the battery compartment of the game," said Chris, tasting the rain on his lips. The Lemon Peeler was peeling faster and faster up the long slope of Telephone Pole Lane. "It's a perfect fit! The green rock fits perfect in the battery compartment of the green game! Green is as good as gold!"

"Somebody likes us," said Dan, focused on getting the Lemon Peeler up to a higher speed. "Let's break through and thank them!"

"The green rock," said Chris, feeling the turbulence in his gut. "It's making the game go crazy ... the field ... the lights ... the buttons ... the scoreboard ... Dan! Dan Man! Dan Buddy! Something's happening to the game! The game is changing! The game is changing! Dan Man, I can see lights I've never seen before! The game is changing! The stadium! The stadium is changing ... getting bigger and bigger ... morphing ... exploding ... we're becoming ... my stomach ... can you feel it? The game is changing, Dan! Things are changing! Can you feel it, Dan ... we're flying! We're in the air and we're flying! I'm flying with my Dan Man! Dan Man is flying with me! Dan, we're flying! We're flying! We're flying! Dan, I can fly with Dan! Dan can fly with me! We're like Zephyrs United! True Gold Zephyrs flying with wings!"

"We might fly better, Brownster buddy, if you take your arms off my face so my eyes can see the sky!" said Dan in the pilot's seat, all patient and calm.

"Sorry, Captain!" said Chris in the copilot's seat. "We're flying! We're in the magnet! The horseshoe magnet stadium of our dreams! The one I drew in the shed! Look at the shed! We're flying over the football shed and the rest of Dreamville!"

"Nice of you to finally open your eyes," said Dan, manning the controls in the cockpit.

"I said I'd go anywhere with you," giggled Chris. "I didn't promise I'd always have my eyes open."

"Hey, Chris," said Dan.

"Yeah, Dan?" said Chris.

"We're flying," said Dan. "Check 'er out, our very own aerial transport."

"True Gold," said Chris, looking beyond the cockpit window.

"We're magnetized," said Dan, reaching out for Chris' hand.

True Gold, the Bearcat Boyz' personal horseshoe magnet stadium.

True Gold, the stadium of their dreams, complete with everything needed to dream their lives away. The cockpit sits atop the closed end of the magnet and rotates 360 degrees. Currently, the cockpit is facing away from the stadium below. True Gold is hurtling through space, flying like the wind in TURBO MODE (as opposed to GO-CART MODE).

"We've got so much to learn about all the gizmos on here," said Chris, browsing the big thick driver's manual. "Says here: we have ... transcontinental, cross-dimensional travel capabilities ... but I can't find anything about that eggbeater-like thing behind the far end zone. Or what it's supposed to do."

"With our amazing minds, it'll be a snap," said Dan, hitting some button, resulting in the sound of a duck quacking. "And fun!"

"The only way to fly," laughed Chris, watching the sky whiz by.

"Anytime you wanna fly this puppy, you let me know," said Dan.

"That was gonna be my line to you!" said Chris.

"Sweet," said Dan.

"GAME PLAN," said Chris. "There's still that pesky little dissolving issue, and I definitely don't wanna dissolve now that we've found True Gold."

"Tell me about it," said Dan. "But first, we need to make a little stop ... bust up a little legal proceeding in the hills of Malibu ... hold on now ... remember I'm new at flying this newfangled stadium *slash* aerial transport ..."

CHRISTOPHER BROWN, AKA THE BROWNSTER, WAS A DOLL of a guy, resting motionless on top of a table in the middle of a legal proceeding.

"So what exactly is a Bearcat?" asked the arbitrator.

"Your Honor, if Bear—the original Bearcat—were here, he could explain it better," said Walter, seated at the table with a lawyer by his side.

"Where is this Mr. Marcus 'Bearcat' Coleman?" asked the arbitrator, looking through his notes for the full legal name. "And you can stop calling me Your Honor."

"It's *Bear*—not Bearcat—Coleman, Your Honor," said Hail Larry's Wife, seated on the McPherson side.

"Where is Bumble Bear?" asked Hail Larry, seated on the McPherson side.

"Detained," said Walter, turning to the arbitrator. "Not legally, Your Honor. He sent an email saying he'd be here."

Silence ensued in the gymnasium. The arbitration was being held at the former junior high in the hills above Malibu, the proposed site for either Hail Larry's Wife's Complex Gym or Bearcat Studios. At stake: the Complex properties in Malibu and Chicago, as well as Bearcat Studios and its properties, including the current topic: the half-developed, half-produced, animated storytelling project known as *The Bearcat Boyz*.

"So what exactly is a Bearcat Boy?" asked the arbitrator. "And you can stop calling me Your Honor."

"*A Bearcat Boy, Your Honor,*" began Walter and the Hail Larrys, speaking at once. Walter cleared his throat like a floor general and took control.

"A Bearcat Boy," said Walter. "Your Honor, think of it as a next generation ... a new kinda ... well, you see, they're guys who ... are ... cool ... and ..."

"Make their own golden rules," said Hail Larry's Wife.

"And do fun shit," said Hail Larry. "Like play football and cheerlead. It's a sports thing."

"Spirit lead," said Walter, trying to score one for the absent Bear. "Bearcat Boyz don't do labels like gay, straight, or even bi. They're just sexual, and looking for a soul mate, another Bearcat Boy just like them, someone cool, accepting and looking for a True Gold buddy-for-life."

"Can a Bearcat Boy be a girl?" asked the arbitrator.

"That's a Tigercat, Your Honor," said Hail Larry's Wife. "*Growlllllll.*"

"A Tigercat?" asked the arbitrator. "What is a Tigercat?"

"Says here, a Tigercat doesn't have to be female," noted Walter's Lawyer, reading from a thick stack of court documents.

"We're trying not to look at these as male/female elements so much as energies, Your Honor," said Walter.

"What is an Energy?" asked the arbitrator.

Walter and the Hail Larrys wore blank expressions.

"Where's Bear?" asked the three.

"What about these props?" asked the arbitrator, eyeing the props spread about the table.

"*I* came up with a lot of the toys, Your Honor," claimed Hail Larry.

"Like hell, McPherson," said Walter. "It's been mostly Bear, Your Honor, from the Cool and Dreamy Music Button, to the green rock, to the flying stadium known as True Gold, and all the other stuff we've barely looked at yet. Like the statue of me and Bear that rides around the rings of the eggbeater, as if on a roller coaster. And the living quarters called the Jaw. Guess where? On the jaw of the horseshoe."

"Hot Lava was our own concept for our own aerial transport, Your Honor," said Hail Larry, arms wrapped around his toy stadium like a protective parent. "We're more the oval types, my wife and I, and our two lovely children."

"And the chill zone is ours, too, Your Honor," said Hail Larry's Wife. "And the portable nursery that can be wheeled down to the locker room."

"What about this eggbeater on the stadium? Where does that fit in?" asked the arbitrator, eyeing a mound of documents related to that device alone. "Who can tell me about the eggbeater, other than the fact it has a statue on it?"

Walter and the Hail Larrys wore blank expressions.

"Where's Bear?" asked the three.

"There's no eggbeater on Hot Lava, Your Honor," said Hail Larry's Wife. "They can keep that creepy ole thing."

"Your Honor," said Walter. "We just want to dissolve this as quickly as possible. Most of this is from the imagination of my partner, Marcus 'Bear' Coleman … wherever he is at the moment, God only knows."

"What's this I hear about another Marcus Coleman claiming to have thought up all of this stuff?" asked Hail Larry's Wife.

"Haven't heard that one," said Walter. *Mild laugh.*

"So do we get to keep Hot Lava and the McPherson dolls—I mean, action figures—or what, Your Honor?" asked an impatient Hail Larry.

"Mr. Coleman designed the McPherson dolls," noted Walter's Lawyer, reading from a thin stack of court documents.

"I object!" said Hail Larry's Wife.

"It's not a court of law, *b—*" said Walter, stopping just short of name-calling.

"Don't talk to the wife like that," said Hail Larry. The three started arguing in front of their lawyers and the arbitration staff, not stopping until they heard the shattering of a window high up in the gymnasium.

"We're under attack!" yelled Hail Larry's Wife. Some in the gym scrambled above the table. Others scrambled below. The arbitration staff swirled in panic. Papers swirled in the swirl. The gadgets and toys on the table rocked and rolled. Then Walter aimed to play hero and tried to restore calm.

"We're okay!" said Walter. "Just a bird or something hitting the window and passing through."

"Looked to me like a greenish, goldish rock of some kind," said Walter's Lawyer, prompting Walter to eye his lawyer curiously.

"Here it comes again!" yelled Hail Larry's Wife, pointing to a swirling object near the rafters. Everyone re-scrambled, above and below. More papers swirled in the swirl. The gadgets and toys stirred again. Then Walter aimed to play hero and tried to restore calm.

"Threat's past!" shouted Walter. "Just another bird passing through, probably two love birds playing tag. At least somebody believes in still having a little fun."

"Looked to me like a white volcano or flying oval stadium or something," said Walter's Lawyer, prompting Walter to eye his lawyer curiously.

"Enough!" said the arbitrator. "Enough for one crazy, miserable day where the alleged main creator of these fantasies isn't even here to represent himself. Call me, *if* and when you people ever grow up. But don't call me Your Honor!"

The arbitration staff and the lawyers packed up and vanished, leaving Walter alone with the McPhersons in the otherwise empty gymnasium.

"Where's Bear?" asked the three.

COOL AND DREAMY MUSIC BUTTON: *"Love Rollercoaster" by the Red Hot Chili Peppers ... wild, twisted ... dip, watch it! ... ride of your life!*

"Now that's what I call rocking 'n' roaming!" said Chris, amazed at the way Dan steered True Gold in and outta that gymnasium window like that.

"You like?" asked Dan, guiding their aerial transport away from the hills of Malibu and toward the Pacific Ocean.

"I love," said Chris in the copilot's seat.

"Sweet," said Dan. Just then, another aerial transport pulled up alongside the pilot's side of the cockpit window.

"Don't think you can dance this mess around on the Tigercats!" yelled Hail Larry's Girlfriend from her cockpit window.

"I heard something about the school's hot couple getting their own aerial transport over the summer," said Chris, sounding disappointed to hear the dream had come true.

"Called Hot Lava, fools!" yelled Hail Larry, wide receiver for the Dreamville Zephyrs. To emphasize his point, an eruption of something gooey and silvery shot out of the volcano near the back of their transport.

"Colorful, but we ain't got time for kids' games. Punch it!" Dan put True Gold in TURBO MODE and the magnet left the oval in the dust. They would deal with Dreamville's resident hot couple another time. After losing Hot Lava, True Gold cruised to a slower speed near the ocean. "Hold on, while I find a place to land this puppy."

"So you think breaking up the arbitration back there bought us some time before dissolving?" asked Chris, going through the loot they'd lassoed from the table in the gymnasium.

"According to the universal memo I swiped from the creation station @ the Dean Dome, whatever those folks were doing in that gym had to do with dissolving *us*," said Dan, more focused on surveying the coastline below ... *heading north.*

"I hope we caused enough commotion to stop them for now," said Chris, holding the eggbeater lassoed from the table. "This reminds me of the thing on the back of our ship. I wonder what it's for?"

"God knows," said Dan. "But with any luck, we swiped enough of their legal mumble jumble documents, it'll take them weeks—maybe months, maybe years—to straighten out their paperwork ... Hey, there's a nice spot below to land ... an oval park ... coordinates on the dash say: Oxnard State Beach, just north of Malibu ... *hmmm* ... imagine that."

"Somebody already has," said Chris, reading from a large document:

"To meet Walt, Marcus had chosen a gem of a park on the coast in Oxnard. The beach beyond the dunes was clean and friendly, but the huge oval park bordering the dunes was the true scenic treasure."

"Whoa, stop right there," said Dan, looking at the large document in his buddy's lap. "What in the world is that big thing?"

Chris took another look at the cover of the very big and unfinished manuscript or movie script or something. "It's a story called *Walt Loves the Bearcat*."

"Bearcat?" asked Dan. *Mild laugh.* "I'm liking that as a good nickname for the Brownster."

"Dream on," giggled Chris.

"Read on," said Dan, "while I land True Gold, read me the story of *Walt Loves the Bearcat* from the very beginning ..."

DAN JOHNSON AND CHRIS BROWN LAY ON THEIR BACKS, gazing toward the clear and sunny sky above Oxnard State Beach.

"Wow," said Dan, still stunned.

"Tell me about it," said Chris, still stunned.

The boys had just finished reading *Walt Loves the Bearcat* up until this very point in the story ... and were astonished to have arrived at this very point in the story.

"Talk about a long and winding road," said Dan. "And a wordy dude!"

"Apparently, somebody had something very important they wanted to tell somebody else," said Chris, almost sounding defensive.

"I never knew one person could use so many words," said Dan.

"Apparently, somebody else never knew one person could use so few words," said Chris, almost sounding defensive. "If you read the story from my point of view."

"Yeah, but I never knew one person could verbally express so many feelings in one lifetime," said Dan.

"Apparently, somebody else never knew one person could verbally express so few feelings in one lifetime," said Chris, almost sounding defensive. "If you read the story from my point of view."

"Yeah, but they sure sound like cool guys, eh?" said Dan.

"No doubt!" giggled Chris.

"I like that Coleman," said Dan.

"I like that Yeager," said Chris.

"Sweet, let's save their asses," said Dan. "All of them. My gut tells me that's the only way to save Dreamville and give me a chance to *ki*—kick your ass in the game again. And forever."

"Dream on," giggled Chris. "But first, wanna jump off this sun deck? I'm getting kinda hot."

The boys were riding on the rooftop of a surrey circumnavigating the oval pathway at Oxnard State Beach. Beneath them, a lovely Indian family of four was enjoying a tour around the road of life, which resembles an oval.

An oval ... our energy travels our universe in an oval, like rings on the atom. This much is true, and this much is part of the pretty picture slash *equation the non-rocket scientist, childlike brain @ the creation station is trying to paint for his hero and the world.*

Dan and Chris hopped off the surrey and ducked into the bushes where they got down to business. Chris reached inside his pocket and pulled out the game otherwise known as Mattel Electronics Football. Dan reached inside his pocket and pulled out the green rock, ready for insertion into the battery compartment.

ROCK INTO GAME

NEVER TOO OLD

BUDDIES FOR LIFE

ALWAYS TRUE GOLD ...

"*The green rock,*" said Chris, feeling the turbulence. "*It's making the game go crazy ... the field ... the lights ... the buttons ... the scoreboard ... Dan!*"

"*Yeah, bud,*" said Dan. "*I get the feeling that's gonna happen every time we jet somewhere ... Sweet, huh? Hold tight, gotta get True Gold over these palm trees! Hang on, little Bearcat!*"

"*You called me little Bearcat! Things are changing! Can you feel it, Dan ... we're flying! Dan, I can fly with Dan! Dan can fly with me! We're like Zephyrs United! True Gold Zephyrs flying with wings!*"

True Gold was soaring high above Pacific Coast Highway ... *heading south.*

"Where we flying to?" asked Chris from the copilot's seat, settling down once they reached cruising altitude.

"According to that big notebook we swiped called THE NOTEBOOK OF NOTES, our next stop is not far from here," said Dan, punching in some coordinates on the dash.

"We're gonna visit this Marcus Coleman guy?" asked Chris, thumbing through the notebook of notes.

"Yes and no," said Dan. "I have a feeling our ticket is gonna be our imagination."

"He's kinda cute, from the description in the notebook," giggled Chris.

"No doubt!" said Dan, checking out the canyons below.

"Check this out," said Chris, indicating the notebook of notes. "Marcus Coleman's role models were two guys named Chris and Dan, who lived in Tulsa back in the day, but who didn't know how to be True Gold buddies."

"*Whoa,*" said Dan. "Talk about cross-dimensional."

"Says here that *that* Chris and Dan were from a time when it was harder for guys to be buddies-for-life," said Chris.

"I can't imagine not having a buddy," said Dan. "Lucky I don't have to."

"But *buddy,* we're gonna dissolve soon if we don't get Yeager and Coleman together," said Chris. "They're our dreamers; they hold the key to our whole lives."

"Yeah, but both sets of Yeager and Coleman?" asked Dan.

"Says here: the famous boys and infamous boys are four parts of the same atom," said Chris, reading from the notebook of notes. "I'm gonna guess in non-rocket science terms, that means yes."

"Talk about a tough first assignment," said Dan.

"GAME PLAN," said Chris. "But first, let's review for us more analytical thinkers—those of us who work better when taking our time to absorb the facts."

"We got four original cool and dreamy dudes," said Dan.

Marcus Coleman ... waiting in the bleachers of the football stadium in the hills of Malibu. To see if Walt's coming back. Or to give up on the idea that Walt's coming back. Or to see if the note that blew away will mysteriously come back. For any kind of inspiration telling his soul where to turn next. At the heart of his dilemma lies one question: does he truly believe he deserves the man of his dreams and happily-ever-after, however both are defined?

"Poor bastard," said Chris. "How'd he end up this way?"

"Dunno," said Dan, "but I have a feeling we'll find out if we keep going. We'll save his ass. Who's next in the notebook of notes?"

Bear Coleman ... emotionally-absent buddy of Walter Yeager. For the first time in his life, the original little Bearcat is consumed with self-doubt. The Bear in the Plastic Bubble went out into the post-hibernation world and the bubble burst. Now he often feels retarded, or a Jerry Lewis nightmare come true. At the heart of his dilemma lies one question: does he truly believe he deserves the man of his dreams and happily-ever-after, however both are defined?

"I don't know who's the poorer bastard," said Chris. "Marcus or Bear."

"What's it say for the Yeagers?" asked Dan, glancing down at the Santa Monica Pier.

Walter Yeager ... retired NFL football star. CEO of Bearcat Studios and president of the Bearcat Investment Group and the Bearcat Charity Foundation. The three-time Super Bowl champ is still feeling his way around his new life as a retired athlete still in the public eye as football's first "openly sexual" quarterback. Hurts for his hurting Bear but doesn't know what to do except to keep on loving his buddy, always and forever, and pray that it helps.

"Talk about a tough transition," said Dan, sounding rather empathetic.

"And then there's Walt," said Chris, looking at the notebook of notes.

Walt Yeager ... single, divorced father and successful financial wizard. Retired from football in college due to back problems that were never reversed via Bass the Dane. Whereabouts: unknown. True nature: unknown. Thoughts about black spirit leaders with fantastical ideas about being his soul mate: unknown.

Unless somebody can dream a better dream.

... After a phone mix-up in Chicago, Marcus met Walt in California. It was like a dream come true for Marcus, meeting the man from the photograph that inspired so many beautiful dreams—the two of them laughing, joking, connecting, getting along so well, as if ... *that's the way the gods drew it up ...*

... *the joy, the connection, the realization that they were magnetized, at least in Marcus' dreams.*

... *Then came* ... the realization that Walt wasn't there. The little red sports car was gone, the note blew away, and Marcus was alone in his whole new world.

"And so he waits," said Chris, looking up from the notebook. "That bites."

"Ah, every cowboy's gotta have some mystery about him," shrugged Dan, flying over the Pacific.

"This is me over here rolling my eyes, but don't take it personally," said Chris, eyeing the red button on the control panel. "I just feel for Marcus. He needs what everybody needs."

COOL AND DREAMY MUSIC BUTTON: *"Somebody To Love" by Queen ... a lonely boy's prayer to his universe. Bearcat Boyz ain't too proud to beg. This much is true.*

"Now descending onto the makeshift offices of Bearcat Studios in West LA," said Dan, slowing down True Gold and going into STEALTH MODE. Moments later, they were hovering next to the second-story window of a small brick building. "STORY MEETING. Bear Coleman's talking to his small staff about Marcus Coleman in *My Whole Other Life.*"

"So this is where he's spending his time," said Chris, instinctively knowing which buttons on the panel to push to use his imagination:

"So what happens next to Marcus?" asked a male assistant in the office.

"Thinking," said Bear.

"Why can't I see the rest of Bear?" asked Chris, straining to get a better look at the window. "I can only see his elbow. Move in the picture, Coleman, you double dawg!"

"Ha!" laughed Dan, turning up the music. "He's not budging. Listen up."

"I've got it!" said Bear. "It just came to me. *That* Marcus finally gets a dog and we show them together in a montage to that song by Queen."

"Is this before or after he's met Walt?" asked a female assistant.

"Way before," said Bear. "In the present, Marcus is still stuck at the old junior high in Malibu, waiting to see if Walt's coming back. He'll be waiting in the bleachers until the end of the movie. We're not changing that. We're going back a few years in the story now. Picture it: it's the new millennium. Marcus is surviving with AIDS, miracle of miracles. There's no scientific rhyme or reason. He's like one of those homes spared in a tornado or earthquake—you know, like when the rest of the neighborhood is wiped out."

"He's a survivor," said a female assistant. "Like Duncan McDuncan."

"Exactly," said Bear. "With all the same challenges of being a generation's worst nightmare who hasn't withered away and died, as predicted by the world."

"Still feeling like a stigma, or really an enigma now," said a male assistant, looking at his notes.

"Still an *AIDS aura* to everybody," said a female assistant, "but kind of a *freakish AIDS aura* now, like, *why is* he *still alive?*"

"Tell me and I'll be the second to know," said Bear. *Mild laugh.* "So anyway, Marcus is alive. He's writing novels—good ones, I might add. Kind of a halfway decent life—not rich, not poor, no buddy yet—but he's got a dog now!"

"A dog just like Hip," said a female assistant, petting Hip, who was napping at her feet, "and Walter, too," she added with a giggle.

"Exactly," said Bear. "An adorable, golden blond, swift and agile, panther-like dog that is the most sensitive creature Marcus has ever known. So in *My Whole Other Life,* cut to the song 'Somebody to Love' by Queen, the sweetest serenade to the world to *help me find my buddy, people!*"

"I love it," said a male assistant.

"Picture Marcus, playing in a seaside dog park," said Bear, elbow moving excitedly in the window. "He's chasing his dog, laughing with the other dog owners, connecting as friends. Queen is singing about how, *I'm just trying to be a good boy, getting down on my knees, praying to God, working hard every day*—all that shit— and Marcus is having a ball being a man of the new millennium, whatever that means."

"Like a newborn kid," said a female assistant.

"Exactly," said Bear, "but he's a lonely newborn boy. We show him writing his novels with his dog by his side at his seaside pad. *Find him ... somebody to love!* We show him playing in a gay basketball league, huffing and puffing up and down the court with guys half his age. *Find him ... somebody to love!* We show him getting his horny gay sex, that double dawg!"

"Where?" asked a male assistant.

"Where else? The gay world!" laughed Bear. "But it's a game he's ready to stop playing. Meanwhile, the song is still going: *Find him ... somebody to love!* We show him spending most of his time alone with his dog. *Find him ... somebody to love!* We see him dancing to the song in his bedroom—through the years—starting when he's a little boy in Mama Rent's house, then a teenager, then a college kid in the dorm, then in his thirties, and now, in his forties. He's still singing and dancing like a cute and goofy kid in his bedroom. *Find him ... somebody to love!* Marcus Coleman, a man who's still alive, still hopeful, but still searching for answers and love. And better dreams. Get it?"

"The dog is cool and all," said a male assistant, "but how about waking up his romantic soul?"

"We're gonna have to go there, sooner or later, huh?" asked Bear, trailing off and moving away from the window. "Do I smell nachos for lunch?"

"I think he's on his way again," laughed Dan, flying away from the two-story brick building.

"It's a good thing that song worked," said Chris, indicating the universal memo coming over the dash.

"Trouble back in Malibu. Punch it!" said Dan, putting True Gold in TURBO MODE and zooming away from West LA.

COOL AND DREAMY MUSIC BUTTON: *"Trust" by Prince ... a hard-thumpin' joy ride to the promised land!*

True Gold was a model of a stadium, resting motionless on top of a table in the middle of a legal proceeding.

"So what exactly is True Gold?" asked the arbitrator. "And what about the motto outside the stadium's granite walls: ROCKS, BLOCKS, BODIES?"

"Your Honor," said Walter, seated at the table with a lawyer by his side, "Bear could explain it better, if he were here, but: we throw *rocks,* meaning sports, build *blocks,* meaning words and letters, and take care of our celestial *bodies,* more or less, give or take."

"Where is Mr. Marcus Coleman?" asked the arbitrator, looking through his notes. "And you can stop calling me Your Honor."

"It's Marcus 'Bear' Coleman, Your Honor," said Hail Larry's Wife, seated on the McPherson side. "Not to be confused with some freakin' guy with a similar name claiming to have thought this all up."

"Where is Bear anyway?" asked Hail Larry, seated on the McPherson side. "I kinda miss the kid. So do the kids."

"Working at the office," said Walter, "then scouting locations for a home in Oxnard for his mother and her new fiancé, our old coach ... Coach Renteria. Imagine that. Bear and Reggie are gonna be related. And Bear's mom is gonna become Mama Renteria. Or Mama Rent for short. *Ha!* Man, I miss my Bear."

Silence ensued in the gymnasium.

"So why is there a ticket window," asked the arbitrator, "but it says here, the ticket booth is always unoccupied. How do these Bearcat People get into the true golden stadium?"

"Your ticket is your imagination, Your Honor," said Hail Larry's Wife.

"I don't get it," said the arbitrator.

Silence ensued in the gymnasium.

"So why exactly is there so much profanity in these scripts for *The Bearcat Boyz?*" asked the arbitrator. "And you don't have to call me Your Honor. I really wish you wouldn't."

"*The reason for the profanity, Your Honor,*" began Walter and the Hail Larrys, speaking at once. Walter cleared his throat like a floor general and took control.

"The profanity, Your Honor," said Walter, "is part of the concept of depowering certain words, while understanding the power of the everyday things we say."

"Like how just saying *heaven* or *hell* in a sentence affects the energy you bring into your world," said Hail Larry's Wife. "Heavenly energy or hellish energy."

"The Bear is a damned genius," said Hail Larry. "I mean, blessed genius."

"With an amazing mind that feels underappreciated right now," said Walter. "But he's got these fascinating theories about soul mates, and bonds between blacks and whites that go back to the beginning of time on Earth, and the map of life being as easy as the game of football, or any sport, or just the freakin' alphabet. People need to listen to my Bear ... I probably need to listen to my Bear."

"It all makes so much sense when he explains it on the beach at night," said Hail Larry's Wife.

"And that's the stuff he wants to deal with in *The Bearcat Boyz,* Your Honor," said Walter.

"But with a lot of fun shit in between, Your Honor," said Hail Larry. "Football, spirit leading, stadiums flying like freakin' spaceships, kids stuff."

"What about this thing called Dean Durrett Syndrome?" asked the arbitrator, looking at his notes.

Walter and the Hail Larrys wore blank expressions.

"Where's Bear?" asked the three.

"McPhersons, what all do you want?" asked a resigned Walter. "I don't think my Bear cares anymore."

"So are we ready to forge an agreement?" asked the hopeful arbitrator. Just then, they heard the shattering of a window high up in the gymnasium.

"They're back!" yelled Hail Larry's Wife. Some in the gym scrambled above the table. Others scrambled below. The arbitration staff swirled in panic. Papers swirled in the swirl. The gadgets and toys on the table rocked and rolled. Then Walter aimed to play hero and tried to restore calm.

"All clear!" said Walter. "Just birds again."

"Are we sure that wasn't an unidentified flying object of some sort?" asked Walter's Lawyer, looking through his notes.

"What—like a flying horseshoe stadium?" scoffed Walter.

"Enough for one crazy, miserable day!" said Hail Larry. "Let's table this for another time, maybe when Bear's here, so we don't have to hear him bitch and moan later about squeezing him out."

"Good idea, you might be right, I second that boom, sounds good, okay, cool, meeting postponed, sorry, arbitrator people," said Walter and the Hail Larrys.

A bewildered and agitated arbitration staff swirled out of the gym in a hurry.

"Not bad, Brownster, for your first swoop 'n' grab from behind the wheel," said Dan from the copilot's seat as True Gold sped away from the Complex in Malibu.

"Practicing on that Wal-Mart on the way up here really helped big time," said Chris from the pilot's seat. "So now what? I mean ... Game Plan."

"Reverse it," said Dan, reading the universal memo coming over the dashboard. "Marcus of *My Whole Other Life* needs us."

"Again?" said Chris.

"You doubt the Dan Man?" asked Dan.

"No way!" said Chris, then he said into the engine mic: "Reverse it!"

"Coleman—Marcus—is alive and dreaming again," said Dan, looking at the notes just swiped, "but he's not dreaming big enough to help us save Dreamville. He still has no idea he's meant to be with Walt."

"What a dope! Hasn't he ever seen a Julia Roberts movie?" asked Chris. "She always gets her Richard Gere in the end—you know what I mean."

"Yeah, but the poor bastard Marcus Coleman has never felt as special as Julia Roberts," said Dan. "He's only been the supportive best friend who provides the shoulder for Julia to cry on while agonizing for two hours over whether or not Richard Gere is going to finally fall for her—hook, line and happy ending."

"At which point the best friend gets shuttled back to central casting to do sitcoms and infomercials," said Chris. "What a horrible way for Marcus Coleman to feel."

"The very definition of a poor bastard, according to these notes," said Dan. *A poor bastard is a man who feels his heart has no home other than his own.*

"Deep," said Chris.

"Tell me about it," said Dan.

"There's Bear now," said Chris, descending down to the two-story brick building that was Bearcat Studios and hovering next to the window outside Bear's office. "All I can see is the back of him."

"Coleman's sitting at his desk," said Dan, reading from the notebook of notes. "He's working on the script for *My Whole Other Life* while watching hoops on TV. The NBA playoffs. Says here: Coleman's in the middle of a personal sports miracle: his favorite childhood team, the Indiana Pacers in their glory years in the NBA, to date."

"Looks like he's having a great time!" said Chris. "He's cheering for his Pacers against the giants of the NBA. Like a dream come true."

"Look what he's typing in his notes for *My Whole Other Life*," said Dan.

Marcus used to cheerlead for Reggie Miller at UCLA, so seeing Reggie right-backatcha in the form of leading the Pacers to Spiked-glory is another way Marcus is reawakening to the dreams of his soul and the miracles of life. The more passion he finds in his world, the more alive he feels. The more alive he feels, the more in touch he becomes with his deepest dreams.

"Ah, the power of sports dreams, no matter the dreamer," said Dan.

"Coleman's gonna need more inspiration than that," said Chris, "something to wake him up."

"He's about to get it," said Dan, eyeing the golden sunset straight ahead ...

Mama Rent Dreams Bigger Dreams.
Cool and Dreamy Music Button: *"Fields of Gold" by Sting ... wistful wondering as you wander the landscape of your own field of dreams.*

Retired from her job as a librarian, Mama Rent dreams of living near the beach and enjoying a cozy seaside life. Mama Rent is already living two other dreams come true: her chocolate Lab puppy and her chocolate fiancé, Ernie Renteria, the retired football coach. The Rents-to-be dream of selling the family home in Hayward and moving to Oxnard Bay, a sleepy senior community a few miles north of Malibu. Mama Rent offers all her children one last chance to retrieve any old belongings from the old homestead before the purge and move.

"There's Bear now, or at least, the back of him." Chris put True Gold in stealth mode and cruised to a hovering position just outside the Coleman family garage, which was open and flooded with hazy sunlight (the stuff of blurry dreams).

"Coleman makes the journey home," read Dan from the notebook of notes. "In the garage, amidst his old college boxes, he finds the program. UCLA @ Georgia. The original game. He thumbs through and sees the photo, Yellow Polo Shirt Walt Yeager. Let's zoom in and see wassup."

The photo is so tiny, thought Bear. *You can barely see Walter, his face, his eyes. He still looks perfect, still represents perfect to me. Has he ever not been perfect to me? At the core? His aura? His beautiful, strong, healthy, friendly, masculine, warm, half-smiling, golden blond aura? Would Marcus fall for the buddy of my dreams from one little photo? Could one photo be that powerful? Then again, look at what one pissant Bearcat photo did in my life.*

Bear decided to check his old college journal, the one he kept for a couple of months in the blur. He wanted to see if he had ever written anything about Walter. He found one entry:

> I love this dream buddy and hope it's not too good to be
> true. It's too frustrating to think he'll fade away, like all
> the guys before him. I have faith though. Knowing I have
> a buddy makes all the difference in the world when I go
> to sleep at night, thinking about how much Walt loves the
> Bearcat.

Could he ever be anything but perfect to me? Why is he so perfect to me? For me? No matter what else matters. No matter what kind of life. No matter what life? How would Marcus experience this moment?

Bear decided to buy a ticket and use his imagination.

The photo is so tiny, thought Marcus. *You can barely see Walt, his face, his eyes. Haven't seen this picture in years. Never needed to see it much. His aura resided in my heart—his beautiful golden blond aura, always representing my deepest dreams: a duo that brought out the best in each other, buddies united. Would Bear have fallen for my dream buddy from one little glance at a frat party? Can one glance be that powerful? Then again, look at what one little pissant glance at a photo in a game program did in my life.*

Marcus decided to check his old college journal, the one he kept for a couple of months in the blur. He wanted to see if he had ever written anything about Walt. He found one entry:

> I love this dream buddy, but conversely, I wish I could
> get over him. It's too frustrating, knowing I can never
> have him, like all the guys before him. I shouldn't worry
> though. Walt's immortality is battling a strong tradition
> of easy-come, easy-go dream buddies and buddy dreams.
> Still, for now, the Bearcat very much loves Walt.

Could he ever be anything but perfect to me? Why is he so perfect to me? For me? No matter what else matters? No matter what kind of life. No matter what life? How would Bear experience this moment?

"Attention, Bearcat People," said Dan, using his fist as a mock PA system, "before we go deeper into Coleman's spiraling, cross-dimensional vortex, there's trouble in another part of the Bearcat Universe."

"I'm on it," said Chris, zooming away from the garage of the Coleman home in Hayward. "Good thing, too. I was about to get dizzy."

"Hang on, we're almost home, little Bearcat," said Dan.

"GAME PLAN," giggled Chris.

"Malibu again," said Dan.

"Reverse it!" said Chris into the engine mic of True Gold.

REELS UPON REELS OF FOOTAGE for the movie *Walt Loves the Bearcat* sat piled on the table in the middle of a legal proceeding.

"So what exactly is this partially-completed *Walt Loves the Bearcat* film about?" asked the arbitrator, reading from his notes. "The story of parallel fantasy universes? Four lifetimes going around the same atomic particle in reverse directions? A pretty picture a young boy is trying to paint to explain something? A mathematical equation a wounded adolescent genius is trying to share with the world that broke his heart in ninth grade, the very year his young black mind was about to take off into untapped scientific territories, territories buried in his wounded soul until now? A launching pad for a new generation of sexually confident Bearcat Boyz who create their own golden rules? The beginning of the truth about race relations and golden soul mates in America? *Huh?*"

"Your Honor, if Bear were here, he'd fill you in, trust me," said Walter, having a slice of wedding cake.

"Does he plan on leaving the reception elsewhere on the grounds to join us?" asked the arbitrator, having a slice of wedding cake.

"Knowing him, he'll be dancing all night," said Hail Larry's Wife, having a slice of wedding cake. "I think he's the one who hired Prince."

"At least, he'll tire the kids," said Hail Larry, having a slice of wedding cake. "Bear, I mean, not Prince."

Silence ensued in the gymnasium in the hills of Malibu. On the grounds beyond the gym, Prince was jamming a live version of "Let's Pretend We're Married" for the newlyweds, Coach Renteria and Mama Rent, aka the Rents.

"I'm going to take it as an encouraging sign," said the arbitrator to the McPhersons, "that you were willing to allow Mr. Coleman's mother to have her wedding and reception here at the disputed property in question. Now, if I could just get you to stop calling me Your Honor."

"*Your Honor, we thought this might—*" began Walter and the Hail Larrys, speaking at once. Walter cleared his throat like a floor general and took control.

"We were hoping, Your Honor," said Walter, "that Bear might take some time out from the reception to join the arbitration."

"But Bear just doesn't seem interested in resolving anything," said Hail Larry's Wife, "or talking to anyone."

"Barely spoke to me," said Hail Larry. "And I love Prince."

"Join the club," said Walter.

"Then I'm going to recommend the complete dissolution of this dream— I mean, endeavor—immediately," said the arbitrator. Just then, they heard the shattering of a window high up in the gymnasium.

"Yes!" shouted Hail Larry's Wife, sounding like a bad actress. "I mean: yes-I-hear-an-attack-again-oh-my-God!"

The arbitration staff swirled in panic. Papers swirled in the swirl. The gadgets rocked. Then Walter aimed to play hero.

"Probably the doves Bear ordered, just doing a drive-by," said Walter, then turned to his lawyer. *"Nothing legal!* Sounded like they were crying though."

"Why did Bear just leave us standing alone in a world so cold?" asked Hail Larry.

"Enough!" said Hail Larry's Wife. "When doves cry, it's a sign. We shouldn't dissolve anything. For now, maybe ever. I believe in signs like that."

"Good idea, me, too, I second and third that boom, let's not do it, we're clear, you might be right, sounds good, sorry arbitrator people," said Walter and the Hail Larrys. The arbitration staff up and left in a huff.

"What'd we say?" asked Walter. *Mild laugh.* "I thought the point was to resolve things outta court. We kinda did. Sorta."

"Freakin' Yeager, pay up." Hail Larry extended his hand across the table.

"What? Oh," said Walter, remembering their bet and reaching for his wallet. "I thought for sure that guy was gonna explode and go off on us."

"What do you think the arbitrator would do if we keep calling him Your Honor?" wondered Hail Larry while outside the gym before the first arbitration meeting.

"A hundred bucks says, eventually he'll blow his top," said Walter.

"You're on," said Hail Larry, extending his hand to shake on it.

"Easiest C-note I've made in months," said Hail Larry, eagerly swiping Yeager's cash.

"Hell, Larry, about time you won a bet with me," said Walter, never happy losing at anything.

"Guys, are we ever gonna be a foursome again?" asked Hail Larry's Wife. "Seeing Coach and the Colemans and Yeagers today—and Grace and her girls, and Tank, and the Asian lesbos, and Roberto A. Selladito, and even Reverend Reggie Snowman, and everybody else—really makes me miss the old days."

"Reverend Reggie did a great job with the ceremony," said Hail Larry. "And Yeager's old supermodel girlfriend Ivanya Elle M'vanya still looks freakin' hot! Man, I still love women!"

Walter sighed. "Think you guys can help me get Bear back in the fold?"

"How?" asked the Hail Larrys.

"Dream of it," said Walter. "And pray for a miracle."

"I THINK WE JUST SAVED OUR ASSES, not to mention our cool and dreamy lives!" said Dan from the pilot's seat as True Gold soared above the hills of Malibu.

"I think you're right!" said Chris from the copilot's seat.

The boys hooted and hollered, then fell silent.

"So why don't we feel so good?" asked Chris.

"Because our dreamers don't," said Dan.

At the Complex in the hills below, Bear Coleman sat in the stands of the football stadium, contemplating his life as the wedding reception went on elsewhere on the grounds.

In a different world, Marcus Coleman sat in those same stands, contemplating his life as he waited in the darkness for Walt.

"Time to do what Dean Dome hired and fired us for," said Chris. "Make sure they dream the better dream."

"Onward!" said Dan.

"Where to?" asked Chris and Dan together.

"Look what it says here in the notebook of notes," said Chris.

When your mind's in a quandary, go wandering elsewhere in your dreams.

"I'll take you there," said Dan, putting True Gold in TURBO MODE.

COOL AND DREAMY MUSIC BUTTON: *"Countin' on Miracle" by Bruce Springsteen ... hard drivin', soul pleadin', gettin' ready to throw another Hail Mary ...*

True Gold went tripping through the sky, the planets, the galaxies, even a parallel fantasy universe or two, all while Dan, and sometimes Chris, steered the horseshoe magnet through the universal space known as God's country. At least the parts the fallible gods on Earth have dreamed up so far. Most of outer space was dark, so it was like flying through, over and around an endless parade of stars and suns, stardust and planets, rocks and blocks, and all kinds of squiggly, indescribable strings and things that neither Chris nor Dan had ever seen before. But it was all a whole lotta fun. Like a sweet dream. When they had enough, they came back down to Earth, refreshed, reenergized and full of hope.

Dreamin'. The true power of True Gold.

"Hold on, re-entering Earth's atmosphere," said Dan, swooping down on the home planet.

"And getting a universal memo," said Chris, indicating the dash. "Sometime later, Bear Coleman is waking up from a nap at Bearcat Studios."

"Let's see what he's been dreaming of," said Dan, steering True Gold toward the small brick building, then going into STEALTH MODE while hovering next to the second-story window outside Coleman's office.

"Why can't I see more of Bear?" asked Chris, straining to get a better look at the window. "I can only see a part of his back!"

"STORY MEETING," said Bear to the small staff in his office. *"I'm Marcus Coleman. I'm waiting in these junior high bleachers in Malibu. I'm sitting up here, dreaming about celebrating my mom's wedding. The night's wearing on. I got no Walt. I got no fun, no buddy, nobody. I'm a nobody. In a world without Walt, I'm a nobody. Just a body. But nobody loves me ... like that ... I've never felt special that way ..."*

"Bear, you okay?" asked a male assistant.

"*Huh?*" asked Bear, rejoining the room, mind, body and soul. "Sorry ... lost me for a second. Okay ... so we're near the end of *My Whole Other Life*. And I still haven't figured out why Walt left, and more importantly, if he's coming back. And why? Or how? And what for?"

"He left to attend a function in Chicago," suggested a male assistant.

"He had to think about things," said a female assistant, "sort out his feelings, deal with his own 'Complex' issues before such a big ... decision."

"Are we sure it's not Walter just pretending to be Walt?" asked a male assistant. "Like in some therapeutic exercise to help his buddy work things out?"

"You mean, like, role-playing?" asked a female assistant.

"We are talking happy ending, right?" asked another female assistant.

"Of course," said Bear, not sounding so sure, "but why would a guy like Walt fall for a guy like Marcus?"

"He's a survivor," said a female assistant. "They're both survivors. Not of AIDS necessarily, but of life and life's challenges. Of dreams denied. Or at least, deferred."

"They relate to one another," said another female assistant. "They're amazingly just like Walter and Bear. It's chemistry. It's magic. Movie magic."

"Movie magic," repeated Bear.

"Come on, Bear-man," laughed the female assistant. "How many movies have you seen where people fall in love like magic?"

"Then fly off into the sunset without worrying about all the details," said a male assistant.

"Don't sweat the details in your fantasies," said a female assistant. "A friend of mine named Benchley once told me that."

"So Walt's not tied down to this whole 'heterosexual' thing?" asked Bear. "Even though he's gone the traditional 'straight' route so far?"

"Why can't he be just ... sexual, like you and Walter?" asked a female assistant, "without any other labels. Like a bearcat boy."

"Or he could be straight as an arrow, and fall head over heels for Bear," said a male assistant. "I mean, Marcus, not Bear—I mean, I'm sure it's happened before."

"Frankly," said a female assistant, "if a man who's basically a carbon copy of the real-life Walter Yeager was dreaming of me, I wouldn't be worried about which sexual box to put him in. I'd just enjoy the package."

"Ah, ha! What about the HIV?" said Bear, as if stumping them.

"What about it?" asked a female assistant.

"Walt knows," said Bear. "Marcus told him. Maybe Walt freaked out and ran from that alone?"

"Walt could be educated and open-minded," shrugged a male assistant.

"Or able to see beyond an *AIDS aura*," said a female assistant.

"Or not see an *AIDS aura* at all," said a male assistant.

"Duncan's right," said a female assistant. "Walt could just see the golden brown aura that matches his own golden blond aura."

"Sergeant Holly's right," said a male assistant. "Walt could be flattered by Marcus' dreams of Walter and Bear in this life."

"He could see a friend in Marcus, an admirer, a buddy," said a female assistant.

"Maybe Walt can relate," said a male assistant. "Maybe Walt's had his own personal challenges, like, his back injury that never got reversed by the Dane. And he *has* been divorced a time or two, so the man's had his share of rocky road, as opposed to Bob & Jimmy's Yeager-meister."

"I love it," said a female assistant. "They've both had their challenges since college—starting in college—talk about something in common. They're survivors!"

"Just like Walter and Bear," shrugged a male assistant. "Nothing's gonna stop them now."

"So Marcus is supposed to just count on a miracle? And believe a white man from the North Pole is gonna make all his dreams come true?" asked Bear, suddenly reminded of his days with Santa and the ER Wife.

"Maybe Marcus makes some of Walt's dreams come true," shrugged a male assistant. "Nobody's even mentioning that."

"Meaning?" asked Bear.

"Look at what Walt's getting out of this," said a male assistant. "A great companion in Marcus—kinda like you, Bear, with a less charmed life."

He's getting something outta the deal, too, thought Bear.

Marcus has a lot to offer Walt.

I have a lot to offer Walter.

I've had a lot to offer Walter all these years.

He's gotten something outta the deal, too, thought Bear.

"So cut to the end of the movie," said a doubtful Bear, "and Marcus is just supposed to ... count on the fact that, by some miracle of fate, some ... miracle is gonna happen?"

"Isn't that called two people falling in love?" asked a female assistant. "And movie magic?"

"The real miracle is staying together, " said a male assistant, prompting a round of laughter.

"Yeah, but—" said Bear.

"Didn't Romeo and Juliet meet, fall in love and die for that love, all in, like, a few days?" asked a male assistant.

"A million Hollywood movies have been made where the couple falls in love and rides off into the sunset after, like, a couple of hours or days," said a female assistant. "That's what Lucy or Lacy—I can never remember which—did in *Freeways*—well, before she lost it all after honking her horn at the wrong old lady driver that one day. Poor Lacy. Or Lucy."

"I know how movies work," said Bear. "*Duh?* It's just that ... for the audience to believe in Walt, this white, upstanding icon of a financial wizard, falling for Marcus, this black, HIV-positive-whatever ... maybe we should have had Marcus going for someone completely different from Walt: a black guy, a Jewish guy, a *gay* guy."

"In other words, create a whole different Marcus Coleman," said a female assistant.

"Why should Marcus want to be with a man like Walt anyway?" asked Bear.

"Because maybe that's what resonates in his soul?" said the same female assistant.

"We're talking a huge Hollywood miracle here, folks," said Bear.

"Does Marcus believe in miracles?" asked a female assistant.

"Remember, he's had a tough road," said Bear. "Buddyless. Hard to believe in the miracle of love when you've been buddyless your whole life."

"What would it take for Marcus to believe?" asked a male assistant.

"Walt to show up for one," said a female assistant.

"I think the bigger question is, what would it take for Bear to believe," said a male assistant.

"What do you mean?" asked Bear.

"It ain't gonna happen unless you believe," said the male assistant, "no matter what we say, or what's good for the audience."

"Duncan's right," said a female assistant, patting Duncan McDuncan on the shoulder. "Coleman's fate is up to Coleman."

"Good one, I like that," said a male assistant.

"Is that lunch I smell?" asked Bear. "Better hurry. I think it's tacos today."

The staff swirled out and headed for the kitchen. Bear stayed behind, sitting at his desk, back to the window.

"He's calling something up on his monitor," said Chris, looking through the notebook of notes in the cockpit of True Gold.

"Something about a guy named Dean," said Dan from the pilot's seat.

"Dean Durrett Syndrome," said Chris. He read aloud from the notebook of notes what Bear Coleman read to himself on his monitor: "when you don't believe you deserve the beauty God has placed before your eyes."

Dean Durrett ... the most beautiful boy at Hayward Central High, always and forever. To this day, one of the most beautiful souls to Marcus Coleman's soul, and a man unseen since high school.

Dean Durrett ... tall, blond, seemingly carefree, a prototype quarterback from a prototype family of prototype successful white kids. Dean was a god to young Marcus Coleman in the halls of Hayward Central High. Dean was also untouchable. After the quarterback of Marcus' freshman dreams called Marcus a "Bubba Retard," no way was Marcus "Bubba Retard" Coleman gonna even look Dean Durrett's way. The ungraceful, unathletic, bearish black boy had learned his lesson. The gods of the world were off-limits to his dreams, even though all he dreamed of were the gods.

Marcus put Dean in a dome and kept him safe and pure, an immaculate conception of a dream that could never cause injury or pain, yet still remind Marcus of the existence of perfection to his soul's eyes.

Dean Durrett ... a man with whom Marcus shared one brief glance throughout high school, a moment which Marcus remembers to this day: the wide-eyed look in Dean's eyes, the flickering glimpse inside the windows to a young man's soul.

"You never know what impact you really have on the rest of the world and every single person in it," said Dan.

A photo, a smile, a thought, a word, a look, an act of kindness, an act of unkindness. An act you may or may not ever be aware of.

"People you may never meet or never know may be thinking of you right now," said Chris, reading from the notebook of notes, "dreaming of you, dreaming of a wonderful loving life with you. Somebody may be loving you in all kinds of special ways tonight in their dreams. Anything is possible."

"If I were Walt, I'd be amazed," said Dan. "Stunned but amazed."

"But Marcus has this Dean Durrett Syndrome," said Chris, indicating the notes. "Marcus has never even conceived of the possibility of a man as special in his eyes as Walt Yeager, or Dean Durrett, ever falling in love with him, wanting him, needing him. Says here: in his real life, Marcus has rarely dreamed of *any* man treating him special. Check this out ..."

In the gay world, the question is:

"Hey, you, where can we go fuck?"

As opposed to:

"Hi, what's your name? And what makes your soul resonate with joy?"

"Glad we're not gay like those poor bastards!" said Dan, watching as Bear shut off his monitor and headed for lunch.

"I guess that's how it was back in the olden days," said Chris, reading from the notebook of notes. "A lotta black guys and guys who called themselves gay didn't feel good about themselves. Says: guys like Coleman grew up thinking they were ... faggy dorks unworthy of love that was True Gold."

"Man, that bites," said Dan.

"Glad we weren't around then, or during those *Tulsa* days," said Chris.

"Tell me about it," said Dan. "Let's hook these guys up."

"GAME PLAN," said Chris.

"Feel like a Milky Way run?" asked Dan. "I think we could use the fuel."

"Sure, I'll drive," said Chris. "Love tripping the galaxies with my bud."

"HARD TO BELIEVE WE THOUGHT THIS would be fun without Bear," said Hail Larry's Wife, sitting poolside at the Jaw on a starry night. "Kids, don't hold the dogs' mouths underwater, please!"

"Freakin' Yeager, where's your buddy?" asked Hail Larry, floating on a raft in the pool. "He used to keep better track of you. Wait, did I say that right?"

"What's today, Thursday?" asked Walter. He was standing on the upper deck, looking down at the pool in the backyard. "The note on his creation station said he was doing research in West Hollywood tonight."

"He sure is doing a lot of research these days," said Hail Larry's Wife.

COOL AND DREAMY MUSIC BUTTON: *"It's Raining Men" by The Weather Girls ... Bear Coleman lets loose!*

"Come on, Roberto, scream!" yelled Bear.

The six million men in the big gay club screamed at the top of their lungs!

Bear and Roberto the Celibate—the boys' personal assistant—were in the hottest new club in WeHo, that place young Bear left behind so many years ago to be Walter Yeager's buddy.

"Tonight *he's* Mr. Bear Coleman, wherever *he* is!" yelled Bear.

"Who's Mr. Bear Coleman, sir?" yelled Roberto, looking cramped and uncomfortable next to the bar.

"My husband, fool!" yelled Bear. "Drinks for all the boys on that side of the room! Where's the people of color?"

"This is a whites-and-Latins-only night," said Roberto.

"Then why'd they let my black ass in?" Bear suddenly remembered who he was and who he was buddies with. "Oh ... let's go."

COOL AND DREAMY MUSIC BUTTON: *"I Try" by Macy Gray ... story of a sorrowful soul stumbling around without the one who makes it all ... balanced.*

"Lovely song, eh?" said Roberto, turning down the Macy Gray tune coming over his radio. He was sitting in the driver's seat of his ground transport with the window rolled down. "Did you get enough?"

"Plenty," said Bear, standing in the parking lot of the big gay club. "I think eight seconds in a gay bar is plenty. Any more, and it will drag the film. I'll make that 'one little cut' before the screening this weekend. That and the title change. It'll take five minutes to do, tops."

"If you say so, sir." Roberto's transport moved away in the LA night. When Bear was alone, he eased into his own SUV in the shadows of the big gay club.

So I didn't miss anything in the last 21 years ... whew!

Bear eased onto the highway for the ride to the Rents in Oxnard. Daddy Rent—formerly Coach Renteria, aka Black Coach—would be catching up on *All My Loves,* his soap. Or maybe Bear would head home to Moose Jaw and Walter. Or maybe Bear would fall asleep while spiraling down the freeway at a highly dangerous—

—Bear blurred awake in time to right the ground transport and avoid crashing into an already-nightmarish plethora of red lights on the other side of the road ...

"That would have been a good sequence for *Freeways Claim Bodies That Fade,*" said Marcus Coleman, riding in the passenger seat all of a sudden.

"*Or* I could dream up a scene where the protagonist talks to his alter ego while driving home delirious one night," said Bear.

"Nice to see you haven't lost your wit, even if you've lost interest in what makes your heart tick," said Marcus.

"Walter still makes my heart tick, you damned well know that," said Bear. "*Oops.* You blessed well know that."

"Then why are you wandering all over creation, wondering what kind of creations you can dream up without your buddy?" asked Marcus.

"I have no idea what you mean," said Bear.

"You're absent emotionally, Bear-man," said Marcus. "Even to the Hail Larrys."

"We made up already!" insisted Bear.

A tropical beach, circa recent big league dreams ...

"Surprise! Our own personal Let's Make Up Super Duper Luau, courtesy Walter and Bear. Oh, and here's that tape from the Dane's research. The good tape. It was in Bear's old jacket pocket all this time!"

"I arranged the damned—*blessed*—thing!" said Bear. "Who else in the damned—*blessed*—gang ever does shit like that but the retard?"

"Surprise! We already knew about the luau and here's our gift in return, from the McPhersons to Walter and Bear: the two Complex properties in Malibu and Chicago! The whole reason we bought them in the first place was to give them to you!"

"Still playing the emotional retard card, I see," said Marcus.

"What's that freakin' mean?" asked Bear.

"I thought I taught both you big league boys about not giving a fuck about the labels the world creates for your horny and famous asses," said Marcus. "That's what I dreamed of for the last 21 years."

"Bullshit," said Bear. "And I don't need Julio the Bullfighter to tell me that you stopped focusing on Walter and me a long time ago, like around the time you saw Walt's name on the Internet and your dream man became a real person."

"Excuse me for wanting my own damned Walt—my own *blessed* Walt in my own life—and letting the damned—the *blessed*—big league boys romp into the Super Sunset without me," said Marcus. "Lousy job of it, by the way."

"Meaning?" asked Bear.

"You've spent these last years wondering if your whole life would have been better with or without Walter," said Marcus.

"And you've spent these last years wondering why you've spent a lifetime dreaming of a stranger, not to mention why you can't find your own True Gold buddy," said Bear. "That's why I never dreamed of you settling for just anyone, you know."

"I know why I never settled for anything less than true love. I'm not that much of a fool," said Marcus. "Or retard. I can fake a lot of things in my life, but true love isn't one of them."

"What's the point of getting in the game unless you're going for True Gold?" recited Marcus and Bear. *"Together, as buddies on the same team, always and forever. This much is true."*

"I thought about leaving him years ago, you know," said Bear.

"Ah, yes," said Marcus. "'Setting Free the Bearcats,' a chapter I planned to write but just couldn't see it through, even for a New York minute."

Setting Free the Bearcats: Bear leaves Walter for an agreed-upon, six-month separation, so Bear can prove to himself he can survive without his buddy.

"Glad I never did that," said Bear. "I imagined it slicing a wound in both our hearts, especially my buddy's."

"I'm living proof you can survive without Walter," said Marcus. "Besides, I couldn't put it in your DNA to leave *or* cheat on your man. We made a promise to God, remember?"

"So now you understand why, back in your gay 90s, you wondered about having a genetic predisposition to not being in a relationship," said Bear.

"Because it was the polar opposite?" asked Marcus.

"That's the way the gods drew it up. We're supposed to have buds," said Bear.

"Twisted," said Marcus.

Silence ensued in the ground transport blurring northbound on Pacific Coast Highway.

"I know about the movie you're finishing up for the special screening this weekend," said Marcus.

"So," said Bear.

My Whole Other Life by Bear Coleman, the story of a former college cheerleader who dreams of a lifelong romance with a handsome college quarterback he once saw in a photograph. Poor bastard Marcus Coleman is alone for life unless he can overcome Dean Durrett Syndrome and believe he's worthy of true love from another truly golden soul.

"I think it's heartwarming," said Bear.

"If Walter Yeager were my husband all these years," said Marcus, "I'd be focused on creating *The Walter Yeager Story,* not a movie that could be subtitled, *Solo Flight: Marcus Coleman's Sucky Single Life.* Where's the love story of your life? What happened to you and your sexy and famous hero QB who changed history?"

"Apparently, somebody else has the option on that little pissant ditty," said Bear.

"Meaning?" asked Marcus.

"I know about the novel you're finishing up," said Bear.

"So," said Marcus.

Walt Loves the Bearcat by Marcus Coleman, the lifelong romance of a college cheerleader and quarterback, from the Sugar Bowl to the Super Bowl, a story of love, football and wacky adventures. The big league boys are happy together until they begin to question themselves and their love, as seen through the eyes of the Image Keepers—the media, from tabloids to television.

"I think it's heartwarming," said Marcus.

"Your novel is my life!" cried Bear.

"Your movie is *my* life!" cried Marcus. "You promised your husband *The Walter Yeager Story.* On the field in Athens that first magical weekend."

"*The Walter Yeager Story* has been all over the news, haven't you heard?" said Bear.

"That's not *The Walter Yeager Story* you know," said Marcus. "Nor is that the Walter Yeager you know."

"What do you know about my Walter Yeager?" laughed Bear, hearing for the first time the radio in the transport.

Cool and Dreamy Music Button: *"You're the Best Thing That Ever Happened To Me" by Gladys Knight and the Pips ('nuff said, almost).*

"Walter Yeager has been there every single time I needed him," said Marcus. "Every. Single. Time. I've had as much sex as any other human being, especially of the male variety. But I've slept alone just about every night I've ever slept on this planet. That's over 15,000 nights and counting. You have no idea how lonely that is until you wake up alone on the morning of your 32nd birthday and the very ground beneath you is too busy rumbling to let you stand upright."

Everything around you is crumbling, literally, so violent, so loud. There's nowhere to go. It's not just your dreams, your bed, your house, your world … it's the entire universe as far as you can see, rearranging itself without a care as to how you're going to survive.

"At 4:30 a.m.," said Marcus, "a minute before the 4:31 a.m. Northridge quake, I would have made a pact with God or the devil to be anybody's buddy—a quarterback, a serial killer, Mr. Right, Mr. Wrong, an abusive boyfriend, anybody—just to be with somebody that hellish morning. Not to mention trying to get to sleep again alone that hellish night. And the hellish weeks after."

But I could never settle. I could never fake it. Somewhere inside me, I knew that I, God, made a promise to Big Light in the Sky … I will not bear false idols. I will only worship the idol you send me, should you ever send me my very own personal idol to worship … as I worship you, Big Light in the Sky … as I love myself … as I learn to worship myself through worshipping another, just like me and you …

"Since I saw Walt's picture during my Hep B rehab, no other dream has brought me more joy," said Marcus. "No single person has comforted me more in my bed at night—not having sex, not watching TV, not talking, not even touching. Walt gave me comfort just by being there in my dreams, offering unconditional acceptance for who I was, what I did, what I dreamt of, what I felt, what I needed … for all that I am. I'd feel that acceptance, then I'd feel peace, then I'd fall asleep with a better dream in my mind, my heart, my soul. All that from dreaming of Walt, a man I never imagined to be perfect, just perfect for me."

Between every second of pain and glory, there was a moment spent just loving you and me in my dreams.

"Some might look at my fantasies and think: how sad or pathetic," said Marcus. "They may see my actions as those of a lonely boy, a sad man, an emotionally retarded soul, whatever. We know all the labels the Image Keepers are good at coming up with. Some might think: how crazy of him to share all this now. How crazy would I be if I didn't share the single most joyous thing in my life? Learning to love a man unconditionally by loving him unconditionally for 21 years has been the greatest gift life has ever given me, come what may with my dreams for my pissant little ditty."

"Is that it?" asked Bear, looking in Marcus' lap.

"Just some notes and drawings," said Marcus. "I'm on my way outta town for a writer's conference, thought maybe I'd do some work on the plane. See if I can figure out this fuzzy equation that keeps appearing in my head."

"Me, too!" said Bear.

"But I only see half," said both Marcus and Bear.

Earth, life, humans, energy, soul mates—are all like a single atom, complete with orbiting rings. Each ring is energy flowing in one direction or the other. Life flows in two directions, forward and reverse, one direction no more or less valuable to the journey.

It's not the direction. It's not the details. It's the feelings. Energy is nothing more than feelings. Feelings are nothing more than energy. Life ends and begins there. The rest is details.

"Is there anything to all this?" asked one Coleman.

"Dunno," said the other Coleman. "I do know I started off trying to paint a cute little picture, the way a kid might. But the story feels like an equation, and now it seems as if my non-rocket scientist brain—the one that shut off part of itself during junior high—that brain is trying to get some air and communicate something very special my soul learned by loving the man of my dreams unconditionally for 21 years."

"I feel like I'm trying to tell people something based on my ... somewhat childlike mind being infatuated with him all this time," said Coleman.

"What about the eggbeater?" asked Coleman.

"Kinda like the rings on an atom," said Coleman.

"And at least we know where it goes now," said Coleman. "On top of the building behind the bleachers in the end zone."

"The Archives," said Coleman, "or engine room, where we store all the artifacts and memories that power True Gold, literally and figuratively."

"But what's the eggbeater for? What are any of these dreams for?" asked Coleman.

The highway blurred by a gillion miles an hour. Or was that just space and the universe going its normal speed?

"Is there anything magical or scientific to any of this? Did I recognize my soul mate from one glance 21 years ago? Are we bonded like the iron core of the Earth and the magnetic poles emanating from that core? What would be the implications of such a powerful bond between two golden boys of their race? Are we living in a world with so much perfect grace that our souls can find truly golden perfection in another soul, as if God drew it up that way, if we only believe? Or am I just a crazy fucker who's got skillz in the dream department? All I know is, there exists a man whose beauty inspired a lifetime of memories and dreams, and each and every cool and dreamy moment with the man of my dreams has helped keep me alive as much as anything else in this universe. Loving him has given me hope when I didn't have hope, blessed me with dreams when I was running out of dreams, given me somewhere to go where life wasn't perfect, but life was perfect between me and my buddy. And we never doubted our love, not like most fallible gods. Walt Yeager has been my hero, not because he's some perfect man in other people's eyes, or his own eyes, or even in my own eyes. Walt Yeager has been my hero because of the way I feel when I think about him. Good. Pure and simple. The love I have for him never runs out. It's as boundless as my spirit, so boundless that when I truly feel the power of that love, I'm able to love more and more about myself and the world around me. This much is true. That alone gives me hope that someday, I'll truly feel worthy of that kind of powerful love, and that I truly deserve the kind of happiness most of us only dream about. Like Daddy Coleman used to say, anything is possible. True?"

The transport fell silent for the remainder of the journey, pulling into the driveway of the Jaw just after dawn. An eager Bear jumped out and hurried into the house, ready to tell his buddy the good news: the spirit leader was back. But all Bear saw of his man was a note on Bear's creation station in the home office.

> Boys with Mama Rent.
> Had to leave for Chicago.
> Waited as long as I could.
> No fun without you. #13

Nothing is fun without Walter, thought Bear, racing to the backyard deck and dialing his cell. "Location," said Bear upon getting an answer.

"Nanna Helen's in Oxnard," said Hail Larry's Wife. "The kids are next door, playing with the dogs. Larry's on the patio, having some long-winded discussion with his grandmother and Mama Rent. More importantly, where are you? And where are you showing up this weekend?"

Tomorrow night, the boys had a conflict in their schedule.

Saturday night in Chicago, the West Winnetka Warriors United Football Club (Boys 10-18), was christening its new facility at Walter's former junior high, highlighted by the unveiling of the Warriors United Walk of Fame, featuring honorary member, Number 13, Walter Yeager.

Saturday night in Malibu, Bear was holding a special advanced screening of his new movie, *My Whole Other Life,* for family and friends at the future site of the Bearcat Studios *slash* Dream Games Complex (where people play games that help them get in touch with their deepest dreams).

"Walt's gonna kill me for saying this," said Hail Larry's Wife, "but he's made sure everybody—I mean, Colemans, Yeagers, Tank, everybody!—is showing up for your movie in Malibu."

"No, he *did-n't,*" said Bear, "as the kids say."

"Yes, he *did'ed,*" said Hail Larry's Wife, "as *I'm* saying."

"Oh, QB," said Bear with a soft sigh.

"Don't tell him I told you," said Hail Larry's Wife. "It's supposed to be a surprise."

"Oh, I've got the surprise," said Bear. "For him. Here's the game plan." After telling his best pal the game plan, he added: "Can't wait to see you again."

"You just saw us last weekend in Cabo," laughed Hail Larry's Wife.

"Can't wait to see you again," repeated Bear, hanging up and heading for the kitchen. In his hurry, he bumped into the patio table, causing papers and stuff to fall to the deck. One item was a homemade CD.

Good song for "Whole Other Life," said the handwriting of Hail Larry's Wife. Bear swiped up the CD and headed out the door. There was much work to be done.

Cool and Dreamy Music Button: *"World Without You" by Belinda Carlisle ... Here we go 'round again ...*

"Way to swoop in and outta there, Brownster!" said Dan from the copilot's seat of True Gold. "Causing all that commotion so Coleman saw the CD."

"I'd like to thank my teacher, Dan the Man Johnson, who taught me all I know about flying True Gold while tripping on the far side of the universe last night," said Chris.

"*Ha!*" said Dan, acting like he didn't want to take credit.

"There's Bear now!" said Chris, following Bear's ground transport down below on Pacific Coast Highway. "He's so handsome, if I say so myself!"

"I second that emotion!" said Dan. "I'm not sure who's cuter, Bear, Marcus, or the Brownster."

"Dream on," giggled Chris. "I could say the same about you and those Yeager boys. You guys are practically triplets. You sure one of them ain't Dan's daddy?"

"Tell me about it," laughed Dan. "But first, check this out from the notebook of notes: we're entering something called the *pas de finale ... hmmm ...* better stay close to these guys ... might need to spread some more zephyr winds on them."

"Working great so far," said Chris. "They're finally listening to the music we're sending their way."

"Music is the way to the soul, kid," said Dan, kickin' back with his feet on the dash ...

In a world without you ...

... Bear Coleman had a lot to do, starting with doing away with the title *My Whole Other Life,* and turning *Walt Loves the Bearcat* into a better dream and movie before tomorrow night's screening in Malibu.

... where would I be?

... To re-edit and re-assemble the movie, Bear hunkered down at Wendy Jiu and Lisa Wu's Tigercat Studios in the Valley. With the help of the lesbo cheergirls, Coleman spent hours repackaging his film in a whole new light, combining *My Whole Other Life* with *The Walter Yeager Story,* hoping the re-cut would be just one of several miracles happening over the weekend ...

In a world without you ...

... In Chicago, a man named Yeager, the greatest quarterback in the world, prepared for his inauguration into the Warriors United Walk of Fame at the new home of the West Winnetka Warriors United Football Club (Boys 10-18).

... where would I be?

... In LA, a man named Coleman, lover of the greatest quarterback in the world, prepared for the debut of his new movie, *Walt Loves the Bearcat,* to be screened in a junior high gymnasium, soon to become the Bearcat Studios Theater at the Complex in the hills of Malibu.

In a world without you ...

... In Chicago, a man named Yeager busied himself amidst the chaos and construction on the grounds of his old junior high *slash* new football club *slash* site of this weekend's inauguration ceremony.

... where would I be?

... In LA, a man named Coleman missed a man named Yeager very deeply. He missed the feeling of holding him, smiling at him, feeling him, loving him ... a breath away from his heart and soul.

In a world without you ...

... All over America, Bearcat People mobilized to their next destination in life: Malibu.

... where would I be?

... While Yeager and Coleman prepared for their big nights, dreaming of their family and friends in transit.

In a world without you ...

... The Yeagers, the Colemans, the Renterias, the McPhersons, Tank, the college student, Grace and her grown and growing girls—everyone in their world was going to be in their world on Saturday night.

... where would I be?

... Coleman didn't care which world he was in. Coleman just wanted to be in a world with his buddy. Sometime on Friday, Coleman left Tigercat Studios in LA and headed for Chicago to surprise Yeager. To keep the re-cut of the movie going, Coleman left film editor Wendy Jiu or Lisa Wu in charge.

... Her partner, Lisa Wu or Wendy Jiu, wanted to come to Chicago, which she had never seen. Lisa Wu or Wendy Jiu thought Chicago looked like a pretty picture on postcards. She wanted to see what magic she could find in the city on her own.

... *Fine, said Coleman. But when we get to the airport, I gotta split. This is a journey young Skywalker must take alone ... for a while anyway ... True?*

"There's Coleman now, getting off the plane in Chicago!" said Chris, cruising by the terminal window at O'Hare. "Man, is he ever in one big hurry."

"Didn't even pay attention to Lisa Wu or Wendy Jiu," said Dan. "*Whoa ... hold on ... these Chicago winds are much stronger than ... Stop that song! Oh, shit ... I think I hit the music button too hard ...*"

"Zephyrs!" yelled Chris, pointing to the gigantic wind coming their way.

True Gold blew away in the Chicago sky, swirling and spinning outta control in a gigantic zephyr, all while the song "World Without You" by Belinda Carlisle remained stuck in perpetual play on the Cool and Dreamy Music Button ...

"AND NOW, LET ME INTRODUCE OUR distinguished guests," said the dark-haired lesbian at the podium. Marcus put his smile on autopilot and glanced at the other panelists. Initially, he had declined the offer to speak at the writer's conference on a Friday afternoon before most of the participants had arrived. But once he realized he'd be free for the remainder of the weekend, he was just fine with being part of the warm-up act. That way, he could be ready on a moment's notice should he need to leave the hotel in downtown Chicago, say, for example, to meet Walt Yeager—should Marcus get up the nerve to call this total stranger.

"... author of some 'unique' novels so far," said the dark-haired lesbian at the podium, reining in his attention, "Marcus Coleman hails from the LA area and has been nominated for several book awards. So far, he has been *Lucci'd* at every award ceremony—his words, not mine."

Laughter rippled across the small gathering in the large conference room. The turnout belied the topic of the panel: WHY GAY AMERICA CARES ABOUT GAY LITERATURE. Marcus sat the farthest away from the podium. His mind stayed in the room for a little while, and even heard an interesting point or two. But eventually, as it so often did, his imagination took him elsewhere. He envisioned a handsome blond man in his early forties, driving a sedan or luxury SUV down the highways of Chicago on a late Friday afternoon. He figured Walt to be a white-collar professional who made lots of money the way white, ex-college quarterbacks do. Maybe Walt was on his cell phone that very moment, checking with his secretary, or giving his wife and kids an update on his arrival time. Then again, maybe he was single. Divorced, single and hetero. Or maybe he was a lover of men, and single and heading home from a tough day at the office, dreaming of an adventurous weekend in the city, not far from the conference hotel ...

"Chris Brown, do something to turn off that music button! The song is driving me crazy now!"

"I'm trying, Dan ... whoa ... watch out for that flock of seagulls!"

"Trying to get a shot of Coleman in the window of that conference room ... whoa ... another zephyr ... why couldn't they have had this gig in Philadelphia? Whoaaaaa!"

"We conquered the world, or tried to," said Marcus aloud to the audience at the writer's conference. "In my dreams, we did great things, and stood by one another like warriors united, always and forever. This much is true."

You tell 'em, handsome black stud, thought Bear Coleman, sitting in the back of the large conference room, imagining the speaker to be Marcus of My Whole Other Life.

Instead of surprising Walter right away, Bear decided to check into a hotel that was coincidentally hosting a writer's conference. Bear pictured Marcus traveling to Chicago and speaking as an esteemed novelist. In My Whole Other Life, *Walt would also be in Chicago, just like Walter, about to be inducted into the War-*

riors United Walk of Fame. Bear pictured Walt of My Whole Other Life *on the grounds of his former junior high turned boys' football club. Walt Yeager wouldn't possess the long and glorious stat sheet of Walter Yeager, but Walt would be honored by the Warriors United just the same, for his earlier accomplishments in high school and college alone. On or off the field, both Walts had quarterback in their veins. Their DNA was programmed to take care of business, lead the way, make sure everything was nailed down before the weekend's big event.*

Maybe I should call my buddy, thought Bear. Hey, Yeager-man, I'm in Chicago for your Walk of Fame ceremony, not my movie screening in Malibu. Or am I a total retard for following him wherever he goes once again? I gotta get outta here.

"Thank you very much. Enjoy your weekend," said Marcus Coleman.

"Uh, excuse me," said the dark-haired lesbian at the podium. "Just exactly how does this relate to WHY GAY AMERICA CARES ABOUT GAY LITERATURE?"

Marcus collected himself. "It's not about literature. Or film or books or paintings. It's about pretty pictures that resonate in your soul, beautiful imaginings that light up your heart and make your whole being want to sing the most glorious songs of your deepest dreams. Those pretty pictures can come from literature, film, paintings, a song, a sunset, the heavens, even ... a photo. Pretty pictures are everywhere, Bearcat People ... your ticket is your imagination."

Marcus paused, smiling at the dark-haired lesbian, who still didn't seem convinced.

"Perhaps we'll leave that discussion for the Q&A," she said, sounding quite bewildered.

In a world without you ...

"*Chris Brown, if I have to hear that song one more time!" yelled Dan from the cockpit of* True Gold.

"*Trying, Dan," said Chris from the copilot's seat. "You and your Super Arm jammed the music button big time! Here, lemme see what happens if I use this hammer ... whoa! ... the button flew off the control panel and out of the back of the cockpit window ... it's heading straight for the eggbeater above the end zone bleachers!*"

... where would I be?

BEAR SAT ON THE BED IN HIS HOTEL ROOM and wondered what the rest of Chicago was doing on an early Saturday morning. He imagined Walter running errands for his mom, chauffeuring his sister's kids to soccer, or arriving back at his parents' house, sweaty and pumped after a good session of cardio in the park.

What else could my buddy possibly be doing?

He decided to raid the minibar. "This is my movie and I'll have a cliché shot of courage if I want." He poured himself a shot of tequila in a plastic cup, then retrieved his cell phone, sat on the bed and cleared his esophagus. The hacking made him dizzy but he continued onward.

"Dan, the music button is being tossed around inside the eggbeater which is spinning a gillion miles an hour!"

"Chris, see if there's a button to turn the goddamned thing off!"

"Dan, I think we'd better bless the goddamned thing first!"

Bear dialed the number and pressed TALK. The combustion within his soul forced him to stand. A wave of nausea boomeranged in his head, followed by a sudden eruption of blaring music and a shrill female voice:

"—oooooooooo ..."

He spun around in a panic. The clock radio on the nightstand had turned itself on, drowning out the cell phone in the process.

"... where would I be?" sang the female. It was Belinda Carlisle, the former lead singer for the Go-Gos.

"This is ... not gonna work," said Walter's voice as he answered the phone. "Hey, Bear-man, where's my buddy?"

Bear reached for the radio's cord, traced it behind the nightstand, and yanked it out of its socket, getting the silence he wanted. Walter had answered the phone and was waiting for a reply, but Bear remained mute. Belinda Carlisle had thrown him off.

"I'm in ..." came out of his mouth, just as he realized: I didn't have my shot of courage!

"Dan, the eggbeater is swirling like mad now with the music button going off inside like a firecracker!"

"Chris, what do you suppose that means on the dash?"

FOUR-PART DISHARMONY

"Well, Dan, judging by all the lights on True Gold going crazy, I'd say some-body's got their wires crossed."

"Wow, Chris ... this is definitely a case of bad cell phone reception in dueling parallel universes!"

"Marcus ..." said Walter, "... sorry, Bear, someone was asking my partner's real first name. When you coming home, Bearcat? Do I get a hint? Are you still there?"

"I'm still here," said Bear, trying to summon up the nerve to tell his buddy he was in Chicago, not Malibu.

"Lotta construction here at the Warriors site ... get me another nail please ... are you coming home ... to the folks for dinner ... Sis, did you hear me?"

"Are ... are you talking to me, Walter?"

"You're Marcus ... when ... Sis ... are you coming home?"

"Walt ... you're asking me if I, Marcus Coleman ... am coming home?"

"Yeager, yes, that's how you spell it. Yes ... married twice, divorced twice, retired from football after back surgery in college ... hold on ... someone on the line ... where are you now?"

"Chicago, but I've just come ... home near Malibu."

"... breaking up ... more nails, please ... upsetting ... so much to do before tonight's ceremony. Hey, I may not get to the pro football Hall of Fame, but Walt Yeager's one lucky bastard to make the Walk of Fame, eh?"

"... home near Malibu ..."

"Bear! ... grin and bear it ... I love Malibu. I love Malibu and ... you need to get me more nails! As many as you ... can bear."

"Did you ... call me Bear?"

"Bear ... look, there's goes a cat ... your name ... right? I love Malibu and ... you."

"You know about Malibu? And the Bearcat? Is this Walt or Walter?"

"This is twisted. Hold on, Bear ... Do we know each other?"

"I think I have the wrong number. I was looking for someone, but I think I screwed up. Sorry to bother you."

"You're busy, QB, see you back in Malibu."

"See if this helps!" said Dan from underneath the control panel. He unplugged a cord and the eggbeater came to a halt. The Cool and Dreamy Music Button hurtled into space, luckily toward the cockpit at the other end of True Gold. Using his quick-thinking mind and panther-like skills, Dan leaned out of the cockpit window and caught the music button just as it was flying by, heading toward outer space.

... Bear Coleman pressed END, frustrated at the lousy reception. Even more disturbing was the fact that he had flown to Chicago for Walter's ceremony instead of staying in Malibu for his own big night. *Only an emotional retard who's still infatuated with his man after 21 years, right?* thought Bear. With that, he decided to retreat to California as soon as possible.

... Marcus Coleman pressed END twice, then pressed it again to make sure the connection was severed. Whatever had just happened killed any visions of having a beer with a golden blond stranger. Now the bigger priority was his own sanity. With that, he decided to retreat to California as soon as possible.

"THAT'S WHAT I CALL a *pas de duh!*" said Dan from the pilot's seat. True Gold was in GO-CART MODE, drag racing a commercial airliner a hundred times the size of their aerial transport.

"Was that reception malfunction our fault because of the music button?" asked Chris.

"Is that why I feel kinda lousy?" asked Dan.

"How can we help them?" asked Chris.

"Dream of it," said Dan.

2000 earth miles and a few time warps later ...

"Saturday night at the Complex," said Chris, reading from the notebook of notes as True Gold began its descent into the hills of Malibu. "Friends and family gather to watch Bear's new movie, *Walt Loves the Bearcat*—look, there's the old junior high gym turned movie house for the night."

Dan circled the gym, peeking through the windows at the movie screen. "Looks like the actor playing Bear is running around in a Chicago Zephyrs' uniform, playing both offense and defense in the Super Bowl. What a lovable dope."

"He runs funny," giggled Chris.

"Almost as cute as somebody else I know," said Dan. *Somebody I wanna kiss.*

"What's that you just said?" asked Chris.

"*Shh* ... better not talk during the movie," said Dan, taking True Gold over the gymnasium roof toward the canyon.

... Inside the theater, the audience gasped at the very last Upon Further Reveal. Or was it the very first Upon Further Reveal? "*Sometimes, you have to go back to the beginning to get to the end,*" whispered a boy's voice in the theater.

"There's Bear Coleman now!" said Chris, pointing to the bleachers of the football stadium. "Or is that Marcus?"

"What's it say in the notebook of notes?" asked Dan.

"*Coleman* sits alone in the bleachers, playing Mattel Electronics Football," said Chris, reading from the notes.

"Which Coleman?" asked Dan.

"Doesn't say," said Chris, flipping through the notebook. "But here's something: as *Coleman* sits in the bleachers, playing the game, he remembers his life and his dreams. On one hand, he envisions it all happening as it does in *Walt Loves the Bearcat* by Bear Coleman, a combination of *My Whole Other Life* and *The Walter Yeager Story*. On the other hand, he envisions it all happening as it does in *Walt Loves the Bearcat* by Marcus Coleman, a combination of *The Walter Yeager Story* and *My Whole Other Life.*"

"Whoa, sounds cross-dimensional," said Dan, "and overwhelming."

"Try whelming," said Chris, reading from the notes. "Because once you can handle whelming, you can get to the welding."

"Welding?" asked Dan. *Mild laugh.*

"Putting all the pieces together, even the twisted ones," said Chris, reading from the notes.

In God's universe, everything fits, especially, if you try whelming.

"Sweet," said Dan. "Let's park 'er on top of the press box and see what happens."

True Gold came to a hover landing on the small wooden press box atop the bleachers, directly opposite the storage shed across the field ...

THE SCREEN ON THE LITTLE GREEN BOX went blank. Mattel Electronics Football was outta batteries once and for all. Coleman stared at the bleachers beneath his feet and sighed, then he arched his head toward the starry night, his gaze roaming the universe above ...

Try whelming, whispered the universe.

Coleman giggled in his own headspace, which suddenly became a little more cool and dreamy. He scanned the infinite universe surrounding him, reaching out in all directions, not just the directions he could see and that humanity was aware of. He felt like a tiny speck of creation amidst all there was, and suddenly his dreams weren't all that monumental, all that earth-shattering, all that important. Except to him. To him, they were everything. His dreams had kept him alive—all his dreams: the dreams that came true, the dreams that didn't, the dreams that were still out there, waiting to be conceived. They had all kept him alive. His deepest dreams had created his soul and kept that soul alive.

That soul deserves happiness, he whispered back to the universe. My soul deserves its deepest dreams. I deserve my deepest dreams. No matter my skin color, my height, my weight, my age, my athletic ability, my mental capacity, my "lifestyle." No matter my HIV status, my sexual habits, my choice of sex partners. No matter my deepest dreams and my deepest dreams for me and my soul mate. No matter all else, we all deserve life's biggest miracles and our deepest dreams come true.

... Like a text message from Walter to Bear: DON'T WANNA INTERRUPT THE MOVIE. JUST LANDED IN LA, ON MY WAY. GUESS WHAT I'M DRIVING?

... Or the note from Walt to Marcus—the one that blew away—suddenly blowing back into view, landing on the bleachers in plain sight: BACK IN A FLASH ... OF LIGHT. GET IT?

We all deserve miracles, thought Coleman. Who would have dreamed a boy named Marcus would become his generation's worst nightmare, then survive AIDS for over 20 years, still believing in his deepest dreams?

Who would have dreamed a boy named Bear would become buddies with

one of the greatest quarterbacks that ever lived, then go through heaven and back,
still believing in his deepest dreams?

"I want my freakin' C-note for the freakin' Sox bet," said a man's voice passing in the blur between the bleachers and the gymnasium.

Who would have dreamed the Boston Red Sox would be down 0-3 to the New
York Yankees in the American League Championship, then come back to win that
series, along with their first World Series in 86 years? Who would have dreamed a
man named Coleman would be rooting for a team from Boston—the sports town
he hated—because the more impossible the dreams that happen in your lifetime,
the less impossible your dreams become to you. He cried tears of joy watching the
Red Sox celebration. Who would have dreamed of such a thing? Fallible gods, that's
who. Fallible gods who dream their deepest dreams and believe in the miracles that
make them happen. Thank God there's space for us, thought Coleman as a flash of
headlights wiped across his face. Thank God, god showed up.

In the blurry distance, just beyond the end zone of the football field, a little red sports car was coming to a halt. After a moment, a golden blond aura
emerged, his half-smile beaming, even from far away.

The man of my dreams, thought Coleman with a relaxed smile. *The rest is*
details.

The blond aura moved down the opposite sideline toward the shed near
the 50-yard line. Coleman gathered himself, descended the bleachers and moved
across his very own field of dreams, heading straight toward the most beautiful
man his soul had ever loved. They came together near the shed, nice and easy,
warm and friendly.

"*Did I dream you showed up? Or did you show up and now I'm dreaming?*"

"Does it matter as long as I'm here?" asked Yeager. *Mild laugh.*

"Where have you been all day?" asked Coleman.

"Long story. Back and forth, here and there, around, Chicago, LA, your
wacky dreams," said Yeager. "You?"

"LA, Chicago, around, here and there, back and forth, my wacky dreams,"
said Coleman. "I can skip the details for now. I'm just glad you showed up."

"I'm glad *you* showed up," said Yeager.

"If you show up, I'll show up," said Coleman. "Didn't somebody once say
that?"

"*Ha!*" said Yeager, looking off into the hills. "So you've really gone all out
with *Walt Loves the Bearcat.*"

"If you were there, you'd know," said Coleman.

"Seems so real," said Yeager, "like it all really happened that way, all of it.

You know, I'm hoping to spend a lot more quality time with the dreamer man behind the dream."

The admission prompted Coleman to blush toward the canyon. He could live for eternity and this man could still cause a gentle quaking in his soul.

"So how does it end?" asked Yeager.

"How does Yeager want it to end?" asked Coleman.

"I know two buddies who, at least in one of their lives, made a deal," said Yeager. "Or did I just dream that up?"

"First I've heard about a deal," laughed Coleman.

"You remember," said Yeager, nodding toward the coast, "the deal."

"Oh, that deal," said Coleman.

Seaside Inn, Malibu, 21 years ago. Walter told Bear: "Gimme 21 years to figure out if I wanna hang forever, little Bearcat. I should know something by then."

"The option is up," said Yeager. "It's been 21 years, give or take a couple of months."

"No doubt," said Coleman.

"And here I feel like I'm just getting started," said Yeager. "But I tell you what: Yeager called it the last time. This one's on Coleman. True?"

"I don't care," said Coleman.

"You don't care who calls it?" asked Yeager.

"I don't care what you have or haven't done to anyone else in this world," said Coleman. "I don't care what they call me or you, from faggot to nigger to hero to psycho crazy to sexual to homo to retard to genius to just another fallible god in a universe full of nothing but fallible gods. I'm not a rocket scientist or a photogenic chiropractor or anything, but I believe we're supposed to be buds, that we're made for one another. I can't remember who, but someone once asked me to define what resonates in my soul. The answer is you—whoever you are, no matter what you want me to call you, no matter what you want to call me—it's you. You resonate in my soul. You have since the day I first laid eyes on you in your pale yellow polo shirt. You'll always resonate within my soul. I still believe we're soul mates, always and forever. I still believe I asked God for you, and God sent you to me, and now I wanna continue fulfilling the promise I made to God, to love you forever, come what may. I've had my sampling of Yeager-meister and his cool and dreamy soul. You better believe I'll take another 21 years, every single which way I can."

"Sweet," said Yeager. "*Rightbackatcha.*"

"I only have one other request," said Coleman. "Actually two."

"Marcus *slash* Bear *slash* Bearcat Coleman with only two requests? What happened to your usual one million?" laughed Yeager.

"I guess you broke me down," said Coleman. "Now I know what's important and what's details."

"Go for it," said Yeager. *Mild laugh.*

"Request number one: hold me?" said Coleman.

Yes, that's it ... just how I dreamed. Just how it's supposed to feel, only much, much, much more heavenly than I ever imagined. Seems that way each and every time.

"Request number two?" asked Yeager, holding onto his buddy.

"Chicago," said Coleman. "I'm dreaming of seeing my buddy's name on his Walk of Fame."

"I'll take you there," said Yeager.

Coleman and Yeager circled the telephone pole near the shed, noses to the ground, searching then finding *it* at the same time. *It* was a tiny football, slightly bigger than a man's thumb. *It* looked more like a smooth and shiny rock, perfectly shaped and polished with a slight greenish tint. *It* was the football Walt had thrown at the telephone pole in the hills of Malibu earlier that morning, when Walt and Marcus were trying to get a grip on their sanity. The football had hit the top of the telephone pole and caused a mini-lightning storm. Yep, *it* had been a very long and winding day on one side of the universe.

Yeager picked up the rock, or football, or rock-shaped football or football-shaped— "The green rock?" said Yeager, as if to clarify the name.

"Whatever Walt wants," giggled Coleman.

"Walt or Walter?" asked Yeager.

"Whatever Yeager wants," said Coleman.

Yeager put his arm around his buddy and led him to the football shed on the sideline near the 50-yard line. The boys went inside, barely noticing anything but one another in the blurry darkness.

"Ready?" asked Yeager, sitting on one bench.

"Let's do dis," said Coleman, sitting on the other bench.

ROCK INTO GAME

NEVER TOO OLD

BUDDIES FOR LIFE

ALWAYS TRUE GOLD ...

"*The green rock,*" said Coleman, feeling the turbulence in his gut. "*It's making the game go crazy ... the field ... the lights ... the buttons ... the scoreboard ... Big Norse!*"

"Never get tired of that, do you, little Bearcat?" laughed Yeager. "Hold tight, gotta get True Gold over the gym. Hang on, Soul Man!"

"Look at all the people running out of the Bearcat Studios Theater to see what the blast was all about!" said Coleman. "I wish they could enjoy the fireworks in Chicago."

"Dream of it, little Bearcat!"

True Gold soared over America, heading straight for the heart.

"WE'RE EXPECTING MR. YEAGER any moment now," said the nervous man at the podium in the middle of the football field at the former junior high football stadium in Chicago.

"Freakin' Yeager owes me for the Red Sox winning it all before the Pacers," said Hail Larry.

"Freakin' Yeager and the Bearcat are probably off somewhere swapping Sugar," said Hail Larry's Wife.

"It's about freakin' time," said Hail Larry. "Maybe they'll give our kids some little Bearcats to play with."

Hail Larry's Wife shot him a look that asked: Have you gone insane?

"Dream of it," said Hail Larry, then nodded to the football shed on the sideline near the 50-yard line. "There's the freakin' happy homos now."

In the distance, Yeager and Coleman emerged from the football shed, rearranging themselves as if they had been up to something quite mischievous and infamous inside.

"Was that little shack there before?" asked Hail Larry's Wife.

"No, woman," said Hail Larry. "It just fell from the sky and landed there when we had our backs turned to the bleachers, geez! You think True Gold has Hot Lava's transcontinental, cross-dimensional capabilities? No freakin' way! Open your beautiful brown eyes sometimes, wife of mine ... like our darling two angels here ... yes, aren't you angels, big Oscar and little Ariel? Did you enjoy the movie in Malibu?"

"Here he is now," said the nervous man at the podium, "Walt Yeager, West Winnetka Warrior United!"

The hundreds in attendance applauded. Yeager took the podium and smiled his gorgeous half-smile, looking like the coolest cowboy hero a boy named Coleman could have ever dreamt up. QB spoke some dreamy words about a football career full of hopes and dreams. What Coleman felt was:

"... nothing in this life is worth achieving if you can't share it with the people you love most ... my football career, no matter how long or short, no matter how famous or infamous, glorious or glory-less—that career takes a backseat to the experiences I have shared with my loved ones and my teammates ... that is why Walt Yeager is alive today, to share the glory of the love I have felt with all of you ... may we always be Warriors United ... thank you."

Other Warriors spoke and accepted a miniature version of their plaque on the Walk of Fame. Whole families and contingents of loved ones applauded as each Warrior was honored for achieving some measure of his boyhood dream of being a football hero. As usual, Coleman's mind wandered when the subject wasn't his man. As the others spoke, Coleman imagined what he himself might say (were he the type to verbally express his feelings for his True Gold buddy):

I am not a religious man. Not in the "dress up and go to church every Sunday" sense, not in the "pray before meals and bedtime" sense, and certainly not in the "eternal damnation" sense. But I do consider myself spiritual. And I do believe that there are forces greater than mankind, and powers far beyond our confused little brains' ability to comprehend. Sometimes, I give these forces a name, not a very original one, but a name just the same: God.

To me, God's not a man. Or a woman. Or a tree or a dog. God's not even a He. God is everything beautiful, powerful and majestic. Everything worldly and otherworldly, and everything in between. God truly is ... All That.

With that preface, I say the following:

As a young child, when I gazed into the big pupils of our family dog, a black beagle named Benito, I saw the eyes of God.

As a preteen, standing on the swaying deck of a tour boat, my aging grandmother holding my hand, I stared up at Niagara Falls, its vast expanse consuming my entire line of sight, and I saw the face of God.

As a 21-year-old college student, when I saw Walt for the very first time, his golden blond aura brighter than his pale yellow polo shirt, I saw the soul of God. No matter where the road of life takes me, no matter anything else about who I am and the world in which I live, breathe and dream, this much is true.

"Ready for blast-off again?" whispered Yeager later into the evening.

"Where to?" asked Coleman.

"Whatever Marcus wants," said Yeager.

"Marcus or Bear?" asked Coleman.

"Whatever Coleman wants," said Yeager. *Mild laugh.*

"That's my QB," said Coleman.

"What's in a name, eh?" said Yeager, trying to be sly. "By the way, what was that guy's name, the slick and oily dude who was always causing trouble? I was just trying to remember that. His name was ..."

"Yeah, right," said Coleman, as if *he* would ever lose the Bet. *(First person ever to say that Evil Announcer Guy's name has to do something really heinous.)*

"Some other time," laughed Yeager, leading his buddy back to the football shed. "Some other time, I'm gonna get you real good with that one."

"Dream of it," said Coleman. "But first, how about dreaming of some Sugar in the skybox?"

"Sweet," said Yeager.

"THE SKYBOX," SAID CHRIS BROWN, reading from the big thick driver's manual, "a special compartment that detaches from the cockpit and floats in space, giving one total privacy in stealth mode."

"Sweet," said Dan, steering them over the Chicago skyline, following Yeager and Coleman's bigger version of True Gold. "Check out the universal memo coming over the dash."

"Bearcat Boyz needed in Dreamville," said Chris, reading the memo. "Entire town may soon implode. The controversial movie *Road of Life* is opening at the movie house, and nobody is dreaming a better dream about race relations."

"Sounds like a new adventure," said Dan. "And a job for us."

"So all our dreams *can* still come true," said Chris.

"Sweet," said Dan. *I hope that means this Bearcat Boy gets to kiss the Brownster someday.*

"What was that, Dan?" asked Chris.

"I said I hope it means I'm still gonna kick your ass in Mattel Electronics Football for the rest of eternity," said Dan.

"Dream on!" giggled Chris, turning up the music.

COOL AND DREAMY MUSIC BUTTON: *"Love Rollercoaster" by the Red Hot Chili Peppers ... wild, twisted ... dip, watch it! ... ride of your life! Or two or three or four!*

"Look," said Chris. "Yeager and Coleman have the stadium scoreboard on the exterior walls of their True Gold all lit up and working! Look what it says."

Reborn to be wild!

"We haven't even begun to mess with our scoreboard yet!" said Chris.

"There's a lot we haven't done," said Dan. "I had a dream I was as big as the whole stadium and throwing long bombs to cool and dreamy receivers that run like gazelles. And you were dancing and cheering for me in front of 80,000 people. When does that get to happen?"

"Tell me about it," said Chris. "Hey, what's that little red thing inside their eggbeater, popping around like a piece of popcorn?"

"I got a feeling it's the little red sports car Yeager was driving earlier today," said Dan.

"Hold on, let's go to the replay board," said Chris. "DATELINE: a few minutes ago."

"The green rock," said Coleman, feeling the turbulence in his gut. "It's making the game go crazy ... the field ... the lights ... the scoreboard ... buddy!"

"Never tire of that, do you?" laughed Yeager. "Hold tight, gotta get True Gold over the Sears Tower if we're gonna go tripping around the galaxies tonight."

"Look at all the people running out of the Walk of Fame dinner to see what the blast was all about!" said Coleman. "I wish they could enjoy the fireworks in Malibu."

"Dream of it," said Yeager. "And turn on the eggbeater, since we finally figured the blessed thing out."

"Speaking of, did we remember to take care of the car you were driving?" asked Coleman.

"As we fly," said Yeager, putting True Gold in TURBO MODE.

"While we're at it," said Coleman. "Think I'll change the scoreboard, in case any universal space travelers wonder what the deal is with us two wacky kids."

"Sweet," said Yeager. "Let's jet."

True Gold soared into space. The eggbeater behind the bleachers swirled away, churning up the little red sports car inside. In its place, fireworks shot out of the eggbeater, filling up the universe with the most spectacular light show the boys had ever seen, all the boys in all worlds, from True Gold to True Gold to every Bearcat Boy that ever dreamed of having a True Gold buddy-for-life.

"So *that's* what the eggbeaters for!" said Dan, amazed at the fireworks going off all over creation. "Recycling!"

"Life is recycling," said Chris, reading the universal memo coming over the dash. "Taking energy from the universe, using it and putting it back. The more blessed the ways you recycle, the more blessed the ways the universe says, *Rightbackatcha*. Works the same for soda cans, feelings, love, hate and all forms of energy. Wow. Who would have dreamed up such a thing?"

"Tell me about it," said Dan. "But first, look at the cool and dreamy messages on Yeager and Coleman's exterior scoreboard. Then we gotta get home, see if Dean Dome will reinstate us on the Dream Force."

"Dream of it," said Chris. "And punch it!"

The smaller True Gold took off for Dreamville. Meanwhile, Yeager and Coleman's aerial transport soared higher into space, ready to roam the cool and dreamy universe, never to need anything again but zephyrs and song. And maybe an occasional game, just to make life interesting.

Walt Loves the Bearcat
The Bearcat Loves Walt
Walter Loves Marcus Loves Walt Loves Bear
Coleman Loves Yeager Loves Coleman Loves Yeager
Walt loves the Bearcat loves Walt loves god loves god
And God Loves Them All
This much is always and forever True Gold.

Gratitudes

Individually thanking every celestial body in my life would require another long and winding road. One per lifetime, please (so far). Sincerest gratitude to all in my universe, you know who you are (just to name a few): the superstars, the shooting stars, the imploding stars, the exploding stars, the comets, the galaxies, the planets, the stardust, the energy fields, the time warps, the black holes, the white lights, the moons, the satellites, the flickering flames, the flaming flames, the asteroids, the space invaders, the smoke, the fires, the quakes, the floods and all the indestructible forces of All There Is.

Sincerest gratitude to my teammates and opponents on all sides of the universe, you know who you are (just to name a few): the energies, the biologicals, the infatuations, the relatives, the counterpoints, the refs, the panthers, the bruins, the trojans, the dawgs, and by extension, all their teammates, opponents and loved ones. Sincerest gratitude to that which has sent me a thought, a dream or a moment in my life, no matter the content of that thought, dream or moment. Your energy helps power my world and aids me in living my dreams.

Amazingly. Gracefully.

Most of all, in every moment of every moment for all time, sincerest gratitude to god, who knows exactly who god is, the one who inspires me to dream the better dream each and every day. This much is True Gold, always and forever.

About Randy Boyd

RANDY BOYD loves to dream, especially of dreams involving heroic sports teams, athletes and spirit leaders. And buddies.

RANDY BOYD has never been gay, straight or bi, just a boy *slash* man in need of one True Gold buddy.

RANDY BOYD loves to tell stories to his buddy in their dreams.

RANDY BOYD loves all sides of his soul.

RANDY BOYD loves all sides of his soul's mate.

RANDY BOYD loves God but does not understand all of God.

RANDY BOYD can be knocked off his ass by God at any moment in time. Especially when Randy thinks he knows it all (02/05).

RANDY BOYD exists because somebody dreamed him up.

RANDY BOYD thanks all those who dreamed him up.

RANDY BOYD thanks his buddy, come what may. This much is True Gold, always and forever.

Novels by Randy Boyd

Uprising: The Suspense Thriller—Three closeted celebrities. One homophobic U.S. Senator. A deadly plan of assassination. A straight FBI agent out to stop it. Which side will you be on? A Literary Award Finalist for Best Men's Mystery and Best Small Press Title.

Bridge Across the Ocean—A friendship between a black gay man with HIV and two straight, white teenage brothers changes all of their lives forever during one magical summer in Cancun. A Literary Award Finalist for Best Small Press Title.

The Devil Inside—A respected businessman must figure out whether the new man in his life is a dream lover or date from hell with strange ties to a bizarre and twisted underworld. A Lambda Literary Award Finalist for Best Science Fiction Novel.

Walt Loves the Bearcat—Black, gay, UCLA cheerleader copes with the 1980s AIDS crisis by dreaming up a "whole other life" with a white quarterback who becomes the first openly gay, superstar athlete of his time. A Lambda Literary Award Finalist for Best Romance.

Available wherever most books and ebooks are sold.

For more information,
visit randyboydauthor.com